The Blessed Coterie

Venus Cox

Divine Desires Press

The Blessed Coterie

Copyright © 2023 by Venus Cox

All rights reserved. Printed in the United States of America. No part of this book may be used or reproduced in any manner whatsoever without written permission except in the case of brief quotations embodied in critical articles or reviews.

This book is a work of fiction. Names, characters, businesses, organizations, places, events and incidents either are the product of the author's imagination or are used fictitiously. Any resemblance to actual persons, living or dead, events, or locales is entirely coincidental.

Character & scenery illustrations by Aga

ISBNs:

Ebook 979-8-9883470-3-3

Paperback 979-8-9883470-2-6

First Edition: October 2023

10 9 8 7 6 5 4 3 2 1

For all the ladies who've been told they were 'hard to work with' or 'too abrasive' when they simply wanted to be heard and respected.

For all the gals who've been called 'moody' or 'bitchy' for having big emotions and hearts.

For the readers who agree a woman deserves to be just as morally grey as a man, and also agree there's nothing wrong with being sweet and kind.

For the people who don't always know who to trust.

And if you're just here for the quality smut and to explore the rich realm of Colsia, this is for you too!

Content Warning

This book is intended for an adult audience.
It has explicit sex and foul language. Lots of it.

Kinks & Tropes

Arranged Marriage
Blood Play
Breeding/Pregnancy (mild symptoms)
Consensual Nonconsent
Dom/Sub Dynamics
Double Penetration
Dubious Consent
Fire Play
Group Activities
Knife Play
Praise/Degradation
Voyeurism & Exhibitionism
"Good girl."
"I would burn the realm for you."
"Touch her/him and die."
"Who do you belong to?"

Possible Triggers

Abandonment
Alcoholism
Discussion of infertility
Kink-shaming
Mention of death of a woman and unborn child
General racism/stereotyping between the different fantasy races
Violence (mild)

GREATER COLSIA SEA

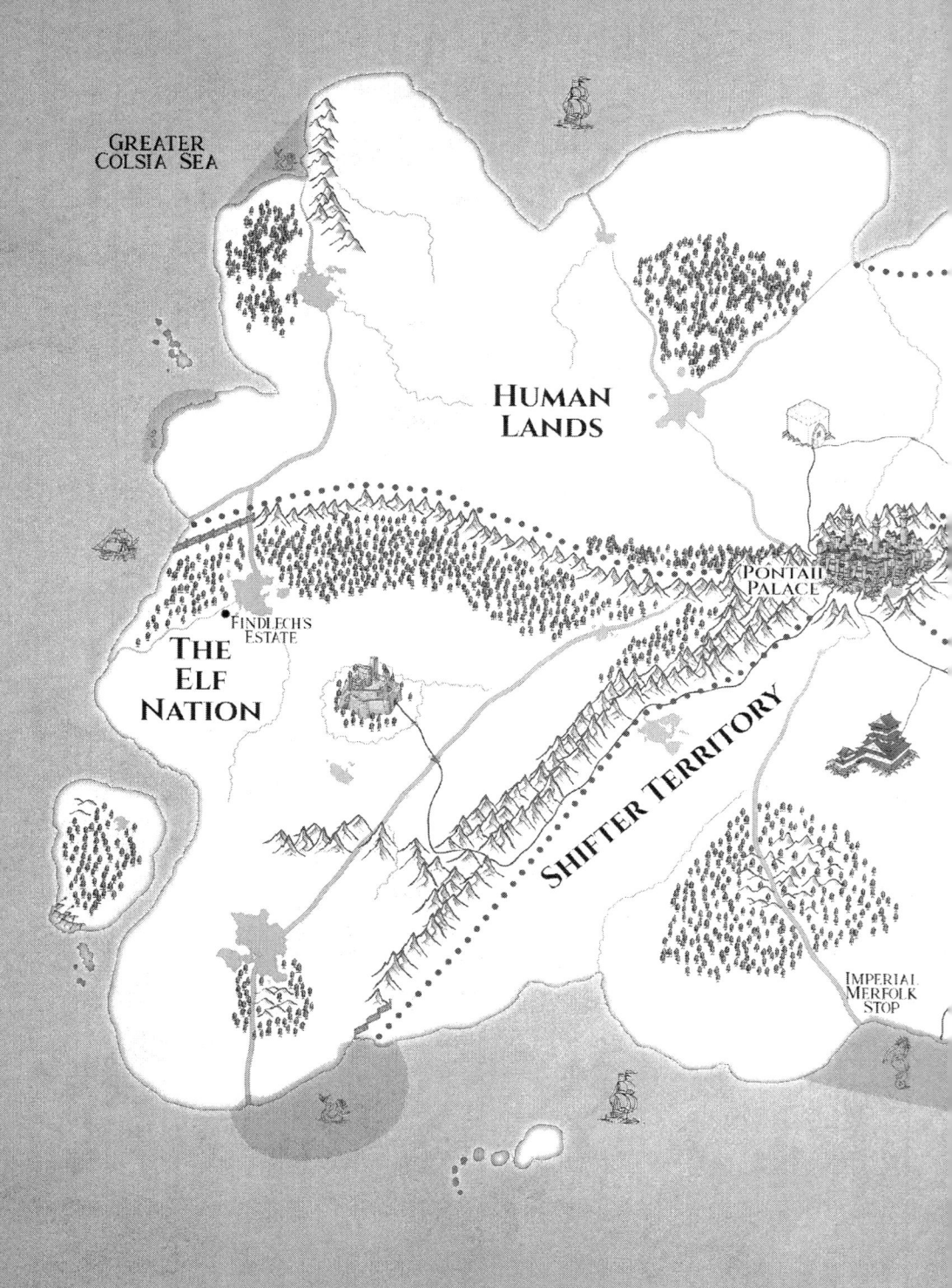

HUMAN LANDS

FINDLECH'S ESTATE

THE ELF NATION

PONTAII PALACE

SHIFTER TERRITORY

IMPERIAL MERFOLK STOP

The Realm of Colsia

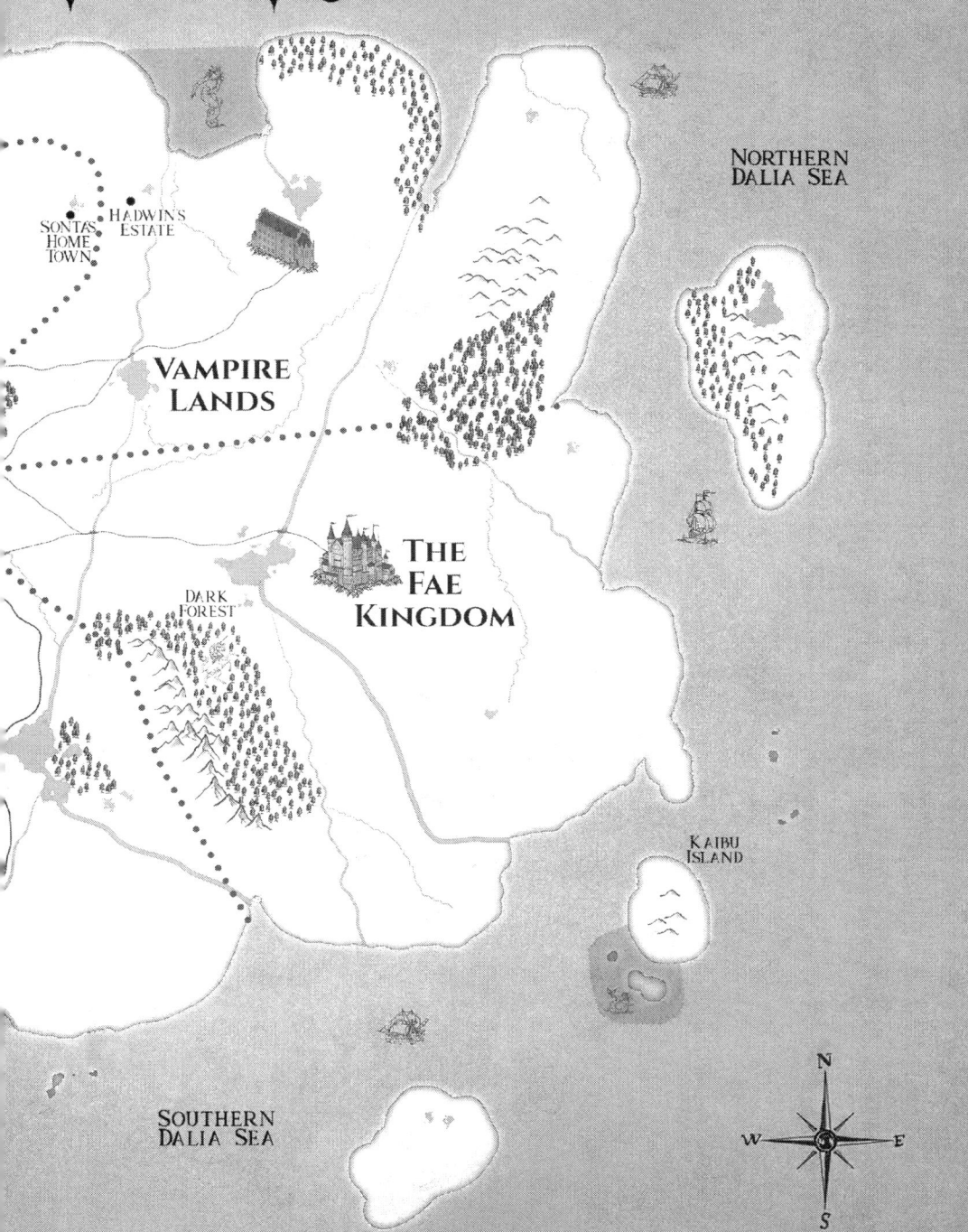

- Sontas Home Town
- Hadwin's Estate
- Vampire Lands
- Northern Dalia Sea
- Dark Forest
- The Fae Kingdom
- Kaibu Island
- Southern Dalia Sea

Within the Pontail Palace

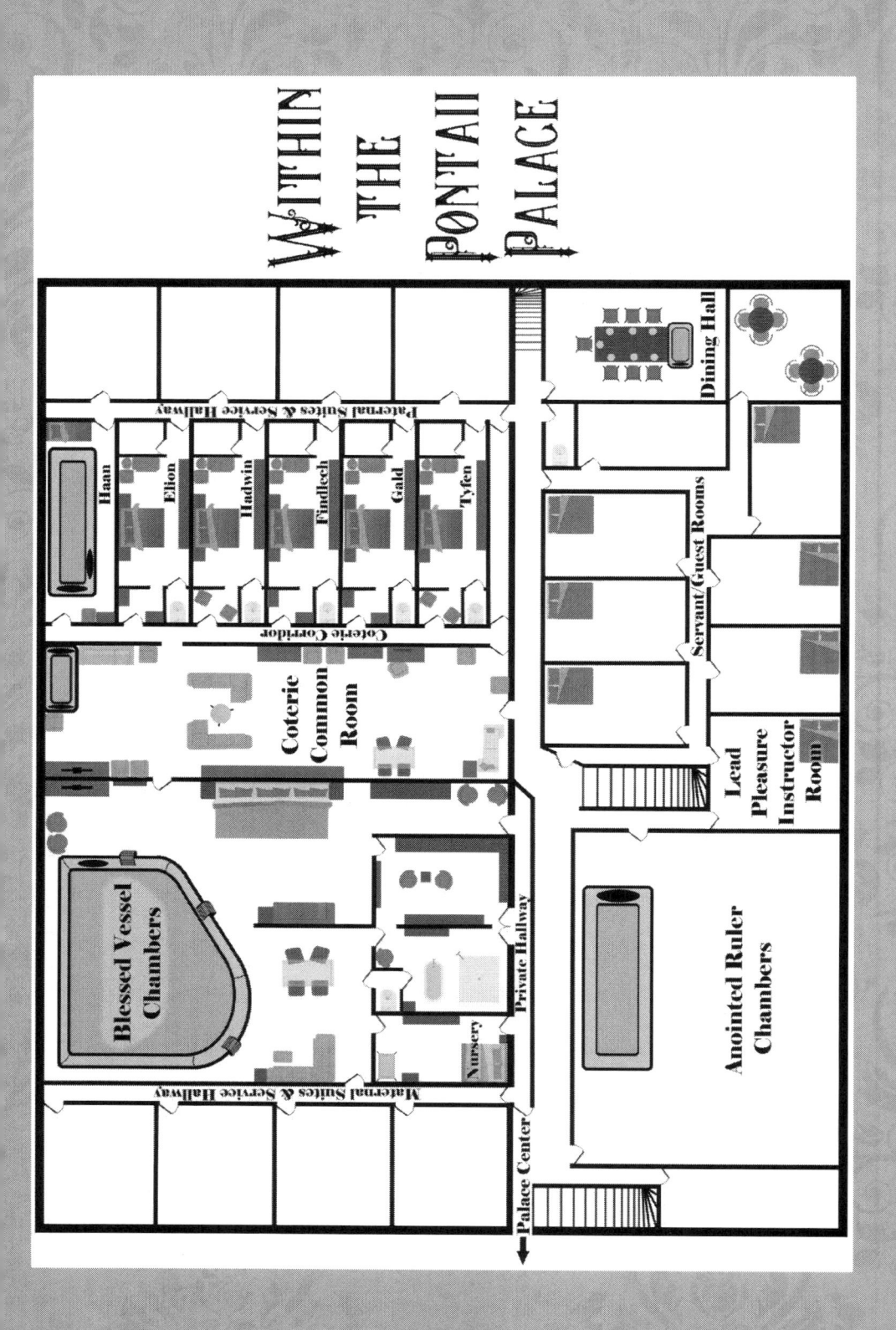

- Dining Hall
- Paternal Suites & Service Hallway
  - Haun
  - Ellon
  - Hadwin
  - Findlech
  - Gald
  - Tyfen
- Coterie Corridor
- Coterie Common Room
- Servant/Guest Rooms
- Lead Pleasure Instructor Room
- Blessed Vessel Chambers
- Nursery
- Maternal Suites & Service Hallway
- Private Hallway
- Anointed Ruler Chambers
- Palace Center

Pronunciation Guide

Alana: uh-LAWN-uh

Allister: AL-iss-ter

Baylana: BAY-lawn-uh

Blantue: BLAWN-two-eh

Blantui: BLAWN-two-eye

Bretton: bret-un

Casten: CAST-en

Cataray: CAT-uh-ray

Colsia: COAL-sea-uh

Coterie: KO-teh-ree

Danah: duh-NAW

Day'niair: DAY-knee-are

Dayton: DAY-tun

Demali: de-MAUL-ee

Elion: EL-ee-on

Elout: ee-LOWT

Falauay: FALL-oh-way

Feintal: FAINT-all

Findlech/Findie: fin-DLECK/fin-DEE

Gaffey: GAF-ee

Gald: GAWLD

Haan: HAWN

Hadwin: had-WIN

Hajba: HAI-buh

Hilta: HILL-tuh

Hoku: HO-koo

Hoy: hoy

Jaylin: JAY-lin

Kaibu: KAI-boo

Kernov: CARE-naw-v

Klaum: klaum

Koitah: COY-tah

Leonte: lee-ON-tee

Lilah: LIE-luh

Lourel: LOUW-rel

Malaya: muh-LIE-uh

Mallon: mal-lun

Mammi: mam-EE

Marsone: mar-SEWN

Mebana: meh-bawn-uh

Nil: kneel

Pontaii: PAWN-tie

Schamoi: s-chuh-MOY

Sonta Gwynriel: SAWN-tuh gwin-REE-el

Syinth: sigh-INTH

Tailar: TAYL-are

Talphus: TAL-fuss

Tyfen: TIE-fen

Velant: VEH-lawnt

Vesta: VEST-uh

1
Tyfen's Bedroom

Tyfen twisted the door handle to his room, carrying me over his shoulder. Stunned at what he'd just said and done, I remained silent.

'What I *want* to now that I don't *have* to,' he'd said…

I'd just been confirmed pregnant. Now, he didn't *have* to bed me anymore, but here we were…

I barely got a decent view of his entryway before he set me on his bed and left to lock the door.

The walls were practically bare, the room lackluster. What had I expected? A shrine to himself as a fae prince? Elaborate décor centering on his people? Honestly, I *had* expected a bit of that.

Tyfen returned, crossing his arms. He said nothing.

After an uncomfortable moment of us locking eyes, I swallowed. "Why?" Why had he finally brought me to his bed? He'd never once invited me over the last month. Why the sudden change?

His gaze raked over me, my bare legs and all. "My loyalty is sworn to you, isn't it?"

Yes, he'd taken an oath in front of a thousand before claiming me, but we'd never talked politics, had never even really been civil with each other.

"You've made it abundantly clear you never wanted to be here with me. But *now* you want to be? After your initial duty is done…?"

"Yes," he answered softly. "I'm just… I'm tired of pretending we don't make a great pair, or at least that we couldn't make a great pair." His dazzling green eyes were so sharp, so handsome. "We're good at this."

My stomach fluttered. Yes, we were phenomenal at fucking, despite how much we fought. But I was exhausted from the constant put-downs. "We're good in bed, but I'm tired of you treating me like shit, Tyfen."

He frowned, his posture relaxing a hair. "I'm sorry," he whispered. "You never deserved that. I'll be good to you."

Once upon a time, as old lore held, the fae had been incapable of lies and deceit, but those bonds had been broken long ago. Still, Tyfen had never been this way with me, and I wanted to give him the chance to explain himself, to grow our relationship.

"I just want to enjoy the time we have together," he added.

"Okay." I'd expected minutes ago for us to agree he was done with his sexual duty in my Coterie. Now, we'd actually agreed to be lovers?

Tyfen rolled his shoulders, then clasped his hands in front of him. "How would you like it?"

My mouth went dry as I gazed at his chiseled form. He'd never asked me what I wanted, and I wasn't even sure how to answer. Despite his faults, Tyfen and his cock had always pleased me. "I'd like to see whatever you want to show me."

His lips twitched into a grin. "You're sure about that? I have a wide variety of interests."

I smiled, fiddling with the end of my robe, which now fell midthigh on me with the way I sat. "As do I."

"Lie down, Sonta," he ordered, narrowing his eyes.

"Do you want me to remove my robe?" I slid my hand onto the knot.

"Did I stutter?" He angled his head. "I don't recall saying anything about your robe." His tone was firm and commanding, but not truly belittling.

My core heated. Just because he wasn't going to be an asshole anymore didn't mean he would suddenly become a sentimental lover. I followed directions, lying down.

"Good girl."

Goddess help me—I loved it when he said that.

Tyfen approached the bed, reached down, and grabbed the knot himself.

I didn't say anything as he unknotted it, still trying to wrap my head around this new Tyfen, this new arrangement.

"You should pick a word you can use if you want me to stop," he said.

I swallowed. My five pleasure instructors had taught me plenty over the last five years. "I trust you," I said, testing him.

Once the knot in my robe was undone, he opened the robe, letting the fabric fall to my sides. "I want a word, Sonta." He stepped back. "I will *not* hurt you or your child. So give me a word."

Never had I heard him more serious. Perhaps in a couple of our arguments, but not when calm like this. It was sexy, and I believed him. "My child will be safe. As for me..." I bit my lip. "I sometimes like a little pain with my sex."

Tyfen folded his arms, unamused. "Pick a word, or get out and go back to your room."

Okay... It took me a moment as I searched his all-too-serious face. "Red."

"The color?"

I smiled. "The opposite of your eyes."

His gaze slid to my breasts. "Good." He returned to the bedside, took my arm and pulled it out of the robe, then the other. The simple sensation of his hands holding mine made me giddy.

I arched my back as he slid the robe out from underneath me. I was completely naked, and he was still completely clothed—that wouldn't do. "Do you want help with anything?"

"No. I'll tell you if I want something from you."

Tyfen opened his bedside drawer. My eyes widened as he pulled out a yellow cord—a soft, thick rope I knew all too well.

"*That's* where you were when you went missing during the Coterie interviews?" He'd left the common room to go to my playroom.

He wrapped the cord around his hand, glancing at me. "You took me into that room to fuck for the better part of a month. Now that we're on better terms, I think it's time to have more fun."

Was I wet for him? Yes.

Tyfen took my hand, wrapping the cord around my wrist. He expertly tied a strong knot, then stretched the cord up to the slats in his headboard.

"You're really going to tie me up?"

He didn't skip a beat as he straddled me, holding the rest of the cord. He peered down at me. "You're required to make a lot of decisions on a daily basis. I imagine you sometimes want to surrender control."

I did, and I was surprised he realized. I enjoyed both dominance and submission, depending on the day, situation, and partner. I bucked my hips, rubbing against him while smiling my reply.

"Stop it," he growled.

I didn't stop. "Why?"

He rested more of his weight on me. "Because I said so."

This time I did obey, grinning as he took my other hand and tied it to the headboard. He was going to fuck me restrained, and I would enjoy it.

Tyfen checked his knots, satisfied with his work. He glanced at my breasts again, then slid his hands to fondle them softly. If he kept this up, I would be positively drenched before he even got naked.

This was the first time he had caressed me as proper foreplay, not just aiming to get me started for a quick fuck.

"One thing, Tyfen."

He looked up, his thumbs on my nipples. "You don't get to make demands, Sonta."

I could. I could revoke my consent by giving my word. "If we're going to do this, I want you to look me in the eyes. No more cold finishes."

Averting his gaze, Tyfen leaned down and tickled my nipple with his tongue, then switched to the other. I panted a breath of ecstasy.

He met my eyes again. "I can do that."

"Kiss me."

He instantly smirked. "Don't be greedy. You're not the boss right now."

I could wait.

Tyfen got off me, grabbing another bundle of cord from his drawer. He closed the drawer and set the cord on the bed near my feet. Instead of tying up my ankles right away, he tugged off his shirt.

I wanted to kiss his pecs and abs, trace every tattoo to his cock. He kicked off his shoes and socks, then unbuckled his belt. He slowly, *painfully slowly*, took off his pants, folded them, and set them on a chair. He glanced at me, keeping eye contact as he removed his shorts.

He was already large, and despite all the sex I'd previously had today, I wanted him inside me. As he turned and set his shorts down, I admired his ass.

He stood tall, facing away from me, flexing and stretching. My brain lost all capacity for higher thinking.

"That's not fair." I pouted. "I can't even touch you tied up." He'd waited until my damn hands were bound.

Turning, he wore a look of satisfaction. "Consider it a punishment for your greed, and for not obeying me right away."

I rolled my eyes.

"Really? You're going to roll your eyes at me right now?"

My only reply was a toothy, cheesy smile.

This time *he* rolled his eyes. "You're such a bitch."

The insult didn't hurt, not with the way he'd said it. I wanted to egg him on, but I also was ready for our foreplay to be done with already.

Instead of retorting, I enjoyed the view of his cock as he knelt on the bed. I spread my legs, eager for him.

"Close your legs," he demanded. When I didn't right away, he grabbed my knees and closed them for me.

"Or what?" I opened my legs again.

He crawled onto me—every inch of skin that touched was divine.

"Or what?" he repeated, his tone firm. "I'm sure I can come up with a list of punishments to convince you."

I simply smiled.

Somewhat gently, he lifted his hand, then rested it on my throat with a light grip. Despite his serious face, my smile only grew at the pressure. I closed my eyes and tilted my chin back, adding to the pressure of his hand.

He reciprocated, choking me a little harder. I sighed, relaxing under him.

"You're such a dirty whore, Sonta."

My elation faded, as did my smile. I kept my eyes closed, willing myself to push past that sinking feeling in my gut.

"Don't pretend you're hurt by that."

But I *was* hurt by it. Because my mother had been a lowly prostitute—a whore. And Tyfen himself had made me feel that way in the bedding chamber. I couldn't chase away that feeling, so I opened my eyes. I didn't mind insults when submitting during sex, as long as it wasn't that one.

"Red," I whispered, gazing into his handsome eyes.

Without hesitation, Tyfen recoiled, removing his hand from my throat. He searched my face. "Are you okay? I wasn't even pressing that hard…"

I swallowed the lump in my throat. I felt so weak and pathetic using a safety word over something so minor, but I wanted to enjoy my time with him, not suffer through it.

"Don't call me a whore," I said, terrified he'd mock me. "Anything but a whore."

He squinted as though he wanted to know why. "Okay. Not a whore."

"Thank you."

Tyfen nodded, still huddled over me. "You want me to fuck you, right?"

"Yes."

"Okay. Then stop being a bitch and let me do as I please."

I grinned again, easily falling back into line.

He shook his head. "You're such a greedy cunt." He said it with less conviction than before, assessing my reaction.

Arching my back, I ground against him.

Grabbing my knees, he forced my legs down. "You're hopeless."

I was.

He shifted, reaching to the foot of the bed. It wasn't the rope he grabbed, but another tool from the playroom. Tyfen kept surprising me.

"What's that for?" I asked innocently.

He furrowed his brow. "Play dumb all you want. I'm happy to educate you."

My cheeks were going to hurt from all the smiling.

Tyfen palmed the tool, spreading my legs with his own legs and hands. He slid two fingers inside me, rubbing me. I held back a moan.

"Nice and wet," he said. "Not really surprising for a greedy cunt who likes my ass and cock." His look was absolutely arrogant.

I blushed, offering no reply.

Using my natural lubrication, Tyfen prepared the tool intended for my ass. He hiked me up and dipped another finger into my center as he aimed for my back entrance with the tool. Spreading my cheeks, he gently slid it in. My anticipation grew. It wasn't two men inside me, but it simulated it well enough.

Tyfen's gaze kept darting to check on me. He was so different, and it made me recall the first time he'd tried to make me wet and had reopened Hadwin's blood play wound on my nipple. He'd almost seemed concerned about me.

Perhaps it hadn't just been disgust about getting blood in his mouth.

"Do you dislike blood?" I asked cautiously.

He scrunched his face in confusion, lowering me back to the bed. "I'm not squeamish about it, if that's what you mean. I'm sure I don't get off on it like … Duke Hadwin does…"

I didn't have the courage to clarify, to ask how much he really cared about me. "Okay."

Tyfen teased me with a quick rub on my clit, then trailed his hands down my legs as he backed up. With the rest of the cord, he proceeded to tie my ankles up, latching them to the bedposts.

Finally.

After checking the knots, he stood. "I'm thirsty." He grabbed a water bottle and emptied it as I watched. He again took his time.

I almost yelled for him to hurry the fuck up, but he'd only take longer to torture me. Instead, I closed my eyes and waited. I flexed and unflexed my pelvic muscles, savoring the tightness of the tool he'd left inside me.

Before I knew it, Tyfen returned, hovering over me. "I won't go easy on you."

"I wouldn't ask you to."

He wasn't yet fully erect. Such a pity, because I would have happily offered to help with that…

Sliding up my body, he dipped his head and kissed my neck. His lips were thorough as his cock further hardened against me, as I wished I had free hands to explore his body, to rub his sensitive ear arches.

With each kiss, Tyfen's lips roamed lower. He passed where he'd given me a massive hickey once. I had to know… "How much do you remember from the night you showed up to my chambers drunk?"

Tyfen halted, his gorgeous green eyes slowly meeting mine. "All of it," he said softly.

All of it… He remembered giving me two orgasms, and claiming me with a sloppy hickey, and insulting me by telling me he hated how much he enjoyed being inside me. He remembered making love to me, and me grasping his cock.

I had every right to be angry or embarrassed, or any number of other things.

"We're starting something new, right?" he asked. "You and me?"

We could both use a fresh start, whether or not the child in my womb ended up being his. I nodded.

"Good." He really did have a handsome smile, though it didn't last long as he continued his descent, his lips and hands brushing my skin in ways they never had.

Finally, he reached my pussy and prepared himself, peeling back his foreskin. "You remember your word, right?" A challenge glinted in his eye.

"Yes." I could barely breathe, my anticipation so high.

He pressed his tip to my opening. The warmth was welcome, the pressure as he slowly entered—beautiful. I couldn't hold back a moan as he eased in, the pressure of the tool in my backside rubbing as he did so. It *might* be too much with how large he was. We'd soon find out.

For all his talk, the way he entered was surprisingly kind. He was strong, though apparently aware of how human women weren't *quite* as sturdy as the immortal fae ladies…

He looked up, his cock fully inside me. "I'd say to hold on, but we've already taken care of that, haven't we?" He pulled almost all the way out, then plunged into me.

I gasped. The ache was incomparable, the pleasure divine. As promised, Tyfen kept his eyes on me most of the time as he drove into me. In and out, so forcefully I was grateful for the secure ropes tugging at my ankles. Were it not for them, my head would have been beaten against the headboard.

With the extra tool aiding Tyfen, I came quickly and forcefully. My core was on fire, my legs trembling. It was a damn good thing these walls were thicker than the wall between the common room and the hallway.

Tyfen followed right after me, not hiding his shaking as he came. His breathing ragged, he drove deeper, huddling over me. He rested his forehead on my stomach, sliding his hands under my back.

He kissed my bare stomach, his panting tickling my skin.

I wanted nothing more than to run my fingers through his dark brown hair. It was cruel to be tied up.

He lazily pressed his lips to my skin a few times as we cooled. I ate it up.

While he'd done a good job looking at me as he'd thrust, I craved that connection so much in the moment. "Look at me, Tyfen."

He sucked in a breath, but did not lift his head.

"Please," I whispered.

With one more kiss to my belly, he looked up, a soft smile on his face. His eyes, his ears, his muscular physique… I loved it all.

"How was it?" he asked.

"Great."

Tyfen nodded. "Me too."

That may very well have been the most honesty we'd ever had between us.

"I could go again," he said. He was still inside me, still huge.

I was screwed if he wanted to go again already. "If we can take out the tool in my ass, then I'm okay with that."

He arched an eyebrow. "Why? You have quite the selection in your sex room. I'm sure you're used to them."

Perhaps in the sweet glow following great sex where he actually met my eyes and didn't run off, he wouldn't shove my response in my face. "It's too much. You're too big."

His smirk was instant.

"Arrogant ass."

His look darkened. "Excuse me? Did you or did you not want me to remove that before I take you again?"

Swallowing, I reminded myself I was tied up and he was in charge. It really would be too much to go twice with it in, and I could tap out with my safety word, but I'd rather not. I bit my lip. "Please?"

After taking a moment to consider, he reached down and slowly pulled it out. I got instant relief from the oppressive tightness. Staying inside me, he chucked it to the ground.

"Ready?"

I rolled my wrists and ankles. "I'll do my best to hold on tight."

2

The Invitation

Every single muscle in my body shook after Tyfen took me a second time. He was just as spent, straddling me, pressing his sweaty forehead to my sweaty chest.

After moans and gasps of pleasure, we now hushed, our lungs and hearts finding a softer rhythm. Bondage was fun, but I wanted to cuddle.

Were we really the type to cuddle? We never had before…

After another minute, Tyfen lifted his head, acknowledging me. He carefully reached behind him and grabbed a towel to catch the cum that gushed out of me as he pulled out. He was gentle as he wiped us both off.

Setting the towel down, he crawled up, leaning over me. "You wanted a kiss?"

My heart danced. "Yes."

"I suppose you were good enough."

He dipped his head, but I interrupted him. "Actually, can you untie my hands first?"

"Why?" His lips lingered just above mine, his minty breath mixing with mine.

I lied. "It's kind of hurting…" My ankles *did* hurt, but not my wrists.

"Sure." He sat up and untied them.

I smiled at the sweet way he checked my wrists, running a hand over each one.

"There." He resumed his descent to kiss me.

Tyfen's lips were strong yet soft. I could have kissed him all night. Though, I did want more from this as he kissed me again and again.

I broke free, turning my head.

"Sorry," he said.

"No, it's fine. I'm just a little sore with my back." I wriggled a little to adjust my position, and he spread his legs, heightening himself to give me space.

"Of course," he said. "I haven't been with a human in a couple of decades, so just let me know when you need something different."

My brain caught on that little nugget of volunteered information. Like Hadwin, Tyfen really hadn't bedded a human to prepare to enter my Coterie? Elion had admitted he had. Gald openly admitted to 'whoring around the realm' for fun and politics, and mages were more human than not, anyway. Of course Haan wouldn't have dared to have sex with a land-walker, and I couldn't imagine Findlech bedding a mortal woman just to practice.

It didn't really matter all that much in the end, but it was intriguing.

I finished shifting, happy to still be under Tyfen. He dipped and kissed me again, gliding his tongue against mine. I delayed my ulterior motives for a moment while I savored his weight on me, his warmth and touch, while I fought for dominance with my mouth.

Only then did I make my move.

While Tyfen had touched my ass a couple of times, I had never once had the pleasure of holding his, and it was perfectly muscled. *That* was why I'd asked to have my hands freed.

I slid my hands to his firm cheeks, grabbing them and moaning.

Tyfen took his tongue back, gazing into my eyes. His lips still grazed mine. "You are such a greedy lying cunt."

I giggled. "Come on… You had to untie me eventually…"

He sighed, then continued to kiss me as I groped him, appreciating his mouth's work at the same time my hands explored the curves and angles of his ass and thighs.

Eventually, I did need to take a piss, though. "Hey, can I get up? To use the washroom?"

Tyfen drew a breath. "I suppose I can manage that."

I enjoyed each of his flexed muscles as he slid off the bed and walked around to untie my ankles. He frowned as he undid the first one. My ankle was tender as he ran a finger across it.

"You're bruised," he whispered. Regret laced his tone.

"I heal fast. It's fine."

He glanced at me. "It's fine? Like when you lied to the entire Coterie about how you hurt yourself, then made us all panic by downing an *entire* bottle of—"

"Stop it," I snapped, fully sitting up. "I'll make sure the others don't get angry, and I won't make that mistake again."

"That's not the point, Sonta." He was not happy with me. My ankles hadn't really even hurt that much until he'd been halfway through taking me the second time, and everything else had felt too good to use my safety word.

"The midwife said I get to determine what's too much for me. This isn't."

He averted his gaze, shaking his head while untying the second cord.

I stretched and rolled out of bed, meeting him at the end, where he wound up the cord we'd used.

"I told you I like it rough," I said, standing tall next to him.

He still towered over me. "I told you I wouldn't hurt you or your child."

"I told you I like a little pain during sex."

Tyfen glared.

"Don't go soft on me." I grinned. "I don't want to keep calling you an asshole for the wrong reasons."

He rolled his eyes, walking around me to the headboard for the rest of the rope.

A water pitcher and empty cups called to me from a side table near his sitting area. "Mind if I have some water?"

"Go for it."

He busied himself, straightening things up. I poured some water and drank it while admiring his crown on a shelf. It sat atop a green tufted pillow, a shade or two darker than his eyes. One of the few decorations in here, his crown glinted in the sconce light of the room.

Like I sometimes did, I stretched my muscles as I drank the water, standing on my tippy-toes, then tipping back onto flat feet. It worked wonders for the calves.

About to ask Tyfen about his crown, I turned my head, only to find him biting his lower lip, staring at my ass. I stopped my flexing, and his eyes met mine. Embarrassed, he grinned, then set to making his bed. "I thought you needed to use the washroom."

I downed the rest of my water. "It's possible to both need to intake *and* expel liquid all at once." I smiled sarcastically, setting down the glass, and headed to his washroom. All the mens' rooms were more or less the same, so it wasn't hard to find.

Part of me was tempted to snoop, but I didn't want to jeopardize what we were starting. I did sniff a bottle of his cologne, though. I liked his earthy scent as much as his body.

When I emerged from the washroom, Tyfen sat on his bed, his eyes closed as he pinched the bridge of his nose. His sheets had been pulled up to his waist, but his chest was still exposed. Were he a statue, I'd title it 'beautiful and broken.' I could reassure him I hadn't been hurt that badly. But that might not be the problem.

My stomach twisted as the memory of all his abandonments over the last month flooded me. He'd always been quick to leave me after sex. While I didn't want him to change completely, it killed me that he may still regret sleeping with me.

Where was this going?

"Thanks for letting me use your washroom." I bit my lip, spotting my robe on his bedside table and making a beeline for it. "I'll get out of your hair."

"Yeah," he muttered, watching me put on my robe.

My chest ached at the easy dismissal.

"I'm guessing you already have someone lined up for your bed," he said as I tied the knot.

With all my pride, I wanted to lie and say yes. While I had planned on surprising Hadwin in his room, I hadn't *formally* made those plans or any others. "I don't."

"You ... could stay," he said.

Cautiously, I met his gaze. "For how long?"

"All night if you'd like." There *was* plenty of space on the bed next to him... "No clothes allowed, though," he said more confidently, a hint of a smile showing.

While I should have played more coy, I didn't. "Okay." I undid the knot, slipping my robe off again.

Tyfen lifted the covers. "Come on, greedy cunt."

I smirked, taking the sheets from his hand. "How very gentlemanly of you, *asshole*."

He chuckled. "Don't accuse me of being a gentleman."

I slid into bed. The familiarity of the intimacy was so foreign. I stopped near him, but not touching.

"I only bite during foreplay and sex," he crooned.

I grabbed his muscled arm and bit it softly.

He furrowed his brow. "Are you rabid? Or do we need to order you food?"

I clamped down harder.

"Ouch!"

Letting him go, I smiled. "There. Now you don't have to feel bad about hurting me, since I hurt you."

His mouth hung open. "You're an odd little human. You know that, right?"

I frowned, genuinely not sure if I should be insulted. "I'm not little." Well, compared to him I certainly was, but I was average enough for a human woman...

He surveyed his arm where my canines had left an indent. "I might make you pay for this."

I batted my eyelashes. "Please do."

His smiles were so rarely soft and sweet, but this one was. He wrapped an arm around me, pulling me to his side. Our hips kissed as he rested his hand on my waist.

We both had our knees up, but he straightened one of his legs, hooking it under mine and raising it again. Butterflies flitted in my stomach.

"So..." he said.

He was holding me, sweet and salty. Mostly sweet.

"So," I echoed. "You were checking out my ass a few minutes ago."

Tyfen shrugged. "You were flexing. I'm sure you're aware how that accentuates your curves."

I shyly bit the insides of my cheeks. Unlike he'd done by flexing earlier, I hadn't actually done it to draw his eyes. But it was still nice to be admired. "More than ... *sufficient*?"

"Why do you always say that to me? And that way?" He narrowed his eyes.

"You really don't remember?" A cold memory settled in my heart.

"Obviously not."

"The bedding chamber." I pursed my lips. "You stripped me down when you didn't need to, after making a display of yourself. You intentionally caused a scene and humiliated me, then after assessing my body, you simply told me I was 'sufficient.'"

His throat bobbed as he pulled back his arm. "I... I'm sorry, Sonta. You never deserved my anger. It was never really aimed at you."

"For a hunter, you have poor aim."

Frowning, he gave no response.

I shouldn't open the wound that had festered when we were just starting a cute moment, but I couldn't help myself. "You constantly made me feel like shit. You made me wait in the middle of the dance floor when others were watching, expecting you to be there. You've insulted me time and time again. You always leave me right after sex, like I don't have feelings. I do."

Tyfen blew out a breath, ruffling his hair. I half expected him to kick me out of his room. "I can't undo that. All I can do is say I'm sorry. I was an ass. I didn't want to be here. At first, it was to embarrass and anger my parents."

He'd succeeded. "Like a petulant child... You're two hundred and what?"

He glared. "It's more complicated than that."

"You didn't want to join my Coterie, so you threw a fit, and I became your target. How is it more complicated? Wait, because you didn't like Lilah's scent on me, right?"

"Damn you, Sonta. No." He huffed. "Yes, it was rude for you to start the Great Ritual with her on you, but I just used that to fuel my anger, okay? It wasn't you. It wasn't her. It's just ... complicated."

"Then uncomplicate it for me, Tyfen!" My ears were warming. I deserved a better explanation after all he'd done to hurt me.

His jaw clenched, his eyes boring into me. "I'm not ready to talk about it, least of all with *you*." He looked away. "Fucking take it or leave it."

We sat in silence, both staring forward. Maybe I shouldn't have brought any of it up. Or *maybe* I should have demanded answers before we'd had sex tonight and started something cozier. I recalled Findlech's words about Tyfen having a right to his feelings, and how he was somehow involved in a thwarted war between the elves and fae.

Maybe we had moved too fast tonight. Tyfen wasn't ready to give me what I wanted from him.

"Do you want me to leave?" I whispered.

The silence was long, far too long. Whether I should be angry or sad, I didn't know. I was a bit of both.

As soon as I started to slide my leg off Tyfen's, he grabbed my knee, holding it in place. "Stay. Please."

It wasn't just the words, but the way he'd said it that stopped me in my tracks. My memory floated to a watercolor painting up in my studio—a sorrowful one with green the color of his eyes, and autumn leaves around an ancient elf structure. That vision had happened after he'd left my chambers, begging on his knees to be allowed to bed me for his people. He'd even teared up.

"I can't keep doing this," I said. "Great sex, then left to feel like crap."

He shook his head. "I promise to do better. Please. I'm just not ready to talk about some things. And I need you to respect that. You deserve answers, but I can't give them right now."

Against my better judgment, I allowed my desire for the man I hoped he'd become to motivate me. "Okay. I expect answers *someday*."

Swallowing, he nodded.

I slid my hand onto his. "I *am* kind of hungry... Assuming you're okay with staying up to talk about some things?" I shrugged one shoulder. "We've never even talked about politics. Or what your favorite color is. Or how you fit all your ego into your hulking body and scrawny dick."

He grinned. "Let's order some food."

I got out of bed and put my robe on. It would be best for me to order since I'd be eating some of it. I went to the small back servants' door—each of the men had one for easy service and cleaning so the Coterie corridor remained uncluttered.

I opened the door, and a single attendant hopped up. "Your Holiness."

Luckily, they wouldn't say anything about whose room I was in, and I was grateful. I hadn't yet processed how to approach this new situation.

I told the servant my chef could prepare what was easiest from the kitchens at this time of night. Just before I finished, Tyfen's large hand rested on my back. I startled, looking up at him. He wore a robe as well. "Her Holiness would like to order some wine."

The servant looked no less than shocked.

I elbowed Tyfen. "No, I don't. *Obviously*." The Great Ritual didn't end until I gave birth, and I was *pregnant*.

"What she means is she wants to order wine for *me*."

Riiiiight... I had forbidden servants from serving him alcohol in his room. He thought I'd let him drink away our conversation and sex? "No. No wine."

Tyfen pouted, drifting his hand down my back to my ass. "Just a little? There's a lot to celebrate..." Not that the servant could see it, but he reached his hand up my robe, aiming for goddess knows where.

"Go back to your room." I gave him a stern look.

He winked. "Yes, ma'am."

After finishing my order, I returned to his bedroom. He lounged in his seating area, on a chair.

I rested my hands on my hips. "Really? You *are* allowed to drink at group meals."

He pouted again. "Do you limit the others this way?"

No. None of the others had knocked on my chamber door drunk, either. I softened. "Do you have a drinking problem?"

Pouring a glass of water, Tyfen offered me a disingenuous smile. "The only problem I have with drinking is that you don't let me do it when and where I want…"

I approached him, then sat on his lap.

"Did I say you could sit there?" he asked.

"Oh…" I went to stand, but he grabbed me and put me back.

"Did I say to get up?"

I rolled my eyes.

"You have a great motherly look already, Sonta. The bitchy kind that terrifies a child into obeying."

Despite the mixed insult and praise, I smiled. That thought warmed a special place in my heart. I held a hand to my stomach.

"You're excited," he said wistfully.

I nodded.

He didn't seem excited. I couldn't blame him since his behavior had cost him several opportunities to bed me. "It *could* be yours," I said encouragingly. "You were the first, and sometimes once is all it takes."

Tyfen rested his chin on my shoulder. "I know," he whispered.

No matter the outcome, nothing could be done about the past. We'd agreed to move forward.

3
Tracing His Tattoos

Tyfen and I chatted for a while as we waited for the servant to bring our food. He let me hold his crown. I placed it on his head—he really was dashing with it on.

His smile was charming, his eyes beguiling. "We both wear crowns..."

My cheeks warmed. "Yes, we do." We could make a great pair if we worked at it. I'd been attracted to him from the moment I'd met him, despite all his flaws.

I took his large hand, tracing his fingers. Most of his tattoos were on his torso, but some extended onto his arms. Both of his inner forearms were bare, though. When a fae found their mate and they both accepted the bond, a similar tattoo would be inked on one of the forearms of each partner. He hadn't found his mate yet.

"You were chosen for my Coterie because your uncle found his mate, right?" His uncle had been assigned to the last few Blessed Vessels.

Tyfen nodded. "I was assigned this position forty years ago."

"Was that odd to know you were arranged to be with someone who hadn't even been born yet?" I more cautiously added, "Have you always resented this assignment?"

He pursed his lips, placing his crown to the side. "Immortals expect large age gaps, and we have to learn to be patient."

A sinking ache in my stomach reminded me how insignificant I was. He would easily outlive me, and if he was patient, this obligation would be over soon enough, and he could go back to searching for his mate.

He continued. "As for resenting this assignment... I didn't at first."

I shifted on his lap, intertwining our fingers. "You don't resent me for the loyalty you've sworn despite possibly having a mate out there somewhere?"

He took a moment to respond. "I'm not worried about that. I don't resent you for that."

His response was distant.

"Do you have another lover out there waiting for you?" It was highly unlikely he'd been celibate while waiting for me to be ready. He'd already admitted to sharing a bed with a human a couple of decades ago. "If what you want is freedom, I would never hold you here against your will. And … I'm willing to share if need be… If there's someone else…" It would be infinitely more complicated if my child ended up being his, but I wanted him to be happy, and I wanted to give us a chance.

He rubbed my knee with his free hand. "There's no one else out there, Sonta."

How was that possible with him being so handsome? He seemed more than tolerable when he wasn't taking his anger out on me.

"If that's not why you started to resent your assignment to my Coterie…" I was broaching a sensitive topic again.

We locked eyes for a moment.

"Pass," he said.

I could only nod. If he needed boundaries, I could respect that. At least he hadn't gotten angry about it.

"I'm sorry you're here against your will," I said gently. "But I'm glad we're trying to make the best of it."

He slid his arms around me and held me tight.

"Do you have a thing for pregnant women?"

"What?" His voice was full of confusion. "No. Why would you think that?"

I shrugged. "I guess I'm wondering if it's part of why you now want to be with me. I know some men love it. I don't mind, but I don't plan to be pregnant forever…"

He let out a soft breath. "I'm happy you're happy to be pregnant. And you're expected to have a safe pregnancy, so that's great… But I… I like someone who *happens* to be pregnant; I don't like her *because* she's pregnant."

I wanted to know so badly why he'd despised being assigned to me, and also what had changed. It was probably simpler than my mind allowed me to believe. Just like he'd said—he now wanted to be with me because he didn't *have* to.

Forcing my curiosity down, I gave him a smile. "Okay."

Not much later, the servant knocked at the door, and Tyfen and I brought in our food on trays. We sat on his bed, next to each other again, surveying the trays.

"Oh." I picked up a small shot glass of deep purple liquid and set it on his tray. "I special ordered this for you."

He raised an eyebrow. "Dipping sauce?"

I couldn't hold back a grin. "You wanted wine."

Tyfen sighed. "Seriously, this tiny thing?" He picked it up.

I giggled. "I'm not a tyrant. You're welcome."

He tipped the shot glass back, then set it down. "How *generous* of you."

My smug grin couldn't be wiped off my face.

"I'll make you pay for that," he threatened, his tone that of the dominant lover who'd tied me up earlier.

I picked up my fork and pushed around some chopped fruit. "I enjoy both dominance and submission, and sometimes just lovemaking," I admitted. "I don't *always* want to do things this way."

He took a fork to his own food. "I can appreciate that. I'm the same way. We'll sort it out."

My heart swelled at the promise of us making plans.

The food was decent, the conversation enlightening. While he did choose to pass on some topics, he had lived over 200 years—he had a wealth of stories. His relationship with his parents and some of his siblings was strained, but that sounded like a more recent issue. He enjoyed all the responsibilities he held in his kingdom, though he admitted he didn't really want to be there right now, either. When asked where he'd prefer to be if not in the empire's capital or in his homeland, he passed.

While I would not betray Findlech's confidence in me by naming him as my source, I tiptoed around my knowledge of the almost-war he claimed Tyfen had had some involvement in. The emperor's and magistrate's staff had filled me in, after all.

Tyfen passed.

It wasn't just an interrogation, though. Tyfen asked a lot about me. Unlike Hadwin and Gald, he had never really taken the time to learn much about his intended. It was fun to start from a blank slate.

Tyfen asked about my father, as had most of my men. Officially, the public believed my father had died before I was born. My mother had been too afraid the truth of my origins would tarnish me. She hadn't wanted to endure the public's scrutiny, either. A widow was more loveable and pitiable than a lowly prostitute. All the important people in the palace knew the truth, though. The emperor and magistrate had always followed the story, in part because we feared any sort of drama arising. Any number of human men may appear professing to be my birth father, claiming status, asking for money, or trying to influence me.

"He died before I was born," I said.

"I know." Tyfen set down his utensils, picking up a glass of water. "But what kind of stories has your mother told you about him?"

I swallowed my bite of dessert, wiping my hand on a napkin. I wasn't really a fan of lying when it wasn't necessary. Could Tyfen be trusted? Would I be opening myself to his scorn? Or would my uncomfortable truth induce him to be more forthcoming with me in return?

Resting my hands on my full stomach, I sighed. "Can I trust you with a secret?"

"I don't see why not."

I scanned his face. "My mother doesn't know who my father is. She was a prostitute…"

He blinked. "Oh. Well, she was lovely when I met her at the poolside…"

They'd both been civil, but Tyfen had still been moody that day, and my mother had only partially concealed her dislike of him—a dislike born solely out of support for me.

"Is that why you don't want me to call you a…"

"A whore?"

He nodded.

"Yes." Despite myself, I smiled. "Greedy cunt *is* pretty accurate, though, with how much I crave sex." My core heated at the simple admission.

His smile mirrored mine.

I was genuinely surprised a highborn prince didn't balk at his assignment to a prostitute's daughter. Higher class sex workers like Schamoi were never looked down on, but lowly prostitutes usually held a negative place in the public eye. "What do you think of a Blessed Vessel born of a whore? Does that tarnish my tiara?" I handed him my heart and reputation, possibly too hastily.

"Hmm…" Grabbing his tray, he stood and set it on a table in the corner. "Done with yours?" I nodded, and he took mine as well.

I straightened the bedsheets around me while waiting for his response.

Tyfen returned to bed and sat on top of the blankets. "Honestly, I can't blame you for concealing it. But sex work has its levels. The only reason your mother would have a different reputation than your pleasure instructors is because of the clientele they serviced, right?"

"Yes."

"Either way, it would take a lot more than questionable parentage for the millions of citizens in this realm to fall out of love with one of Hoku's daughters. Very little could tarnish your tiara."

I didn't care as much about the public's opinion as I did his opinion of me. I already agreed with him about the public's adoration. "Does it tarnish me in *your* eyes?"

He took a moment to consider again. "I've lived a lot longer than you. I've had a variety of companions. While most have held status befitting a prince's companion, they haven't all. And your status is still higher than mine, as Hoku's daughter."

It somehow wasn't reassuring. I wanted more depth, something more personal.

My expression must have given away some of my disappointment because he continued. "I'm barely allowing myself to get to know you now, but your tiara is not tarnished with me. You're a good soul, Sonta. The heart wants what it wants. The body craves what it will." He looked away distantly. "Even when the fates deal you an unfavorable hand…"

Another riddle that made me question how he felt about me.

"What does your heart want, Tyfen?"

He paused, still not looking at me. "It wants … me to get comfortable again as we talk some more. I'm going to take care of the sconces if that's all right with you."

"Sure." Some people were better at casual sex than I was. I wished I didn't crave a deeper bond. I hadn't always, not with the young men I'd slept with in my teenage years. "I'm going to get more comfortable, too."

I took off my robe and returned it to the bedside table. The bed was warm, and I slipped under the sheets to my neck. With only the candle flickering on his bedside table, Tyfen also took off his robe.

The only gods of this realm were minor deities, gaining the title through union with female goddesses. But Tyfen—with that physique, he was something of a god in his own right.

"For fuck's sake, Sonta. You seriously have no shame."

My cheeks warmed again at him catching me staring at his cock. "It's not my fault your tattoos practically point to it!"

Chuckling, he joined me in bed. He sweetly caressed my ass. "I guess I can't blame you."

"I want to hear the stories behind your tattoos."

"Sure. Starting with which?"

"Roll onto your stomach for me. I'll trace them as we go."

He hummed his approval, facing down with his arms to his sides, his head turned on his pillow.

I slid onto him, making sure to grasp his ass a minute before sitting on it. I wanted him again already. I first lay on him, pressing my breasts to his back. I could sleep in this position. He was so sturdy. I loved our skin touching, and the way his breaths lifted me.

"Interesting tracing method."

Smiling, I sat back up. "Don't be a prick when I'm cuddling."

Starting with the small of his back, I pressed my fingers to his skin, following the black ink. "What's this one?"

Story by story, moment by moment, I traced his marks while he told me about each one. Much like mage tattoos, fae ones generally meant something and were usually permanently inked with magic. Most fae had tattoos based on important bargains they'd made and their family heritage and status.

Tyfen's were no different. He had marks indicating he was royal-born; others pointed to serious promises he'd made over the years. His official titles had also been inked upon him. He was a commander in his kingdom's royal guard, a sworn protector of his people. As he'd always lived in times of peace, his main responsibility had to do with hunting in their deep forests. Lost to time in the centuries after their creation, oni, monstrous vampiric creations—likely shifters or fae having suffered a venomous bite—still plagued dark forests, feeding upon lost travelers and local fauna, unicorns included.

It made me sad. I was impressed by Tyfen's skills, but he wasn't the only member of my Coterie. In nearby rooms, my two mates slept. Hadwin was a victim of his own people, a vampire who had not volunteered to become one. His progenitors had created the oni, who now roamed without masters. Hadwin had my heart without question. He was a good man, but not all would see him that way.

And then there was Elion. As my shifter mate, his loyalty was unmatched. We'd never had conflict between us the way Tyfen and I did. Shifters had historically been the most innocent in all the conflicts, often losing their lives and freedom to the more brutal fae and elves.

Massaging Tyfen's shoulders, I tried not to dwell too much on history. I wasn't here to condemn these men for the mistakes of their ancestors, nor to seek justice for the same. We had peace, and the life in my womb was part of the plan to keep that peace. My Coterie was designed to help us move forward. My heart could keep them separate, cherishing the part we each played.

I pressed a kiss to Tyfen's back. "Okay, roll over and tell me about the tattoos on your front." I knelt to the side to allow him to move.

We both ignored how quickly he became engorged as my naked pussy rested on his cock. By the time he finished telling me his tattoo stories, my hands rested near his groin. That last tattoo that pointed to his cock? Apparently, it had been etched into his skin when we'd taken our oaths of loyalty in the bedding chamber. It was a special and sacred bond. I was fully wet, ready for more of him.

"I guess we should probably go to sleep," I kidded.

His hands kept stroking my thighs. "And here I thought you only asked me about my marks for another chance at fucking me..."

Grinning, I leaned forward. I brushed my lips to his, kissing him once, twice. "You're worth getting to know without ulterior motives."

He held my ass. "Thank you for saying so." He claimed my mouth. I was wholly his for this moment, for this night.

My core was on fire with need, my lungs and heart racing. "Can I?" I panted.

"Yes."

I scooted back, wrapping my hands around his massive cock, slowly peeling back his foreskin. Delight danced in his eyes. Tonight featured a lot of firsts for us, including me taking him, being on top.

Positioning myself, I slowly eased him into my entrance. He stretched me with each inch, and I didn't hold back a moan at how exquisite simple penetration was with Tyfen. He slid his hands from my hips to my breasts and groped them. "Show me what you can do," he whispered.

I didn't want wild fucking. I wanted to make love to Tyfen.

Rolling my hips, I pulled back, then took him in deeper. He let out a groan of pleasure. I was already tight, my nerves sensitive.

I rolled back again, and he thrust up as I descended.

"Fuck," I whispered.

With each rise and descent, my pleasure built, as did his. I savored each moment his face laxed as I took him in deep.

He kept groping my breasts, and as I neared release, he pinched my nipples. The pain drove me over the edge.

"Shit!" I clutched his hips, gasping and holding myself up as he finished the work to bring himself to completion.

While my sounds may have mimicked prey fighting for its life, his were of the strong commander and hunter he was.

I lingered there, fighting for air and clear thinking to return to my body.

Tyfen rested his hands on my thighs again. "You're…"

Rolling my hips and taking him in again, I gave him inspiration to finish his sentence. Not that he did, since he was busy shuddering.

After blowing out a few breaths, he met my eyes again. "How often do I get to have you?"

The simple question flooded me with emotion. Elion had asked me that multiple times when he'd been in the thick of his mating fever. Tyfen had all but demanded once a day with me after claiming me in the bedding chamber. A petty part of me wanted to point out the tables had turned, my heart still hesitant to accept a changed Tyfen, but I didn't want to spoil what we'd just shared.

I rested my hands on the marks that symbolized his oath of loyalty to me. "Not half-bad for a greedy cunt?" I grinned.

He didn't return the grin as he gingerly ran his thumbs over my knees. "Not at all bad for a skilled lover."

My heart was full, and I couldn't ignore that. "Thank you. You too." I shifted a bit; this time he wasn't staying as hard for as long. "I imagine I could … squeeze … you in once a day." I flexed my pelvic muscles as I said it.

He panted out a breath and a curse. I beamed. Six orgasms a day was easy for me. I usually preferred at least three or four. Between Hadwin, Elion, Tyfen, and Gald when he wasn't busy with Findlech, my needs were easily met.

"Thank you," he said. "And I wouldn't demand more than that, well… I wouldn't demand at all, I mean…" He stuttered, and it healed a part of my broken heart to have him acknowledge how wrong it had been for him to demand sex from me in the first place.

He gathered himself. "I mean to say … I would never turn you down if you wanted more. And I'm grateful you're giving me a chance after I was such an ass."

I needed to visit Lilah soon to help deflate my ego. Coteries didn't usually go so well. Not that Findlech had worked out in the 'loving and adoring me' part, and Haan and I were more friends than anything, but I was blessed to still want to share a bed with four of my Coterie even after it was no longer required. I had Haan on the back burner for a distant date after giving birth, too.

I took in each shadow of Tyfen's handsome face as the candle on his bedside table flickered low. "I'll let you know."

4
A New Normal

Tyfen and I cuddled, eventually falling asleep in his room. I loved being the naked little spoon with him. I usually slept deeply, but I was also an early riser. After waking, I slid out from underneath Tyfen's arm and used his washroom. I was tempted to wake him and have a little more fun, but I couldn't do it. He was so adorable, so at peace as he snoozed soundly. Instead, I found a pad of paper and scratched out a note, thanking him for a nice night. I left it on the bed next to him and pressed a kiss to his forehead before putting on my robe and crossing the common room to bathe in my own chambers.

As I bathed, dressed, and had a servant help me with my hair, I couldn't help but replay the entire last day.

I was pregnant. With the realm's next empress or emperor. And one of these six men was the father.

There wasn't one among them I'd be upset to have as the father. Obviously, some held a closer place in my heart like Elion, Gald, and Hadwin, and some relationships were more complicated or cautious, like with Findlech, Haan, and Tyfen. But we were all on fairly good terms, and all were seemingly honorable and kind men.

All smiles, I entered the common room once I was ready. Elion, as he often did, eagerly greeted me first with a hug and kiss. I made my rounds, and the men congratulated me. I hung back, though, when it came to Tyfen. He was clean and handsome, reading a book in his usual chair. He hadn't so much as lifted his eyes to acknowledge me so far.

I was hungry for breakfast, and announced I was ready to head to the dining hall. Haan swam away, and most of the men strode out of the common room. Hadwin lingered, holding my hand. We walked to the door together.

Tyfen still sat in place, unfazed. My anxiety rose. "Are you going to join us for breakfast?"

His voice dripping with disdain, Tyfen responded as he flipped a page in his book. "If things change and I care to spend time with you, I'll let you know."

My heart ached at his return to callous insults.

"Come on, darling." Hadwin trailed his fingers through mine before stepping out the door with a smile.

I looked at Tyfen a moment longer. "Fine. Be that way." I choked back my crashing hopes.

As I took a step toward the door, Tyfen quietly uttered, "Greedy cunt."

My heart skipped a beat. He'd only ever used that nickname, that insult, in bed last night. I glanced back.

His bright green eyes met mine for the briefest of moments, a tiny grin on his lips before he dropped his gaze and turned another page.

A game. He wanted to play. The smile in my voice was veiled as I returned the insult. "Asshole." Just before I crossed the threshold, I hiked up my dress to expose my bare ass to Tyfen.

"Fuck," he whispered.

Today was going to be a good day after all.

Despite yesterday's confirmation of my pregnancy, nothing unusual disrupted my routine. Hoku blessed her daughters with mild symptoms and healthy wombs. I had mates and partners I still enjoyed time with—in and out of the bedroom. I still had important meetings, too.

I had one such meeting with the emperor and magistrate right after dinner. We discussed how the news of my conception had already been sent out to the territory leaders, and spoke about upcoming events. Nothing groundbreaking, really.

As I strolled the long distance to my chambers, my mind rested on Tyfen again. After our little playful moment before breakfast, he'd joined the rest of us to eat. We hadn't spoken a single word to each other since then, not at lunch or dinner or between. He had glanced at me a couple of times in the common room, though. If Tyfen wanted to play the game of us still loathing each other, I'd let him be in charge.

I exited the last corridor on my return from the center of the palace, entering my private tower, then rounded the corner.

None other than Tyfen stood in the hallway, his arms folded as he leaned back against the wall.

I stopped in my tracks. "Hi."

He turned, eyeing me. "Finally."

I was giddy but nervous. "You've been waiting for me?"

Tyfen nodded. "Let me show you something." He held out his hand, grinning.

With an arched eyebrow, I stepped forward and took his hand. We passed a few lit sconces. His hand caressed mine, strong and warm. Without warning, he opened a small door, pulled me into the dark room, and closed us in.

"This is a storage closet..." I said.

He held my chin. "That it is." His lips pressed to mine.

My chest tightened. "You want to show me a storage closet?" I kidded.

"I want to show you a good time in one." He kissed me again.

I giggled. He was adorable when he wanted to be. I no longer cared why he'd so abruptly changed, so long as he continued to be this way with me.

One kiss became two, then four and more. His hand moved to my dress, sliding its way in to caress my breast. I panted, tingling with want.

"It was"—he kissed me—"a long day … waiting … to get you alone," he said between stolen kisses.

I nibbled on his lip, wrapping my arms around his neck. "You could have asked earlier."

His other hand slid my dress strap off, making it easier to fondle my other tit. "And your stupid meeting took so long."

He tasted good and felt great. Still, I pulled back. "We need to talk politics… You and me."

"Not right now, we don't." He released my breast and glided his hands down my body until he reached his belt.

I drew a deep breath. "This morning and now… Do you not want the others to know we're…" What exactly were we? What exactly were we doing?

The closet quieted. "I'm not sure. I think it's more fun this way. I guess if you want, I don't mind the others knowing." He added with more of a grumble, "Granted, I'd rather Findlech keep his pointy ears out of my business."

Ah, yes—the one-sided hatred neither would tell me about…

Regardless, it was kind of fun having a secret affair with Tyfen to spice things up. "I'm fine keeping it between us, as long as you don't plan to always fuck me in dark closets."

His chuckle was deep and sexy. "I can work with that." His pants fell to the floor.

I put a hand on his deliciously thick cock as his hand went up my short dress.

"Why did you put underwear on?" Commanding and bossy, he pressed me to himself.

I kissed him again. "I think they're pretty."

His lips were against mine. "Take them off."

If he was going to order me around, I would give him some grief. "No."

"Fucking take them off, or I'll tear them off," he uttered through clenched teeth.

My smile only grew. I whispered against his lips again. "Such a demanding asshole. *Some* underwear is more accessible than others…"

His hand shot from my ass to my pussy and teased at the opening of my crotchless underwear. "Why didn't you say so?"

I hummed my reply as I reached up and rubbed the pointed arch of his ear. He shuddered, one hand flicking up to hold my back as the other hiked my knee up, leaning me against him.

My core was on fire, my breathing heavy in this silly little room. I wrapped my arms around his neck again as he glided his cock inside me.

VENUS COX

***

The next week was a whirlwind of activity and organization. I sent my mother a letter and quickly got a reply of congratulations.

Despite my and Findlech's differences, his idea to coordinate time with lovers wasn't horrible. I tried to be a little less impulsive, planning specific nights with my men, sometimes sharing and other times one-on-one. I claimed two nights a week to myself, though one of those was secretly for Tyfen in his room.

Gald and Elion shared me in bed one night—I loved that the two of them were willing to coordinate. Lilah painted me nude to mark the announcement of my conception, and then sketched Gald fucking me for the first time. The painting was beautiful, the sketch hot. The long kiss I stole with Lilah set my core ablaze.

Hadwin and I experimented with trickier bite locations for blood play. His cold cock and warm smile were always welcome in my life.

My anxiety about Haan grew, that he'd lost out on the chance to be my child's sire. The different races had different lengths of pregnancies, though it didn't exactly look the same for a Blessed Vessel. At the shortest, a merfolk mixling would probably have a six-month gestation. At the longest, fae and elf mixling gestations ran around a year.

Since a pregnancy with Haan's child would be so short, that meant the cravings would usually hit before any others would. I hadn't started craving fish any more than usual, especially not raw. It wouldn't be conclusive until the mage midwife confirmed the paternity, but my hope for Haan started to slip away. We didn't speak of it, but it hung in the air as we carried on.

As for Tyfen, I loved our dynamic. We still didn't see eye to eye a lot. He got defensive and dismissive at times when we did finally delve into the political nature of our duties with each other. He swore his father's unicorn adornments had all been harvested before the laws had changed, and he didn't like the accusations both vampires and shifters laid at the fae's doorstep about encroaching upon their lands. He especially didn't like the mention of merchildren being netted in fae waters and sold.

We traded barb for barb. I thought he should be better prepared to answer those questions; he thought I shouldn't expect him to single-handedly stand trial or make reparations for his parents' and people's actions. It was true he wasn't a policymaker as the second-born prince, but it was the responsibility of a Coterie member to navigate these issues, to strive for change and to prepare the next ruler to have a healthy mindset.

As usual, we yelled it out, then fucked it out, then calmed and spoke more rationally. It wasn't exactly hate sex, and while I tried to be civil, I didn't exactly dislike when things went that route either.

Despite the occasional disagreement-turned-argument, we were growing closer, still in secret. It was fun sneaking into his room or hiding somewhere new for sex. Between my time with Gald and my time with Tyfen, my playroom got plenty of use.

I also concealed the truth from my Coterie a lot. I sometimes felt guilty, but not too much. I frequently used Lilah as an alibi to meet up with Tyfen. While Lilah didn't realize I was doing it, I still visited her after Tyfen and I went our own ways, just to keep the story up. She was happy for the visits.

After the first week of our new arrangement, Tyfen gifted me a bracelet. It was simple compared to my other jewelry—twisted black leather strands that wrapped around my wrist. It was more than jewelry—like our relationship, it had a secret. When undone, the strands became a great tool for punishment. Since I didn't always want to be submissive, even with my own bratty style, I wore it on days I wanted him to be in full control. The way he subtly checked my wrist every morning…

Soon enough, two weeks had flown by after the confirmation of my pregnancy. My Coterie and I had been together for six weeks. Lilah left the palace for a few days to visit family and a girlfriend. She gave me the sweetest hug and kiss before going. It made me feel even guiltier that I still hadn't told her about Tyfen and me. I would … soon… For the time being, Tyfen and I got a little more creative with our lies to meet up once or twice a day for sex.

He still wasn't terribly open about himself, but I kept trying. He had the brightest smile and sexiest laugh when it was the two of us trading stories of our childhoods and how different our upbringing had been. He had the darkest scowl on bad days, and those were the days he clammed up the most. I tried to not take it personally.

5
The Challenge

Tyfen liked a good challenge, and in more than one way was good at rising to the occasion. I'd been forced to use my safety word a couple more times since coming up with it.

This time, I may have bitten off more than I could chew. He would try to prove me wrong about his endurance, and I would try to prove to myself I could actually handle my own challenge without tapping out.

"Eyes on mine," he ordered as I knelt on a mat in the playroom. I wasn't allowed to admire the rest of his body as he stripped.

I soaked up every moment we got together. My pleasure instructors had taught me tons of positions to work around a swollen belly, so I wasn't concerned about continuing to enjoy sex. But I was worried Tyfen may not be as rough with me as I wanted when things progressed. Gald and Elion were still both good about not holding back, but Hadwin and Tyfen had both become more cautious. Hadwin took less blood, though he didn't need to hold back. Tyfen switched from dominant asshole to practically panicked sweetheart when I used my safety word.

I no longer feared a loveless life—I was lucky; I had love in spades. Now, I feared them all using kid gloves with me.

So, I gazed into Tyfen's beautiful green eyes as he slowly took off his clothes, one item at a time. He barely blinked as he did the job. Unable to help myself after he reached down, after cloth hit the mat, I stole a peek at his cock.

"That's once," he chastised.

I looked away, blushing.

"Looking away is also against the rules, Sonta."

My eyes snapped to his. I pursed my lips.

Tyfen angled his head. "Greedy fucking cunt. We're barely getting started…"

I held back a laugh. I was trying to be less of a brat today.

"Eyes on mine and stand up."

I followed directions, and he approached me. "No touching."

Groaning, I frowned.

His smile only grew. "Fine. Turn around if it's so hard to control yourself."

I did, and he pulled my dress straps down, allowing my dress to fall to the floor. He set to work on my corset, roughly tugging it. Each jostle made me wetter for him. After he got it off, he tossed it to the side, then pulled my underwear down.

"Take your hair down."

I followed orders, my hair cascading over my shoulders and back.

Tyfen pulled my hair to the side, then slid his arms around me to caress my breasts. I couldn't help but lean into him as his cock pressed against my ass. In the smallest whisper, he asked me how I was feeling.

"Great." It took everything I had to not grind against him. "You forgot my bracelet."

A deep purr rolled in his throat. "That stays on in case we need it."

He glided a hand down and slipped a finger through my labia, straight to my entrance. He fingered me, and my breathing picked up. He gave a satisfied hum as he hardened against me. "You earned your nickname, didn't you?"

I nodded.

After taking his finger out, he licked it clean. "Sweet almond."

It was a silly thing the public didn't know about, but something I'd learned from the Blessed Vessel diaries passed down over the centuries. We tasted and smelled different to the different races, something that appealed to each of them. I'd enjoyed finding out what I was like for each of them—Findlech and Haan obviously excluded. Lilah and my pleasure instructors had agreed I tasted more like strawberries.

"Turn around and on your knees again." He backed up, and I obeyed.

My mouth watered at the brief glimpse I got of his cock before he turned to grab a chair from the corner. Then I stared at his ass until he returned. With his typical swagger, he sat on the chair, his legs open.

"First round."

I wanted him inside me already, and not just in my mouth, but this was my own fault. I'd taunted him, saying he couldn't *possibly* come three times in a row. He'd met my challenge by saying he'd do it his way in my mouth, pussy, and ass. We'd actually shaken on it, then I'd giggled.

Tyfen gestured to his cock. "Show me what that big mouth can do."

I scowled, and he scowled right back to put me in my place. Scooting forward, I grasped him at his base. I'd already sucked him off once, but it hadn't gone all that well. I'd never before struggled to give a man head until Tyfen, but he was genuinely just that big.

Licking his tip, I gently pumped with my hands. We kept eye contact, and I loved it as my tongue explored him, as it caressed the underside of his cock each time I took him deeper, then pulled back.

His hands rested on his thighs. I loved his groans and increased tension as I took my time, as I quickened my pace.

When we were halfway there, I glided a hand up his inner thigh and ever so lightly massaged his balls.

The more he tensed, the faster and harder I sucked. I took him in deep as he came, his salty seed draining down my throat.

"That's my good girl," he panted.

I smiled, lazily sucking him clean. He went to pull out, but I couldn't resist softly closing my teeth on his cock.

His eyes widened. "Let me go."

I ran my tongue over him again as his expression darkened. Then I freed him. Straightening in his chair, he grasped my jaw. "No games."

I pouted. He was sexy when he was angry or flustered.

"Give me your wrist," he muttered.

Biting my lip, I held it up. He unwrapped my bracelet and stood. "Bend over."

Smirking, I obeyed, and I enjoyed the sting on my ass both times he whipped me with the leather.

"Are you going to cooperate now?"

"I think so..."

"You *think* so?"

While I was having fun, I didn't want to make him too mad tonight. "Yes. I'll cooperate."

"Good. Sit up."

I did, crossing my legs and licking my lips. One of three penetrations down.

Tyfen set my bracelet on a nearby table. He offered me water, but wouldn't let me hold the glass. He poured the water into my mouth.

I didn't mind following Tyfen's rules during sex. He was fun.

"Ready to go ahead?" he asked.

Fidgeting with my hands, I stood on my tiptoes. "Could I have a kiss first?"

He squinted. "I have a hard time trusting you after your teeth scraped my cock..."

I couldn't blame him, but I frowned.

He pressed his hand to my throat, applying barely any pressure at all. "One kiss. No touching me."

I clasped my hands despite my desire to explore him. He leaned in and gave me a soft kiss. Even after he pulled away, his hand stayed on my neck, his thumb softly grazing my skin. After stealing a second kiss, he let me go.

He strode to a set of drawers and pulled out a blindfold. I admired his ass again when he turned away from me, then met his eyes on his return.

After blindfolding me, he picked me up. There were a lot of activities to do in here…

He was careful with his placement when he eased me down, and I instantly recognized the setup. One of my pleasure instructors had enjoyed this, affectionately calling it 'the spreader.'

A narrow seat had been mounted to the wall, making my pussy easily accessible. My legs rested in stirrups.

Tyfen quickly discovered how to adjust the height. Blindfolded, I had fun simply listening as he prepared me.

After he had me as high as he wanted, he took my hands and cuffed them above my head with restraints secured to the wall. No seeing, no touching. I would surrender it all to him.

"You remember your word?" he whispered.

"Yes." I smiled at the challenge. I never took my safety word lightly.

With a click of the chair, my legs opened wider. And another click. And another. I was snug in the spreader, my hips gently opening as Tyfen adjusted it.

I was flexible, but even I had my limit. It started to get painful.

He clicked again.

I didn't use my safety word, but my grimace betrayed me. He took it down a notch, then caressed my hips, massaging me to loosen me further.

Tyfen could never be *just* an asshole to me anymore. Not when his torture was tinted with sweetness.

After I'd had time to relax my muscles, he retightened that last setting.

Without warning, his finger slid into my entrance. I panted out a breath. His lips circled my nipple as he gently pumped me. I moaned as he warmed me. I was already wet for him, but I wouldn't turn down the extra attention.

Not that I had much of a choice in the matter.

He didn't linger too long, withdrawing his finger and barely grazing my clit. His mouth worked both of my tits in turn.

Sliding his hands onto my waist, he pressed his chest against mine, claiming my mouth again. His tongue could do no wrong, not even when there was an insult on the end of it.

"Is my greedy cunt ready?" he asked.

My whole body ached for him. "Yes."

One of his hands left my waist, and my anticipation grew. My hands tied, my legs splayed, there wasn't a lot I could do in the way of thrusting or grinding. I was his plaything.

With his first powerful thrust, I gasped.

This fae was a muscled trained soldier. A man who drove into me as if starved for more depth inside me.

As much as I normally enjoyed eye contact during sex, I also loved the surprise and mystery of being blindfolded. Our breath and pleasure mingled as he kept plunging into me, and each time he changed his angle, he adjusted his hand placement. On my waist, my breasts, my thighs, and on the wall behind me, his fingers caught in my hair.

"Tell me how much you love it, Sonta."

It was hard to form words or even thoughts. "I love it." Something akin to a whimper escaped my lips.

His voice was gravelly as he plunged into me again. "How much?"

Every nerve screamed for release, pushed to the edge. "Fuck. I…"

His cock hit that place deep inside me that tickled a special kind of buildup, a soul-shattering release.

My orgasm was explosive, intensifying as he thrust a couple more times.

I couldn't find my breath as he filled me, as he called my name, as we shook together.

Not a single woman in this realm could be angry about filling the role of Blessed Vessel, not when she was assigned the best of the best.

Tyfen pressed against me, still inside me, his breath sweet in my ears as we cooled. He lazily kissed my neck.

After another minute there, his lips grazed my ear. "Ready for round three?"

I unsuccessfully fought a smirk. "You still think you can manage it?"

He pinched my nipple, and I yelped.

"What did you just say?" he asked.

"I'm ready."

He freed my hands. "Hold my neck."

Why did he always smell good? I slid my arms around him as he released the tension of the spreader and picked me up. My legs hugged him as he carried me back to the mat. I found his lips and kissed him without permission. He didn't bark at that.

After he set me down, I asked if I could take off the blindfold. He said no.

So, I waited patiently on the floor, my pussy tender. He moved the mats around me, then repositioned me on all fours. I was already pretty spent, so I was grateful for the soft pillow to lean over.

The mat rustled behind me as he knelt. His large hands roamed my curves, one caressing the cheek he'd punished me on. "Does it hurt?"

I hummed. It still stung a little as he touched it, but the welt wouldn't last long.

He kissed it. "You're fucking beautiful, you know that?"

My smile was soft. "Thank you." I considered making a snide remark to tease him, but I didn't. "You're gorgeous."

He didn't give a cocky reply. "Are you ready for me to fuck you one more time?"

I adjusted my position, presenting my ass. "Yes."

He nudged my legs open, then slid himself into my center again. He was already dripping from the last penetration, but I was grateful he made sure he was topped up for this one.

Now he pressed his cock to my back entrance and eased in, allowing me to stretch as he did so.

He had two more centuries of experience than me, and it was laughable I'd mocked him once for not knowing how to get me wet. The tables had turned.

Gently, he thrust in and out. It took a while for him to build up, having already given himself to me twice so recently. I made sure to let him know it felt good, and he repaid the favor.

He grew close to his third release, and me my second. As he neared, he slid a hand to my clit. I shuddered, and his friction brought me to completion. He followed soon after.

Tyfen held me, buried inside me. We were sticky and sweaty, both spent and both successful in our challenge. After another minute, he withdrew, holding my hips.

He took off my blindfold. "Get comfortable. I'll clean up."

After washing himself, he wiped me down. I hadn't moved a muscle, just hugging my giant pillow while on my knees.

Joining me on the mat, he pulled me to him, kissing my forehead. I smiled and wrapped a leg over him. "I like this Tyfen."

His smile was sexy, his eyes dazzling. "I like my Sonta."

My heart fluttered. I wasn't just Sonta; I was *his* Sonta.

"How do you feel?" His hand lingered on my waist, a thumb stroking my stomach.

Spiritually and emotionally, I was completely fulfilled. I was blessed in more than one way. If he was talking about my unborn child, worried about my safety again—things were fine there, too.

"Happy and healthy."

He searched my eyes, moving a strand of hair away from my face. "Good."

I loved Tyfen. Not just for the sex and the fun secrecy. Not just because he was sworn to me and we were political allies. I loved the part of him that bossed me around when he needed control, but also the part of him that was quick to respond to my needs. He was flexible and strong. He was sweet and playful in his own way.

I hadn't actually said the words 'I love you.' He hadn't either. My heart was still cautious with him, and it might always stay that way, with him closed off the way he was. I prayed he'd find the courage to fully trust me with his heart and life someday. For now, I kept reaching out to him, kept trying to be patient.

"Did you enjoy yourself?" I asked, gently rubbing his sensitive arched ears.

He closed his eyes, moaning. "Hell yes." He angled his head away to stop me from touching his ear. "Fucking you is my favorite battlefield."

I chuckled, kissing him. We lay there on the playroom mat for some time, wrapped up in each other.

"My bedroom?" he eventually confirmed. It was one of my 'sleep alone in my chambers' nights where I secretly planned to be with him.

"Yes. Mind if I do one last thing first?" I traced the tattoos on his neck and pecs. "I had a vision earlier today, and I always like to paint them the same day."

I'd invited most of the men up to my studio already. Even Haan had swum up to check it out, though the tank in the room was quite small. I'd never been comfortable inviting Findlech up, though. Not after he'd been oddly cold about one of my vision sketches, saying Hoku never should have blessed me with that.

Part of me still feared I was too sensitive with Tyfen. If I took him up there and he mocked my lack of skill, my pride couldn't take the blow. But in the moment, I felt strong. We'd come far. "Would you like to join me? I can show you my paintings…"

He planted one more kiss on my lips. "I'd love that."

6

The Haunted Painting

Tyfen and I dressed, then cleaned up the playroom. The servants always had their hands full, but I didn't want to constantly traumatize them with my lifestyle. I liked that Tyfen didn't mind getting his hands dirty. Having grown up poor, I was used to dressing myself and keeping things tidy when my mother had to work, but Tyfen had been born and raised a prince. He wasn't just a pampered asshole. He worked hard in his responsibilities to his kingdom, and didn't hesitate to help me with these menial tasks.

Before we left the playroom, he pulled me in for another kiss, soft and sweet. "I love—" He stole another kiss, and my heart fluttered. Was he going to say it? "—spending so much time with you."

His smile was genuine, and my hopes only stuttered a little. Time and patience—that was all he needed. At least he no longer said he hated how much he loved being with me…

"Me too." I caressed his cheek. "Let's check out my studio."

We were usually much sneakier than this when meeting up, but it was late. While we took the back stairs to get to the level my studio was on, we didn't hide that we were together. We held hands the whole way.

I led Tyfen into my studio. His eyes lit up instantly, staring at the walls covered with my paintings. "This is amazing."

I threw my arms around him. "Thank you."

He gently rubbed my back, his gaze slowly taking it in. "These are all your paintings?"

"Yes."

"All from visions Hoku's given you?"

I nodded. "Do you want to look at them while I paint my vision, or do you want a bit of a tour?"

"I'd love a tour from the artist." He smiled.

"Your wish is my command." I hooked my arm through his, and we walked to the far side of the room. I explained how the rougher ones were obviously from my childhood. He asked why I organized them by color instead of chronologically. I simply liked it that way.

His face and voice exuded adoration. "It reminds me of your first dress at the banquet before the Great Ritual. That sparkly colorful number."

I raised an eyebrow. He'd acted so indifferent, so disinterested. "You were paying attention?"

He looked away, uncharacteristically shy. "Of course I paid attention."

I leaned into him. "Lilah suggested I make copies of the paintings and bind them into a book for the baby."

"That's a wonderful idea, Sonta." His voice was soft as his gaze roamed the paintings.

Not all my paintings were easy to group into a specific color, so I usually went with the predominant color, or the mood of the vision that had inspired it.

We stood in front of the green section. I pointed to one I'd painted over a month ago. "This one still bugs me." Findlech had been so elusive about it—the one with ancient Elvish pertaining to the high lord's family. Neither Gald nor Hadwin had been able to help me understand the mystery behind it.

I'd grouped it with the green paintings—despite the partially brown mountains, the autumn leaf colors, and the grey stone—because of the still-bright green grass. The green grass, kissed by morning dew in my vision, matched Tyfen's eyes.

I turned to him to say so. Tyfen stared at the painting, his breathing uneasy, his face pale, as if he stared into the face of merciless death itself.

"Are you okay?" I asked.

"That…" His throat bobbed. "That…" He pointed at it. "You saw *this* in a vision?"

All confusion, I nodded.

"From Hoku?"

"Yes… The visions are a gift to her mortal daughters."

Tyfen's eyes were glued to it. He shook his head.

I narrowed my eyes. "You know this place?"

He snatched it off the wall, tearing it where the pin had held it in place.

"Hey!"

His expression a rush of confusion and anger, he glanced from the painting to me. "When? When did she show you this place?"

Did it matter? She showed me the past and present, all of it soft impressions. Why was a fae getting so worked up about an elven site?

I tried to calm him, resting a hand on his arm. I smiled a bit as I recalled the exact night I'd had that vision. "I had it after you left my room. That first night after the celebration when you came into my room, begging me for sex."

He looked positively ill. Like he may vomit.

Tyfen recoiled from my touch. "No. You're the last person this vision should have been given to. She had no *fucking* right."

I gaped.

He crumpled the paper in his fist.

"Tyfen!" So few people had access to my visions and the paintings of them. None of them had ever disrespected or damaged them this way. "Give that to me now!"

His fist tightened as he backed up. "No." He searched my eyes, panicked. "Why? Why would she send this to you? I thought she was kind, not cruel."

I blinked. "She *is* kind…"

"No." He shook his head again, his grip tight on the wad of paper. "No. No. No."

I stepped forward. "What's wrong?"

He stepped away again. "No." With each repetition of the word, he became a shell of the strong and dominant man I'd come to love. Tears coated his eyes.

"Please," I pleaded. "I can help."

Swallowing, he turned and strode to the door. He kept muttering "no" as he opened it. I flinched as he slammed it shut behind him.

I stood there, alone, incapable of understanding what the hell had just happened. Hugging myself, I stared at the closed door. Should I go after him? Let him cool off and sort things himself before discussing it?

Seeing him that way made me hollow. It wouldn't go well, though, if I chased after him to demand more answers, to try to calm him.

I sank onto my chair, staring at the wall for a while. I was numb, my heart hurting. My fingers trailed over the leather bracelet he'd given me.

Tears came to my eyes. While I still had hope we'd sort things out, I hated this feeling. His claiming hickey had disappeared. His leather bracelet was removable. I didn't need a permanent mark to signify a relationship just because I had one with Hadwin, Elion, and Gald, but the lack of permanence with Tyfen twisted my stomach. Would he get tired of me? Was what we had still too shallow?

My hands rested on my stomach. *What if this child isn't his?* Would he leave me?

I drew a few deep breaths. I needed to be calm. Whatever had bothered him didn't change who I was or my calling. He'd been spooked by something, but he would come around.

Maybe. As an immortal being, he perceived time differently. He'd alluded to him eventually opening up to discuss things from his past, but what was his timeline? When I was on my deathbed and he still looked like a strapping, youthful man?

Needing a distraction, hoping he'd return in a while to explain, I forced myself to face the task I'd come here for in the first place. I prepped my painting table with my water paints, my actions slow as though I crawled through a vat of honey.

It wasn't my best painting, but the scenic cavern was beautiful, a yellow sun bright in the sky. I blew on it to help it dry, tired and worn both physically and emotionally.

VENUS COX

 Tyfen never returned with my painting or an explanation. I picked a spot in the brown section for this new vision and pinned it there. The soil and rock were like my heart and mind at the moment—muddy.

 Sconces crackled softly as I walked the corridors alone. I peeked into the common room, not surprised to find it empty. He would have gone to his room to hide from me and whatever feelings he had. I resisted the urge to go see him; I couldn't bear him shutting me out again or getting angry for pressing the issue.

 I went to my room, my heart hurting more as I removed his bracelet to bathe. My bed was entirely too large as I slipped under the sheets alone.

 No matter how much I analyzed Tyfen's actions and reactions, I never made progress. Eventually, the trickle of the pond in my room lulled me to solo slumber.

7
Back at the Bottle

When I entered the common room in the morning, Tyfen was a no-show. That hollowness in my heart from the night before lingered despite the warm greetings from the rest of my Coterie.

Hadwin's hug and kiss were sweet, his hazel eyes divine. Haan was friendly, as was Findlech. Gald grabbed my ass and made a vulgar comment I would normally have laughed at.

After breakfast, Elion made love to me, then took me on a walk around the grounds. He asked me what was wrong, but I didn't know how to explain myself. My relationship with Tyfen was still new, complicated, and secret. But he'd stolen my painting and crumpled it up. It was almost as if it were my heart he'd stolen and crumpled.

In the end, I evaded the question, snuggling up to Elion and talking about the summer weather.

Tyfen still didn't show by lunchtime. I let Gald fuck me after that. The panting and moans occupied my mind and body for a time, and I did my best to focus on our relationship alone while we were together. But my mind lingered on Tyfen's absence after we parted ways.

Hadwin's cold cock and loving gaze after dinnertime helped me better remember I was very loved, and that one man's irrational behavior shouldn't topple me. I sat on his lap after we rejoined the others in the common room. We chatted with Haan, who regaled us with the most charming stories about his youth amidst the deep-sea merfolk. Hadwin's arms around me, Elion's watchful smile as he sat near, and Haan's sexy voice couldn't be beat.

It was Hadwin's turn to share my bed. He knew something was wrong and was respectful when I declined to talk about it. He'd already voiced how he didn't like the way Tyfen treated me; I wouldn't shame myself by admitting I'd trusted Tyfen with my heart and he'd crumpled it.

I was being too dramatic, anyway. It wasn't like he'd left me for good. He was just hiding out in his room while he sorted his emotions…

I hoped.

Either way, Hadwin offered to make love to me again, and I took the opportunity. The way he worshiped me, filled me, and caressed me was incomparable.

He held me after we blew out the candles and went to bed.

I couldn't fall asleep. After an hour of tossing and turning, I kissed Hadwin. "I need to go take care of something."

He caressed my hip. "Anything I can help with?"

"No, but thank you." I didn't want him walking into Tyfen's and my drama, and I didn't know how long I'd be up with Tyfen. "Stay here? I might be a while, but I'll be back."

He stole another kiss. "Okay. Love you, darling."

My heart fluttered as it always did with him. "Love you too."

After throwing on a robe, I strode to Tyfen's door. I knocked, but no answer came.

I waited, hugging myself. After a minute, I knocked again, a little louder and longer. I leaned in close. "Tyfen?"

No response.

Please don't do this.

A third time, I knocked. "Tyfen? I know you're in there." I actually didn't, but it stood to reason he was.

"Go away, Sonta," he called from the other side of the door.

I frowned. "I just want to talk."

"Please. Leave me alone."

I held my hand to the door for a moment, my feelings stuck in my throat. "Please don't push me away."

His response was little more than a murmur. "I'm not in the mood to talk. Go to bed."

I lingered. Usually, Coterie members clamored at the chance to be with the Blessed Vessel, to get in her good graces, even if it was solely for politics. Tyfen had never done a good job of that.

Sighing, I resigned myself to leave. "Good night."

He didn't speak again, and I left.

Hadwin welcomed me back to bed with a kiss and a cuddle. "That was a quicker errand than I expected."

"Yeah," I whispered as I nuzzled his neck.

***

Tyfen didn't leave his room the next day either. I tried to keep up my mood and let him work through whatever he needed to. I let Elion have his way with me at bedtime, and I gasped through the pleasure and pain. We chatted as we grew tired. While I liked his naked form huddled around mine as we slept, I wanted something a little different.

"Would you mind if I cuddled you in your wolf form?"

He eagerly agreed, shifting and cuddling up to me again. I stroked his soft fur. He had a calming presence when he wasn't overprotective or desperate to bed me.

"I love my mate," I whispered, running my fingers through his fur again.

He licked my hand; it brought a smile to my face.

On the third day with Tyfen holed up in his room, Findlech said something at dinner, wondering if someone should check on him.

Of course, all eyes turned to me. "I'll take care of it." After eating, I spoke with a servant to confirm Tyfen was at least having food delivered to his room. She confirmed he had been ordering and receiving some.

It was Haan's night to share a room with me. I asked him privately if he was all right skipping this week, just in case. He was always thoughtful and generous. Granted, we never actually shared a bed, so when he slumbered in either of our ponds, there wasn't much we actually shared.

A group of us sat together in the common room, trading stories. The long couch easily fit four of us. It was sweet having Elion's hand on one of my thighs and Gald's on the other. To add to it, Gald's other hand was on Findlech's thigh. They still didn't generally show any outward flirtation or affection around us, but this small instance was truly endearing.

A knock sounded at the common room door from the main hallway. Hadwin jumped up and opened it.

A servant girl popped her head in. "Your Holiness, you asked to be notified?"

My heart pumped faster. "Yes, thank you. I'll be right out."

I kissed Gald and wished him a good night. As I pulled back, my eye caught on his hands. He'd taken his hand off Findlech's leg while the servant was near. I tried not to frown as I bid Findlech good night.

"Good night," Findlech wished with his small type of smile.

Elion gave me a giant hug and kiss, as did Hadwin on my way out.

I followed the servant girl, grateful for the timing. I'd asked the Coterie servants to notify me if Tyfen ordered any deliveries to his room. I wouldn't risk him turning me down at his regular door again.

She led me to the paternal service hallway that led to each of the men's doors.

Tyfen's food order sat on a tray next to his servants' door. The servant stayed back at my request as I knocked and picked up the tray.

It didn't take long for Tyfen to open his door. He only wore his shorts. Surprise was painted on his face at seeing me. "Sonta…" His breath carried alcohol to my nose.

Before he could deny me entrance or shut the door in my face, I ducked under his arm, squeezing into his chambers.

He spun. "I don't want to talk."

I shrugged, setting his tray on a small table. "Then we won't talk. I'll just sit with you while you enjoy your late dinner."

Narrowing his eyes, he grunted. "Is that a hobby I don't know about? Watching people eat?"

I smiled wryly. "Yes. Very erotic." Not giving him an option, I walked into his bedroom to sit. It was … not pretty. In his three days of isolation, he'd obviously had a rough go of it. He hadn't let the cleaning staff in—the bed was unmade, his clothes from when we'd been in my painting studio were strewn on the floor, a couple of things were also askew, and several uncorked wine bottles had collected on a side table.

My heart twisted at the sight, but I eased myself down onto a chair.

The servants' door latched, and Tyfen stalked back into the room, carrying his tray of food. Instead of sitting with me, he sat on his bed, ignoring me.

I watched in silence, fighting the urge to scold him for acting this way, as he cut into a steak. He was handsome as ever, even with his hair a mess. Continuing to ignore me, he ate a few mouthfuls. He grabbed an open wine bottle by his bed and took a healthy swig.

Sighing, I stood. After finding a pitcher for water, I filled it from the tap, then poured a glass. I carried it to him. "Here. I'll trade you for the bottle."

He glared at me, dark and threatening. "I'm finishing this bottle."

One would have thought I'd tried to steal fresh prey from a wolf, or me from Elion in the bedding chamber. I was tempted to try to take the bottle as I had before. The knife and fork in his hand made me think twice. Tyfen wouldn't actually hurt me, but it gave me pause…

"Fine. But you should still drink water for hydration." I gingerly set it on his bedside table.

"Thanks," he whispered.

"You're welcome." The table was crowded. Three wine bottles sat on it, all empty. The man could certainly hold his liquor.

I grabbed the three bottles and their corks in an attempt to tidy the room.

"What are you doing?"

I didn't respond, carrying them to the sitting area to join the other two empty bottles in there. I sighed. "Who do we need to fire for bringing these to your room?"

His cutlery clanged on his plate. "Are you really that much of a bitch?"

I squinted. "Excuse me?"

"You'd fire a servant for bringing me wine? You'd be so callous?"

"I ordered them not to bring any to your room." I gestured at him. "For your own fucking good, *asshole*!"

He rolled his eyes. "What if it was my aide? Will you fire a servant who's not your own?"

I hadn't really considered an aide sneaking it in. I had no authority over the servants he'd brought with him, at least not regarding their employ over something like this. "*Was* it one of your people? I deserve to know if one of my own people would betray me."

He picked up his cutlery again. "It was neither my servants nor the palace-assigned Coterie servants."

Plopping on a chair again, I glanced at him skeptically. "Magic?" The kind of magic that could bring objects into or through the palace was extremely limited, kept at bay by wards.

"No… You may have tainted the Coterie servants against me, but the kitchen staff doesn't know about the restriction." He took a healthy bite of fried potato.

I pinched the bridge of my nose. "You nicked a half dozen bottles from the kitchens?"

He gave me a bright, disingenuous smile.

"Lovely," I drawled.

"Thank you. As a commander, I'd hope I have a *few* techniques for achieving my goals."

"What are your goals?" I asked softly. "With me? With us?" This behavior was a massive leap backward for us.

He locked eyes with me, his brow furrowed. "I told you I don't want to talk." His tone oozed warning. I wanted to push him. Maybe if he screamed at me, at least he'd scream something that made sense. But I wasn't ready for him to hurt me further, or to have him kick me out.

I stayed put as he devoured his meal. My eyes trailed across the messy and damaged room. There was a small dent in the wall. Underneath it lay his crown. I couldn't bear to see it on the floor like that. A crown or tiara should never be left that way.

I walked to it and picked it up. I frowned as I inspected it. One of the metal spires was bent. "I'm sure the emperor's blacksmith can make quick work of repairing this."

"I don't give a shit about that crown," Tyfen muttered.

My gaze shot to him, and he looked away. He wasn't the *crown* prince of the fae kingdom, but he was still a *much-loved* prince. He held official duties in his kingdom, and had a major place as a representative for his people by default as my Coterie partner.

He had begged on his knees to be allowed to bed me for the sake of his people. "You don't mean that," I said.

"I do. Don't tell me what I do or don't mean."

"I thought you loved your people."

He cut up the last piece of his steak. "Maybe I deserve to be happy, Sonta. I deserve to *fucking* be happy. I've done enough. I've paid enough." His voice rose. "I want to be happy! Is that so wrong?"

"Of course it's not."

"That's not what Hoku thinks."

I arched an eyebrow. "Why not? What feud does a goddess have with a fae prince?"

He shook his head. "Why don't you ask her?"

It didn't work that way, and he knew it. For now, I replaced his crown on the cushion it usually sat on, then tidied a couple more things.

"Stop cleaning my room. You're not a servant."

"No. I'm not. But you don't want to talk, so I'm keeping busy."

After finishing his food, he placed his tray on the floor by his bed, then grabbed his wine bottle again.

I dared to approach, sliding onto the bed beside him.

He tipped back the bottle.

"I already miss the taste," I said. "Though I prefer white wine."

He barely acknowledged me with a grunt.

"You really went to the kitchen on your own, and they handed you six bottles of wine?"

"Yep. Told them the Coterie was celebrating. No one questions anything in the Coterie—they all imagine we're having fantastic orgies all day every day."

I chuckled. "They probably do." I scooted closer to him, laying my head on his shoulder. "You deserve to be happy, Tyfen."

Silence was his response.

"We don't have to talk if you don't want to. Just…" I didn't want to sleep in this mess, and it would do him good to get out of it. "Just come to my chambers and cuddle with me." I gingerly rested a hand on his thigh.

He said nothing.

I rolled my head to look at him. "We can do more than cuddle. Would you like to fuck me?"

He met my gaze, taking another swig of wine. "Can I fuck you with this bottle?"

I grinned at the hint of playfulness in his voice. "Sure. It wouldn't be the first item shoved up my pussy, and it certainly won't be the last." I lightly trailed my fingernails up and down his thigh.

He let out the smallest smile, though it quickly faded. "I just want to cuddle."

"Okay. No talking, no fucking, all cuddling."

Tyfen blew out a long breath, setting down his bottle. "I need to bathe."

I wasn't going to leave him again in case it was a ploy, and he really needed out of this room. "My large bathtub is bigger than yours."

It took some coaxing, but he agreed to sneak to my room with me. He dressed in a robe, and I gestured to his room on the way out, asking the servant to please tend to it while we were out. We left through the servants' hallways to avoid the common room in case the others were still awake.

We hopped into the bath together, but he wouldn't kiss me or even allow me on his lap. So, I soaked up the warmth and fragrance, running my hands through the water and bubbles as he scrubbed himself down. To avoid utter silence, I tried small talk, and he obliged. We discussed fragrances and colors, though he scarcely looked at me, scarcely spoke in response.

He was a broken man, and I had no idea how to help him mend himself. I didn't know the problem, and I didn't know the solution.

After rinsing and toweling off, he dressed in clean shorts, and I put on a nightie. This time I held him in bed.

I ran a hand through his hair as we lay there. "This is your first time alone with me in my bed," I mused. The first night, he'd slept on the far end away from me, and I hadn't invited him to join me since then.

"Good night, Sonta," he whispered.

I kissed his bare shoulder. "Good night, Tyfen."

8
My Dearest

Despite normally being a sound sleeper, I startled awake in the middle of the night. Tyfen thrashed in bed next to me, yelling something in his native Fae tongue. I knew hardly any Fae words, so I had no idea what he was shouting.

"Tyfen!" I shook him hard. "Tyfen!"

He kept jerking and muttering. What kind of nightmarish beasts had he faced over the years in the deep forests of his kingdom?

I shook harder. "It's okay."

After I repeated his name, his eyes finally shot open. He gasped.

I cradled his face in my hands. "You're all right."

He still seemed dazed as his eyes searched my face in the dark, the room only lit by the faint glow of the twin moons on a cloudy night.

"Nil Day'niair," he whispered.

I still had absolutely no idea what he was saying. "I'm right here."

Drowsy and relieved, he sighed. His eyelids drooped closed as he settled back onto the bed, holding me tight.

He hadn't had nightmares when we'd slept in his room, though he also hadn't been drunk those nights…

Either way, I enjoyed the cuddles, and my own heart calmed as his breathing slowed in peaceful slumber.

He kissed me awake in the morning. I wore the biggest smile and slid a hand under the waistband of his shorts, be he recoiled.

"Sorry. I'm just not feeling it," he said.

I sat up, running a hand through my hair. "That's fine." I wasn't used to rejection, least of all from Tyfen. I wanted release, and I wanted to rekindle things with him, but he'd had a rough night, and a rough few days.

"Do you often have nightmares?"

He pursed his lips. "I woke you."

"It's fine."

"Did I hurt you?" Regret and worry laced his words.

"I'm fine. I promise."

"Okay."

For a minute, the pond's trickle was the only noise in the room. If he didn't want to explain his nightmare, I wouldn't push.

"How about we have breakfast in here? Just the two of us."

He sat up too. "You don't have to coddle me, Sonta. I'm fine. You can spend your time with the others."

I interlaced our fingers. "I can spend my time with you, too. And I wouldn't make the offer if I wasn't keen to…"

The tiniest smile graced his lips.

"Then we're set. I'll order, then let the others know I'm taking breakfast alone." I snuck another kiss and did just that.

The servant at my private door assured me the kitchen would be swift with my order, and I got all the cuddles, kisses, and gropes I could ask for from some of my favorite men in the common room while waiting. Since Tyfen didn't want to bed me, I told Elion he could have me sometime before lunch. He was always happy to assist his mate when it came to that.

Tyfen was still in a somber mood as we sat at my small table to eat in my chambers. He was buzzed, and I wasn't sure what was safe to bring up, considering how things had soured this week.

We talked about the food—I'd ordered some of his favorite fae dishes. The egg dish was a bit undercooked for my liking, but everything else was spot on.

I speared a wedge of peeled citrus. "Would you be up to teaching me some things in Fae?" It was a neutral topic, a way we could possibly spend more time building our relationship. "I was too embarrassed to speak any during the celebration because I know so little, and I'm sure my accent is atrocious."

He guzzled some water. "If you'd like."

Our breakfast had to be short, as I had meetings to attend to. I made him swear to not nick any alcohol from the kitchens. He grumbled and rolled his eyes, but finally agreed. He was going to take a long stroll across the palace grounds to clear his head. Anything was better than the solitude of his room.

***

Some women might resent being predestined to take a lot of cock for the sake of their empire. I mostly resented the constant meetings and tutors, though they wouldn't be so intensive had my identity as Hoku's daughter been recognized at a younger age. It was what it was.

Returning to my tower, I passed a young fae woman. While much of the staff was human or mage-human, we still had several of the other races employed here. My mind had wandered during the dull meeting, fixating on what Tyfen had said to me in bed.

I turned. "You there…"

The girl faced me, her soft features and arched pointy ears all delicate. "Your Holiness?"

"Could I ask you a quick question?"

She smiled. "Of course."

"What does Nil Day'niair mean?" I likely butchered the pronunciation.

But probably not too badly, because her face lit up. "Does our handsome prince call you that?"

My cheeks were instantly on fire. It wasn't right to gossip with the servants, especially when I didn't even know what it meant. *Surely* he hadn't sweetly called me his greedy cunt in Fae amidst a chaotic nightmare…

I just shrugged my response.

"It means 'my dearest,'" she said, positively giddy.

My heart fluttered, and I looked down. I honestly didn't mind his degrading nicknames for me, depending on how and when they were said. But it felt nice to have a sweet one now, too.

"Thank you. That's all I wanted to know."

She curtsied. "Always happy to serve the Blessed Vessel. May Hoku multiply her blessings on you, and on the child in your womb." Her smile was bright as her gaze slid to my stomach.

My brain stuttered for a moment. Would she be this excited and wish me well so readily if the child ended up not belonging to that handsome prince of hers? I quickly recovered, though. Her employment here at the palace meant she was disconnected enough from the service of her own kingdom that hopefully she was of the right mindset of unity.

"Thank you," I said. "May she multiply her blessings on you as well."

We both returned to our business, but I had a skip to my step the entire way back to the common room.

As much as I wanted to be with Tyfen when I returned, he wasn't in the common room. Haan said he'd recently spotted him out by the palace lake while on a swim.

Sometimes, my heart and mind stuck with one of my partners, but I tried to give them an equal amount of my time and affection. While Elion's mating fever had all but subsided, his urges for me still tugged me to him daily.

He held me from behind as we chatted with the others. His swelling cock against my ass certainly helped wet me. He kissed my neck. "Are you getting hungry for lunch?" he whispered.

I grinned. I *had* promised him we'd have sex before lunch. "In a few minutes…" I took his hand, leading him to my chambers.

Gald looked up from the sofa, giving me a wink.

As always, Elion was perfect. Passionate, sweet, happy to be with me. We didn't dawdle long, though, and I was surprised that Tyfen returned to the common room as we were all leaving for the dining hall.

He joined us. Not that he spoke to the others, but it was still good to have him here.

I cut into a slice of ham. Maybe Tyfen could use some encouragement around the others? It would also be nice to not have to sneak around just to convey a message to him.

"Tyfen, would you be up for those Fae lessons we discussed, after lunch?"

He didn't look up from his plate. "Sure."

All the others glanced between Tyfen and me, confused at our civility. Then their gazes drifted to my plate.

Seriously?

I slammed my cutlery on the table. "Will you all please stop that! Stop watching what I'm eating!"

After several days of them studying my food intake, it was getting on my nerves.

"If you can't let me enjoy meals with you in peace, then I'll have to eat by myself until we all learn who the father is together in the paternity reading."

Guilty looks crossed their faces, and a couple of them mumbled apologies.

"There are no surprises here," I added. "I like cock, and I like food."

Gald snickered.

I continued. "So I'll eat my regular meals when we're all together. For all you lot know, I'm secretly downing a buffet of raw prawns and fish when I sneak away, or I'm guzzling gallons of blood nightly. Pregnancy cravings, if there are any, will be between my chef and myself until my midwife's reading."

More guilty looks and nods responded.

Hadwin shrugged. "We meant nothing by it, darling."

If I were in their shoes, my curiosity would be killing me, too. I of course wanted to know, but I was also afraid to find out. It would change our dynamic, and I wasn't ready for that yet.

Then again, it was a little silly for them to assume I'd have cravings with Tyfen's child. Blessed Vessels generally had more consistent cravings when the father was a merman, shifter, or vampire. But, I could understand the men's confusion to some extent. They weren't used to me being civil with Tyfen, or spending special time with him. Everything we did together was a secret since the pregnancy confirmation.

"I promise I'll spend more time learning each of your tongues," I assured the others. "I just thought it would be good to start with Tyfen's, that's all."

"Yep," Tyfen said, dripping disinterest. "It's only right she start with Fae, given the ghastly incident at the celebration and the way she insulted my mother. She has some ass-kissing to do…"

I took a sip of water, my stomach churning. I'd insulted the queen? I genuinely couldn't recall anything of the like.

He looked up from his food, holding a spoonful of seasoned barley. "Sonta attempted to say something to my mother—goddess knows what—but her Fae was so poor, she called my mother a bottom-dwelling whore."

I spat my water out. "You asshole!" He knew damn well I hadn't attempted to utter a single Fae word to his parents.

Tyfen glared at me; only I would recognize that glint in his eye. "Don't blame me for your incompetence, bitch. *You're* the one who insulted my mother!"

I clenched my teeth and swallowed the absolutely traitorous laughter that fought to come out. We played this game well around the others.

Though, they didn't always enjoy it…

"Stop calling her that," Hadwin bit out.

Elion scowled at Tyfen, too. "Sonta would never do that on purpose. Maybe if you got to know her better and stopped being a prick, you'd know that."

I pressed my lips into a thin line, heavy with guilt. Even Gald, Findlech, and Haan flashed Tyfen a look of disapproval. It wasn't right for them to all hate him just because we played this way.

"Fine," Tyfen replied. "I'm sorry, *Your Holiness*. If you'll please stop insulting my mother, I'll try harder to give you the respect the others think you deserve."

I rolled my eyes to lean into it. "Get over yourself."

Findlech piped up. "I, for one, am astounded by how delectable this meal is today."

It was comical how Findlech chose to deflect drama at times, though judging by Tyfen's genuine scowl, he found it less comical.

Drawing a deep breath and letting it out, I sopped up my mess of water. Tyfen's walk had done him some good if he was not only in a mood to eat with us, but also to joke. I obviously owed him a *sincere* apology for the imaginary offense to his mother, and I hoped it would be a naked apology.

Crossing his arms as we left the dining hall, he kept silent. We decided to study in the library. With each footstep, I waited for him to pull me into another closet for fun, but he didn't.

"I'm sorry for offending your mother," I said, grabbing the railing in the last stairwell.

He smirked. "Good."

We climbed the stairs together. "I didn't *actually* offend her, did I?"

"No…" His tone was humorous. "If you'll recall, *I* did my best to offend my parents for the both of us. I'm sure they found you charming."

Right… He'd intentionally made them mad because he hadn't wanted to be assigned to me, for some reason I still didn't understand.

A day at a time…

After we entered the library, he turned to me and held my chin. "I enjoy your wit." His expression was soft.

"Same." I hugged him, and we held each other a moment. "I take it your walk was good?"

"It was."

I smiled, then led him to a couple of chairs in the corner. "So… Learning Fae…"

He ruffled his hair, claiming a chair. "You're sure you want to learn from me? I'm not a teacher. I don't really know where to start…"

I shrugged as I took the chair next to him. "Basic things that would be good for me to know when we're in your kingdom for the imperial tour."

He nodded. "Sure."

"Plus, it's more fun to learn from someone I like." I winked.

His smile was genuine. "I'm happy to help." He stood and grabbed a pad of paper and a pencil. "To keep track."

I lovingly ran a finger across his arm. "You've already taught me a couple of words; that's why I know you'll be a great teacher."

He crossed his legs, furrowing his brow. "I haven't taught you any Fae…"

"Yes you have." I beamed. "Nil Day'niair."

What I *expected* was another cute smirk to acknowledge he'd called me that. Instead, all color drained from his face.

"Did I say it wrong? I asked one of the fae servants. She told me it means 'my dearest.'"

"Yes, it means that." He looked down, still unsettled. "But I didn't teach you that."

"Well, no… We didn't sit down so formally, but you said it to me." I frowned, coaxing him by rubbing his arm. "Last night, when you woke from your nightmare…"

His throat bobbed. "I didn't teach you that. I never would have. And I never would have intentionally called you that."

That was a punch to the gut. "Why not?"

He scrunched his eyes closed, then looked at me. "It's…" He set down the paper and pencil. "We… All of us … in the Coterie… Even young Elion… Even you. We all have pasts. Former … lovers."

My heart stopped beating at precisely the moment my stomach dropped. "That's what you used to call another lover…"

The shame covering his face confirmed just that. My eyes instantly welled up.

Remorse was woven into every bit of his tone, every pore on his handsome face. "I'm so sorry. I don't even remember saying that. I wasn't fully awake. I didn't mean to hurt you."

I wiped away a tear.

"Shit," he whispered.

I couldn't stop the tears, couldn't stop the way it made me feel. I stood and walked toward the door.

"Please, Sonta," he weakly pleaded.

Sniffling, I didn't answer as I left. "Fuck." The waterworks kept pace with my feet as I stormed away—no plan in sight. I'd just needed out of there.

I wasn't mad at him. How could I be? He hadn't been malicious. And I certainly didn't expect him to have never loved someone before. He'd been fairly open about having multiple lovers over his more than two centuries.

If anything, I was mad at myself. I was a stupid girl who had latched on to the idea of him giving me that name. Of me having more importance than I actually had in his eyes. I was mortified to have so proudly told him I knew he thought of me that way. I was ill knowing that servant girl imagined he called me that when he never truly had.

I took the stairs upward. At the top of the stairwell, I crumpled to the floor, holding my knees and sobbing.

I hated this. I hated that Tyfen and I kept hurting each other. Intentionally and unintentionally. Hadwin, Elion, Gald, and Lilah all had pieces of my heart. Even Haan and Findlech had small corners as friends. But their love and friendship could not heal the portion I'd already given Tyfen. That part of my heart was his to deal with. I wished we weren't so mercurial in our relationship.

Naturally, a servant needed to use the stairs. He panicked and wouldn't leave me alone until I told him several times I was fine and didn't need help. He gave me a handkerchief before hesitantly leaving me like I'd asked.

Not ten minutes later, Gald crouched next to me.

"Sonta? Are you okay? What's wrong?"

"I'm fine. Leave me alone, please." I'd finally stopped crying, but my eyes were puffy, my voice nasal.

"Not when you're like this, I won't." He pushed his curls out of his face. "What did Tyfen do?"

"Nothing," I replied weakly.

"That's a load of shit. You left to go study with him less than half an hour ago, and now I stumble across you like this?"

My shoulders slumped. "It's not like that."

"Stop letting him treat you this way."

I looked into Gald's beautiful blue eyes. "Do you love me?"

"You know I do."

"Then trust I can handle myself. And please go. I just want to be alone right now."

He wrinkled his nose. "It's not fair to demand things that way."

I wiped my nose with the tiniest bit of my handkerchief.

Gald sighed, pulling out his own handkerchief and handing it to me. "I'll go. I'll be in the common room if you want to talk. And I'm packing my wand if you need me to find Tyfen…"

"I'll let you know if I want to talk."

He sighed again, then kissed me on the forehead and left.

I was pathetic. Utterly pathetic. I'd never been so emotionally fragile before. I was made of tougher stuff.

The facts didn't lie, though. Perhaps it was pregnancy hormones? That was a thing, though it didn't happen to every woman, and I hadn't really read in the Blessed Vessel journals about previous daughters of Hoku struggling with it. They were usually pretty frank.

I blew out a breath and told myself I could only wallow a few more minutes before picking myself up.

And that was exactly what I did. I sat back, running my hand over my belly. Soon, I would discover whose child this was. I was excited and terrified all at once.

I sat there for maybe fifteen minutes, and then footsteps thudded on the stairs below me.

"Doesn't anyone use the other stairwells?"

Tyfen rounded the corner. "Not when they're looking for you."

9
A New Name

Tyfen frowned.

I looked down. "Hi."

"Hi." His voice was soft.

He climbed the stairs and sat next to me.

I played with the handkerchief Gald had given me, speechless.

"I'm *so* sorry," Tyfen repeated.

Burying my face in my hands, I shook my head. "You have nothing to apologize for. You didn't do it on purpose, and I overreacted."

He rested a hand on my back. "I still made you feel bad. I'm tired of this. I'm tired of hurting you." And he sounded tired.

A heavy weight settled into the pit of my stomach. I sat back, and he removed his arm. "I want to understand you. I want…" What did I want? When was it helpful to push someone out of their comfort zone when they weren't ready for that? At the very least, I needed some confirmation. "You said you have no other lovers out there waiting for you."

"I don't."

I gazed into his eyes. "If you did, we could work with it…"

"I promise," he said. "I have no one else in my life like you."

I nodded. "I'm sorry I overreacted."

"You *didn't*."

I wished I believed him.

"Will you please give me one more chance?" he asked.

One more? The fool I was, I knew in my heart I'd give Tyfen a thousand chances. I did like pain in my own way, though not usually this sort…

"Of course."

Gingerly, he laid his hand on my knee and stroked it with his thumb. "I'd like to give you your own nickname, though."

Despite the lingering numbness, I smiled playfully. "You already call me plenty of things. Sonta… Your Holiness… Bitch and greedy cunt."

He bit his lip; he was damn hot whenever he did that. "A sweeter name, just for you. Something in Fae, but only if you want."

I adjusted my position, considering it. "Run it by me, and we'll see."

"Hoy Falauay."

It had a bit of a ring to it… "What does it mean?"

"Great beauty."

Perhaps I was too demanding, but I'd hoped for more, for something deeper. I shrugged.

"You don't like it?"

"I just… You like me for more than sex and looks, right?"

He furrowed his brow. "Yes…" He pondered briefly. "Blantui. Strength."

I liked the sound of it on his lips, and the meaning behind it. "It's nice."

He arched an eyebrow. "Just nice?"

"I love it."

His eyes were the most beautiful piercing green, his smile a bit of a smirk. "Okay, then, Blantui."

Everything in me fluttered. "Would it be weird if I used the same nickname for you?"

"Hmm…"

I poked his arm. "I mean … look at those muscles. That's strength if I've ever seen it."

He cocked his head. "Excuse me? You didn't want a superficial nickname, so I gave you one that describes your heart, mind, and spirit." He sweetly brushed his finger along my thigh, instantly warming my core. "Yes, you're also physically strong, but that isn't the only reason I want to call you that."

I took his hand, intertwining our fingers. "You're strong in multiple ways, too. You're smart, and you have a strong spirit and heart."

His expression fell. "I can't agree with you on all that."

"Then I'll keep calling you it until you believe it yourself."

He processed for a moment, opening and closing his mouth. "You could call me anything and I'd be happy."

He was so kissable. I shouldn't be turned on so soon after becoming a wreck so easily, but here I was.

"But," he added, "for me it would be Blantue, since Fae is gendered."

"Right. Thanks for the lesson."

He stroked me again with his thumb. I was weak for him.

"Do you want to go back to the library for your lesson?"

When we fought, we fucked it out. I wanted to make up by making love. But he hadn't wanted to bed me last night or this morning, and I didn't want to push him. "Yeah, let's go back to the library."

He narrowed his eyes. "It doesn't sound like that's really what you want."

My cheeks warmed. "You don't want to do what I want."

"And what's that?"

I slid his hand up my thigh, under my dress. "I'd rather have you teach me Fae words in my chambers, the kind that *won't* be helpful on the imperial tour."

His voice was gruff. "I'd be okay with that."

We stood, and I straightened my dress.

"Can I hug you?" I asked.

He answered by pulling me in, threading his fingers through my hair.

After a moment, he spoke again, still holding me. "You have a lot of people who care about you. You're strong and blessed."

"Thank you."

He pulled back, pursing his lips. "For a scrawny guy, Gald can be intimidating when he has his wand."

It was laughable—as if Gald could terrify a muscular commander of the fae royal guard. Then again, their magical advantages depended on the circumstances. Gald's elemental abilities were innate, and his skills only grew more impressive with his wand, his knowledge of spells and potions.

"What did he say?"

"Not much. We barely crossed paths when I was searching for you. He thinks I'm a waste of space, like the others do."

I frowned. "Maybe we should be more open around everyone. It's not like we're not already in the Coterie together…"

He looked down, hesitating. "I… I think I underestimated how much… It's not everyone." He met my gaze. "I don't mind getting yelled at or having them hate me—I really don't. But I didn't realize how much I *don't* want Findlech knowing I'm happy. He wouldn't want me to be happy."

I scrunched my face. That made absolutely no sense. Tyfen didn't like Findlech, so wouldn't he want to rub his happiness in Findlech's face if he thought it would make him upset?

"You lost me," I said.

Tyfen balled his fists, then stretched his hands out. "I just don't want him in my business."

"Okay…" I still didn't get it, but it didn't bug me all that much to continue our charade. "For the record, Findlech can be a bit self-righteous, but I genuinely don't think he'd want you to be unhappy…"

Tyfen looked down again. "I promise you you're wrong." He said it so certainly, so factually, as though he stated the sky was blue.

What I wouldn't do to be a fly on the wall and figure out how they'd both played into the war that had never happened... To learn what they *really* thought of each other and why...

Tyfen drew a deep breath, taking my hand again. "Did you still want your lesson in your chambers?"

I instantly smirked. "Yes."

"Great." He released my hand. "I think we should aim for neutral."

I arched an eyebrow.

"Not cozy in front of the others, but perhaps fewer arguments." He let out a breathy chuckle. "In our short exchange, Gald told me I needed to straighten the fuck up in case your child is mine. He thinks I'll be a horrible father."

"Oh..."

"Yeah."

We agreed to be more neutral, just not showing affection around the others. Which meant we took different paths to the private entryway of my room.

The moment I shut the door, I kissed him hard, unbuttoning the top of his shirt.

He pulled back. "Can I ask a question?"

"Anything." *One* of us was an open book.

"Would you get your bracelet?" He ran his finger across my wrist.

I squinted, half in jest. "You had that made for me to wear on days *I* want that dynamic." I hadn't put it on today...

"I know. I won't make you wear it. I just want to see it."

Skeptically, I retrieved it from my dressing room. "Here."

He took it from me and undid the clasp. After uncoiling it, he put it around his own neck, then clasped it shut.

I blinked. "Did you..." I always wore it wrapped around my wrist three times... "You had it made long enough for you to wear it too?"

He grinned. "I want you to be in charge."

Fuck, he was hot.

"Fine." I resumed my work on his buttons. "You don't get to touch me until I say so."

"Yes, Your Holiness." He actually said it respectfully for once.

"You don't get to touch yourself, either."

"As you wish."

The last buttons swiftly slid out of place. I freed him of his shirt and dropped it to the floor.

Still as a statue, he stood there, simply watching me.

I wrapped my hands around the back of his neck, then traced his tattoos down his marvelous chest. His eyes were greedy as I unlatched his belt.

Not genuinely planning anything physically rough, I almost let myself forget. "Give me a word, Tyfen."

He took a moment to consider as I undid his pants and let them drop to the floor.

"Koitah," he said.

I furrowed my brow. "And what does that mean in the imperial tongue?"

His smirk was sexy. "It's a shame you haven't learned that yet, isn't it?"

I pursed my lips, resting my hands on my hips. "Excuse me?" He was having too much fun turning the tables on me. He wasn't going to be completely submissive.

He didn't respond; his expression only grew more arrogant.

Trailing a hand along his chest, I held his gaze, then pinched and twisted his nipple.

"Shit!"

"Koitah means shit?"

He laughed. "No. It's the smell of the air after rain and lightning."

I had to laugh too. There was definitely no reason I would have ever learned that Fae word. "Okay. Koitah it is."

I kissed his nipple before continuing to undress him. We kept eye contact as I pulled his shorts down. Then I wrapped my arms around him and palmed his perfect ass. "Thank you for giving me my own name."

"You deserve it, Blantui."

Him calling me that would never sound wrong, not in a decade, not in a lifetime. I locked eyes with him, then stroked his cock with the back of my finger.

"Fuck," he panted.

Grinning, I stroked him again, then glanced at his hands. They were clenched at his sides. "It's a shame you can't touch me back, isn't it?"

He refused to respond.

"Fae lessons … like I mentioned earlier. I now know what blantui and koitah are." Another stroke as he hardened. "What's the name for this?"

He shuddered. "Syinth."

"Interesting." After another moment feeling him up, I stepped back and slowly slipped out of my dress. The bra I wore today came off easily enough without assistance, and like a lot of days since the Great Ritual started, I wore no underwear.

Tyfen licked his lips, and I stepped up to him, pressing my naked body against his. "You look hungry," I said.

His hand slid onto my hips. "Yes."

"Are you touching me without permission?"

"Sorry." The smile on his lips as he removed his hand said anything but.

I stood on my tiptoes, throwing my arms around his neck. Not quite kissing, I brushed his lips with mine. "You *will* be sorry."

A satisfied groan rumbled in his throat.

I released him and crawled onto my bed. I beckoned him to join me with my finger.

He readily hopped onto the bed.

"Hold on." I gestured for him to get back. "On your knees, at the end. This way you don't forget you haven't been given permission to touch me."

He did as ordered. I loved the sight of him kneeling before me—a fae prince, collared, and I wasn't even wearing my tiara.

"Back to our lesson," I continued. "What's this in Fae?" I circled my nipple with a finger.

"Klaum." He bit his lip, staring. I could almost feel his lips on me. I was ready for him, but that leather number on his neck wasn't for simple or sweet fucking—there needed to be a bit more pain.

"We're going to take some time on a few words…"

I had a little fun, making him repeat himself a few times. I intentionally butchered the word for lips five times, and he glared at me as he repeated it each time.

"We might have to go slower if you're going to look at me that way." I pouted.

He pressed his lips into a thin line. "My *deepest* apologies, Your Holiness."

I beamed, adjusting my position with a pillow behind my back. He taught me all the female anatomy I could touch; I stroked myself and gave him a good view while I did so.

There was almost pain in his expression at his restraint. His generous cock was as ready as I was.

I dipped my finger into my center. "Do you want to be in here?"

His green eyes met mine. "Yes," he breathed.

"That's unfortunate. You get to watch me enjoy myself."

He grumbled, setting his hands on his thighs.

"Hands on the bed. You don't get to touch yourself."

Those handsome eyes danced with challenge as he slid his hands back onto the bed. Later, he would make me pay.

And I would love it.

I pumped my finger inside myself, moaning. I was well practiced, especially after all the times I'd had to please myself between my discovery as the Blessed Daughter and when I'd moved into the palace and had pleasure instructors assigned to me.

Still, I had stage fright. I closed my eyes, imagining Tyfen inside me. As much as my moans likely tortured him, they helped me grow tighter.

Only when I was close to completion did I open my eyes. He looked properly desperate.

I peaked, exaggerating my gasps. Pleasure rippled through my core.

Sighing, I relaxed my body. I could go again and love it just as much, especially with that damned cock of his.

"My fingers are wet," I said, withdrawing them. "What should I do about that?"

His throat bobbed.

"You wouldn't want to taste them, would you?"

"Yes." His voice was strained.

I tipped my knees to the side, gesturing to a spot next to me. "No touching other than your mouth on my fingers."

He didn't hesitate to crawl over and take me in deep just like I intended to with him in a minute.

Tyfen sucked, licking my fingers clean. I removed my fingers. "Good boy."

He gave me another dark look. I laughed. Truthfully, it just didn't roll off the tongue the same way.

"What else can you do with your mouth?" I asked.

His gaze quickly slid to my pussy.

"I was thinking a kiss."

He chuckled. "I can do that, too." He stopped himself as he leaned in. "Can I hold your breast?"

I almost said yes. *Almost.* "I'm sorry, I don't know what a breast is... I'm practically fluent in Fae now, and I've simply forgotten that word in my native tongue."

Squinting, he repeated his request. "Can I hold your mebana?" I would have said yes had he not also added a couple of extra words under his breath. The second translated into cunt.

"You did not just call me that!" At least I now knew the word for greedy, too. I fought a grin.

He lowered his head. "Sorry, Blantui. Can I hold you?"

I couldn't refuse him when he called me that. "Yes."

His large hand fondled me as he leaned in and kissed me. I loved every part of him, his warm hands on me, his strong tongue wrestling with mine, the wet tip of his firm cock pressed against me as he scooted closer.

As we kissed, I repositioned myself.

Tyfen came up for air. "What else can I do?" His pupils were so big, so dilated.

I searched his handsome face. "I don't know, Commander. Your soldier's been at attention for a while now. What *can* he do for me?"

With a smirk, he straddled me, easing himself in. After a moment, a sigh escaped his lips, relief in his eyes, as if he'd been dying of thirst, and my wetness had spared him.

He leaned in, holding me by the nape of the neck, and placed the sweetest kiss on my lips. "Are you ready?"

"Yes, Blantue." I so rarely teased him by squeezing like I did with the others when they were inside me—he stretched me so fully. But I did, and he went feral.

We were both too worked up for soft lovemaking. Tyfen barely even pulled out any before plunging back into me. I bucked my hips to meet him with each thrust.

We panted and moaned, groped and kissed.

Tyfen and I had only one speed and two directions—forward fast, and falling out fast.

I clawed his back, desperate for him.

Everything was exquisite—his size, weight, pressure. The gasp of his own release as mine barreled through me in record time.

Exhausted, he nestled his forehead between my breasts, the both of us catching our breath.

"Thank you for everything." He gazed up. "You truly are blantui for putting up with my shit."

"It's a small price."

He smiled softly. "Can I kiss you again?"

"Yes."

As he did so, I removed the leather from his neck and tossed it aside. Only the stars knew how long we stayed there, lips entangled, him still buried inside me. Eventually, we did pull apart, though.

He cuddled up with me, running a hand over my stomach. "You're still okay?"

How could I not love him when he acted this way? "We're both fine. I'm tough."

He nodded, entranced.

"Have you always wanted children?" I asked. The two of us had never really talked about it.

Silently, he removed his hand from my belly, gliding it to my hip. "Pass."

Pass? How could he pass on such a simple yet important question? "You…" It was a yes or no question, right?

A dark corner of my heart trembled because he had never really told me why he'd resented coming here. "Do you not like children?" Politics be damned, if one of these men didn't actually *want* to be a father…

"I like children," he plainly replied.

"Then why would you pass on that?"

Sometimes, it was as if he looked past my eyes rather than into them. "Pass," he repeated.

I couldn't accept it this time. "Will you be angry if this isn't yours?"

He narrowed his eyes. "Of course not."

"So, then you'll be happy if it is? Or isn't?" Yet again, he'd confused me.

His tone was sincere. "Mine or not, I'm here for you and for your child. For my empire and my kingdom. I…" This was one of those moments where it almost sounded like a declaration of love was about to spill out. Instead, he averted his gaze. "I swore an oath, didn't I? And I… I love spending time with you."

I couldn't say it if he wasn't courageous enough to, not yet. "We should probably get ready for dinner soon."

"Don't want to make the others wait," he said distantly.

"It's not like we can't take a *little* more time to cuddle…" Part of me felt guilty for giving him so much of my attention the last few weeks, but at the same time, we'd had a lot of catching up to do compared to how my relationships with the others had progressed.

He kissed my forehead. "How do you do it? I don't mean balancing the time between your mates or coordinating what you have with Gald or even all your other duties. How do you have space in your heart for so many? Even Lilah—forcing yourself to be apart during your pregnancy."

It was sweet he acknowledged that, especially given the offense of her scent on me in the bedding chamber. "I don't know… I was born with a heart that can expand to find a place for everyone." I smiled. "Each of you have a special corner in here." I placed his hand over my heart.

He smiled. "A rare gift, I think."

"What of your heart?" I asked. "You don't think you could share?"

Nuzzling my neck, he kissed it. "What heart? I have none. I'm a heartless asshole."

I giggled. "No you're not."

"Yes I am." He groped my breasts. "My heart is a cold, dark fortress."

I tried to not be offended by the implication. Did he not love me because he allowed no one in at all? "Where does that leave me?"

He stopped what he was doing. "I… I didn't mean it that way. Sorry," he whispered.

I didn't respond, waiting to see if he would add anything.

"Did I just ruin everything again?" he murmured against my neck.

My heart started to deflate. I fought with all I had to simply stay happy, to turn back time a few moments.

"Kiss me," I said.

And he did. It was soft and prolonged. He kissed me until I felt better, until that pain melted away, until I remembered some people were better at showing than speaking when it came to matters of the heart…

10
CRAVINGS

I had to admit I was not doing the best job at balancing my time and attention. Tyfen was a shiny, exciting thing, not even one of my mates.

I did my best over the next couple of days to devote more attention to the others. Elion and Hadwin were always happy for more time—in or out of bed, and I loved them both. Gald and I were half friends, half lovers. He didn't command as much of my time in the bedroom, but the flirtations and jokes kept coming. The kinky sex was still amazing.

Haan and Findlech were becoming closer friends of mine, and it was fun to sit together and talk about the different languages. Vampire, shifters, and humans—mages included—all defaulted to the imperial language, with small regional dialectal variations. Elves and fae had their own languages, but pretty much everyone was also fluent in the imperial tongue.

Merfolk, however, were exciting to learn about. Few spoke our language, for obvious reasons, and our attempts to learn their language were always rather pitiful. The vocal cords were a funny thing above and below the water. Merfolk used a combination of spoken word and hand gestures. It was becoming a sweet tradition for the Coterie to gather around Haan's tank to learn and swap stories.

Tyfen hung back, still eluding the group, in his chair in the common room, but there was a softness now. He remained quiet, reading books, jotting in a diary, and rarely gave any of us attitude.

A week before the paternity reading, my nerves started to set in. Everything was going to be madness. My mother would arrive soon, Lilah had returned to the palace, and I would be discovering who the father of my child was. My head spun when I considered it all.

Unlike the pregnancy confirmation, the paternal reading would not be as private. All the realm's leaders would be in attendance, just like at the beginning of the Great Ritual, and there would be a celebration, though much smaller than the grand ball.

A day after the revelation of the father, the imperial tour would begin, starting with a visit to the territory of the father. We would be on the road for weeks.

As we all sat at dinner one day, my mind wandered, tuning out the others. My venison was dry and bland, the rest of the food rather bland too. Perhaps it wasn't the food. It was just my stress getting to me, and the somber mood brought by today's rainstorm.

My chef approached me. "Not to your liking, Your Holiness?"

Embarrassed, I took another bite of my venison. "It's lovely."

"Is there anything else I can add to further your enjoyment?" he asked.

I chewed slowly, surveying the table and thinking. Everyone chatted and ate, throwing the occasional glance my way when my chef and I spoke.

This meal really *wasn't* that great, considering we had the best chefs in the realm. And if I was honest, the last day's worth of food hadn't hit quite right.

My gaze rested on Elion's plate. His steak was nearly raw, and it looked good—beautifully moist and tender.

I choked down a lump in my throat, and glanced at the other dishes. Hadwin's goblet of blood called to me as well.

Fuck.

The food I'd been served wasn't bland; I just wasn't fully satiating a craving. A craving given to me by the child in my womb—the child of one of my mates.

I blinked, swallowing my food. "It's lovely. I mean it. I've just got so much on my mind."

He sketched a bow. "Very well. Don't hesitate to call."

"Thank you." My heart raced as he left, as I forced myself to eat more for show.

Despite us avoiding the topic, it was clear Haan all but expected the child to not be his. I felt guilty for my relief that it was a child of a land-walker, simply because it made my life easier. It was a shitty thing to feel relief over.

Findlech and Gald would be fine, though a little sorrow grazed my heart about Gald. This was the only child he would have wanted. He'd already talked about getting himself altered like Schamoi and my other pleasure instructors, so we could remain lovers without the stress of him accidentally impregnating me.

Any bonus children I chose to have wouldn't automatically be the next in line for the throne, even if something tragic happened to my firstborn—it was a complicated hierarchy, and only once had a replacement been needed, when an empress died before the next Blessed Vessel was discovered.

My heart was worried about Tyfen, but I ignored it as I scooped some steamed peas and ate them. He was a good man. Troubled, but good.

As for Elion and Hadwin... One was about to be ecstatic he was a father, the other disappointed. They each wanted a child with me, for both political and personal reasons. I prayed in my heart the one whose seed hadn't won would be gracious, and that the blow would not be too harsh.

A shifter–Blessed Vessel pregnancy lasted just over nine months, and a vampire–Blessed Vessel pregnancy lasted around ten. At least there was a bit of relief that it wasn't a fae or elf pregnancy, since those usually lasted a full year.

After dinner, I excused myself and walked the many stairways to the very top of the tower. I paced in the quiet cool of the evening, the ground still wet from the earlier shower.

I wanted to tell Lilah, but it was tradition to keep it secret. I didn't want funny looks or any slipups. It was important this didn't get out. The leaders of the realm all needed to know at the same time.

I hugged myself as I chilled, the trickle of rain starting again.

Over hundreds of years of Blessed Vessels keeping track of their lives in journals they passed down, many had recognized cravings before the official paternity readings. Some had distracted themselves to minimize their obsession and to conceal their suspicions. Others had faced their cravings, confirming them by trying different foods in private.

Which did I want?

I was drenched by the time I went back inside. After strolling the hallways alone, I ducked into the library, unlocked my Blessed Vessel cabinet, and sat down to write.

Not even a month ago, my pregnancy had been confirmed—I'd been overjoyed. But this… This news brought more complex emotions, and much more complication. I jotted them down.

At least I could share my news with my journal.

After a few paragraphs, I kept tapping my pen against the pages. Blessed Vessel journal entries were generally short, so I kept mine that way. But I couldn't shake off the need to *know*.

I couldn't pretend not to care who the father was. Nor could I distract myself for the whole week before the ceremony.

Lilah could be trusted, but just like I hadn't broken my oath to not have sex with her, it didn't feel right to burden her with this knowledge. She would find out with the others.

There was one person I could confide in, though. It wasn't really even confiding. It was a two-for-one scratch for my itch.

My dress only slightly damp now, I locked up my journal and headed down to the kitchens.

It was a bit irregular for me to make the journey there myself instead of ordering food through a servant, but it wasn't like I'd *never* done it.

The staff greeted me, bowing and wishing me Hoku's blessings. I strode to my personal chef's office, and they fetched him for me. Pots and pans clinked as I waited.

"Your Holiness." A short human man, he wore casual clothes, which was to be expected at this time of the night.

"Please close the door."

A spark of recognition, or perhaps curiosity, danced in his eyes. "Happy to."

He sat across from me at his desk—a sturdy oak piece covered with recipes and ledgers.

"I need to make a special request." I fidgeted with the hem of my dress.

"I'm always happy to serve."

I swallowed. "I ... need this to be confidential."

His gaze drifted to my still-flat stomach for a moment. A smile tugged at his lips. "I've sworn on my life. Hoku's daughter and anointed are my priority, and their secrets will be kept."

"Thank you." I blew out a breath. "I'd like rare steak and pig's blood delivered to my chambers."

"Of course. I'll do so quickly and discreetly, Your Holiness."

"Thank you again."

My visit was brief but successful. I returned to my chambers and paced again.

I wanted to know. Knowing would help prepare me for the repercussions.

The wait was short; the chef knocked on my door minutes later. I allowed him entrance.

"The freshest." He set the tray on my private dining table. "Would you like me to step outside, or would you like to have a servant fetch me later? I will of course conceal any remnants and wash the dishes myself, Your Holiness."

The pond trickled to my left as I sat, the wall to my right concealing my bathing room and the nursery I hadn't yet shown anyone. "Would you mind keeping me company?"

He smiled softly. "It's my honor."

I gestured at the seat across the table, and he sat.

He removed the cloche for me, and I stared at the two dishes. At the same time I salivated, my gut twisted. He'd seasoned the steak, barely giving it a sear—it was still hot. The blood was in a small chilled ornate bowl. "This is pig's blood, right?"

"Yes."

Blood. Bloody steak and plain blood. Before I'd ever let either of my mates bed me, I'd detested blood. Luckily, after I gave birth, the cravings would go away. And even during my pregnancy, it wasn't like I *had* to eat this way, but it would help satiate the cravings.

Since it was the more benign of the two, I selected the steak first, cutting a thin strip from it. Blood wept onto the plate.

I held the fork up, staring again.

Breathe in. Breathe out.

"Here's to finding out..."

I stuck it in my mouth and chewed. I slumped in my chair, closing my eyes and letting out a soft moan. The steak was juicy and flavorful. Then again, the texture was a little off-putting... It was kind of squidgy.

Instead of chewing, I found myself sucking the moisture from it. The meat was nice enough, but the juices…

The chef and I exchanged cautious glances. I could take it or leave it with the steak, though I didn't love the texture.

Setting down my fork, I picked up the blood. I salivated again. The blood was thick and dark. A small smirk crossed my lips as I recalled Schamoi sitting across from me at this very table, teasing me with a bowl of blood like this once. I'd become more comfortable with blood with how often I let Hadwin feed on me during sex, but I'd still never tasted any beyond what I'd been required to take from him in the bedding chamber.

I pressed the chilled bowl to my lips and tipped it up. The blood was rich, salty in all the right ways, a tad sweet, and a bit metallic. Normally, the metallic flavor would have been too bitter for my liking, but I found it tangy. I gulped the entire bowl down.

The chef wore a grin. "Now we know."

I set the bowl down, stunned, staring into it. I was tempted to lick up the dregs.

"Fuck," I whispered. Tears came to my eyes. Hadwin. My sweet Hadwin was the father of my child.

"Are you okay?" The chef was all kindness and concern.

Confused by his question, I furrowed my brow as I wiped away a tear. "Yes…" I couldn't stop crying, though. Hadwin so desperately wanted to be a father, and had lost that chance when his mortality had been stolen by an evil man. Only a Blessed Vessel could do this for him.

"You're disappointed?" the chef gently asked.

I wiped away more tears. "No. Sorry. I'm happy. Very happy. He's a great man."

His smile bounced back. "Congratulations."

Drawing a deep breath, I sat straighter, trying to collect my emotions.

"Would you like more of the steak?" he asked.

I didn't, and that made me sad. Poor Elion would be disappointed. "No thank you."

"Very well." The chef replaced the cloches. "Would you like to discuss plans for the concealment of any craving orders and deliveries?"

Now that I had actually tasted the blood, it would be hard to go without it. My head was still spinning at the news, though. "I… I don't know."

"You've got a lot on your mind. We can discuss it at another time. For now, would you like an approved servant to deliver some to your chambers in the morning?" He looked embarrassed. "I don't know what your activities look like in the morning with your Coterie, but…"

Tonight was supposed to be my night alone. "You can have one deliver some before breakfast. If I don't answer, they can leave it in the tall closet in my dressing room. There's an empty shelf in there."

"Will do. And will you want human or pig's blood?"

"Pig's," I swiftly answered. While human blood would satiate me more fully, I couldn't wrap my head around consuming it.

He nodded, congratulating me again and wishing Hoku's blessings on me before leaving with the tray.

I sat alone for a minute, taking it all in.

Hadwin.

The man I so fully loved, falling for him almost as quickly as I'd admitted to Elion that I loved him as his mate.

Hadwin had been sweet in the bedding chamber, distracting me, choosing to not take offense when I'd panicked at him sucking my blood and me sucking his. Would he have a good laugh about the prospect of me now joining him in blood consumption?

Too antsy to sleep, I shed my clothes and swam in my pond. I loved being one with the water. I allowed it to caress me, easing my anxiety, helping the joy settle into the cracks that anxiety had formed.

Things would be okay. I knew in my heart things would work out. I just had to remind myself of that fact, and not overthink it all. The emperor and magistrate and their advisors were wise and much more prepared than I was to handle the political ramifications of the reveal. They would help.

For now, I swam. And processed the news the best I could.

I tossed and turned in bed for a while, trying to fall asleep. It wouldn't do.

Hadwin had issued me an open invitation to his room anytime for any reason. I craved nearness with him.

Wearing a robe, I snuck out of my chambers through the dark common room. I slipped into Hadwin's room and laid the robe on a chair in his sitting area.

I approached the bed, but didn't climb on. Despite his sweet disposition, I had to remember he was a predator. One who had endured two decades of torture and hell. I tried to never startle him awake.

"Hadwin," I whispered.

"Hello, darling." He shifted in bed.

I smiled, crawling onto the bed. "Were you already awake?" He was a light sleeper, but I'd tried to be careful when sneaking in.

He wrapped a chilled arm around me as I got under the covers. "Your heartbeat," he whispered.

It always surprised me how well he could hear my heart. "Sorry to wake you."

"Nonsense." His voice was groggy as he pulled me closer. His chest to my back, my ass to his groin, his hand on my breast. "Sleep always takes a backseat to you."

I was tempted to seize the invitation to ignore sleep, to make love to him—the father of my child.

I didn't, instead letting myself enjoy his cool embrace. We fell asleep together; I belonged in his arms.

Early in the morning, I woke to his smile—that perfect fanged smile.

"How are you, darling?" He slid a hand to my stomach. "And your child?"

My heart skipped a beat. *Our child*. I wanted to scream the good news, but I didn't. "We're good."

I ran a thumb over his soft beard. "How are you?"

His hand massaged my hip. "Any day I wake to my mate in bed is a good day."

"I love you," I said. "All of you. Your cold skin, your blond hair and hazel eyes. Your heart and scars. All of it."

He searched my eyes. "I love you too, Sonta."

"I like your hazel eyes," I repeated, taking his hand. I moved it down to my pussy, then I stroked his cool cock. "But I often prefer them red."

Red bloomed in them already. He slid a finger to my clit. "So do I."

11
Picnics

Hadwin brought me to completion three times before breakfast. That was a record for us. Granted, we were also running extremely late for breakfast. He kissed me while I tied my robe.

"Love you. I'll see you soon," I said.

His hand rested on my ass. "I love you, darling." His eyes were so dark, so deep, his voice soft and sexy.

I pulled back, pointing a finger at him. "No. I need to go."

He smirked. "We can have meals delivered to the room…"

Fuck, I wanted that. I was astoundingly horny for him. I wanted that connection more than ever. His veins also appealed to me—an odd fixation. Previous Blessed Vessels who had carried vampire mixlings had reported that. It wasn't just human or pig blood they craved, but also the father's.

Hadwin had nice blue veins, something I hadn't appreciated before now.

I took another step back. "We should eat with the others."

He stood naked, a statue of sex and perfection, licking his lips. "If you say so…" He enjoyed taunting me.

Did he know? He had to know, right? Then again, like Elion, Hadwin never turned down sex with me.

Summoning every ounce of my self-control, I spun. "I'm going. I'll see you in a few minutes."

His chuckle was barely resistible as I left his room.

And then I had to do the walk of shame, or more like sprint of shame, through the common room. Everyone else was already in here. Gald whistled as I passed.

"Sorry. I'll hurry. Or you can get started without me."

Before anything else, I rushed to my dressing room to check for my morning delivery of blood. Relief flooded me as I tipped back the vial a servant had left.

It was silky and salty, quenching some of the outrageous thirst I had for Hadwin. While we'd worked up quite a sweat, I didn't have time for a full bath, instead wiping down with damp cloths. After throwing together an outfit and brushing my teeth, I ran back to the common room.

"Sorry again." Everyone sat waiting. Hadwin stood against the wall, his still-red eyes raking over me.

Were my knees weak? They might be. I dispensed with the individual pleasantries since we were so late. "Come on, I'm starved."

Breakfast tasted better. It was a smidge bland, but much better than the day before. But my mind lingered on Hadwin. I avoided looking at him. Instead, I glanced around at the others. My heart was in such conflict. They all deserved to know, but I couldn't give them that yet. While I couldn't divulge my knowledge of my child's paternity, I could make a goal to give them individual attention before everything changed again.

"Can I make a suggestion?" I asked during a lull in conversation.

Everyone gave me their attention.

"I guess I don't know if it's really a suggestion... I love these meals and how they bring us together."

Gald smiled.

"But it's going to be a crazy week with the paternity reading."

That acknowledgement prompted mixed responses—hopeful and nervous glances.

"I'll be busy, and my mother is coming. I don't want to stress too much, and I don't want to neglect anyone."

"Sonta, we're grown men," Findlech reminded me. "Your job isn't to take care of us."

I appreciated the reminder. "Thanks. I just mean I know things are changing, and I'm planning on taking my meals alone until the paternity reading. Well, not alone, really." I sipped some juice. "I may spend a few meals with my mother or Lilah, and I'd like to spend several with you all. One-on-one picnics and the like."

I got warm smiles. Tyfen even failed to hide a small one.

"Great. And nights I share my bed may change with everything going on. I'll keep you all in the loop."

After breakfast, I snuck away to speak to my chef. I ordered more pig's blood, and discussed the two meals I wanted to share for lunch and dinner.

I met with Elion one-on-one for lunch in the gardens. We discussed his hopes and fears fairly openly. While he wanted my child to be his, he had to consider it may not be. He tactfully let me know which of the others he hoped was the father and which he didn't—purely for the sake of politics and how his people were concerned.

His feelings about the elves were rather ambivalent, and about the fae much less optimistic. Rightly so, given his territory was sandwiched between the cousin races, and there had been lots of tension throughout their history.

It gutted me when he also ranked vampires low on the list. I did my best to keep a neutral expression.

Coterie life in the palace, thus far, had its ups and downs, but it was overall pretty great. The men were generally respectful of each other on a personal level, even when politics came up. But I wasn't always in the common room.

I ate a bite of salad. "Has Hadwin been unkind?"

Elion shook his head, finishing a rather rare bite of meat. "There was that unfortunate first morning together where he wanted to kill me for taking you."

I blushed. It admittedly hadn't been a great start to Coterie life, but that didn't mean the sex had been subpar. I regularly enjoyed Elion tossing me around, and waking me with him already knotted inside me when it was just the two of us in bed.

Elion continued. "It's just hard to feel good about vampires given what they did to us, and others, in the past."

"The oni?" The former fae, elves, and shifters who had been envenomated.

"Yes."

My stomach twisted. Despite my joy with Hadwin, I could not forget the bedding ceremony. The crowd's cheers for the vampires had been the lowest. Hadwin himself had acknowledged his and his people's place in this realm.

"Hadwin would be fair, and it's not like he's directly responsible for the oni…"

We chatted more. It wasn't just ancient grievances that bothered Elion, but the closed-off nature of vampires in general. As much as I wanted to rebut that, I didn't. Technically, shifters were some of the most open with their borders and privacy, so vampires were no more closed off than the fae or elves. In the end, I didn't want to defend Hadwin too much; I didn't want to give anything away. Elion would be joining me for the entire imperial tour. We had time to ease his worries.

I dabbed my lips with a napkin. "And you're certain none of this is jealousy for having to share your mate? How often do you want to kill them all and fuck me all day?"

He smirked, and damn if he wasn't sexy when he looked mischievous. "Of course I'm a bit jealous. As for killing the rest of the Coterie, that's only a mild desire, like my desire to throttle one of the others when I see you run across the common room barely clothed, leaving from their room." Placing his plate in the picnic basket, he drew a breath. "As for wanting to constantly fuck you…" His narrow silver eyes met mine. "How is it possible I've left you questioning that?"

I bit my lip. "I asked the garden staff to keep the area clear while my mate and I picnicked."

"Really?" he growled. His expression and stance quickly became that of a predator.

I backed away on the picnic blanket. "Really…"

***

After great sex, we kissed and stayed in our embrace. I loved being with Elion, and I assured him no matter who the father was, I would raise my child to respect shifters.

He didn't ask if I knew who the father was—none of the men had, to their credit. They weren't supposed to know, and they respected me enough to not put that pressure on me.

I did feel like shit, though, when my mind wandered as we kissed. I kept imagining Hadwin. I had never once let myself do that when I was with Elion. The pull of my child's father was much stronger, now that I knew who it was, now that I had tasted blood. I did my best to stay in the moment.

After our lunch date, I returned to my chambers and found relief from my cravings thanks to the vial of blood the staff had left me. Before my dinner date, I had a fitting with Madam Gaffey for the paternity reveal. As usual, she kept things professional, not prying.

Having returned from visiting our childhood hometown, Lilah joined me. She had a spark in her eye as I unashamedly changed dresses. We continued to pine for more intimacy, but I trusted the abstinence between us would make it that much more special when I was free to lie with her again.

Lilah caught me up on her trip, passing along her parents' well-wishes for me. I wanted to burst with the paternity news, but this wasn't the time or place. She would be happy it was Hadwin, though, given he'd been the first to offer her a place in bed with us. Granted, she got along with most of the Coterie, and that was a blessing I didn't take for granted.

After we left Madam Gaffey's workroom, Lilah and I chatted more privately in the hallway. We held each other by the waist.

"I missed you," I confessed.

Her smile was so breathtaking. "I missed you too." She glanced at my stomach. "I won't ask all the questions I want to, but are you happy? It's still wild to think you're pregnant."

My heart could burst. "I'm happy."

"Good." She glanced at my lips.

"You can join me on the imperial tour…" Though she'd have to do as she did now, pretending to exclusively be my friend. In the palace, at least we had *some* freedom to be us, but the realm may still view her as a distraction from my duties. We'd have to be more careful when visiting the various territories.

She pursed her lips. "Cataray is back from vacation and will be visiting me here."

"Aha…" Cataray hadn't come to visit since before the Great Ritual began. "Have fun while I'm out, then."

"Thanks." Her eyes drifted to my lips for just a moment.

"Just kiss me," I said.

And she did. My heart pounded every time we stole a moment to ourselves like this. I cherished her full, soft lips, her warm tongue as we deepened the kiss.

After a minute, she pulled back. "I… I can't wait until we can share a bed alone again, just the two of us." She looked down, embarrassed. "Obviously, I can wait, and I will, but you know what I mean."

I took her hand, rubbing her palm. "Me too."

***

The look Hadwin gave me when I emerged from my chambers... His giant fanged smile had my heart racing already. I'd changed, getting specially dressed up for our dinner date. He had been on my mind constantly.

He slid his arms around me, stealing a peek at my chest. I couldn't blame him with how revealing my dress was.

"You look lovely, darling."

I adjusted his jacket. "And you look rather dashing." I kissed him, then took his hand.

As we headed down the corridor, a battle raged between my heart and mind. I shouldn't do what I wanted to, what I'd come prepared to do... I hadn't fully made the decision; I could still back out.

No matter what, we were going to enjoy a nice dinner. A dinner in a special place I'd never brought the men in my Coterie. The open skies were gorgeous as we stepped onto the terrace of my tower.

I thanked the servant waiting for us, specially tasked with bringing me my food safely. They bowed and took their leave.

"This is an amazing viewpoint," Hadwin whispered, admiring the view from the railing. "Were it not for the mountains, we could see the whole realm, couldn't we?"

I looked forward to seeing more of this realm, traveling it. All of it, with him on the imperial tour, since the father of the future ruler always accompanied the Blessed Vessel. It would be more than Hoku's visions had ever given me, yet everything they had prepared me for.

I slid my arms around him. "Yes. It's magnificent."

After a few minutes, we sat to eat. Hadwin was visibly confused by the spread since he usually kept to human blood.

"Human blood, pig's blood, and liquor... You don't remember that's what you ordered poolside when we were all together?" I hedged, not wanting to spoil the surprise.

He chuckled. "Okay. I remember now."

It was the truth, just not the complete truth... I anticipated he'd enjoy his vampire cocktail, but part of me hoped he would leave some pig's blood. He preferred human blood anyway.

He mixed his drink, oblivious to the reason for the special treat, while I chose from a fruit, cheese, and cracker tray the kitchen had prepared. While it all tasted great, I could smell the blood from his cup, and my mouth watered.

Later.

I had the same conversation with Hadwin that I'd had with Elion—the 'what if it's not yours' discussion. He didn't have an immediate answer; he really had to think about it.

While he had his personal opinions of the men in the Coterie, he separated that from his overarching political concerns. His answers surprised me. He worried Gald being the father would make the next emperor or empress too human-centered, since the capital was already teeming with human representation, and the magistrates were all elected from the human population. He was hesitant about the idea of Findlech or Tyfen being the father, simply because we didn't have the best or closest relationships, so he feared my child growing up with their influences. I didn't vocalize my disagreement.

None of our relationships were perfect. Of course, Hadwin didn't know how close Tyfen and I were, though even I still worried about how closed-off he was. And Findlech was closed-off in his own way, and there was no romantic affection between us. But I truly believed in my heart I could have worked things out with any of these men had they become the father.

Hadwin shook his head. "Granted, it might be better for the child if the father isn't me or Haan."

I frowned. "Don't talk like that."

He grinned. "We're the outcasts." They'd become good friends over the last several weeks.

"Who both have kind hearts and good heads on their shoulders," I rebutted.

Hadwin shrugged. "True, but association with either of us will make it an uphill battle for your child."

I dusted cracker crumbs off my dress, giving him a scowl. "He or she will have a pampered life in the palace and an uphill battle to be a good ruler no matter the father." I cocked my head. "People will worship the literal shits my child takes, solely because they will be Hoku-blessed."

Cringing, Hadwin laughed. "Fuck, Sonta. While we're eating?"

I joined him, laughing as well. "I'm just making a point." I took a sip of water. "And you're squeamish about that kind of thing? I'll have nursemaids in spades, but I intend to change my child's messes myself as much as possible. I suppose I should have asked about baby messes before letting anyone bed me."

Hadwin dug into the dessert berries and popped one into his mouth. "Of course I'll help. I'm not afraid to get my hands dirty." He looked down as he chewed another berry. "Granted, that depends on whether I have permission from the father to help in that capacity … if I'm not lucky enough to be the one."

My heart quaked. I wanted to tell him so badly. Despite it going against tradition and my better judgment, I was genuinely considering divulging that tidbit.

"No matter what"—I rested a hand on his thigh—"I love you."

His smile was beguiling. "I love you too, darling." He leaned in and kissed me.

Done with my food, I shifted, resting my head on his shoulder. The sunset was almost complete, the skies clear.

Hadwin placed another kiss on my head. "How good are you at keeping secrets?"

12
SWAPPING SECRETS

"Secrets?" I asked. Was I good at keeping secrets? My accidental outing of Lilah, myself, and Findlech wasn't promising evidence… Though I wasn't exactly a gossip… "I suppose I'm good with secrets. What would you like to tell me?"

Hadwin faced me, holding my hands. "There are things you don't know about me, things I'm not supposed to tell you…"

That wasn't a fantastic confession to hear from the father of my unborn child… "Like what?"

He glanced at our hands. "I need to know you won't speak of this to anyone. Not Lilah or your mother, not the emperor or magistrate."

It sounded serious, and I found myself echoing something Gald had told me once. "I can't blindly promise not to tell something to the emperor or magistrate. My loyalty is sworn, as is yours…"

He gently sighed, stroking my hand. "It's not that kind of secret. It's more of a … vampiric secret. There's a complicated process to picking out who gets to join a Blessed Vessel's Coterie…"

He searched my eyes. "I imagine there are secrets Blessed Daughters and Vessels keep amongst themselves… Part of why you lock those journals up?"

I bit my lip, nodding. There were, but for the most part, it was about privacy of a public figure rather than keeping the public in the dark. There was one secret, though, about our visions. It was a gift we never told anyone about. I looked forward to the day I could experience it for myself.

"I trust you, Hadwin. If it's not a harmful secret, I'll keep it."

He smiled. "It's not." His gaze returned to our hands. "I'm young for a vampire, especially considering how short a time I've been free, been a duke."

He'd only been a duke for ten years. Many more important vampires could have been selected for my Coterie, most of whom were centuries old.

"We don't have to get into it all right now, but part of the reason I was allowed to join your Coterie is because of my youth, my lack of time spent in vampire society."

I furrowed my brow. "Your people picked you because you're inexperienced? That's an odd choice."

His voice was hesitant. "Not when you realize most titled people already have mates, and many of the others are hesitant to bind themselves to a Blessed Vessel."

A good portion of vampires were monogamous. "They don't want to share?"

He hesitated. "Yes and no. You know how it works, right? Bonds between vampire mates are very strong. They're generally much weaker with a human mate."

I nodded. I'd witnessed it myself when it came to how Elion and Hadwin affected me. Hadwin's emotional and physical tugs were usually much softer.

Hadwin lifted my hand and kissed it. "This next part, I'm forbidden from telling you, but I don't like having secrets between us. And it's been eating at me the way I hesitated to tell you I loved you when you first said it to me."

I'd almost forgotten he had; he'd shown me dozens of times since then that he loved me. "You were nervous. I understand how you would be because of your past."

"That was only a small part of it," he replied. "I'm supposed to … not act how I feel, and it's a daily battle."

I squinted. "And how do you feel?"

He pressed his lips into a thin line. "The secret held by the vampire high court is that the mating bond to a Blessed Vessel is stronger than with a normal human, and even stronger than with another vampire. It's the strongest kind of bond we have."

My eyes widened. "Really?"

"Yes." His hazel eyes were kind and sweet. "And it binds me to you even when your time as a mortal is up."

Fuck… I didn't constantly consider the immortality of some of my Coterie members. Vampiric mating bonds dissolved when one of the partners died, but if this type didn't…

"You don't think you'll be able to … move on?"

His smile was coy. "I know in my heart I never could. And most in vampire politics do not wish for that kind of restriction—they're content with their riches and associations and influence, despite the honor being in a Coterie brings."

It made sense. Hadwin hadn't been tied to many people—human or vampire—after turning into a vampire. I tried not to pity him for being bound to me so permanently; he didn't want my pity.

"I understand why they may not want to join a Coterie, but why would they keep that a secret?"

"Like I said, the bond is stronger… Insanely strong. I do my best to hide it, but…" He glanced down. "You're all I think about. I understand more than people realize how Elion felt in the heat of his mating fever."

I blinked. No wonder he hadn't batted an eye at how horny I'd been this morning.

"But…" he continued. "Hoku dampens your mating bond to Elion, right? Well, it's unequal for vampires. It's very one-sided."

It was hard not to frown. "I don't know what it feels like to be you, but I *do* love you."

"I know. And I'm grateful for that. But we keep that a secret because it could be used against us."

"The strength of the bond?"

"Yes." He looked me dead in the eyes. "If you asked me to use my venom to create an oni, I would…"

My stomach churned. An oni? An undead monster?

"I would burn the realm for you," he said.

I bit the insides of my cheeks. "No you wouldn't. You have too kind a heart."

His unflinching gaze told me he didn't agree. It reminded me he'd tortured and murdered people in revenge instead of turning them in to the emperor's enforcers.

"For me, for all of us, darling … we're lucky *you* have a good heart. Now that I know you, I don't worry about you manipulating the bond."

"I would never. Hoku's daughters are here to help *keep* the peace."

With a slight grin, Hadwin held my chin. "But you're not infallible, not immune to influence. And Hoku herself, when she was mortal, lived a life rife with violence and manipulation, did she not?"

I smiled. Despite my mother and I never having worshiped Hoku faithfully when I was younger, I still knew all the stories from ancient history. Hoku had been a cunning and talented mage, taking on challenges I could only imagine. "True."

I got up and straddled him, sitting on his lap. We shared a smile as I wrapped my arms around his neck, and he wrapped his arms around my waist.

"Thank you for telling me," I said. "Your secret is safe with me, and I promise to not ask you to start a war."

He kissed me. "I appreciate that."

"Honestly, I can't be too angry to hear you're even more madly in love with me than I thought."

He chuckled. "It's nice to get it off my chest. And … I thought you'd be interested in something else…"

I hummed my curiosity.

"That bond is why I can so easily wake you from deep sleep, like when you had that terrifying night vision."

My jaw dropped. "Wow."

"And why I hear your heartbeat so loudly."

"That makes sense."

He didn't break eye contact. "And I thought you'd like to know that's why I can also hear your child's heartbeat."

I gaped. "You can..."

His smile was charming. "Yes."

He kept saying *your* child, not *our* child. Was he respecting my boundaries, or did he just not know? "I'd imagine the different races might sound a little different... Do you have any inkling?"

"No. I don't know that my predecessors have tracked it well enough to differentiate a mixling fetal heartbeat like that."

My own heart raced. I shouldn't tell him. I shouldn't.

He narrowed his eyes the way he always did when my heart rate changed without explanation.

So I kissed him, hard. Each time our lips met, I fought the urge to tell him. He would find out soon...

As they often did when we made out, his hands found my ass. He was hard underneath me, and I was wet.

Wet and craving. Craving blood, mostly his.

"I love you," I panted out between kisses.

"I love you too." His fingers roamed, discovering my underwear was the crotchless kind. His growl of approval set my core on fire.

I wanted to bite him, suck him, taste him. And, honestly, part of me believed *all* the men deserved to know in private whether my child was theirs. I wished I could gently let the others down before their leadership stood in that paternity reading.

As much as I wanted to let them down in my own way, I couldn't. But I could share this secret with Hadwin; he would keep the secret. He would protect his child.

My temptation grew too large, and I kept kissing him as I reached a hand up to my hair and carefully freed the spiked ritual claiming ring I'd used on him in the bedding chamber. I'd had a trusted servant attach it with a clip in case I couldn't help myself.

Hadwin slid his hands to his belt, his lips busy with mine. I pulled away from the kiss and sucked on his earlobe.

"You think you're going to get lucky?" I asked, slipping the ring on.

He stopped working on his belt as I kissed his neck. "I ... assumed..."

I grinned and kissed his beautifully veined neck. I found the spot for puncturing. "You're not wrong." This time, I didn't hesitate as I pierced his flesh, then swiftly covered it with my lips.

"Fuck!" he whispered. In a heartbeat, he pulled me away from his neck, holding my shoulders, staring at me. "It's mine?"

I'd barely tasted his blood, but I swallowed, smiling. Hadwin knew I would not drink blood, especially his, unless I was experiencing pregnancy cravings.

His red eyes were wide, his face somehow paler than usual. "It's mine? It's really mine?"

I nodded. "You *are* happy, right?" His shock made it hard to tell.

"Of course I am. I just... I can't believe... Darling..."

My heart fluttered at his inability to form a complete sentence.

"You're craving me." He angled his head, giving me access to his neck again.

I accepted the offering, sucking gently. His blood was so much more satisfying than pig's blood for my pregnancy cravings. It was cold, thick, sweet and salty. It was like a perfect dessert, coating my mouth and settling my soul.

I wanted more of him, grinding against him. He resumed his work on his belt as I finished feeding on him and swallowed. It didn't take much for me to be satiated.

Hadwin freed his cock and kissed me. "I love you."

Shifting, I took him in, savoring every inch of his coldness inside me. We stole kisses as I rolled my hips, as he thrust up.

I loved the friction, his chill slowing the buildup. His gaze was so fierce, and I almost predicted his next movement. He wanted faster, harder.

Hadwin held me tight, rolling us both so he landed on top. I tightened my pelvic muscles around his cock, making him shudder. His eyes were so dark red they were almost black.

He drove into me, and I panted out my approval. With his free hand, he tried to slip my dress strap off, but it didn't easily budge.

"Just rip it off," I breathed.

It only took one quick tug, and then he had access to my breasts. A great multitasker, he kept thrusting as he lowered his lips and sucked each of my nipples. They would someday feed his child.

But for now, they were for him.

He pierced me, his saliva rapidly numbing the pain, and then he fed.

I came quickly, forcefully, moaning and gasping as he kept going. After a few more deep thrusts, he followed.

Normally, Hadwin stayed inside me as we cooled, but he pulled out, spilling his seed out of me. He immediately backed up, spreading my legs further. With a sinister grin, he lowered his head.

He didn't lick me, though. First, he used his fangs to tear off my underwear, then he went for the move Lilah had sworn was the best she'd ever experienced at the Suck and Fuck, the move Hadwin had been too timid to try since he hadn't been formally trained.

His tongue grazed my swollen clit, then his fang clamped down on it. A small scream escaped my lips as my body tensed.

And then he sucked.

Blood rushed to my clit, his thirsty sucks strong.

I instantly climaxed again, gasping.

He didn't stop, greedily taking more. My back arched as I orgasmed again.

And again.

I gulped air, my whole body tight. What a normal man could perhaps do with some skill in one finger and a few minutes of time, Hadwin could do countless times with his fangs and lips in the blink of an eye.

Obscenities flew out of my mouth with each new crest of pleasure. He kept monitoring me, kept enjoying me.

I stopped counting, my breath ragged, my energy spent. "Stop," I said, my voice hoarse.

Hadwin halted, gently licking up any remaining blood. "You're all right? It wasn't too much?"

Stars winked in my vision as my body slowly relaxed.

"Darling?"

I waved a hand, blinking.

"Too much blood?" He pivoted and grabbed the remaining blood from our meal.

"I'm fine." My heart still pounded, my muscles weak. "I just… Even I have limits…"

He wore a gentle smile, brushing hair away from my face. "But you're okay? Our baby's okay?"

Our baby.

Tears pooled in my eyes. "Yes, we're great."

He settled down next to me, giving me the sweetest kiss. His hand stroked my stomach. "It's really mine?"

"Yes."

Now *his* eyes glazed over with tears. "I'm a…"

"A father." Something he had wished for for the better part of eighty-four years—something he could now only be with the help of a Blessed Vessel.

His throat bobbed. "Yes." He kissed me softly a few times. "I know you didn't get to choose, but thank you."

My energy exhausted, I found the strength to reach up and run my hand through his blond hair. "I'm glad it's you."

If I could've captured and bottled the sincerity and joy on his face, I would have. I was glad I'd chosen to tell him. It would have been a crime to force him to contain himself in the name of decorum amidst the most important people in this realm.

He held me tighter. "I should care about what this means for my people, but I don't right now. I'm just happy."

"Congratulations."

We cuddled and kissed longer as we discussed our child. Obviously, we would both have to pretend we didn't know who the father was. Hadwin was happy to let me drink from him whenever I needed for my cravings. We discussed names. I hadn't given it a single consideration, and he wasn't set on any, but he had a few ideas, depending on the gender.

After a while, the night grew cold, and I mentioned I'd like to return to my room, obviously sharing it with him.

I grunted sitting up, my whole body sore from the repeated and intense orgasms. "Sorry. I can carry you."

Grinning, I contemplated. Normally, if a man was lifting me, it was to throw me over his shoulder or to toss me on the bed. "You plan to carry me down several flights of stairs?"

He popped the top off the bottle of human blood. "Don't underestimate me."

I chuckled as he guzzled the rest of the blood. "Sure. You can carry me."

It took us a few minutes to locate the puncturing ring I'd discarded in the dark, but we found it, and he picked me up. I wrapped my arms around his neck and couldn't stop smiling as he carried me back down to my chambers. We used my private entrance. I could barely stand when he set me down.

"I can draw you a bath and help you stretch," he offered.

I accepted. He was the sweetest and gentlest as he helped me remove my clothes, and poured the hot water with soaking salts. My nipple and clit stung a bit from the open wounds as I eased myself into the water, but not much thanks to the numbing of his bites. Hadwin joined me, stretching me. I particularly liked the part where he stretched my thighs and groin, holding the position while kissing me.

"If you're not too sore after a while..." He licked his lips. "I could order more blood to give me some strength if you want to celebrate more... But only if you really want to."

I grinned again. The bath had done me wonders, and as long as he didn't feed on me again tonight, I was sure I would enjoy some more lovemaking. "Order me some tea and snacks while you're at it."

13

The Nursery

Hadwin and I dressed in robes and ate snacks on the daybed. He'd ordered some pig's blood for me, but I didn't even have the smallest hankering for it after drinking his.

He couldn't keep a smile from his face, his eyes constantly darting to my stomach. My cheeks hurt from smiling, too.

"Do you … want more sex tonight?" he asked. "Or would you rather sleep?"

My core still ached from the repeated orgasms he'd given me. "Let's maybe wait a while and see?"

"Okay."

I took his hand, standing us both up. "Let me show you something."

He followed, his cool hand in mine the whole way as we walked behind my partition wall.

A good portion of my floor hadn't been used in decades, and some of it may not be used in my lifetime. The floor plan provided privacy and protection ideal for a complex familial living situation like mine with my Coterie. While my firstborn would have their own larger chambers as they grew, they'd start things off in the nursery attached to my personal chambers.

I'd never let anyone in this room. I turned and leaned back against the door. "Want to see the nursery?"

Hadwin's eyes lit up. "Yes."

Opening the door, I tapped a fae light to illuminate the room.

In the corner sat a cradle, all ready for the next Anointed Ruler, the next emperor or empress. Aside from a dresser and side table, the only other object in the room was an adult bed.

Sliding an arm around me, Hadwin kissed my cheek. "I still can't believe it…" His smile was enchanting. "Smart to have a bed for you in here."

I leaned into him. "Yeah. Nice for when I don't want to have a bassinet in the main bedroom." While my bedroom was beautifully set up for entertaining my lovers, it wasn't ideal for waking in the middle of the night and stumbling across the place to go feed my child. This also gave us some privacy. While things would no doubt change with motherhood, I planned to continue having an active sex life, and needed some separation. This was a family home, not a sex worker's establishment.

"Notice the bed is large enough for two?" I asked. "The size is right, just like any of the Coterie beds."

Every word he uttered was like a cherished prayer. "I look forward to joining you there. As the light sleeper between us, I promise to be the one to get up and bring them to you for feeding."

My heart melted. "I love you."

"I love you too."

My mind focused on the adult bed, and my nerves tightened a bit. Hadwin's seed had won. While I had the final say over my firstborn, he had many rights as the father.

"What do you think? About the bed and it being ... shared?" I cleared my throat. "You'll have more say now..." He still couldn't make demands like dismissing the other Coterie members, but he had rights over who had access to our child.

Hadwin pursed his lips, eyeing me. "I guess we have some time, right?"

I nodded. We had about eight months to see how my relationships with the others panned out. Right now, I trusted all the men, and of course Lilah, to be around our child.

"I'm just planning on this bed for sleeping. The other bed is for activities I enjoy when awake."

He grinned. "I like that."

I smiled at the way his eyes betrayed him, at the flicker of red running through the hazel at the mention of sex. "Do you want more sex tonight?"

His eyes grew even hungrier. "You're ready?"

Wrapping my arms around his neck, I gave him a light kiss. "Soon. I vote we pull an all-nighter. Starting with something else we haven't done before..."

He let me lead him out of the nursery. I stripped off my robe and tossed it on the daybed, his eyes raking over me.

Then I backed away to stand at the edge of the pond. "My child is going to learn to swim. It would be a shame if their father never relearned."

Holding the railing, I took the stairs into the tepid water. Hadwin's struggle was apparent as his eyes dashed between the water, my face, and my bare chest.

His hand went to the knot in his robe. "I guess I should dedicate some time to learn."

I took in every pale inch of him as he entered, then pressed myself against him. "After we get in a few laps, I'm sure I can find a way to reward you for your leap of faith."

We did swim. Hadwin was awkward for a while, having not even attempted it in the fifty years since he'd become a vampire. He picked it up quickly, though. I didn't swim too hard, saving my energy and letting my muscles further relax.

For over an hour, we swam and chatted about our future as parents. He was excited to have the imperial tour start in his lands, and to show me his estate along the route. I was excited to see it.

Eventually, we left the water and made love. The way he caressed my belly and kissed it afterward brought tears to my eyes.

"Would you..." He hesitated.

I ran my fingers through his hair. "Why do you get so shy sometimes? I'm not going to bite your head off. Just ask what you want."

He still took a moment. "Would you consider ... someday, obviously down the road quite a bit ... becoming immortal?"

Blinking, I gaped. The fae and elves were so long-lived because of an ancient blessing from one of their goddesses. No one knew exactly how vampirism had come about, though by the way their venom corrupted the other races ... unsavory beginnings were usually assumed.

"You don't have to answer right away," he added. "Just something to consider..."

"I... You'd like me to become a vampire?"

He averted his gaze, kissing my stomach again. "I wouldn't be opposed to it..."

My mind whirled at the question. There was nothing about it in the divine edicts, nor in the previous Blessed Vessels' journals left for me. "Can it even be done? I'm human, but different... Aren't you afraid I wouldn't be safe?" What if I was just different enough to turn into an oni—a mindless creature—instead of a vampire?

Hadwin was quick to answer, confidence in his voice. "It would be safe. I would never suggest it otherwise."

He spoke with such authority that I smiled. But only for a moment. "What of the political ramifications?"

"Once our child sits at the head of the empire, you're allowed to fade into a private life... No one could accuse you of favoritism. Granted, I'm sure immortality would be more appealing if you got along better with the other immortals..."

Despite my friendship with Findlech, I wouldn't give up my humanity to chum around with him forever. Though I *would* get more time with Tyfen, and the thought brought butterflies to my stomach as much as endless days with Hadwin did.

Then again... "I would outlive most of the people I love." I frowned. "My mother, Lilah, Elion, Gald... Our child..."

He nodded. "It's a big decision. One you won't have to make for years. I just wanted to put it out there."

And why wouldn't he? He'd just told me how strong and long-lasting his mating bond to me was.

"Just think about it," he said.

I nodded in return, then smirked. "You're sure you'd want to put up with my shit for that long?"

Narrowing his eyes, he pushed himself up, then straddled me. "I don't know... I *might* get tired of making love to you. You're not all that good at it."

I belted out a laugh. He was actually really great in bed, considering I had so much more experience than he did.

Hadwin leaned down and kissed my love bite. "But, darling, with a few extra centuries, I may be able to teach you how it's meant to be done."

Sliding my hands to his strong thighs, I beamed. "I'm ready for my next lesson if you are."

With the help of blood for Hadwin and invigorating tea for me, we made love throughout the night. I might have even surpassed my personal goal of how many times I'd orgasmed in a single day, and that was quite a feat considering my five pleasure instructors and I had made a challenge of it once. But none of them could bring wave after wave of ecstasy like Hadwin could, like he had on the roof earlier.

When the early morning rays peeked through my window, we were both spent, and both excited for our future plans.

And both going to have to put on our best act about not knowing who the father was...

I drank a little more of Hadwin's blood to curb any cravings before he took off for his own room. We didn't want to raise any suspicions with the others, since we'd spent two nights in a row together.

After he left by my private door, I ordered breakfast to my room, had a servant notify the others to eat without me, and bathed myself, then allowed a servant to help me dress.

It was going to be a great day.

14
Counting Down the Days

It took everything I had to act casual when I entered the common room. Hadwin did well with his nonchalant attitude while perusing a book in his usual place.

I greeted the others first, and Tyfen and I even gave each other a curt morning greeting. His voice and expression said one thing. His eyes said another.

I finally made it to Hadwin and sat on his lap.

"How was your solo breakfast this morning?" he asked, resting a hand on my thigh.

"Lovely. And your breakfast?"

"Always great. And how did you sleep, darling?" A playful smile tugged at his lips. Despite the copious amounts of invigorating tea I'd gulped down, I was still tired from pulling an all-nighter with him.

I mirrored his grin. "So-so."

His hand gripped me tighter, and I fought a laugh.

Elion joined us for more conversation, and I was forced to plan out my day. The next few days were going to be nothing short of chaotic.

I turned to the room. "I have lunch and dinner free for picnics again." Pausing, I considered. I didn't doubt Hadwin and I would sneak in another hookup, and Tyfen and I would, too. Elion would want to be with me. As much as I loved copious amounts of cock and bonding, I needed to pace myself.

"Haan, would you like lunch with me out at the lake? And Gald, would you like dinner?"

They both agreed.

Lunch with Haan was delightful. I met him out at the palace lake, soaking up the summer rays. He caught himself a couple of fish while I ate out of a picnic basket on the shore.

I asked him the same questions I'd asked the others. He obviously wished my child would be his, but he quickly conceded to preferring the shifters after that. Historically and biologically, it made sense.

After eating and chatting for a while, I joined him for a swim in the lake. It was a beautiful outing.

When dinner approached, Gald and I ended up in my painting studio, for old times' sake.

It killed me how much he wanted my child to be his, but when asked how he felt about the others, he shared his preferences. Unsurprisingly, his closeness with Findlech swayed his opinion that way. After that, he favored Haan, then Elion and Hadwin. As much fun as it was to sneak around with Tyfen, it hurt to hear him picked last.

For once, Gald and I didn't even have sex on our date. We did actually paint this time, on paper. He wasn't half-bad. We also rated the sketches Lilah had made of us fucking, and we ended our time with lots of kissing and cuddling. I loved having a partner with lip and tongue rings. He had already decided to get a cock piercing as well, after I gave birth. He'd heal while I healed, then we'd have a hell of a good time breaking it in…

In the late evening, my mother arrived from her cottage. I got the biggest hug, and we joined Lilah for dessert. As much as I wanted to avoid the topic of the paternity reading because of my building anxiety, it was kind of unavoidable. I did keep changing the topic back to Mother and Lilah, though. Lilah was excited to have Cataray visit in a few days, and my mother was planning on staying here at the palace for the foreseeable future.

As it grew late and my energy waned from the all-nighter I'd pulled, Lilah walked me back to my chambers. We held hands, not saying much.

"Do you want to talk?" she asked.

I bit my lip. "I'm just nervous." I hesitated at my door. "Want to come inside?"

She smiled softly. "Sure."

After entering my dressing room, I stripped down and grabbed a nightie. "I don't want to disappoint anyone. And five out of six men in my Coterie will be disappointed."

Lilah eased herself down on the edge of my bed. "Do you think any of them will be mad at you?"

"No. That would be silly." I sauntered up to her, and she held me by the waist.

"Exactly. Imagine the horror of carrying six inside you right now."

I gulped. "No thank you."

She giggled. "And all the various cravings. How would that even work, with merfolk pregnancies being so short and the immortals so long?"

Cringing, I fussed with her curly brown hair. "I have no idea. And thankfully, Hoku has never allowed something like that."

Lilah's hands were delicate on my waist, her rich brown eyes soft. "No matter the outcome, the realm will accept the paternity. They understand you didn't personally choose, and the men will, too."

I nodded. My eyelids were droopy, my movements sluggish.

She gestured with her head. "Come on. Lie down, and we'll talk some more."

I snuffed out all but one of the candles and joined her on the bed. I fit perfectly in her arms as we chatted further.

"I'll still be sad to see the disappointment on their faces…"

"I know." She hooked a leg around me. "It'll be fine."

As I nuzzled her shoulder, my heart calmed.

"Do you know whose it is?" she whispered.

I paused. "You can't ask me that."

"You don't have to tell me who…"

"Yes," I whispered.

"And are you content with who it is?"

Thinking of Hadwin, I couldn't hold back a smile. "Yes."

She threaded her fingers through my hair. "Good. You're happy, and he'll be happy. Keep your focus on that."

She always had a way of helping me refocus. "You're right." I leaned in and kissed her gently.

We made several passes with our kisses. They didn't have to be passionate, nor did they have to lead to something more, to pull my heart to her.

"I love you," I said, forcing my heavy eyelids to stay open.

"I love you, too."

I woke in Lilah's arms in the morning. She was still out cold, a thing of beauty. The morning rays kissed her darker skin. I couldn't help but reflect on our childhoods. She and I had taken countless naps together as little girls; her parents had helped my mother and I find a safe and healthier path.

As much as my mother had wished to leave prostitution after I was born, it wasn't something she could afford. She barely made rent for our tiny apartment. Once I started to ask why so many different uncles visited, none of them paying me any attention, my mother recognized I was old enough to notice.

But not old enough to be left at home alone if she took her clients elsewhere.

Through word of mouth, my mother found a woman not far from us who was looking to take on paid childcare. She already stayed home caring for a few of her own, and her husband owned a shop but had hurt himself. Their income had taken a hit while he healed. Lilah was their youngest. I was shy the first day, but we were inseparable after that. Her home was bigger, her toys more plentiful, her big busy family such a change from what I was used to. I'd never even met my grandparents.

Lilah's mother eventually discovered what my mother's job really was. Instead of ostracizing my mother and kicking me out, she and her husband took action. They kept watching me, refusing to take payment, and her husband hired my mother at his shop. They eventually helped us move out of the hovel we'd been living in, too.

I'd understood very little of that as a young girl. I'd just known I had a new friend, and her older siblings, and more people to care about me. I'd seen my mother happier.

Lilah was my beacon, my safe place. We'd frazzled our parents by finding scissors and cutting each other's hair into jagged mops when we were little, giggling nonstop. We'd covered for each other more than once as teens when I'd snuck out with a boy or she'd sneakily gone off to the Suck and Fuck.

She had taken it hard when the temple confirmed me as Hoku's daughter. A spark of joy had left her eye when I first broke the news to her. We would never open a shop together.

But we would always be close.

I dared to wake her, brushing her hair out of her face and placing a gentle kiss on her lips.

She moaned, stretching, tightening her grip on me. She kissed back, sleepy morning kisses.

"Good morning, sunshine." I smiled.

Her eyes fluttered open. "Good morning." She glanced at the lace curtains at the top of the bedposts. "I meant to go back to my own room last night…"

I kissed her again, holding her closer. "But isn't this better?"

"Yes."

My stomach tightened as our kiss deepened, as our tongues playfully roamed each other's mouths. We didn't take it further, though, despite the fire building in my core, despite my desire to trace her curves.

I was tempted to invite her to breakfast with the Coterie, but given the building nerves as a collective, I decided against it.

My lunch picnic was spent with Findlech. He taught me a few utilitarian words in Elvish as we sat on a picnic bench in my gardens, and we discussed the standard questions. He conceded that, like any of the men, he wished my child were his own for the sake of his people, but he was rather level-headed about the possibility of it not being. He wouldn't be disappointed, nor did he think his people would be all that much. We currently had a half-elf emperor, and the other races in the realm were always chomping at the bit for representation.

In the way he sometimes would, Findlech paused at my question, considering who he would prefer to be the father if not him, and who he hoped the father wasn't. Shifters and mages were fairly neutral to the elves, and merfolk were, too, though he feared they may not care enough about land-walker issues to be engaged enough in rulership. Like the others, he ranked vampires lower on the list, and it saddened me further.

"I think…" He cleared his throat. "I think it would be best for the realm if Tyfen isn't the father."

I adjusted my seat. "Because you don't think he'd be a good father? Or because of the fae in general?"

Findlech opened and closed his mouth, fighting for words. "I ... have no personal intuition about how he would be as a father. I also don't say that based on his people as a whole. The timing is just not right for a fae ruler."

I shrugged. "And why not?"

He straightened, giving me his closed-off expression. That noble, lordly look with his dark brown eyes, long black locks, and dark skin. "I have my reasons for saying so."

Vague contention was such a *lovely* thing... The issues between Findlech and Tyfen were so nebulous...

As much as I wanted to pry, I didn't. I was getting used to being stonewalled, and their armies weren't gathering at their borders, so it couldn't be all that terribly important of an issue...

So, I forced a smile. "Noted."

For my dinner picnic with Tyfen, I took him up to the terrace atop the tower. I'd saved it as a special place for the father of my child, but now that Hadwin and I had been up here, I wanted to share it with others. It afforded lots of privacy, while being romantic.

The moment we closed and locked the door behind us, Tyfen set down our food basket and pinned me against the brick.

"Blantui," he whispered, kissing my neck.

I was putty as he grasped my hips.

"Skipping to dessert?"

He moaned, pressing against me. "I want you for all the courses."

I grinned, running my hands over the muscles beneath his shirt.

"You're not wearing your bracelet today."

"No..." I'd been far too stressed, craving connection and tenderness more than wicked submission. But the way he commented on it made me question. "Do you wish I'd worn it today?" We both switched things up, balancing our need for control and release of control. He usually craved control in the bedroom. Or playroom. Or storage closet...

Either way, Tyfen usually was the dominant one between us, and I liked it. How could I ever forget he was here against his will? No matter what secret pains he withheld from me, I at least understood that much. He craved control to balance out a big part of his life where he had none. And as much as we were growing closer, the inception of our relationship had not been his choice.

In the moment, I struggled to not feel helpless about the way the next few days would go, but I wasn't in the mood to reclaim my peace with a submissive role today. But I'd be willing to bend if he needed it.

Tyfen didn't skip a beat, kissing me hard. "It's fine. I'll take you either way, Sonta."

Despite my empty stomach, I let Tyfen have me first, up against the wall. I didn't have to worry about my gasps carrying on the cooling wind, because he covered my mouth as I came.

Something about Tyfen filled me in a way no one else could, and not just his impressive size inside me. It had to be the eyes. Those stunning green eyes always drew me in.

And right now, they were piercing as we panted together, him still inside me.

Tyfen searched my face. "You're beautiful."

I smiled. The sun was setting, the sky painted vibrantly beyond the mountains surrounding the palace. He hadn't even taken a glance at the view. "The landscape's really beautiful from up here, too."

He glanced to his left. "I suppose it is." His gaze snapped back to me, and he kissed me sweetly, lazily.

After more than a minute, I pulled back. "Do we want to eat before all light is gone?"

Resting his forehead against mine, he breathed softly. "Yes, let's eat."

After a quick cleanup, we sat down to our picnic.

I fed Tyfen a strawberry first. He had the sexiest grin as he took it from me.

"How are you doing?" I asked.

Chewing, he shrugged, then picked up another strawberry. "Fine." He held up a strawberry for me. "You?"

Now that I knew him better, I could better spot his lies. He'd been tense the last couple of days. Needy, hungry, anxious. He showed me a vulnerability he never dared to show the rest of the world.

"I think we're all a little nervous, aren't we?" I bit the strawberry.

He smiled. "Perhaps."

I finished my bite, fiddling with the greens on another berry. "Are you nervous it won't be yours?" Not a single one of the others had listed Tyfen as their most-liked backup, but that wasn't surprising with the way we carried on.

Tyfen averted his gaze. "There's no point in being nervous about something you can't change, right? It's either mine or it's not."

While he'd made that clear after my pregnancy had been confirmed, that didn't mean his people wouldn't be disappointed. Didn't mean *he* wouldn't still be disappointed.

What should I say? When the truth came to light about how sweet Tyfen really could be, the others would like him. Hadwin may not ever be best friends with him, but he'd come to see how good of an uncle Tyfen would be to our child...

"I know it's fun to sneak around, and you don't want Findlech to see you happy, but what do you think about letting the others know we're actually a couple?"

Tyfen pressed his lips together, his expression distant and calculating. He finally looked at me. "I'm ... not ready for that. Things will probably go to shit either way, but..."

I frowned. "What do you mean, things will go to shit? You and me?"

He was quick to respond. "No. I mean overall." His voice and expression were so forlorn. "I just want to enjoy time with you, Sonta."

But wouldn't we be able to share more time together if we were public?

"How long do you want to keep this up? You want to *always* keep us a secret?"

Sighing, Tyfen grabbed another strawberry as well. "Not forever." He searched my face. "After the paternity reading. How about that? When things have calmed down again?"

I smiled wide. "Really?"

He gave me a tiny smile in return. "Really."

"Okay." I took a bite of my strawberry, imagining us finally cuddling in the common room like I did with the others.

Tyfen stared at me, shaking his head. "I'll never understand how you like me after the shit I put you through."

I didn't just like him. I loved him. I just didn't know how to say that to him yet.

"You weren't *that* bad."

His voice was soft. "I don't deserve you. Not in a thousand lifetimes."

My heart broke at that. He'd been an ass, a bully, but I'd never found anything irredeemable in Tyfen. "That's not true. Why would you say that?"

His throat bobbed, and he looked down at his strawberry, turning it in his hand. "Pass."

We sat in silence a moment while he ate his berry. I was at a loss for how to navigate these moments with Tyfen, and this was a more somber one than usual.

He balled his fists. "Sorry. I… We're supposed to be enjoying our time. I'm just in a weird mood today."

I adjusted my seat, crossing my legs and wrapping my hands around his fists. I kissed them. "I haven't stopped enjoying my dinner with you. We started the night off with a *bang*. We have lovely food, and my companion is … decent enough for me to overlook his arrogance…"

He grinned a little.

"And if things go well, I don't see why we can't end the night with a bang as well."

His grin grew. "What kind of a bang?"

I licked my lips. "I'll let you use your imagination."

"Greedy cunt," he whispered.

I giggled, and he relaxed his fists in my hands.

"Let's eat," I said.

He nodded, and we divvied up a few of the little sandwiches the kitchen had made for us. We ate and drank in silence. Despite my love for Tyfen, it was hard to walk on eggshells when his mood was so volatile.

Eventually, he commented on the nice view and location. And a minute later I broached the same subject as with all the men of my Coterie on these individual picnics.

"If my child isn't yours, who would you prefer the father to be?"

Tyfen took a swig of mead and shook his head. "I'd rather not play a guessing game. We'll all find out in a couple of days, right?"

"It's not a game."

"But it does no good to dwell on something that can't be changed."

"I'm not dwelling on it, Tyfen. It's a simple question. And an important one. Things will change forever in a couple of days, and our lives will move in a distinct direction beyond the bedroom. I need to know where everyone stands. I need to know where *you* stand."

He furrowed his brow. "My loyalty is to you and your child. That's all you need to know. Does there have to be a lineup?"

It felt like I was ramming my head into a wall, like we were speaking a different language. We both understood the political ramifications of the paternity results, so this wasn't a matter of simple curiosity.

"Surely there are some of the men you'd rather have as the father than others…"

"Why is it so important to you?" he asked. "Are you so insistent because you know already it's not mine?"

I blinked. "You all have a one in six chance. I've asked everyone the same question. It's not a ridiculous thing to want to know…"

He read my face but said nothing.

"You'd be equally happy if *any* of the others sired my child? You'd be happy if Hadwin or Findlech was the father?"

Tyfen tensed with a scrutinizing expression. "Are one of those two the father?"

I gaped. "What?" None of the others had put me on the spot like this.

"Why would you bring those two up specifically?"

Rolling my eyes, I huffed. "Because no one seems all that fond of Hadwin being the father, solely because he's a vampire, and because you and Findlech aren't exactly the best of friends."

He nodded, relaxing a little. "I won't give you a lineup when it doesn't matter, when I've sworn my loyalty to you and your child." He pursed his lips. "But I hope like hell it's not Findlech's."

I could at least breathe easy that we wouldn't start another realm-wide war over my child, since it was neither fae nor elf.

Closing my eyes, I tried to find that happy place again. That place where Tyfen wasn't tense and closed off, wasn't angry or hurting. "Thank you for answering." I opened my eyes and forced a smile.

He focused on another little sandwich. "Sure."

I watched him a moment, appreciating his muscles, his tattoos, the gentle curve of his ears.

"Blantue?" I said.

A hint of a genuine smile graced his lips. "Yes?"

"Look at me."

He did, angling his head.

"I don't want to do this. Tiptoeing around things while we're eating. Either we fight and fuck this out, or we agree to talk about something amiable beyond the weather."

He beamed. "I thought we were supposed to *end* things with a bang."

I grinned back. "Those are your two options. Get out what you need to say and fuck me until we're happy again, or pick a topic we won't argue about, and make love to me at the end."

Taking a bite of his sandwich, he considered. "What would you like me to teach you in Fae?"

A hair better than discussing the weather… I selected another little sandwich. "What is 'bread'?"

By the end of the night, I knew a few more Fae words, all of them food and drink. Before leaving the rooftop, he made love to me. Though perhaps it wasn't quite lovemaking. He drove into me with a desperation, a need stronger than he usually showed. We both came twice more.

Worn out, we lay on the rooftop, gazing at the stars, his hand on my breast.

I got lost in my thoughts as the cool breeze kissed my exposed skin.

"No matter the results, I think you'll be a great father or uncle."

He held me tighter, his hand roaming to my stomach. "I just want you and your little one to be safe and happy."

I smiled. My heart was safe with Tyfen. All of me was.

"Can I ask you something?" I whispered. If tonight was evidence of anything, it was that Tyfen was on the edge of spiraling again. He needed control. And I… I'd wanted to try something for years, but had been too afraid to ask a partner to participate. Not even Gald or my pleasure instructors.

"What's that?" Tyfen asked.

Anxious, I leaned forward and whispered in his ear.

15

SHATTERED BONES

I woke the next morning, smiling, my mind replaying the conversation I'd had with Tyfen last night. We were going to try something new. But for now, everything was business as usual.

Two mornings from now, I would be in a room full of rulers again, 'learning' the paternity results. I enjoyed Hadwin and fed from him before breakfast, and promised Elion a hell of a good time later in the day.

But right now, I wanted to have fun as a group. Delegations were already arriving, the palace was bustling, and every single one of us was wound tightly.

Back in the common room and changed, I sauntered up to Gald and kissed him. He ran his hands over my skin, tracing my ass in my barely there swimming bottoms. "Your mother won't be at the pool this time, right?"

Smirking, I kissed him again. "Nope."

I made the rest of my rounds, giving Haan a warm smile and approaching Elion. He wrapped his arms around me. "No shifting this time."

I had to chuckle, stealing a glance at his swimming shorts.

"Gald and I have spoken about a spell for my clothes... For that sort of thing..."

That took me by surprise. Most shifters didn't approve of using outsider magic like that, especially because many viewed it as straying from who they really were. But I couldn't deny the benefit. Bonded clothing spells could be done relatively easily to keep clothing from tearing or falling off a shifter. The clothes would fade, then reappear depending on the shifter's form. It would be mighty handy when I had a child running around, so I didn't have to worry about my mate shifting and giving my child an eyeful by accident.

I ran a hand across Elion's bare abs. "I'm for that, as long as the spell doesn't prevent *me* from removing my mate's clothes." I kissed his cheek, and he growled in approval.

Then I visited Hadwin. His arms were rigid, and he was uncharacteristically uncomfortable as he stood there, his scarred white chest bare for the world to see.

No one said anything, but I was immensely proud of Hadwin. This was only the second time the group had seen his scars. He'd told me this morning he wanted to take a leap, to step out of his comfort zone. He was going to swim at the pool with us today, and he was going to go without a shirt.

I kissed his cold lips. "Love you."

His fanged smile was bright. "Love you too."

Someone knocked on the common room door, and Gald got it.

"You look lovely, Lilah."

She grinned, positively gorgeous. "I know."

Findlech loosed a breath. "We're all ready?"

I fought to not roll my eyes. It wasn't like he needed to join us if he didn't want to, but he was here for Gald, and I couldn't blame him with the small tight swimming shorts Gald wore.

"Let's go," I said.

Most everyone filed out before me. I stopped at the door, glancing at Tyfen. "You're sure you don't want to join us?"

He gave me a glare dripping with feigned disinterest. "Didn't really enjoy it last time…"

I fought a smile. We wouldn't be playing this game after the paternity reveal; we were going public after that.

"Fine. Be an antisocial asshole."

"I do what I can, Your Holiness."

Hadwin pulled me along. I barely noticed Tyfen's gaze flash to the bracelet at my wrist before I left the room. My heart fluttered at that look.

Our plans were still on.

I strolled out into the sun and joined the others poolside. Only long enough to 'realize' I must have dropped my hair tie.

After excusing myself, I walked back inside solo. My anticipation grew as I fiddled with my leather bracelet.

Tyfen had agreed to roleplay with me, though he'd been hesitant about the scenario. Had he been too excited about this, I wouldn't have felt comfortable.

But I couldn't keep a smile from my face. I wanted his dominance. I wanted to try something new. And I wanted to share something special with him.

Our relationship had started off so far behind what I had with everyone else. I hadn't ever shared a truly special or unique place with Tyfen—his bedroom and a couple of storage closets didn't really count.

I wouldn't be gone from the pool party for long; we could be quick.

At the top of the stairs to my level, I took a moment to catch my breath and prepare myself. All I had to do if I changed my mind was use my safety word or remove my bracelet. If I didn't do either, Tyfen would take me.

I bit my lip, giddy, then strode down the hallway to the common room. Closing the door behind me, I stole a glance in Tyfen's direction. He still sat, staring at a book.

Aiming for the sofa I'd hidden my hair tie in, I ignored him.

"What are you back for?" he asked.

"I lost my hair tie, not that it's any of your business." I bent over to 'search' between some cushions, giving him a view of my ass.

"You could have had a servant come up for it." His voice was closer.

My heart sped up. "I'm capable of getting it myself…" I straightened, grabbing a pillow to the side as I continued my fake search.

Tyfen's large hand rested on my hip. "Why don't I help?"

My breath caught. "Leave me alone."

His other hand grazed my bracelet. "I'd rather not." He pressed against me; he was already hard. "I think you wanted to see what I could do for you."

"I think you're a conceited asshole."

He tugged on one of the strings holding my swimming bottoms up, undoing the knot. Without hesitation, he pulled my bottoms off and tossed them to the side. "It's about time you get what you deserve."

My heart fluttered again. A threat, no doubt, were it not coming from a lover.

I spun, reaching for my discarded bottoms. "Don't fucking touch me!"

Before I fully stood again, Tyfen knocked me off my feet, onto the sofa. His green eyes bored into mine as he grasped his belt. "I'll touch you if I want to." Every part of him was commanding, from his elegant fae ears to his dark hair, to his tattoos and thick muscles.

As much as I desperately wanted to help him with his belt, wanted to hold his cock, that wasn't how we were playing this time. I'd offered him control, and I'd promised him *some* kind of fight.

I tried to stand, and he pushed me down. If this were a real scenario, he would easily overpower me every time.

As much as we'd planned to be quick so I could return to the pool without suspicion, I wanted to know what this whole experience felt like.

I fought again to get up, but Tyfen pinned me, his hands restraining my arms, his knees wedging between mine to spread my legs.

He gritted his teeth as I writhed under him. "Stop fighting it, or I'll fuck you so hard you forget your own name."

Please do. "Get off me," I shot back, wiggling my hips up as he reached for his belt and held my hands back with his other hand.

Tyfen freed his cock, and my mouth ran dry. My pussy, however, was already wet with anticipation.

"I'll scream," I threatened as he pressed his tip to my entrance.

With his available hand, he grasped my throat. "Good. I'm sure the guards would believe you came up here for a stupid hair tie, and not to enjoy one of the men assigned to fuck you."

He plunged into me, and I gasped.

Why did he feel perfect inside me no matter what he did?

Tyfen pulled halfway out, then drove into me again.

"Please stop," I begged.

He pulled out again, then hesitated, his eyes searching mine. I reassured him by pressing my neck harder against his hand, by lifting my hips.

Taking the cue, he tightened his grip on my throat, plunging into me again.

Goddess save me, I loved this. It felt right to share my first time in the common room with Tyfen. With each thrust from him, I traded my moans, pants, and gasps for a plea to stop.

Faster and harder, Tyfen thrust into me.

"Please stop," I said again, just above a whisper.

"I'll stop when *I'm* done, you greedy cunt."

I fought a smile at the nickname, at the building tightness in my core.

"GET THE FUCK OFF HER!" Hadwin roared, appearing out of nowhere, his blindingly white hands tearing Tyfen off me, out of me, and into the nearest wall.

A sickening snap rang through the room as Tyfen let out a bloodcurdling holler.

"Hadwin!" I screamed.

His irises were deep red, the whites of his eyes bloodshot. He breathed heavy, surveying me for injuries.

Before I could say anything, he spun toward Tyfen, who sat on the floor, dazed, clutching his arm.

Lightning fast, Hadwin reached him, grabbing the injured arm, twisting and yanking. Tyfen screamed as another crack sounded.

I launched at Hadwin. "Stop it!" I tried to pull him away. "STOP IT!"

Hadwin was immovable, the monster many feared coming to life. "I'm done with you!" he growled at Tyfen, ignoring me completely.

"No!" I threw myself between them, covering Tyfen. He gasped in more pain, but it forced Hadwin to look me in the eyes.

"Get away, Sonta." His fangs were bared.

"No! Stop it! He wasn't hurting me!"

Hadwin's confusion registered through his rage. "He was *raping* you!"

"No he wasn't!"

"Your Holiness?" a concerned voice called at the open doorway. A servant who must have heard the commotion.

And what a sight we were... Tyfen bloody, gasping in pain; me half-naked, and Hadwin with blood on his hands.

"Get a healer!" I yelled.

The servant hesitated despite Tyfen's moaning and my order, unsure if it was safe to leave the Blessed Vessel.

"I'm fine. Get a healer now!"

They nodded and darted away.

I returned my focus to Hadwin, who eyed Tyfen like the fae was a fattened pig ready to be drained of blood.

"He wasn't hurting me. I asked him to do this!"

Hadwin's attention snapped to me. He furrowed his brow. "I heard enough. You asked him to *stop*."

My shoulders slumped as tears pricked at my eyes. "We were ... pretending, Hadwin."

His eyes darted, searching me. "You're just covering for him. You said no. He was choking you!"

Never mind me being partially naked; I felt wholly bare now. There was a reason I'd never had the courage to ask a lover to try out this kink with me.

"I liked it." I swallowed.

Hadwin was still bewildered. "He could have hurt you." His eyes flicked to my stomach. "Could have hurt our ... hurt your child!"

"He wouldn't have."

Tyfen groaned behind me.

What's taking that servant so long?

I pointed at a throw blanket. "Get me that!"

Slowly, Hadwin obeyed, bringing it to me.

Wincing, I got off Tyfen and tried to stop the bleeding and assess his injuries. He was still rather dazed. Minding the bones sticking out, I tucked a corner of the blanket behind his head, then draped the rest down, pressing a portion against a wound on his arm that bled badly. With my free hand, I covered his cock with another corner of the blanket.

If we were going to have a brawl, *naturally* it would happen this way.

"Go grab me another blanket," I told Hadwin.

"I'm not leaving you alone with him."

What the hell was Tyfen going to do in this state? "Unless you want the entire palace to see your pregnant mate half-naked, you can stop being *fucking* useless and go get me one!"

He glanced down at me, then stomped away to grab one.

I caressed Tyfen's face. "It'll be okay. We'll have a healer here soon."

Tyfen gritted his teeth. "That fucker's stronger than he looks."

No sooner had Hadwin returned and I'd wrapped a blanket around myself than guards burst into the room, wands and swords at the ready.

"Your Holiness?" A couple of healers stood behind them.

"I'm fine. Prince Tyfen is badly hurt."

The guards parted, allowing the healers to enter.

They quickly assessed Tyfen's arm. "What happened?" one asked.

I gulped. How much did they really need to know? "He... His arm is broken..." As if that wasn't obvious from the copious amounts of blood and the bones...

The healer looked between Hadwin and me. We both had blood on us, but only one of us was strong enough to have done this to Tyfen. Only one of us had red eyes. Only one of us had a menacing scar on their chest.

"Was he bitten?" the healer asked Hadwin.

"No." Hadwin took a half step back.

Tyfen sucked in heavy breaths, glaring at Hadwin. "He was about to."

My heart dropped into my stomach. Everything had gone from playful experimentation to panic to *this*, all in the blink of an eye.

A member of my Coterie had assaulted another member.

The guards faced Hadwin. "You'll need to come with us, Your Grace."

I could barely look at Hadwin, everything a hot blur.

"Can I..." he started. "Can I please dress properly before being paraded around the palace?"

He was only in his swimming trunks, his scar on full display.

The guards looked to me. I was the head of the Coterie, their primary concern. No matter that I wished for privacy, this wouldn't end here. This wouldn't stay a secret like my bruised ribs. Hadwin had to be detained while things were sorted out.

The healers were actively working on Tyfen. There was no more threat.

"Yes, please allow Hadwin to dress first."

A guard nodded and followed Hadwin to the Coterie corridor.

My midwife ran in the door, worry on her face. "Are you hurt?"

"I'm fine." I tugged on my blanket to make sure it was closed properly.

Her gaze traveled between Tyfen and me. "Is that his blood on you?"

I nodded, tears coating my eyes.

She held a hand out. "Come now, let's get you cleaned up and inspected."

"No. I'm not leaving Tyfen."

Tyfen grunted in pain as the healers stabilized his bones, the bleeding having stopped.

"Can't you give him a sleeping tea?"

"No!" Tyfen panted. "I have to stay awake. My delegation is due any minute."

I bit the insides of my cheeks. That had been part of why we'd picked now to sneak away. The fae king and queen expected him to join them for dinner, and Tyfen had been sure they'd demand a lot of his time.

How the hell were we going to explain to the king and queen that my vampire Coterie member had assaulted their son?

"Please, Your Holiness," my midwife implored. "Sit down and let me have a look at you while they do their work."

I nodded again, taking a seat.

She crouched, meeting my eyes. "You swear you're not harmed?" she whispered.

"I'm fine. Just rattled. I don't need to be fussed over."

Sighing, she scanned my face. "I still need to do my duty. Can I please see under your blanket?"

I averted my gaze. "I'm not decent." The strings of my top were visible, but I wasn't ready for the guards and healers to see me this way.

"We can go to your chambers, or we can do this here, discreetly."

I nodded. "Here."

Carefully opening my blanket, she blocked the view with her body. She rested a hand on my stomach. "No pain? No symptoms?"

"No. Like I said—I'm not hurt." Other than perhaps my broken pride and heart, a heart that still thumped at a quickened pace.

Her gaze focused on her hand, the way it had when she'd detected my pregnancy in the first place. "Everything seems fine."

Hadwin walked back in behind me, now dressed, the guard escorting him to the main hallway. His blank expression was like a slap in the face.

My midwife looked between Hadwin and me, then down to my belly again, a spark of recognition in her eyes.

She knew who the father was.

"Please don't…" I begged, barely audible.

She nodded, then covered me back up. "I'm going to stay and monitor you for a bit."

Hadwin followed two guards out, and two remained at the hallway door.

I was numb, slumping in my seat as they patched up Tyfen. He wouldn't even look at me, gazing down, gritting through the pain of them straightening his bones and temporarily binding them into place.

Tears streamed down my face, and my future—my child's future—became a blur.

I fucked up.

16
Thin Lies

"Would you like your hair braided?" a servant asked.

I stared into the mirror, hating myself. "No."

The healers had stabilized Tyfen and carted him away to a palace infirmary, and my midwife and a servant helped bathe me to get Tyfen's blood off me.

Guards had already passed news of the incident to the emperor and magistrate, and I was requested in the emperor's study for questioning.

The entire Coterie and Lilah had already returned to the common room; I couldn't face them yet. Luckily, Elion calmed enough with reassurance from the midwife that I was fine.

I'd never been more scared to meet with the emperor and magistrate, but I didn't have any other choice than to walk into the emperor's study. The moment I did, they looked me over, asking if I was well.

I sighed. "As I've said a thousand times already—I'm not hurt."

"What happened?" the emperor asked. "Duke Hadwin claims he acted out of a belief Prince Tyfen was hurting you."

Swallowing hard, I took a seat. "Hadwin was mistaken. Tyfen wasn't hurting me. It was all a misunderstanding."

The emperor's hard eyes stared back. "Tyfen claimed Hadwin was ready to bite him?"

"I don't know."

Magistrate Leonte adjusted in his seat. "Have the two had problems before now? We should have been apprised earlier of any serious conflicts."

The back-and-forth was painful. No, they hadn't had any serious conflicts. No, I didn't think either man was trying to make a political statement. No, I wasn't covering for either of them.

The emperor asked me for my account of the entire incident. I clammed up. Neither of these rulers seemed the type to understand my varied tastes in the bedroom...

"It was a private matter," I deflected. "A ... relationship thing..."

The emperor leaned back in his chair, eyeing me. "A relationship thing? Your calling is to keep this empire together with your Coterie, not to sow division in your bedchambers."

That was a low blow. "The empire hasn't fallen. It was a simple misunderstanding we can sort out and keep quiet."

Leonte winced. "Sonta ... the delegations have already started to arrive. Tyfen's healing won't happen overnight."

The emperor sat forward abruptly. "Do you know who the father is?"

I cowered. Normally, they wouldn't find out before the others. But these weren't normal circumstances.

"Yes," I whispered. "Hadwin is the father."

The men exchanged a look.

"Does he know that?" Leonte asked.

My stomach turned, and I nodded.

The emperor's expression darkened. "Do any of the others know that?"

"No. We've been careful."

Not in all my time around the man had I ever heard the emperor curse, but he did now. I certainly wasn't fluent in Elvish, but what youth didn't grow up learning curses in foreign languages for fun?

"Even if it is not true, if claims that Prince Tyfen tried to hurt you came to light..." the emperor warned. His tone was grave.

"Never mind him," Leonte added. "While Hadwin protecting his mate and child is understandable, him attacking someone could do far more harm than good for his people, especially if it was only a 'simple' misunderstanding."

For the next few minutes, the two of them explained the possible consequences and scolded me for breaking the tradition of not sharing my knowledge with the father, and of course for not doing a better job at keeping things under control. Each concern was a brick on my shoulders. My shame and anxiety compounded as the weight grew, as everything threatened to topple.

I stood. "You know what I am. My mother and I had no formal education on diplomacy. I'm doing my *best*. And I can still control this situation!"

"Your best?" the emperor chided.

"Hoku chose me. She trusts me. Maybe you should too." My ears heated. "If you'll excuse me, I'm going to speak to the men to keep this under wraps, because this conversation is doing nothing to help."

Neither protested as I walked out.

The moment the door closed behind me, I leaned against the wall and fell apart. Tears trailed down my cheeks, my breathing forced.

Hoku had chosen me for this task. Perhaps she had chosen wrong.

"Sonta?" Kernov asked cautiously.

I glanced to my left, wiping my tears. "Hi."

"How can I help?"

I looked away. "I don't need help. I'll fix it."

"I... Well, all I know is a meeting I was in got cut short because there was a ... fight?"

Hugging myself, I nodded. "I'll fix things."

His voice was as soft and kind as usual. "I'm at your disposal."

No, I needed to do this on my own. I needed to speak to Hadwin and Tyfen, and we needed to come up with a resolution, a story.

"Thank you, Kernov." I wanted to hug him. "I'll send word if there's anything you can do."

He nodded.

"Please make sure my mother doesn't hear of this."

He pursed his lips. "I think she would like to know."

I gave him a stern look, wiping away the last of my tears. "She worries too much already."

Hesitating only a moment more, he nodded again. "I can separate my personal and professional life. I won't mention it, and the rest of the staff understands the need for discretion with this kind of conflict."

"Thank you."

He offered me one more forlorn look before I excused myself and made my way to the palace dungeon.

***

I'd never been to the palace dungeon before, save the tour I'd gotten of the entire palace upon my arrival a few years back. Hadwin sat on the ground despite the bed and chair in the room. It broke my heart to have him here.

He stirred but did not stand, even when I approached the bars. We stared at each other a moment. His eyes were no longer bloodshot, but a rim of red remained around his irises. He was so unduke-like.

"You're well?" he asked softly.

My anger flared. Everyone needed to stop asking me that, needed to stop treating me like I was something so fragile. And I'd already answered him that, had already made it abundantly clear I'd consented to what Tyfen had done to me.

"I'm not the one you should be asking about, Hadwin. I'm not the one with a head injury, a broken arm, and goddess knows what other injuries they're treating on Tyfen right now."

"*You're* my priority," Hadwin said coldly, blandly.

Me? Or the child within me? It was romantic that he prioritized me and our child, but our pairing was so much more than that.

"You have obligations within the Coterie. Obligations to your peers—I shouldn't have to remind you of that!"

He stood and approached the bars. "The Coterie is nothing without the Blessed Vessel. My life is nothing without my mate. If you're looking for an apology from me, you won't be getting it. I saw what I saw, and I heard what I heard."

I clenched my teeth. "Were you going to bite him? Going to envenomate him?"

Hadwin looked down, pursing his lips. "I don't know. It was all a blur. My vampire instincts kicked in."

My chest tightened, the horror of what may have happened to Tyfen had I not gotten between them tearing across my mind.

"That's not okay." I'd kept Hadwin's secrets so far, his illegal actions of revenge in his own lands. But this... "It makes me feel like I don't really know you."

Hadwin's gaze darkened. "Like *you* don't know *me*? The Sonta I know is strong and sweet, not ... whatever that was in the common room and what you claim it was." His hands gripped the bars. "Since when does the woman I love, the *fucking* Blessed Vessel, want to be with a man who hurts her? Who debases her?"

My ears warmed. My roleplay with Tyfen was just that—a roleplay. That kind of sex satiated a complex craving for me, and Hadwin wasn't the type to fill that need. "You've made it clear you have no desire to know about my relationships with the others, so you can't be angry with me when you learn about them."

Taking a step back, Hadwin cocked his head. "Do I displease you in bed?"

I narrowed my eyes. "Seriously?" Hadwin did other things no one else could. His blood play was mind blowing. His desire to please me was top tier. His cold touch always sent shivers down my spine.

And romantically, out of the men in my Coterie, I'd always had the deepest connection with him.

"This isn't about comparison, Hadwin. Just because I love Tyfen, and express it in a different way, doesn't mean I love you or any of the others less." I straightened. "I don't have time for your fragile ego. I need you to be a representative of your people and a father to your child. Neither of which look promising from where I stand right now."

His jaw worked as he processed that. This was so much bigger than us, larger than a lovers' spat. He'd attacked the fae's representative. He could be deemed unfit. The fae could seek retribution. Our child may suffer from the fallout.

"Maybe you shouldn't have chosen the common room to play out your scenario," he muttered.

We shouldn't have. There was a thrill to public sex where one may get caught. And we'd considered elsewhere, but none of the other options had felt right. And Tyfen... I'd wanted him to be the first to take me in the common room.

But we still should have been smarter.

Then again, we'd planned for everyone else to be out at the pool.

Heat rose in my cheeks again. "Why were you following me in the first place?" Would Hadwin always be like this now that my child was his? Overbearing? Overprotective? "You have no right to stalk me. I'm still allowed to do as I please within the divine edicts when it comes to lovers."

A distant look came over him as he backed up further. "Stalking?" His voice was filled with the hurt of a man who'd been scorned and discarded by a woman he'd loved before. "I wasn't stalking you, Sonta."

He balled his fists, then opened them. "If you must call me something, let's make it accurate. I'm a coward, not a stalker. I thought I was brave enough to go without a shirt at the pool today, but one unnerved look from a servant at my scars, and I decided to return to my room for a shirt."

Despite my anger, I couldn't ignore how gutting that was to hear.

He surveyed my face. "I felt my mate's elevated heartbeat as I approached, and then I opened the door to…"

He ran a hand through his soft blond locks. "What should I have done? Cleared my throat? Politely ask if when you begged him to stop, you didn't *actually* mean it?"

I fidgeted with my hands, fighting the painful truth. Hadwin was a victim of his nature and his trauma, and of my stupidity and all our bad timing. Of course I'd wish him to protect me were I actually in harm's way.

I had no words, my head swimming with guilt and anger and worry, with regret and fear and the need to form a plan to fix this before it got out of control.

"I need to go check on Tyfen," I whispered.

Hadwin's sigh was gentle. "I pose no threat. When can I get out of here?"

I hugged myself. "That's up to the emperor and magistrate, depending on how the situation plays out."

"My delegation arrives in the morning…"

Swallowing the lump in my throat, I nodded. "I know."

***

My walk to the infirmary was a somber one. How would we contain this, with the most important people in the empire flooding the palace?

The Coterie already safeguarded secrets amongst ourselves… The palace staff had been selected with extreme care. Hadwin would no doubt want to hide the issue now that he realized he'd been mistaken.

Tyfen… It all came down to Tyfen.

I was greeted by servants and a healer apprentice at the infirmary. I tried to ignore their obvious looks of concern for my well-being.

"How is he?" I asked.

The healer folded his arms. "Those breaks won't heal overnight, and he'll have a nasty headache for some time… But we got to him in time; we'll be able to piece him back together."

He wouldn't die, but he certainly wasn't ready to greet his parents—the king and queen—who expected him anytime now.

I forced a weak smile. "Thank you for taking care of him. Can I see him?"

"Of course. Follow me."

He led me to a private room where Tyfen sat in a bed, propped up by pillows. His arm was wrapped from shoulder to wrist.

His eyes closed, he rested his head against a pillow between him and the headboard.

It gutted me to see him this way. "Can we talk?" I asked.

He opened his eyes and smiled. "I'm not in any condition to finish what we started earlier, so talking is about all you'll get from me."

The healers and guards excused themselves, letting us know they'd be right outside if they were needed.

I gently joined Tyfen on the bed, on his good side. "They tell me you'll heal well."

Tyfen nodded.

"How's the pain?"

He shrugged, then winced. "I'll be fine. If anything, my pride is the most severely wounded." He lightheartedly added, "I'll never live it down if people find out a scrawny vamp got me so well."

Rolling my eyes, I hooked my arm through his. "*That's* what you're worried about? Your reputation as a commander getting his ass handed to him by an average-sized vampire? Not anything else?"

Tyfen wore a crooked grin. "My concerns *might* be a bit bigger than that."

I rested a hand on his thigh under the blanket covering him at the waist. Meeting skin, I dared to explore a bit more. He wasn't wearing a stitch of clothing under these blankets.

He gazed down at me, still playful despite his injuries, despite the humiliation of the guards and healers finding him with his pants down. "I'm sure the nurses would let you bathe me while I recover. You won't be too busy over the next few days, right?"

The irony was that I *would* bathe him, had the next few days not been packed already. I wanted to say something clever and witty back, but the pressure was mounting on me to right this, to sweep it under the rug.

"Hadwin realizes his mistake." He refused to apologize for hurting Tyfen or accept blame for any aspect of the situation, but we'd parted in the dungeon with an understanding… "And he knows how serious this is."

There was a sliver of hope this could be smoothed out still, but if Tyfen demanded an apology from Hadwin, this might go further to shit.

Tyfen blew out a breath, his playful expression waning. "We messed up. And I can't fault a man for wanting to protect his mate and child."

I blinked, surprised Tyfen was so quick to forgive and forget.

"So … what are you saying?"

"I've failed you and my people in many ways, but I'm not ignorant. I understand the repercussions. I comprehend how a simple act of arrogance or misunderstanding, no matter the intention, can blow up in our positions." He adjusted himself slightly, cringing as he did so. "This isn't the first secret within the Coterie, and I doubt it will be the last."

Tyfen was willing to sweep it under the rug? Was willing to let it go just like that?

I glanced at his wrapped arm. "Even if you can glamour that away, what are you supposed to do about hiding the pain?" His every movement was rigid. "Your parents are expecting you tonight, and you'll only have one day to heal before the paternity reveal and celebration ball…"

"I have an idea on that," he said. "And the lie to my parents won't have to be too creative." He smiled to himself briefly. "I haven't always taken care of myself all that well…" He looked away. "I drank too much and tumbled down the stairs."

I frowned, both at the darker recognition of his past and at the flimsy lie. The only reason Hadwin had thrashed Tyfen so well was because he'd snuck up on us. He could be stealthy, and he could be strong when motivated. Had it been a fair fight, Tyfen could've held his ground.

"Tumbled down the stairs?" I asked skeptically. "You're built like a brick, Blantue. If I were your parents, I'd expect the stairs to be hurt worse than you."

He smiled again at that. "I can glamour it to look more consistent with a tumble… And I have a plan."

I kissed his bare shoulder. "Let's hear it."

17
The Mother Majesty

I sat with Tyfen, cuddling, plotting and planning. He'd sent for an aide to request his mother's presence for a private visit once the fae delegation arrived. *Only* his mother, not his father.

I tensed the instant word arrived that they were settling into their guest chambers. Tyfen and I rehearsed our plans, our thinly veiled lies. I trusted the emperor and magistrate were okay with our plans to cover this up, because I'd sent them a letter while waiting for the fae king and queen to arrive, and they hadn't sent a letter back forbidding our approach.

Tyfen kissed me tenderly. "It'll be fine, Blantui."

My heart warmed and calmed a touch.

A few moments later, Queen Lourel herself entered the room. Shock covered her face. "What's the meaning of this?"

Tyfen had glamoured away his head wound and added a couple of cosmetic bruises to be more consistent with a fall down stairs.

"I'm fine, Mother."

"Like hell you are. What happened?" Despite her long journey from the heart of fae lands, not a hair was out of place around her crown and delicate arched ears.

I let Tyfen do the talking.

"You know me," Tyfen drawled. "A little wine, a misstep on the stairs…"

Her nose twitched—her fae senses must have picked up on the strong wine we'd had him drink to make the story more believable.

"You shame us again." Her expression hardened, just like it had when he'd flashed the onlookers from the bedding chamber. "After *everything*…"

Her eyes bored into Tyfen as she let the vague response hang in the air. I felt Tyfen's soul shrink. His mother knew he had a drinking problem, knew he'd gotten into trouble before, and she was displeased with him—a grown man in a precarious position.

"I know," he admitted humbly. "I'm sorry."

It broke my heart how easily she accepted the excuse. At how he took the blame so readily, just like he'd been fine with the rest of the Coterie thinking poorly of him.

"We were celebrating, Your Majesty," I lied. I'd only known him two months; she'd known him over two hundred years… I'd never seen a side of Tyfen that involved merriment and true open joy, but it was obvious he turned to the bottle when upset. Perhaps I could improve his standing with his mother by implying a more benign reason for his drunkenness…

Her expression softened as she glanced at me. "Your Holiness." She gave me a slight bow, then her gaze shifted to my stomach. "Is there … something to celebrate?"

Fuck. Did I just give her hope that Tyfen was the father?

"The entire Coterie, Your Majesty. We're *all* excited for the paternity reveal." I forced a smile. "I obviously was not drinking, though…"

She nodded, then assessed Tyfen further. "Why did your aide only want *me* to come? Why not your father?"

I swallowed hard. Tyfen's relationship with his father was apparently much more strained.

Tyfen drew a deep breath. "He might overreact. Might make things messier. I was hoping you could help."

She hesitated, a regal and scrutinizing expression settling onto her face. Looking at me again, she addressed me. "Would it be possible to have a moment alone with my son, Your Holiness?"

Tyfen gripped my hand tighter under the blanket. I'd sworn I would stay with him; he'd said my presence would help with our cover story. "I want her here. Anything you have to say can be said in front of Sonta."

As the queen's gaze shifted between us, I wished I had glamouring magic to disappear.

Straightening, the queen clasped her hands. "You were celebrating. You got drunk. You fell down the stairs?"

"Yes."

Her expression was harsh. "Did Lord Findlech play a part in this?"

My jaw dropped, and I quickly clamped my mouth closed. She jumped to assuming Findlech had tried to assassinate Tyfen? That he'd pushed him down the stairs?

"No," Tyfen replied curtly. "It was an accident, Mother. He was nowhere near me."

"The Coterie gets along well, Your Majesty."

My lie was received with an expression from the queen that warned she did not appreciate dishonesty. Whatever secret feud Findlech and Tyfen had, she obviously knew about it.

Part of me was grateful, though, that Findlech distracted her from seeking out the truth—that Hadwin had assaulted Tyfen. That would lighten the blow and help smooth things over when Hadwin was revealed as the father.

Still, I wanted to soothe and distract her. Tyfen had playfully joked about needing his parents to believe I cared for him despite having botched things so thoroughly at the opening of the Great Ritual.

I leaned into the romance angle, snuggling Tyfen's arm more, my hand on his exposed chest. "I swear, Your Majesty, our great nations and territories have all sent good men. Especially the noble fae kingdom." I kissed his shoulder again, and he smiled. "Tyfen and I had a rough start, but we're in a good place. We're *all* in a good place to bring the next Anointed Ruler into a happy home."

The lie burned as it rolled off my tongue, as I envisioned the blood in the common room, as I recalled what it felt like to argue with Hadwin from the other side of bars in the dungeon.

Despite my internal pain, the distraction landed well. The queen seemed genuinely happy as she glanced between us.

Tyfen said something in Fae, including my name. I didn't understand it, but it was a calm assurance.

The queen's smile grew as she gave her son a nod and knowing look.

I continued, "I'm terribly sorry this accident happened, and at such an inopportune time, but there was no malice, no conspiracy."

Tyfen spoke up. "But we know imaginations can run wild, which is why we're asking for your help to conceal my injuries, Mother."

She nodded her understanding. "I'll tell your father your plans changed, that you're spending your time with Her Holiness instead of us, while you heal further. I don't like lying to your father…" She scrutinized Tyfen's injuries again. "But you're right to want to keep him out of this."

"Thank you," Tyfen replied.

We briefly discussed how long the healers thought it would take for Tyfen to be completely well. To conceal his pain and injuries, extra magic would need to be added to our façade, magic we needed the approval of the emperor and magistrate to use within the walls of the palace.

The queen tucked a curl behind her arched ear. "I shouldn't be gone long, or my husband will worry." She addressed me specifically. "Let's get this taken care of."

"Yes, Your Majesty."

Tyfen squeezed my hand. "Can I have another moment alone with Sonta before you two go?"

"I'll be right outside waiting."

After she left, I faced Tyfen. "We might just pull this off…"

His smile was sweet. "Wouldn't be the first time I've lied to my parents."

I kissed him. "What did you say in Fae to your mother?"

He furrowed his brow, then remembered. "Oh. I assured her I was happy here."

My heart was lighter.

He smirked. "I told her your tits are incomparable and your pussy tastes like the finest dessert I've ever had."

I glared, balling my fist. Were he not injured, I would have socked him in the arm. It was obviously a lie—he'd barely said anything to her.

"That's it—no sponge baths for you."

He pouted with his perfectly kissable lips.

I stole another smooch. "I really do need to go."

"Okay. I'll take some of that tea now we've got everything sorted."

"Yes. Sleep off the pain. I'll join you in bed tonight."

"I'd love that."

***

The queen's pace was quick as we turned down a corridor, escorted by a few guards.

"I'm sorry he got hurt," I whispered.

She stopped abruptly, sizing me up. Then she glanced at the guards. "Could we please have some privacy?"

The guards looked to me, and I nodded, nervous.

"What don't I know?" she asked me.

I gaped. "Your Majesty?"

"Why would you say you're sorry he got hurt, instead of sorry he hurt himself? Or better yet, why apologize at all if he was foolish enough to hurt himself?"

My stomach knotted. She was a perceptive woman.

I held my hands over my stomach. "You're a mother. I imagine it's hard to see your son hurt, no matter how or why it happened."

She searched my face. "I'm not a perfect mother, but I love my son. Do you love him? Can you truly say you respect him after what he did in the bedding chamber and ballroom?"

He'd no doubt earned himself a tongue-lashing behind closed doors for his performance. The queen's anger had been written all over her face.

"I've forgiven him," I said truthfully. "We're still working through things, but I *do* love your son. I want what is best for him."

She pursed her lips. "And do you love them all?"

That was really none of her business, and rather impertinent of her to ask. Our stations were uniquely different, neither technically above nor below the other.

"You'll have to forgive me, Your Majesty, but I don't openly share such private details about my Coterie."

She looked flustered. "I... I'm not asking for intimate details, but if you favor one over my son... And if you're covering for him..."

My heart froze. I could have sworn she'd bought our lie about the stairs earlier. Perhaps we had a leak amongst the servants after all... "Your Majesty?" Normally, the concern was that one of the men would try to hurt me or my child, not that I would collude to off one of my men...

"Lord Findlech," she blurted. "Did he play any part in this?"

What the... "No..."

"Were you there when it happened?"

"Yes! And I assure you Findlech was nowhere near Tyfen when he got hurt. When he hurt himself..."

"How much do you like Lord Findlech?"

I sure as hell wasn't going to answer honestly. We were friends. "Does Her Majesty know something I should be aware of? For all I know of Lord Findlech, he is a good and kind man."

Her tone and expression calmed slightly. "I'm not trying to make false accusations. In truth, I never met the man before the Great Ritual. But I have my reasons for worrying about him hurting my son."

My brain stuttered. At worst, Findlech was an arrogant elitist, but I could never imagine him taking part in foul play.

I stood firm in my assertion. "Findlech has never once shown any hostility toward Tyfen. Not once. Not in word or action." Ironically, Findlech had been the one to ask—on two separate occasions—if we should check on Tyfen when he'd locked himself in his room. "If anything, Lord Findlech has been more of a friend to Tyfen than the other men in my Coterie."

She looked shocked and disbelieving.

And why shouldn't she? Tyfen seemed to think Findlech was an enemy who wanted him miserable.

The queen knew more than she was letting on.

"What..." I stopped myself. I *needed* to understand what was going on between them. Why these fae hated Findlech so much. How Tyfen was involved in a war that had almost happened. Why both sides were keeping secrets from me.

I couldn't ask her, no matter how much I wanted to. I didn't know the woman on that kind of level, and asking would confirm any ignorance I held, would betray Tyfen. Because if she realized he was keeping secrets from me, she may not buy our love story and our distraction. She may change her mind about agreeing to cover up Tyfen's injuries.

While it was a happy turn of events to not have any accusations thrown Hadwin's way, it wasn't okay for any of the others to endure unjust scrutiny.

"Findlech is not out to get your son. I swear on my life, Your Majesty." My compassion as a mother turned to anger over her accusation of a friend whom she admitted she knew practically nothing about. "I swear on the life of my child, on the name of my divine mother. And I *will not* allow slander of a member of my Coterie."

The hallway was quiet as she gathered a breath. "I meant no offense, Your Holiness." She averted her gaze. "Let's go see the emperor and magistrate about sorting out Tyfen's healing."

Before we entered the emperor's office, Queen Lourel uttered an apology for having upset me earlier, and it put my heart more at ease. I accepted.

Despite that ease, the conspiratorial meeting kept me nervous. Especially because one of us was ... being misled, and then partaking in misleading others.

As people of politics, we did our dance—saying a lot of the niceties and skirting some of the issues. The emperor and magistrate both expressed their apologies about Tyfen getting hurt on the premises, wishing him a speedy recovery. The queen graciously accepted, and apologized for any untoward behavior Tyfen had exhibited to bring about the accident.

The men in charge let me do most of the important talking, allowing me to confirm the half-truths and full lies the queen had been fed and believed. It went smoother than I'd expected. My gut twisted, though, when the topic turned to feintal magic.

"Only during necessary public appearances until he's healed enough to conceal the pain himself," the emperor consented grimly.

"Of course," the queen replied.

"Do you have a servant in mind?" he asked.

She pursed her lips. "I'm not sure yet. I'll have to let you know."

Feintal magic... It was a gruesome thing, usually frowned upon. It allowed a willing volunteer to take on the pain of someone else. Tyfen could glamour away his injuries for the sake of appearances, but his cautious movements and pained reactions would give away the injury. If someone else took on his pain during the paternity reveal ceremony and during the celebration ball, Tyfen could hug me, could dance with me, and no one would be any the wiser.

Except the poor volunteer who would endure the inevitable excruciating pain that would otherwise radiate through Tyfen with each bend and bump of his still-injured arm.

The meeting was brief and to the point.

"Thank you for your discretion." Magistrate Leonte sketched a quick bow to the queen. "We wouldn't want a misunderstanding over the unfortunate timing of Prince Tyfen's injury."

Queen Lourel gave him a nod in reply, and a curt smile. She turned to the emperor. "I appreciate my son being looked after. And I'm grateful for the *impartiality* of our emperor on serious issues." Not a word of her statement rang with true gratitude. If anything, her words were clipped, almost threatening to the emperor.

As always, the emperor was calm and collected, never flinching. "Regardless of my parentage, and *thanks* to my parentage, I do my best to balance the needs and concerns of all the people in this empire."

After another moment of eye contact with him, the queen excused herself, commenting she needed to get back to her husband to lie about why she'd gone missing.

The emperor held me back, and I shrank again under his eyes, and under Leonte's eyes.

"Your lovers' quarrel has made us complicit in this deception," the emperor said.

I gulped. "I know. I'm sorry."

"Surely we don't have to tell you how serious it is to use feintal magic…"

Hadn't we just put this to bed? I should be celebrated with a pat on the back for fixing my problem, not be scolded more. "I understand that. And if you'll excuse me, I should get going, too."

The emperor took a seat behind his desk, and Leonte sat near him.

I should have left immediately. I *did* have urgent things to see to. But I couldn't let the feeling go that *everyone* knew something I didn't.

"Why did Queen Lourel just question your impartiality?" I dared to ask.

He gave me a tiny smile. "That's a good lesson for you to learn, and Hadwin. Something to pass on to your child… The people will always suspect him or her of favoritism to the vampires. Prepare your child to face that scrutiny."

It was true, and I wasn't exactly sure how to help my child face that scrutiny, but we'd tackle that together as a family.

But there was something more here.

"The fae don't like Findlech. I didn't realize they don't trust their own emperor, either."

His aged gaze didn't betray him one bit. "The war that was prevented—just because it didn't happen doesn't mean it can't still happen. When immortal races are at odds, they don't easily shed grudges. The best we can do right now is keep the peace until searing emotions cool with time."

Leonte spoke. "What of Hadwin? In the dungeon… Is he a threat to Tyfen?"

I shook my head. "He can be released."

"Very well. Please get on with your day, and work to keep this under wraps."

18
The Coterie's Reaction

Tyfen would likely be snoozing away his pain anyway, so I made haste back to the Coterie common room. I had yet to address the others.

The moment I opened the door, three of the men and Lilah all jumped from their seats. Haan floating at attention in his tank.

"You're okay?" Elion rushed to me.

"What the fuck happened?" Gald asked.

Lilah said nothing, but wrapped her arms around me, squeezing me tight.

I pulled away, nervous. "Everything's fine."

"*Fine?*" Gald asked in full disbelief, pointing to where Tyfen had almost been murdered by Hadwin. "Whose blood was that? And where are Tyfen and Hadwin?"

Tears pooled in my eyes. "Let's sit down."

Gathering near Haan's tank, we land-walkers eased down onto the sofas, all eyes on me. Fresh paint now covered the wall where Tyfen had been flung.

"This is another one of those things that has to stay within the Coterie. The servants, the emperor, and the magistrate are all keeping this silent, and we need to as well."

Today was supposed to be fun. A release for our anxiety, a last chance to come together before I broke most of their hearts with the paternity results. I resented that I craved a taste of Hadwin's blood in the moment.

"Right now, Tyfen's in the infirmary. And Hadwin's in the dungeon." I quickly added, "But he's being released any minute, and I need you all to just … pretend this didn't happen…"

Five sets of unblinking eyes stared back at me.

"We're going to need more than that," Gald said.

"It was a misunderstanding. Hadwin hurt Tyfen."

They all waited for more. And it hurt my heart to remember none of them had favored Tyfen in my picnic polls. None of them realized we were even an item.

"Tyfen and I had a rough start..."

Lilah held my hand, stroking it. I didn't deserve her love after using her without her knowledge as an alibi when Tyfen and I were sneaking around.

I continued. "But things changed a while ago... And Tyfen and I... We like each other. I love him."

Awkward glances passed around the room, and I couldn't blame them with the elaborate ruse we'd put on.

How much did I have to tell them? I sighed. I'd rather get it out of the way.

"Some of you understand I have ... interesting tastes sometimes..." I cleared my throat. "In the bedroom." *Or in a variety of rooms...*

At least Gald would understand me, being so kinky himself. "I snuck away from the pool to meet up with Tyfen. And we ... were doing some, um..."

I hated this. I hated the judgment and the humiliation of my failure.

"I consented to what Tyfen was doing to me, but Hadwin walked in on it. What he heard and saw didn't reflect my consent." I stared at my shoes. "He thought Tyfen was hurting me. He... Yeah."

Lilah laid her head on my shoulder.

"How badly injured is Tyfen?" Findlech asked.

I couldn't hold back the tears. "He's pretty beat up. You saw the blood." I sniffled. "His arm is broken in a few places. He's..." I drew a shaky breath as Elion handed me a handkerchief.

"He'll be okay. It was just a misunderstanding, a stupid mistake. I can't have people blaming Hadwin for what he did."

I especially couldn't have them hating the father of my child, the future ruler.

"And I don't want anyone to blame Tyfen, either."

I explained how his healing was going, and the concealment of the truth from his mother to dissuade any suspicion, and the planned use of feintal magic.

The room was quiet. I let the silence swallow me. Elion had learned a harsh lesson about consent on our first night when Hadwin had ... threatened him for taking me without permission. Haan understood consent despite it not being a big concern in his culture—how did he view Tyfen and me pretending it didn't matter to us?

Lilah broke the silence. "How can we help?"

I dabbed away my tears. "Just keep this quiet. Try to treat them normally. We just need to get through the next few days..."

"Your secret is safe," Findlech answered, and the others mumbled their agreement.

"Thank you. I'm going to spend the rest of the evening with Tyfen, if anyone needs me." I turned to Lilah and made her swear to not tell my mother. She agreed.

I stood, but Findlech's last words lingered with me. *Your secret is safe.*

Too many secrets for my liking.

"Findlech, can we speak in private?"

"Of course."

I led him to my room and shut the door. "I need to know what's going on between you and Tyfen."

He shook his head. "What happened today doesn't concern me. This is an issue between Tyfen and Hadwin."

I was done mincing words. "Queen Lourel was convinced you were the one to hurt Tyfen. Why would she jump to that conclusion?"

Uncharacteristically, he smiled. "That doesn't surprise me one bit. A rather impulsive leap."

That was a shit answer.

"She didn't suspect anyone else. Only you. I assured her you are a good man who would never hurt Tyfen. I swore on the life of my child. You better pray I never find something that betrays the trust I have in you."

He didn't like the implied threat. "If there are prayers to be uttered, Sonta, let them be to your divine mother. Let them be that this ruse of yours works and no one in this realm accuses Tyfen of trying to hurt a woman. Of hurting the Blessed Vessel and jeopardizing peace for the sake of a quick thrill."

The insult hurt differently than Hadwin's about our roleplay.

"Tyfen would never hurt me, and I will always vouch for him on that."

"It doesn't have to be true for the accusation to spark a fire we cannot stamp out." His tone and expression were severe.

Why was this the focus? Tyfen hurting me? I could easily refute it. Why did Findlech think my word was so meaningless in the public's eye?

"It's not like Tyfen's known for hurting women. I don't see why someone would give any credence to such an outlandish claim."

Silence was Findlech's answer. He clasped his hands. "Some would give credence, I assure you. I have a clear enough head to step back from the situation and acknowledge he's likely not in the wrong, and he's paid more than enough for past mistakes. But not everyone thinks like me. To many, Tyfen of the fae is nothing more than a selfish villain."

To whom? I'd never once heard this slander, and it wasn't like Coterie members were casual nobodies who wandered in from the street to bed me.

Findlech held his hands up. "I'm not trying to stir things up. But I do hope this incident never becomes public to the masses, for Tyfen's sake."

Which was Tyfen to Findlech? A villain or a victim? Maybe I could help if he didn't insist on being so cryptic.

"For Tyfen's sake? And what if people find out about what happened today? That sounds like a threat, Findlech."

"I don't make threats, Sonta. I give warnings. You prying into things can only make them worse. That's all I have to say on the matter."

I was going to lose it. If not today, someday soon. "You know, Hadwin wouldn't have assumed the worst of Tyfen if Tyfen and I hadn't kept our relationship a secret."

Findlech nodded. "I'm sure you're right. And Tyfen should have known better."

What an asshole! Blaming Tyfen? "Do you know why Tyfen wanted to keep our relationship a secret?" I jabbed a finger at Findlech. "*You*. He thinks you want him to be miserable. And for some fucking stupid reason, he thought it would be best to not let you see him happy."

Tyfen's logic still made no sense to me, but it was the truth. Findlech furrowed his brow at my proclamation.

I continued my tirade. "So you can pretend you're superior here, but part of this has to do with you."

Findlech took a moment to chew on his thoughts. "I'm sorry he feels that way. I've already told you I hold no malice for him, and I've tried to talk to him since the Coterie has come together. He's not ready to have the conversation that needs to be had between us. But I assure you, I have never intended to push him down. Nor his happiness with you."

His gaze grew colder. "Nor would I push him down the stairs... No matter the queen's unwarranted suspicions."

I wanted to strangle him with his own long hair. I wanted to painfully twist his pointed ears. This conversation had gotten us nowhere. Today felt like someone had taken a wine bottle and spun it in the middle of the room, laying blame on whomever the corked end landed at.

"If you won't help me understand, then leave me alone." I pointed to the door.

Without another word, he turned and left.

I flopped onto my bed and rubbed my face. Some Coteries were doomed from the start with bad matches. I had thought so well of ours recently...

Soon, I gathered my strength and got up. Hoping I wouldn't cross paths with Hadwin, I left for the infirmary via my private hallway. I couldn't take more stress today.

The infirmary was quiet and dark as Tyfen slumbered, only the faint glow of some fae lights shining in the room. I carefully crawled under the sheets with him and kissed his arm.

Sleeping peacefully, he didn't stir.

I allowed my body to relax, to mold to him. "I love you," I whispered.

The steady in and out of his lungs was his only reply.

I lay there for an eternity, unable to fall asleep. The healer came in at one point to check on his patient and bring me food. I was starving. After munching a bit, I was left with a tray of good things I could snack on later, and the healer pointed out fresh tea, should Tyfen wake and I want to administer it myself.

My pregnancy cravings got the better of me, though. I wanted blood.

The healer fetched a specific trusted servant for me. I requested pig's blood, and they delivered it discreetly.

After downing a dose and lying back down to the silence of the room, I cuddled with Tyfen again.

I still couldn't sleep, couldn't stop my racing mind. At any moment, our lies might crumble around us and snuff out my hope of resolving this situation.

Tyfen's warmth radiated to me, comforting me. He was an ethereal beauty. I traced his tattoos with my finger, along his neck, down his chiseled chest to the magical tattoo for the vow he'd made upon joining my Coterie.

I smirked as I stroked it. Fate had painted it upon his skin rather suggestively, pointing to his massive size. It wasn't the mark of a mate as would appear on a fae's inner forearm, but it was just as special to me.

It was intimate, unique.

I became wet as my finger wandered an inch down and lingered at the base of his generous cock.

Tyfen took a deep breath. "Taking advantage of me while I sleep?" he whispered, groggy.

Startled, I yanked my hand back. "No! Well, sorry. My mind wandered."

He chuckled, then groaned in pain.

"Sorry," I repeated. "I wouldn't do that to you."

He gave me a hazy smile. "You like my cock. You have my permission to enjoy it anytime you want."

I balked. "You're still injured. I'm not going to take advantage of you."

He chuckled and groaned again.

"Let me get you more tea." I stood and grabbed it, then poured some.

"This is a travesty, you know." His sweet, sleepy voice was music to my ears, but it was hard to fight a frown.

"I know. But the good news is we're all on board for the feintal magic and everything."

His eyes opening wider, he grinned as I handed him his cup. "That's good, but not what I was talking about."

"What were you talking about?"

"We're sharing a bed, and you're clothed. That's the greatest travesty in the history books."

I giggled. "You're wicked. Drink your tea." I sat next to him, making sure he could drink propped up at this half-sitting, half-lying-down angle. "I'd happily strip down to cuddle, but I'd rather not be found that way by the nurses or healers."

He sipped his tea. "They're used to nudity."

I scowled, and he winked.

The playful moment dissipated as he sipped more. When he was drunk, he was a *bit* more honest and open with me… Maybe he'd share some secrets in this sleepy state. "Tyfen, have you ever … taken advantage of a woman?"

He looked at me, confused. "No… I told you… It's not like I haven't shared a bed with a paid woman over the last two centuries, but I never…"

Perhaps Findlech hadn't meant it literally, insinuating Tyfen had possibly 'hurt' a woman in that way.

"Have you ever hurt a woman at all?" I asked more directly.

Tyfen lowered his tea, furrowing his brow. "Why would you ask me that, Sonta?"

I sure as hell wasn't going to stir up more drama by mentioning my conversation with Findlech. Instead, I shrugged. "My mind's all over the place. You just joked about me taking advantage of you, so…" I read his kind green eyes in the dim fae light. "I know you're a good man."

Blinking, he nodded. "I'd never intentionally hurt someone. Not even if I hated them." He sipped his tea. "Well … I am a commander, so it's not something I would always have a choice in. The only creatures I aim to harm are oni in our forests." His sleepy gaze was haunted. "And they deserve rest, so I'm happy to dispatch them."

He was drifting off again already.

"Finish your tea," I urged.

He did so, and I took the cup. After setting it on its tray, I turned back to Tyfen. I still had so many questions. "Your mother stopped me in the hallway after our group chat."

"Yeah?" His eyelids drooped.

"She was persistent in thinking Findlech may have wanted to harm you."

Tyfen laughed, his breath catching in pain but his smile didn't waver.

"I wish I could laugh at that," I said softly. "I'm already worried about the repercussions of Hadwin hurting you. I don't need to fight off escalating trouble between you and Findlech."

Sighing, Tyfen gestured for me to rejoin him on the bed. "My mother worries. She jumped to conclusions. Findlech's too concerned about people finding out he sticks his cock in men to worry about torturing me further."

I arched an eyebrow. "Torturing?"

He was exhausted, fading. "For fuck's sake, Sonta. We're fine."

I nodded. "Your mother seemed suspicious of the emperor as well, about him not being impartial about … something?"

Barely shrugging his healthy shoulder, he dismissed her concerns. "I haven't ever been summoned for a private meeting with the man, so I count that as a good sign."

Not the answer I'd expected. Coterie members didn't normally get summoned to speak with the emperor or magistrate without an important reason. Not being summoned was neither a good nor a bad sign—it was just normal.

It didn't matter, since Tyfen was already out before I could utter another word.

I fluffed my pillow and slid against him in bed again. This time I rested my hand over his heart. "Someday," I whispered. "Someday you'll let me in."

His heart was a dark vault, or so he'd said. When would he unlock that vault and let me in? We'd come so far in the last month, but at times it still felt like I only peered into his heart, his life, from the cold distance of an onlooker through a window.

I tried not to dwell, instead replaying the good times we'd shared. Our challenges and nicknames. The way he tied me up. The bracelet he'd given me. The unadulterated smile he wore with the sweetest praise on his lips.

His lips on mine. On my nipples. On my everything.

My mind wandered, and my hand roamed. I found myself gently grasping his cock, taking my time to feel every devastating inch of him.

Fuck, I wanted him. I wanted to finish what we'd started earlier. Sharing panted breaths between lovers.

I ached, wet as I stroked him.

I couldn't. Even with Tyfen's permission, I wouldn't enjoy him so fully while he was injured like this.

My desire fought the decision for several minutes as I lay there, staring at the ceiling. I was so ridiculously horny.

My pregnancy craving for blood had been satiated for the time being. I had food and water. But now that my nerves had calmed, I needed the release I hadn't gotten all day.

I fought my urges for nearly an hour, even as a healer apprentice checked up on Tyfen.

After she left, I was crawling in my skin. I could see to my needs quickly. No one would need to know. No one could object to that.

Giving in, I slid a hand up my dress and down my underwear. I gently rubbed my clit, sighing. My core was already on fire.

A knock sounded at the door, and I yanked my hand back out.

"Sorry, Your Holiness," the healer apprentice whispered. "Elion is out here. He wishes to speak with you."

Elion? What time was it? I'd walked miles in the palace today, spent hours already in this bed with Tyfen. "I'll be right out."

I instinctively gave Tyfen another kiss, this time on the cheek.

After I walked outside the room and shut the door, the apprentice and guards made themselves scarce at my request.

"Hi, mate." I smiled.

His silver eyes lit up at the greeting. "Hi. How's Tyfen doing?"

Elion always had a way of warming my heart. It reminded me of how he'd offered to switch spots at the dining table with Gald when the truth came out about Gald and Findlech being a couple.

"Tyfen's sleeping. It'll be a few days before he's all better, but he'll be okay. I'll let him know you checked on him."

Elion nodded, then kissed me on the forehead. "Let's go for a walk."

My heart froze, wary after the eventful day. "What's wrong?"

Unfazed, he held my chin. "Nothing. I just thought you might like a few minutes away." He pulled me into a tight, comforting hug. "When's the last time you … had your needs met?" He pressed against me, his bulge telling.

I almost laughed. "You came down here for *that?*"

He snickered in my ear. "I've been pacing the next hallway over for hours, worried about you. I didn't have the courage to intrude until I ... sensed your need."

I bit my lip.

"I'm assuming he's not really doing anything for you in his current state."

I pulled back, unable to hide a smile. "Like I said—he's sleeping."

Elion took my hand, an expectant expression on his face.

"I'd feel guilty." I frowned.

Taking my other hand, Elion angled his head. "He's sleeping. And if you love each other like you said earlier, then he would want you satisfied..."

Despite his erection, Elion's offer came across unselfish—not from a need on his part.

He kissed me softly. "My mate took care of my needs when I was desperate. I want to repay the favor."

And just like that, I was putty in his arms. "Okay. Let's make it quick."

Elion led me to an empty room. Without a word, he removed my underwear and dress. His gaze was so loving, so tender as he stripped and took me to the bed.

He laid me down, kissing me.

It wasn't feral fucking. He didn't ask how I wanted it—he understood what I needed without any direction. I couldn't love him any more in that moment as he caressed my lips time and time again, as he rubbed my nipples.

He wasn't taking me in his preferred position, but in a way we could see each other's eyes as he spread my legs and gently entered me.

Every goddess-damned inch of him was a gift. I panted, desperate, already loving his knot growing inside me. "Thank you."

He pulled halfway out, then thrust. I moaned.

"You're welcome."

He withdrew, and plunged in again.

I was so tight, so desperate, so on fire. But I also needed connection, reassurance, comfort. With each stroke of Elion inside me, I found that. His eyes practically glowed with pleasure in his duty, at hearing me pant and moan under him.

With a playful tug, he sucked my nipple, harder with each gasp.

Having lacked all day, I violently careened over the edge of ecstasy, all the while meeting Elion at the hip as he picked up speed, as he found his release.

"I love you, Sonta," he uttered, pounding into me as he filled me.

"I love you, too, Elion."

Panting, he stopped, then stole a kiss. "Better?" he smiled.

I returned the smile, relaxing everywhere save my pelvic muscles, where I squeezed him. "Better."

He growled with pleasure, leaning in and claiming my lips, my tongue, my heart more fully. He ground into me as he did so.

Eventually he stopped again, smiling. "I know you've had a hard day, but it brings me joy to see you pleased."

I ran my hands down his bare sides. "I love that your charming face and perfect cock bring me pleasure."

He nipped at my neck playfully, then pulled out. "Can I?" he asked, his hands on my thighs.

"Sure." I always looked forward to what came next with him.

Without hesitation, he tasted me. I was still so sensitive. He circled my clit with his tongue, and I arched my back.

He growled again. "My mate is *very* tight today." He accepted the unspoken challenge, not just cleaning his mate, but sending me over the edge again as he fully ate me out.

I gasped shallow breaths, my legs trembling as he licked his lips.

"More?" he asked.

"Two is fantastic." I laughed. "Come here." While I'd planned to keep this quick, I wanted to enjoy a brief naked cuddle.

Elion held me, caressing my underbreast. "You really love Tyfen?"

I swallowed. "Yes."

Elion nodded. "I don't have to understand it to accept it."

"Really?" I raised a skeptical eyebrow.

"When he made you unhappy, I wanted to slaughter him. If he makes you happy, the realm is better off." Elion grinned.

I couldn't hold back a chuckle. "Thank you for being so understanding."

Elion searched my face. "What you two were doing when Hadwin walked in on you… You *did* want it? He wasn't hurting you?"

My jovial mood chilled a degree. "Yes." Had it been Elion instead of Hadwin, he would have tried to rip Tyfen's head off too, to protect his mate. "I know not everyone in the Coterie gets why I'd ask Tyfen to pretend that way with me…"

"I do," Elion answered innocently.

"You do?"

"It's like when you run from me and I get to chase you. Or when you're on the bed and back away so I have to grab your hair." He fisted a handful of my hair, tilting my head. "You pretend you don't want it, but you do."

My heart…

"You let me fuck you awake when it's just the two of us," he added. "We have an agreement."

I ran a hand over Elion's chest. "Exactly." I'd never considered how similar Elion and Tyfen could be. If anything, I always compared Gald to Tyfen because of our shared kinks. But Elion liked it rough, liked dominance.

"Thank you for believing me about Tyfen," I said.

"I have no reason to not believe you."

I hesitated to ask, but I needed to know… "How were things when Hadwin returned?"

Elion pressed his lips together. "He didn't really say much. He went straight to his room."

"Yeah…"

After a little more cuddling, I admitted I wanted to go back to Tyfen. He would expect me by his side should the tea wear off again. Elion left me with a kiss and no protest after we dressed.

The realm was upside down as I meandered back to Tyfen's private room. It was true having so many partners could create drama. But … it was also true I could find solace and love in multiple places when I needed it.

Tyfen was still sound asleep when I nuzzled up to him in bed.

My eyelids fluttered in the morning.

"You took me up on my offer…" Tyfen whispered.

I glanced at him. He smirked, wide awake. My hand had found its way to his cock during my sleep.

"Goddess damn me—I'm hopeless." I removed my hand. "How are you doing?"

He sighed. "Stronger. My mother's going to visit soon, then they're going to knock me out to do some more adjusting and healing."

I nodded. "I should go. My mother wants to meet up, and I should check on everyone. Fittings, all that, with the paternity reveal tomorrow…"

"I understand. Don't worry about me."

I left him with a kiss and a promise I would visit him again before nightfall, even if he was too asleep to note my presence.

19

Paternity Reveal

Tyfen was cute and flirtatious when I visited, at least when he was awake.

I had a dress fitting with Madam Gaffey, and I lunched with my mother. Mother was so encouraging, so excited to join me on this journey—one where her only daughter would become a mother, and she herself a grandmother.

With her, Lilah, and the men, I did my best to hide my bubbling stress. I choked it down, hoping and praying—literally praying to Hoku—that the threat of Hadwin's attack becoming public would disappear like snow in spring weather.

I had follow-up meetings with the emperor and magistrate to confirm everything was going well. I wasn't allowed to meet the servant who would be taking Tyfen's pain through the feintal magic—they didn't want to muddy things further.

Hadwin tried to approach me at one point, but I turned him away. He reasoned that, at minimum, I should swallow my pride and feed off him to satiate my cravings.

I coldly turned him down, opting to go the harder route of regular secret doses of pig's blood. Despite our agreement to cover this incident up, I was still upset about his attitude, his unwillingness to simply apologize to Tyfen. I couldn't imagine being happy with Hadwin while Tyfen still suffered.

And I still loved Hadwin, so fully that I feared I'd say or do the wrong thing in my anger to spoil things between us. I'd rather remain apart and silent on the matter until things had calmed and my temper had cooled.

To avoid complications while the palace buzzed in preparations for the reveal, I wasn't allowed to stay the night with Tyfen. Instead, I slept alone in my room, taking care of myself with a new charmed tool Lilah had gifted me.

Granted, 'slept' was too generous of a word. I tossed and turned all night. I *wished* I now only worried about the disappointment five of the men would soon go through.

Now, I was hoping we all made it out in one piece.

***

My morning was as calm as it could be. Tyfen looked like a dream, but he wouldn't be joining us until he needed to because deeper healing was still happening.

I took breakfast in my room, but made a point to join the Coterie for lunch. Everyone but Tyfen was here, even Hadwin. Only the clink of cutlery on plates punctuated the tense silence. Haan kept sending me sweet, encouraging smiles from his tank—somehow, they only managed to make me feel worse.

"You know…" Gald broke the ice. "It's a beautiful day outside. And Sonta looks breathtaking."

The men all glanced at me with a kind nod, save Hadwin, who stared at the goblet in his hands.

"And I know things aren't … ideal right now," Gald continued. "But it's still a great day. Sonta will be a great mother." He raised his glass. "We don't even know the paternity results yet, but I'd like to be the first to congratulate you, Sonta. And whomever the father may be."

The other men raised their glasses in agreement, even Hadwin, though his congratulations were mumbled.

Tears flooded my eyes as my heart sank. "Thanks," I choked out.

Gald frowned.

I couldn't stop crying. If this was how the paternity reveal was going to go, how would my birth go? Would there be magic duels and sword fights while I was pushing my child out?

"I need to … prepare," I lied. Head high, I walked out of the dining hall, and was grateful no one followed.

A crew of servants and attendants helped ready me for the events of the evening.

Madam Gaffey primped me, applying the final touches of my look. The magenta gown was beautiful, but failed to brighten my mood. I was all jitters.

She took my hands, gazing into my eyes. "Nervous for the realm to learn the results? Or excited?"

I drew a deep, shaky breath. "Both?"

Her smile was warm. "You are Hoku's daughter. You can handle any task given you."

Hoku had been an extraordinary mage during her mortality. I was nothing like her. I wasn't as strong, and I couldn't unite this realm.

I could barely keep my own personal shit together. Not even my Coterie was unified.

"I'd like to think so," I lied, forcing a smile and holding back fresh tears.

First, we'd have the paternity reveal, then a banquet and a ball. This would be less public than the claimings had been, but there would still be a few hundred attendees between all the important dignitaries.

This time, Lilah and my mother escorted me to the small ballroom where the reveal would take place. I clung to them with each step.

"Don't be nervous," my mother soothed. "No matter what, you'll always be able to look back fondly on this special day."

Fondly? I already wanted to forget it.

We stopped before the large double doors. My mother hugged me gently.

Lilah took my hands. She looked ravishing, her purple eyeshadow highlighting her brown eyes. "You can do this." She knew the truth of everything going on right now. I'd even confessed to her earlier today about Hadwin being the father and him already knowing.

She was my rock.

Leaning her forehead against mine, her words were firm yet gentle. "Just remember to breathe."

I squeezed her hands. "Thank you."

Kernov greeted us, giving me a knowing look. He now understood the stakes and lies. "Sonta." He nodded. "You'll be marvelous."

He took my mother's hand and kissed it, offering her an extra smile. "You're all ready for your entrance?"

The three of us nodded.

"Very well. May Hoku multiply her blessings on you."

My breath was again shaky, my underarms sweating. As the ballroom was being quieted beyond the doors, I forced myself to focus on my child—nothing and no one else. Not the Coterie, not politics—just the sweet life within me.

I am Hoku's daughter. I may not be like her, but I was chosen by her.

My mind fluttered away in a vision. I lay in a field of lavender as it swayed in a summer evening's breeze. The aroma filled me, soothing me. A songbird chirped nearby.

The vision was short, like they sometimes were. Just enough to show me a glimpse of this beautiful realm, to ease my frayed nerves.

I wore a smile, grateful for the timing.

"Accompanied by her mortal mother, Vesta Gwynriel, and her childhood friend, Lilah Casten," an announcer started.

In comparison, it was odd hearing Lilah announced without a formal title of any sort, but I was grateful both she and my mother were allowed to escort me, and that they'd agreed to it.

The announcer continued. "Her Holiness, the Blessed Vessel, Sonta Gwynriel."

I wore my best regal face, and both my mother and Lilah clasped their hands in front of them.

The double doors opened, all eyes inside on us.

Striding in, I tried to acknowledge the different groups with my eyes. It was much like my initial meeting with the men of my Coterie, though a bit more formal. Mother and Lilah followed a pace after me on either side.

A stage had been erected at one end of the ballroom, and I walked to it. Lilah and my mother took their places at the base of the stairs.

VENUS COX

I passed Magistrate Leonte on my way up. He stood on the middle stair for the reveal ceremony. While the magistrate and Anointed Ruler were often balanced in their power, their places tonight were very different. Leonte had been elected for a limited term, not a lifetime. The emperor was front and center for this announcement.

Leonte gave me a warm smile and nod as I passed, and I returned it.

I met the emperor at the top, and he welcomed me in like fashion, though not quite as warmly. It wouldn't be him if he did.

"Your Holiness," he said.

To the world, we exchanged niceties and respect. In my heart, I knew we both panicked about our lies and collusion shredding this event and this realm.

Then again, I couldn't imagine what it would look like to see him or any elf actually panic.

The emperor turned to the room full of dignitaries and gave a speech about how this was another important step in the process of passing the torch. He went on about unity, and accepting change, and Hoku's edicts, and all the stuff needed to prepare five-sixths of the people in this room for disappointment while remaining compliant.

My mind wandered, taking in my men. They were all so well put together. I got kind looks from each of them, though Hadwin's gaze was more of longing and lingering hurt than anything.

Tyfen was the picture of health, his injuries all healed or glamoured away for the event. His posture was somewhat casual, and it gutted me to know the way he stood—just for appearance's sake—was causing someone else in this palace excruciating pain.

The emperor ended his speech. "Would you like to add anything, Your Holiness?"

I swallowed, standing straighter. "I'm honored to be your Blessed Vessel. I'm not a perfect person, but I'm dedicated to my calling as the mother of the next Anointed Ruler. I'm dedicated to you and your people.

"I wish I could make you all happy today, because I know each territory has their concerns they wish were closer to the heart of the ruling emperor or empress. But Hoku sends one ruler."

It wasn't always customary to make a formal declaration, but I wanted to. Perhaps as insurance in case things fell apart, or just to bolster the morale of the Coterie.

"The leadership of the territories in this realm picked well. I will be happy no matter the father, because you all sent good men. And I'll continue to be grateful to have them in my life and my child's life. They'll help me raise a mindful ruler."

I gave them a genuine smile, meeting Queen Lourel's gaze for a moment.

"I've been taking more lessons from Prince Tyfen and Lord Findlech, trying to learn your tongues better."

Happy looks acknowledged their gratitude for the effort.

I glanced at Gald. "As a human, it's been a treat to have Gald by my side. He brings me a smile every day, and a little piece of my childhood home."

His dashing blue eyes twinkled.

"Chancellor Haan…"

The merfolk all listened intently to what the land-walker would say about him.

"Chancellor Haan is a wise and wonderful man, and someone I will always cherish and call my friend and family."

His turquoise tail gleamed in the fae lights as he nodded from his tank.

"I've loved hearing all his stories of the deep seas," I added.

I turned my attention to Hadwin and his people. "Duke Hadwin and I have been spending some time trying to sharpen my dancing skills to your traditional songs." I bobbed my head. "Granted, we've been pretty busy, so please don't fault him if I still butcher things."

They chuckled, and Hadwin even cracked a smile.

"And Elion…" I met his grey eyes. "Elion has helped me appreciate the shifters even more. Their loyalty and kindness are astounding, and they remind me that simplicity isn't a bad thing."

I cleared my throat. "I'll do my best to continue to learn and then share with the next Anointed Ruler as much of each culture and their concerns as I can. We'll keep the peace. We'll make Hoku proud as we keep the grand tradition according to her laws."

Nervous about how things could go in the next few minutes, hours, and days… Fully aware their obligations to me—Hadwin excepted as the father—were now lessened after this reveal… I more formally and clearly repeated my invitation.

I couldn't handle my Coterie crumbling. Privately or publicly. Politically or in my heart.

"I welcome all six of these men to stand with me in this cause, to live at the palace in my Coterie. As they wish, and as they're able to."

Most of these men still had other responsibilities back in their homelands they needed to tend to.

I ended my speech, my nerves on edge again. "May Hoku multiply her blessings on us all."

They repeated the blessing in a chorus.

As I drew a deep breath, my midwife climbed the stairs to the stage. "Ready?"

There was no going back now. I couldn't change anything.

"Yes."

My dress was specially tailored like the one I'd worn for my initial conception reading.

The midwife slipped her hands onto my belly.

My stomach churned at the deception. A half dozen people in this room already knew Hadwin was the father, her included. But we put on our act.

After a minute, she met my eyes again. "Are you ready for them to know?"

My heart pounded in my chest. It wasn't like I could pass and just return to my chambers for a nap. "Yes."

She pulled her hands back, nodding to the emperor. Confidently, she addressed the room. "I'm pleased to announce the next emperor or empress of Colsia will be half vampire."

My eyes snapped to Hadwin, and he wore a strained smile amidst the sea of excited chatter from his delegation.

I couldn't bear that look from him, the strain of his fake expression like the strain of our relationship.

My gaze shot to Elion. He pursed his lips, nodding, obviously disappointed. I wanted to hug him, but for now, his father's hand on his shoulder would have to do.

The merfolk seemed resigned to the news, disappointed despite my speech to make sure I'd consider their people's needs.

At least Gald smiled encouragingly at me despite the unkind subtle glances his group gave the vampires.

A look like that to Hadwin and his people cut me deep. They were scorning my child as much as my mate.

I glanced at Tyfen, anxious for his response.

He didn't make eye contact, instead gazing off into the distance, nodding as though he was numb inside. Would he hit the bottle and beat himself up because he'd lost chances to sire my child early on?

And then his father, the fae king, raised a finger into the air.

My heart stuttered.

I glanced at Findlech and his party. His eyes were on the fae king as his own high lord raised a finger in contest as well.

Although I'd known this might happen, although contests at paternity reveals were historically common, it still hurt.

Findlech returned his attention to me with a soft and confident look. "It's all right," he mouthed.

Was it all right? Would it be? From the man who'd given me a vague warning about Tyfen two nights ago… It didn't soothe my soul as much as it could have. Then again, Findlech understood the situation between Tyfen and Hadwin, and he still made a point of comforting me.

The emperor spoke. "I see we have a contest, as is your right. While Magistrate Leonte and I ensure the screening and competency of the empire's head midwife are top tier, we of course have another midwife to confirm the results."

A male mage took to the stairs, having waited on standby. I felt horrible for my midwife, that her competency was being questioned. She was the most skilled person in the entire empire to confirm the father, but the pride of the cousin races…

Lilah and my mother wore expressions of secondhand embarrassment, and the vampires' elation at the results had cooled.

The room went silent as the new mage midwife approached me. "Your Holiness."

"Please, go ahead." I clamped my mouth closed while he slid his hands onto my stomach. I wanted to tell the fae king and elf high lord where they could shove their contests.

I knew who the father was. And they fucking had to know that I knew. It was common knowledge I would have had vampiric cravings by this point in my pregnancy.

But I kept my mouth closed, trying to honor the official order of things.

The second midwife took his time with his reading, then straightened, facing the group.

"I confirm the results. A vampire life grows within the Blessed Vessel."

The king and high lord nodded their resignation, and some of the tension dissipated.

"A time of celebration," the emperor said. "Hoku picks as she best sees fit, and my full support backs the results." He gestured to the room. "We'll adjourn to the grand ballroom for our banquet shortly. I'm sure Her Holiness is eager to receive the attention of her Coterie at this time."

The room buzzed with excitement, and I quickly thanked the midwives for their services. I faced the emperor, and we shook hands.

"Congratulations, Sonta." His elderly voice hummed with a level of warmth I rarely heard from him.

I was still rattled by the contest. "Tyfen's father contested…" I whispered.

The emperor wrinkled his nose. "Be calm. I expected no less on this occasion, no matter the results."

"Okay."

"Go," he urged. "Go celebrate with your loved ones."

As I took the stairs down, I got a hearty congratulation from Leonte.

Since Lilah and my mother were right there at the base of the stairs, I gave them a moment of my time next.

My mother pulled me into a tight hug. "Congratulations!" She whispered into my ear, "Hadwin is such a sweetheart. I'm glad it was him for your sake."

A dull ache filled my chest. Yes, a sweetheart. *A sweetheart who nearly murdered another man I love two days ago…*

"Thank you, Mammi."

Not even thinking about it, I hugged Kernov as he stood next to me. It wasn't until his arms reciprocated that I realized we'd never hugged before, and it wasn't entirely appropriate for me to hug the magistrate's advisor in the moment.

I pulled back, and he offered his congratulations.

Lilah hugged me, not saying a word.

While the room had stirred and conversation buzzed within the delegations, my Coterie had all stayed in their places.

Hadwin looked at me expectantly, and I met him.

He took my hand. "Hello, darling." Never had he said it with reservation like this.

"You're going to be a father." I wore a bright smile as though this were all new to him.

He wrapped his arms around me, and I leaned into the embrace.

"I'm sorry for making today more stressful," he whispered.

It was a shit apology…

As much as Hadwin and I loved each other, we weren't just a couple. We were in a Coterie, and that carried certain expectations. The fact that Tyfen so easily forgave him, not blowing this up the way he could be, spoke more to *his* character than it justified Hadwin's lack of cooperation and compassion. As a representative for his people, he still should have apologized to Tyfen.

He was only sorry I was obviously on the verge of losing it. And I might still lose it. The emperor and magistrate had laid all the blame at my feet, and I'd done a fair job so far of keeping the peace, but this house of cards might fall with the slightest change in the winds.

Perhaps I was taking out my anger too much on Hadwin, but it was hard to be with him at the moment, knowing Tyfen still wasn't well, and that a poor stranger was in agony right now.

I was on edge, breaking under the weight of my responsibilities. It was up to me and me alone right now to ensure each of my partners and their nations felt properly supported, consoled, represented, and celebrated. All while making sure my posture and words were befitting the occasion, and my smile was on point.

I may not be thriving in the moment, but I was surviving. What was Hadwin doing? He couldn't so much as swallow his pride to utter a fucking simple apology to smooth things over and help with the burden crushing me.

He wasn't sorry for hurting Tyfen, for risking peace and possible harm to his mate and child. He was only sorry I was obviously on the verge of losing it.

I said nothing.

"I love you," he whispered.

As I released him from the hug, I could barely meet his hazel eyes. "I should see to the others. Congratulations."

Making a concerted effort to match the mood I ought to have, I greeted each of the other members of my Coterie, accepting congratulations. It took everything I had to not console them, to not offer apologies that the results had not been in their favor.

Now was not the time or place. To console the others would be to insult the vampires.

I received warmth from each of the men in turn.

Tyfen's hug was short. "Hadwin…" he said.

I gulped, praying he still felt the ruse we were all putting on was worth it now that he knew who the father was.

"I…" A packed room of people watched us. I couldn't explain, not here and now.

"Don't worry about me," he answered.

A measure of relief washed over me. "Thank you."

I lingered in Elion's arms just a little longer. He hurt the most.

I quickly met with the others, then joined the vampires. They were eager to start up conversation about the imperial tour already, since it would begin in their territory. Hadwin took my hand as we talked.

Appearances. Riches and power were lovely things until your life was on display, until you had to pretend you weren't at odds with the father of your unborn child in such a volatile situation.

A bell rang, claiming everyone's attention. Someone announced the grand ballroom was now ready for the banquet, welcoming us all to head that way.

20

Threats

The servants had hustled to make last-minute changes to the ballroom for the banquet, now that the paternity results were known. Lilah, my mother, and I would be sitting with the vampires for more opportunities to mingle.

The food on our tables was much more sparse than on the others. Most of the vampires drank blood from goblets, occasionally munching on regular food as a delicacy. I had a loaded plate, though, as did Lilah and my mother. Kernov sat with the emperor and magistrate at their head table.

My personal chef approached, delivering a cordial glass of pig's blood for me.

"Thank you," I sighed.

"Congratulations, Your Holiness." We would both be happy to not have to sneak around when it came to satiating my cravings.

He sketched a bow and retreated. Lilah and Mother fell easily into conversation with the vampires around them, who were eager to learn more, eager to win over the people most important to me.

I downed the pig's blood, savoring the saltiness on my tongue, soothed as it satiated my craving.

Hadwin sat to my left, the vampire countess directly across from me.

"Is that your first taste?" she asked, grinning. "Or have you been sating your cravings for a while?"

The more lies I told, the more I had to keep track of. "I confess, I've been secretly having blood for a bit now."

She approved. The countess was an elegant and intimidating woman with long pointed nails to mirror her fangs.

"Pig's blood or human?" she asked, her tone honey-smooth.

My face flushed. "Pig's."

"Hmm." She glanced at Hadwin. "Do you look forward to tasting Duke Hadwin? I hear the father's blood is rather hypnotic for Blessed Vessels."

I glanced at Hadwin, and he smirked. "I look forward to it, darling."

He seemed more at ease now that we sat with his people, better at putting on an act. Like I hadn't rejected his offer of tasting his blood earlier today.

He searched my eyes as if dredging for our usual connection.

My anger still smoldered within me, but I was wise enough to remember my place and the delicate balance I needed to maintain.

I couldn't have the vampires assuming I didn't love Hadwin. They wanted proper representation, and I planned to give it to them. "I'm excited to try new things, to immerse myself more in vampire ways."

Hadwin rested a hand on my thigh under the table, and I ignored it as I took a bite of food.

"Don't say that too loudly," the countess's mate drawled. "The others might whine about the results." He scowled at the fae and elves at their distant tables. "Oh wait, they already did that."

I gulped down some water.

The countess kept her eyes on me, scrutinizing. "That flustered you when they did that."

"Yes," I admitted. "I just... We're here to celebrate, is all."

The countess's mate rolled his eyes. "You'd think as fellow immortals, the cousins would care a little more for our kind, but they're *better* than us because they come by their immortality differently."

The countess kept eyeing me. "What are your thoughts on that, Your Holiness? Your child will face less compliance and more discrimination because of the fae and elves…"

This felt like an interview as they waited with bated breath to know what I thought. But why the hell should *I* need *their* approval? They were lucky I was giving the realm a half-vampire child. What would they do if they didn't like my answer? Get another Blessed Vessel to pop out a child for them?

I didn't like the tone or arrogance.

Remembering my diplomacy, I flashed them both a polite smile as I cut into a spear of asparagus. "My aim is to raise my child with a balanced view of the realm. Each of our territories has its share of treasures and tragedies, right?"

The woman shrugged. "How are we to move past our differences if their stubbornness always deludes them into thinking they're superior? What do *they* do for sick humans? Mages and vampires handle them well enough, don't we?"

I blinked. Yes, mages and vampires cured humans, but she wasn't going to make me fawn over vampires by simply appealing to my humanity. Nor would she by playing a victim. We were all victims and perpetrators in our own ways throughout history, and she was being willfully ignorant of the harm her own people had done.

"Respectfully, milady, there's still a lot of growth to be had by us all... I'm sure the cousins would soften more if their ancestors who had been turned into oni all rested in peace."

Hadwin's hand on my thigh clamped down as if to warn me to shut up.

Perhaps I'd been a little firm in my assertion, but I'd tried to be rational. Who the hell was he to try to silence me?

The countess's gaze flicked to Hadwin, her lips twitching slightly. "Interesting perspective."

"Sonta didn't mean anything by it," Hadwin responded.

The fuck I didn't... If I wasn't going to kiss Queen Lourel's ass, I certainly wasn't going to kiss this woman's, either.

I gave her another smile. "I speak my mind. And I won't apologize for it. But I assure you I hold no malice toward vampires."

She nodded and took a sip from her goblet.

Hadwin's hand still gripped me, and I wanted it off. I also could use a moment to decompress on my own.

"Not to be indelicate—"

"Darling..." Hadwin said, applying more pressure.

I stared at him. If he ever tried to do this to me again, I'd stab his hand with my steak knife.

Doing my best to contain my composure, I ignored him. "I'd like to excuse myself for a quick moment... Washrooms and human pregnancies..."

She flourished a hand in the air. "Of course. I'm sure it's been a busy day for you."

I stood and strode to the private hallway for a break. Leaning against the wall, I took deep breaths.

"Sonta?" Lilah entered and grabbed me in an embrace. "Hey, you've got this."

"Fuck the realm." When was this going to get better? Being the Blessed Vessel was fun in the bedroom, but...

"Sorry. You're *only* allowed to fuck six men right now, not the entire realm."

I let out an airy chuckle. "Screw you."

"I'd take you up on that offer." Her voice was as playful as ever, her hug still tight. "What happened? I couldn't hear with all the chatter, but it looked a little tense."

"I just... I'm not the right person for this."

"You are, love."

I calmed in her arms. I wanted to beg her to come with me on tour, but she had plans with Cataray.

Sighing, I pulled back. "I don't mean to whine. Hadwin was just being an asshole..."

She frowned. "Very unlike him. Granted, I thought we'd agreed that descriptor belonged to Tyfen until recently…" She'd been forgiving about me keeping secrets from her, but she wouldn't forget it easily.

"Yeah…"

Kissing me sweetly, she distracted me. Maybe I should have taken her up on her joke of an offer to run away with her long ago.

"I miss you," I whispered.

"I miss you more."

She kissed me again, softly, sensually, her tongue sliding against mine. I was starved for gentleness and sex. "We can't do this again, Lilah."

She stepped back. "I know. Sorry. I just wanted to make you feel better."

I took her hands. "And you have."

"Sonta?" Hadwin called from the end of the hallway.

I grunted, and Lilah pouted.

"I can't even piss alone?"

"Go. I'll tell him to wait."

I thanked her and went to the washroom. If I hadn't been wearing copious amounts of beautiful cosmetics, I would have splashed my face with cool water. Instead, I finished my business and walked out, greeted by Hadwin.

"Are you all right?" he asked, almost his normal self.

"We've had this discussion about stalking, right?" I now understood why he'd returned to the common room the day he hurt Tyfen, but he knew I was stressed right now. Following me when I left to get a tiny moment to myself was suffocating; his attempts to silence me uncharacteristically overbearing.

In our relationship, we both needed to work on a few things, but politically, he was out of line.

"That's not what happened, and you fucking know it," he snarled.

"Call it what you like. I'm allowed to take a few minutes to myself amidst getting fucked physically and emotionally for this realm, okay?" I stood tall. "And don't you dare ever try to silence me like that again. Remember your place."

"You can't just disrespect the countess like that."

"She started it. Her and her mate." I recalled so many lessons, so many entries from previous Blessed Vessels in their journals. Despite our divinity, many immortals still tried to dominate us because of our mortality. I refused to let that happen to me. "I'm not going to play the coward just because my child will be one of you!"

"I am *not* a coward," he said through clenched teeth. "I just understand the hierarchy of vampires better. There are things we need to discuss, and perhaps we would have had time to today had you swallowed your pride earlier."

My jaw dropped. "Me? Swallow *my* pride? Coming from the asshole who won't lower himself to offer a simple apology to Tyfen after nearly killing him." I jabbed Hadwin in the chest. "Coming from the man who may very well have turned him into an oni had I not intervened. You're lucky the fae aren't planning for battle right now. That is all thanks to *his* generosity."

Hadwin huffed.

"I'm *not* starting my legacy this way, Hadwin. Bowing and muttering niceties to stroke an immortal's ego when they should know better. My child—"

"*Our* child."

"*Our* child's legacy will not begin this way."

He furrowed his brow. "Why are you being this way?"

This was going nowhere. "I'm going back to dinner now. I'll be civil and excited about today's announcement, but don't push me."

"Please…" he practically begged.

I ignored him, strolling into the ballroom with a bright smile, acknowledging everyone I passed.

The rest of dinner luckily passed rather peacefully. Perhaps the countess had gotten the hint from my brief departure.

After a while, plates were cleared and the groups mingled more. Unsurprisingly, many shifters had drifted over to the merfolk tanks. That warmed my heart. Elion and Haan even spied me watching them and waved. I blushed.

While the fae and elves had stood in solidarity about contesting the paternity results, they did not mingle even a little, both choosing to stay with their own kind. A few humans and mages wandered over to talk with my party and the vampires.

The orchestra struck up a tune, and I let it lull me to a safer place in my soul.

Kernov approached and rested a hand on my mother's shoulder. I loved that they weren't hiding their affection for each other now. I wished she could join me for the tour, though I'd told her I wanted to do it alone.

Honestly, I wanted it both ways. But I wanted to prove to myself that I could handle my calling. I was a grown woman. She was staying here while I toured.

Kernov looked at me. "I've claimed a few dances with your mother once it all begins."

It was a subtle prod. No one could dance until I did with Hadwin. I couldn't avoid him all night, despite our whole five words uttered to each other after returning from the washroom.

I turned to Hadwin. "Let's dance."

He obliged, and everyone watched as a vampire tune started.

His hands were cold against my skin as he led me in the steps we'd practiced on romantic candlelit evenings in the library.

"You're doing really well," he said softly.

I averted my gaze. "Thank you."

Silence reigned, and I tried to smile for all the onlookers. As the parents of the next ruler, we were attempting to paint a picture of love and loyalty the people could have hope and confidence in.

Hadwin was handsome, his blond hair and beard, those hazel eyes. "You look great tonight," I offered.

"Thank you."

I told myself I was refraining from conversation while dancing because Gald knew how to lip-read, and others might as well. The truth of it was I kept wondering what it was like for Hadwin to be bound to me eternally. He could sense my heartbeat. Our child's heartbeat.

Did it feel any different as my heart broke over this distance between us?

The song was nearing its end.

"Can I kiss you?" he asked, his voice full of hesitation. "For … appearances?"

Why did a simple request make me almost cry again? He'd been too shy to ask for a kiss in the bedding chamber, had told me I deserved to be made love to for the sake of it and not for politics.

But here we were. Kissing. For appearances.

I choked down the hurt. "Sure."

His kiss was soft as the song ended, as the people clapped for us.

"Thank you," he said.

We didn't linger long as others took to the floor with a new song. I danced with Elion, Gald, and Findlech. They were understanding and sensitive about my mood. Tyfen was being shepherded around by his father to greet all the fae dignitaries, so I sought out Haan. Although we didn't dance, it wasn't awkward. I took extra care to meet each member of his delegation.

I glanced in Tyfen's direction to see if he wanted to dance, but he was gone. I scanned the room and still couldn't find him. Wouldn't it be my luck if he stood me up for our dance again?

Excusing myself, I left the merfolk and found Kernov. "You haven't seen Tyfen recently, have you?"

He pointed to a set of doors. "He walked out with his father a few minutes ago." He added in a whisper, "They didn't seem too keen on each other…"

It was a private family affair, I told myself. But my intuition and curiosity got the better of me. "Thank you."

I exited the room through those same doors, and a guard steered me in the right direction.

Raised voices down a small hallway stopped me around the corner.

"It's not that much to ask for, Tyfen," King Bretton snipped.

"I understand that," Tyfen replied, annoyed.

The king muttered something in fae that sounded a lot like cursing. "Constant disappointment. This was your chance to redeem yourself."

"This was a disaster from the beginning, and you have no one to blame but yourself," Tyfen shot back.

"Really? *I'm* to blame for this failure? You were to come here to win her heart, to bed her, to bear a fae child. You got lucky in the drawing to be the first to claim her, and then you made a spectacle of yourself, went out of your way to earn her scorn. Did she even let you fuck her after that?"

I didn't particularly enjoy hearing them talk about me that way, but I couldn't stop listening.

"Yes," Tyfen ground out. "I fucked her plenty. I've done my job to the best of my ability. Please tell me my own father understands how conception works..."

"Don't patronize me," the king warned. "Have you been keeping it hidden?"

Keeping what hidden?

"You know I don't even get a choice in that!" Tyfen's tone had swiftly switched from angry to hurt and exasperated.

"So you say."

"Just because you..." Tyfen paused. "Go to hell."

"Watch it," the king growled. "I have plenty of sons and daughters who don't almost start *fucking* wars. Who don't sully my name and cost me dearly. Who don't constantly disappoint me. You're replaceable."

I stood there, wide-eyed. Who the hell talked to their children that way? If Tyfen was really that bad, the realm would know. He was the most high-profile of any in the Coterie.

No wonder Tyfen had only wanted to loop his mother in on his injuries. Thank the stars we'd kept his father out of the loop.

The king continued. "I wouldn't lose a wink of sleep to cut you off or cut out your tongue, so watch what you say to your king."

I couldn't listen any longer.

Rounding the corner, I beamed. "Tyfen!" I called excitedly. "I've been looking *everywhere* for you!"

The king straightened, gazing at me, putting on a façade of regality. "Your Holiness. Congratulations on the fruit of your womb."

A sack of horse shit was more appealing than speaking to him at the moment.

"Thank you so much, Your Majesty." I hooked my arm through Tyfen's, and he smiled at me.

"I hope you took no offense to the contest..." the king said.

Like hell I didn't...

"Of course not. It's a formality. I know you and your wife and people are faithful and trusting of Hoku." I laid it on thick, giving Tyfen an adoring glance. "Though I wouldn't have been upset at all if the results had swayed another way..."

Tyfen acknowledged my flattery with a twinkle in his eye.

I turned back to the king. "But I wouldn't slight the vampires by saying I'm upset. I have a lovely Coterie, truly."

Tyfen's hand rested on my hip.

"I'm elated to hear that," King Bretton crooned.

I laid a hand on Tyfen's chest. "I came searching for you to dance. I wouldn't want anyone doubting how much I care for a certain handsome fae prince, especially given the … unfortunate way things started."

"You should go," the king quickly answered.

Naturally, he was beyond happy to shove his son off for the sake of appearances and duty… He'd forced Tyfen to join my Coterie in the first place.

"Thank you." I kept my smile. "And I'm terribly sorry I've kept Tyfen all to myself while you've been here." I stroked Tyfen's chest, and looked down, coy. "I guess I enjoy having him to myself too much."

Perhaps that was a bit excessive.

"No trouble at all," the king replied. He stood there as if waiting for us to run off to dance, but I wanted a word with Tyfen first.

"Speaking of having him to myself, would you mind if we had a moment alone first?"

"Of course." He shot Tyfen a look, then excused himself.

Tyfen's lovestruck mask dropped, his gaze trailing after his father until he turned the corner.

"So…" I said.

Tyfen shook his head. "Not here." He took my hand and led me further down the hallway, eventually pulling me into a storage closet.

"This feels familiar," I mused.

He chuckled. "Greedy cunt. If I weren't hurt, I'd reenact that right here and now."

I hummed my desire, and he kissed me.

"Are you okay?" I asked in the dark.

"I'm fine," he answered plainly. "How much did you hear?"

"Enough to dislike him for eternity."

Tyfen sighed. "He's not usually this bad."

"He threatened you. He called you replaceable."

"I'd rather not talk about it," Tyfen replied softly.

It took me a moment to gather my thoughts. Picking his good hand, I intertwined our fingers. "Ever?"

"Just not now."

That gave me hope he was letting me in instead of pushing me away.

"Okay. But for the record—you're not replaceable to me."

Tyfen held me tight against him, hip to hip, resting his chin on my head. "Thank you, Blantui."

My heart leapt.

We finally had a moment alone, so I dared to ask, "Is our secret still safe, about what happened the other day? Because your father contesting…"

"We're fine," he soothed. "Ironically, that's why he pulled me from the ball. He was angry I was being standoffish about socializing. He doesn't know how fun this all is with a dull ache in my body and head, and the knowledge that every time I raise my arm to shake someone's goddess-damned hand, I'm probably making that poor sap somewhere in this palace scream in agony."

I frowned, and Tyfen removed the hand of his injured arm from my hip. The feintal magic transferred only Tyfen's pain, and the recipient had to be awake to suffer it. While Tyfen's arm and head injury had healed a great deal, delicate tissues and bone had been pieced together, and each movement likely strained the injury, opening things back up. Once the feintal spell was lifted, Tyfen would not only be in agony, but his healing may be set back for days.

"I'm sorry this happened," I whispered.

His voice was far too cheerful as he tried to help the situation. "Just tell your mate next time he breaks me to try and do it on my nondominant hand."

I grunted. "That's not funny."

"It's a *little* funny, Sonta."

"Does it hurt them if I kiss you?"

"Groping is probably out, but a kiss is fine…" His voice was sexy, the dark little closet intimate.

I leaned in and caressed his lips with my own, stealing a bit of sunshine on my rainy day.

His good hand roamed, tracing my underwear lines. He offered his tongue as we kissed, and I accepted, pressing myself against him, minding his injured arm.

He became hard against me.

Fuck. I was wet. Each stolen second was a gift, a relief, a memory in the making of how far we'd come, what kind of shit we could get through together when the fate of the realm danced precariously on the tip of a pin.

Two months ago, we'd been snapping insults at each other and meaning them. Now, I wanted to claw his clothes off and claim every inch of him.

But… I pulled myself away. "We should go dance." I smirked. "And you may be a commander, but you should probably hide your salute."

He chuckled. "Yes, we should go. I'll address that minor issue."

Nothing about Tyfen or his cock was *minor*.

We emerged from the closet, hand in hand. My emotions had been everywhere today, though most of them were much more somber than they should be for the joyous celebration of the life within me.

For the first time all day, my smile was genuine as I strode next to Tyfen down the hallway.

Before we turned the last corner, Tyfen stopped. "One thing…" He wasn't smiling anymore.

"Yes?"

He grappled for words. "I … grateful … you've helped convince my parents you care for me."

"I *do* care for you, Tyfen…"

He rested a hand on my hip. "I know. I just mean it's good for all of us men to have our people see us winning the heart of the Blessed Vessel."

I pursed my lips. "I heard you and your father mention that…"

"You *know* you mean the world to me, right? That it started out as duty, but…"

But did he love me? I loved him, but had been too afraid to say it with how much we pushed and pulled as we navigated what it meant to be a couple.

"I know, Tyfen. I don't hold it against you. It's not exactly every woman's dream to be bedded out of duty, but I'm grateful for where we're at and where we're going."

He smiled. "Good."

"Anything else?"

His throat bobbed. "Like I was saying… I'm happy for my kingdom to know we're together, but I'm not ready for the realm to know yet."

A stake through the heart.

"Why?" I asked, fully disheartened. Why would Tyfen want to hide our relationship? "People know you're in my Coterie… And you promised we could stop sneaking around after the paternity results…"

He averted his gaze. "I meant we could let the Coterie know…"

My heart was a pincushion today, a target on an archery field full of the emperor's best archers.

"Why?" I asked again, my lip quivering. I didn't consider myself too arrogant, but nothing about Tyfen wanting to keep me a secret made sense. He was ashamed of me? After how close we'd grown?

Men around the realm would sell their souls to fuck me. I was a goddess's daughter, skilled in the bedroom, decent with my heart and mind… I held a unique place of power, and I understood that.

Tyfen hesitated, closing his eyes.

He wore that look. The look he often gave before he uttered 'pass' because he wasn't ready to talk about something from his past.

"You know"—he opened his eyes—"I just think with everything that's gone on, it would be disrespectful for you and me to look too cozy as we dance. It's obvious to everyone your relationship with Hadwin is strained right now. And it wouldn't be right to look happier with me than with the father of your child."

Tyfen was being generous by sweeping Hadwin's assault under the rug.

But he wasn't *this* generous.

The problem was, despite the blatant lie, it was also a truth. It would be wholly inappropriate to show up giddy with Tyfen while I'd been terse with Hadwin, especially after Tyfen's father had contested the results.

I accepted the lie. "Okay. We'll dance as friends, just like I did with Findlech."

Tyfen wouldn't meet my eyes. "Thank you."

We returned to the ballroom, and attention immediately landed on us. Tyfen guided me to the dance floor, and the orchestra started.

He led me, and we both smiled for the people.

"I hate this song," he said, the corner of his mouth twitching as he tried to ease the new tension between us. It was the same song they'd played at the previous ball, the one he'd insulted and the only fae one I knew well.

The inside joke wasn't lost on me, but all I could muster was a brighter fake smile.

A moment of silence passed, then Tyfen tried again. "My mother said she was impressed with your accent earlier."

I nodded. While making my rounds, I'd bumped into her and had remembered to practice some of the new Fae Tyfen had taught me.

He angled his head. "It's a good sign she wasn't insulted this time, right?"

Another inside joke, about our ruse with the others. Our ruse of not being a couple, just like we pretended to not be right now.

Tyfen spun me, then pulled me back in. "You're angry with me." His voice and expression were strained.

I kept my happy little fucking lie of a mask up. "No. It's fine."

I wasn't angry.

I was disappointed. Disappointed that on one of the most important days of my life, of my child's life, I had to pretend I was happy with their father when we were at odds, and pretend I *wasn't* madly in love with Tyfen when I was.

21

The Painful Goodbye

I sat in my room, wearing my golden nightie, hugging my legs and staring at the giant windows onto my gardens. A heavy wind whipped at the curtains.

Every part of my heart and soul was numb.

Luckily, I'd been able to leave the celebration ball without all the pomp and circumstance like we'd had at the last one. I'd excused myself, claiming I was too tired from the excitement.

Hopefully people had bought the lie, assuming any tension between myself and the others was purely out of exhaustion.

Two hours after returning, bathing, and readying for bed, I still sat here, drowning in my heartache.

Someone knocked at my door to the common room, and I ignored it. I didn't even have it in me to tell them to go away.

After a long silence, they knocked again. I ignored them again.

The doorknob twisted—I rarely locked that door because they usually respected my boundaries.

"Sonta?" Elion stuck his head in.

"I want to be alone."

He stepped all the way in. "Okay…" He frowned. "Can I do something for you? Do you want to talk? Or… I can help you in other ways…"

No one's cock or any other body part could console me right now.

"Or I could fetch you some blood from the kitchens…" he offered.

Why did he have to be such a sweet and considerate mate? And why did that offer make me instantly tear up?

"I'm fine," I choked out.

Elion closed the door, crossed the room, and scooped me up into his arms. "Come on."

A day full of forced smiles and repressed anger and hurt and fear all came to a head. I sobbed.

"I fucked up," I whimpered. If I hadn't asked Tyfen to take me in the common room, none of this would have happened. Hadwin and I wouldn't be fighting, I wouldn't be biting my nails about the lies we were piling on, and Tyfen wouldn't be back in the infirmary right now, sleeping away the agony of his healing with the feintal spell removed.

I couldn't stop crying.

"It'll be okay." Elion laid me on the bed, holding me tight and kissing my cheek. "Mistakes happen."

Not this big, not to people in places of power. They had their shit together.

I was inconsolable as I continued to bawl.

He didn't freak out, just holding me, stroking my arm and planting the occasional kiss on my skin. "Get it all out."

After a few minutes, I calmed a degree, sniffling.

Elion's hand rested on my stomach. "I'm excited for you, Sonta. I'm sure it's nice to have some certainty…"

"I'm sorry it's not yours," I whispered. Not that I truly wished my child weren't Hadwin's, but Elion had clearly been the most devastated to have the results not in his favor.

"Me too," he whispered back. I'd genuinely never heard him so sad. He nuzzled my neck, breathing softly.

Another tear rolled down my cheek onto my pillow.

"We'll be fine," he assured me. "No matter what any of the rest of the Coterie does, I'm here for you and your child. Even if Hadwin left, I'd be here to help you raise this little one."

That didn't help. Hadwin—leave? He was legally the *only* one who couldn't leave me now. "Please don't talk like that."

He rubbed my shoulder. "Sorry, I didn't mean… I just wanted to let you know I'm here."

I drew a deep breath and let it out. "I know. And I love you for it."

He gave a tiny growl of approval. "Would you like to cuddle with me in the flesh or the fur?"

I was spent. "Either way."

Another knock sounded, this time from my private door.

"I'll get it." He scooted off the bed and greeted the person. "Oh… Hi…"

"Hi…" It was Lilah. "I… Sorry, I thought she'd be alone."

"We're just cuddling…"

"Can I come in?"

"Sonta?" Elion asked.

I sighed. My 'I want to be alone to wallow in my pain' plans weren't going all that great. "Sure."

She entered the room, frowning as I sniffled. My eyes were puffy, and I didn't care how pathetic I looked.

After passing me a handkerchief, she folded her arms. "Can I join in on the cuddling?"

"Sure."

She beamed. "Great!" Glancing down at her ball gown, she added, "I'm going to borrow one of your nighties, though. This isn't exactly cuddleable."

I weakly nodded.

"Hey, Lilah—" Elion started as she went to my dressing room. "Actually, uh, Sonta, are you okay with me staying the night? Just cuddles and sleep?"

My vocabulary was extensive in this worn-out state. "Sure."

He turned back to Lilah. "Then, Lilah, are you okay if I sleep in my shorts?" The three of us hadn't yet shared a bed.

Lilah chuckled. "Elion, I know you were clueless at the time about who I was, but I saw your ass and cock in the bedding chamber... Between that and our time at the pool, is there much to be shy about?"

He snickered in return. "True."

I didn't even turn to watch them strip, just lying there.

"You know, speaking of not being shy..." Lilah said. "Could you get these buttons for me? I had a servant help me dress earlier."

"Of course. You're one of us now."

Lilah gasped playfully. "Excuse you! How *dare* you group me with you men. My tits and beauty routine are *far* too marvelous to casually throw me in with the lot of you."

Elion laughed again, and their ability to carry on this way despite the chaos soothed my aching heart a degree. The Coterie was accepting Lilah.

A minute later, Elion crawled into bed behind me again, then Lilah joined us after snuffing the last candle.

She brushed wisps of hair away from my face. "Thanks for letting me join you." She snuggled up, and I settled comfortably between the two of them.

"Why would Tyfen be ashamed of me?" I whispered to Lilah. I prided myself on being self-aware, but I really didn't understand him right now.

"He said that?" Her tone was defensive on my behalf.

"He doesn't want the realm to know we're together..."

"But you *are* together... He's in your Coterie..."

I filled my lungs. "He didn't want anyone to see us happy together tonight, romantic."

She sighed, kissing my forehead. "I don't know, love. But that's a shitty thing to do to someone you care about."

Yes. It was.

***

The next day, the hours were short and the minutes long as I stumbled through my to-do list. Tyfen spent another day in the infirmary, sleeping and healing. Hadwin didn't bother with me, steering clear. As for the others, we finalized plans and said preliminary goodbyes.

I guided my servants on things to pack.

Unavoidably, I also had another meeting with the emperor and magistrate. So far, it looked like any major repercussions had been avoided regarding Hadwin hurting Tyfen, and regarding the paternity results.

So far.

I had a lovely goodbye with my mother—she cried about watching her little girl grow up, become a mother, and travel the realm.

I slept alone this time, again tossing and turning about starting the imperial tour in the morning.

Another large banquet was held for breakfast, celebrating the paternity reveal. It gave everyone the chance to swap political chatter, to plan for the life and influence of my child, who hadn't even been born yet.

I would teach my child to respect these people and to protect these people. But I would also protect my child *from* these people, from those who would plot and plan to use him or her as a pawn.

Having cried it out, I did a better job of smiling and conversing, of being civil with Hadwin.

The fae king was annoyed about the results of the coin flip for the imperial tour rotation. We would be traveling counterclockwise through the territories. Not only had the paternity results not been in their favor, but now they would be the last to receive me and Hadwin.

Good. His anger brought me satisfaction after having heard him threaten Tyfen.

Once the breakfast came to a close, the emperor and magistrate both gave speeches. Hoku's blessings were uttered.

My heart raced as soon as I left that banquet hall. This was *actually* happening. I'd looked forward to this day for ages. After all my training and tutoring, I would meet the people. I would travel across the realm and see some of those beautiful landmarks I'd encountered only in visions.

A spark of excitement guided my every footstep as my Coterie and I strode out of the palace toward the main gates.

Servants and dignitaries were everywhere, excited to see us all off. By now, word had traveled by magic and messengers to every corner of the empire with the news of a vampiric Blessed Vessel pregnancy. Regardless of people's opinions on it, there would be parades and celebrations galore. I let the bright colors and attitudes lift my spirits further.

Hadwin, Gald, and Elion all went to the carriages right away, Hadwin in his travel cloak to shield him from the sun. His people were traveling to their territory ahead of us, so they'd left after breakfast instead of dawdling in the uncomfortable rays to join us.

It was time to say my official goodbyes to the others, even if they were only temporary. The magistrate was traveling with us on this first leg of the tour, so he was getting situated in his carriage. The emperor was gracious in wishing me well, reminding me to use any imperial resources I needed should trouble arise.

I gave my mother a giant hug, and Kernov a handshake. I lingered a moment in Lilah's arms, though we'd had a more tender farewell in private this morning.

Out of my Coterie, I first bid Haan and his people farewell, the merfolk gathered in a reception pool near the end of the lane.

No matter what, I would always welcome Haan into my life. His slitted purple eyes, gorgeous turquoise tail, his handsome smile and bronzy muscles… Even those shell and sea urchin spine earrings, which always made me think of how much I loved swimming. He was kind, and his curiosity to learn about us land-walkers was ever so endearing.

"I'll miss you," I said with a smile.

He matched my smile. "As will I miss you. I'll do my best to be back here for your resting visit." Each of the three legs of the tour to the six territories would take about five weeks with travel time and celebrations. Between each leg, we would stop at the palace to rest for a week.

"I look forward to it."

He used his impressive strength to lift himself higher and gave me a kiss. I loved it.

Haan was going to visit his home in the southern sea, reporting to his people and fulfilling duties.

I turned my attention to Findlech. While Gald had wanted him to join us on this portion of the tour, Findlech would be hanging back and joining us later. He had some official duties to handle with his delegation, and would also be traveling to his own territory. As a still-active lord, he had duties he'd entrusted to others, but wanted to check in.

"You're welcome to join us whenever you're ready," I told him, and offered a hug. While he wasn't a hugger in general, and especially not affectionate with me, we kept up the ruse for the sake of concealing his sexuality with all the people watching.

"Thank you. I will." He really was a decent hugger when he wanted to be.

While we were in a more or less good place, there were still unresolved issues, unanswered questions.

"Is there anything I should know?" I asked. About this drama with Tyfen, the fae, the elves, *anything*…

"Enjoy your time. You deserve to celebrate, Sonta."

"Thanks again."

Tyfen had hung back a bit, devastatingly handsome but shyer than normal.

I approached him, forcing myself to not take his hands. "How are you feeling?"

He wrinkled his nose. "I'll be grateful to get this spell off me and just finish the healing."

I couldn't ask him to join us on this first leg of the journey. Not only did he need to heal, but putting him and Hadwin together in such close proximity, and under these circumstances...

Still... "After the vampire stop is our visit to human lands." I rocked on the balls of my feet. "I can make sure Hadwin behaves. Or that he's not around. And you could just winnow in for a visit. I could show you my hometown..."

Tyfen pressed his lips together. "We'll see."

I hid a frown. "Will you write? Send me updates on how you're doing?" He planned to stay at the palace while I was gone, even after his delegation left, unless he was called back to his kingdom for official duties.

Scratching his arm, Tyfen shrugged. "We'll see."

Why did he have to be so standoffish? No one could hear us right now. They were all a good distance away.

"What's wrong?"

"I'm just tired, Sonta."

It wasn't that.

"How are things with your father?"

Tyfen smirked and shook his head. "I told you—don't worry about that."

We stood a minute, and my heart thundered. I hated leaving him this way. "I know you're not ready for people to see us as a couple..."

He frowned.

I continued. "But know that I am. And I..." I'd never had the courage to tell him I loved him, not when he was awake. And in so many ways at so many times, it had felt like he'd been close to saying it. I couldn't imagine leaving him for five weeks without the assurance that I cared. That I accepted him. That unlike his father, I didn't consider him replaceable.

"You mean the world to me, Blantue." I smiled softly. "I love you."

He instantly looked down, tucking his hands into his pockets, his arms rigid. "I..."

The silence was long, but I was patient.

Suddenly, his face hardened, and he locked eyes with me. "I think it's interesting Hadwin knew the child was his before the reveal."

My eyes widened.

"Exactly. You knew and you told him. He slipped on that tidbit after trying to murder me. That was rather generous of you to let him know and then put me in danger."

My jaw dropped. "What? I..." My brain stumbled and stuttered. "Tyfen, he would have protected me like that even if he weren't the father of my child, given what he walked in on!"

"Still." Tyfen's tone was unforgiving. "Don't tell me you love me when ... when you set me up to get hurt."

I grabbed his hand. "I didn't! We *both* agreed on the location and timing."

He took his hand back. "But you asked me to do that. You suggested the activity and location."

We couldn't be having this conversation. Not here, not now. With hundreds watching on, with dozens waiting for me at the carriages.

"Please don't do this, Tyfen."

Chewing on his lip, he shook his head. "Enjoy your tour with your mate." He turned, and strode toward the palace.

Leaving me here.

My heart raced, my lungs fighting to keep pace. Everything blurred as he walked away.

I no longer cared that everyone was watching him slight me. Or that he might go announce to his delegation the truth of what had happened with Hadwin.

I *should* have cared, but I didn't.

I couldn't bear to see him leave me. He had told me I meant the world to him. He had praised my wit; he matched my body and soul in so many ways. And he was walking away.

"Tyfen!" I called.

He kept walking.

"Tyfen!" I shouted louder.

He ignored me.

As every good memory of our time together collided with his rejection, my heart shattered. Tears pricked at my eyes.

I panicked. Glancing at a guard close to Tyfen, I gestured for him to stop him. The guard stepped in his way, and Tyfen spun.

"What the fuck are you doing?" he ground out, shocked that I would have an imperial official intervene.

My breathing was ragged, too quick as I trembled at the thought of losing him, of leaving him like this. "Don't. Don't do this."

He returned to me, his expression still terse. "You need to go on your tour, not stir up more problems."

"I can't do this," I whimpered, a tear streaking down my cheek. "I can't. I can't leave things like this with us."

"Sonta..." he said a hair more gently.

"No. We *both* know it was just bad timing, so don't *fucking* push me away." I stared into those beautiful green eyes I loved so much. "I can't do it," I repeated.

His sudden mood shift and reveal about his knowledge of Hadwin's fatherhood only came out when? After I told Tyfen I loved him.

Tyfen and his dark vault of a heart that I'd thought we were slowly making progress on.

"Please," I begged. "I can't go on tour leaving you like this." My lip trembled, more tears cascading. "You can't make me love you then keep shutting me out."

He instantly frowned. He knew he'd fucked up.

"When I said I love you…"

He flinched. Why was that such a horrible thing for him to hear?

"I *do*," I continued. "I didn't say it to manipulate you or…"

I could barely breathe. "Please don't do this," I squeaked.

Tyfen grabbed me, pulling me into his arms. "I'm sorry. Fuck, I… I'm sorry, Sonta." He threaded fingers through my hair. "Shit," he whispered. "I'm sorry."

His shoulder muffled my sobs. I couldn't leave Tyfen this way. He had my heart.

"You're right," he admitted quietly. "I just…" His arms squeezed tighter.

I held him a moment, calming simply by being in his presence.

After a minute, Tyfen pulled back, holding my shoulders and gazing into my eyes. His eyes were coated in tears too, his expression full of regret. "You don't deserve this. I fucked up, okay? But I…" He struggled to talk, his face screwed up.

"I'm going to get my shit together. I promise. I mean it." His tone was earnest, urgent. "I don't want to keep hurting you." He wiped away a stray tear from my cheek. "I *promise*. I'm going to get my shit together, okay? I'm sorry."

I nodded. He needed to work his way through his troubled heart, and if he was really willing to put in the work, it finally gave me a light at the end of the tunnel for our volatile relationship.

He caressed my cheek. "You're Blantui—you can do this tour. And when you come back to visit…" He offered me a sad smile. "Things will be different. I swear it."

"Thank you," I whispered. Tyfen had to heal. His body, his heart, maybe more. No matter what his primary problem was right now, I still worried about leaving him here. "Promise me you won't drink while I'm gone."

He pressed his lips together, looking down in shame. "I promise. No booze." He looked up again, a tear on his own cheek. "I'm really sorry."

I smiled encouragingly. "You're Blantue, too. You can sort this out." I took his hand. "I know you can."

I hugged him again, and we stood there for hundreds to see. I certainly hadn't planned to 'out' our relationship this way, but I would have endured hell for every moment of my tour if the last image I had at the palace was him walking away. I would have worried about him every moment.

"I guess people know now…" I said.

He held my chin, biting his lip. "What's a few hundred in on the secret, huh?"

I smiled as I wiped away the last of my tears. "Please send word. I want to hear how you're doing."

Swallowing, he nodded. "But you should go. Everyone's waiting on you, and I don't want you getting stuck in the narrow pass, all right?"

"Yeah." The goodbyes weren't supposed to be long. "Can I kiss you?"

He smiled gently. "Yes." He caressed my lips with his own. It was soft, sweet, and short. It was perfect, because it was Tyfen.

I blew out a breath as we separated. "I'll miss you."

Tyfen squeezed my hand. "Go on, Your Holiness. Go make the people as happy as you make me."

I let him go. Only now did all the eyes on us press in on me. "I'll see you before you know it." I turned and walked toward the carriages.

At the edge of the gate, I turned back. Tyfen stood there, his arms crossed, and he gave me an encouraging smile.

A ways beyond him stood Findlech, still in place to wave us all off. He kept a sharp and curious eye on Tyfen, then glanced between us. It put me on guard. I flashed Findlech a look, imploring him. He likely hadn't heard the conversation, but I'd just had a guard stop the fae prince, had argued with him, had kissed him. In front of everyone.

Findlech understood my worried look, offering me a smile, a single nod and a raised hand of assurance.

Things would be okay.

Several carriages had lined up; soldiers on horseback and supply carts were already prepared further down the road.

My party had two carriages for comfort and privacy. I approached the first. The door had been left open, the late summer heat radiating off the thin metal plating.

"Honestly," Elion said to either Gald or Hadwin, "I don't blame you. If I'd walked in on that, I would have killed him first and asked questions later. No one hurts my mate."

Elion... My sweet, loyal mate... The one who had *acted* like he'd cared about Tyfen's well-being. If he was happy to share his true feelings when he thought I was out of earshot...

I quietly took a step closer, peering in. Gald sat on the far bench, polishing his wand. He glanced up.

"Even if it wasn't what it looked like," Elion added. "Your mate comes first."

My face heated at the betrayal.

Gald looked properly awkward at me hearing that, at me eavesdropping. "Gentlemen—" he started.

I shot a finger to my lips to shush him. If they were going to have a bonding session that involved bashing Tyfen after Hadwin tried to kill him, I wanted to hear it all. I wanted to know where things stood as they casually chummed around about my relationship with Tyfen while I was fighting tooth and nail to keep him.

Hadwin sighed. "I'm not really interested in conversation right now, Elion. But thank you."

"Yeah, of course."

It fell silent as they waited for my arrival. Gald pursed his lips and stayed quiet.

I stepped into view of Elion and Hadwin. "I'm glad to know how you really feel about Tyfen, Elion. So very grateful for your support while I'm struggling with every last wisp of sanity I have to…" I shook my head. "You can fuck yourself."

Elion slumped in his seat. Hadwin said nothing, rubbing his beard.

I faced Gald. "Would you like to join me in the other carriage?"

Gald swallowed, avoiding eye contact with the others. "Um, yeah. Of course."

I stepped aside, and he got out, then hopped into the carriage behind this one. I glared at Elion and Hadwin. "Enjoy your journey." And then I slammed the door closed.

I was barely halfway to the next carriage before Hadwin jumped out of his.

"Sonta," he implored.

Glaring, I faced him. "What?"

"We should share a carriage," he said matter-of-factly.

"Later."

"We have a lot to discuss on the road."

"I. Don't. Care."

He frowned, his hazel eyes tinting red. "I love you. We're starting a family. We need to be able to talk."

I hugged myself. "I love you too, Hadwin. But right now, I don't really like you much. Get back in your carriage."

I left him there, joining Gald in the second carriage, and closed the door.

22
Face to Face

I sat opposite Gald, and soon enough the carriages lurched forward. Servants and delegates waved, all still excited for the imperial tour to be on its way. I put on a smile as we passed and waved.

Gald wore a cute expression as he met eyes with Findlech.

"Hopefully he can join us soon," I said.

Gald blushed.

It wouldn't be all that traditional for Findlech to join us on the first leg of this tour, but no one would pry. Findlech wasn't the father, nor was he my mate, and his nation wasn't on this leg of the tour, but people could assume all they wanted that he and I were madly in love and that was his reason for accompanying me.

After our entourage left the palace grounds, Gald and I settled in more comfortably on our benches.

Now that the smiles—real or fake—were gone, all we had between us was the quiet ambiance filtering in from outside the carriage. Horse hooves clopped around us, both from our draft horses and the steeds of the soldiers flanking us.

The longer we rode, the more awkward the silence got.

"Sorry if I made things uncomfortable back there," I said.

He pursed his lips. "No problem." He bobbed his head, but kept his mouth closed. It was obvious he wanted to say something.

"Say what's on your mind."

Gald wrinkled his nose. "I don't want to upset you."

I sighed. "I won't bite your head off. You can be honest with me."

He rubbed the knee of his pants. "I think you may have been a bit harsh back there, especially with Elion…"

I frowned. He was right. I shouldn't take out my stress on the wrong man. This was primarily a Hadwin and Tyfen issue.

Still, I was defensive. "He told me he believed me, supported me. He even asked about Tyfen like he cared, but then I find out he's gossiping behind my back?"

Gald shrugged. "They weren't really gossiping. I think Elion was just trying to comfort Hadwin, trying to be kind and keep the peace. It has to be hard to have his joy tamped down by everything, to have his mate and the mother of his child mad at him for simply trying to protect her."

I scowled. "It's not that simple with Hadwin."

Holding up his hands to soothe me, Gald added, "Sorry. I shouldn't comment on what I don't know. But unless there's something more with Elion, I do think you were a bit harsh. Keeping the peace in this Coterie is not your job alone. I really do think he was trying to help."

I bit my lip, nodding. "You're probably right." I slumped in my seat. "Sorry for being so bitchy."

His smile was warm and sexy. "I'm glad you've got spunk. No matter how great your pussy is, I would have been disappointed to be partnered with someone dull."

As usual, he lightened my mood by making me chuckle.

Gald stretched out his legs in the aisle. "Everything okay with Tyfen?"

"He's healing."

"That's not what I mean." He eyed me. "I knew something changed between you a while back, but I couldn't put my finger on it."

I nodded, thinking of the promises Tyfen had made me at our parting. Yes, I'd just had a breakdown in front of the most important people in the realm, but my heart was at peace that he was going to face what he needed instead of avoiding it. He cared for me. He loved me.

"Tyfen's amazing. I hope everyone gives him a chance when we get back."

Gald nodded in reply.

The carriage jolted with a bump in the road, startling me. I grabbed on to some straps near the doors to support me. "I've slept like shit for nights on end. I was hoping to get some sleep."

"I think it's just a rough stretch here until we hit the main pass," Gald replied. He scooted to the far side of his bench. "Come lie down."

I accepted his offer, nestling my head in his lap. Gald sweetly ran his fingers through my hair and over my face. He gave me that adoring look he often wore after we had sex, his curly red hair swaying with the carriage.

It was so calming, so soothing, and I quickly fell asleep.

Some time later, I woke to another lurch of the carriage. We were stopping for rest and meals, already winding through the mountain passes.

I took time to relieve myself. Elion shyly approached me afterward while I waited for a servant to fetch a satchel that had been packed for me. He apologized about me overhearing him and Hadwin earlier, but I was the one who apologized more. I couldn't fault his protectiveness of me nor his kindness to Hadwin. At least he hadn't tried to shut me up the way Hadwin had.

Hadwin didn't approach me, but he did stand outside his carriage, shielded by his hooded cloak, just looking at me with invitation. We needed to talk to prepare for the celebrations in vampire lands, but I wasn't ready.

I had Elion rejoin Hadwin for now, and the entourage continued. We had time to sort things. Right now, I needed time to reflect and calm.

***

The first day's travel went well. I'd packed a painting pad and notebook for travel. I hadn't found time to paint the brief lavender field vision I'd been given recently, so I kept up my tradition and did that. It was more abstract than usual, owing to the bumpy roads, but it was lovely to complete.

In my notebook I also started a list, my thoughts back on Tyfen. Hopefully, he was taking it easy, healing, and happy. My list was full of questions to ask him when I got back for my first rest week. I wouldn't throw them all at him at once, but there were things I needed to know, and his promise to open up brightened my hopes. For such a popular public figure, he was still such a puzzle.

A god in the bedroom, but a puzzle in my heart still.

Our entourage stopped in a good, defensible clearing within the mountains, and set up simple tents for the night. My Coterie members and I all slept in a tent together. I allowed Elion and Gald to cuddle me—Gald had already seen to my sexual needs in the carriage. My first time in a carriage was a fun adventure.

The next day, I chose to ride with Elion, and gave Gald a choice. Gald chose to ride with Hadwin, and it pricked at my heart, knowing he was doing it to support Hadwin while we were at odds.

I wasn't ready to hash things out with Hadwin, but Elion and I had already mended things after our little spat. He *also* enjoyed the adventure of fucking in a moving carriage.

The sun was setting—vibrant orange, pink, and red streaking across the sky. It was a long travel day, but we pushed further for a better place to set up camp and water the horses.

I expected another half hour of travel as Elion and I cuddled in our carriage, his arm slung around me, his hand holding mine.

A rumble roared outside, freezing my lungs and heart.

Soldiers shouted, several from behind our carriage racing past us on horseback.

Another roar shook through the air.

"Fuck," Elion whispered, jumping up to peer out the window.

The carriage abruptly stopped, throwing Elion off-balance, and nearly tossing me off the bench.

"Shit!" Elion and I looked outside both doors as the commotion became louder, trying to find the source.

Hadwin and Gald rushed to our carriage and yanked the door open.

"Is that what I think it is?" Elion asked.

Gald was no less than rattled, and Hadwin's expression was grim.

"Oni," Hadwin replied. "Cut us off at the front—a rather large pack by the looks of it." He started to shrug off his travel cloak, his pale skin now safe from the sun in the fading light.

Gald was spooked, but rallied his courage, glancing over his shoulder. "I've never fought an oni," he confessed. "I can try to help, or I can standby to transport Sonta to safety."

"Keep Sonta safe," Hadwin ordered. He pointed at me. "Stay with Gald."

I didn't have to be told twice. My only gifts involved mostly sweet visions, fast healing, a wild sex drive, and great birthing hips. I had nothing compared to an oni...

These oni had survived for centuries in woods like the ones we passed. A vampire had bitten a fae, elf, or shifter that long ago to turn it, to corrupt it. An innate magic shielded them, making them hard to take down. Without a master, they mindlessly wandered for eternity, brutally feeding upon anything that moved.

Gald got into the carriage with Elion and me, and Elion squeezed by him to get out.

Hadwin blocked him, preventing him from exiting. "What the hell do you think you're doing, Elion?"

"I can hunt," he said firmly.

"No," Hadwin ground out just as firmly. "You're a pack hunter, currently without your pack. You haven't trained with the emperor's men."

The commotion rose ahead in the distance as soldiers shouted orders. They formed lines between the carriages and the beasts.

"I can still help," Elion insisted.

Hadwin leaned in, his eyes bloodred. "Stay. With. Our. *Mate.*"

It only took Elion a moment to straighten, obeying the order. "I'll keep her safe."

Hadwin reached for his blade's sheath. None of my men wore weapons in the palace—we were all safe there. It was actually rather sexy, his dagger strapped to him like that, or so I'd thought earlier this morning when he'd dressed, when we weren't all in danger...

"What are you doing?" I asked.

He pulled the blade out of its sheath. "Helping."

My heart raced. "You... No! Stay here with us. The emperor's men have it under control."

Just then, a soldier screamed, and a horse whinnied.

"I'll be fine." There was fear etched on his face, but absolute determination in his tone.

"Hadwin," Gald chastised. "That's practically a steak knife. Not even a proper sword. Get your ass in here and let the emperor's men handle it."

"I don't need a sword," Hadwin scoffed. He stole a glance at my stomach, his lips firming.

"Hadwin!" I yelled as he darted away.

Elion furrowed his brow. "Does he have battle training?"

I gaped, watching the father of my child go to throw his life away. "No. Not that he's ever mentioned…" He'd never been in the army. He'd survived decades of torture and had killed several vampires, but fighting wild beasts?

Gald pressed his face to the glass of the side window, and I leaned out the door to watch. Elion held me back by the wrist.

The Blessed Vessel's entourage was always well guarded. We didn't need Hadwin out there.

I spotted my first oni in the distance, and my stomach churned.

The venom that created oni didn't take long to corrupt the body of its victim, but the mind was the first to go, relinquishing any higher thought and subjecting it to the whim of its master. These oni, however, were not freshly turned. Centuries of wandering and exposure to the elements had turned them into sickening sights.

This oni's skin was bloated—a shade of bruise purple. Its jaw hung loose as it snarled, snatching at the horse of a soldier trying to land a blow with his sword.

Their thickened skin and magical protection made them hard to take down by sword, and even harder by wand. Luckily, they weren't as fast as a horse; unluckily, they could easily throw a horse several yards without any effort at all should they grab one.

Hadwin reached the line of soldiers, and my heart calmed a little when one soldier turned to him, yelling and gesturing for him to get back.

He could play the hero all he wanted, but they weren't going to let a member of my Coterie—the father of the next ruler, no less—get killed by doing so.

But Hadwin argued with the man, refusing to turn back.

A second oni charged the section of the line Hadwin was near.

I opened my mouth to yell for him to come back, to get as far away as possible, but nothing came out.

The oni grabbed a man, and the man screamed as the oni bit his shoulder and tossed him aside to swing at another soldier attacking him.

Hadwin stood firm as the soldiers ignored his protests, not letting him cross the line. He lifted a hand, a subtle gesture to the closest oni. The oni stopped its attack and looked at him.

Slowly, Hadwin dragged his hand through the air, and the oni turned as if following orders.

It's following orders…

As if it had a master.

Oni only answered to vampire masters.

The three of us in the carriage stared in shock as the one under his control attacked the nearest oni from its own pack.

"*Shit,*" Gald whispered in awe.

Hadwin and the soldiers had no time to stop and celebrate. Hadwin lifted his hand to another one, a little to his right, beyond the line of soldiers.

Its attention snapped to him like the other's had.

To the left, soldiers had started attacking the two oni Hadwin had turned on each other. The oni promptly remembered that tastier, fresher flesh stood before them, rounding on the men.

Hadwin yelled at the soldiers, and they backed up. He used his ability to reengage the two oni into fighting each other.

The men to the right ganged up on the solo attacker, but stopped once the beast did, once Hadwin had it back under his control.

Hadwin could direct these oni—one at a time.

With the solo beast staring Hadwin down, no longer attacking, Hadwin approached, and the soldiers made an opening in the line for him to walk through.

My heart rate doubled. "He can't just… He should stay back and keep it dazed while the soldiers handle it."

But he didn't. He walked right up to the thing.

"Is he trying to get himself killed?" Elion asked in shock.

That image gutted me. Surely he wasn't so upset about us fighting that he'd be careless on purpose…

My nerves frayed with each cautious step Hadwin took toward the thing. He stood within inches of it—if he lost its loyalty for even a split second, it could kill him with a single swipe of its grubby paws.

Hadwin lifted his hand higher, and the oni raised its head, exposing folds of skin gathered at the neck. Firmly grasping his dagger, Hadwin plunged it up, through the neck, into the skull of the thing.

Its expression slacked, and it slumped to the ground as Hadwin backed up.

I blinked. He'd killed it. Just like that, he'd commanded it to stop attacking, to make itself vulnerable, and to allow him to kill it.

"That's rather handy," Gald said.

Hadwin shouted and gestured at the soldiers; this time they listened. He seized control of one of the two fighting oni and had it approach him while a dozen soldiers took on the other. Hadwin's work was slow and intentional, but more effective than the soldiers' attacks. Once he dispatched his second oni, he finished off the one the soldiers had mostly taken care of.

Hadwin joined the soldiers farther up the path, facing the rest of the oni pack somewhere I could not see from the carriage.

I kept looking, my heart racing. Just because the first few had gone down easily didn't mean Hadwin was invincible.

Several minutes later, the roars had all silenced, though the emperor's men still shouted orders.

My heart leapt when Hadwin ran back to the carriage.

"You're safe?" he panted. His concerned gaze covered me, then the others.

"Yes," I answered. "Are you okay?"

He nodded, watery black blood splattered all over his clothes.

A soldier on horseback galloped up to us. "The path's cleared. We're riding on!" he barked out.

Hadwin joined us in the carriage and plopped down. We shut the door and a minute later were already on the road again.

Mage soldiers helped heal injured comrades on the sides as we passed, slaughtered oni sprawled on the ground next to them.

Hadwin stared into the distance, dazed.

"Are you okay?" I asked again.

He looked at me, his gaze dropping to my stomach, then lifting to my eyes. Slowly, he nodded. "I will be."

"I didn't think you had battle training," Elion said. "You could lead your own army with those skills."

Hadwin glanced down, not replying. A chill ran down my spine. He'd been ordered to never tell me how strong the mating bond was for him, for fear a Blessed Vessel may be corrupted. 'I would burn the realm for you,' he'd told me...

After a second of tense silence, Hadwin spoke. "I belong to the Coterie, to the empire now, not to my people. No one would want me as a soldier."

"We're all grateful you stepped up, though," Elion said.

Hadwin met his gaze. "Perhaps in this carriage. You didn't see the soldiers' looks. They saw a monster, and I don't mean the oni. They didn't have to say anything for me to know exactly what they were thinking. Maybe I drew in those oni in the first place..."

I swallowed, my mouth dry. It was too far-fetched for someone to imagine any vampire would have my entourage attacked when I was about to give them a ruler to represent them. Then again, in the game of politics, it sometimes behooved the attacker to appear the hero or the victim to twist the narrative. And I wasn't the only important person in this procession. Elion and Gald were here, and the magistrate in his own carriage.

Still, Hadwin was not to blame, and his continued state of shock made that apparent.

"Either way, we're grateful you took charge," Gald said.

Hadwin continued to stare at the floor. "Well, at least I'm not a useless coward again."

"No one would ever dare call you that," I reassured him.

His eyes drifted to mine. "No one?" It was a pointed accusation, and it took me a moment.

I'd screamed at him after he'd attacked Tyfen, calling him useless. I'd called him a coward for not standing up to his countess about the oni.

"I'm sorry," I whispered.

Gald handed Hadwin a handkerchief to wipe up some of the blood on him. "I thought oni only obeyed the master who created them."

Hadwin swiped at his face and neck. "Their allegiance can be usurped, especially if they've been separated from their last master long enough."

Next, Hadwin took care of the blood on his hands. We all sat in silence as night fell, the realm darkening around us, only lit by the twin moons in the sky.

"I'm sorry, Elion," Hadwin murmured.

Oni usually traveled alone, but the rare pack popped up now and then, thought to have been a pack of shifters in their former lives, still clinging to instinct.

Elion fidgeted with his hands, a slight frown on his lips. "Thank you. At least they're now at peace."

We rode—quiet, alert, and jittery—for at least a couple of hours. Servants quickly set up tents for rest once we stopped. Hadwin and I had a brief private meeting with the magistrate. We all agreed it was likely just bad timing—oni were known to roam forests like the one we'd been passing, and in the nearby mountains. Hadwin did confess, though, that he believed the vampires were intentionally lax about patrolling and dealing with oni on the fae borders compared to those on the human borders.

They wouldn't want humans to feel unsafe entering their lands to work, to sell their blood. But the fae...

The magistrate took note to discuss the issue with the emperor at a later time.

Hadwin went to a nearby stream to fully wash the blood off him and change, and he returned to the Coterie tent with damp hair.

Elion and Gald had settled in for the night, and I had moved Hadwin's bedroll next to mine.

He glanced at me, a question in his gaze.

I was in a nightie, sitting on my bedroll. "Come on." I nodded at his place.

Blowing out a breath, he joined me. I cuddled up to him, sliding a hand up his shirt. "I was terrified when you took off like that."

"So was I," he admitted. "I've never dealt with that many oni before."

That many oni? I wasn't aware he'd ever dealt with *any*. Before I could ask, he spoke again.

"I'm sure the soldiers wouldn't have ignored *Tyfen* if he'd tried to help them." There was a bitterness, a distant tone to his words. "Born royal, a commander who regularly hunts them in his own forests."

I frowned. "Hadwin ... I'm sorry for insulting you. I panicked, and I was angry, and I shouldn't have treated you the way I did." I took his hand and slid it to my stomach. "You thought we needed help."

His breath shuddered.

"I love you," I whispered. "And I love Tyfen—differently, but not more."

Hadwin sighed. "I know." He stroked my hair a moment, then kissed my forehead. "I'll apologize to him when we get back, okay?"

My heart rested more easily than it had in a while. We'd just needed time to calm from the events. "Thank you." I kissed his cool lips, latching my leg around his.

23

SHARED BY MATES

I stirred early in the morning, the crickets still playing their chorus outside the tent. Half my body was chilled. I smiled, because that half touched Hadwin.

Unable to help myself, I stroked his light beard. His veins called to me, so close, so thick and juicy. I'd downed pig's blood last night, but that never satiated my pregnancy cravings as well or as long as Hadwin's blood did.

Hadwin moaned softly.

I kissed his neck, sweetly at first. He gripped my hip more firmly. "Good morning, darling."

I loved that. I kissed his neck again, sucking a bit, then gently pinching with my canines.

He let out a breathy chuckle, his hand now up my nightie, on my ass. "Would you like a drink?" he offered.

My mouth was dry; I was starved. "I ... don't have my piercing ring with me." I'd rashly made a point of *not* packing it at the palace because I'd been so angry with Hadwin. It had been childish of me to assume I could be so mad at him that I wouldn't give in during our five weeks on this leg of the tour.

"I cleaned my dagger well," he said.

I blinked, meeting his honey-hazel eyes. "A knife?"

He shrugged. "It gets the job done. I know you wouldn't hurt me on purpose." Grinning, he added, "I don't feel much physical pain anyway, right?"

No, he didn't.

I straddled him, carefully picking up his dagger. It was perfectly cleaned and polished. He quickly hardened under me, and I wanted him even more.

"Here..." I set the dagger down, then lifted his shirt; he helped me remove it. "In case I drip some blood on you..."

Really, I'd just wanted to have more skin contact. I picked up the dagger again. It was sharp on both edges of the blade. "You really trust me?"

Hadwin took my hand and guided the blade to his chest, right over his heart. "With all that I am."

That spoke volumes, considering the gnarled scar on the other side of his chest, where he'd been impaled and tortured for the better part of two decades.

The flat of the dagger against his skin, I dragged it down to his navel. "Where should I puncture you?"

His hazel eyes tinted red, his cock thrumming under my pussy. "Wherever you wish."

With a smirk, I set the dagger down yet again and quietly scooted back, slipping his shorts off him. My mouth watered, my heart unsure whether I wanted his blood or his cock more in the moment.

Picking up the blade, I sat on his thighs. "*Wherever* I wish?"

Hadwin swallowed. "I trust you."

I wouldn't dare pierce his cock. Unlike Schamoi's new mistress, I wasn't a vampire skilled at blood play of that sort. But I did have fun, dragging the flat of the blade down him again, just above his cock and to the right. "Would this be safe?"

His breathing was a bit more ragged. "Depends on how deep you go, doesn't it?"

With a smile, I carefully placed the tip to his pale skin. It might be absolutely horrible placement, but I wouldn't drive deep. I gently pushed into his flesh, just the tip. It created a wider hole than my piercing ring would have, but I didn't dig much deeper than it would have.

I withdrew the blade, and his thick, rich blood called to me. I backed up, supporting myself with my hands, and pressed my lips to him. I took a suck, coating my mouth in perfection. How had I gone days without it?

His cock hardened further, his tip wet against my shoulder as I took a couple more sucks from his wound.

His breathing was labored, his irises fully red now.

I licked his wound clean of the blood, then grasped his cock with both hands. I licked up his wetness, which mirrored my own, and wrapped my lips around him. Hadwin's cock was perfectly cold in my mouth as I ran my tongue along it, as I sucked.

Hadwin shuddered with restraint. The other two were still sleeping, and only a few soldiers stirred in the distance outside the tent. Keeping quiet while fully stimulated was part of the fun.

After a minute, I'd thoroughly worked Hadwin up. I sucked as I removed my mouth. "This way, or would you like me on top?"

I prayed he'd choose the latter, because I was incredibly tight, desperate. But I could wait if needed.

"On top," he answered.

Hiking up my nightie further, I crawled back up, positioning myself to take him in.

Just then, a different tug pulled on my desires.

Fuck. Despite his eyelids being closed, Elion was awake. Hadwin's desire for me always ran through me differently, like a frigid stream snaking through my sensitive veins, tickling and taunting my senses. Elion's cravings were more of a warm torrent, ramming me into a hard rock.

I glanced at Elion again, then looked at Hadwin, frowning. "He's awake," I mouthed. Hadwin had never been interested in being watched, though options were limited when we were traveling like this.

Hadwin glanced between us. "Would you like to join us, Elion?"

My eyes widened. Hadwin was offering to share? Fucking with an audience was one thing, but this....

Elion opened his eyes, his gaze landing on me, hungry. "I'd love to."

I stared at Hadwin again, tilting my head, still curious.

"Tell me you haven't dreamed of your mates taking you at the same time..." he crooned.

I blushed, biting my lip.

His tone was a bit softer. "Maybe it's time I branched out a little."

"Only if you want to," I whispered.

He nodded.

Elion pulled off his blanket, yanking off his shorts. "How do you want it, Sonta?"

My core heated. I was already on top of Hadwin... "You take the back?"

His growl was a purr as he crouched behind me. "Whatever you want, mate."

I couldn't stop smiling. "Let's be quiet," I whispered. "I don't want to wake Gald." He faced away from us on his side.

"What if Gald is already awake?" He turned over, a sleepy sexy grin on his face. He licked his lips. The way his tongue tip glided over his lip piercing always got me.

I'd entertained three men at once, though neither Hadwin nor Elion would be all that excited for direct intercourse with Gald.

I was lost for a response, but Gald quickly added, "I'm excited to see a mates-only display. Do I get to watch? I can polish my own wand..."

I almost giggled. Ever the voyeur, ever the flirt—Gald had my heart.

"Sure," Hadwin answered.

"That's fine," Elion echoed.

"Can I make a request and a suggestion?" Gald offered.

A bit of impatience rose in Hadwin's voice; he was already testing his limits of sexual comfort. "What's that?"

"Take off Sonta's nightie. Her tits are wasted right now. I want to see it all."

My cheeks burned.

"I certainly don't mind that," Hadwin replied, helping strip me. He, Elion, and I were all bare now.

"And I suggest she be gagged," Gald said.

Hadwin hesitated on that one.

"She's a rather vocal creature, and these tent walls are mighty thin. We wouldn't want the soldiers outside thinking she's distressed."

Elion pressed his erection against my back as he knelt close, his lips grazing my ear. "She is rather vocal, isn't she? Especially when she's shared."

I could barely breathe. He was absolutely right. He and Gald had shared me twice now, so he would know.

"Not a bad idea," Hadwin admitted.

Gald got up, folding a handkerchief. He knelt to the side of us. "Kiss first," he demanded.

Smiling, I kissed him. He took his time, enjoying it, fondling my breast with his free hand. I repaid the favor by stroking his length beneath his shorts.

He pulled back, his dazzling blue eyes sparkling. "Open your mouth for me, beautiful."

I did, keeping my eyes on his as he inserted the handkerchief. I bit down, and Gald retreated. With not an ounce of shame, he lay back down, taking off his shorts and holding himself.

"Ready?" Hadwin asked.

I nodded, grasping his cock more firmly and easing myself onto it. Each cold inch massaged me, building the anticipation.

Elion held my hips, and I bent forward, giving him more access to my ass. The shifter mating bond was a beautiful thing with the way he naturally lubricated to penetrate me.

He took his time positioning himself, then slowly pushed his way in, his cock knot growing and rubbing within me.

It was fantastically filling to have them both inside me, my mates. One cold, one warmer than most, both great lovers. My heart skipped a beat when I thought of the frigid order Hadwin had issued Elion last night. 'Stay with our mate.' *Our* mate—he'd never talked that way before.

Hadwin palmed my breasts, smiling with his fangs on display as he thrust up.

Elion followed with a thrust of his own.

I clamped my teeth down on the handkerchief, a moan already betraying me.

Hadwin rather liked that, thrusting again.

It took a minute for the two to work in tandem, but they were quick learners. I hardly did anything, supported by them, relying on my handkerchief to muffle my ecstasy.

Hadwin slid his hands to hold my sides.

"See how nicely her tits bounce without that nightie," Gald said.

I glanced at him, and his grin was as mischievous as ever while he pumped himself.

Hadwin's thrusting became more fevered, and Elion matched him thrust for thrust. As I returned my attention to Hadwin, his eyes weren't on mine, but on my breasts. I couldn't help but remember our first time, when he'd claimed me, when he'd shyly and lustily peeked at my breasts in my revealing dress.

Lust filled his expression now, but not a hint of that shyness.

And me, I was just along for the ride, breathing through my nose, biting down on that cloth to muffle the moans.

Hadwin met my gaze as he came, shuttering and panting. I more actively rode him, Elion still slamming into me as my tightness built, as every muscle within me burned and tingled and trembled.

As I gasped in relief.

Elion's well-timed pounding brought him satisfaction soon after, his fingers like claws digging into my flesh, his body pressed to mine as he filled me, a growl of pleasure on his lips.

I was dazed, barely able to keep myself in place. My mates held me up well, Elion wrapping his arms around me, now palming my breasts. Hadwin grasped my thighs, his finger slipping in to massage my clit.

Tensing and shuddering again, I was grateful I hadn't dropped that gag yet as another orgasm rocked me...

Elion kissed my neck, still worshiping me as his knot eventually shrank. I spat out the gag, and Hadwin kept his eyes on me. We shared a smile.

From the side, Gald softly groaned his own relief, and he gave me a satisfied grin, holding another handkerchief to catch his cum.

I soaked up the intimacy of the moment despite the growing noise outside the tent. After a minute, Elion pulled out and cleaned himself up. I gave Hadwin a kiss then dismounted him. He wiped up quickly and redressed, offering to let the servants know we were up and to get breakfast cooking.

After taking a moment to wipe myself clean, I joined Gald on his bedroll, straddling him. His smile was adorable, his mop of red hair charming. "Thanks for the suggestions."

He caressed my ass as I leaned down and pressed my breasts to his bare chest. "Anytime. I aim to please."

Our noses touching, my lips hovering above his, I giggled. We took a minute for our own intimacy, simply naked and happy, our tongues tangling, me remembering how much I loved his piercings.

Gald sighed when we pulled our lips apart, one hand on my lower back, another tucking a strand of my hair behind my ear. "I told you things would get better, right?"

Things were still messy, and my life would always be a blend of chaos amidst comfort, but this morning was a perfect one. "You're right."

Elion finished dressing. Hadwin returned and changed into his travel clothes and cloak. Gald and I couldn't dawdle naked all day either; the servants needed to pack the tent, and we needed to get on the road.

Hadwin watched as I dressed, sheathing his dagger again. He stood as I finished slipping my dress on and tying up my hair. "Mind if I have a moment alone with Sonta?"

Elion and Gald both agreed, ducking out of the tent.

"What's on your mind?" I asked.

Hadwin pulled me to him, wrapping his arms tight around me. "You. You're always on my mind. I love you so much it hurts."

I kissed him. "I love you too." I held the nape of his neck. "What did you think? Sharing me for the first time?"

His lips twitched. "I thought it would be awkward, but it really wasn't. Not the way we did it, at least."

My heart fluttered. "I enjoy when my men get along. When my *people* get along." It brought me so much joy that the Coterie had accepted Lilah, too, though any sexual pairings with her would have to wait.

He nodded, caressing my ass.

I smiled. "Does that mean you'd be interested in doing it again? I was rather shocked you offered…"

Hadwin hummed. "I could see it happening again, at least after near-death experiences." He winked. "And I didn't hate the part where you sliced into me to drink…"

"Mmm…" I ran a thumb down his neck. "We'll need to pick up a new piercing ring along the road."

"Or I could simply use my fangs to pierce my own arm or wrist for you to drink."

I blinked. "Why didn't you suggest that instead of having me cut you?"

His smile was seductive and playful. He'd enjoyed the blade on his skin. Going through what he had last night with the oni really did make him adventurous.

I tilted my head to the side, offering my neck. "Would you like a little something before breakfast?"

Sliding a hand to my breast, Hadwin leaned into my neck and placed his fangs on my permanent bite mark. Instead of piercing and drinking, he kissed me. "Maybe for a treat on the road? Will you share a carriage with me today?"

I nodded. We still had important matters to discuss.

Before leaving the tent, we stole a moment, kissing and reconnecting alone, then joined the others at the firepit for breakfast. As we finished eating, a soft hum sounded in the air in front of Gald. He smiled as a letter materialized in front of him, from Findlech. Findlech's magic was typical for his elven lineage, and I'd seen him send and receive official mail like this throughout our time at the palace.

It was cute to think of Findlech sending him a letter so soon—a private couple's thing. While Tyfen could winnow, he couldn't send letters this way, but he could get letters to me easily enough. I looked forward to receiving some, looked forward to hearing how he was doing as he 'worked on his shit.'

Gald read his letter, his anticipation quickly melting. His jaw tightened as he read, disappointment or anger taking over.

"What's wrong?" I asked.

Shaking his head, he finished reading his letter, then he crumpled it up so tight his knuckles turned white. He stared into the dying fire, not acknowledging me.

A burst of flame shot out to Gald and encircled his fist. He opened his hand, and the letter—now ashes—flew away in the breeze.

Even for Gald, it was a bit dramatic for his emotions to switch so rapidly, for him to so coldly destroy a letter from his other lover.

"Nothing's wrong," he said.

Maybe the letter had been from someone else, not Findlech? "What was the letter about?"

He met my gaze, playing with his tongue ring on the edge of his teeth. "Findlech has to ... take care of something. He might not make it for this leg of the tour."

I frowned. Gald wanted him here so badly, especially for the human portion. "We won't be in human lands for almost three weeks. There's still hope he might make it, right?"

Looking down, Gald blew out a breath. "You're right."

**

It was a more somber morning after that, with us learning how badly mangled a couple of soldiers were after the oni encounter. Luckily, no lives had been lost.

Still, I was happy to have made up with Hadwin, at least most of the way. His promise to apologize to Tyfen on our return meant a great deal to me, but I still couldn't overlook the way he'd tried to shut me up during our encounter with the countess.

We rode together, just the two of us in one of the carriages. We held hands for a while, still clinging on to the joy between us from the morning feeding and sex. But the road was long, bumpy, and quiet.

"We should talk," I said. I didn't want things to sour between us again, but sex and the promise of an apology weren't enough. We weren't simple people having a petty spat.

"What about?" he asked.

I tried not to sound defensive. "We're going to deal with the countess more than any of the other rulers, and soonest, and we need to talk about how that dinner went where you tried to silence me."

He took his hand back and ran it through his hair—not angrily, but frustrated. "That was a bit of a disaster; I'll give you that. But we still have to be careful how we speak, Sonta. That was a direct attack about a ... sensitive subject."

I tilted my head. "It was a statement of fact, not an attack. Is an ancient countess so fragile she can't hear the faults of her own people?"

Hadwin balled his hands into fists, then stretched them out. "It was just horrible timing to discuss oni, okay? That criticism from you with the news of me being the father so fresh…" He met my gaze. "I had to work my ass off, had to agree to things I wasn't all that keen on in order to win the place of joining your Coterie."

I nodded, and it hurt my heart a little to hear it. Some of my men had been assigned to me mostly due to privilege and nepotism—a prince, a lord, the high alpha's son. Some of the men had been required to work for it more—Gald and Hadwin. Haan was somewhere in the middle with the way merfolk society approached the Coterie.

"Especially after your hesitation in the bedding chamber," Hadwin said. "I lied to you to spare your feelings. They… They noticed you weren't fond of me."

My heart sank further. "It was just the blood…"

"Still…" he whispered. "It's just added pressure to smooth things out, to prove I'm capable at my job."

"You're beyond capable, Hadwin."

"I…" He hesitated. "I have someone I'd like you to meet when we're at the main celebration. She's eager to meet you, and I think she could give you some perspective."

"Who's that?"

He flashed a shy smile. "It's kind of a surprise." He cleared his throat, adjusting his posture. "For now, I need my people to think you're madly in love with me and that you trust me implicitly."

I sighed softly. "I *am* madly in love with you, Hadwin. And I *do* trust you."

He took my hand again, sweetly intertwining his fingers with mine. "Thank you. That's all we need. And no mention of oni for now… If they've roamed the land for centuries, we can wait a little while before tackling the issue, right?"

"Okay," I conceded.

He kissed my forehead.

"I was really proud of you last night. And terrified of losing you."

He slid a hand to my stomach. "I'd rather have your two heartbeats than my solo one any day."

"Were you scared?"

A hint of his dazed expression from the night prior showed on his face. "I was. That many…"

I searched his face, curious. "You've dealt with them before? How did you come to learn how to master an oni?" He'd only been a vampire for five decades, a drop in the bucket compared to most vampires. "Or is it a natural skill?"

He pursed his lips. "I doubt many fresh vampires know how to control an oni, or even new age vampires."

'Fresh' vampires were a century old or less. 'New age' vampires had been born as humans sometime during or after Hoku's mortal reign. Vampires older than that were generally referred to as 'ancient,' though many classified themselves by more specific timeframes associated with different rulers.

Hadwin was a fresh vampire, so new to the game.

"So, how did you learn?"

He chewed his lip, looking at our clasped hands. "I'd like my friend to explain it. I think she could help you understand better than I could."

I eyed him, and he returned a look pleading for peace. Ultimately, I *did* trust Hadwin. He was shy and uneducated in a way the others weren't, but I couldn't imagine him with malicious intentions.

"All right," I said. "No more talk of oni, and I look forward to meeting your friend."

As the carriage bobbled along, I rested easy with the assurance that Hadwin and I were in a good place. We had a truce on the topics of tension, and while I was gutted to learn the vampire leaders had been offended by my behavior in the bedding chamber, I was up to the task of proving my respect for them.

24

The Vampire Reception

It took us a full week to reach the vampire capital. We stopped or slowed at small celebrations for Hadwin and me along the path. Gald was down in spirits for a day about Findlech's letter, but he bounced back.

We were all in pretty good spirits, though in the quiet hours in the carriage, my mind often wandered to the palace. Lilah's girlfriend was there to visit her. Mother was there ... probably spending time with Kernov. Tyfen was waiting for me, taking care of himself as promised. I still hoped he'd at least send word.

An enormous parade welcomed our entourage as we rode into the capital of vampire lands. We didn't have a ton of say over our timing; it was midday, so the people wore cloaks or held shades to protect themselves from the sun. Save the random human now and then, that is, easily spotted by their warmer skin tone and lack of cloak—they were fun to pick out. It was odd not to see children, though. The laws regarding fresh vampire creation were strict and nuanced. Most fresh vampires became such out of necessity, to live longer due to disease or injury, but the empire forbade the creation of vampire youths, as it would be more cruel to lock them in that state for eternity.

An entire week had been set aside for our time in vampire lands, starting with a ball and reception the next evening.

The countess and her mate greeted us graciously at their castle and apologized profusely for the unfortunate run-in with the oni along the way. I clamped my mouth closed, hanging on Hadwin's arm, letting Magistrate Leonte make it clear with his politician's words and tone how disappointed he was, how it could have been a great tragedy and we'd gotten lucky, how the empire would like to see a more concerted effort to clean up the oni in that region.

The countess gave him a sickeningly sweet smile that made me want to wring her neck, assuring Leonte it was at the top of her to-do list.

They were respectful to Gald, as they were with most humans. And they put on a good show of kindness for Elion, though I could see right through it. He was useless to them. Vampires didn't like shifter blood and didn't want distractions that might pull my attention from Hadwin.

We got a tour of the grand ancient castle, then enjoyed dinner with the countess, her mate, and a dozen members of her court.

It was more awkward than I'd thought it would be. I had to stop myself a dozen times when I almost asked an offensive question in an attempt at small talk. Vampiric families were almost always chosen families. No children, parents, siblings... Some clung to their ancestry by staying close to their sire, but that wasn't always the case. And it wasn't appropriate to ask about their envenomation story in case it was too sensitive or personal, just like Hadwin's story was. For the most part, I let them lead the conversation.

The way we ate was also awkward. My chef accompanied us on the journey, but it was too much to ask for him to take over private kitchens such as this one, so I ate what the vampire court served me, but a food taster ensured it was safe. It was a requirement for the entire tour.

Elion and Gald had the option of food tasters as well, since they were more likely to be harmed than myself here, though they declined.

At the end of the night, I was ready for rest and proud of myself for the reception I'd gotten, having hopefully proven I like vampires despite the impression I'd given in the bedding chamber.

The countess herself escorted us to our guest rooms. Hadwin and I were assigned a grand suite by ourselves in a long corridor.

I had done my best all day to be overly grateful, overly excited to be here, compensating, but I couldn't ignore the passive aggressive moves. Perhaps Elion's steak had been cooked poorly by accident, though it wasn't likely. But it was a bit over the top to separate our group.

The suite was beautiful and ornate, with a large bed front and center.

Hadwin held my hand. "Thank you so much, milady. We're very grateful for your hospitality."

I smiled. "We truly are." I fought myself but quickly lost. "All the doors along this corridor... What do they lead to?"

She smiled in turn. "Spare rooms. No one is staying in them, so you won't be disturbed."

Right...

"Then it wouldn't be a problem if my other Coterie members slept closer?"

She glanced at Hadwin, then me. "I assumed you would enjoy some privacy with the father of your child. An extra measure of safety for your unborn child, the next Anointed Ruler."

"I see. It would mean a great deal to me to have them closer, all the same. I know better than anyone—"

Hadwin tightened his grip on my hand, but I ignored him.

I continued. "I assure you when it comes to my child—Hadwin's and my child—and matters within my Coterie, I know who I can trust. I appreciate you moving them into the rooms next to us."

She pressed her lips into a thin line. "Of course, Your Holiness. We'll have that done right away."

"Thank you *so* much," I said.

With a curt smile, she left the room, ordering the servants to ready the rooms for Elion and Gald.

I closed the door, then turned to Hadwin, crossing my arms. "You did it again."

He swallowed, looking down. "Sorry. I just don't like confrontation between the two of you."

Forcing myself to let it go, I sighed. "I'm sure a woman of her status and age will survive a simple request for room changes when she's intentionally slighting other members of the Coterie."

He nodded. "Again, I'm sorry."

After we readied for bed, I straddled Hadwin and massaged his cock under his shorts.

"Darling... Let's just go to bed tonight..."

I pouted. "I'm utterly insulted you don't want to rail me."

He groaned. "It's just weird to do it here, in the countess's castle..."

My jaw dropped. "You plan to not have sex all week?"

"Aren't you tired after all the travel?"

I sat back. "Was she one of your former lovers or something?"

Hadwin's face screwed up in shock. "What? No!"

"Then why are you acting so weird?"

"I just want sleep, Sonta."

My shoulders slumped. "And I want sex before sleep." He wasn't turning me down just because he was tired. He was turning me down because of that goddess-damned countess. I shook my head, getting off the bed. "I'll be in Elion's room."

Hadwin sat up. "Really? I turn you down once, and you skulk off to make me feel bad?"

My face burned. "No, Hadwin. I want sex. It's as *simple* as sex. And do you or don't you want your people to think we're all over each other? Your signals are all a mess. I'm going to spend some time with Elion while you sort that out."

Hadwin huffed. "If someone finds out you went to Elion's room instead of staying here..."

I raised my voice, done with the conversation. "The people know I share a bed with six men. I'm *assigned* to fuck six men. No one would be shocked. And no one's going to even know, given the part of the castle we're in, Hadwin!" I threw my hands in the air. "I'm going to go blow off some steam. You can stay here and get your shit together, and I'll come back when I'm done."

And I did just that. Elion was an enjoyable ride. When I came back to Hadwin's bed, he faced away from me, his attitude as cold as his body. He didn't respond when I tried to start a conversation. We slept with a good deal of space between us.

In the morning, Hadwin offered a generic apology and offered to make love to me. I was still angry he was acting so standoffish, so I declined.

While there was tension between us, at least it wasn't as bad as everything had been at the paternity reveal.

We had a lovely day, getting a tour of the expansive grounds from a human servant, especially the part where we learned about the variety of flowers that only bloomed in the moonlight, ideal for vampires to enjoy.

Later, the large banquet, reception, and ball were held at a grand hall in the center of town. People lined the streets in anticipation, and I enjoyed walking the latter part of the path to greet them, even with the annoyance of added security.

The hall was bursting at the seams with vampire nobility, members of the countess's high court and representatives from the different clans.

The countess had dressed elegantly, her sharp makeup accentuating her high cheekbones, her tall curled updo commanding. Her dress was lavish, yet still simple enough to complement the belt she wore with an ancient dagger sheathed on it—the True Blade. Her display of the dagger spoke volumes. It had been a gift from Hoku to a vampire lover during her lifetime, something cherished by the vampires. Instead of being in a temple or museum, the countess wore it as an accessory, much as she wished my child and I would be.

After dinner, there was loads of socializing—everyone wanted a moment with the Blessed Vessel and her triumphant mate, to meet me and congratulate us.

Once the tables were fully cleared, music played, the ball starting. The room was rather gothic, with a few viewing boxes on an upper level.

Hadwin guided me to the floor, and we danced. He was skilled, leading me well. I tried to ignore the eyes on me, so oppressive from every side.

I smiled—for them, for Hadwin. Our anger had mostly dissipated throughout the day.

As we spun, I kept feeling a particular set of eyes on me, those of a woman I'd yet to meet. And then my gaze caught on a pair of icy blue eyes in the corner, accompanied by bronze hair.

"Schamoi's here," I whispered excitedly to Hadwin.

"I told you I'd offer the invitation."

I beamed. "I know... I just wasn't sure it would work out."

While most of the invitations had been issued by the countess herself, Hadwin was allowed to invite a few personal guests. He'd confessed he didn't have a lot of friends in vampire society—he was close with his servants, who took care of his empty manor, but hadn't branched out a ton in his freedom.

I'd been worried about Schamoi taking employment with a vampire mistress, and wanted to make sure she was the right sort. Hadwin had looked into her for me and assured me she was known to be a kind woman. While she was indeed wealthy and important in her clan, she wouldn't have made the cut to be invited to this event on her own.

"Thank you. This means a lot to me." I gave Hadwin a sad sort of smile.

"I know, darling." Sweetness twinkled in his hazel eyes. He could get so jealous, so overly protective at times, but he could also be generous.

After the dance came to an end, he kissed me, his hands on my lower back. Another song started, and others took their places on the dance floor.

"Shall we go visit with our special guests?"

I hesitated, raising an eyebrow. "What will people think?" He certainly seemed to care a great deal about that lately.

The jab wasn't lost on him, his voice a controlled calm. "You wanted him here. I invited them. It would be rude to not address our guests." His tone softened further. "Please don't mock me when I'm making an effort here, Sonta."

I tasted my humble pie, nodding. "You're right. Thank you. Let's go meet them."

Hadwin guided me to Schamoi and his mistress, his arm around my waist, and I made sure to hold him.

"So kind of you to join us," Hadwin began, taking the woman's hand.

I stole a glance at Schamoi, but we didn't greet each other. His wide-banded golden collar told me all I needed to know. She was a possessive mistress, and their dynamic had a sense of ownership to it.

The woman smiled politely at Hadwin. "I'm honored. It's not every day the Blessed Vessel's mate extends such an invitation."

I kept a grin to myself. I'd noticed how some of these vampires referred to Hadwin. While some addressed him by his title of duke, most stressed his place as my mate, as the father of the future Anointed Ruler. It was a higher position than a simple duke, especially one who had recently risen from obscurity.

And this woman, who gave me a hesitant side eye, she was a collector, but also intimidated by me. I was a threat, the former lover of her new lover, a woman much higher in position. She'd probably only accepted the invitation as a stepping stone for her status, her draw to power. That was no doubt why she'd zeroed in on Schamoi so quickly. Other men had applied to be pleasure instructors, but those who had not been granted the positions to serve me had gone away in obscurity. Schamoi was her trophy.

"Your Holiness," she addressed me, offering a bow. "I pray Hoku multiplies your blessings. Congratulations on your pregnancy."

"Thank you so much." I smiled adoringly at Hadwin to ease her worries about me stealing back my former lover. "Hadwin's going to make a fantastic father."

The way his eyes glistened made my heart pound. He cleared his throat, then addressed Schamoi. "I don't believe we've been properly introduced." They'd been in the same room for my pregnancy reading and for my claimings, but had never spoken.

Schamoi nodded stiffly. "It's an honor."

We stood there awkwardly for a moment. What were we supposed to say? Was my former lover to congratulate my new one for knocking me up? Or my new lover to thank my former for teaching me to fuck well?

Luckily, Hadwin cut to the chase. "You wouldn't mind swapping partners for a dance, would you?"

Schamoi shyly gave me a smile, then looked away. His mistress hesitated. I even hesitated a bit. It was extremely unorthodox, but I'd been open with Hadwin from the beginning about loving Schamoi, and missing him, and I'd even mentioned that we may never get to dance like he'd promised two months ago, before he'd contracted himself to this woman.

"I think it's a grand thing," Hadwin added, "that old lovers can remain friends. And that we're all here to meet new people. I'd love to get to know more about you and your clan." He was all charm, and I loved him dearly for it.

She lightly scoffed. "Of course a dance would be fine. I have no reason to be jealous."

And she didn't. She had been envenomated in her forties, a beautiful woman. As much as Schamoi still held a place in my heart, we did not belong to each other anymore.

Schamoi finally spoke to me. "Shall we?"

I contained my excitement. "Yes, let's."

First, Schamoi kissed his mistress's hand, then he took me to the dance floor. Hadwin led her to the floor as well.

"That collar..." I said.

He smirked. "Don't pretend you don't like some weird shit, Sonta."

The sound of my name on his lips was fantastic, and I chuckled. "True."

"How are you doing?" The warmth of his hands on my body was so familiar.

I blew out a breath. "It's been interesting... Ups and downs."

He glanced at Hadwin. "How do you feel about the results?"

My smile was genuine. "Even amidst the chaos, I recognize how lucky I am. I'm glad it's Hadwin."

Were we still lovers, Schamoi would have kissed me on the forehead, but we weren't anymore. It still ached that he'd found a new woman so soon when I'd envisioned him returning to my side after the birth of my child, but it didn't hurt as much as I had expected it to. "You're still liking it here with her?"

He frowned. "I'm sorry I hurt you by moving on so fast." He spoke softly. "Sonta, I knew I had to let you go. And I needed to move on, so when the offer came..."

"I know." I let my pain go. "You deserve to be happy." I wasn't his little dove anymore. He was loyal to his new partner, and I couldn't fault him for that.

He swallowed, keeping our steps in time with the music. "I am happy. And I hope you are too."

"I am." I chuckled again, this time to myself. "Honestly, I can barely keep my Coterie from imploding some days, so I'm quite content with all I have on my plate."

He raised an eyebrow. "What does that mean for you and Lilah?"

"She fits in perfectly."

He simply responded with a grin.

We danced and chatted for the whole song, peace I hadn't felt in our last goodbyes settling into my soul. I realized a few things I never had before...

I was quick to fully invest my heart, though I really already knew that, given how quickly I'd fallen for the men of my Coterie.

I'd never had a male friend around my age before. Never. At least not since puberty. But I was at peace with Schamoi as my friend.

Some relationships had beginnings and endings, and that was okay. Though, I hoped we weren't ending things in *all* ways.

"I'd love for you, and your mistress, of course, to come visit after the birth, to come see my child for yourselves. As friends."

His smile was wide. "I'd love that, too." He bobbed his head. "It would be best if the invitation came from you and your duke, though, directly to her." He whispered, "She *is* a little threatened by you."

I couldn't hide my smile. "I'll make sure we extend the offer directly. And I'm not ashamed that I'm glad she feels threatened. Not something young little Sonta would have ever imagined."

He was adorable, sweet, and gracious. As much as I wanted to hug him at the end of the song, I respected his new boundaries. We rejoined Hadwin and Schamoi's mistress. Schamoi kissed her hand again in greeting.

I made sure to lay on the affection for Hadwin, too. I wrapped my arms around him, kissing him. "I missed you. And you're a *much* better dancer than Schamoi."

Schamoi belted out a laugh. "Goddess damn you, Sonta."

I feigned a gasp. "You're lucky I still consider you a friend. Not just anyone calls me by my given name."

His mistress eyed us.

I wanted to put her at ease that we truly were friends, that I wouldn't try to steal him back. "I'm glad he's enjoying his new situation. He's loyal. As am I."

Hadwin slid a hand to my stomach, kissing my cheek.

She seemed more content. "I'm happy to hear it." She glanced at Schamoi, a smile on her lips. "He tells me he's happy, but a woman never knows."

He gave her eyes I recognized well, eyes that said he'd make sure she never had that doubt again once he had her alone.

Hadwin and I stayed by their side for another moment, chatting more easily.

Eventually, a tall handsome man approached Hadwin, another vampire. "She's ready whenever you are."

Hadwin glanced up at the viewing boxes on the next floor, where a woman watched us. I'd felt her stares all night, which was silly considering *everyone* had been staring at me and scrutinizing me all night. But something was different about her. She looked vaguely familiar.

Hadwin grinned. "We'll be right up," he told the man, who simply acknowledged the statement and went his way.

"Who is that?" I asked.

He held my chin. "Are you ready to meet that friend I spoke of?"

25

Hadwin's Friend

Hadwin took my hand and led me to a narrow set of stairs while people danced and mingled on the main floor. Extra security guarded the base of the stairs, but they moved aside without prompting to allow us passage. It was kind of exciting, sneaking off to meet a friend of Hadwin's.

At the top of the stairs, another beefy security man stood with his arms folded, simply gesturing with his chin at a hallway that led to the various viewing boxes. Hadwin gave him a courtesy nod back as I continued to grip his hand.

"Who is she?" I whispered as he pulled me down the hallway.

His smile was bright, his fangs showing. "You'll find out soon…"

About halfway down the hallway, a tall figure blocked the doorway leading to a viewing box. He perked up, leaning out as we approached.

I blinked. He wasn't a vampire or a human. This man was an elf, his youthful light skin and tall, pointed ears hard to miss. It wasn't like the other races in the empire *couldn't* be found in vampire lands; it was just irregular.

"Here they are." He spoke to his right, then greeted us with a bow. "Hadwin. Your Holiness."

Hadwin still gave no introduction, but acknowledged him with a handshake.

The elf held out his hands to me, too, and I took them. "It's truly a *singular honor* to meet a Blessed Vessel," he crooned.

Before I could say anything, the woman piped up. "Oh, fuck off, Mallon." Her tone was more playful than full of censure, and the elf chuckled. It was far from a belly laugh, but more jovial than most stiff elves I'd met.

"I'll make myself scarce," he said before bowing and heading the other direction.

"Come in," the woman beckoned.

Hadwin and I entered the viewing box. The box had two levels, and the woman sat in a chair at the base of a small set of stairs that led to the actual viewing area.

Her smile was bright, her fangs sharp, her brown eyes beautiful. "Sit, Sonta." She gestured to a chair opposite her.

I did, though it was a bit awkward to have her address me so informally, and for me to not even know her name or station.

She looked up at Hadwin, giving him a different kind of friendly smile. "It's good to see you."

He beamed. "You as well."

It was heartwarming seeing him this way, to meet his first true friend. She was so elegant as she sat there, and so familiar. I still couldn't put a finger on it. She probably just had one of those faces... Her hair was black, in tight curls. Her skin had the typical vampiric pallor, a toned-down look to it, but it was obvious from her coloring and features that she had been a beautifully dark-skinned woman in her human days.

"We'll talk later," she told Hadwin. "I want time alone with Sonta."

Hadwin glanced between us, pursing his lips.

She cocked her head, crossing her legs and straightening her deep blue gown. "You don't trust me with her?"

He straightened. "Of course I do." His response was swift and unguarded, ringing true.

"Then run along. We'll have time to catch up."

I sat there, stunned that Hadwin would just ... drop me off with a stranger like this. But he did. He leaned down and planted a kiss on my cheek. "I'll see you soon, darling."

I gaped as he pulled away and closed a curtain behind him.

The woman surveyed me. "Congratulations on your pregnancy."

"Thank you."

Though the room below was full of merriment, only silence hung between the two of us as she looked me over.

"I'm sorry... Hadwin didn't tell me who you are. And I'm curious why there would be any doubt about trusting us alone together..."

She wore a knowing smile again. "I'm known by a few names." She leaned forward and held out her hand. "And Hadwin may hesitate to leave us alone because I keep his secrets."

I blinked. She was known by a few names, but wasn't going to tell me any of them? And how had she come by Hadwin's secrets? "Hadwin and I don't keep secrets from each other..." I asserted.

Her smirk was feral. "I highly doubt that, Your Holiness."

I swallowed. "I'm sorry, I still don't know your name."

"My apologies, so rude of me." She sat back, straightening her posture. "At the moment, most people know me as Duchess Jaylin, though you'd likely know me by another name."

I waited, but she didn't give me anything more. There were dozens of duchesses throughout the different clans and courts in vampire territory. "And what name would *I* know you by?"

Amusement danced on her face. "I bet you've read something I've written."

"I ... don't usually make time to read," I confessed. "You're an author?"

"Most people wouldn't consider me one, but I'm certain you've read my words before." Her tone was as confident as her words.

If she wanted an ego boost, I couldn't offer that. I didn't know any famous authors by name, vampire or human. I shrugged. "Sorry. I have a terribly busy schedule."

She examined her nails. "Too busy to read the journals locked up in your private library?"

My jaw dropped, my recognition instant. *Goddess save me.*

"*Baylana?*" No wonder she looked so familiar—her portrait hung in museums, in the very palace itself in a gallery of the Blessed Vessels of our realm.

"Yes." She had walked the realm two generations ago, having served by bearing a half-shifter mixling, a well-loved empress.

"You..." I sat, stunned and flooded with a million questions. "You're dead."

She chuckled. "I like my privacy. Vampire lands are a good place to hide and fade into obscurity." She swatted a hand through the air. "Plus, depending on who you ask, part of me *is* dead, though most vampires don't take kindly to that sort of talk."

I was still shocked, trying to take in the news. She'd faked her death, because it was most certainly in the records that she *had* died. And now it made sense that Hadwin had been so confident about my safety when offering to turn me into a vampire someday. It had already been done once. "Are there any more of us who have chosen to become immortal?"

Her voice was calm, soft. "Not that I'm aware of. But it was a risk I was willing to make to spend more time with the men I love."

I smiled. The elf gentleman had to be from her Coterie, and the vampire who had fetched us from the dance floor may very well be her mate. I couldn't ignore the fact Elion and Gald were with us, though. "But hasn't it been hard to see the mortals you love die? Your family, your daughter, your other partners?" Even if I chose to become a vampire down the road, Elion could not. Envenomation would turn him into an oni. And I didn't think Gald would accept the offer, since eternal bites stripped mages of their magic, though he may be swayed someday, considering his relationship with Findlech...

Baylana sighed. "It's not an easy choice. Has Hadwin made the offer already?"

My cheeks warmed. "Yes."

She hummed with satisfaction. "You have time to sort that out."

My mind leapt to the others. Haan wouldn't take the offer or risk. Findlech was already immortal.

Tyfen… My heart fluttered at the thought of sharing eternity with him. I yearned for a letter from him, and looked forward to seeing him again in a month's time.

And there was Lilah… We'd never discussed eternity this way, and I genuinely wasn't sure what her feelings would be.

I plucked a question from the many racing through my mind. I'd never imagined I would have the chance to sit with one of my divine sisters. "Who all knows you're still alive?"

"The countess and I have an agreement… She and her people keep my identity concealed as well as they can, and I … look the other way on some of her policies."

I wasn't sure how to feel about that…

"My daughter knew, and we visited often in secret." Her voice softened, reflective. "And my wonderful shifter mate spent the rest of his days by my side."

I smiled, grateful for Elion. "What about your fae partner?" Tyfen's uncle had been in her Coterie, the same one I would have been paired with had he not found his fae mate.

Baylana wrinkled her nose. "We didn't get along all that well. We barely kept in touch after my daughter was crowned, and I'm sure he didn't mourn me when I 'died.'" She arched an eyebrow. "How are things with his nephew? Are they all the same?"

My cheeks warmed again. "Tyfen's … complicated. But he's great, and I…" I barely knew this woman, but we had an instant connection and bond. "I love him. I love them all in my own way."

"Lucky," she said.

Drawing a deep breath, I considered what all I could ask her. I wanted to know about her time in the palace, her time since, her visions and all aspects of her life. I could spend days with her, learning and soaking it up, but I couldn't be missing all night—we were at a ball celebrating Hadwin and me, our child.

"How is it you and Hadwin became friends?"

Fondness gleamed in her eyes. Either that or mischief; it was honestly hard to tell. "What has he told you about himself and his journey to join your Coterie?"

Hesitating, I kept my mouth closed. I didn't know what she knew, and I wouldn't betray him. "Well…"

"I'm assuming you've seen his scars and he's told you from whence they came? Who gave him an eternal bite?"

I nodded.

"A wretched man, though I confess I only knew him by name before Hadwin disposed of him."

My stomach churned like it always did when I considered the hell Hadwin had been through.

"My duke and I take a special interest in the comings and goings of vampire nobility. These lands are perfect for concealing yourself, but are the least tamed in the empire. It can be cutthroat here, and people just aren't as loyal to each other as they are in the other territories. We try to get to know anyone like Hadwin, someone who rises to nobility after killing the previous owner of the title. Especially when they come from obscurity like him."

It made sense. With her vampire mate holding a ducal title, they did have some power, but she was retired from her Blessed Vessel role. They didn't technically have the authority to sway politics even here when it came to their equals, but it was endearing to hear they kept a finger on the pulse of the situation.

"You have to be cautious," she said. "With the cults, and old ways still pervasive in some circles. But Hadwin..." She grinned. "Hadwin was a breath of fresh air." Then she cringed. "Well, not at the beginning, mind you. He was quite unwell."

He had described himself as practically feral, hinting he'd not been a pretty drunk before. He hadn't walked out of his sire's dungeon and instantly cleaned up and taken his place in vampire nobility. It had taken him twenty-one years to fully make his claim.

"How long have you known him?" I asked.

"Since a few years before he actually claimed his title. My mate had business dealings with his sire, and as much as Hadwin tried to conceal his absence, we noticed. We took him under our wing."

She went on, telling me how they'd gotten to know him, and tried to point him in the right direction once they realized he was a good man to hold a title here. What a gift it had been for Hadwin to be discovered by the right people, for a former Blessed Vessel and her partners to nurture and guide him.

"I'm grateful he had you."

She rocked her head with reluctance. "We could only do so much. Even after he formally claimed his place as a duke, he didn't fit in."

I frowned. "He told me he only ever had two lovers after being turned."

"Yes. He tried working things out with a servant girl he'd spared, who he'd worked with, but it just wasn't the right fit. And then I set him up with a woman whose own wealth and station would have complemented and better cemented his place, but it didn't work out either." She eyed me, a gentleness settling into her expression. "He was too soft for a place like this," she admitted.

I pursed my lips. "He's kind, but he's not weak." He'd killed several vampires, and had almost killed Tyfen.

"No, not weak. But ... comparatively, it would have been easy for a more established vampire to conspire against him. He wasn't happy here. He couldn't have his former human life back, and he didn't want to sit here in his new wealth. So, I gave him a push. Blessed Vessels deserve good lovers, not just assertive political ones. He would be a good representative, bringing healthy views to the table. And being a Coterie member would give him a chance to leave here and move on, especially with the ... strength ... of the bond." She hesitated on that one, giving me a questioning look.

"He's told me about the strength of the bond with me." I rolled my eyes. "It's ridiculous they expect them to keep that from us."

She shrugged. "It's a strong bond. They like control. I doubt many vampire Coterie members actually keep that promise."

Likely not, not when their loyalty was so strictly to their mate. "But…" I paused, not wanting to speak ill of Hadwin to a stranger, even though she was who she was. "He's loyal to me, but sometimes I feel his loyalty still lies with the countess. He's so anxious around her…"

Closing her eyes, she nodded. "I didn't recommend the Coterie position without reservations. It's not an easy process."

Hadwin had once made it sound like it was, that it was a position many in vampire nobility didn't even want.

She continued. "He wasn't particularly fond of having to bed her…"

My eyes widened. "What?"

Baylana cleared her throat. "He didn't tell you that? All vampires volunteering for a Coterie have a long process of proving themselves, and the top few candidates are required to lie with the countess. They have to prove they're good in bed."

My mind whirled. He hadn't bedded humans to prepare, but the countess herself. "It's meant to ensure he can please *you*."

"She may very well have different tastes than I do. That's a *ridiculous* requirement."

"The countess has her power plays, and while Hadwin didn't enjoy it, he entered knowing it would be required."

There wasn't much I could say to that. I at least appreciated the assurance he hadn't enjoyed it. "So his anxiety around her isn't an old lover's thing?"

Baylana chortled. "Not in the slightest. Hadwin and *her*? No." She sobered. "I imagine he still lacks confidence, feels his position is more precarious than it is, his loyalty pulling from both directions."

She wasn't anywhere close to laughing now. "He went through hell and back with his sire. And I regret he was further stressed by the Coterie trials. I'd hoped he would be more relieved once he won the chance to join."

He *was* confident most of the time. "When we're at the palace and she's not around, he's fine." The countess was a trigger for him. She made him feel unsafe. I regretted being so harsh with him last night.

Baylana spoke so matter-of-factly. "He almost quit, more than once, but he was in a bind when it came to the oni test."

Oni test?

"I don't blame him for dispatching his own; I just wish we'd realized sooner. It was quite a scramble to find a replacement in time." She sighed. "But honestly, who could blame him? Had I been turned that way, I would have let my oni feed on my sire, too."

My stomach churned, bile rising in my throat. I choked it down. "What?"

She bit her lip, averting her gaze. "He didn't tell you about that, either?"

"Hadwin owned an oni? And he let it…"

Her words were cautious as she tried to calm me. "Most vampire nobles own oni, as a reminder of strength and as a safety measure. And Hadwin inherited his from his sire…"

I swallowed, trying not to vomit. No wonder Hadwin and the countess had been touchy about oni. It wasn't simply that they selectively patrolled for them in the wild, but they actively kept them as … guard dogs. "That's disgusting!"

She raised her hands soothingly. "My mate and I do not keep one, and not *all* nobles do. I've made my sentiments clear, but my position is precarious. To join a Coterie, the men must prove they can control one, and from what I've heard, it was a mighty helpful skill on your journey here…"

I rested a hand on my stomach, my mind still spinning. I could go off on how our rescue wouldn't have been necessary if they weren't selectively permissive to the oni wandering about, or I could argue how every single one of those was an oni and a soul who deserved peace after centuries of numbness. My last meal kept trying to rise, though, at the image of what Hadwin had done…

"He fed his sire to his own oni?"

"Yes," Baylana said without hesitation. "His sire fed the servant he'd killed in front of Hadwin to the oni, and he made Hadwin watch, so it was fair to repay the favor."

The servant had been dead, not fed upon alive… Hadwin had implied I hadn't been imaginative enough about how vicious he'd been with the man who'd taken his life from him and tortured him…

Baylana tilted her head. "You think it was too harsh?"

I gulped. Did I? I hadn't realized how far gone, how filled with hate and despair Hadwin had been as a survivor. He didn't like talking about it, even now. But was it wrong, what he'd done? He'd gone through hell after hell. Losing his family to a plague when he was still a child. Scorned by a woman he'd loved. Losing his humanity, then enduring decades of torture. Even the freedom he'd brutally fought for hadn't released him from it all—he hadn't fit into society, and had been forced to prove himself to have a chance with me.

"I guess I'm just shocked. Please, I want to hear more. I want to understand Hadwin."

Baylana obliged.

Hadwin and the other remaining servants had tried to dispatch the oni on their own after they'd taken over the estate, but taking down an oni was difficult, even for skilled soldiers. And with the right proximity, their sire could control the oni to free himself. Hadwin had searched out all the material he could find on what to do with an oni. There weren't exactly how-to manuals floating around, as they'd been expressly forbidden during Hoku's reign, and most ancient vampires passed down that knowledge orally. But Hadwin had been the right mix of clever and desperate, researching everything he could, testing for years how to usurp an oni's loyalty.

He'd finally gotten it down. Crudely, nothing like the skill he'd exhibited on our journey here, he'd learned oni control well enough to get the beast to follow him. With the help of his servants, he'd led it to the cellar holding their old master. The beast was starving badly enough, its loyalty won thoroughly enough by Hadwin, that the master's screams could be heard across the estate.

I really was fighting to keep my food down. Hadwin continued to impress me with his resolve, the fight in him. He'd eventually burned his old manor down, his sire and the oni turned to ashes with it.

But his fight still hadn't been won. Baylana had mentored him as best she could to fill his role, and when she pivoted to the Coterie route, it came with dangers. Hadwin's lack of an oni and his rudimentary control of one made him vulnerable to the countess and her court. It wouldn't take much for those high in power to lop off his head and bestow his shiny new estate and title on someone else. Baylana and her mate had trained Hadwin, as they'd been trained by others, to fully master oni control. He'd had to demonstrate in front of the countess herself.

Hadwin had given so much, had gone through so much.

"I know you don't approve of the way I do things," Baylana added. "The agreement I have with the countess is a precarious one. But perhaps this is one of the issues you can address more head-on in your place, something you can help your child understand."

I smiled again. I could recall journal entries in Baylana's own handwriting. She'd always sounded courageous to me in the way she'd faced her duties. It was true her position and influence were much changed since then, but her words still rang true in my heart. "A Blessed Vessel bows out of courtesy, not in submission."

She beamed at me quoting her. "I told you you've read some of my writings."

I wanted to soak up all her knowledge, but this evening wasn't all about meeting my divine sister and swapping secrets, and her vampire mate soon reminded us of that as he interrupted.

"I think they're getting restless about her being gone so long."

Baylana nodded.

"When can we talk more?" I begged.

"We'll make arrangements."

My heart warmed. "Thank you for meeting with me, and thank you to both of you, and your elf partner, for helping Hadwin get where he is."

"You're welcome."

I stood, straightening my dress, but couldn't resist asking one more question—one that demanded more privacy. "Could I have just one more moment alone with Baylana?"

Her mate nodded. "I'll be at the end of the hallway."

I made sure to give him time to walk away, peeking out of the curtain to ensure we had no eavesdroppers. "Have you ever ... told anyone about Hoku's great gift to her daughters? *The* gift?" I didn't need to elaborate.

"I have not. Not even my mates know of that. Some things are too sacred to speak of." She lifted an eyebrow. "Have you told anyone?"

"No. And I won't." I blushed. "I was just checking…" I agreed it was a sacred gift, and it could carry consequences. "Is it as great as the journals make it out to be?"

The fondest of looks graced her beautiful face. "It's even better. It makes the journey worth it."

I took her hand and squeezed it as my heart was near bursting. "Thank you. For everything. I look forward to chatting again."

"As do I."

26

Solid Foundation

My mind raced as I took the stairs back down to the ground floor, but it quickly calmed at the sight of Hadwin at the bottom. He socialized with people, sending them away once he spotted me.

His look betrayed his hesitance. What had Baylana divulged about him? And how had I received it? He'd taken artistic license when it came to his history.

He held out his hand for me, and I took it, savoring that cool eternal touch. "Darling…" He said it more as a question than a greeting.

I raised a hand and caressed his blond beard, his cheek. "I love you."

Relief oozed from him as he pulled me into a hug. "You're not angry with me?" he whispered into my ear.

"I like your friend," I said. "You were wise to trust her. And she picked the right man."

He pulled back, his eyes reddening. "I love you," he breathed.

I kept smiling, and we went to the dance floor to make sure we were seen again. With so many onlookers, we didn't discuss much about my encounter with Baylana, but I expressed how excited I was to spend more time with her. After our dance ended, Hadwin gave me a kiss worthy of a victor, something to make his people proud. Then I took a turn with Gald, then Elion.

Like most celebrations, this one would last for hours, especially given the nightlife of vampire society. I talked with so many people, my mind spun. While I detested being near the countess, I kept my head high.

Blessed Vessels bow out of courtesy, not in submission.

I shared another dance with Hadwin later, and I couldn't stop trying to read his mind as we locked eyes. We both wanted to talk about how my meeting with Baylana had gone, and wanted to know where we'd landed in our relationship. It didn't take me long to concoct an idea.

Having learned my lesson, I roped Gald and Elion into my plans. I led my three men upstairs, and we approached an empty viewing box. I had Hadwin go in first, then I turned to the other two. "Why don't you check out the view in the one next to us?"

Elion opened the curtain and stepped in, but Gald lingered. "These viewing boxes are large enough for all of us…"

I smirked. "Rather observant, but I have something in mind." I pressed against him, tangling my fingers in his curly red hair. "Be a doll and make sure no one comes into my box? I don't want any repeats of what happened at the palace."

Gald nodded. "What if *I* need to check on you?"

I leaned in and kissed him softly, then sucked on his lower lip piercing. He moaned. "Not this time, Gald."

"Okay," he panted out. "But I want you soon."

I winked my promise, then entered the viewing box, closing the curtain behind me. Hadwin stood on the higher level, gripping the railing and looking down. "Quite the celebration."

I grinned again as I stood next to him. The room was lively as ever. "Funny how people come together to make toasts to the success of your cold cock in my warm pussy."

He chuckled. "So crude, Sonta."

Leaning against his arm, I mused, "Which time do you think it was? In the bedding chamber?"

"I don't know."

"I'd like to think it was our first time in the library. Do you remember how hard you made my ass hit the table? Or how well you sucked me off for your first time?"

He properly blushed, at least as much as a vampire could.

"You could have had a *thriving* career at a Suck and Fuck, but you threw it all away!"

He shot me a playful look of reproach.

I turned, facing away from the crowded room. I pulled him to me, and he held the railing on either side of me. "About my meeting with Baylana…"

Hadwin swallowed. "Yes?"

"I'll speak to the countess as I see fit, because I know my place, and I've had training of my own."

Averting his gaze, Hadwin nodded. "I'm sorry I keep… It's just hard for me to be back."

I held the lapels of his suit jacket. "Your countess and I won't ever agree on some things, but apparently we agree on one thing…"

"What's that?"

"You're a great lover, Hadwin."

He instantly frowned in shame. "Baylana told you about that?"

No one else, at least to my knowledge, had been forced to bed their leader to prove their worthiness for my Coterie. Most of them hadn't had to prove anything at all, having already earned their place through nepotism or a role they already held.

"She's a shit ruler for that," I said. "And you don't have to prove yourself anymore. Not to me, not to them. Do you hear me?"

His jaw worked. "It's easy to say that. Harder to accept."

I cradled his face. "Put your trust in me."

He nodded.

"You promise? You trust me?"

"Yes."

"Okay." I lowered my hands. "Slide my dress strap off this shoulder." I shrugged my right shoulder.

He narrowed his eyes. "Why?"

"You said you trust me."

He accepted the challenge, sliding it off. His fingers glided against my skin sensually.

"Kiss my shoulder," I ordered.

He smiled, only breaking eye contact to lean forward and do so.

People were watching us, always keeping an eye on the couple they were here to celebrate.

His cold kiss was soft, and before his lips left my skin, I added another demand. "Kiss my neck like you mean it."

A growl rumbled in his throat as his lips trailed up my neck. I was already wet.

"And the other side…" I said.

I only got a flash of his now-red eyes as he switched sides, slipping off my strap and worshiping my neck. I panted my approval, stroking him below the belt.

"You know, darling… I didn't get a choice as to having spectators in the bedding chamber, and Gald watching the other day was stretching my comfort zone enough… So whatever you have planned"—his lips grazed my ear—"I'll have to cap it somewhere."

"They don't need to see more than this," I assured him.

He met my gaze, smiling. "Thank you for the special public attention, though."

We were only getting started…

I kissed him, hard, pushing him back down the narrow aisle between the seats. He held me tight, kissing back. Our lips parted for a moment as we made sure we didn't stumble down the two stairs that took us out of sight.

I guided him to a chair like the one I'd used when speaking to Baylana a few boxes over, then sat him down.

Hadwin was all smiles. "Maybe I *should* have you and Baylana speak more often…"

Crouching, I reached for his belt.

Wincing, Hadwin moved his hand to intercept mine. "They already got a sneak peek. But if we stay in here, everyone's going to…"

He needed this to get over that hill he kept stumbling on.

"They'll what?" I tilted my head. "Assume your mate, the mother of your child, is fucking you in the middle of an important ball?"

"Well… Yes."

I stood, hiking up my dress, then straddled him on the chair. "Where's the harm in that? Where's the harm in your people seeing their Duke Hadwin is so adept, so charming and handsome that I couldn't keep my hands off him for a few goddess-damned hours? Let them assume. Let them *know*. Feed off me. Let fresh wounds on my neck be their proof."

He swallowed, his hands resting on my backside. "I… You have a point."

This was more than giving the people a good show.

"We're not walking out of here until you feel safe, Hadwin."

"I'm safe."

I pressed a palm to his heart. "You are." I searched his eyes, and said the words, what he needed to hear from me.

"You're mine, and you're safe. I'm not your parents and brother—I heal fast, and have the best healers the realm can afford."

He looked down at that. He'd lost his parents and only sibling to a plague decades ago.

"I'm not leaving you alone," I said. "I'm not a money-seeking woman only interested in your wealth."

"I know you're not," he whispered.

"And if you ever went missing, I would send the emperor's men to tear the realm apart until I found you."

Hadwin's shoulders slumped. The human woman he'd loved decades ago had abandoned him, had never looked for him when he left to sell his blood for her and went missing.

I grasped his chin, forcing him to look at me. "I am not a wicked person who would hold you against your will, who would knowingly hurt you, who would deprive you of anything you want."

"I know," he whispered again.

"Nor am I a prize you need to keep proving you're worthy of. Not to your countess, not to *anyone*."

He didn't respond, but he kept eye contact.

Hadwin still feared losing me, losing his place in society. No matter how hard he'd tried over the years, all he ever did was lose.

"You told the rest of us after you killed those oni that you belonged to the empire now, that no one would want you in their army."

"It's true," he answered.

But he'd said it like it was a bad thing. Like he was homeless.

"Exactly. You belong to me. To the empire." Now that Hadwin was in my Coterie, his position as duke was solid. No one could take that from him so long as he was with me. "I protect what is mine, Hadwin. Take a moment to think about that. Take a moment to think about who you are. *You cower to no one.*"

"You're right." A shade of confidence grew in his expression.

"I'm carrying your child."

His smile could melt the snow from the highest mountaintop midwinter.

"And should the emperor's health fail him before this child takes his place, you and I will rule together alongside the magistrate. I need you to be confident."

Fierce resolve settled into his features. Unlike the others, he hadn't come for his people or for power. Hadwin had primarily signed up to be in my Coterie out of self-interest, to escape. No matter his reason for joining me, he needed to step into the role of the next Anointed Ruler's father.

"I can do anything with you by my side, darling."

We shared a smile. "Good. Now…" I shifted my hips. "I'm going to show you how much I love you. I don't actually give a shit what all those people think. I'd want to fuck you either way."

His smile grew. "Okay."

I stood, and he didn't even let me remove his pants and shorts; he quickly dispensed of them himself.

While I wore more underwear on tour than I did at the palace, I made sure it was the kind with easy access.

He was erect, ready for me as I traced the veins on his cock. I was tempted to lick him, but his hands were already grasping my hips to guide me closer.

His hands shifted to my waist as I peeled his foreskin back and positioned myself. Every chilled inch of him slid into me perfectly. I panted out a breath at the shock.

"If I become a vampire, I'll miss the difference in our temperatures, won't I?"

His eyes red, he met my gaze. Both hands held my hips under my dress. "If you become a vampire, I won't ever have to miss *you*."

I rolled my hips, and his eyes fluttered, his grip tightening. He thrust up, and I rolled my hips again, riding him. "Show me what you can do, Hadwin."

He accepted the challenge, thrusting and plunging with fervor, perfectly timed to each of my movements.

"I love you," he gasped.

Nothing intelligible left my lips as I tried to quiet my own moans and gasps. I found his lips with mine, marrying our tongues as we built our pleasure and pressure.

"Hadwin," I panted.

He plunged harder.

A traitorous moan escaped my lips.

I flexed around him and presented my neck. He clamped down and sucked, barely tasting any blood before that sweet tickle in my veins sent me over the edge. He joined me in ecstasy.

I tried to catch my breath, whispering into his ear, "Who do you belong to?"

His voice was gravelly. "You."

Grinning, I leaned back, meeting his gaze. "And what would happen if we walked downstairs, and your countess told you to keep another secret from me?"

His eyes darkened. "She can fuck off."

I smiled. "But what of the repercussions?"

He spoke softly but confidently. "No one can hurt me anymore."

"That's right." I kissed him again, and his hands roamed happily on my ass.

"Do we *have* to go back down?" he asked.

I beamed. "Afraid so." I rocked my hips. "But you know there's always more of this to come."

He liked that reminder.

Despite the incomparable joy and strength we shared, we truly couldn't stay here forever. Our cleanup was quick, our smiles stuck in place. Dressed again, Hadwin caressed my cheeks, then replaced one of my dress straps. I stopped him from sliding the other up. "Leave it."

As we opened the curtain to the hallway, both Elion and Gald stood there, leaning against the wall, staring at us. They'd been close enough to hear at least the gasps, and Elion would have sensed my desire. Elion was calm; he was doing well keeping his head down in vampire territory, letting Hadwin have the spotlight. Gald grinned knowingly, ever the flirt.

"I'm sure I can make time for you two, tonight," I said.

Hadwin wrapped his arms around me from behind. "No. She's mine tonight. You can have her in the morning."

I loved that confidence, that assertiveness.

"In the morning," I echoed. After drawing a breath, I added, "Do you two mind staying up here a couple more minutes?"

They agreed to, and Hadwin and I took the nearest stairs down. Eyes immediately caught on us, including the countess's. Only then did my smile fully bloom, the fresh red bite marks on my neck visible, and I pushed my strap up, as if I'd forgotten to finish dressing myself after our heated moment.

Her grin of approval was too selfish, as though she had selected her puppet wisely. She'd never understood how much Baylana had mentored Hadwin, that she had urged him to apply for the Coterie. Right now, the countess patted herself on the back—I let her. She and I would never be friends, not with her attitude and policies, but we would do this dance for the rest of our lives as I mentored my child.

Someday, maybe tonight, maybe a decade from now, she'd be humbled as Hadwin and I stood together, doing what was best for us, for our child, for our Coterie, and our realm—not giving two shits about the fear she struck in so many in her own lands.

***

The rest of the celebration ball was lovely. Honestly, the rest of the week was lovely. Hadwin ravaged me, made love to me, and asserted himself when needed. The vampires showed us great hospitality and curated wonderful views for us to visit. Naturally, we didn't see the slums or the oni hidden in people's basements, but we appreciated the vampire lands for what they were—imperfectly beautiful. The people here struggled to be united, often lashed together by the need to cure their diseases, or as victims of evil sires. They were a messy bunch, oft forced to look out for themselves, forced to scratch someone else's back to keep their place.

Vampire lands were the best place to disappear to, the most dangerous of the entire empire. It was fitting my child was half vampire, because there was work to be done here.

Baylana and her elf and vampire partners joined us as we traveled away from the capital, bringing along their own carriage. They escorted us to Hadwin's estate before turning back. It gave me countless hours to discuss things with her, subjects both important and more personal. She didn't like sending letters in case they were intercepted, but she promised they'd visit us at the palace after my child was born. I couldn't wait.

Hadwin's estate was expansive and well kept, though not opulent or flashy. He kept it simply, his servants a skeleton crew. It was a bit somber. The manor was too tidy, too unlived in—evidence he'd never fully settled in. A path still led to the site on the far end of the property, where the ashes of his agony lay. He took me there, holding my hand tightly.

In the end, I was happy to lead him away, not a word spoken between us about it.

His estate wasn't *all* gloomy. He was coy when he shared he'd never made love to anyone in his master suite. He'd saved it for me, and the night we spent worshiping each other there was divine. We painted each other with pig's blood in his large tub, then licked it off each other. Not something I'd ever imagined myself doing, but it was beyond gratifying.

Hadwin made me the official offer to move into his estate someday, when we wanted to retire from the palace. 'The entire Coterie,' he said. In truth, that offer couldn't properly include Haan, as it wasn't built to accommodate merfolk, and I didn't dare ask if he would genuinely accept Tyfen here.

I still yearned for a letter from Tyfen.

Like Hadwin had told me shortly after joining the Coterie, we'd lived fairly close to each other. The human–vampire border definitely had its own socioeconomic dynamic. Humans tended to be poorer here, not able to afford nicer places away from their natural predator. The blood trade was popular, and we paid a hefty price for Suck and Fucks, whereas rich humans could rest safer far away, paying more exorbitant prices for private vampire escort services.

Vampire lands were similar. Hadwin had been sired by a wealthy duke who was able to afford fresh local human blood on a regular basis. The further a vampire lived from human lands, the poorer they usually were, many barely subsisting off pig's blood. Either that, or they were ultrawealthy, able to entice humans to move all the way to their estates.

It was humbling rolling our carriages into my hometown. Honestly, a large part of me wished we didn't have to visit here. I missed parts of it, but not all. Gald, Elion, and Hadwin wouldn't judge me for my humble beginnings, nor did the magistrate, but none of them had lived quite this low, other than Hadwin for a while when he'd been orphaned.

The streets were lined, packed full, the crowd raucous. I swallowed, forcing a smile. My biological father may very well be in the crowd somewhere, not even knowing his seed had become Hoku's daughter through a woman he'd hired to lie with him. Whomever he was, he probably hadn't even remembered my mother's name by the time the deed was done.

Fonder thoughts warmed my smile. Mother had sent a letter. It wasn't like she'd gushed about her time with Kernov at the palace, but she'd mentioned him.

The carriages slowed as we approached the part of town I'd directed them to. Once they stopped, we waited inside our carriages while soldiers secured the area.

Gald exited first, taking the lead in human lands, but not overshadowing Hadwin. He helped me down the steps, and I stole a kiss.

"How does it feel to be home?" I asked. He didn't hail from this region, but they were human lands, nonetheless.

His smile was somewhat strained. "Good."

He'd been getting regular letters from Findlech. What I wouldn't do for that from Tyfen… Granted, Gald was never happy with Findlech's letters, quickly burning them, announcing Findlech still couldn't join us, and insisting we put on a happy face and move on.

"I'm sure he'll make it," I assured Gald.

"Thank you." He stole another kiss. "Come on."

Having diverted from the main route through town, away from the parade, we first stopped at Lilah's family home. Her mother squeezed me within an inch of my life, her father had the heartiest mustached smile, and her siblings were their usual friendly and goofy selves, just more grown up than I remembered.

They were timid meeting Gald, Hadwin, and Elion, though they quickly warmed up. Magistrate Leonte had ridden on. While he ruled in tandem with the emperor, he was also the primary ruler of human society, so he had plenty of official business to attend to while we had our side trip.

Lilah's family invited the men to take tea, and none of them balked. We gathered, sipping and chatting. I sat between Gald and Hadwin.

Lilah's family congratulated Hadwin, and his smile was wide as he thanked them.

"I have a letter for you from Lilah," her mother informed me. "She sent it here so it wouldn't go astray while you traveled."

I giddily took it from her but waited to open it. "I've told her a thousand times the palace's magic mail can get it to me directly." She could have sent it the same way Findlech sent his own letters.

Either way, I was happy for news.

"Is she enjoying things at the palace still?" her mother asked cautiously. "Everything's ... good?"

My heart warmed. She wanted to know if my men were giving her daughter any trouble. "My Coterie respects Lilah."

"She's lovely," Hadwin said.

"They know we're together," I added.

Her mother beamed. "I'm glad of it." Lilah's older brother even gave an approving nod.

"Yeah, we love having her around," Gald said. "And her skill at sketching is unmatched."

My mouth went dry. She didn't normally sketch, but she had done a few of Gald and me fucking. He pointedly did *not* look at me.

Elion spoke up more innocently. "She really is a great artist. When Sonta and I were up in the studio... That portrait..." He stopped himself, then sipped his tea. "She's a great painter."

My core heated at Elion's arousal, my cheeks flushing. The portrait was of me, nude.

Lilah *did* paint things beyond me...

Hadwin leaned in and whispered in my ear, "I didn't lie when I said she snored louder than thunder."

I choked on my tea, then belted out a laugh.

Hadwin hid his smile, addressing her perplexed family. "Lilah is *lovely*," he repeated.

Our visit was sweet, endearing, and far too short for my liking. I hugged them all, then we took our leave. I clutched Lilah's letter, excited to read it in the carriage. We first took a short detour. I hadn't really wanted to show my men the place my mother and I had last occupied, but they'd been so curious.

"There." I gestured to the building, then glanced at my boots, cringing and shaking off some mud.

"Sonta," a slimy voice from my past crooned.

I tensed, my heart racing. I turned, facing one of the boys—now a man—who I'd fucked nonstop as a teenager.

"Why are you here?" I asked.

Hadwin, wearing his day cloak, slid his arm behind my back possessively. He could sense my heart. "Who is this?" he growled, his voice low.

Elion swiftly picked up on the tension, his arm going around me too.

Gald glanced between us and Dayton, the man who'd made my heart race in all the wrong ways.

"Not even a hello for your former lover?" Dayton asked.

"I don't refer to you that way. My Coterie doesn't even know who you are."

He looked at my men, weighing his options. "Are they that jealous? Or are you trying to tell me you didn't come back home to rekindle old flames?"

"Dayton, you don't get to wear a badge because you fucked me. You were low-hanging fruit." It may not be kind, but it was true. The only reason we'd humped like animals as teens was because we were both horny. But when my identity as Hoku's daughter had been discovered, he'd become prideful and aggressive. He was one of the reasons I'd been cut off from the young men I had been with until I'd come to the palace. He hadn't hurt me, but the attention for being involved with the Blessed Daughter had gone to his head, and he'd scared me.

A menacing gleam flashed in Dayton's eye as he responded to my jab. "As were you, Sonta. Before your discovery."

Hadwin and Elion both tightened their grips on me, and Elion snarled quietly.

Gald stepped forward. Even without brandishing his wand, he was commanding in his distinguished mage's cloak. He wouldn't normally wear it to walk the streets, but today was special.

"You dare talk to Hoku's daughter that way? Most people know their place and bow. You're not even worthy to lick her boots."

Quickly humbled, Dayton did sketch a hesitant bow. "She's a servant of the people, one of us. I'm allowed—"

"Run along," Gald said, stepping even closer. "It's pretty clear she's done with you, and she's performing her service to the realm. If she wants to perform more community service, I'm sure she knows how to find you."

Dayton threw him a dark look, then another at me. "Fuck off, *Your Holiness*."

He walked away, and I held back a laugh.

Still defensive, Gald faced me. "Are we going to allow that?"

I beamed, my heart full. "Let him go."

We returned to our carriage, and no one spoke a word as we settled in.

The carriage lurched forward, and I stared at the folded letter from Lilah in my hands. I was so lucky. So loved. A childish prick like Dayton really had no ability to frighten me anymore.

I looked up at my men. Hadwin sat next to me, his arm around me, and Elion and Gald sat opposite us. They all sprawled out like this carriage was home.

Shyly, I glanced back down at my letter. "I love you. All of you."

Hadwin traced a cold finger down my arm. "It's mutual."

I took them in again. They wore grins, having enjoyed themselves, having kept me safe even if it was only from a small threat like Dayton. Their ferocity filled the carriage, Hadwin's mating urges running through my veins, Elion's hormonal tug warming my core. Gald even had the balls to expose his bond tattoo and run his tongue ring across it before folding his arms behind his head and slouching more comfortably.

Goddess damn me, I wanted them all inside me right now.

"Fuck you all," I spat, flustered, hot and bothered.

"This carriage is a little tight for that dynamic, but maybe when we make it to the inn tonight." Gald had zero shame in accepting a four-way, but I blushed.

"I'm game," Elion said, his eyes flashing silver as they bored into me.

Hadwin hesitated. "We'll talk logistics… I'm not as wild as you two."

More than my excitement for the possibility of such a group activity was the peace in my soul. I radiated it as I rested a hand on my stomach.

This was what I'd dreamed of for my Coterie. Unity, camaraderie. This group had come so far. And honestly, most of the Coterie was there. I was excited to see Haan again at the palace, and I still hoped Findlech could join us since Gald wanted him to so badly.

Tyfen… He was the odd man out, requiring the most work to integrate. I hoped with all my heart he would get the courage to winnow here for a visit, but at the very least I wanted a letter.

Tonight, sometime between whatever we settled on for sex and when we turned in for slumber, I would respond to Lilah's letter and write a new one for Tyfen.

My heart was full today.

27

The Fertility Rite

It took us a full week to travel from my hometown to the capital of human lands. The celebrations along the way were bright and cheery. The four of us in our carriages got along well. Enough cities dotted the entire route that we didn't need to pitch tents anywhere, either.

Lilah's letter was brief, but it made me yearn for her beautiful smile. The lack of a letter from Tyfen hurt. I tried to push away my worries that he'd lied about his promise to not drink while I was gone. Obviously, he would have healed of his injuries, and the palace would have told me if there were a major problem.

Maybe he needed time alone to sort out whatever held him back in our relationship. I could give him that time, though I hated not hearing from him. Just the smallest update would have made my day.

I didn't allow myself to dwell, though. There was too much excitement amongst the humans and mage-humans. Some were naturally shy around vampires, but many were welcoming. Honestly, the human leg of our tour was likely to be the friendliest for Hadwin, and the most friendly for my whole traveling party.

Gald kept getting letters from Findlech—they always brought a frown to his tender lips. It broke my heart. Gald confessed he didn't care that we wouldn't be swinging by his hometown, but he would have cared more if both Findlech and I were there with him. Whatever Findlech was doing, it had to be important to disappoint Gald like this... Findlech would have been well received here, too, since humans would have loved an elf Coterie member touring in their lands; so many humans had a fascination with our neighbors to the south.

Instead of being miserable together about our absent lovers on our home territory stop, Gald and I agreed to make the best of it. Making the best of it included participating in the Fertility Rite.

I had to admit, participating in the Fertility Rite wasn't my first choice. I'd had enough exhibitionism for the Great Ritual, but Baylana had spoken well of the Rite, and Gald practically begged to participate.

We had our main celebration in the human capital—a festival from sunrise to sunset—with all the food, drink, and merriment people could ask for. I danced with my men, letting all my worries float away as they twirled me.

It was less formal here, perhaps because of all the children who ran through the streets, a stark contrast from life at the palace and from our visit in vampire lands.

I couldn't be more in love with Hadwin as we slow-danced, his cloak shed as the sun set.

The Fertility Rite, however, was not an event for children, and not open to everyone.

It was frowned on for Elion to come; he was a little disappointed because he was curious, but he accepted it and planned to stay at our accommodations.

Hadwin would have been allowed to come as the father of my child, but he also opted to stay behind since he was 'allowed' but not explicitly 'invited.' Some traditions were solely for myself and the Coterie member of the territory we were in.

Gald and I dressed, both less formally than we had for the Great Ritual claimings, but in slightly nicer clothing than what we'd worn to the daytime celebrations.

I hadn't brought Tyfen's leather bracelet with me, and it wouldn't have even matched this dress, but I ached for him as I slid on a pearl bracelet to complete my look.

"You look amazing, as ever, Sonta." Gald stood behind me, caressing my hips.

His touch sent a shiver down my spine.

"Thank you. And you look dashing." I smiled into the mirror we both faced as he rested his chin on my shoulder.

"Are you ready?"

I sighed. "I'm … nervous?" Was that what I was feeling? It was hard to say. While I understood the Fertility Rite, and people's expectations for it, and the sense of community it brought, I still worried people may be disappointed. I wanted everyone to be happy and successful, and I had no magic of my own to make that happen. My role was solely an honorary one, though more devout extremists may interpret it to be more than it was.

"Do me a favor?" Gald asked.

"What?"

He slid his hands down my arms. "Actually, two."

"Okay…"

"First: switch which arm that bracelet is on? I want everyone to see that beautiful bond mark."

"Oh…" I unclasped it right away. "Sorry. It's not like I mean to cover it up. It's just easier to put bracelets on that wrist." I usually remembered to put Tyfen's leather bracelet on my other wrist out of respect for my bond with Gald.

Smiling, he helped me clasp it on my other wrist, then kissed my bond tattoo.

"Second?" I asked.

He held my chin. "Second." His blue eyes were dazzling as he brushed his thumb against my lips. "Tonight is going to be about you…" He kissed me the way a partner does when they want to make your knees instantly weak. Slow. Lingering. Tender. "And me." He kissed me again, and my heart raced, my core heating.

"No one else," he added. One more kiss.

My lips followed his as he pulled away. He smirked, then admired my earrings. "Do you think we can manage that?"

Smiling, I wrapped my arms around his neck. "Yes." I stole a few more kisses as his hands roamed. We weren't going to dwell on Tyfen or Findlech. I wasn't going to feel guilty leaving Hadwin and Elion for the evening. And I wasn't going to make the outcome of the Rite my personal burden, because it truly wasn't.

I missed Gald more than I realized, having to share him, but it made moments like this that much more special.

Finally pulling back, I gazed into his eyes once more. "Let's go."

It was so quiet as soldiers escorted us to a solo carriage. We rode mostly in silence, holding hands. My nerves slowly gave way to excitement as we approached the temple the Rite was taking place at. One of the biggest temples built to honor Hoku.

I had been brought here once before, prior to moving to the palace.

Dozens of spectators who wouldn't be participating still lined up outside the temple for a glimpse of us. I did my best to acknowledge and greet them as we ascended the large stone steps up to the temple.

A Demali mage priestess greeted us with a smile at the top of the stairs. Demali were a special kind of mage, their magic the rarest in the realm. Demali magic was wild and powerful, though it could be catastrophically dangerous. They were revered, always in charge of Hoku's temples, though in darker days, their treatment had been anything but kind.

Hoku had been a Demali before her ascension.

While I'd always been in awe of Demali, I'd instantly felt a greater connection with them after my discovery as Hoku's daughter. Many called the Demali her mortal children as well, though she shared no blood with them and had never called them that herself; they walked in her legacy almost as I did.

"Your Holiness." The mage extended her hands, and I took them. Many people shied away from even touching a Demali for fear of their magic, though that was purely out of superstition. "We're excited you could join us this evening," she added. Her long blonde hair stirred in a breeze. Her green eyes were piercing, though her most notable feature was of course her Demali mark on her face. It was hard to not stare at the birthmark.

"Thank you so much," I answered.

She turned her focus to Gald, extending her hands to him. He took them without hesitation. "Master Gald." Her smile grew.

While Gald wasn't yet a *grand* master in his order, he was a master. "It's an honor."

She glanced between us. "Everything has been prepared to your specifications."

A twinge of guilt streaked through me, but I quashed it. We could have arrived earlier, could have greeted the people, but I hadn't wanted to. Each Blessed Vessel handled the Rite differently. If I greeted these people in this temple right now, they would all want to touch me. Hold my hand, press their forehead to mine, touch my stomach. It would be for luck. As far as I knew, doing so didn't actually give them luck. And as much as I willingly gave my body for the service of this realm, being felt up for superstition and to give these people false hope wasn't something I wanted to be a part of.

Twice a year in human lands, Hoku's temples opened for the Fertility Rite. Always when one of the moons was full. It was a special event to have one of the moons aligned during my tour.

It was said the ebb and flow of the tides and the magic within the realm danced with Goddess Danah's magic. Fertility Rites in shifter lands were vastly different, and held in Danah's temples. But I was the human icon of fertility, and the goddesses were a peaceful chorus, so humans held the Rite in Hoku's temples.

Gald and I held hands as we entered the temple, and the main room hushed as the doors opened.

The priestess before us announced our arrival. "We welcome Hoku's daughter, the Blessed Vessel, the mother of Hoku's heir—the next Anointed Ruler, Sonta Gwynriel. And her Coterie partner, Master Gald."

It felt a little awkward to have a dozen titles and Gald only one…

"May Hoku multiply her blessings on us all this sacred evening."

Everyone chanted the blessing, bright eyes and smiles filled with hope.

A crude, misunderstanding person would label the Fertility Rite an orgy, but it really wasn't. It was more special than that. We weren't drunkards going at it for the sake of pleasure alone. There *was* pleasure to be had, but this was an important opportunity for so many couples in their journey of conception. Many here struggled to conceive, though some were just excited to start their journey of building a family, taking it outside their private bedrooms. Fertility Rites where a Blessed Vessel participated were *always* well attended, especially when she was with child.

The giant hall had been cleared of the usual benches, but it was now packed with at least a couple hundred participants. Their eyes were on Gald and me, whispers filling the air as we strode through the room to the front. A giant chair—more of a throne—sat there for the two of us.

Couples had brought chairs, stools, or soft pads to participate.

Gald sat first, and I took my place on his lap.

A priestess stood in the middle of the hall, commanding everyone's attention. She gave a beautiful speech, quoting scripture and poems. Hands around the rooms squeezed tight around their loved one's, everyone's anticipation growing.

Her smile was sweet as she ended. "May the blessings of Hoku, Danah, and the rest of our Divine Fates fall upon you all."

As she retreated to the side of the room, a harpist strummed a few chords for ambiance music.

My stomach knotted. *Performance time...*

Couples around the room took their positions, ready to get to business. Some more shyly hung back. Others eagerly waited for Gald and me to start.

He rubbed my knee, his voice soothing. "How are you feeling?"

I blushed. "I'm fine. I don't know why I'm shy after the claimings." I angled my head. "How about you?"

"I'm happy to be here with you."

I admired his freckles, his nose and lip piercing, caressing his cheek. "I..." I drew a breath, mentally drowning out the whispers and occasional moans and giggles of those in the room getting their partners ready. "I'm sorry you didn't end up being the father." He had wanted it so badly, and this Rite would have been that much more special had he been the father.

His expression was contemplative as he interlaced our fingers. "Don't be sorry. I'm happy for you. And for Hadwin. I'm grateful that, even though it isn't mine or that of one of the men I favored more, you're happy. You love Hadwin. He's the right mix of kind and strong." He pursed his lips. "Hadwin treats you right, so the outcome could have been worse."

The subtle dig hurt. To Gald, Tyfen would have been the worst outcome. Flashbacks played in my mind of Gald finding me in a stairwell after I'd cried over Tyfen. Tyfen had told me Gald confronted him, wand out, telling him to get his shit together and that he would be a terrible father.

No one understood Tyfen the way I did. No one knew his tender and vulnerable side like I did.

"That's not fair," I whispered. "And what happened to tonight just being about me and you?"

Gald looked down. "Sorry." He squeezed my hand, then met my eyes again. "Just know that, no matter what happens, I'm here for you, okay?"

I furrowed my brow. No matter what happens? Was there some possible scenario that may play out I couldn't think of? It would have made sense for him to say that before the paternity results, but now...

I shook it off, accepting the kind words and assurance. He'd probably switched trains of thought, now referring to the uphill battle of having a half-vampire mixling.

"Thank you, Gald."

He smiled encouragingly. "And don't get me wrong... I may not have won the paternity, but I still fully intend to be the fun and clever uncle, winning favorite uncle points with your child."

I giggled.

A woman gasped in the audience, drawing our attention.

"I guess we should get started," Gald whispered in my ear.

I beamed. "Yes."

My dress's skirt was large and long, but the top fairly sheer, the sides open. I wore no undergarments. Gald glided a finger to my side, grazing my skin as he leaned in for a kiss.

I kissed back, tender at first, then paying special attention to his lip ring, sucking on it, then his tongue ring. He let out a moan as our tongues tangled. I was plenty warm for him as his other hand went up my dress, tickling my thighs.

I panted out a breath as I claimed his mouth more vigorously, as I wetted and warmed and tightened. As his cock swelled under my weight.

The room grew louder as partners came together, the harp still playing a lulling tune in the background.

"Are you ready?" Gald asked, his voice thick.

"Sure." I stood in front of him, facing the room, and he pulled his cloak over his lap for privacy as he freed himself from his shorts.

"Okay, love," he said as he grasped my hips.

We'd practiced this position a couple of times to get the angle right. He slumped in his chair a bit, gathering the back of my skirt as I eased down. He held his cock, guiding me onto it.

Fuck, it felt nice to have him in me, and this angle just hit differently.

I carefully eased down, slowly taking him in all the way.

"Nice job," he praised as he straightened my skirt around us. Were a stranger to not know, they'd think we were just sitting here, me on his lap.

Gald thrust up, his hands roaming to the open sides of my dress. He palmed my breasts, fondling them as he continued to thrust, as I rolled my hips.

His lips grazed my ear. "Make sure to let the people know how much you enjoy it."

I smirked. This was Gald's turn to shine in his own lands, and I didn't mind the people knowing their Blessed Vessel was *very* satisfied with our relationship.

For Gald, for the people, and for myself as the pleasure built in my core, I moaned his name.

He worshiped my neck with his lips as he circled my nipples and thrust. I had to admit this was a rather passive position for me, but still a fun one.

He plunged into me with increasing speed, his hips lifting me with each thrust.

Gald pinched my nipples, and I shuddered, a gasp escaping my lips.

The room dissolved as I focused on the nerves sparking around the friction of his perfect warm cock. As I leaned into Gald, rocking my hips, savoring the attention and pressure on my tits. As I relished his labored breath kissing my ear and neck from behind.

He panted with the effort of each upward thrust, my moans punctuating every one. The moans mingled as he barreled into me, holding me to his chest with hands assaulting my breasts.

I came, arching my back as I gasped.

Gald held me tight, and kept going. The angle with my arched back brought a fresh kind of pleasure and pain.

"Fuck," I squeaked.

Groping and grinding, Gald finally found his release, filling me, shaking and gasping.

I kept my eyes closed, my neck pressed against his. The warmth and pressure where we connected—it was divine.

After gulping some air, Gald returned his attention to my breasts, sweetly caressing them now. "How did you like it?"

I hummed my ecstasy. "You deserve to be promoted to Grand Master just for that."

He chuckled, holding me by the waist with one hand while continuing his attention with his other.

"You're marvelous." He kissed my neck as we watched the room before us. Many couples had already completed, also soaking in their togetherness, though a great deal still went at it.

I wasn't a voyeur in the way of regularly craving it, but I enjoyed watching now. There were beautiful unions taking place. There was so much love in the room, so many different positions.

There was also a healthy amount of groups bedding each other. Inevitably, some couples showed up here as swingers, having met another couple and getting experimental while here. A dirty smile graced my lips as a pair of men exchanged their women, each looking like they hoped to get hard again for another go.

Some were obvious throuples, a man showing attention to two women, or two men to one woman. I tried not to smile too much, remembering some of these people were more desperate in their desire to conceive. For many of these women, taking multiple partners during the Rite wasn't out of fun; rather it was done to maximize her chances of conceiving.

In some instances, men kissed, taking turns with a mostly dressed woman. She may only be there as a willing surrogate for the couple, and the same went for pairs of women kissing, allowing men to take them solely for the purpose of conceiving a child to nurture with their lover, wife, or hajba partner.

The Fertility Rite was optional for Blessed Vessels to attend, not explicitly part of our duties, but the sentimentality here echoed my purpose. In a sea of people fucking, there were any number of pairings. We had any number of beliefs. But we valued Hoku, each other, tradition, and family. There was unity here.

I was at peace.

Gald shifted a bit, sliding a cloth between us to catch his cum as he shrank, but he kept holding me as we watched on. I gave people encouraging smiles as they glanced at us.

There wasn't an exact ending time for the Rite. Some women accepted multiple partners, and some just took their time, but eventually people started to file out.

I whispered to Gald. "Is it nice not having someone inspect you this time?"

He snickered. "I've never been shy about my cock. It didn't bother me."

And he really wasn't shy. I'd been a little nervous about this part of the tour being awkward because of flirtations or pressure on Gald. He'd admitted to me that, aside from his reputation for being studious and hardworking, he *had* exchanged sexual favors to win the opportunity of joining my Coterie. I'd noticed a bit of flirtation directed his way by certain leaders, but nothing too awkward.

He was mine now, at least for the foreseeable future.

Gald adjusted his seat again, and we agreed to clean up. I helped cover him again as he wiped up and put himself back. Then I returned to his lap.

He kissed my shoulder, and we admired the harp music in the background.

"You still aren't interested in having any children now?" I asked, just to be sure.

Gald shook his head. "Not for me. I'm happy." He turned me sideways on his lap, making eye contact. "I'm happy. Content. More than I even thought I'd be." His smile was so warm, his voice so sincere. For my pride's sake, I didn't ask how much of that had to do with me, and how much had to do with Findlech. We were happy, and that was enough.

"I love you." I kissed him again. We carried on that way again—kissing and cuddling, whispering sweet nothings as the night waxed late, as the room grew quieter.

Eventually, even Gald got bored with how long some of the couples were taking. We tried to be patient, but I didn't turn him down when he slid a hand under my dress and fingered me to a second orgasm just for fun. Like with his piercings—current and intended—he aimed to please his partner, and I would never fault him for that.

✳✳✳

The rest of our time in human lands was genuinely amazing. Even the travel went smoothly. The only damper was Gald's mood. He did his best to hide it, especially when I had the wonderful opportunity to meet his family, but he was stressed.

Findlech never joined us, but he sent letters. Letters Gald seemed both angry and distraught about. He always burned them right after reading them, then took a moment to process before pretending everything was fine.

I wasn't used to Gald acting this way; he was always so chipper and positive.

The last night before hitting the mountain trails back to the palace, we stayed at a large inn. I requested two rooms for my party, and left Elion and Hadwin to share a room to give Gald more of my attention before returning home.

A blaze crackled in the fireplace, warming the room against the rainy autumn weather. I sat on the bed in a short nightie, brushing out my wet hair after a bath. Gald eased down onto the end of the bed, pinching the bridge of his nose, still tense about a new letter.

I crawled to him and massaged his bare shoulders. "Hey."

"Hey," he whispered.

"So tight..." I dug into his muscles.

"Yeah." His voice was so flat, his spirits deflated.

I wrapped my arms around his midsection. "We'll be home soon. Letters can be ... rather impersonal. Won't it be nice to be home? You said Findlech's going to be back from his lands..."

Gald sighed. "Yeah..."

I pulled back, frowning. "Look at me."

He scooted further onto the bed, crossing his legs and facing me.

"You can talk to me about anything," I said. "I hate seeing you this way."

He bit his lip, looking down. "Right..."

I took his hand. "Is this... Are you and Findlech having problems in your relationship?" Things were still new, and a breakup would definitely add complications within the Coterie, but we could navigate it.

Gald lightly ran his thumb across my skin. "No. Findlech and I are fine."

"I can't help but feel like it's more than just disappointment he never made it on this leg..." I could be wrong, but Gald seemed the type to get over that sort of thing quicker than this.

He met my gaze, his brilliant blue eyes troubled. "You're strong, Sonta."

I furrowed my brow. "Okay..." My heart fluttered a bit at the thought of Tyfen calling me Blantui again.

"I love you," Gald said.

I smiled. "I already know that."

He swallowed, reading my face. "I just want you to remember that."

"And...?"

The pause was long before he looked down, turning my hand over and tracing my bond mark on my wrist. "And I'm sorry I've been in a bad mood. I think we should end this leg of the tour on a good note." He lifted his head. "Don't you?"

I perked up. "And what did you have in mind?"

A softer grin than usual grew on his lips. "For starters, we need to get rid of that useless nightie."

I giggled. He lunged forward and pinned me as he worked my nightie up my body and over my head. I freed a hand, reached down his shorts, and grasped his strong cock.

Gald pressed his lips to mine. "Not yet."

Pulling my hand out, I pouted. "No?"

He gave me a deep, carnal gaze. "No." He fully straddled me, tucking his curly locks behind his ears. "When was the last time I gave your perfect breasts the full attention they deserve?"

I giggled again. "I don't remember..."

Letting out a loud, dramatic sigh, he shook his head. "That won't do. Let's remedy that situation right now."

He huddled over me, his lips encircling my right nipple. The tip of his tongue tickled my areola, the metal ball piercing applying pressure. I squirmed at the pleasure.

Gald took a deep breath, lit his tongue on fire, and breathed on my breast, the hot flame kissing my skin. It ached and warmed and wetted me. Then he gazed into my eyes, both hands around that single breast. "I'm going to make you come at least twice before I take you. Do you think you have that in you?"

"Yes," I murmured, aching for the fulfillment of that promise.

"We'll soon see…" With another flame on his tongue, he dragged it on the underside of my breast. The tickle surged through my body, my skin tight from the heat. Opening wide, Gald fit as much of my breast into his mouth as he could, grinding against me, and sucked. Hard.

Fuck.

28

THE EMPTY ROOM

The ride through the mountains to the palace was relatively uneventful. The leaves were turning with the season, and autumn drizzle accompanied us.

I couldn't keep my mind off the people I loved who I hadn't seen for five weeks now. I was excited to hear about Lilah's time with her girlfriend, and my mother's time with Kernov.

I had mixed feelings about seeing Tyfen. I wanted to rip his clothes off and ride him. I missed his eyes, his ears, his muscles and tattoos. I missed his voice. The feel of his hand on my ass, his cock inside me. His whispered threats and sweet nothings.

But he had not written to me even once. I'd written twice. As much as I wanted to reunite in bed, I worried for him. I set my resolve and prepared myself. If he'd hidden himself away, collecting wine bottles for the last five weeks, I'd have a hefty chore ahead of me to help him.

But he was worth it. Now that I knew the goodness and sweetness in Tyfen, the *real* Tyfen, I wasn't going to let him go. We fit too well together.

I prepared myself to spend most of my rest week with him. If he actually was all right and just a jerk about not writing, he'd feel the sting of my leather bracelet on his ass—he owed me.

As we rolled up to the palace, we received warm greetings from servants galore. My mother gave me a giant hug, inspecting me to make sure I'd returned in one piece. Lilah hugged me as well.

Kernov's greeting was barely a short acknowledgement, as he had to attend to the magistrate right away.

My heart hurt that Tyfen hadn't come out to greet us. Then again, Findlech hadn't either.

"Have you talked to Tyfen or Findlech?" I asked Lilah. "Or Haan?" He was going to try to return for my rest week.

She winced. "I've been pretty busy. And, you know… I'd rather chum around with the ones you took on this leg, if you know what I mean."

I couldn't blame her. I'd bring her and Tyfen together. I'd help everyone see the loveable Tyfen I did, now that our relationship was finally out in the open.

We left the servants to unload the carriages as we strode to the castle, and I told Lilah I'd come find her to catch up later. Elion eagerly looped his arm through mine. "I'm excited to sleep in my bed again." He grinned. "Or yours."

I nudged him.

"Agreed," Hadwin said, taking my other hand. Dead silent, Gald trailed behind us as we made our way up the stairs.

I had a bit of a skip to my step as I opened the common room door.

Findlech paced in the middle of the long room.

"Hi, Findlech." I smiled. "I thought you'd be outside to greet us."

Extremely standoffish, he eyed me. "Sonta…"

Tired from all the travel, I didn't have it in me to sort through Findlech's oddness. I wanted to see and hold Tyfen.

"Is Tyfen in his room?"

With a stern expression, Findlech's gaze snapped to Gald. "Gald!"

"I couldn't find the time…" Gald replied, exasperated.

"Couldn't find the time?!" Findlech asked, his words clipped, his tone reproachful.

"Couldn't find the *right* time," Gald defended.

There was no play, only anger and defense, and I was at a loss.

"What's going on?"

Findlech straightened, eyeing me. "Tyfen's gone."

My brain stuttered for a second. "Oh." He still could have sent a letter… "His parents called him back to his kingdom to take care of duties?"

"No." Findlech frowned. "He… He wasn't even properly discharged from the infirmary before he left the palace, walked to the edge of the property wards, handed a note to a guard, and winnowed out." Findlech's throat bobbed. "The note only said to send his things home. He hasn't been seen or heard from since."

I couldn't breathe, my heart aching, my mind whirling.

"No…" Tears gathered in my eyes. "No, he… Why would he do that?"

"I can't say."

Hadwin rested a hand on my arm, and I shrugged him off. "No. I don't believe you."

I stormed to the Coterie corridor, and no one moved to stop me. After throwing Tyfen's door open, I peered in. My heart nearly shattered.

The room was completely empty. The bed was stripped, and there wasn't a single sign of Tyfen. No crown, no décor, no wine bottles or clothing. Nothing. It was like he'd never even been here.

I couldn't stop the tears.

He had *promised* me he was going to get his shit together. That he was going to sort himself out. That he wanted to stop hurting me. He'd said he cared for me.

He'd promised he'd be here to see me when I got back.

"I'm sorry, Sonta," Findlech whispered behind me.

My lip quivered. "Why? Why did he go?"

"I can't say." Findlech's expression was somber, regretful. "I'm sorry."

I grappled for words, fighting to understand. "He left before he was even healed?"

Findlech tugged on his vest. "He was decently healed. He probably didn't have more than a scratch on him. But it was right after his delegation left."

Hugging myself, I shook my head.

He'd promised…

I turned and walked through the room, as if I could find a clue, a note for me. My eye caught on a couple of notes on his bedside table, and I snatched them up.

They were from me. They'd been opened, the seals broken.

"But … I didn't send these until well after he would have been fully healed." I glanced at Findlech. "Who opened my mail?"

Findlech cleared his throat. "I needed to make sure there wasn't something you kept private that would help us explain his behavior and find him."

My heart chilled, but my blood was on fire. "You opened my mail?"

He swallowed. "It was necessary. I'm sorry."

"You had no fucking right to read my personal mail!" Was this payback for accidentally outing him? For catching him in a vulnerable position in Gald's bed?

These two letters had things intended only for Tyfen's eyes. Things sweet and sexy. Me urging him not to drink—none of the others knew he had that problem.

My eyes burned as I clutched the letters and walked up to Findlech.

He straightened.

I felt so incredibly violated, and with every part of my soul, I wanted Findlech gone. I wanted to dismiss him from my Coterie, and I could. The divine edict allowed it at this point. He'd pretended to be my friend, but a friend wouldn't do this.

"I hate you, Findlech." My words squeaked out, far too weak to convey how completely livid I was.

"Sonta," Gald softly chastised at the doorway.

I jabbed a finger in his direction. "Don't you dare stand up for him. If it weren't for Findlech, none of this would have happened, and he knows it." Their stupid secrets and weird tension had contributed to Tyfen being miserable here, and the eventual lead-up to Hadwin nearly killing him.

"He was trying to help," Gald said. "Findlech's barely even been able to tend to his duties. He's been here trying to help the emperor sort out Tyfen's shitty disappearance and keep it a secret. So don't blame him for Tyfen's behavior."

I blinked, just now realizing the emperor had known this whole time, and Findlech had been here instead of visiting his homeland.

Tyfen had no legal obligation to be with me now since he wasn't the father, but *never* in history had a Coterie member not at least stuck around for the birth. It would be a massive scandal, and the palace would want it hushed.

"He still had no right to read my personal mail, Gald!" I spun and stared at Findlech. "If you needed information from me, you didn't have to open my private mail. You could have—"

And then it clicked, the depth of the betrayal. Findlech could have sent me a letter letting me know what had happened, asking if I had any idea why Tyfen would have left.

Findlech *had* sent letters. Several of them. All to Gald.

Gald had been disappointed. He'd known Findlech wasn't able to come. He'd understood why.

"How long have you known, Gald?" My voice was low and threatening.

"It was for your own good, Sonta. The bastard left you without a second thought, without a single concern for your happiness. Right after he found out he wasn't the father."

"He loves me!" He'd never said those words. He'd freaked out and pushed me away when I'd used them, but I knew his heart…

Didn't I?

"Findlech and I were looking out for you," he reasoned.

I was beyond reasoning. My ears burned more than Gald's flames had ever burned my skin. I knew exactly when Gald had learned about Tyfen's disappearance.

He'd gotten his first letter from Findlech as we'd sat around the breakfast campfire. He'd known just a couple of days into our five-week journey. The bastard had distracted me the whole time, making love to me and hiding the truth.

Before I even realized what I was doing, I marched up to him, my hand flying through the air, and smacked him.

I jolted back in shock at the sting in my own cheek. I'd slapped him hard, and had forgotten about our bond, which tied us together.

Gald's expression darkened, his face reddening—even more so where my hand had landed. "What the fuck was that for?"

"You're a selfish bastard."

He leaned in, his eyes boring right through me. "*I'm* selfish? I've only ever been good to you, Sonta."

"Hiding things from me is not how you show you care." The immortal rulers of this realm looking down on me and having their power plays—that I understood.

But Gald should be more understanding. He should respect my need to stand on my own and not be coddled, to not be overshadowed and treated like I was weak.

He stepped even closer. "Who did you the decency of covering you in the bedding chamber after that *asshole* made a mockery of the Great Ritual and intentionally humiliated you? Who offered to let you have another chance with Haan when it might have impacted my chances of being the victor? Who kept your secret about Lilah being your lover? And comforted you after the *bastard* you're defending left you in tears in the stairway?"

Gald balled his fists. "Fuck, you're blind when you want to be."

He was right about all those, but I was angry and hurting. "So I'm supposed to just let him go like that? Because you think you know him?" I pointed at Gald. "Don't pretend you're not a self-serving, selfish asshole yourself, Gald. Lie to me. Tell me you didn't know I would be hurt by you *fucking* Findlech behind my back, not even doing me the courtesy of asking."

A twinge of guilt crossed his face.

"And why were you the first to ask me to dance at the Great Ritual celebration? Don't pretend every motivation of yours isn't about you climbing the ladder, Gald. You wanted everyone to see me breaking tradition. You wanted everyone to see *which* Coterie member I danced with first. You made your statement."

"Yes, I did," he shot back. "I didn't think it was a crime to make a statement by dancing."

"And what did that mean for Elion while he was suffering from mating fever? And Haan? You put me in a no-win situation, all for your arrogance."

He pursed his lips. "I hadn't really thought about that."

"That's because you're a selfish asshole."

His face hardened again. "One mistake negates everything else?"

"It's a pattern, Gald. Why did you keep the news of Tyfen's departure from me?"

"Look at you, Sonta. You're a mess. You wanted to spend the last five weeks this way?"

I could throttle him. "Every time you fucked me. Every time you made love to me with your words to hide the truth... What was on your mind? Concern for me? Or concern for your own goddess-damned career? What would the people say if the Blessed Vessel wasn't happy and fawning over her mage partner, right?"

Calmly, perhaps too calmly, Gald drew a breath. "You don't want to believe I love you. Fine—it's your choice to be blind to Tyfen's flaws and allow him to tear this Coterie apart. You want me to admit I kept the truth from you to keep you happy for appearances? Okay. I did."

Finally, some honesty.

Gald shook his head. "But I did do it for you, too. If you had been miserable for that leg of the tour, you would have regretted it. This is your first impression, going out into the realm and being with the people."

My voice was weak, my energy spent. "The realm already gets my child and my time. I don't owe them my heart."

"No, but every dance we shared, every smile and laugh, every time you crouched to greet a child along our path… You wouldn't have those memories, Sonta."

I hugged myself. "Thanks to your lies, I do have all those memories. And they're all tainted." I choked down the lump in my throat as fresh tears emerged. "All of them. I deserved to know. I deserved to have my privacy respected."

I pushed past him, walking to the common room.

Hadwin frowned. "Sonta…" He spoke softly. "Tyfen isn't—"

"Don't," I warned. "You have no right to speak, either, after almost killing him."

"I was going to apologize," Hadwin defended.

"Too little, too late. You should have done it immediately."

Hadwin's eyes reddened. "I shouldn't even have to. I still wasn't in the wrong for trying to protect you."

I gnawed on my lip, visions of Tyfen in the infirmary racing through my mind. "He was so quick to hide what you did. He did that for me. For you. For the Coterie. He swept it under the rug without hesitation, Hadwin. And no matter how justified you were when you saw him with me, you *almost* killed him. He saved your ass."

"But it's not like it's my fault he left," Hadwin whispered.

"You don't even know the half of it," I whimpered. "He knew you knew about being the father. You let it slip after attacking him. He still saved you. But when we were getting ready to leave on tour…"

I was there again, hesitantly standing with Tyfen the last time I saw his sweet face. Things had been rocky, but I'd had hope. I'd told him I loved him.

His response had been to blame me for putting him in harm's way, for putting him in a bad position. I'd recognized it as a ploy to push me away because he wasn't fully ready to open his heart to love. But now… Maybe I'd been wrong.

Because he'd sworn he'd be here. He'd backtracked and promised me the world. Only after I'd fallen apart and made a scene. He'd told me what I'd wanted to hear, to make me go.

"No one liked Tyfen, Hadwin. Findlech's bullshit forced our relationship to stay a secret. Yes, Tyfen had problems, and he wasn't always great to me, but you don't know the side of him I do. You drove him away. I'm trying to make a family here, and you helped drive him away."

"How much did he love you if he left without a word, and so quickly?"

"How can you stand there and ask that? How can someone with a strong mating bond make demands of an average man whose pain they don't know?"

"Darling, you can't seriously—"

I held up my hands to stop him. My Coterie was crumbling around me, and Hadwin was the last person I could lose right now. We had come too far, grown too much on tour to backtrack now.

"I'm walking away, Hadwin. We're not having this conversation."

And I did just that, making a beeline for my chambers.

Elion sprinted to me. "Sonta!"

I nearly closed the door before he put a foot in to stop me.

"I…" His expression was full of worry. My sweet, unproblematic mate.

"Elion, I need some time alone. I mean it this time."

Frowning, he nodded. "I love you."

Tears streamed down my face as he removed his foot, as I closed the door and locked it.

I leaned against the wall, gulping air, my veins on fire, my mind a muddy mess.

Tyfen left me.

He left me.

He's gone.

He…

He hadn't just gone on a short vacation or left to complete his princely duties. He'd left, without a word, and had his belongings sent after him.

My stomach churned, my anxiety growing. My brain turned to mush.

Why did he leave me?

My room was bright, the sunset blazing outside the open windows to the garden. Everything was tidy.

Such a large room for such an empty heart.

Maybe… Maybe he had left a note, and no one had found it? Something private for me?

Wiping away my tears, I set to scouring my room and dressing room. I looked in every drawer and cabinet, even though I knew he wouldn't have opened some of them.

The only thing I had tying me to Tyfen was the leather bracelet he'd gifted me.

Perched on the edge of my bed, I held it, fiddling with it.

And I bawled.

Why would he let me get so close, fall so hard, just to hurt me? What could have been so bad, so important, that he'd left so scandalously?

I crawled onto my bed, staring at the bracelet, lost in my grief.

Nearly five weeks without word.

I'd worried he was drinking again, but this? What was I supposed to do with this? Had he left me a letter… An explanation…

Tired from travel, exhausted by my emotions, I fell asleep clutching the bracelet.

29

Lost

"Your Holiness!" a woman's voice woke me, her slender warm fingers holding my chin.

My eyelids fluttered. My midwife sat next to me, concern written on her face. "Are you unwell?"

"I…" I was still groggy, and starving, and worn out. My eyes were puffy, my heart broken. At least my cheek no longer hurt from slapping Gald. But she wasn't really asking about me. Like everyone else in this realm, she cared about Hadwin's child, Hoku's heir.

"I'm fine. Just tired…"

"The servants are bringing a late supper and some blood," Lilah whispered as she stepped into view behind my midwife. She frowned.

I sat up. "Thank you," I croaked.

"Is there anything I can get you?" the midwife asked.

Did she even know about Tyfen? How much had the palace locked down that tidbit?

"No. I think some supper would be great, and then I just need to rest after all this traveling."

She nodded. "Before I leave, can I do an examination?"

"Of course."

She took her time examining me physically, then doing a reading on my slowly growing stomach.

Lilah and I looked at each other, and her frown spoke volumes.

"You didn't come see me, and then you didn't open your door… So I went to the common room to see if you were there."

My frown matched hers.

"Elion's sitting in there. He told me about…"

A whimper escaped my lips, and Lilah's sweet expression only deepened in sympathy.

The midwife didn't pry. "Everything seems all right. You know how to find me should you need me."

I sniffled. "Thank you."

Lilah climbed onto the bed with me after the midwife left. "Are you okay?"

Fresh tears came. "No. Not even a little."

She held me tight, not saying a word for the longest time.

After a while, she drew a breath. "I'm sorry."

"Me too," I squeaked.

A servant knocked on my private door, and Lilah left my side to bring in a tray of food.

She watched as I ate and drank. "Elion wanted to make sure you knew he and Hadwin didn't know about Tyfen leaving."

I swallowed a bite of noodles, numb. "Yeah, I figured. Just my two traitors."

Lilah fidgeted with her hands. "I feel bad I didn't even know, but I never come down here unless you're here…"

I shook my head. "You were busy, anyway."

"Was the tour nice? Your letters made it sound lovely."

A barely there smile graced my lips. "It had its moments. It was great seeing your family, but I could have done without getting attacked by oni."

Her eyes widened. "What?"

I caught her up on a few details, but didn't really feel like going into it all, especially anything that involved Gald. Those memories were tainted, bitter.

She rubbed my knee. "I'm glad you're safe. After talking to Elion, I told your mother you were too tired from travel, so she wouldn't worry."

"Thank you."

Lilah hesitated. "You know… With Tyfen, just like you told me after that last ball, what he said to—"

"Please don't," I begged.

"But I…"

"I can't hear another bad thing about Tyfen today. Everyone hates him, but I can't handle someone else I love speaking poorly of him."

It was unfair of me to ask. Tyfen *had* done shitty things now and then. I'd even encouraged Lilah to dislike him from the beginning, but everything had changed. Unfortunately, they just hadn't gotten the opportunities to get to know him like I had.

No one else heard the softness in his voice as he asked me about my paintings. Or his devastatingly handsome laughter when we poked fun. No one else saw that haunting look in his eyes when something weighed him down. Or understood what it was like to have a pause where we just looked into each other's eyes and *knew* we fit.

"Okay," Lilah said. "You love him. I … won't talk about him."

"Thank you," I whispered.

Perhaps he *was* just an asshole. He *may* have left because he was a heartless jerk who'd lost the paternity race. Perhaps he'd left for a completely different reason we just didn't understand. Perhaps he'd gone missing under more nefarious circumstances than we believed. Details of his vague departure could have been fabricated.

No matter the reason for Tyfen's disappearance, I couldn't bear more criticism of him before I'd hashed it out for myself. He wasn't here to explain or defend himself.

I'd spent too much time holding my hand out to him to give up now.

My brain was too crammed to work it out at the moment. I needed a distraction, and I was being selfish by talking all about myself.

"What about you?" I asked. "How was Cataray's visit?"

Lilah looked down, skimming her hand across the bedspread. "It… She…" Her voice softened further. "We broke up."

Could my heart take more? "Are *you* okay?" She'd been seeing Cataray for two years. She loved her…

Tears gleamed in Lilah's eyes now. I pushed my meal tray away and scooped her up into a hug. "What happened?" They were supposed to have a great time together for a good portion of my first leg on the tour.

Lilah's words were strained. "I don't really want to talk about it."

"Okay." I squeezed her tighter. I wouldn't push if she wasn't ready, but I did need to know. "Are we talking … taking a break, or…"

She sniffled. "We're done."

I frowned. Cataray had always been cordial to me, but not really my type.

Burying my face in the crook of Lilah's neck, I held her. "We're quite the pair, aren't we?"

She let out a muffled chuckle, pulling back. "Yeah. I guess so."

I reached into the bedside table drawer and pulled us each out a handkerchief. "When did you two decide?"

She dabbed up her tears. "She wasn't even here a week."

I gnawed on my lip. Lilah hadn't mentioned anything of the sort in her letters, nor had her parents said anything when I'd seen them. "Why didn't you say something? Do your parents know?"

"I didn't want to stress you. You're busy, and there's nothing you could have done… I haven't told my parents yet."

Looking down, I played with my handkerchief. Her keeping this secret from me didn't sting as badly as Gald and Findlech's actions did, but it hurt that everyone thought I was so fragile. Despite my calling as Hoku's daughter, I constantly fought for my place because everyone viewed a younger mortal without significant magic as weak. And when it came down to it, when it came to Tyfen—if Findlech and Gald's story was true—I had to admit there was nothing I could have done. It wasn't like he'd announced he was leaving and I could have found a way to stop him. He'd intentionally left before anyone could halt his departure.

But I could have been here for Lilah.

"I'm never too busy for you."

She gave me a disbelieving look. "Your every moment is planned on that tour. I wasn't dying. I managed."

I took her soft hand into mine. "I can't always be here in the blink of an eye, but I can make sacrifices for the people I love. I would have sacrificed sleep and asked Gald to perform a travel spell just so I could be back here and hold you for a night."

"I love you," she whispered.

We cuddled for another few minutes, and once our tears dried up and my stomach protested again, I slid my tray back to finish my food.

"Can I do anything for you?" she asked.

"No. I'm just hungry and tired. I have a meeting with the emperor in the morning, and with the magistrate. So I'm going back to sleep after finishing this."

I ate a spoonful of pudding, then reconsidered my plan. "I'm not ready to see the men, but I dropped my letters to Tyfen when I…" Somewhere in the blur of this evening's revelation, probably when I'd slapped Gald. "If you'd be willing to slip into the common room and grab them for me… They might actually be in the Coterie corridor."

"Sure. I'll be in and out before they know it." She kissed my forehead and opened my door to the common room.

"Oh." She stood there, her voice surprised. "Hello."

Someone was in the common room? It was getting late, and the day hadn't exactly ended in the 'let's all gather to chum around' kind of way.

"I was just going to grab something real quick."

No one responded, but Lilah glanced at me. "I'll be right back." She closed the door behind her as I polished off my pudding.

No sooner had I finished my meal with a vial of pig's blood and washed it down with water, than she returned, letters in hand.

My privacy had been violated once already, and I didn't want them floating around.

"Thank you."

She smiled. "You're welcome." She handed them to me. "The men put them back in Tyfen's room. It kind of felt naughty walking in there. I hope that's okay…"

I swallowed, trying not to let my spirits plummet again. "It's fine. Right now, it's just an empty room…"

She stood, hands clasped in front of her.

"Who's in the common room?" I asked.

"Oh…" She pursed her lips. "Elion's in there. He's … sleeping by your door. In his wolf form."

I frowned. Goddess, I loved him. My sweetheart, my protector. I should invite him in, but I simply needed a break from my entire Coterie.

"He'll be fine out there," I said. "Do you want to stay the night?" We could both use someone to cuddle with.

Her smile was beautiful. "I'd love to."

Blowing out a breath, I pushed myself up off the bed. "I really want to be comfortable… Is that okay?" I hated doing this dance, as though sometimes people couldn't just cuddle naked without having sex, but I was who I was, and we were doing our best to follow the edicts.

"Get comfortable," Lilah said. "Do you want me to borrow one of your nighties?"

I swallowed. "Do what makes *you* comfortable." In truth, I really did want that skin-to-skin contact, but I'd let her choose.

I stripped down, completely bare, and slipped under the covers. She was more hesitant, but eventually slipped off her dress and bra and set them on the daybed.

Lilah was gorgeous, and even in my depressed state, I couldn't ignore it. The curve of her hips, her ass, her breasts.

Yes, I was wet and wanting, but I could control myself.

Though, my breath hitched as she lifted her arms to remove some pins from her dark brown hair. The candlelight in the room danced on her darker skin, and her nipples were perky with her arms raised like that.

She turned, catching me staring. Her smile was the sweetest. "What's on your mind?"

I blushed. "I'm thinking Cataray is a fucking idiot for ever letting you go."

Lilah pressed her lips together. "So is Tyfen."

I looked down. It wasn't the same. I refused to accept it could be the same. Lilah and Cataray were over, done. I couldn't believe Tyfen and I were done. He had a piece of my heart I wasn't willing to let go. And that was without considering the massive political ramifications we may face…

I had to remind myself that, despite me only finding out today he'd left, he'd actually left five weeks ago.

In five weeks, he could have sent a letter. Could have winnowed to me. Could have returned.

Five weeks wasn't an insignificant amount of time…

My heart reminded me Tyfen was immortal, and the passage of time for him worked differently. My mind replied that I was just making excuses for him.

"Sorry," Lilah said. "I promised I wouldn't speak ill of him."

She snuffed out the candle and climbed into bed with me. Our bodies molded together perfectly as our arms touched, as our breasts pressed to each other, as our legs intertwined.

"Can you even tell I'm pregnant yet? I think some of my tighter stuff is getting more snug."

She cuddled even closer. "You're starting to look like you ate too much at a banquet."

I giggled. "My little food baby will rule the realm someday."

She hummed her sleepy agreement.

I kissed Lilah's cheek. "Thank you for staying with me."

Her fingers caressed my hip. "I'll stay with you for as long as you'll have me, Sonta."

She always spoke peace to my soul. "Then I'll keep you forever."

The morning was difficult, my sexual urges inflamed by waking with Lilah pressed to me. She was beautiful, and sweet, and clever. Her hair smelled like lilacs and honey.

It wasn't like Hoku would strike me down for making love to her, but it went against the spirit of the Great Ritual. She wasn't in my Coterie, and I should be dedicated to them right now.

Not that there was much reciprocal dedication with Tyfen gone and Gald looking after his own, and Findlech betraying me.

I blew out a breath.

What was Tyfen doing at this very moment? Maybe he was visiting his old lover, the one he'd called 'My Dearest'? My guts twisted at the thought, and I had to force myself to breathe and hold back tears.

Lilah woke to a servant ringing my call bell. I ordered breakfast for us in my room, then hastily dressed.

"I'm sorry I have my meeting, but we can spend time together later."

"I'll be up in the studio," she said. "I haven't been moping the *whole* time you've been gone. I've had a lot of time to do some soul searching." She gave me a soft smile with her beautiful lips as she caressed my cheek. "I think you'd be proud of me. I'm working on a new project."

I was immensely proud of her for picking herself back up. "I'm excited to see it."

Her kiss was lingering but far too short as I had to pull myself away to go to my meeting.

As I strode to the emperor's study, a million questions streamed through my mind. Mostly about Tyfen, but also about the collusion to keep me in the dark.

The emperor and magistrate already sat, and the emperor gestured to a chair.

I eased myself down.

"I trust you slept well after all your travels?" the emperor asked.

I eyed the men. "You both knew Tyfen left."

Magistrate Leonte looked down.

"Very well, then, we'll dispense with the pleasantries," the emperor said. "Yes. We both knew."

I glanced at Leonte. "Did you order Gald and Findlech to keep it from me?"

His face was apologetic but not submissive. "I didn't need to. They understood the fiasco Tyfen's disappearance could cause. It needed to stay under wraps. As it must continue to until we get to the bottom of this."

"I deserved to know. As the person who would be shamed for being abandoned by one of her Coterie members so early, I obviously wouldn't have shared that information."

Leonte acknowledged with a brief nod. "Most people prefer to suffer in private. This was the best move for everyone, you included."

Crossing my arms, I looked between them again. "Did you both read my letters as well? In your 'investigation'?" I would die on the spot if they had.

"No," the emperor answered. "Only Findlech."

"My mail is *personal*," I snapped. "And since when did a member of my Coterie become a personal servant to our emperor? I gave no credence to what Queen Lourel said when she implied you may be struggling with impartiality, but the elf member of my Coterie invading my privacy at my half-elf emperor's behest when my fae partner has gone missing is a rather dangerous connection."

He didn't skip a beat, didn't change his tone one bit. "Findlech was the first person to witness Prince Tyfen's aides packing his things. He was still here on business with his delegation and was the first to alert me to this scandal. He's done you a great service, Sonta."

He adjusted in his seat, leaning back. "As for impartiality, I caution you to not draw conclusions. Tyfen's parents know he's missing. We've been in contact and have tried working with them." Sighing, he added, "And I'm sorry about your privacy being invaded. I would not normally condone that, but we had little choice without disturbing the work you were doing. Without knowing Tyfen's motivations and intentions, we don't…"

The emperor took a moment. "We don't know if this could snowball into something bigger. We had to take the risk. Plus, we'd hoped we could locate him before your return."

Was life always to be like this in my position? Constantly hearing that the balance of the realm rested on an unstable head of a pin?

No matter what, I couldn't undo what had been done. I just wanted Tyfen back, safe and happy by my side.

"What did the king and queen say?"

"They were surprised. They don't know why he left or why he sent for his things. He never returned home and never sent word."

My hopes drained. He wasn't just gone to me. He was gone to his family?

"They are certain he's alive," the emperor added. "They've been searching and have declined our help at this point. They're confident he can be found. They know he's within the borders of their kingdom."

He was alive. Tyfen was alive. I could breathe.

"Is there a reason to be concerned for his safety?"

"One possibility is that the vampires might have learned about the debacle with Duke Hadwin. The elves have their own old grievances with him. For all I know, he may be a threat to himself. Pick one."

My heart thudded harder. "But they're sure he is safe? He's within their borders?"

"Yes. They're trying to trace him." The emperor folded his hands on his crossed knee. "It's not easy to pinpoint him. I'm sure you can imagine why, given how magic plays a greater role outside the palace wards."

I nodded, a ball of nerves. Tyfen had masking and winnowing powers. Others did too.

But he was alive, presumed safe… It gave me something to hold on to.

"I want to know everything. I want to see the note he left. I want all the details."

"We still need to discuss details of your tour thus far and preparations for the next leg," the emperor reminded me.

"Tyfen first."

The meeting ran much later than I'd expected it to, but we discussed much of the first leg of my imperial tour, and prepared for the next. I asked every question I could think of, as did they.

I didn't know why Tyfen had left. He hadn't given me any indication. I confessed he'd told me he hadn't wanted to come here in the first place, but we'd grown close. I relayed how he'd told me he also didn't want to go back to his kingdom, but there he apparently was. I warned them about Tyfen's own father threatening him; Leonte dismissed it as the king's temper, but assured me they'd keep that under advisement.

They asked me about what had happened during our goodbye when I was leaving for the tour. I was too ashamed to go into detail, but it hadn't gone unnoticed that I'd ordered a guard to intervene when Tyfen was walking away.

Tyfen had pushed me away after I told him I loved him. I didn't tell them that part; my heart couldn't bear that truth.

"He promised he would be here when I got back…"

They let me see the letter he'd handed a guard seconds before winnowing away.

It was nothing more than a torn piece of parchment addressed to his head aide with a scribble and his signature. 'Go home and take my things.'

The guard attested to Tyfen only winnowing away with the clothes on his back and his sword in its sheath. The fae king and queen relayed that none of Tyfen's possessions seemed to be missing beyond that.

I was numb, my head racing with all the 'what-ifs' as I left the emperor's study. As soon as I clicked the door closed behind me, my stomach growled.

"Lunchtime?" Kernov asked.

I spooked, a hand to my heart. "Goddess damn you, Kernov. Don't surprise me like that."

He stood from a chair in the hallway. "Sorry. I've been waiting for you."

I'd missed his friendly eyes, and the way his salt-and-pepper hair complemented his dark skin.

"How are you doing?" His voice was all kindness, and as the magistrate's top advisor, he would of course know about Tyfen's absence.

It was like I had a direct line from my heart to my tear ducts. I fought that burning. "Please don't ask me that."

He nodded. "Very well. Your mother and Lilah have conspired to share lunch. They're waiting for us in your mother's chambers, if you're up to it."

I smiled. "I'd love that."

With the click of each of my footsteps in the palace hallways, I thought of Tyfen. Right now, he was lost to me like a leaf in the autumn wind. As much as I wished for him to be here, wished to make sense of this whole scenario, I couldn't grasp him and pin him down.

30

One Short Week

Lunch was lovely with my mother, Lilah, and Kernov. Mother didn't know Tyfen had gone missing, and we would keep it that way. She was already nervous about my happiness and safety, and she had her own anxieties about being away from her cottage. Though, all things considered, she seemed rather happy, rather cozy with Kernov. It was a warm spot in my dreary autumn heart.

My rest week was simultaneously too busy and too quiet.

I had fittings with Madam Gaffey for current elf and shifter fashions for the next leg of the tour, and for any alterations needed for my growing belly.

I spent time with my mother and Lilah, together and separately.

When I didn't have meetings or time with Mother or Lilah, I moped. I'd snuck into Tyfen's room to search for anything that may have been missed. I cried on his bed when I realized—despite how silly it was—that his servants had packed up and shipped off the rope he'd borrowed from my playroom. I wanted to trace his tattoos, to taste him, to feel him inside me. To hear him call me any of the nicknames he had for me. I wanted to see his gorgeous green eyes and hold his hand.

Since I didn't talk to my Coterie all week, my pleasure tools got a great deal of use, and I always envisioned Tyfen when I used them. Tyfen or Lilah, since she was keeping me company in my room and the temptations were strong.

The one exception to my no-contact-with-my-Coterie rule was when Haan pulled on my call string. I was genuinely happy he had returned. He was kind and sympathetic. That airily husky voice and those slitted purple eyes got me every time. We swam in my pond, and I let him distract me with stories of his visit to his home in the southern sea.

Mostly, I missed Tyfen. I analyzed everything he'd said and done in our time together. I smiled and sobbed through the various memories, yearning for anything of him. The leather bracelet around my wrist became a constant accessory just to feel near him.

I stared for an hour straight at the journal I'd been writing in on my tour, at a list of questions to ask Tyfen. Then I set to work on writing more. Instead of questions to get to know him, now most questions began and ended with the theme of 'why.'

Why was it so scary to be loved by me?

Why had he left without a goodbye?

Why had he left at all?

I didn't go up to my studio until five days into my rest week. Lilah had forbidden me from coming up without announcing myself. She'd decided the big project she was working on was going to be a secret. So, when I did make it up there, I was strictly forbidden from looking under a canvas she'd draped over some projects.

I'd had two visions on tour, which meant two paintings to hang, plus the lavender one. I found places for them all, then froze at the empty spot in the green section.

The painting Tyfen had stolen. The dewy grass in the vision had matched his green eyes. That feeling of loss ached viciously as I touched the tack still stuck in the wall where he'd ripped it off.

I'd yet to repaint it, but the image remained sharp in my mind. I hadn't asked him about it after that day, hadn't gotten it back. He'd been too sensitive about it for me to dare to.

Tears stung in my eyes as I stared at that pin.

"Hey, love," Lilah said. "You ready?"

We'd agreed to paint a number of portraits throughout my pregnancy, and it was best to squeeze it in during my rest weeks for now.

"Yes, I'm ready." I disrobed and sat on a bay window bench, my back to colorful stained glass this time.

Lilah coached me on how to position myself. We finally settled on a pose. She picked up a pencil and began sketching me.

"I'm going to need a more genuine smile than that. This is for posterity."

My strained smile drooped to a frown. "Isn't it a lie to paint an expression that doesn't represent the truth of the moment?"

"Sonta…" She spoke softly. "This isn't about you and your Coterie. This is to celebrate your journey with your child."

I looked down, my hands on my naked stomach. How was it possible to just think of my child without his or her father and uncles? Hadwin and the others hadn't even tried to speak to me since I'd locked myself in my room, which I was actually grateful for, but still…

Lilah sauntered up to me. "Do you need help forming a genuine smile?" Her tone was playful as she slipped a strap off her low-cut dress.

I hid a grin. "Seducing me won't get you the kind of smile that says 'I'm thinking of my child.'"

She giggled. "But we could try…"

Sitting next to me, she caressed my face, her expression tender. "I've always admired you, Sonta. Your boldness and sweetness." Her thumb ran over my lips, and my core lit ablaze. "Your adventurous side."

"Yeah?" I didn't always see those things in myself; they kind of ebbed and flowed...

"Yeah." She smirked. She looked so goddess-damned gorgeous right now with her hair tied up in a messy bun. Her long eyelashes were always beguiling.

Lilah leaned in and pressed her lips to mine. I held her by the nape of the neck, savoring it. As I stole another kiss, she moaned, leaning further into me, her hand resting on my bare thigh.

"I'm glad you're back," she whispered against my lips.

"Me too." I pulled her in, and she straddled me.

Her tongue glided against mine slowly and intentionally as she worked her fingers through my hair.

My hands slid up her dress to grope her ass.

Fuck.

She wore no underwear, and I hadn't a stitch of clothing on me.

Lilah's hands roamed to my breasts as our breath quickened. I wanted her mouth on them, my fingers inside her, and hers inside me.

I tightened my grip on her hips, panting her name as she kissed my nipple. "We shouldn't."

She stopped sucking on my tit and pulled away. Swallowing, she frowned. "I'm sorry. I keep doing this to you."

I was so wet, so desperate, so on the edge of not keeping that part of my vow. "Don't be sorry for wanting to be with me."

Lilah pressed her forehead to mine. "I do, but I'm still sorry. You have enough pressure on you. I think ... I'm going to need a few more cold baths when you're back."

She got off me and straightened her dress. "It's selfish, but I wish Haan's seed had won, because you'd be closer to popping his child out."

I couldn't help but chuckle.

"At least I got you to smile..."

I sighed. "How about a different look? Something contemplative..."

She nodded. "Like you, the idea is lovely."

I took a few cooling breaths, my heartbeat still pulsing in my pussy with desperation, my nipples still perky. Then I got back into my pose, holding my stomach, this time gazing at my collection of paintings.

I focused on my child and their future. I set aside my pain over Tyfen. My guilt over being ostracized from my Coterie and doing a piss-poor job as the Blessed Vessel. I set aside my resentment for the things I couldn't have.

And I focused on the beauty. Even in these paintings and accompanying visions, both sorrow and horror were found, but as they hung on the wall, they made a gorgeous rainbow, the amalgamation a thing of true art.

I prayed to Hoku, asking for her strength, for clarity. I imagined the little one in my womb. Allowing my mind to quiet, I pictured them as a newborn babe, as a small child, and as a regal ruler. I remembered the promised gift Hoku gave her daughters—our secret—and a genuine smile graced my lips.

After a while, Lilah called me over to approve the sketch. She had a natural talent. She'd captured the pose well, and even the smile mirrored how I'd felt while pondering my child.

"I love it."

She beamed. "I already painted swatches of the colors of the first portrait, and since we don't have pesky clothes to color match..." She winked. "It will be done up and dried for you to see when you return from your next leg of the tour."

I drew a deep breath. "Do you want to come with me this time?"

She hesitated. "I'll come if you want me to."

"Which means you'd prefer to stay here?"

"My big project has a time commitment, but I could push it back if you wish me to be with you. They would understand."

No... She didn't want to travel as the secret lover, and I was proud she had some big project she was excited about.

"Stay. Elion might be sad you're not joining us, but I don't have a great feeling about how things will go with Findlech's stop. Stay here and make me proud, and stay out of that chaos."

"Okay. We'll write?"

I nodded.

"And I'm a travel spell away if you change your mind."

I appreciated the offer more than she knew. "Thank you."

Glancing at the sketch one more time, I smiled. "Do you have any paintings of Cataray sitting around?"

"Umm... No. I never painted her. Why?"

I shrugged. "Just thought I'd see if you wanted to go bother the palace archers by asking to borrow their bows for target practice."

"Sonta!"

I laughed. "Sorry, that's wicked of me." Lilah still hadn't wanted to talk about their breakup, so I shouldn't assume the worst of Cataray.

As I grabbed my dress and slipped it back on, Lilah spoke again. "You know, I learned many women's breasts change with childbirth and breastfeeding. The color and size of their areolas." Her finger grazed my sketched breasts on the paper as she bit her lip. I was still wet, and that look on her face wasn't fair in the slightest.

"I don't think mine have changed yet."

She stole a peek at my chest. "I'll notice when they do." Her lips twitched. "We'll do a color match on your next visit, just in case."

I kissed her again. "Look at my artist, being so thorough with her details."

She giggled.

Sighing, I forced myself away from her. "I think I'm going to share my bed with Elion tonight."

Lilah frowned. "Sorry."

"No, it's not just you. I mean … the more time I'm with you, the harder it is to keep my vows, but I feel bad Elion's been sleeping outside my room." He didn't deserve it, and I'd had enough space and time to myself to calm.

"I understand."

"He'd probably be fine sharing with you again on another night, but…"

Her grin echoed my knowledge. "He'll want to make up for lost time."

I left her with one more kiss—keeping it short to stop tempting myself.

Once back in my chambers, I settled down for an early night. Granted, 'settling down' didn't usually equate to 'getting fucked out of my mind'…

The common room was empty when I opened the door, save for sweet Elion huddled up to the door, his massive grey wolf form curled into a ball. His ears instantly perked up, and his tail wagged.

His tail slowed as he got to all fours, awaiting word from me.

"Come inside."

He leapt into my chambers, and I locked the door behind him. He transformed into his usual self, naked.

Goddess, I loved those narrow silvery lycan eyes, that black hair and his loving expression.

"Are you okay?" He took my hands. "Can I hug you?"

I wrapped my arms around his neck, and he pulled me in tight.

I hated people asking me if I was okay lately. It forced me to ask myself the same question. It made me think about Tyfen and all the other problems, and it made me remember that I was not okay.

Instead of the truth, I gave Elion an answer I hoped would become the truth. "I will be."

He inhaled deeply, his cock already hard against me. His mating fever had gone away, but absence made the heart grow fonder… And the cock harder.

"What can I do for you?" he asked. Despite his hard-on, his voice was as tender and thoughtful as ever.

I pulled back. "I want my mate to show me how much he loves me."

His eyes flashed silver as he slid a hand up my dress to caress my ass. "If that's what you really want, you're going to need water to hydrate, an understanding that you're not getting any sleep tonight, and a promise that you'll tell me when it's too much."

My insides tingled at the threat and promise.

"*When* it becomes too much? Or *if* it becomes too much?"

He yanked me to him, pressing his erect cock hard against me. "What does my mate think I'm going to answer to that?"

A growl rumbled in his throat as he claimed my mouth.

I was going to be ravaged, and I already wanted to moan my pleasure at the thought of it. "I'm yours to do with as you please," I whispered against his lips.

Elion made quick work of freeing me from my dress, and he circled me, his hands groping as he went. "Let's see how flexible you still are with that child in you."

He backed me up onto the bed, our flesh kissing as he guided me to the middle. His look was intense, his breathing nearing a predatory growl.

I lay there, waiting for a command. He didn't command me, instead spreading my legs enough to kneel between them, then grasping my knees and bending my legs up. A smile quirked on my lips. Soon, I'd no longer be able to easily do some positions, but I could do this one still.

Relaxing my legs, I allowed Elion to fold me in half, giving him fantastic access to my pussy. As fevered as he was with want, he was a gentle enough mate to ease me into the position, to stretch my muscles as I hooked my ankles behind my head.

His grin was wicked as he leaned down and plunged his tongue inside me, then dragged it up, circling my clit.

Fuck.

That was all the tenderness and preparation I needed, and all he gave me, before he pressed his tip to my entrance, and drove deep.

My first moan betrayed me.

His hands grasping my legs, he stayed on his knees for the first few thrusts. He was thick, knotted, rubbing me just right.

The harder and faster he plunged into me, the quicker our pants as he took me, the deeper his penetration.

I squeezed around him, savoring the friction as his feet clawed at the bed to get more leverage.

Deeper.

Harder.

Needier.

Those goddess-damned noises I always made with him announced my joy, my tightness, only inciting more fervor as he slammed into me, something of a howl on his breath as he found his release, and I found mine.

Panting, Elion rested his hands on my stomach, and I eased my legs down onto his shoulders with him still knotted inside me. We shared a smile.

"I love you," he said.

I grinned wider, soaking up the moment of us, just us. "I love you too."

He glanced back. "I might have torn the sheets with my claws…"

While he always respected my wishes not to fuck an animal, he did sometimes partially shift, his back feet becoming large paws so he could dig in for better leverage.

My smile remained as I slid my hands to his. "Sometimes, sacrifices must be made." I drew a circle on his hand with my fingertip. "Do you want to call it a night? Or do you have more in you?"

The look he gave me for insulting his ravaging abilities…

31

The Snake

My throat was sore the next morning. Partially from some rather vigorous oral I'd given Elion when my pussy and ass had needed a break, but mostly from how much he'd made me gasp and scream.

Elion and I may choose to abstain every now and then just to have a wild night like that again…

On the last day before leaving on tour again, my guilt grew about not having spoken two words to Findlech, Gald, or Hadwin during the week, despite running into each other a few times in the hallways.

Maybe I was overreacting, being childish, but my heart and pride wouldn't allow me to offer an ounce of apology when I worried so much about Tyfen.

But my lack of being with the men all week did soften the blow of our arguments, and part of me looked forward to being with them again. I was nervous, knowing this could get worse, but I missed them.

I let Elion take me a couple of times during the day, and he spent a few hours in the evening counseling with his aides and ensuring he packed everything well. He was nervous and excited to have his home visit on this second leg of the tour.

Tonight, I would share my bed with both Elion and Lilah—just cuddling.

As I slid my nightie on in my dressing room, the private entrance to my chambers opened and closed.

"I brought a surprise," Lilah called.

I smiled as I removed an earring. "I hope it involves chocolate, and that you brought enough to share with Elion."

"I don't think Elion would be interested in sharing," Gald said.

My mood deflating, I huffed, tossing my other earring onto the vanity. I rounded the corner to my chambers' entryway. They both stood shyly.

Scowling at Lilah, I rested my hands on my hips. "I thought you said you brought a surprise, not a snake."

She pouted. "He may be a snake, but I really don't think he's a venomous one."

"Thanks for the vote of confidence, Lilah..." Gald gave her a look.

"Don't give me that look. I said I'd let you in. The rest is up to you."

"What do you want, Gald?" I had a decent guess, but I let him speak since he was the one desperate enough to rope Lilah into it. He wanted to make sure I'd still approve of him coming on this leg of the tour. He had no need to, but he wanted to be with Findlech and see more of elven lands.

"I want to offer my help," he said.

I raised an eyebrow. "How?"

"A tracing spell for Tyfen."

My heart skipped a beat just at the mention of him.

"His parents have already reported he's in their kingdom."

"Has the *palace* performed a tracing spell on him?"

I rolled my eyes. "I don't know. But he's not easily traceable." I wouldn't betray Tyfen's magic, which he'd shared with me in confidence, but it was more than him simply being able to mask, glamour, and winnow. "The fae have strong magical borders."

"And I was chosen for your Coterie because I'm a damn good mage, Sonta. I can at least *try*. Do you want a confirmation or not?"

I clasped my hands before me. "I do."

"Good." He passed Lilah and headed straight for my bed with a scroll in hand. He unrolled it to reveal a map of the realm.

Gald reached into his pockets, pulling out a small bowl, a pouch of herbs, and a divining pendulum.

Lilah and I gathered on either side of him as he set the bowl in the middle where the palace lay, and dumped the herbs in.

"This works much better if I have something of his." Gald faced me, hesitant. "I didn't really feel comfortable approaching the emperor for that note Tyfen left, but maybe we could try with the letters you sent him?"

My stomach squirmed. My privacy had already been invaded with regard to those letters. "He never even read them or touched them. I doubt they qualify."

Gald shrugged. "His room was emptied. I don't have anything else."

I held the leather bracelet on my wrist. "What about a gift from him? Something we shared?"

"That would be perfect."

I unsnapped the bracelet and unwound it, then handed it to Gald.

He glanced at it, his eyebrows lifted in surprise. He'd noticed me wearing it before, had playfully made some innuendo about understanding its possibilities as a lover's whip, but I'd never used it with him since it was only intended for Tyfen. Now Gald knew a bit more about how Tyfen and I played.

To his credit, Gald said nothing, simply resting it on the edge of the map.

Speaking in an ancient mage tongue, Gald touched the map, bracelet, and pendulum, then sparked a fire from his finger and ignited the herbs. As the herbs smoked, he picked up the pendulum and went to work.

Dangling from a chain, it swung. It gyrated wildly over the fae kingdom, though not over any particular area. The moment Gald moved it past fae borders, the pendulum all but stilled. He did a quick pass over the rest of the realm, then focused again on the fae kingdom, trying to pinpoint a more precise location.

It was disheartening to simply have confirmation of what we already knew, but it was reassuring to know Tyfen's heart still beat.

"Sorry," Gald said. "I'm not able to get anything more specific."

"There may be other magic at play beyond the fae's magical borders, too. At least you were able to pierce the borders enough to confirm he's there still, and alive." The disturbing thing was if Tyfen was using his masking magic to hide himself from a tracing spell, it meant he *wanted* to stay hidden. Or worse yet, if someone else was concealing him, there may be other problems we'd yet to consider. Someone may have coerced him to leave the palace.

"Thanks for trying," I whispered.

"Yeah..." Gald set to work, putting out the flame and cleaning everything up. I picked up my bracelet and snapped it back on.

As soon as Gald's supplies were packed up, he faced me. "I ... also wanted to ask you..."

"Should have just cut to the chase, right? You want to make sure you can come tomorrow?"

Lilah casually retreated to the dressing room.

He looked down. "I can't help that you're mad at me, but I need to know if you changed your mind about me coming. I need to know if I'm packing tonight or not."

My broken heart wanted to tell him no, that he could fuck off, that if I couldn't be fully happy, he couldn't either. My words caught in my throat, though; I couldn't commit either way.

Frowning, Gald met my gaze. "I didn't realize you've been so angry about my relationship with Findlech. You said you forgave us, and gave us your blessing, Sonta."

I swallowed. "I didn't realize it bothered me as much as it does." It had been shitty for them to sneak around behind my back, and I hadn't realized how much that still ached until they'd colluded to lie to me again.

"Are you going to make us choose?" he asked. "Because I don't want to. I love you both. I miss you, and I hate seeing him this way."

"What way is that?"

"Findlech *does* respect you. He values you for your calling, and he values you as a friend. And he's sorry he invaded your privacy, but hearing you tell him you *hate* him..."

Tears pricked at my eyes. "If Findlech respected me, he wouldn't have done that. He would give me more credit. He wouldn't keep secrets from me. And neither would you."

Gald shook his head. "I don't know what's going on between Findlech and Tyfen and all that. He assures me he doesn't know more than we do about Tyfen's disappearance. I trust him, Sonta. And I trust if there's something he's not confiding to us, that he's doing it for the right reasons. He's looking out for your best interests." Gald took my hand, his dazzling blue eyes pleading with my own.

I missed his touch and friendship, his frivolity, his everything. I hated being at odds, but I also hated the sour feeling in my gut about Findlech's secrets.

"It's easy for you to trust him, because he's never betrayed *your* trust."

Gald sighed. "Fair. Still…" He grasped his rolled-up map tighter. "If you allow me to come, I'd be willing to do a tracking spell every day, just to see if there are any updates along the way."

That offer certainly swayed my decision. I was hesitant to rely solely on Tyfen's parents for regular updates, or even the palace after their deceptions.

"Fine. You can come."

He smiled gently. "Thank you."

I released his hand. "Go on. Go pack."

"You won't regret this." He headed for the common room door.

Part of me already did. Elves could be snobbish, and I didn't imagine many would appreciate that Gald would be joining us on the tour as an extra.

"Gald?"

He halted, turning. "Yes?"

"Please don't make me regret this."

He frowned again. "Of course not. I'm there for you as much as I am for Findlech."

My hurt pride couldn't accept that. "You only came here tonight to demonstrate your magic so I'd invite you along. Don't pretend you did it out of concern for Tyfen or for my benefit."

Gald shook his head. "When two truths exist, they don't have to be exclusive, Sonta. I want to be there for Findlech, and I want to be there for you."

No mention, of course, of being there for Tyfen.

"You don't want to have to choose between Findlech and me? Then don't ask me to choose between *my* lovers, Gald."

Drawing a deep breath, Gald nodded contemplatively. Message received. He held up his map again. "Let's bring him home and go from there."

Bring him home.

"Thank you," I whispered.

Elion knocked at the common room door, then opened it, surprised to find Gald in here. Gald simply bid him good night, and Elion shut the door after entering.

Lilah came back into my room. "Well … shall I fetch some chocolate from the kitchens for a sweet treat? Or do we just want to head to bed?"

As much as I wanted a sweet treat, I needed my strength for whatever chaos the next day may bring me. "Let's go to bed."

32

Findlech's Warning

Luckily, the farewell for this leg of the imperial tour was not as well attended as the one right after the paternity reveal. Still, servants excitedly gathered outside the palace to wave us off. This time, no Coterie members stood at the end of the lane for farewells. Attendees must have noticed Tyfen wasn't present. Some surely knew he was missing, while others would speculate.

My saving grace was that it wasn't really their place to gossip about my Coterie. For all they knew, he was in his room or the infirmary with an illness, or he'd been called back to his kingdom for royal duties.

After saying goodbye to Lilah, Mother, and Kernov, I did get one heartwarming farewell.

Haan's smile was sexy and bright as he waited for me at the pool. He kissed me. "I'll miss you, Sonta. And I'm sorry you're still hurting, but know that my heart is with you."

I gave him a half smile. I loved Haan in my own way, and he loved me. Merfolk didn't generally express emotion the same way we did, didn't feel affection like many land-walkers did, but I didn't doubt his words.

"If I believed there was something my people could do about Tyfen..." he offered.

I rested a hand on his muscular arm. "No, it's best this remains silent for now, but thank you."

Had tracing spells indicated Tyfen was on an island or sailing the seas, that would be another issue entirely, but nothing indicated as much.

"I'll miss you too. And I look forward to seeing you during my next rest week."

"As do I."

After kissing him again, I approached the line of carriages. My four attending Coterie members all stood in a line, waiting to hear how I wanted everyone to ride. Before I could say anything, a servant approached.

"Your Holiness, His Magnificence wishes for you to ride with him for the first portion."

I blinked. "Oh. Okay." I shrugged and headed to the emperor's carriage a few up. Let the men sort out their own seating arrangements.

As the emperor was half elf, him attending this leg of the tour was tradition so he could visit his father's homeland. The security was even tighter than it was for the magistrate.

I climbed into the emperor's carriage and sat opposite him. "You wanted me here?"

He waved at a soldier through the closed window, signifying we were ready to take off. "Yes. I know Findlech will be briefing you for your visit in his capital, but I'd like to offer some counsel as well."

I nestled my hands together in my lap. "Certainly. I, uh, didn't prepare for a briefing so quickly, so I don't have anything to take notes with."

Someone outside whistled, and a moment later the carriage lurched forward.

"That's quite all right. I'm sure you can commit these to memory."

Smiling politely, I nodded. "Thank you. I'm all ears." My eyes darted to his actual ears, then away. Was that a rude saying for elves? As a mixling, his ears weren't as tall and pointy as full elves', but it still made me wonder.

"Very well. Let's get started."

While I trusted Findlech's advice on cultural matters more than the emperor's—it wasn't like the emperor had grown up in the elf nation—I did trust the emperor's political advice more. He kept his finger on the pulse of the entire empire, while Findlech's primary concern was his own people.

The emperor listed off bucketloads of advice, and I really did regret that I'd packed my journal away. But I listened intently.

Some of his advice was about etiquette, some about the current political arena. I couldn't forget what he said about the tension between the fae and elves in the last few years.

I needed to remember to not mention a certain member of the high lord's family who had passed away, not even to offer condolences. Elves sometimes grieved for decades, and it was still too touchy of a subject for them.

I had to make sure I—and the members of my Coterie—never took a bite of food before the high lord did at meals. As the head of the nation, he always ate first, and it would be a massive sign of disrespect.

I wasn't to shake anyone's hand through a doorway, as they could be rather superstitious, and the Blessed Vessel making that mistake could be seen as a condemnation and curse for their people.

The list went on and on. Forget understanding all the reasons for the instructions—my mind whirled at trying to remember everything, period. I did my best, though, and repeated the emperor's guidance back to him.

For a man who rarely spoke in small talk, he could talk anyone to sleep when it came to policy and procedure. While we'd never been chummy during the years we'd cohabiting the palace, he'd certainly taken opportunities to mentor me alongside my assigned tutors. As he now regurgitated information I already knew, and piled on more I didn't recall having learned before, I nodded and asked clarifying questions.

Eventually—*finally*—we took a morning break to rest and water the horses, and I was released from our meeting.

Findlech approached me and asked me to join him for a briefing in one of our carriages. We had over a week of travel to take care of it, so I didn't see the rush, but it may help cement some of the advice the emperor had given me. And I could get this unpleasantness over and done with.

"Sure, let me fetch my journal."

My journal and pen rested on my lap, my hands on top, as the carriages moved again.

The silence was supremely awkward.

"Thank you for joining me," Findlech said.

I nodded, taking him in. He was such a clever and handsome man. Wiser than I could ever be in so many ways. I loved his dark skin and long hair, and the fetching circlet he wore for official occasions. But he had hurt me, and I didn't know how to get past that.

"You know, Findlech, when I walked in on you and Gald in his bed, that was an accident. I wasn't prying. My letters to Tyfen were *private*."

Those letters had been meant for Tyfen's eyes only. I'd pleaded for him to not drink, worried because he hadn't written to me. No one in the Coterie knew he had a drinking problem. I'd written some rather suggestive and kinky things, too, trying to entice him to visit me because I'd missed him so much.

I felt so naked, so bare in front of Findlech.

"I'm sorry, Sonta. I assure you I don't judge you or Tyfen for the contents. I read them solely for research."

I scowled.

"As for your anger for Gald and me being together without asking permission, let that blame fall upon me. Gald wanted to be open with you, but I wasn't ready for people to know about my preferences yet, not even you."

Maybe I should have been more forgiving, but it wasn't like either of them were born to be as horny as I was… They could have waited a bit longer…

I didn't answer, sulking.

"You have the power to destroy my happiness, Sonta." His voice was softer than usual, almost even strained…

He continued. "You could make us stop being together. And as much as that would make me *absolutely* miserable, I would still be faithful and loyal to you. I need you to know that."

That twisted my heartstrings. I didn't want to be a villain. For how little emotion Findlech regularly showed, these words cut deep.

Drawing a breath, I crafted my response. "I'm not going to separate you two, Findlech."

I would be gutted if Gald someday decided he wanted to be exclusive with Findlech, but I had to remind myself they were also both my friends and political allies.

I rubbed the bond tattoo on my wrist. Gald had mentioned all three. Friends, lovers, allies.

"Thank you," Findlech responded.

"Do you resent having to share him?" I asked. I had multiple lovers, and if one was busy, I could pick someone else. Findlech only had Gald, and had to share him with me.

Findlech wore a humorous smirk. "How could I? He's in *your* Coterie."

I shrugged. "That doesn't mean anything when it comes to matters of the heart."

He nodded his acknowledgement. "I ... like having my own room. My own time. As much as I love Gald, he can be a bit wild... Something I admire, but..."

My heart warmed as I fought a smile. Gald was our wild stallion, and I loved him for it.

Findlech rubbed his knee. "I love seeing him happy. I think it's ... adorable ... the way he looks at and talks about you, Sonta."

I properly blushed. "Thank you. I guess I get a little insecure at times when it comes to Gald."

"Yours is a precarious place."

"You could say that again."

Findlech straightened, more serious again. "Like I said: I love seeing Gald happy. And he and I have agreed to let each other fight our own battles, but I need to say one thing..."

"What's that?"

"I don't appreciate you hitting the man I love."

I gulped. I wasn't normally violent. I didn't know why Gald had brought that out in me. "I'm sorry. It won't happen again."

"Good."

After a moment of silence, he crossed his legs. "If we're okay to move on, we have a few tour matters to discuss."

We were at that familiar juncture. Still not on the exact same page, but tension had been eased enough to move forward.

"I'm all ears." I bit my lip. "Is that saying offensive to elves? Because if it is, I'll work on not saying it."

Amusement danced in Findlech's dark eyes. "Over several centuries, I've heard many insults, including those about our ears. I don't believe that phrase has been used in a derogatory way."

I rested easy. "Good…" I flipped open my journal and gazed up, ready for more instruction.

The emperor was long-winded, but Findlech was… What's a way of saying worse than long-winded? I wrote everything down. Many things he instructed me on, the emperor had already touched on.

My stomach eventually growled, ready for lunch, but we weren't stopping for another hour.

"I know you don't want to hear this, Sonta, but we also need to discuss Tyfen."

I clenched my teeth and braced myself. "What about him?"

Findlech's face was sober. "You need to not mention him. At all. Not even his name. To anyone in my nation."

"That's a bit of a ridiculous request."

He didn't flinch, didn't move a muscle. "I mean it. It would be better for you, this Coterie, and the entire realm, if the name Tyfen was not uttered in my lands."

"It would help if I understood why your people dislike him so much…" I fished, but he gave me nothing. "Am I not allowed to mention *any* fae? Or just Tyfen?"

"I wouldn't mention his family either, but I forbid you from discussing Tyfen."

Forbid? One of my men was *forbidding* me? It was as if he'd clamped his hand down on my leg to tell me to shut up the way Hadwin had.

"You'll discover, Findlech, that I don't respond well to being ordered to shut up."

Findlech's expression hardened as he shook his head. "You don't have to like it or understand it to agree to it." He looked me dead in the eyes, his voice cold and grave. "I would rather you tell my high lord himself and *all* his court that I share a bed with a young male mortal than have you utter the syllables 'Ty' and 'fen' in the same sentence."

The blood froze in my veins at his sincerity. Findlech's biggest fear—so far as he'd ever shared with me—was being outed to his people. He worried they wouldn't respect him as their lord for loving a man, for changing his sexual preferences after centuries of being with women.

I spoke softly, cautiously. "No matter you and I not seeing eye to eye, Findlech, I wouldn't try to bring Tyfen up to embarrass you. I will still honor you as my Coterie member in front of your people."

"Of course we all wish the Blessed Vessel to honor us in our homelands on this tour, but that is not what I speak of. Honor me all week. Show the people you respect me. Or don't. Nothing—*nothing*—could be more damaging to everyone than to mention his name."

As usual, I couldn't make heads or tails of these two. "You told me once you hold no grudge against him. Has that changed?"

Findlech looked down. "It's hard to say. Without knowing *why* he left, I can no longer gauge his character. One may say the evidence now sways out of his favor, whereas I have been more generous in the past than others in my position would be." He met my eyes, softening. "I'm not a dreamer the way you are. I don't have visions. I don't fixate on the unseen possibilities of people. I see facts. I use logic. And I form my judgment from there. Tyfen right now is a mystery to me. I can make assumptions all day, but that does no good. He could be a tragedy, or he could be a threat. I can't say which."

My heart hurt at the assessment.

"All that said," Findlech added, "I do not lightly issue my warning. It is based on facts, not opinions. It would not matter whether Tyfen was conspiring to assassinate my high lord or save his life; my plea remains the same. I implore you: if you hold any respect for me at all, and if you want what is best for your child, you won't bring Tyfen up in my lands." He glanced out the window. "I won't be discussing this further."

My child.

"Am I in danger, Findlech? Is my child in danger? I deserve to know if there's a threat."

Findlech rubbed his temple. "Not that I'm aware of. I don't mean to frighten or threaten you, Sonta. All I am saying is if you walk into a forest when there has been a decade-long drought, you don't carry a blazing torch." His eyes met mine. "I am warning you the woods are dry, and I ask that you not light a fire."

Don't bring up Tyfen. Don't spark a fire that could burn the realm down.

"All right. I won't bring up Tyfen."

I hadn't really planned to, anyway…

"Thank you."

The carriage grew uncomfortably quiet again after that. I glanced out the window, watching wispy cattails sway in the breeze by a nearby stream.

"I … would also like to give you this," Findlech uttered.

I glanced at him. He held up a thin, rectangular box with a ribbon tied around it. "I want you to know that this is not solely a political gift. It's not only for appearances, despite the way it may come off."

Intriguing…

He continued. "I'm sorry I've failed you as a romantic partner, and at times as a friend. And I want you to know I *do* respect you. As an individual, and for the divine you are."

I accepted the box and stared at it. I hated that my mind regularly reminded me my Coterie wasn't simply a group of lovers and friends. We were allies, or supposed allies. My men were representatives of their people, here to use me as a surrogate and to afford them the opportunity to shape our realm through my child. The right words and flattery, the best gifts, could simply be tools to manipulate me.

I understood that, and I had to choose whether to let suspicion spoil Findlech's kind words and the gesture he just made.

My cautious heart softened a bit due to the way he'd expressed himself, that he respected me for the divine I was. For all his stuffiness, Findlech was a devout worshipper of the goddesses of our realm. I still knew him the least of the Coterie, but I understood he visited the palace chapel for worship more than any of us in the Coterie. I appreciated the reverence he held for my position, even if he sometimes struggled with me being so young.

"Thank you," I finally said, untying the ribbon. I opened the box, my eyes suddenly widening at the gift before me. Bright silver covered in delicate diamonds, a pair of ear adornments were nestled in the box. I'd seen similar ones worn by elf women on special occasions, including the high lady herself at all the official Great Ritual events thus far.

I picked up the pair, inspecting them. They were deceivingly light and absolutely stunning.

"Very fashionable for a woman of high status," he softly explained. "Specially crafted to fit your shorter, curved ears."

My lips quirked upward. They were structured to look like elf ears. "Thank you, Findlech."

His smile was genuine. "You're welcome."

We stopped for lunch soon after that, joining the others. I absolutely loved my gift, and I did my best to let that happy feeling override the stressful warning Findlech had issued shortly before he gave me that box.

The chatter of soldiers drowned out the sound of my men and I chewing our food. Nothing more than that was going on between us as we munched on delightful finger foods the palace kitchens had prepared.

I downed a vial of pig's blood, and Hadwin's eyes dropped to his food.

He wanted me to feed on him, and I wanted it as well. At least this time I hadn't been so pigheaded as to not bring my puncturing ring. We would find a way to get past this.

"Autumn is my favorite season," Hadwin volunteered. "Less sun, beautiful colors."

Elion pointed at him, finishing his bite. "I'm summer all the way. Give me that sun, those hot nights and great hunts, drinking straight from a stream when you're too tired."

"I'm a winter man, myself," Findlech said. "Nothing beats sitting in your robe with a steaming beverage in front of a fireplace with a great view of the snowcapped mountains."

Gald cleared his throat. "One must ask... Is there anything on under the robe?"

I bit the insides of my cheeks to hide a smile as Findlech replied.

"*Must* one ask? In public?"

Gald beamed. "Want and need have to meet somewhere, Your Lordship."

Findlech gave him a pointed look of casual censure.

I sliced into an apple, rather stupidly, and nicked myself. "Shit!" It instantly bled.

"Here." Elion stuck my finger in his mouth, his tongue grazing it to apply healing saliva.

"Thanks."

Hadwin's stare landed on my love bite, which hadn't been touched in a week. There was no doubt he would have loved to suck my cut finger first...

I got his attention, gazing into his sweet hazel eyes.

"I love all seasons."

He offered a hesitant smile.

Gald chimed in. "Then it's up to me to correct you all, and share with you an exhaustive list of why spring is the best season."

Elion left my finger with a kiss, and he wrapped a handkerchief around it.

"Gald, my love?" I said.

There was a twinkle in his eye at me addressing him that way despite our recent quarrels. "Yes?"

"I don't care which carriage you ride in, but I've already been assaulted with a morning full of men spouting off exhaustive lists, so whichever carriage you choose, I will have to pick the other."

He snickered, then gave me a soft pleading smile.

Our lunch break wasn't long, but it helped smooth out some sharp edges on our Coterie's corners.

Findlech and Gald did choose a carriage by themselves. I went to the one behind it; Hadwin claimed the spot next to me, and Elion sat across from us.

After a minute back on the road, Hadwin scooted closer, whispering, "How are you?"

Despite the brief levity of lunch, my mind returned to Findlech's warning. If I didn't want to risk peace or my child's future, I had to pretend like one of the men I loved dearly didn't even exist.

I rested my hands on my stomach. "I've been better."

Hadwin wrapped an arm around me, pulling me to himself. He leaned his head against mine. "I've missed your heartbeats," he confessed.

That almost broke me. I took his hand, scooting closer.

Across from us, Elion slouched, getting comfortable, locking eyes with me. His smile was beguiling. It reminded me that, no matter how dark the clouds seemed right now, there would be sun to come. And I was very loved.

33

A Close Call

The weeklong ride to the elf nation took forever. We traveled on the shifter side of the mountain border, and the land was beautiful, but communities scarce. Not that I needed tons of parades and fanfare. It was simply lonely.

That was ridiculous, of course. I had four of my six Coterie members with me, and the emperor, and loads of soldiers.

I had too much time to think and worry. It didn't help that my constant view reminded me of Tyfen. The painting he'd stolen had depicted a vision I believed involved these mountains. Something about it had disturbed Tyfen, and we were rolling right into the territory where the vision had taken place.

Findlech's warning about Tyfen widened the cracks of my anxiety. I had to ask Hadwin and Elion to ignore my tears when I'd randomly start crying.

I'd been so excited—once upon a time—to tour here amongst the elusive and reclusive elves. Now, I just wanted Tyfen back, and to avoid any mistake that could endanger anyone.

Despite the regular silence still between us, I finally shared a bed with Hadwin again. Well … we shared the carriage after dark to feed off each other and fuck. Talk was minimal, our hearts still distant, but at least we could take care of each other in that way.

Elion helped me when I asked, and was so calm and patient.

Gald spent most of his time with Findlech, and I didn't mind. He was cordial with me during meals and other exchanges.

Despite my building nerves about entering the elf nation, I was so tired of the same view while traveling that I was grateful to go through the main pass. In the higher altitudes, we spotted our first snowfall of the year in the peaks already.

Touring amongst elves would be different than with the others. Three people in the empire had full access to all parts of all territories—the emperor, the magistrate, and myself. I could go anywhere I pleased, though my companions may be limited. Someday, I would like to explore the elves' picturesque lands more, but for now, we traveled only to the two locations we'd been officially invited to for the imperial tour.

We would be going to the high lord's grand castle and then to Findlech's estate—nowhere else.

There were a few small gatherings of commoners along the way. It warmed my heart to glimpse seas of pointy ears, their tall owners ethereal. Guessing an adult's age was nearly impossible; so few showed wrinkles.

I tried not to be offended that not only was the tour so limited in scope, but that the general elf population wasn't all that elated to see me. Like Tyfen had told me once—I wasn't the first Blessed Vessel in his lifetime, and I wouldn't be the last. Many of these elves had likely been alive when Baylana was the Blessed Vessel. I wasn't as shiny for them, especially since the mixling in my womb was not one of theirs.

I was a torrent of emotions, but I took it one breath at a time.

While I wouldn't wear them the entire trip, I slipped on my ear adornments for our arrival at the elf castle. The castle was even more massive than I'd imagined, with a moat occupied by merfolk. That brought me a fond smile as I imagined Haan.

Findlech, Hadwin, and I made sure we were all in the same carriage for our arrival, Gald and Elion as my guests in the carriage behind us.

I straightened my dress, stretching my legs as High Lord Elout and High Lady Marsone approached.

Findlech snatched my wrist, leaning down to whisper in my ear. "I almost forgot. That sketch you once showed me, with ancient Elvish, did you bring it?"

He'd startled me with his abrupt action, his urgent tone. "No…"

"Good. Do not mention it. To do so would be as bad as mentioning … you know who."

My heart raced, and Hadwin glanced at me, concerned.

"Welcome!" High Lady Marsone said, her gaze catching on Findlech's gift, a small smile acknowledging it.

Findlech released my wrist, and I slid on the best smile I could muster.

No mentioning my painting… One more stressor to add to the pile.

The three of us bowed, as did Gald and Elion behind us.

"Findlech." The high lord greeted him as though speaking to an old friend. "And Your Holiness." His voice and expression gave off an air of reverence.

His tone wavered the smallest amount. "Duke Hadwin—we extend our congratulations."

The high lord glanced behind us. "And of course more members of your Coterie."

I offered him a sickeningly sweet smile. He knew damn well what their names and titles were, and it was rude to address them so dismissively.

"Yes. I always appreciate your hospitality extending to my Coterie. You of course know Elion as the high alpha's son, and Master Gald?"

"Yes," the high lord replied with a curt smile.

So rarely did men and women of power fight with swords, arrows, and magic when they could do so with the right words.

"We're excited for your stay," the high lady added. "We'd like to show you around personally and get you settled after your long journey."

And they did just that. They led us through the giant elegant rooms of the castle. When the hallways were wide enough, Findlech was on my left, with Hadwin on my right. In more narrow places, Hadwin walked behind us. There were so many traditions, rules, and superstitions to remember.

After showing us the main ballroom, the high lady turned to us. "Of course, anytime you and Findlech need a room for a coitus break, it can be arranged. We understand the Blessed Vessel has specific needs."

I gulped. I'd rather not have people acknowledge my sex drive, and I certainly had no plans for 'coitus breaks' with Findlech.

"That's so very thoughtful. Though, I'm able to take care of myself without interruption to others."

Her smile was sweet, her face round and her light brown braided hair long. "Nonsense. I'm sure Findlech does the job quite well, doesn't he?"

Findlech slid an arm around me, pulling me closer. "I take care of Sonta well enough, though I assure you she knows what's best for her."

His arm around me was so foreign, but it made me realize I hadn't shown an ounce of affection for him yet. We'd discussed the level of attention I needed to show. Luckily, he was regularly stiff about public affection to begin with, so it wasn't like I needed to fawn over him to conceal his sexuality or to build him up in his people's eyes.

I slid an arm around him as well, resting a hand on his chest.

Fuck, I forgot how solid he is under his clothes...

"I'm grateful you sent such a great match."

The high lord and lady looked pleased.

"Before we continue, perhaps we should discuss sleeping arrangements so the servants can finish unpacking your things," the high lord offered.

I smiled. "Fantastic."

Like in the countess's manor, we had our own corridor, but we were led to a large room at the end.

"We don't have any beds so giant as the one in your personal chambers in the palace is rumored to be," the high lady said, "but we hope this may meet your needs."

The room had two large beds with a small space between them.

"We can all stay in here," Findlech answered.

"Lovely. If you'd like to take a moment to freshen up, I'll go speak to the servants now."

Findlech offered her a courtesy bow. "I think we'd all appreciate that." He closed the door behind him and locked us inside.

"It's ... almost like our first night together," Elion said.

Hadwin pursed his lips. "We're sure we all want to share one room?"

Gald simply looked between Findlech and me.

Findlech answered. "I think it would be best. Fewer questions if a servant accidentally drops into the wrong room."

I fidgeted with my fingers. "I agree. I ... just feel like it's best to stick together on this stop." I looked to Findlech, a question in my expression that I couldn't quite form.

There was a tension here I couldn't put my finger on. The way servants had looked at me, and glanced at Findlech. Maybe they were questioning if he'd done his job well enough since he hadn't been the one to knock me up?

"Everything is fine," he assured me.

I calmed a hair after that, and we all freshened up before the events of the evening. There was a banquet in our honor this evening with dozens of lords of parliament and their partners in attendance.

Music was lively, the candlelight casting lovely shadows in corners of the room. A massive wall-to-wall tank took up a portion of the room, and merfolk swam and mingled.

All the merfolk in the moat and indoor tank swam freely, though only by explicit invitation of the high lord and lady. They weren't imprisoned, though Haan had mentioned once he considered them sellouts. They were rather gluttonous and disconnected from their own people and culture, living trophies to stroke the high lord's ego.

It was hard for me to pass judgment when I didn't fully understand what it felt like to swim with their tails.

The evening was genuinely nice, with the exception of the introduction to the high lord's eldest son. He gave me looks that sent unwelcome shivers down my spine.

It probably had to do with the fact he was my original intended Coterie partner. He'd been selected long ago, but last minute, before the members were finalized by each territory, Findlech had replaced him.

The next night, when we'd all rested and toured the grounds extensively, there was a grand ball. The dancing was elegant, and I had to smile when dancing with Findlech this time. In so many ways, I wanted to wring his neck, but I couldn't ignore the kindnesses he paid me. He constantly complimented me in front of his people, perhaps more than I even did him.

I enjoyed dancing with the others, too. I couldn't ignore the subtle slights the elves offered Elion, Hadwin, and Gald, but I made sure to give them each my utmost attention while dancing to make up for it.

Hadwin's goddess-damned hazel eyes melted my heart. His closed-mouth smile twisted it.

Elion dressed so smart, paying more attention to his attire, posture, and speech amongst the elves to boost his image with this race; elves really could be such snobs. I was impressed by how hard Elion worked to fit in and stand out, even if it pained me to see him depart from the more animalistic lover and mate I knew.

Even Gald was more tame than usual. As he led me across the dance floor, I refrained from asking all the questions I wanted to: Was it hard to see Findlech fronting as my lover instead of his? Was he trying to make a good impression for human and mage-kind alone? Or for himself as Findlech's lover with the hope they'd go public someday?

Either way, Gald was mine and mine alone for this dance. His dazzling blue eyes and mop of curly hair were nothing but a complement to his dashing outfit, his charm unmatched. He kissed my hand when the dance was done, and my smile was firmly in place.

The room was rather warm, though. I excused myself from the ballroom and found a place with a view on a balcony. Findlech joined me. From the position of the rising moons, we faced southeast. I cocked my head, focusing on the mountains in the distance. Something clicked in my mind, a reminder of my elusive vision. The placement of the mountains ... the skyline... They'd been the background in my vision.

"You've been doing great, Sonta," Findlech said.

I straightened. "Thank you." I faced him. "When we first arrived at this castle, you said you trusted that I knew what was best for me."

"Yes?"

"I appreciate that."

He gave me a reassuring smile.

"So I'd like you to trust me enough to tell me what I'd bump into if I walked straight in that direction and kept going." I gestured to the mountains.

He glanced that direction, his expression hardening when he realized I was talking about the location of my vision.

I prodded. "I know what's best for me. You either trust me or you don't. Hoku gives me visions for a reason."

Findlech drew a breath. "You're not ready, Sonta."

"And when will I be ready?"

He shook his head, contemplative. "I don't know. But I promise you it's not right now."

I sighed. "I'm not accustomed to people gatekeeping my own visions from me."

"It's a marvelous skill to be able to adapt to new and uncomfortable situations."

I glared at him.

He shrugged. "How about I get us some water?"

"Sure..."

The moment he left, I went back to cocking my head, imagining myself miles away at a secret location.

"Is Her Holiness looking for something in particular?"

I startled. "Shit!" I spun.

The high lord's son stood before me.

"Sorry," I sputtered. "Didn't mean to swear."

He smirked. "No trouble. This is your first time here. I'm sure our level of culture takes some getting used to."

I could vomit on the spot. It was certainly elegant here, but he honestly thought this drafty castle was better than the Pontaii Palace?

He joined me at the balcony edge. "You didn't bring your full Coterie with you."

My train of thought derailed. "Here I thought bringing Elion and Master Gald was too much for elven tastes. I didn't realize I should be traveling with the full set."

His smile was unsettling. "Why not? If you're bringing the spares, might as well invite the whole party." He tugged on his jacket sleeve. "Or did you? Did either of your two missing lovers turn down the offer to come?"

"Umm..." What game was he playing? "It's not exactly convenient for everyone, is it?"

He shrugged. "Your merfolk chancellor may have liked his surroundings here."

Aha. Not the approach I'd thought he was taking. It was generally assumed spares on tour weren't really wanted. But he wanted to know if the elves had been slighted? I certainly wouldn't tell him Haan had no desire to come.

"Chancellor Haan is very busy with his duties in the southern sea while I'm on tour. I'm sure he meant no offense by his absence. I'll relay to him that his presence was missed."

"Lovely. And what of Tyfen of the fae? Did he turn down your offer to come?"

Fuck.

Double fuck.

"Um... What?" Findlech hadn't told me what to do if *someone else* brought up Tyfen...

The high lord's son narrowed his eyes ever so slightly. "Prince Tyfen. He didn't want to come? I very much would have liked him to be here."

Where the hell was Hadwin? Apparently too far away to sense my pounding heart. This all felt like a trap.

"I ... can't really say, Your Lordship."

He angled his head. "Do you like Tyfen? Does he please you in bed? Or perhaps you're too shy to admit you detest him. I hear he made quite the display of arrogance before bedding you."

My ears burned. "I assure you what happens in my chambers is not a concern of yours. The public may speculate for sport, but a lord should know better than to question a lady, never mind the Blessed Vessel, about such things."

Unbothered, he lifted an eyebrow. "I of course meant no offense. But I'm curious. Is this anger in defense of your prince lover alone? Or are you so vigilant in your defense of all your Coterie?"

"I will stand up for each of my Coterie members. I know they each have goodness in them despite any faults. I truly don't know what you're fishing for, but Tyfen—"

"Sonta!" Findlech barked out behind us.

I whirled, staring at him and a servant who was approved to bring me safe food and drink.

I stepped away from the high lord's son, pointing at him. "He started it!" I sounded like a child again, fighting over a toy with Lilah.

Findlech's hard gaze turned to the high lord's son as he handed his goblet of water to the servant. "Go away."

The servant hesitated, but followed orders.

"I'm surprised at you," Findlech told the high lord's son.

"Can you really be?" he smoothly defended.

"Rather impertinent." Findlech's words were clipped.

"What's the harm in discussing our Blessed Vessel's Coterie?" he asked innocently.

Findlech gave him another look of warning. "Distasteful and disgraceful." I couldn't imagine Findlech speaking so boldly to his high lord, but the high lord's son was a lower lord just like Findlech.

"You're quite feral, Findlech. I didn't realize you were so fond of your new mortal partner. It's a shame you didn't put a child in her."

I stood there, hands on my stomach, feeling every bit the political pawn so many rulers wanted me to be.

Findlech smirked a bit. "I've proven myself many times. Hoku's will is carried out as she wishes in these things." He held out a hand to me. "As for my lovely partner, I *am* rather fond of her."

I walked to him, taking his hand, and the out.

Findlech slid a hand to my hip and ass, and I blinked. "What do you say, my sweet? I was coming to fetch you for a coitus break."

My cheeks instantly warmed. "I ... would love that." I leaned into it, aiming to give him a kiss on the cheek, but Findlech kissed me fully on the lips. It was weird. Not bad, just... It was Findlech.

"Come, my sweet."

I forced a smile and looked back at the high lord's son. "I need to thank your parents for sending me Findlech. I can't imagine a better elf for my Coterie."

He scowled at the dig, since Findlech had replaced him.

Findlech tugged on my waist, guiding me away. We found a narrow hallway and kept opening doors until we discovered an empty room. He shut the door and locked it behind us. It was a cozy little sitting room.

Findlech pinched the bridge of his nose.

"Next time we get into an argument, remind me to be grateful your people sent you, okay? Because I'd hate to have to share a bed with that man!"

Blowing out a breath, Findlech stared at me. "What. Happened? What all did you two discuss?"

I cowered. "I was being honest. I didn't bring Tyfen up. *He* did. He cornered me, and I didn't know what to say."

Findlech rolled his eyes. "I'm shocked he would do that. Then again, I shouldn't be."

Nervous given Findlech's prior warning, I hugged myself. "What does this mean?"

"I need you to tell me *exactly* what the two of you said."

I recounted it to him as best I could remember.

"You did well. Neutrality is ideal should someone be bold enough to bring him up again."

My shoulders slumped, my heart still uneasy. "I deserve to know why Tyfen is such a taboo topic here. What he has to do with the war that never happened. That's what this is about, right?"

Findlech didn't answer.

"I *deserve* to know. I love him, and he's missing. Throw me a goddess-damned bone, Findlech."

His rich brown eyes searched mine. "If Tyfen sets foot on elven soil, his life is forfeit."

My heart dropped into my stomach. "What? Could he... Could your people be the reason he's missing?"

Findlech angled his head. "I don't believe so."

"Don't *believe* so? I need a more certain answer than that!"

"I can't give you assurances I don't have. If my people had him, I assume he'd be dead already, or back here at the very least, not in his kingdom. It ... doesn't make sense."

Tears pricked at my eyes. I would give anything for Tyfen right now. If I thought I could make a difference, I'd resign as the Blessed Vessel here and now to ensure his safety, and let Hoku's contingency laws kick in.

"I need more than that, Findlech. I need Tyfen back in one piece."

Sighing, Findlech frowned. "I'm doing all I can, Sonta. Contrary to popular belief, I didn't volunteer for your Coterie to become your lover, obviously. And I didn't do it to further my political career. I'm doing the best I can with the resources I have."

Doing the best he can? I didn't understand what exactly Findlech was doing. What kind of strategy he had. "If you tell me more, I can help. I have the resources of the emperor."

Findlech shook his head.

I gaped, trying to sort out this information. Perhaps I shouldn't have been so surprised to hear Tyfen had a price on his head, given Findlech's implications about him being central to the thwarted war a few years back. But...

"Does Tyfen *know* he has a target on his back?"

Findlech's answer was deep and final. "Yes."

"So ... he would have never come on this leg of the tour with me."

"I certainly hope he would not have been that foolish."

I furrowed my brow. "My Coterie is protected by imperial law. No matter your quarrel with Tyfen, he would be immune."

Findlech looked away as though he might not be as certain of that.

"That's the law, Findlech. You don't think your people would be compliant?"

He again would not answer.

"What if the paternity results had been in the fae's favor? The father is required on all legs of the tour. Your people wouldn't have killed him..."

Findlech swallowed, then met my eyes. "Aren't we grateful we don't have to find out?"

I couldn't hold back tears. It had been days since I'd had a proper breakdown over Tyfen. I wanted him and needed him. I needed him to be okay, and not to have a death sentence on his head.

"Whatever he did, it couldn't be so bad he deserves to die," I squeaked out.

Findlech strode to me and took me into his arms. "I'm sorry, Sonta. I'm sure we'll find him and sort this all out."

I cried. Sniffling and struggling for air, all while Findlech held me.

When I calmed a degree, I pulled back, locking eyes with Findlech. "Imagine it were Gald."

Sincerity was etched into every word, his every feature, as he handed me a handkerchief. "I'm trying. The emperor's trying. Tyfen's parents are trying. We're doing all we can to bring him back to the palace."

I nodded, blowing my nose. Gathering myself, I breathed deeply. "How much longer should we be in here? For them to assume we..." I folded the handkerchief. "I don't want to insult you by being too quick..."

He gave me an uncomfortable grin. "I'd say it's usually best to err on the side of taking longer to please one's partner, but I'd be more concerned about bringing you out looking like you've just been crying." He nodded to the chairs. "Let's take a breather for a few minutes."

"Okay."

We sat, and I stared at the handkerchief as silence kept us company.

"Like I said," Findlech began. "If one of my people brings him up again, which I'd be shocked if they did, then I don't expect you to bad-mouth Tyfen."

I wouldn't.

"I'm sure young Lord Elout was simply fishing to learn if you'd side with us or a criminal. Neutrality is your friend right now."

I nodded. "I really am grateful for you, Findlech. I would have been miserable with that asshole in my Coterie."

He offered me a polite smile.

"Why were you chosen? I would imagine the high lord would want his son to keep more power by being in a Coterie again." It wouldn't have been his first time. "Why were you chosen instead?"

Findlech pressed his lips into a thin line. "The parliament urged the high lord to put me into your Coterie."

I nodded again. The elf high lord worked more closely with his parliament of lords than the fae king did with his lessers.

As we sat, Findlech assured me he would do everything in his power to make my stay here more comfortable, and that I could relax completely once we were at his estate. I breathed easier with the assurance.

Once we agreed it was time to get back to the celebration, we stood, and I picked a piece of lint off Findlech's dress coat. "You know, you have shared your body for the sake of your people, and I share mine for the sake of the empire." It wasn't like his cock hadn't been in me a couple dozen times. "If you need to kiss me again or grab my ass, or anything else to sell it to your parliament that they chose correctly, then don't hesitate to do so."

Findlech gave me a genuine smile as my friend. "I appreciate the offer."

34
The Travel Arch

The rest of the ball went swimmingly, honestly, other than some uncomfortable glances from the high lord's son. I made sure to cling to Findlech a bit more visibly.

That night, the five of us went to bed as we had before—Gald and Findlech sharing a bed a couple of feet away, and Hadwin and Elion wrapping around me in my bed.

I was nearly four months into my pregnancy, and while Hoku's daughters were blessed with easy pregnancies, it wasn't like we didn't still have changes happening in our bodies. My growing child was starting to wake me during the night, forcing me to use the washroom.

I got up at one point, careful to mind the unfamiliar layout. After returning to the bedroom, I couldn't help but steal a peek at Gald and Findlech on their bed. Findlech was the big spoon, holding Gald. Gald was so sweet and boyishly handsome, drained of manly swagger and mischief when he surrendered to sleep.

Findlech stirred, his eyes fluttering. He blinked and spotted me.

"Sorry," I whispered. "I just... He's cute when he sleeps."

Findlech's smile was soft. "Why don't you join us? He'd like that."

I honestly hadn't expected the offer, but I loved it. With a glance at Hadwin and Elion, I agreed. I slid into bed next to Gald, and Findlech and I worked out whose arms and legs went where.

We bid each other good night, and I smiled at the warmth of Gald. He wore only his shorts, and I'd forgotten how much I loved his touch.

In the morning, a surprised Gald was happy I'd joined them. His sleepy kisses were enough to get my core burning, and his gropes as Findlech still rested certainly helped. "I can't tell you how many times I've dreamed of sharing my bed with both my favorite people."

I brushed a curl out of his face. "I love you. And I'm sorry I hit you the other day."

His stunning blue eyes took in my face. "Thank you. You just need to remember what I told you before. Slapping has to be part of foreplay." He slid his hand under my nightie to firmly grasp my ass. "And only as hard as you want to be spanked yourself."

I let out a silent chuckle. We'd definitely played around with that.

"Deal." I touched his lip ring with a finger, frowning. "Would you mind trying another locating spell this morning?"

I'd already asked him again last night, my anxiety for Tyfen growing.

"Sure." We still didn't see eye to eye on a few matters surrounding Tyfen and his disappearance, but we could find a middle ground.

***

I couldn't remember a time I'd been so tense. Spending time at the elf high court was too formal, and my guard was as high as it could be, given the encounter with the high lord's son the day before.

Focusing on my duties, I carried on with the celebrations, pretending I didn't know they wanted Tyfen dead while I worried about him so much.

We were scheduled to spend four full days at the high lord's castle, then three days in Findlech's territory.

On the fifth morning in the castle, I was beyond ready to move on. Servants bustled, and our security staff made extra preparations. My Coterie and I took different washrooms to get ready.

I let Findlech and Gald use the one connected to the master bedroom we'd stayed in, since they were dragging their feet about getting out of bed.

As I was about to disrobe and dip my feet into my warm bath, I realized I'd forgotten my clothes to change into.

After dashing back to the main bedroom, I tapped on the door, and no answer came. It wasn't locked, so I cautiously opened it.

Findlech sat in bed, his chest bare and his long hair down. "Hi, Sonta."

"Oh, sorry." I pointed at my stack of clothing. "Just grabbing this." I snatched it up, then faced Findlech again. "When Gald is out of the bath, will you send him my way? I'd like to do one more tracking spell before the rest of our things are packed up."

Formal as ever despite his lack of clothing, Findlech nodded. "I'll tell him."

Just then, the wad of blankets around Findlech's waist stirred, and Findlech went rigid, his eyes wide as he looked away.

I guess there's no need to pass on my message... Gald was under that blanket, servicing Findlech with a bit of morning delight.

My face warmed. At least this time I didn't see all of them both as they fucked. "Right... I'll leave you two to..." I hastily left and went back to my bath.

I took my time in the bath, pondering all the little things in life. I was still jealous of those two, and I knew it was wrong. Luckily, that jealousy was softening with time and logic. They loved each other, and I really *was* happy for them. Lilah would probably put me in my place, reminding me the world didn't revolve around me. I'd received sweet letters from her and Mother just yesterday.

And there was no need to feel threatened, especially when it came to Gald. He was bound to me by word and magic. He was still a great and attentive lover. If push came to shove, I would fight for him like I would any of my Coterie members, but not in this way. If his interest leaned toward Findlech more than me someday, I wouldn't whimper and whine, wouldn't throw a fit.

What was the use of a man's affections if he didn't willingly give them? I had to let go of my fear that Gald may choose Findlech over me because his heart led him there; I needed to stop worrying about something that may never happen.

I finished brushing my wet hair, and started pinning it up as someone knocked on the washroom door. Opening it, I found Gald, armed with his spell supplies and a shy, apologetic expression.

"Come in."

He entered, and I closed the door behind him and locked it.

"I'm sorry, Sonta." He set his things on a dresser.

As much as Findlech enjoyed his privacy, it *was* hard not to laugh at the look he'd worn when he'd given himself away. Still, I had to give Gald a hard time.

"You two *do* know how to work a lock, right?"

"Yes..." He frowned. "I'm sorry. It's all my fault, okay? I just... You have all of us, and Findlech only has me. And he's stressed out of his mind. I just want to give him some special attention on this leg of the trip."

I baited Gald further. "A *lot* of special attention. I heard you two fucking two nights ago."

Gald's eyes widened. "Oh, well... We were trying to be quiet, and you always sleep so soundly..."

I smirked. They had been quiet, but Hadwin's child woke me sometimes with cravings or by prodding my full bladder. It was hard to hide the rustle of sheets and gasps of pleasure when you're making love, even if you're trying not to disturb the other occupants of the room.

Gald took my hand, his expression desperate. "I swear, Sonta; I didn't just ask to come here to be with Findlech. I'm here for *you*. I'll do a tracking spell a dozen times a day if you ask me to. That's why you agreed to let me come."

That last reminder made me feel rather shitty. I hadn't intended to dangle their relationship over them.

Resting a hand on Gald's chest, I tried to calm him. "I appreciate that. We're good, Gald. Findlech and I worked things out on the ride here. The three of us—we're good."

He relaxed.

"As long as we keep open communication and honesty, that's what matters to me," I added. That was what our fight had really been about.

Gald nodded.

"Now," I teased, "you said you're here for *me*?" I leaned in to kiss him. "You *did* clean your mouth before coming here, right?" I didn't imagine I'd be that fond of the taste of Findlech's dick.

Gald scowled. "I clean myself thoroughly between you two, thank you very—"

I claimed his mouth, chuckling. He always smelled of mint and soap. Gald wouldn't slack on something like hygiene.

Forcing myself to let the stress melt from my body, I kissed Gald hard, and he reciprocated perfectly, holding me to him, his tongue wrestling with mine.

I finally came up for air, my arms wrapped around his neck. "Thank you for helping ease my anxiety."

Gald gave me a lazy grin. "Is that all you want? Has anyone even taken you this morning?"

"No." I frowned. And now I was craving release more than ever. I glanced at his spell supplies. "But we're in a rush to get out of here, and I really want to make sure Tyfen's still safe in his kingdom."

I hadn't told the others that Tyfen had a target on his back. Some things were best to share with the Coterie, but this didn't feel like one of them.

Gald held my waist with one hand, sliding the other up my skirt and down my underwear. "We have the time. I want to take care of you."

Fuck. Gald really did get off by pleasing his partners. When I'd asked him why he'd never pierced his nipples, he'd told me he just hadn't prioritized it. His tongue piercing brought pleasure to his partners more than nipple piercings could.

Gald's hand gently held my pussy as he waited for permission. I glanced at his spell things, my heart and core in a fight over priorities.

Guiding me back, up against the wall, Gald added, "I wouldn't have been selected as your lover if I wasn't good at completing multiple tasks in a short amount of time."

"Okay," I breathed.

His blue eyes sparkled as his middle and ring fingers penetrated me, his thumb sliding to my clit. "Let me remind you why I'm here."

Gald was great at giving me reminders. His brand of charm was almost always impossible for me to say no to.

Smoothly, he rubbed me, his thumb caressing my clit while his two fingers pumped, instantly massaging me in a tender area.

I was swelling, heating, growing wetter as he plunged as deep as his fingers could go, fast and intentional. Closing my eyes, I savored our stolen moment, grinding against him.

With his free hand, he held the nape of my neck, and he kissed me again, his tongue roaming far too slowly and sensually for the absolute artistry he performed with my pussy. It only made me want him more.

I moaned, not a thought in my head as I let him finger me to ecstasy, as I whimpered at the way he continued to stroke my clit through my entire orgasm.

Gald slowed, smiling.

I blew out a breath. "Thank you."

He gave me the most tender kiss. "You're welcome. No matter what, I'll always have time for you, Sonta."

I returned his smile. "I'll always make time for you, too."

He stole another kiss, then pressed his forehead to mine. "I suppose we should see to that tracking spell?"

"Yes, please."

After a quick wipe-up, he performed the spell for me. Tyfen was still alive, still somewhere in his kingdom. I breathed a little easier.

My relief didn't last long as we gathered in the high lord's travel room. It was a quaint little thing with some sofas situated in the corner, and giant maps of the realm covering the walls. The main focus, however, was the floor-to-ceiling travel arch.

The elven travel arch was an awe-inspiring artifact, something created millennia ago. The fae had a matching one. We didn't even have one at the Pontaii Palace. It worked much like winnowing or travel spells, aiding in swift transport.

It wasn't really *my* nerves, per se, that were frazzled about passing through it. Gald was of course excited, and Findlech was unbothered, having used it before. Elion was sweating and rigid, staring at the thing as though it might swallow him whole. Shifters really didn't appreciate using others' magic.

I wanted to hold his hand and reassure him it would be fine, but I also didn't want to coddle him in front of the others.

Less visibly anxious but still nervous, Hadwin flashed him a reassuring look that melted my heart.

The emperor wished us well; he would be staying at the castle to discuss imperial business. If only that meant clearing Tyfen's name, but the emperor didn't even fully understand the conflict there. He'd simply enjoyed catching up with his kinfolk. I'd had a nice time getting to know his elf father, as well.

One of the high lord's guards stepped forward with a cylindrical crystal, and Findlech held out his hand. The guard drew a slash across Findlech's palm, then handed him the crystal. "Your Lordship." He offered a small bow.

"Thank you." Findlech faced me. "I'll be right back, my sweet."

I was starting to get used to Findlech calling me by a pet name. It was kind of cute in a platonic way.

Findlech approached the arch and walked straight through the middle, swallowed up by the utter darkness of the gateway. It *was* rather unsettling.

A minute later, he emerged from the darkness, smiling. He nodded first at the high lord and lady, thanking them for their hospitality.

"The security team is ready, as expected." He took my hand and kissed it. "Join me." He acknowledged the rest of the Coterie. "You're all very welcome as guests."

The guard withdrew another crystal from the arch, and I held out my hand. He repeated the process, drawing a line across my palm, then handing me the crystal to take with me for our eventual return.

Findlech's estate was far from the castle, and much of the terrain along the way was uninhabited—a waste of our time to trek in this short week on tour. This was the best way to celebrate with the people of his court.

Findlech took my hand again and led me through.

Walking through the arch felt exactly like walking through a doorway, save the breeze on the balcony we now stood on.

We surrendered our crystals to the head of security and waited for the others in my party to come through. Gald was practically giddy, and Hadwin and Elion only slightly relieved to have gotten it over with.

"Welcome to my home," Findlech said, spreading his arms wide.

The view was beyond enchanting, with vineyards and farmland sprawling as far as the eye could see, only interrupted by mountains in the distance. The land was as captivating and ethereal as the people.

"Let the celebrations begin," he said.

35
Findlech's Estate

Things were much more casual and personable with Findlech's people. We took a carriage to the local town hall, where the citizens had already gathered to celebrate their lord and his Blessed Vessel partner.

I admired Findlech in a new light, and the elves as a whole. While his people gave him proper respect, Findlech smiled more than I was used to seeing. He'd known these people for centuries. He'd listened to their pleas when a fire destroyed their home and land, had taken criminals off the streets, and had watched them grow from newborns to adults. Old and young alike, his people loved him.

Taking my first relaxing breaths since arriving in the elf nation, I enjoyed myself. The people stayed up late, drinking mead while I suffered through water and juice. They were still a bit standoffish with my non-elf partners, but they weren't as obviously abrasive.

My favorite part was meeting Findlech's children and their mothers. Findlech had told me all about them in our earlier bonding. His children were all dashing, their skin different hues.

Most lords married or had children strategically. Findlech had never actually married any of these women, though he'd considered it with a couple, had almost thought he'd loved one of the first. It had never taken.

The women were all kind; there was no awkwardness about me being his newest 'lover.' His children were supportive as well.

I ached, though, knowing Gald kept his distance, that he was only 'another man in my Coterie' to Findlech's loved ones. Gald had dreamed his whole life of touring elven territory, and cherished Findlech so much already. I dragged him into the conversation, explaining how much these two always gabbed about politics. It helped warm Findlech's people up to him.

After Gald got wrapped up in conversation, I made my exit, grabbing some fresh grapes from my chef.

Hadwin dared to wrap his arms around me from behind, his hands on my growing belly. "I'm sure Gald appreciates that."

Grinning, I leaned into his embrace. I'd happily be Gald's wingwoman if it made these two happy.

I did have to wonder, though, about Findlech's choice to be in my Coterie. He hadn't joined to find love. He'd said he hadn't done it to boost his status, either. And he *loved* his home and people.

Why had he left it all to be in a loveless arrangement if not for status like he'd done with these women? His relationship with Gald was a happy coincidence.

I'd asked Findlech more directly about why he'd been assigned to my Coterie. He had volunteered, and the elven parliament had urged the high lord to select him over his own son.

Findlech—my puzzling partner—only gave me vague answers.

Having noticed I'd left his side, he glanced at me from across the hall. His dark brown eyes and expression held centuries of secrets. The trouble was, I was never sure how many of those were sweet secrets, and how many were sinister.

In my heart, I knew he was more good than not, just like I knew that of Tyfen. I offered him a smile, and he returned it with a nod.

"I kinda like it here," Elion said from my left. He took another swig from his mug. "Great mead."

My feet ached by the time we returned to Findlech's estate. Elion had definitely drunk too much mead, and was rather frisky with me. I was happy to take that offer, and led him to a guest room.

Like Tyfen, Elion had no problems getting the job done while inebriated. My feet were tired, but I wasn't yet. Elion dozed off next to me, naked. I placed a kiss on his lips and ran my fingers through his hair. "Enjoy your rest, mate."

I slid off the bed and dressed again before joining the others in a massive living room.

A fireplace blazed in the corner, perfect for both the chilly evening and the large sofas and chairs gathered round with a stunning view of the territory through a massive window.

I squeezed in between Hadwin and Gald, sipping a hot cup of raspberry cocoa. Findlech had assured us we could all be at ease in his private home. He even held Gald's other hand as we all sat together.

"Elion won't be joining us?" Findlech asked.

"He's out cold."

"Not surprising. He got a little carried away there…"

I cringed. "A little." He'd gotten fairly loopy and a bit loud at the end of the night.

"We should watch that," Findlech said. "Public drunkenness will do his people no favor when it comes to reputations amongst my people."

I glared at Findlech. Why did he have to ruin this perfect evening with his stuffiness?

He held up a hand in defense. "It wasn't horrible. I just think he should be more mindful of the impression he's giving on this tour. Many of my people haven't encountered a shifter, at least not in a long time."

Rolling my eyes, I huffed. "He was tipsy, not drunk. And your people can take their—"

Gald grabbed my hand and Findlech's hand and lifted them together to his face. "I *love* when my people get along." He kissed each of our hands, giving us each sickeningly sweet smiles of reproach.

His goofy stare and fluttering eyelashes calmed me.

"You suck," I said.

His lips turned up mischievously. "Only the sensitive parts." He dragged his tongue piercing across the back of my hand, and the reminder made my core heat all over again. He could work magic without magic when it came to that tongue and ball at my clit.

I took my hand back and wrapped it around my warm cup of cocoa. "Fine. Truce. I'll remind Elion in the morning." I glanced at Findlech. "Tell your people that's how shifters offer their compliments to the brewer for good mead." I pouted at not being able to sip any. "Not that I would know if it was any good."

"I'll have some sent to the palace as a birthing gift. A few kegs of it."

I giggled. "I'm all for that. Goddess, Lilah would love it too." My heart warmed at the thought of her back at the palace, working on her secret project. She'd probably like it here, as well.

"It is rather good," Hadwin added.

Movement fluttered inside me, and my heart skipped a beat. Hadwin looked at me, a question in his eye.

I smiled. "I think so."

He set down his drink and held his hand to my stomach, feeling for more movement. The movements were still subtle, but his smile was a mile wide.

I loved that smile, this man. And the reminder of how much it meant to him to have a mate, and a child on the way. Despite our differences and quarrels, I would always love Hadwin. He would always have my heart.

The baby kicked again, and my own smile grew. Gald watched, curious.

"Want to feel it?" I was only four months along out of my ten-month term, but the baby had become more active.

"Sure." Gald's expression was sweet as he touched my stomach.

I glanced at Findlech. "I'm not fond of strangers touching me, but I figure anyone who's had their cock inside me can feel it if they'd like."

That embarrassed kind of smile graced his lips. "I'm fine, thank you." He'd probably had more than enough touching and faking with me lately. "I'm well aware of how it feels to have a pregnant partner."

Right. Findlech was the only father in my Coterie other than Hadwin, and this wasn't his child, so I couldn't blame him. Granted, Haan probably was a father, too, but merfolk were … different. They fucked or got fucked at random, not always forming any real connection with their partner. He may have a thousand little offspring for all we knew. He may be fucking a beautiful mermaid at this very moment, his urges kicking in. Either way, he wasn't as sentimental about fatherhood as we land-walkers were.

The baby kicked again, and this time it made me a little nauseous.

Hadwin glanced at me, sensing my discomfort. "I might be able to help with that."

He knew as well as I that vampire mixling babies could often be soothed when the mother fed off the father. Its jumping jacks may be an indicator it wanted some blood. My mouth was instantly dry. "We can try that."

We excused ourselves to a guest room. No one wanted to see me feed on Hadwin, and it almost always led to sex anyway.

Hadwin immediately dropped trou once we entered the room and closed the door behind us.

I raised my eyebrows. "Cutting right to the chase, huh?"

He pursed his lips, shy. "I… I was hoping, um, that you would want to feed off me like you did that one time in the tent…"

Glancing to his left, my eye caught the glimmer of his dagger. He'd set it down amongst his other belongings after claiming the room earlier.

Grinning, I perked up. My gaze lowered to his now-freed cock. I'd pierced him with his own blade just next to it on his thigh before we had our first threesome.

I grasped the handle, inspecting the blade, then pressed the flat side against his cock. "You trust me with something so sharp again?"

His eyes red, he swallowed. "I trust you with everything."

My heart cracked at the reminder of everything between us, good and bad. Weeks ago, I'd begged him to place his trust in me, that I wouldn't let anything or anyone come between us. But for three weeks now, we hadn't discussed what needed to be said about the Tyfen affair. All we'd done is put on a show for the people, and then fucked and fed in private on occasion as our cravings for each other took over.

Our distance was excruciating for Hadwin. He needed that connection.

I searched his vulnerable eyes, my own desire growing, our child dancing more in my womb. "Get on the bed. Sit with your legs crossed."

He smiled, slipping off his shirt and doing as told. I discarded my own clothes, then sat on his lap, facing him, wrapping my legs around him. His cold thighs under mine, my palm resting on his chilled hip.

Part of me had wanted to slice next to his cock again, to suck him. I really did love his unique coldness inside and against every part of me. But the veins in his neck called, and I loved the intimacy we found with our chests pressed together.

I hovered the dagger by his neck and grazed it against his skin. He kept his eyes on me, his breathing heavy and eyes red, but not out of fear.

Holding the blade tip to his neck, I grinned. "For old times' sake." Making sure to poke just right, I found his vein, dug the tip in, then set the dagger aside.

Hadwin grew large under me, his hands on my ass.

I reached down, adjusted him, then enveloped his cock, one beautiful inch at a time.

"I love you," I whispered as I wrapped my arms around his neck and pressed my lips to his fresh injury.

"I love you too," he panted out with my first suck of his perfect thick blood, as I rocked my hips.

He rocked in rhythm with me, holding my ass, moaning with each push and pull.

The more I sucked, the larger he got, and the faster we rocked.

I loved this position. It didn't allow for the most fervent penetration, but it rubbed right and allowed us a closeness we both craved right now.

After I had my fill of his blood, I swallowed it down, then claimed his mouth.

Hadwin didn't hold back, a hand sliding to my breast to fondle it as we kissed, as his tongue explored my mouth, his cock cooling and heating me at the same time.

The buildup was slow, perfectly slow, not a word between us while we lost ourselves, tangled up. It was better than any sex we'd had rocking a carriage in the dark along our tour route.

My tightness built, and Hadwin aimed his lips for my neck. He worshiped my love bite with tender kisses, but said nothing.

"Yes." I answered his unasked question, half begging.

The pinch of his fangs hurt for but a moment, and then the exquisite tug of blood through my body tickled. His breathing was guttural as he sucked, his hips strong as he rocked.

My release wasn't explosive, but it was exquisite, a small whimper escaping my lips as I rode that friction he kept giving me. He stopped sucking, his breath on my neck, his small moans a treasure in my ear while he shook and filled me.

We stayed there a moment, his face in the crook of my neck. "I love you, darling," he whispered.

I pulled back, gazing into his eyes. I could never not love this man. It wasn't just the sex or the mating bond, or even that we were having a child together. I loved his soul. "Would you like to cuddle?"

He gave me a fanged smile. "Yes."

We untangled ourselves, then cuddled a while and shared kisses, whispering sweet nothings. I ran my thumb over his soft beard. "I love you, too."

He moaned in satisfaction. "Stay the night with me?"

I drew a breath, somehow still full of energy. "I'm pretty awake… I'm not sure yet."

"Okay," he whispered, his hand stroking my hip. "I'll leave the door unlocked in case you want to join me. I'm tuckered out."

I savored another kiss, then crawled out of bed and dressed.

As I approached the living room, I hesitated. Findlech and Gald were whispering, and Findlech kissed him. I'd seen Gald fucking him from behind and sucking him off from underneath a blanket, but this somehow felt more intrusive, walking in on a tender moment like this. I took a step backward to rejoin Hadwin, but the floor creaked.

Findlech pulled away from Gald, glancing at me. "You can come in."

"I just…"

"I'm going to bed, too. You're more than welcome to join Gald in here."

I smiled. "Okay…" I stepped forward as Findlech stood.

He rounded the couch and rested his hands on Gald's shoulders. "Sleep where you want, but remember that if you join me, make sure to lock the door when you come in."

Gald chuckled. "Will do."

I appreciated the reminder.

Findlech approached me. "You seemed to enjoy yourself today."

My smile grew. "I really did. And your home is so lovely." I meant every word.

Pride shone on his face. "Good. You're family now. You're welcome to visit anytime. That offer extends to the rest of the Coterie. It's delightful having more people here."

As the fireplace crackled, I couldn't help but think how peaceful it truly was, and how I'd love to come here for a quiet getaway from the stresses of the realm now and then. It was even more hospitable than Hadwin's manor. Most elf lords' manors had accessibility for merfolk to visit. Granted, Haan would feel rather cramped here, and the reason for those tanks and paths often held a darker history from centuries past, but it was an option.

My heart twisted, though, because Findlech was leaving out one person. Someone who held my happiness hostage.

"*All* of the Coterie can come to visit?" I asked in challenge, my eyes threatening to tear up.

Findlech looked down. He hadn't actually meant *everyone*. Tyfen was a wanted man in these parts. He could never drop by for a relaxing vacation. Findlech leaned closer, his expression full of pity. "I'm sorry, Sonta," he whispered. "I understand you love him, but I can't fix the situation he's in."

Findlech was so fetching in this lighting, with his dark skin and hair, even his casual dress. His deep voice was mesmerizing, his offer of friendship kind. But it was like a punch to the gut in the moment for him to enjoy Gald here while I missed Tyfen so terribly.

"Everything all right?" Gald craned his neck to look at us. "Conspiratorial whispering... Or am I about to ruin a birthday surprise?"

His birthday was coming up soon, though we hadn't planned anything concrete yet. Findlech gave me a pleading look to not taint Gald's happiness with my tears.

Swallowing the lump in my throat, I accepted the change of subject. "Celebrate your birthday?" I kidded. "One step toward getting closer to your old man lover here."

Findlech shook his head and rolled his eyes playfully. "How very generous of you."

I cleared my throat. "I think I'll actually get changed into something more comfortable, then I'll join you, Gald."

"Okay."

"Thank you," Findlech whispered.

Forcing a smile, I nodded, then strode back down the hallway to a room I'd claimed. I allowed myself a few tears before changing into a nightie and returning to Gald in the living room.

36
The Burned Nightie

Gald sat alone in the living room, enjoying the dregs of his hot cocoa while staring into the fireplace. He lifted a finger, guiding the fire with his magic to pick up a new log and swallow it.

I smiled and wrapped my arms around his neck from behind. "I'll never get tired of your magic."

He hummed his delight. "Join me."

Rounding the couch, I did just that. I sat next to him, picking up my cocoa, which had grown cold.

"Here, hold it out," he said.

I held the mug in front of me, and he simply gestured with his fingers again. A ball of flames dashed from the fireplace as the liquid swirled out of the cup. They did a dance in the air, intertwining and kissing, eventually raining down into the mug as a steaming drink.

My smile grew, and I put the mug to my lips. "I'm *definitely* going to keep you around."

He snickered while I savored a sip of my perfectly warm raspberry cocoa. It warmed my insides as it slid down my throat.

"I'm glad you want to keep me around," he said softly. "Even when we disagree on things." He slouched more comfortably on the plush sofa. "I … wasn't expecting this outcome when I made my bid to join your Coterie." His voice was contemplative, peaceful. "I guess I expected great sex, and I hoped to like you."

Gald's smile was so cute as he faced me. "I never saw myself really settling down. I may be a jackass for admitting it, but I kind of imagined we'd be more casual, and that once you bore your firstborn, that I'd, you know, keep going out and traveling, meeting new people, and only dropping by the palace now and then."

I sipped my cocoa. It wasn't like most Coteries didn't have some members who carried on that way. While the arrangement was permanent in the way of loyalty, it wasn't always exclusive. Gald admitting his intentions had been as much didn't surprise me, but it did validate some insecurities I'd had about him leaving me. He'd fucked his way across the realm, learning and adventuring. While I planned to travel more frequently after the birth, I *was* a bit of a lead weight as a partner, tied to duty and the palace.

"I'd love for you to stick around, Gald. I'd miss your smiles and your laugh. But you don't think you'll get bored?"

He raked his tongue piercing across his teeth as he thought. "I still plan to travel. With you. With Findlech. I'll visit my family home sometimes. And goddess knows we're just getting started on how you will mold your child and prepare them for their reign, but I really do love it. I love you, and Findlech, and the palace."

He rarely talked so sentimentally, and it filled my heart. "I'm glad to hear it. Maybe you'll be our trip planner of the group. Whenever we have official business somewhere, you can scope out fun side trips."

"Wouldn't it be fun to actually locate where all your visions have taken place?"

Heartache choked back my joy. "Maybe…"

He raised an eyebrow, lifting a hand to massage my neck. "Not that interested after all?"

It was doubtful he even remembered the ancient elven vision that troubled me, and he didn't understand it was somehow linked to Tyfen.

I gave him a smile. "Are you proposing we all go visit where I got attacked and eaten by a murky-water merperson in vision?"

He cringed. "Fair point. Maybe we'll sort through them before choosing which to hunt down."

"Sounds like a good idea." I snuggled up to him and drank the rest of my cocoa, letting the crackle of the fire soothe my soul. Stars twinkled in the sky, and I couldn't help but get lost in the moons' light as it bathed the world below.

Was Tyfen admiring the moons right now, wherever he was in his kingdom?

In my mind, I was back at the palace with him, sharing stories and stealing kisses. Hiding in storage closets and sneaking into each other's rooms.

After a while, I set down my empty mug. Lost in his own thoughts and the silence of the night, Gald sat quietly. I pulled my knees up, hugging them—something that would only get harder with time as my belly grew.

I rubbed my golden pendant, the one with Hoku's image on it, which I wore for official events and now on tour for good luck. I prayed for guidance, for Tyfen. For my heart to be okay no matter the reason he'd left or the outcome of his decision.

"Off on one of your visions?" Gald whispered.

I blinked and gazed at him. "No."

"Gotcha. You just looked like your mind wandered far."

Shrugging, I dismissed him. "I can't imagine many prettier sights than out this window. I could stay here all night."

He pointed at the fireplace, and a trail of fire left it. The flames gathered at the window and followed his finger as he traced the skyline of mountains and the moons.

I smiled again.

"There's one sight more beautiful," he said.

"Yeah?"

He balled his fist, and the flames gathered, shooting right at us.

I yelped and ducked into his arms, but the flames barely licked our skin as they dissipated.

Gald chuckled, and I smacked his thigh. "Not funny."

His arm slid around me as I huddled against him. "A little funny."

I scowled. "Is this your trick to get lovers in your arms?"

He leaned in, wrapping his arms around me even tighter. "It works..." he whispered. Taking advantage of me having already removed my earrings, he sucked on my earlobe, his ball piercing rubbing.

"Mmm..."

His hand slid up my nightie, higher up my thigh. "Or have you had enough today?"

I couldn't contain my smile as my core heated again. "I might be able to *squeeze* you in before we go to bed."

His lips trailed down my neck. "I like it when you squeeze me."

"My room?" I asked. "Or yours?"

"Here and now."

I pulled back, eyebrows arched. "I'm not sure how Findlech's going to feel about us defiling his couch."

Gald grinned. "He gave me permission to use any part of his house. He knows me well enough." His look turned even more mischievous. "Of course, he doesn't want us in the basement."

Findlech had asked us to leave the basement alone when he'd given us the grand tour. It wasn't an unreasonable request given how private he kept most of his life. It wasn't like he had an oni stashed in there like most vampire dukes and duchesses did.

Gald continued. "He's fine sharing me with you, but he's not willing to share his playroom with you."

My eyes went wide. "Findlech has a playroom?" The things people say about the quiet ones...

Gald belted out a laugh.

"So, he doesn't?"

He stole a kiss. "You think he'd let me tell you if he did?"

I didn't really want to know how kinky Findlech got, yet I kind of did...

Caressing my face, Gald kissed me again. "Here and now. I want the fire when I fuck you."

My face warmed, butterflies dancing in my stomach. He could summon fire of his own with his elemental magic, but having a source like that blazing fireplace in the corner definitely helped.

"Fine. Only if you're sure he won't mind."

Without a word, Gald palmed my breast, a flame bursting from his hand.

My nightie caught fire.

"Shit!"

Gald stood, folding his arms and smirking as the flame enveloped my nightie, burning it all away. It was hot but tolerable.

My heart racing a mile a minute, I sat there in shock, completely naked as a magic breeze carried away the ashes.

"Gald!" I scolded.

He bit his lip. "I've wanted to do that to you for ages."

I wrinkled my nose. "Now you owe me a new nightie."

His gaze raked over my body. "Worth the price, beautiful." He started to unbutton his shirt.

I crossed my legs. "That's not fair. Burn your own clothes away."

He feigned taking offense. "I have more clothing on than you did. We wouldn't want to be wasteful."

Gald liked a good game, and so did I. I stood as he finished unbuttoning his shirt. "I'm pretty tired, after all. I think I'm going to bed instead."

I didn't get two steps away before he grabbed me by the waist and pulled my back to his bare chest. "You're going to stay right here."

"Am I?" I fought a smirk of my own.

His free hand worked at his pants and shorts. "I'm giving you a massage, and then I'm going to fuck you to sleep, Sonta."

"Hmm…" Maybe he'd enjoyed a bit too much mead, too.

The moment his shorts hit the floor, his second hand groped my tit, pinching my nipple enough to make me wet. It gave me enough pain that I knew he would also be feeling it in his nipple.

He pressed his erection to my ass. "Tell me you want this."

It was hard to turn Gald down when he offered, and I could always use a little more fun and distraction from the stress of my daily life.

I ground my hips back. "I want this."

He sucked on my earlobe again. "Lie down. Let's start with that massage."

I obeyed, getting comfortable on the large sofa. He straddled me, pushing my hair to the side, then set to work. His hands, kissed with flames, rubbed deep. He was thorough, and the temperature burned a bit, but in all the right ways.

His voice was soothing while he told me stories about learning to use his magic as a little boy. I shared stories of my earliest memories of Hoku's visions. His playfulness turned to sweetness as while rubbed away the knots and tension in my neck, back, and shoulders. Granted, his cock pulsing against my skin kept it from being *too* sweet.

After placing a kiss on my back, he got off me. "Roll over."

I did so, sleepily.

He straddled me again, resting his hands on my baby bump. "I love this for you." Regret still tinged his words, though the sentiment sounded genuine. He hadn't signed up just to find another lover. He'd had them in spades. He'd joined my Coterie to father this child.

Sliding my hands onto his thighs, I couldn't help but think of the argument we'd had. He *was* giving, possibly the most giving of my men. "I'll never forget your selflessness by offering Haan another chance with me. And I don't have to question which of their uncles will be fighting for the place of the most fun one."

He beamed, then glanced at the ceiling in thought. "Is it really a contest, though? Come on. I *am* the fun one."

I wasn't sure about that. Something told me Elion would be vying for that spot, too. "I guess we'll see."

Humming, he narrowed his eyes. "Let's start by showing their mother some fun…"

Giggling, I slid my hands to his perfectly tight ass. "You always win points by doing that."

He took my hands, intertwining our fingers, then pinned them above my head. I loved the way he looked when he made love to me with his hair down in this position, the way his curls hung around his face and tickled my neck while we kissed.

His lips were soft, his piercings warm as he kissed me, as he slowly glided his tongue across mine. I bucked my hips, eager with anticipation, and he deepened the kiss.

Releasing one of my hands, he slithered his free hand to my clit and teased me ever so gently. My core tightened, and I panted out a breath as he leaned down and sucked the very tips of my nipples.

Fuck. Sometimes pain, pressure, and plunging were all I wanted, but the delicate shit melted me too.

His finger dipped inside me, and a satisfied groan left his lips at my wetness. He adjusted himself, pulling back his foreskin, and eased himself into my entrance.

I closed my eyes and savored it while he grasped my free hand again.

Having slid in all the way to his base, he pulled out slowly, then thrust just as slowly.

I joined him, meeting him in the middle for the next thrust.

His face was so sincere as we locked eyes. "I'd die a happy man if you were the last woman I ever made love to."

"I'd be okay with that." I took him in deep as he picked up speed, that sweet friction hitting just right. "Does that mean group fun with Lilah is out?" The two had casually mentioned being open to it once when she'd sketched us fucking.

He halted. "Well ... I'm still happy to fuck around in groups. Taking Lilah would be fun. Just ... together."

I smiled and raised my hips to encourage him to keep going. I'd considered all the pairings, honestly. Lilah and I hadn't talked in depth about it, but I knew her tastes and kinks well enough.

Elion, and maybe even Hadwin someday, would be comfortable in a group, but neither would want to penetrate her. She'd let Gald fuck her just for fun and to try it, but they'd never truly be more than a platonic pair who fucked on occasion.

But Tyfen... Tyfen had had his wild prince days in his youth. He'd tried it all. When in groups, he preferred to take multiple women rather than share men.

Lilah and Tyfen hadn't gotten a chance to grow their friendship to that level yet, but I kept that hope in my heart, because she was the only woman I could imagine sharing him with.

My mind wandered more than it should with Gald inside me, and I stopped myself once I realized what I was doing.

I closed my eyes again, forcing the image of Tyfen out, focusing on Gald's cock, and the pressure as his base met my pussy each time he thrust.

"Harder," I begged.

He plunged with more fervor, and it sent chills down my spine.

I opened my eyes. "As hard as you can."

His blue eyes gleamed with the challenge. "Happy to."

Gald gripped my hands tighter, leaned into it more, and slammed himself into me. Hard and fast, his strokes short and forceful.

I panted and moaned as the pressure built, as I tightened around him, as he reached new depths.

My thoughts were nowhere and nothing as I found my release, my legs shaking, my stomach tight. Gald kept pounding into me, prolonging my orgasm until he found his own.

He filled me, and we shared a smile. Releasing my hands, he dipped down for more kisses. After all was said and done, we exchanged 'I love yous,' and he used his magic to save Findlech's immaculate couch from his cum. Thank goddess for that...

We were both spent. "Which room?" I asked.

He slid between me and the sofa, spooning me and pulling a blanket over us both. "Mmm... Yes."

Sleepy, I giggled. "It wasn't a yes or no question."

He nuzzled and kissed my shoulder. "In a little bit."

A second later, a scuffling sound startled me, and my eyes shot open. The morning's light blinded me, and I squinted.

Shit.

Hadwin sat in a chair beside the giant window, holding a book, though his eyes were firmly fixed on my breasts. The blanket had slipped, and my upper half was on display.

He blushed and focused on his reading when he realized he'd been caught. "Good morning, darling."

Elion hummed from a chair at the other end of the window, eating breakfast. He gave me a smile as I pulled the blanket back up.

Gald stirred behind me, his hand stroking my underbreast.

"Findlech's not awake yet, is he?" I whispered to Elion.

"He *is* awake," Findlech responded from behind the sofa.

Double shit.

"Sorry." I cringed. "We meant to go to one of the rooms."

He sighed, appearing at the end of the couch. He glanced at Gald, arching an eyebrow. "I know what I signed up for."

Gald snickered, fully palming my breasts.

Trying to be quick but careful, I pivoted, taking the blanket with me as I stood. Gald cupped his hands over his groin. "Sonta…"

I smiled wide. "Don't pretend to be shy about your cock with the Coterie."

He narrowed his eyes. "It's cold." The fire had gone out overnight.

"And you expect a lady to be cold instead?" I wrapped myself tighter, rubbing my cheek on the soft fibers.

He gestured at the other sofa with his chin. "Hand me that blanket."

"I'd rather not."

Cocking his head, he looked past me. "Do me a favor, Elion?"

Elion shook his head. "I'm happiest when my mate's happy. She seems pretty happy with you butt naked right now."

I pouted. "That's what you get for burning one of my favorite nighties." I grabbed the second blanket, and he reached for it. I simply flung it over my shoulder. "Enjoy the show, everyone."

I rounded the sofa.

"Share a bath?" he asked eagerly.

"I'd like some alone time."

"Findlech?"

"It's a shame you slept in. I've already bathed."

I laughed far too hard as I entered the hallway. "Maybe Findlech can find you a floating toy to keep you company in your bath, Gald."

Life with Gald would never be boring, not when we had so much fun with our teasing.

37

CLAIMED IN A CARRIAGE

The rest of our time in Findlech's lands was lovely. I still had my anxieties, worries, and sorrows bouncing through my mind and heart, but I did my best to enjoy each moment as it came. Despite us barely talking, I could tell the tour was taking its toll on Hadwin. The subtle aggressions about a vampire siring the next ruler were constant. Findlech did a good job of balancing that, and I spent the last two nights in Hadwin's bed. I was proud of both Hadwin and Findlech.

We returned to the high lord's castle, and my anxiety peaked, but we were eventually sent on our way without conflict, and I breathed easier about the Tyfen issue. The emperor rejoined us, and he didn't even seem concerned when I privately confided the elves wanted Tyfen dead. Tyfen was known to be in his own kingdom, so I should consider that an issue for another day.

The carriage ride back to the elf-shifter border was long, my thoughts drifting every which way. It was tight quarters, as most of the time, the five of us chose to ride in the same carriage. If only for appearances, Hadwin and Findlech remained with me, and it was good for Elion to be here to start putting him in the center of things since we were headed to his portion of the tour. We certainly wouldn't shove Gald off to a carriage by himself.

I often napped between Hadwin and one of the others on the ride, saving my energy. As much as my soul dully ached that we weren't talking the way we used to, it meant the world to me that he held my hand or rested his hand on my thigh.

Leaving behind the mountains in elven territory stirred my pain about Tyfen. The leaves were changing, the greens of summer conceding to the colorful palette of autumn. The vision I'd had that was somehow linked to Tyfen had probably happened around this time of year.

It was impossible to be happy for long, to not let guilt win. Here I was, parading around like nothing was wrong and like I was the happiest woman in the world with my partners, all when a corner of my heart grew cold with cobwebs.

I couldn't decide which was worse. Knowing Tyfen could conceal his location and may be doing so willingly, or knowing people wanted him dead, and may be hiding him.

He had unintentionally called me a pet name for a previous lover in the haze of a nightmare once... Maybe she was less trouble. Perhaps she didn't have other lovers who tried to kill him.

But what if he was being tortured right now? What if he'd been forced from the palace to protect me or someone else?

Tyfen had left the palace and hadn't been seen for two full months now. Each day carved a bit more into my soul, despite the emperor's reports that Tyfen's family was still diligently looking for him.

As we properly entered shifter territory, I promised myself I would give Elion my full attention. My mate needed my undivided time and support.

During our first stop in official shifter lands, we switched things up in the carriages. Elion wanted to share one with me alone.

His clothing was more natural today as he donned his native clothing. He relaxed more than I was used to seeing on this tour, and it made me happy.

He held me as the carriage jostled forward. "I'm excited to finally get my chance with you."

I smiled, caressing his soft cheek. "Me too, mate."

His eyes flashed silver at that, his fingers digging into my hip.

"Remember that while we're here. Whose mate you are. You're mine and mine alone for now."

Running my fingers through his black hair, I considered what he meant by that. He wouldn't intentionally belittle Hadwin to puff himself up with his people—they'd become friends and allies—but Elion would easily be the most vulnerable in his people's eyes solely because his seed hadn't won. Shifters cared very much about virility, and in their culture, it said a lot about a man. It wasn't fair, but it was the way of things. He would have to prove his worth and dominance even more now than he had before joining my Coterie.

I took Elion's hand, intertwining our fingers. I'd never forget how hurt he had looked and sounded when he discovered he wasn't the father of my child. "I'm sorry it's not yours."

Elion drew a deep breath. "We need to talk. Go sit on the other bench."

I swallowed hard, doing as asked. I hugged myself, covering my bare midriff in my new maternity outfit, nervous about his serious tone.

Elion pursed his lips. "I need you to stop doing that."

"Doing what?"

"Treating me like I'm wounded."

"I'm … not," I quietly defended.

He wasn't angry, but his tone was firm. "You are, Sonta. And I love you for your unending kindness and consideration, but as much as I need those, I need your respect."

"You have my respect."

"You constantly look at me as though I'm wounded. You keep apologizing and walking on eggshells around me."

"I…" What did he want me to do? Be dismissive? I tried not to coddle him, but Coterie life *was* hard for him. He had to share me, which was very unnatural for him. He'd gotten a rough start with the group because of his mating fever. He was the youngest of the men. He'd faced passive aggression from loads of people along the tour.

More than anything, he'd wanted me to bear his child, and I hadn't given that to him.

"I'm not a cub, Sonta. I'm a grown man, and I need you to treat me like one."

"I am! I don't know what my mate wants from me…" I huffed, exasperated. We never quarreled, so I didn't know what to say.

He bounced his knee. "I need you to recognize that I can take care of myself. Just because I wasn't in control when we first met doesn't mean I'm that same man now. I'm not a slave to the fever anymore. And I'm disappointed the child isn't mine, but you apologizing and giving me looks of pity only makes it worse. Treat me like a fucking man, not a wounded animal."

I frowned. I hadn't even realized I'd been doing it.

"I sit back on this tour and let the others take front stage as they will because I understand how these things work. I don't demand more of your time because *I understand how these things work*. Just because I'm nice doesn't mean I won't do what it takes to fight for myself, my mate, and my people. If I need something, I will ask or I will take."

I looked down at my hands, fidgeting with them in my lap. "Okay."

His voice softened. "You like my parents?"

My smile recovered as I met his gaze. "I *love* your parents. I've been looking forward to seeing them again." In truth, I was sad they weren't my child's grandparents. I would have loved to have more frequent visits.

Elion smiled back. "And they love you." He gazed at my stomach. "They'll be fair with Hadwin and the child, despite any long-held hostilities between our peoples." He adjusted his seat. "The mistake outsiders make with my parents is assuming their kindness makes them weak. Like me, they understand shows of strength need only be strategic reminders. If you earn your people's loyalty and respect, you have no need to constantly bark orders and demand more than is necessary."

He eyed me a moment. "I'm assuming the emperor and magistrate have told you about a threat a few years back, about the elves and fae gathering at our borders."

I shyly nodded. "It looked as though they were preparing for war."

"Yes. We were ready for the worst again. My people enjoy a simple life, but that doesn't mean we don't understand our place in this realm, and the threats around us. Our packs were ready. No matter how well trained we are, we're also not stupid. We're not mindless brutes. We understand the imbalance of magic and strength. We bow to the emperor for a reason. It was not because of weakness we informed him of the threat. It was because we use our resources wisely."

I loved this side of Elion, the poet and wise soldier who often hid behind his passion and calm sweetness.

"I admire that about your people, Elion."

He smiled again. "Thank you."

I'd sworn to myself I wouldn't bring Tyfen up, but I couldn't help myself. I'd even asked Baylana if she knew how Tyfen was tied to the conflict, but she hadn't known. While she tried to keep her finger on the pulse of the realm, she admittedly spent most of her time hiding and trying to tame the wilder vampire lands. "Do you know how Tyfen's involved with that conflict, with the war that never happened?"

Elion angled his head, his grey eyes narrowing. "I wasn't aware he was involved…"

I certainly hadn't intended to implicate Tyfen as the aggressor and make him seem more of an enemy. "I don't actually know that he was. There was just a vague claim that he might know more, but I have no proof."

Nodding slowly, contemplatively, Elion searched my face. "I deserve to know if he's a threat to my people."

"I really don't think he is. He holds no malice toward you. The emperor and magistrate report no threat."

The tension in Elion's face eased a degree. "Good. My delegation hasn't reported any serious concerns lately, and I hope it stays that way." He rubbed his knee. "And I trust my mate would not choose him over me, should his actions and intentions be harmful to my people."

Elion tried to be neutral in the group, but he had his loyalties. His warning reminded me how little people knew Tyfen's heart like I did.

"I wouldn't have to choose, Elion. It's my job to *not* choose."

His reminder was soft. "But you do choose, Sonta. Every day. You choose who you allow into your heart and bed. Who will be allowed to help form the opinions of your child. I trust that Hoku was wise when it comes to who *she* chose."

I offered him a weak smile. "I love you."

He let out a low growl, crossing his legs. "I love you, too, mate."

"I *am* excited for your portion of the tour, genuinely. And I'm sorry I haven't shown you my respect in the ways you need it. Tell me what you need from me, and I'll do my best." I drew a breath. "I'm yours, mate."

With the air cleared, we discussed his expectations of me around his people. I also expressed my need for him to tell me when I was offending him, to not bottle it up the way he had.

As the afternoon turned to evening, we met another pack of shifters alongside the road. Groups of wolves, foxes, badgers, and all manner of shifters had gathered along the route to steal a glimpse of the Blessed Vessel and her mate. It was heartwarming as we waved, as they chased the line of carriages for a while to keep up with us.

We weren't attending parades on the way to the high alpha's property, but loads of citizens had left their homes to spy us, many camping out for days in their fur.

We stopped for dinner with a large gathering, taking the time to greet them. The adults shifted into human form to visit with us, many quickly donning scant clothing they'd carried, out of their understanding for the other races' sensibilities. The little children ran naked, giggling and free from the stresses of the realm.

I clung to Elion's side, not just for show, but because I loved my mate, and I loved how simple his world could be. Simple by choice.

All the shifters looked at the rest of my Coterie with caution, especially Hadwin. It meant the world to me when, after introducing me as his mate, Elion introduced Hadwin to his people. He introduced him as his brother, a vampire who had respect for the shifters.

I almost cried. While I understood how Elion's choice to do so lifted him as well—to act wounded and petty after losing the paternity race would only solidify that impression with his own people—it was the proof I needed that my Coterie really did stand a chance of staying together. We'd come a long way from Hadwin yelling threats at Elion for fucking me without permission. Now, they'd shared me, and they had their own understanding about how they balanced their dynamic with their mate.

Hadwin accepted the introduction graciously.

After dinner, we resumed our course. My stomach full and the fresh taste of pig's blood washed down with juice, I cuddled up to Elion in our carriage.

He kissed my head, tickling my arm. "Have you given any more thought to extra children after this one?"

I bit my lip. I hadn't really considered it; I had too much on my plate right now. Turning, I read his face in the fading light. "I'm still not sure. I want to say yes to giving you at least one child, Elion, but I don't want to make a promise I can't be sure of."

Along with the many blessings Hoku gave her daughters for their sacrifice for the realm, she made it so we couldn't conceive for the first year after bearing the Anointed Ruler. We could heal and give our full focus to the next emperor or empress. We didn't have to stress about accidental pregnancies.

He rubbed my arm. "I understand. I'm not trying to pressure you."

"You really want to be a father, don't you?"

The warmth of his smile was beguiling. "Yes."

"You'll make a great father."

A growl rumbled in his throat as his hand made its way to my inner thigh and up to his bite mark.

My core heated at the touch and as a response to his own desire.

"Honestly, I'll take as many cubs as you'll give me, Sonta."

I swallowed. "Even though they'll be runts?" That was the trade-off for a shifter mixling. In animal form, they were much smaller than their peers, and in a society where virility, size, and strength meant so much, it wasn't a small matter.

He grasped my chin. "They will be *mine*, so they will be respected."

Fuck, I loved him. The soft side and the possessive dominant side.

Elion stole a kiss. "Do you plan to have more offspring with the others?"

We'd all more or less discussed it. Hadwin was undecided. Gald was a no. Findlech's was an obvious answer. Haan and I planned to fuck after my pregnancy, but neither of us felt that need to bring a life into this world together. Tyfen and I hadn't actually discussed it, though. Our relationship had been too slow-growing to talk of things that far out.

"I don't know, Elion. Bonus children in Coteries require a great deal of planning and cooperation." We had to work out childcare with the different fathers. We also had to work out strategic contraception. We had contraception tea, and then we had barriers. The tea made me unable to conceive at all while I took it. The barriers were of course single use. I didn't imagine Elion and Tyfen would want to constantly wear barriers while I kept popping out children for Hadwin specifically. I couldn't even have sex with Haan when I was trying to conceive for another man, because his barbed cock would pierce right through the barrier. Gald had his reasons for wanting to alter himself so he couldn't accidentally impregnate me—he liked fucking without a barrier as much as I did.

"It's not a competition," I reminded Elion.

His smile hinted at embarrassment. "I didn't mean it that way."

"Then how did you mean it?"

"I … like my mate pregnant."

"Ooooh…" He was so predictable in many ways when it came to his sexual preferences, but he still managed to surprise me. So far, his only kink I knew about other than the obvious shifter preferences was his love of collecting my underwear. The palace dressers *had* to wonder why I constantly needed new pairs. They were a prized possession for Elion—he had a drawer full of them in his room, and when he missed me while I shared my time and bed with the others, he'd dig into that drawer.

"You like your mate pregnant?" I repeated.

He gazed at my growing baby bump. "Yes." His voice was hoarse.

"Why haven't you told me this before?"

He swallowed. "I don't want the others to think poorly of me."

It was a reasonable fear. Hadwin might not be too fond of the idea of Elion being turned on by his child growing within me. I gave Elion a smile. "No one needs to know." It wasn't like the others had even realized I rarely wore underwear twice; they'd never questioned where they disappeared to.

I rested my hands on my stomach. I was four months along out of ten. "I'm not even halfway. I still look like I ate a giant meal and have a bit of bloating."

He slid his hand back up my skirt and brushed my bite mark, then tenderly touched my pussy.

I instinctually spread my legs a bit more, my insides tightening.

He didn't penetrate me, didn't even focus on my clit. He simply grazed my labia, up and down, hinting at dipping his finger in. "I notice the small changes each day. I intimately know *every* curve of my mate's body."

If I hadn't been wet before, I was now.

Just as the sunlight of the day was giving way to the moonlight of night, his pleasantries with his people and our talk of politics were giving way to passion.

"I'm yours," I said.

Another growl rumbled in his throat as he withdrew his hand and closed the curtain on his side of the carriage, and ignited some small fae lights. I closed the curtain on my side as well, then waited for instructions.

"I want all of you," he said, his eyes glowing, his breathing heavier. He gave no command as he kicked off his shoes, undid his belt, and removed his pants and shorts, then shirt.

Elion had the perfect form. Muscled, but not too much. Toned. His cock was beautiful as he turned and crouched before me.

I spread my legs further, but he shook his head. From the floor of the carriage, he reached up and grasped the waistband of my skirt. Lifting my hips, I allowed him to pull it off me. He made quick work of removing my top as well, and the bra I wore. I soaked in the intimacy of his skin against mine as he straddled me.

Elion glanced at my wrist. "All of you bare."

I nodded and took off my bracelet. I still hadn't told anyone other than Gald and Lilah how much my leather bracelet meant to me, but the others had picked it up. I always wore it now to keep Tyfen in my heart, even when it was far too casual for my outfit, and Gald still used it every day in his tracking spell.

I was always conflicted about my bracelet. Hadwin and Elion's claiming marks couldn't be removed from my body, nor could the magical bond tattoo Gald had given me. Why should I have to remove Tyfen's bracelet to make love to my other men?

Then again, it wasn't the mark of a lifelong partner, not really. It had been given as a gift, a symbol of how we wanted to keep our relationship and kinks with each other a secret from the others.

Carefully placing it to the side, I sat bare before Elion, under him as he continued to straddle me on the carriage bench. Especially in Elion's territory, I was going to give him my all.

The carriage jostled as it hit a bump in the road, and Elion with his lightning-fast reflexes grabbed one of the hand straps near the top of the door. He'd already taken me in a carriage a few times, and it sure made for some fun times, and funny times, depending on how bumpy the path had been.

"You're mine in my lands," he said, every word as possessive as a shifter mate's could be. "I'm going to show you what it *really* means to be claimed."

My heart thudded faster at the threat and promise. I'd already anticipated his desire; he planned to fuck me constantly like when he'd had his mating fever, and as we had a few days before we arrived at his hometown, I expected this carriage would get plenty of use.

"I'm yours," I reminded him.

"I'm the only one who gets to fuck you here."

I bit my lip, hesitating. I'd already let Hadwin take me a few times within shifter borders on the route to the elf nation, though that was often considered 'neutral' territory.

"You have to allow Hadwin a few chances with me." By law, Hadwin had more say now. "I have pregnancy cravings you can't take care of."

He huffed. "Fine. I approve each time."

I smiled at his negotiations. "And Gald's birthday is coming up…"

Elion's lip curled. "Birthdays aren't that important to shifters. You don't *need* him in my territory."

I pouted. "They're important to humans and mage-humans. You'd deny your mate her own traditions?"

"Fine," he grumbled. "Once. For his birthday. And only if we share you."

My stomach tingled at the demand. When offered group activities, it was rare for me to not be on board. The same went for Gald. "I'm sure that can be arranged."

Elion grasped my chin again. "Other than that, you're all mine."

"So much talk, Elion… So little action."

He panted out a breath at my tease. "Get up."

As he got off me, I stood, at least as much as I could in the carriage.

"Turn around, on the bench. Use both hand straps."

A grin slid onto my lips as I rested my hands on his chest and kissed him. "If you say so."

His cock pressed into me, the tip already wet as he grabbed my waist and stole another kiss. Then he released the hand strap and forced me to face away from him.

I'd never forget the gasps of shock in the bedding chamber when he'd tossed me around, flipping me on the bed. I loved that feral side of Elion.

I knelt on the bench, facing the back and reaching out to hold the hand straps on either side of the carriage. "Like this?"

Elion's hands grasped my thighs, spreading them further. "There." He slid his hands to my belly as he stood behind me. More gently, he stroked my stomach, growing even harder against my back.

I had to smile again about him liking me pregnant. I'd never feel insecure about my body with him, and I was glad he'd finally told me, so he wasn't ashamed to acknowledge that part of my body while someone else's child was in there.

He took his time feeling me, then glided his hands to my breasts and cupped them.

"Do me the honor of not holding back," he whispered in my ear.

"I never hold back with you…"

"No? I want you loud enough for the guards on either side of us to worry about you, to hear you over the sounds of their horse's shoes."

I fought a giggle. I definitely *did* hold back when it came to that part of sex with Elion. But I was his right now. "If it pleases my mate."

"It does."

His fingers spread, and he pinched my nipples between them. Then he dipped down, pressing his cock to my entrance. Not as forceful as he likely desired because of the unpredictability of the carriage and road, he thrust up and in.

My grip tightened on the straps to hold me up as my body relaxed for him. He kept going, pushing in to the hilt as his knot swelled and anchored his place inside me.

My blood pumped, my heart beating fast.

He adjusted, stabilizing himself now that he was fully inside me. Placing his right foot on the bench next to my knee, he steadied himself. His left foot stayed on the ground, but his knee leaned against the bench. His hands snaked up from my breasts to wrap around my hands, holding the straps with me.

He pulled himself out to where his knot caught inside me. Just the one motion and the way it rubbed me put me in another world.

"Whose are you?" he whispered into my ear.

I shuddered as he thrust. "Yours," I panted. "You're my mate."

He pulled out again with a growl of pleasure, his cock large and rigid, and perfect within me. "That's right." He plunged into me again.

While our preparations to get in a good position had taken some time, he didn't waste any more with his movements now.

With each stroke, my tightness built. With each powerful plunge, he drove me forward. My hands secure on the straps with his covering mine, I didn't lose my balance.

In and out, Elion pleased me, his knot pounding deep as our hands tugged on those sturdy straps, as my knees eventually slid forward on the bench, pushing me against the soft back.

Elion clambered forward to be closer, deeper, to not lose momentum.

And I didn't hold back a single moan or gasp as he reached that place within me that always gave me an explosive finish.

Another stroke and I needed him more than air.

Another thrust and I could cry from the pressure.

His last plunge, needy and forceful, sent me over the edge.

"Fuck!" My legs shook, my entire core on fire.

Elion didn't relent at all.

"*Oh, goddess, Elion...*" I closed my eyes, fighting through the waves of pleasure as they rippled through me.

He kept going, soon finding his release, gasping himself. "Mine," he snarled. "Mine."

With plenty of energy left in him, Elion kept burying himself in me. He dropped his hands to my hips to keep me in place, to get closer and deeper.

I was as loud and vocal as he wanted me to be, and I certainly didn't have to try.

My hands slipped from the straps, and his fingers clutched me like claws.

I leaned forward, giving him a better angle as I pressed my face to the soft back of the bench.

It could have been two more minutes or two more hours for all I knew, but Elion drove into me past the point of pleasure and pain until we each found another release. The second time was softer, but that much sharper.

I could barely breathe by the time he stopped, my hips sore from his firm grip.

Elion gulped for air as well while he wrapped his arms around me and supported me. "All mine," he panted.

We both might as well be drunk, by how we swayed with the carriage.

He kissed my shoulder and grabbed a cloth for the bench under me. He held me tight, gripping one of the straps again to support us both as his knot subsided.

I wasn't even standing, but I could barely keep myself upright, my thighs screaming, my abdomen warm.

"You'd let me know if I took you too hard, right?" he asked.

A sleepy, lazy smile graced my lips. "Sure."

After another minute, he pulled out, his cum dripping down my legs onto the cloth. I blew out a breath and leaned forward again as he cleaned himself off and then wiped my legs down.

His hands held my hips gently this time. "Let's have you sit." He turned me around and eased me down, his lycan eyes bright silver.

Elion nestled into the tight space between the benches, kneeling on the floor. Without a word, he glanced at my pussy, a question in his eye.

I barely remembered my name at this point, but I wanted more of him. "Kiss me first."

He obliged, straddling me again and claiming my mouth as he had the rest of me.

After several minutes, he pulled back. "Can I taste you?"

I stole one more kiss, sucking on his lip. "Yes."

He got back on the ground, spread my legs, and happily lapped up the remaining evidence of our love. I was so tender, so sore. His tongue was so stimulating yet soothing with his healing saliva.

When he'd had his fill, he laid his hands on my thighs, glancing up at me. Both of us looked drunk, our energy expended.

"Come here," I whispered.

He held me on the bench, and I only put my leather bracelet back on so I wouldn't lose it.

At some point, we jolted awake at rather vigorous slamming on the carriage door. The guards woke us from a deep slumber to let us know we'd arrived at our campsite for the night, and the tent was ready. Half-asleep, we sloppily put our clothes back on, our hair unkempt, and we stumbled to the tent and joined the others.

38
COLSIA'S SIMPLER SIDE

It was impossible for me to dwell on the negative in shifter lands. Not with how often and fervently Elion was claiming me. Nor with how welcoming and unproblematic his people were. In all of history, the shifters' greatest fault was disjointed packs, though they'd organized since; they'd rarely ever been the aggressors.

The shifters were near impossible to read when they were in their animal forms, but when in human form, they were also harder for me to read than the other races. So much of their communication was nuanced with glances and the subtlest of gestures that carried over from their animal forms, where they could not speak. While I'd run into several shifters in human lands growing up, I'd never known any well.

As far as I could tell, they all took Hadwin's victory as the father fairly well. Sure, there were hesitations given his vampire nature, but Elion, Hadwin, and I worked harmoniously together as we made our way through the crowds. It would never not wrench my heart to see Hadwin hide his handsome toothy smile when he tried to come off less intimidating. But he did it for his people and his child, and I adored every part of him.

If anything, the shifters were more visibly wary of Findlech, which took me by surprise. Until I recognized how aware the shifters were of the threat elves like him had posed at their borders just a few short years ago. Many of their packs had been ordered away from their homes and families to secure their lands and prepare for the conflict that never came. Or at least hadn't yet... As the emperor had reminded me—the immortal races didn't often drop feuds quickly.

Findlech took it in stride, ever the gentleman and politician. He never once acted offended about the aggressive stares he got.

VENUS COX

We celebrated Gald's birthday on the last day of our travels to the high alpha's home. He was adorable, and so was Findlech as he requested a carriage for them alone that day. Before heading to bed that night, Gald, Elion, and I gathered in the other carriage for our time together. Logistics for three in a carriage were tricky, but we all had a smile on our faces afterward...

My heart fluttered as we rolled into the drive of the high alpha and his mate early the next morning. The whole household stood outside, awaiting our arrival.

They gave the warmest greeting of any of the rulers, and I had to remind myself of Elion's rules. No matter how much I wanted to, I *didn't* apologize that Elion wasn't the father, that I wasn't making them grandparents of the next ruler.

But I finally knew that I *did* want to give Elion a child someday. This was too happy a place and family to not share more.

We were greeted by lower alphas and their mates, who joined us for this week of celebration. The accommodations were humbler than that of the other rulers, but still far grander than anything I'd lived in before moving to the palace.

Elion held his head high. He was even more sexy when he was commanding like this, his arm always around me, letting the people know I was *his*.

We got to tour the alpha's garden. I cried happy tears, getting to see it in person, the first of my visions I knew the location of for certain. Gald was excited to see it, too.

In shifter lands, they'd planned no balls or parades. As much as I loved dressing up and dancing, the lack of formality was a breath of fresh air on this tour.

We left the high alpha's estate each morning, and branched out to a new location for the day. Most shifters didn't even use public transportation, but we still used the carriages so as to not waste any time.

Their open markets were so vibrant, much more lively and full than usual, as the weeklong celebration had extra amenities in the form of a festival.

I sat between Elion and Hadwin as we watched a magnificent shifter performance featuring all the small animals in an outdoor amphitheater. It was mesmerizing, recharging my hope and happiness.

The imperial taster had to keep scolding me for trying foods without having them test it for poison first, but it was hard when I wanted to take it all in.

Throngs gathered in the center of their lands to see us, happy and curious. Each day, I was laden with fresh wildflowers people had picked and woven into crowns and necklaces for me. I was gifted handmade earrings made of acorns. A servant had to carry all the beautiful gifts, there were so many.

On our last day in shifter lands, I ached at the thought of leaving.

Elion held my hand as we walked through the nearest market, strolling to a blacksmith he'd commissioned surprises from. His parents walked ahead, and Hadwin behind us. Gald and Findlech had chosen to stay back at the high alpha's estate for the day.

The blacksmith greeted us all, then reached for a square wooden box. "Sir Elion." He bowed, handing it to him.

Elion gave it to me.

I beamed as I undid the latch. "It's about time I started getting gifts…"

Elion let out a breathy chuckle.

I opened the box, and found a beautifully simple necklace, a large hoop of hammered gold. "I love it," I whispered as I ran a finger along it.

"Let's put it on you." He took it out and set the box down. I lifted my hair, and he opened the hoop enough to put it around my neck and secure it.

Elion pressed his forehead to mine, taking my hands. "I *love* sharing my homeland with my mate."

"And I love having you for a mate. And spending time in your homeland." I kissed him—the onlookers ate that up.

It hadn't been for show, but I was still glad to know it improved his people's opinion of him. He wasn't a failure because he hadn't sired the next ruler. He couldn't have had my heart more securely if he tried, and couldn't have pleased me more, either. He'd fucked me nonstop at his parents' estate, every day before we joined the others in the morning, and after we returned from our outing for the day. We had his parents' lush gardens to ourselves at night, and we had a hell of a time playing adult hide-and-seek.

We had that spark.

Elion accepted the second wooden box from the blacksmith, then turned to Hadwin. Were this at the palace, hundreds would be gathered in fine silks, gold, and pearls for the formality, but we weren't at the palace. Word would spread from the observers who still eagerly followed us.

Elion handed the rectangular box to Hadwin. "For my brother. Congratulations."

Hadwin humbly bowed, taking the gift.

It was as simple as that. The words, the body language, the ceremony. It was like my intentional hesitation at following Elion's orders in the bedding chamber. We did our dance, and we knew what it meant. And so did the people.

Elion accepted Hadwin's place as the father of the next ruler, and so should his people. Hadwin's bow acknowledged their equality.

Hadwin opened the box, a soft smile on his face.

Shifters weren't known for their intricate craftmanship like the elves and even the fae were, but their work was sturdy.

Hadwin withdrew his new dagger, examining it. "A fine blade. Thank you."

Elion smiled as well. "We protect our mate."

Goddess, I loved it when they said that… *Our* mate.

Hadwin replaced the dagger and lid. "That we do." He glanced at the shifters around us. "We'll protect the Blessed Vessel, the emperor and the next Anointed Ruler, and the good people of this realm, no matter the territory or race."

No one would know Hadwin had such humble beginnings, such a traumatic history and limited experience. Baylana and her partners had coached him well on his rise as a new duke, and I loved them for it.

The high alpha and his mate also congratulated Hadwin in front of the people.

It was a beautiful moment in a peaceful place, surrounded by lovely people.

I wished it could stay this way forever...

***

The ride back to the palace for our rest week had me on edge. I didn't want to face reality.

There were no updates on Tyfen. According to Gald's daily tracking spells, he was still somewhere in his own kingdom. According to the emperor's updates, the fae royal family was continually searching for Tyfen, but they were confident they were closing in on his location, and he'd be back before his leg of the tour.

Anger started to fester in my heart because the emperor offered the fae king and queen extra assistance, but they turned him down. They were an arrogant race, too proud to accept help...

I wanted to just move on to the merfolk portion of the imperial tour since we were already halfway to the location, but we pressed onward to the palace for our rest week.

I let Elion continue to fuck me in our carriage, allowing the wild fervor and explosive orgasms to calm my nerves. I slept well each night from the exertion. It was admittedly awkward that one time we hadn't planned well, and the carriages stopped while he was still knotted inside me. Everyone waited on us for lunch while our carriage rocked as he finished me off. It reminded me of how mortifying it had been to have a thousand people hear me gasp under him at our claiming.

I told myself the shy, awkward looks of the soldiers were jealousy, solely to ease my embarrassment. And that embarrassment did ease as he took me in the mountains. The carriage heading up or going down allowed him to plunge to deeper reaches.

Thank Hoku and the stars for my calling. Someone had to do it...

My heart was torn upon our return to the palace. It was home and safety, a place I could truly let my hair down. My mother and Kernov wore the brightest smiles. Lilah... I'd asked her to greet me inside next time, because it was too hard to pretend we were just friends. Some of the servants knew we were together, but not all who gathered for the tour send-offs and receptions.

Our kiss was like lightning once I had her inside. I had cherished her letters and missed her so much. She was doing remarkably well with more time behind her after her breakup with Cataray, and she said she was nearing completion on her secret project.

I wanted to lie with her, hold her, be with her in that way again, and it gutted me we hadn't even hit the halfway mark of my pregnancy yet. The closest we would get was her painting me again sometime this week.

Still, I was happy to see the people I loved, but it hurt to go back to my chambers and to the common room. Tyfen hadn't returned. He had *one* week to return. People would notice if he didn't show up before we left for the last leg of the tour.

Haan's face was also a welcome sight, and his husky airy voice, his purple eyes and turquoise scales helped bolster me. While I didn't think he was all that concerned for Tyfen on a personal level, he was a sweetheart about how it affected me.

I swam with him in my pond a lot as we discussed preparations for my visit to his people. It wasn't like we would have a week in a carriage together to talk.

It kept me occupied.

Until bedtime.

Nearly every night of my rest week, I snuck into Tyfen's empty room and allowed myself to fall apart. I sobbed myself to sleep.

Goddess, I missed him and the piece of my heart he'd taken with him that day. He hadn't given me an explanation or a chance to say goodbye. He'd now been missing for longer than we'd even been together…

He'd called me Blantui—strength. That strength diminished a little more each day without him and his smile and attitude, his eyes and tattoos and heart…

It was tense again with the others, though they abstained from the criticism we all knew they had about Tyfen.

I *knew* I shouldn't be harsh with them, shouldn't take Tyfen's absence out on them. But there was something so deeply etched into me that kept me fighting for him, yearning for him.

My heart was hollow as we readied on the last day of our week, as I numbly had to accept he hadn't returned home. Then again, this wasn't his home. He'd sent all his things back to his kingdom.

The king and queen still refused the emperor's help. I scratched out a letter myself, pleading for them to reconsider. They didn't even deign to respond.

We were all quiet, moving at a snail's pace despite the servants rushing around us at breakfast time. Lilah even ate with us in the dining hall.

We returned to the common room for our private goodbyes. Lilah's hug was impossibly tight, her kiss incredibly soft. She was staying behind again. Her secret project was almost done, and while I craved her presence, I was too uneasy about this next leg to even invite her.

Findlech and Gald bid each other goodbye with a hug and a promise to write. I'd asked Gald to tag along again to keep trying his spells. Perhaps as we got closer to the fae border, his magic would be strong enough to better locate Tyfen.

Findlech wouldn't be welcomed. Not with the queen so suspicious that he'd attacked Tyfen when he'd gotten hurt. Not when the king and queen *knew* the elves had a price on Tyfen's head. Apparently, both nations had closed their borders to each other since the conflict a few years ago, but hadn't made that public. Findlech wouldn't be killed if he joined us in the fae kingdom, but he knew damn well he wasn't actually welcome.

VENUS COX

The emperor was more casual about us colluding to lie this time. Granted, this time it wasn't my fault. Uncharacteristically, he joined us for the last leg of the tour as well. Normally the magistrate would have, but the emperor wanted to be there should anything be afoot as we approached Tyfen's kingdom. He held more authority than Magistrate Leonte in that way.

The lie was weak and unfortunate, but agreed upon with the fae king and queen. Tyfen was not joining us on the merfolk portion of our trip because he had urgent business to attend to in his kingdom. His own people would likely be confused by that, but when it came to royals, you could always say they were vaguely 'busy' with civil service.

Granted, it had to be rather important for him to be so busy as to skip out on this part of the imperial tour...

We got on the road—Hadwin, Elion, Gald, and myself. We rode in the same carriage through the mountain passes. I kept fidgeting with my bracelet, uneasy as I looked out the window. It was properly autumn now, the leaves dropping like my hopes.

Never had a Blessed Vessel been stood up by a Coterie member during an imperial tour. *Never*. There had been that one time where a Coterie member went to his home territory to attend to his duties while she was away on tour, and he'd met an unfortunate end, but he hadn't skipped out on her.

It was our job to put aside any differences, any personal issues, and be there for each other, even if it was only for the sake of appearances. This realm needed the assurance we were united. My divine mother was the goddess of unity, for fuck's sake...

Hadwin's cold hand rested on my knee. "No matter what happens, we'll be fine with or without him."

His words were soft but dismissive. I wouldn't be fine without Tyfen. His loss would be as great to me as the loss of any of the other Coterie members.

I glanced at Hadwin, my gaze hardening. His hazel eyes searched mine, pleading. But in that moment, I only saw the monster who had flung Tyfen into the wall, snapping his arm like a twig. "I won't do this with you again."

He looked down, removing his hand at my warning.

The breeze beating against the carriage glass and the clap of the horses' hooves were rather loud contrasted with the absolute silence inside our carriage.

Perhaps I was a bit too terse on Tyfen's behalf. Perhaps I saw things in a way no one else did. He wasn't bad; he was broken. And every single person in this Coterie had someone watching out for them.

Everyone but Tyfen.

Elion, Gald, Findlech, and Haan all had family and leaders from their homelands who loved them and cheered them on.

Hadwin had Baylana and her partners in his corner, and all the Coterie respected him.

But Tyfen? His own parents constantly berated him, and had forced him into a position he hadn't wanted. No one seemed to care that he was missing, either.

To me, Tyfen wasn't much different than Hadwin. Hadwin had been all alone, left to suffer without anyone caring for him for two decades. No one had ever come to look for him.

Even if Tyfen wasn't in physical danger right now, was Tyfen's dark vault of a heart really that different from the dark basement Hadwin had suffered in, chained to the wall?

The quiet was too much, though, as we continued our journey. I tenderly took Hadwin's hand back, and leaned into him. He rested his head on mine. Hadwin had overcome his madness from his torture decades ago, and was in a much better place. I hoped and prayed I could see that growth from Tyfen someday.

Hadwin kissed my head and slid his hand to my belly, and despite all the conflict in my heart, I smiled.

39

WARMER WATERS

Every day, I checked in with the emperor. Every day, Tyfen's parents reported they were feverishly looking for him. He *would* be there for his hometown visit.

Every day, I fought tears and breathlessness.

We traversed shifter territory to get to our tour location for the merfolk celebration. The merfolk-designated bay rested at the southernmost continental portion of shifter lands. It was one of many protected bays. Land-walkers were not permitted to sail or fish there.

The one blessing upon our arrival was the soothing of the constantly crashing sea waves, the warmer waters and sand despite autumn's full force up north.

A portion of the bay was shared with a settlement of resort merfolk, though they always relinquished the space for imperial tours to allow us to come together.

My party strode to the elegant resort, Elion's arm reassuringly around me. The fresh sea breeze kissed my skin. We first went inside and were shown to our rooms by the humans and shifters charged with the upkeep of the place. Servants hastily started to unpack the carriages, and our guards set up security. The emperor spoke with the head of staff.

I sat in my room—one of the largest—and gazed out the south-facing window. Sunlight danced upon the water for as far as the eye could see. The bay was much more crowded than usual, and I couldn't deny it was an honor that so many of these merfolk had come to see me and celebrate my child. They normally concerned themselves with illegal fishing in their waters, and the preservation of their bays and islands, their way of life. They literally fought off sharks and deep-sea creatures. They were so disconnected from those of us with legs.

I'd never even met the sea king. The emperor himself had only met with him a handful of times, though he'd explained to me we should not take offense to that. The demands on him were unique as the ruler of his own underwater domain.

A knock at the door startled me, and I rose to open it.

Hadwin stood before me and looked me over. "I'm a little overdressed for the occasion, but that's an interesting choice of clothing, darling." I was still fully clothed, in my travel dress, not my beachwear. Things were still tense between us, but I appreciated his soft attempt at levity.

I folded my arms and tapped my foot on the ground. "How dare you judge my clothing."

He grinned. "Do you want help, or do you want me to wait out here?" We were going to walk down to the bay together. He'd changed into clothing better suited for contact with water, though most of him was still covered to protect him from the sun and to conceal his scars.

Did I want him to join me in my room while I changed? Part of me wanted to push him away, but I shouldn't hurt him just because Tyfen had hurt me. It took me far too long to decide as I stared into his sweet honey-hazel eyes. "Come in."

He entered, and we locked the door and drew the curtains. I pulled a swimming suit from my suitcase. "I'm going to change in the washroom."

Hadwin pursed his lips as he eased down onto the edge of my bed. "I can look away if you'd prefer."

That hurt. And while I *was* a bit shy given the distance between us, I hadn't meant it as a slight.

I cocked my head. "Hadwin?"

"Yes?"

"Your spawn thinks my bladder is a toy to squash. I also need to take a piss."

He flashed me an embarrassed smile, a full one with fangs, as he looked down. "Right."

I relieved myself and changed, then admired the suit in the mirror. It definitely had more fabric than I usually wore when swimming, but it was a two-piece that accented my stomach well. I put my hair up and emerged from the washroom.

Hadwin smiled again, his eyes drawn to my stomach. I walked up to him, and he opened his legs, pulling me closer and resting his hands on my sides. He stared at my stomach, the quiet joy of fatherhood in his expression. It made my heart skip a beat to see him so happy.

"You used to admire my breasts that way. They're getting jealous."

He chuckled and kissed my bare midriff. "I'm always happy to show them my attention, too."

"Good. I'd hate to think you only wanted me for my womb."

He met my gaze. "Please don't joke that way. You know it's not like that."

I frowned. "I know."

"Are we all ready to go see Haan and the others?"

I hesitated. I had to drink so much pig's blood to satiate my cravings, when a simple suck from Hadwin would do the trick. "Can I ... feed off you first?" It would last me all day.

Hadwin stood, his voice soft. "No matter our quarrel, I'll never turn you down, Sonta."

I averted my gaze. "Thank you."

He rolled up his loose, semisheer shirtsleeve and bit his forearm, drawing blood. Putting my lips to the wound, I sucked. His blood coated my tongue, the frigid sensation stimulating me. Hadwin's breathing grew ragged as well.

Feeding off each other was always like lighting a fire near dry kindling.

I couldn't help myself as I backed him onto the bed, straddling him and sucking. His cock was already hard under me, and I wanted to ride him with every fiber of my being. His eyes were red as I ground against him, moving my lips to his mouth. He moaned, groping my ass and thrusting up.

We could be quick...

I summoned all the good sense I possessed, pulling my lips away. "We shouldn't. Everyone's waiting."

"I know," he panted.

I forced myself up, sitting back on his thighs. "I mean it. We can't be rude."

He rubbed his face, blowing out a breath. "I know."

He needed a moment for his hard-on to go away and for the red of his eyes to fade. I got off him, hating that I was wet and fighting my urge to take him.

Hadwin propped himself up. "Can I *please* have you tonight?" he whispered. "I miss you."

I gave him an encouraging smile. "Yes."

It took a few minutes of me rubbing my nipples to make them stop pointing and a few minutes of Hadwin *not* rubbing to make his own signs of arousal go away.

In the end, we calmly left my room, joined the others, and descended an enormous set of stairs to the bay.

The resort was elaborate and bright, with sitting and lounging areas for the land-walkers and pools of various sizes, shapes, and depths that both land-walkers and merfolk could access.

We took the long middle path and met the emperor and Haan at the edge of the water where the artificial pools merged with the sea.

"Sonta." The emperor nodded. He hadn't changed his clothes and likely wouldn't. He was here to observe and pay his respects, not swim. A slew of guards already stood around the chair he'd sit in, where the waves would merely lap at his now-sandaled feet.

It made me uncomfortable to have so many guards here, but I'd been reminded it was all for my safety and not a threat to the merfolk. Most of the non-mages had traded their swords for spears, though, and I couldn't imagine it not coming off as threatening. Then again, if someone kidnapped me on land, the emperor's men could give chase. If they kidnapped me in the sea and dragged me under, I would be irreversibly dead, and rather swiftly.

The ridiculousness of the guards' attire at least lightened the mood. Most had stripped to little more than shorts. Should they need to come into the water, they wouldn't want to be weighed down.

I entered the water, my path a long shallow slope, walking a ways out so Haan could rest more comfortably on the sand beneath the waves. I sat, digging my feet into the sand, and properly greeted him.

"I'm so happy to see you," I said.

His smile was hesitant. "I understand Tyfen's not joining us? He got called to his kingdom on urgent business?"

I gulped air, looking down, trying not to spiral about the lie. "Something like that."

"I'm sorry," he whispered, caressing my calf.

A tear forced its way out, and my breathing picked up. I couldn't have a panic attack. Not here. Not now. "I just need to pretend this isn't happening. Please."

"I can abide that." He cocked his head and gave me a warm, salty kiss.

I forced a smile and discreetly wiped away my tear. "Thank you."

We took a minute reacquainting ourselves, and he gestured to different leaders and even family members. All eyes were on us as we huddled together.

After catching back up, I stood, speaking as loudly as I could, thanking the wonderful merfolk for their time and support. I honored Haan, recounting how strong our friendship was, and assured them Hadwin and I considered their concerns as we prepared to raise our child.

I reached my hand out to Hadwin, and he walked toward us. He hid his terror well. He was still reacquainting himself with swimming in a pool or pond, and had never swum in the sea. Not that I had either, but I wasn't the one terrified of being swept out to sea.

He joined us, held my hand, then quickly acknowledged Haan, giving him an imperial handshake.

Haan turned and swam further out to his people. "Let us be merry as we celebrate the Blessed Vessel, Hoku's chosen father, and the next Anointed Ruler." His airy voice didn't carry far above water, but he gestured in his native sign language, and several of his delegation dove, as well as most of the merfolk, relaying our words underwater.

It was cute, but it was also hard to deny that everything about this stop would be a little inconvenient and different than the others.

Excited tails slapped the water, and groups gathered and parted. I walked a little deeper, and Hadwin followed me, holding on to me for dear life. Tons of merfolk came up to meet us, most for the first time. Some didn't speak very well out of water, or weren't well versed in the imperial language, but their smiles were warm, their curiosity often apparent. I did my best to communicate with the signs Haan had taught me. Many merfolk brought handcrafted gifts, like the shifters had. I was laden with all manner of jewelry made of similar materials to what Haan wore—shells and urchin spines. I was excited to try them out with different looks.

When we broke our meet and greet for lunch, Hadwin and I strode back to the resort, where Gald, Elion, and the emperor met us at a table under a large umbrella. Haan joined us in a tall pool next to us. It felt rude to eat while the merfolk weren't being served, but there wasn't really a need for them to be served. They lived in their buffet, and while the bay was overcrowded for the event, and their prey would be scared away or quickly consumed, I'd watched during our entire meet and greet as hungry merfolk would dive, torpedo far away, and return with something like a crustacean or squid. They were self-sufficient.

"Your Holiness." My personal chef set my dish in front of me. He was happy to have full use of a section of the resort kitchen; we wouldn't need food tasters here.

He lifted the cloche. "The finest the southern sea has to offer."

I swallowed, staring at my plate. I *did* like fish, though not that often, and never like this. But I wouldn't dare offend these people. "Lovely, thank you. And so fresh."

Both Hadwin and Elion fought faces of displeasure. They'd still received blood and rare venison, but they'd also been served seafood. I almost laughed.

"What exactly is this?" I asked the chef, pointing to a crystal bowl with chopped-up bits.

"Prawns and three types of local fish, served raw after a light soaking in citrus juice, with salt and a hint of hot pepper sauce."

I pursed my lips. Raw? "Thank you."

Haan watched, eager for my appraisal of his local cuisine. This was my first time at the sea, and I was going to soak it up.

Schamoi would have *loved* this, after teasing me with a raw prawn before.

Here's to you, old friend.

I lifted a spoonful, eyeing it, then took a bite. It was actually rather good. Fresh and sharp.

Haan approved.

As we ate the rest of our meal, the merfolk prepared for their celebration performances. With every part of my heart, I wished I could dive with them and truly come to them, but I was still excited for what they could offer.

The rest of the day, we enjoyed their skills, both above and below water. One private pool off to the side worked a bit like a reverse tank where we land-walkers could gaze into the sea and view them. The movements of the artistic swimmers were nothing short of a masterpiece, their tails turning and flicking in unison, their scales shimmering different colors, their graceful arms and hair flowing with the fluidity of beings who were one with the water.

As the sun set, obscuring underwater activities, we moved elsewhere. In a large man-made pool, we dipped under the soft waves to witness merfolk music. The resort had these contraptions that covered your face so your eyes didn't burn in the saltwater and you could breathe using a tube. Gald mumbled about how he could have just used his elemental magic to help us breathe so we didn't look stupid, but his magic would have frightened the merfolk.

For the first time, I heard merfolk play their instruments and sing. Even though my ears weren't attuned to it, it was beautiful.

As night fully fell, we wished the merfolk good night. They dove to find suitable kelp beds, and we land-walkers retreated indoors. Haan joined us, though. We held a mini Coterie reunion in and around a large circular pool on the lower level. It seeped a measure of peace into my soul. One by one, we left to slumber in our rooms. Haan slept in the indoor pool, and I excused myself to share my bed with Hadwin as promised.

***

It was truly a vacation, a needed rest from the troubles of this tour. There was no political plotting or strategic planning. It was about fun and learning, soaking up the sun's rays and squishing my toes in the sand. Getting to know these people the best I could and as close to their native surroundings as I could.

The next few days, we branched out, covering more of the bay instead of just staying at the resort. We visited with merfolk basking on the beach, and even ventured further into the water on small boats. The further we went, the more security flocked around me. Haan was always at my side, my own personal guide and guard.

I watched underwater, despite the sting in my eyes, as young merchildren played tag, and keep-away with large shells. I saw the people dive and catch live prey, sucking up small octopus tentacles like noodles. I witnessed an adolescent mermaid brush too closely against a male, and she chased him down and fucked him against some rocks.

After that, I kept closer to the boat, reminding myself I shouldn't let my guard down.

I couldn't have asked for more, given my current situation.

Tyfen still hadn't been found, and we didn't have much time left.

The last night of our visit, I joined Haan in the downstairs pool. The servants had lowered a round table into the center. I lay just above the water, and Haan could swim around it. I wanted to do this with my personal pond in my chambers.

I lay on a sleeping pad, smiling at Haan in the soft glow of fae lights.

He rested his arms and chin on the table.

"I love your eyes, Haan. I'll never get tired of them." Purple was one of my favorite colors.

"Yours are lovely, too. Brown is so rare with my people, and the round center of land-walker eyes is charming." Haan never had anything bad to say.

"I miss you when you're gone. Tell me more about what you've been up to."

He caught me up since our last rest week at the palace.

My mind drifted, and I frowned.

"What's wrong?"

"Do you think your people bought the lie about Tyfen?"

Haan looked uncomfortable. "Few land-walkers are of importance to us. Those of us who have gathered here have done so for me, you, the emperor, and your child. Most probably won't even remember Hadwin's name. I'm sorry to say it, but they couldn't care less that a fae prince has gone missing, and they certainly don't concern themselves about his unexpected absence on tour."

I appreciated the harsh honesty. It was one less thing to worry about—gossip about one of my Coterie members abandoning me.

But it was also a spear to the heart. It seemed like no one cared about Tyfen. The elves wanted him dead. My Coterie was ambivalent about his departure. His own parents were too prideful to allow the emperor to send men to help search for him.

He meant nothing to the merfolk, but Tyfen could *never* mean nothing to me. It haunted me, the arguments we'd had. I'd shoved it in his face that he wasn't even the firstborn fae prince, *only* the second-born. What a bitch.

I'd take back every harsh thing, every questionable decision, just to see and hold him again.

Lost in my sorrow, I didn't even notice my tears flowing, that I'd zoned out.

"Would you like a ... hug?" Haan offered.

I sniffled, wiping away my tears. "I want to cuddle."

He glanced at the table. It was large enough and strong enough for the two of us. "I fear the nearness. I'd worry you might ... rub me."

I didn't give a shit right now if I put him into a sexual frenzy. Live or die, at least I'd go out with a hell of a bang. Of course, the sensible side of me won.

"What if we put a pillow between us? No bumping your scale..."

He smiled. "That would work."

I pulled my pillow from under my head, lying on my arm instead, then slid with my back to the edge of the table. His biceps were so impressively carved as he raised himself and swung his tail and torso next to me, in front of me.

Haan wedged the pillow between us, then kissed my cheek.

"I love you, Haan."

He didn't reciprocate, nor did I expect him to. Merfolk didn't speak that way, but I didn't question his friendship or affection. I imagined he sometimes viewed me a bit like a pet, as comical as it may sound. He had deep curiosity about me, a fondness for his cute little friend. I was a shiny new shell with legs.

I occasionally wished our relationship had more emotional depth to it like my relationships with the others in my Coterie did, but I never held his nature against him.

And sometimes it was nice to not have to fret over a delicate relationship with Haan. My men kept me beyond busy trying to cater to their needs and emotions, and Haan was the least demanding of the bunch.

He was my friend and lover, a sexy and sweet man with mesmerizing eyes and scales. I was grateful for all he gave me, for his flexibility, and for his spirit fitting with mine so well.

"Can I get closer?" I asked.

"Sure. I think we're safe with this pil-low." The word sounded foreign coming from his mouth.

I scooted a bit closer, giving him another kiss. "Merfolk really don't have more sensitive spots than your special scales?"

He narrowed his eyes. "Well ... we *can* be somewhat sensitive with gill play, if you're speaking of arousal."

I perked up.

"But I wouldn't risk it with your pregnancy," he warned.

"No. But someday..."

His grin was as adventurous as mine. "I'm happily committed to you, Sonta, and willing to experiment down the stream."

I giggled. I always loved how merfolk adapted land-walker turns of phrase to suit them.

He brushed a hand against my stomach. "So odd to think you'd be nearly ready to deliver if it were mine."

"Yeah."

Gazing into my eyes, he changed back to our previous subject. "You land-walkers have such fascinating quirks."

"Really? Like what?"

"You're so easily aroused. Like with your mouths." It was clear he still only kissed me as a gesture for my benefit, and I still appreciated that he made the effort.

"What else do you enjoy?" he asked.

Had I just become the pleasure instructor? The student had now become the teacher.

"A simple titillating brush of a finger can go a long way." I grazed his arm ever so slightly.

He seemed unfazed. "Like this?" He reciprocated on my arm, and I got goose bumps.

"Yes. Though for better arousal, gentle touch is best in certain areas of the body."

He nodded, a willing student. "Your people seem so focused on the breasts."

I smiled. "Obviously, our women feed with them like yours do, but they're kind of fun, too... Very sensitive." I pushed the pillow out of the way and took off my top. "Especially here, where it's darker."

He circled my nipple with his finger, checking my expression when my nipple hardened.

My core also heated a bit. "Like that, as well as other things."

My mind drifted to Lilah. Fuck, her breasts were great, and the things she could do with mine...

"What else?" Haan asked. "The other Coterie members often grab your tail's back, er, what's it…" He searched for the word.

"My ass?"

"Yes! Is that arousing?"

"Um…" I screwed up my face. "It's more affectionate than arousing."

He leaned closer, whispering. "But … is the ass not also used a lot in land-walker child-making?"

I gaped, blinking.

Haan averted his gaze, suddenly shy. "Sorry if this is inappropriate."

It was sweet, just surprising. But why would a merman, even in his late forties, understand all the nuances and anatomy of a land-walker? Most smart land-walkers didn't get this close to merfolk.

"Haan, you can ask me anything, and I won't mock you. My body and knowledge are yours. Don't be shy."

He gave me a soft smile, then furrowed his brow. "Can I *see* your ass?"

"Sure." I stripped off my bottoms, now bare as I turned to let him see.

Haan grabbed my cheeks, parting them.

My eyes grew wide. "What are you doing back there?"

"Your excrement exit is in here, right?"

It took every ounce of my self-control to not giggle. "Um…Yes. It's part of our asses…"

He spread me wider, and I bit my tongue. I'd had lovers penetrate me there, but none so closely observe it.

"*It's so big!*"

I *lost* it, laughing far harder and louder than I should.

"What did I say?"

I rolled over, facing him, trying to quiet myself. "You can't just tell a land-walker they have a big asshole, Haan. It's … rude. And weird."

He pressed his lips into a thin line. "Sorry. No offense intended."

I grasped his hand. "None taken. I'm sorry; I'm being childish. I've just never been told that before. But I understand why you would say that."

Merfolk were strictly heterosexual. Many assumed it was because they were so fiercely primal, their bodies and urges guided toward reproduction. It may be an ugly truth, but merfolk younglings were often eaten by larger predators…

Others assumed they just didn't peg their own sex because they didn't have as many fixations and stimulation points as we did, and because their 'excrement exits' indeed were *tiny*. Tits, oral, and anal were all out the window with them.

Haan kept asking me questions. I fought to keep a straight face, but it was sweet that he trusted me. Yes, men like Gald and Findlech did make more use of those exits. Yes, I had too, though I warned him it certainly wasn't a beginner technique, and not one I felt comfortable trying with him. The image of his barbed cock planting itself in there…

I also clarified that I could *not* get pregnant through there.

We eventually moved on, past his fascination with asses. I explained foot fetishes, and he was equally curious. I almost pushed him into the water when he tickled my feet. I then explained that feet were ticklish, and that it was most certainly not a stimulating touch when he grazed his fingers on the bottoms.

We eventually moved on to my female anatomy. He understood the basics, but it was interesting as he explored closer, and even explained how it felt different than taking a mermaid under her special scale. Her version of a clit was internal.

My breath hitched as he stroked my clit with curiosity. Haan liked that reaction.

We revisited the breasts. I explained the various ways we enjoyed them being touched, and that we even enjoyed them being sucked on.

He narrowed his eyes. "I haven't suckled a woman since I was a youngling."

I smirked, already aroused. "If you want to give it a try, let me know."

"I would."

I lay on my back, and he leaned in. His lips enveloped my nipple, and he used his hands to grasp my breast, his mouth stretching and taking in an impressive amount of me.

He sucked.

The feeling was so intense, so immediate—I gasped and swore.

Haan immediately stopped.

A guard called out from the hallway. "Your Holiness?" A few had been stationed for my safety in case things went afoul.

"I'm fine. Nothing's wrong. Go back to your station."

"I hurt you?" Haan asked, worried.

"No. But what the fuck was that?"

"What do you mean?"

I couldn't really compare it to Hadwin's blood play; it wasn't like his sucking had pulled the blood in my veins, but it was something similar.

"Can I feel inside your mouth, Haan?"

"Sure…"

With all our kissing practice, we'd barely done anything with tongues. I carefully put my finger in his mouth, first rubbing the roof of his mouth. It was ribbed.

"Do you gag easily?"

He didn't even know what that meant.

I probed further. He'd taken me deep, and the back of his tongue had little knobs. "Your mouth is normal for your people?"

"Yes…"

Land-walkers were missing out… His ridges and knobs probably helped him eat better, and his sucking was *strong*, but not in a sloppy, painful kind of way.

"That felt amazing, Haan."

His smile was bright. "You'd like more?"

"Yes," I panted. "I'll let you know if I need you to stop."

He took me in again, and I gripped the side of the table in preparation. His sucking and rubbing instantly had my core tightening.

An eager learner, he kept going, also remembering I'd said arousal often worked best when multitasking. He slid a finger to my clit, rubbing there as well.

I chomped down on my knuckle to quiet myself, my legs shaking as my orgasm hit. He kept going, and I had to blurt out that I needed him to stop.

It was too much.

I caught my breath, staring at the fae lights. "You… Shit…" Craning my neck, I looked at him. "You do that so well. I'm never letting you go."

He chuckled, and his husky, airy voice was divine. "It's a little harsh for my ears, but I like your squeals of pleasure, Sonta."

"How often will you visit me at the palace?" I asked. "And … I don't just mean for sexual pleasure."

Haan tucked my hair behind my ear. "It will vary with the season. The winter is more brutal for travel, and that lake on the palace grounds isn't much of a treat when it freezes over. In good weather … one to two weeks per month?"

It was generous considering how long it took him to travel back and forth from the sea. "I'll take anything you're comfortable with. And I know it's not all about sex, but you *do* still want to try again, right? With Gald's help after my birth?"

His grin gave his answer. "You're so warm and soft inside. I loved our spin in the water, and I'll take you as many times as you're willing and safe to do so."

I grinned. Our differences may never let us quite hit the level of emotional intimacy I had with the others, but damned if we weren't going to be a great pair at friendship and fucking…

"One last question," he said.

I cocked my head. "What's that?"

"In the bedding chamber, Elion licked you between your female folds. Do you taste good?"

Oh, shit. Was he going to offer?

My cheeks warmed. "Blessed Vessels *do* taste good to their partners…"

"Can I try?"

"Yes."

Oral from a merman hadn't been on my tour to-do list, but if he had even a fraction of the skill he had with my breasts…

I slid down, my ass at the very edge of the table, my knees bent. Haan splashed into the water and came around. His strong hands holding my thighs, he didn't hesitate.

At all.

He so vigorously ate me out, I worried he was starting to get too stimulated himself. Lost in pleasure, I bit my knuckle again to hide my gasps. He stopped after I came, more slowly dragging himself through my center to finish up. I could now confirm he had the longest and largest tongue of any partner who had dared to dip inside me.

I cooled, clutching my abdomen, and Haan swam around to my face.

"You do taste good."

I giggled. "Glad to know."

"Do you know what you taste like?"

Fuck. What would a merman desire? If he said anything fishy… If my pussy tasted like tuna to the man, I would die from that knowledge.

"Sweet sea grapes," he happily reported.

I blew out a breath. *Thank the stars, and each and every goddess amongst them.*

40

The Devastating Double

Before leaving the resort and bidding all the merfolk goodbye, I had my private farewell with Haan. He promised to teach me gill play down the road, and I was excited.

I *wasn't* excited to leave this beautiful paradise, though.

Tyfen hadn't been found. His parents assured the emperor they were closing in on his location and he'd be there for his part of the tour. We were cutting it close.

No matter his reason for leaving, how was I supposed to face him?

I tried to not be weepy and bitchy, and the rest of my Coterie got the hint to just leave me be.

Each day of travel was long and hard, my heart freezing further each mile we traversed without word of him. He could winnow himself to me right away, joining me in my carriage, but he didn't.

The sun set as we approached the fae border wall. We were permitted entrance, and our convoy pulled to the side and stopped. My heart raced as Hadwin helped me out of the carriage. He gave me a cautious smile; he could sense my anticipation and anxiety more than anyone.

"It'll be fine, no matter what." He kissed me on the forehead.

Haan had said that at our parting, too.

Hadwin and Elion each held one of my hands, Gald standing behind us as we approached a security alcove built into the border wall. The emperor and several guards accompanied us.

Fae security bowed, greeting us, and took us inside.

I was too scared to be excited, too fearful of disappointment.

The stone room was dark, the fae lights glowing low.

A handsome man resembling Tyfen stood before us, his crown larger than the one Tyfen owned.

"Talphus…" the emperor said, all hesitance.

Tyfen's older brother, the crown prince.

Talphus sketched a bow. "Your Magnificence." He turned to me. "Your Holiness." He paused longer, his jaw working as he faced Hadwin. "Your Grace."

Lovely. We were starting this way. No Tyfen and all aggression toward Hadwin.

"Where is your brother?" The emperor did not veil his displeasure.

Talphus did not waver. "The family has decided it's best to make a few changes. He'll meet your party at the Crystal City's gates, instead."

I was too stunned, too numb to react much. We still had a few days' travel to reach the fae castle, where our celebration would begin. The castle was situated within a massive area known as the Crystal City.

"That is not how this works," the emperor ground out. "I should have been apprised of changes on such a sensitive issue."

Talphus bowed again. "Our humblest apologies. It was a last-minute decision. All will be well."

The emperor shook his head. "And what of the citizens, parades, and events on the way? Do your people truly believe he's too busy with matters of state for the imperial tour?"

Pursing his lips, Talphus angled his head. "No. We'll be having you travel a different route for your safety."

That put all of us on edge.

"There have been oni attacks along your original route. I'm sure you understand the need to take extra precautions." He gave Hadwin an unwelcome glare.

The emperor grumbled. "I'll be having words with your parents."

"They anticipate that upon your arrival. We appreciate your flexibility, Your Magnificence." Talphus handed the emperor a scroll. "A map of the new route. Your new accommodations are marked on the route. It's still a bit of a drive tonight, so I won't take more of your time."

He turned to me, his brown eyes meeting mine. "I welcome you to the fae kingdom, Your Holiness. I apologize for the less-than-standard circumstances. I assure you we'll do everything to make your time here comfortable."

"Thank you," I whispered, still numb and confused, not sure what to make of this. I dared to ask for clarification where I knew it might hurt me most. He'd said Tyfen would be there when we reached the Crystal City in a few days. "You found him? He's okay?"

"He'll be there," Talphus repeated.

That was a shit answer that iced my soul.

He glanced at Gald. "Your magic is not welcome here. Please keep it to yourself."

"He is in my Coterie. He's here to celebrate, not harm your people."

Talphus gave me a sickeningly sweet smile that reminded me of his asshole father. "Because he's a member of your Coterie, I do not demand he surrenders his wand for the duration of his stay. Nonetheless, we appreciate Master Gald abiding by our request."

"I can help find Tyfen," Gald said. We were within the borders, and his magic wouldn't face as many barriers past those wards.

With the arrogance of his family, Talphus chuckled. "We have a skilled Demali under our employ. I'm sure you can appreciate we're handling things quite well when it comes to mage magic."

The dig was an uncomfortable one, and not just because it was aimed at Gald. Hoku had been a Demali—a rare type of mage. Demali had the ability to become the most powerful beings, though they could also be as powerless as a regular human. It all had to do with how they used the magic they'd been born with.

The prince wouldn't brag if it weren't a powerful Demali, and how Demali gained their power was often rather unsavory.

Gald wasn't fond of the limitation or insult. "You don't have to be a Demali to—"

I gave him a look, and he halted. "Master Gald is very skilled, and I don't find your demand to be in line with Hoku's ideology, but Gald is more than willing to cooperate, as a token of our desire for unity."

Gald shot me a look. "Sure."

"We appreciate that," Talphus said, tugging on his jacket sleeves. "You'll have to excuse me. I must take my leave. Your innkeeper is awaiting your arrival."

He didn't give us much choice other than to leave once he winnowed away.

Gald grumbled, and the emperor looked none too pleased. I squeezed Gald's hand as we all strode toward the carriages.

"You invited me so I could help," Gald complained in my ear.

"And you will. They're lying to us." I didn't know how much, but they were obviously keeping information from us. I faced Gald. "And I think Hoku would approve of us giving them a taste of their own medicine. Just don't get caught."

I was angry, and hurt, and numb, and screaming inside. I couldn't bear the speculation or commentary I knew the others would offer, so I rode in my own carriage, tears rolling down my cheeks in the dark as we took the new route toward the Crystal City.

As expected, the inn was lovely, prepared for us with fine linens and massive amounts of specialty fruits from the different regions of the fae kingdom. I didn't want to be wooed with fruit. I wanted Tyfen.

I ignored the others and wrote letters to Lilah and my mother, telling them how positively lovely the fae lands were so far... They'd forgive me the lies.

Our new route made me uncomfortable, and even the emperor with his normally stony expression showed a hint of anxiety. We all kept our eyes and ears ready over the next few days as we journeyed. No one lined up for parades along our new route; we were actually *closer* to woods where oni might hide than the original route would have taken us. None of us were really fooled by the lie. We were skipping an entire portion of fae celebrations just so the people wouldn't notice Tyfen wasn't with me. I would have been angrier about that had I been ready for the people to know he'd deserted me. But I wasn't ready to be shamed that way.

I clung to my memories of Tyfen. I often didn't understand his motivations and actions, but he was a *good* man. He always made it up to me and saved me in the end. When he went too far during sex, he always felt like shit. When he made me cry, he always did his best to make things better.

When he made me wait in the middle of the ballroom at the Great Ritual celebration ball, he still showed up, swooping in.

He *would* be waiting for me at the gates of the Crystal City.

My confidence waned, naturally, as we eventually approached the gates. I joined my Coterie in a carriage. Elion and Hadwin held my hands, and I squeezed the feeling out of them.

"Calm yourself," Hadwin said gently. "This stress can't be good for our child."

I glared at him. "Tell me to *fucking* calm down again, and see what good that does you."

I was losing my mind. One day at a time, I was losing my ever loving mind.

He quieted quickly, looking away and rubbing my hand with his thumb.

Gald glanced past the curtain. "It's … so unsettling…"

We'd snapped the curtains shut for the last hour of the ride because I couldn't bear to see the people watch us pull up, but it wasn't really necessary. So few had shown up along the road.

I wanted to vomit, so it was good no one was here to scrutinize me.

Eventually, the carriage lurched to a stop. I had to force myself to breathe normally.

A guard opened the door. "Your Holiness, we're going to have you and His Grace gather with His Magnificence here, and the others will ride on through the gates and wait to rejoin you after the victor's loop."

The victor's loop was just another name for a parade. We'd take an open carriage on a long route around the outer walls of the Crystal City, introducing Hadwin as the victor, and allowing the people to see their prince and the Blessed Vessel together.

My heart calmed the smallest degree. They wouldn't have us get out here and switch carriages unless Tyfen was actually here, ready to join me.

What an asshole to wait until the last moment. I'd never forgive him.

Of course, I would forgive him, eventually, but he had a hell of a lot of explaining and groveling to do.

Hadwin helped me out of the carriage, and I sidestepped a puddle and avoided sticking my boots in the mud. It had rained earlier, and I was grateful the skies had cleared.

Hadwin's cool hand gripped mine tightly as we joined the emperor and followed guards to another sort of security outpost by the main gate.

VENUS COX

"I think that's one of my favorite dresses on you," Hadwin whispered. "You're stunning."

My cheeks warmed. I was grateful for the kindness and distraction. It was the longest dress I owned, down to my ankles. It flowed beautifully with my pregnant body, and still gave a nice hint of my chest. I'd even braided my hair today. It was nowhere as fancy or tight as my servants at the palace could do, but I'd done my best.

Perhaps I was overcompensating. While my nerves were frayed, ready to snap, I wanted to at least *look* put together.

We entered the building and were asked to wait. Only fae guards were in attendance.

My heart raced again with each second I waited.

Two tall masculine figures winnowed in. Prince Talphus and one of his younger brothers. The family resemblance to Tyfen was uncanny, though Talphus had brown eyes and the other brother blue. And of course the tattoos peeking out from beneath their clothing differed from Tyfen's.

The princes greeted us.

"How much longer until Tyfen arrives?" the emperor asked.

Talphus clasped his hands in front of him. "With our sincerest apologies, I have to bear the bad news that we were not able to locate him in time."

My breath hitched, and my stomach churned. "He's..." I gulped air, my heart and lungs racing. "He's not..."

I *was* going to be sick.

I fought it, tooth and nail.

Talphus ordered a guard to get me water, and another guided me to a chair. I sat with Hadwin's help.

My breakfast fought its way up as my ragged breathing made me lightheaded.

"It's okay," Hadwin whispered, holding my hand.

"No—" I swallowed as a guard set a glass of water on a small table near me.

Hadwin pressed his forehead to mine, forcing eye contact. "You're strong. You can do this."

I cried. Like hell I was strong. I hated that word now. Tyfen had lied when he'd called me that.

"We're here for you, darling. How can I help?"

I didn't know, and somehow that had been the wrong thing to say. My memory shot to a time Tyfen had mentioned I had a lot of people who loved me.

Why the hell didn't he? Why the fuck had he not had the consideration to break my heart to my face instead of walking away and stringing me along like this?

He didn't show. He'd left me standing in a ballroom, hundreds looking on, my heart shattered on the floor.

Hadwin's concern was evident, his sweetness and calmness soothing. He slid his cold hand to the back of my neck, and it helped ease my nausea.

I was still fighting for air, barely catching snippets of the conversation between the emperor and Talphus. The emperor made it clear none of the other nations had disrespected us this way, and he would be having a serious conversation with the king and queen.

Talphus calmly replied that they had anticipated that, though he defensively admitted they had been certain they could bring Tyfen back in time, that they were close to locating him, and had deceived us to buy time.

"Here," Hadwin said. "Drink some water."

For all I knew, it was poisoned, but I sipped some.

"We were told the victory loop was still happening. You expect the Blessed Vessel to go on like this?" the emperor asked.

Talphus looked at me. "We canceled the initial parades and cleared the main gate, telling the people Her Holiness was having a rough patch with her pregnancy. They'll understand if she remains a little pale."

Red bloomed in Hadwin's eyes as he snarled his disapproval.

How kind of them to pin everything on me and my child as opposed to their royal family for fucking everything up...

Talphus continued. "Surely the Blessed Vessel is capable of putting aside her personal feelings, for the greater good. I trust Hoku chose her mortal surrogate well. Anyone worthy of a title must sacrifice from time to time."

I could rip off his pointy little arched ears and throw them to the crowd like sweets, tear his arrogant body limb from limb.

Hadwin apparently had the same vision as he ground out, more a threat than anything, "How very *giving* of you."

A hint of defensiveness rose in Talphus's callous voice as he told us he was simply trying to remain professional and make the most of the situation.

"So, she and Duke Hadwin are to take the victory loop *alone*?" the emperor asked. "Without your brother? How will you excuse his absence if you've blamed everything on her?"

The younger brother finally spoke again. "I'll stand in for him. I have strong glamour magic."

It was only then I realized he wore Tyfen's crown.

The brother added more shyly, "It's against the law to pretend to be a member of the royal family, but we can break our own rules..."

The emperor sighed, looking at me. They *all* looked at me. *To* me. Waiting for my answer because it was my choice.

They had put me in a shit position. Instead of tainting their own appearances before their own people or the rest of the realm, they'd made me the scapegoat. I could either be complicit in their ruse with his imposter brother, or we could cancel the victory loop and it would be blamed on my 'mortal frailty.' It was already borderline racist to tell the people my pregnancy was taking a toll on me when the public *knew* Blessed Vessels had historically healthy and easy pregnancies. Without a doubt, many fae—many who didn't even recognize their own bias—would think somehow my own child was poisoning me with its 'wicked and unnatural' vampire venom.

As much as I wanted to shrink and hide, I couldn't. I wasn't sure how I felt about Tyfen and his reputation right now, but I needed to preserve my own, and Hadwin's and our child's.

I forced myself to stand, wiping away my tears. "Let's get this over with."

The emperor spoke to Hadwin while Tyfen's younger brother approached me. "Prince Tailar, Your Holiness. It's … nice to meet you. I wish it could have been under better circumstances."

"Thank you," I whispered.

After the briefest chat, we set out for the open carriages. I sat in the front next to Tailar, Hadwin behind us. The emperor, following tradition, took his own carriage behind us.

How does one smile as they spiral into a deep darkness, shards of their heart falling into a pit?

Talphus had one thing right. I did have a title. I'd faked smiles before, and I could do it again. One forced muscle at a time.

It had been chilling to watch Tailar glamour his appearance, putting on the tattoos I'd traced on his brother before and after making love. His new green eyes wedged a knot in my throat.

And that crown. It was wrong for someone to wear another's crown. It felt dirty and abhorrent.

It was as wrong as letting a crown sit on the floor, damaged.

The carriage started, the horses whinnying. The crowd already roared in the distance where the closest citizens spied us.

Tyfen had once been distraught, had holed himself up in his room and damaged his crown, leaving it on the floor. He'd told me he didn't care about serving his people anymore.

Perhaps I should have believed him.

He'd once told me that beyond his task to impregnate me, I meant nothing to him.

Perhaps I should have believed him.

"I really am sorry about this," Tailar said. "It wasn't my choice." His smile mirroring my own didn't match his genuine tone.

"Thank you." We waved as we approached the beginning of the route for the victory loop, and Hadwin rested his hand on my shoulder from the bench behind us.

Happy trumpets announced our start.

"If you're all right with it…" Tailar spoke. "For appearances… You could lean on me, or … some type of mild affection. For the people. For Tyfen." After a moment of silence, he held out his hand.

It *looked* like Tyfen's hand, but it wasn't. I knew the feeling of his body and the soul it housed, and it wasn't Tyfen's.

Tyfen had broken my heart previously, telling me before an important event with onlookers that he was not ready for the realm to know we were together.

Perhaps I should have believed him.

That night, I'd let Tyfen hold me as we danced, forcing a smile for the people. I was a public servant, a vessel, and I could do it again.

I took Tailar's outstretched hand, and he held it up for the fae to see.

41
A Mother's Love

The victory loop took forever. I was genuinely surprised the people were so excited to see us, especially since Hadwin was the father. I asked Tailar about that.

"The people love Tyfen. It's been months since they've seen him. And they're happy to see him settled down with a respected woman."

I choked down fresh tears, and didn't ask more questions. I loved him too. But settled down with me? Apparently not.

It reminded me of the fae servant I'd asked about the nickname Tyfen had called me in his sleep. She'd been *so* excited to hear him calling me a sweet name like that. Granted, he hadn't meant to call me 'my dearest'…

How could the elves want him dead when his own people loved him so much? The fae people's admiration reminded me of Findlech's people's admiration for him…

By the time we finally turned into the Crystal City and parked at the castle, my stomach had calmed from the earlier shock, but I was starving.

The emperor wasted no time, storming into the castle while Hadwin helped me get down and hugged me.

"You did well," he whispered.

He, Tailar, and I strode into the castle, greeted at the main entrance by a hesitantly curious Gald and Elion.

Tailar dropped his glamour, removing Tyfen's crown as the large doors shut behind us.

Gald and Elion instantly gaped. They'd been fooled like the people, assuming Tyfen had actually been at my side.

I turned to Tailar. "I appreciate your kindness and consideration for my feelings, and I … don't want to hurt Tyfen's reputation, but holding hands is as far as I'm willing to take this. I won't kiss you or dance with you. I want your brother."

He nodded. Talphus entered through a grand hallway. "Well done. We'll have time to discuss further alterations to the celebrations planned this week once the emperor and my parents are done hashing it out."

"I deserve to be in that meeting."

Talphus shook his head. "It's a closed-door meeting."

Elion took my hands, kissing my cheek. "You have to be starved."

"Lunch is ready when you are, in the smaller dining hall." Talphus gestured to a servant. "Please do see the Blessed Vessel and her Coterie are made comfortable."

Tailar gave me a shy but friendly smile, holding up Tyfen's crown. "I'm going to return this, then I'll join you all."

Eventually, both Talphus and Tailar met up with us, as well as Tyfen's three sisters—the full set of fae princes and princesses minus the one I cared most for. It was beyond awkward as we picked at our food. It was rich and hit the spot, but not much beyond basic introductions passed between us. I'd quickly explained the circumstances to Gald and Elion before the others had arrived for lunch.

Elion made a valiant attempt to be sociable with the fae royal family as we lunched by commenting on the wonderfully fresh citrus. Talphus muttered that we should enjoy it because most of their citrus crops had been wiped out by a blight. His siblings all averted their gazes at that report, as though they were all ashamed he'd brought up a failing on their part. Gald reminded them there were many mages gifted by Danah who could help heal such agricultural problems, and all he got was a glare from Talphus about using mage magic.

Apparently, they were a sensitive bunch about agriculture…

The emperor, king, and queen were taking their time in their closed meeting, and the rest of us sat twiddling our thumbs as we waited.

Servants showed us to our Coterie rooms, and I took the opportunity to lie down for a bit. My men cuddled with me, very few words exchanged between us.

Eventually, Hadwin and I were summoned. We were taken to the emperor's guest chambers and sat to discuss this disaster with him.

He'd thoroughly reprimanded the king and queen, and they *finally* allowed the emperor to send a small troop of imperial soldiers to help with the search for Tyfen. The king and queen only allowed it under the condition the soldiers wore fae attire, so as to not spook the people. They were still too concerned about their own appearances.

But at least it was something, and if they had more manpower, and were genuine about zeroing in on Tyfen's location, he may be brought back anytime. I couldn't imagine how our conversation would go when they dragged him here and we had it out, but we'd cross that bridge when we got there.

VENUS COX

We discussed the proposed activities Hadwin and I, and Tailar would be attending. I didn't want to do any more fake appearances with Tyfen's body double, but I also didn't want to feed the narrative that I was weak. We met in the middle, with the caveat things may change once Tyfen returned.

We would tour an important park, pay our respects at a few temples, and make a few other minor appearances. Tailar couldn't disguise his voice well to mimic Tyfen, and I'd already noticed a few odd mannerisms that didn't fit Tyfen's personality. I wasn't sure the public would notice all that, though; it may have just been lover's intimacy that granted me those reminders. Either way, all our temporary plans involved distance between us and the public, no big speeches, and minimal shows of affection.

Dinnertime eventually came, and my mouth watered for the divine fae cooking I'd already sampled, but my anxiety remained from the emotionally exhausting day. We were obliged to attend a larger banquet tomorrow, but our reception dinner had been altered to only include my party and the royal family. A relaxation for my 'weak' body...

Gald had secretly performed a tracking spell before dinner, but it had not given us a much more reliable location for Tyfen than we'd already known.

Talk was minimal at the family and Coterie dinner, the food still divine.

The queen spoke, breaking the silence. "We're so terribly sorry, again, Your Holiness, for your first visit to our kingdom. We pray you won't hold this against us."

I chewed my food, looking down at my plate.

"And, of course, we extend our apologies and congratulations to you as well, Duke Hadwin," she added.

My mind raced as I speared another crispy potato wedge. Every single feeling and speck of logic inside me constantly collided. About Tyfen and this whole situation. About my duty. About Hadwin. This wasn't fair to Hadwin, our child, or me. But how much was Hadwin to blame for Tyfen leaving in the first place? Even if his harming Tyfen was only a contributing factor?

After an uncomfortable moment of silence, and Hadwin's soft acceptance of the queen's apologies and congratulations, I looked up.

I forced a smile. "This is some of the finest cuisine I've had in all the realm. I thank you. And it's lovely getting to meet the rest of Tyfen's family..."

Shy smiles shone my way from Tyfen's four younger siblings and a couple of their partners. Talphus more regally nodded, quite content with himself. His proximity to his father at the table reminded me what kind of a man he was, how his father had spent over two hundred years guiding him to be like himself. Had Talphus been a bully to Tyfen the way their father had been at the palace?

The king cleared his throat. "I would like to echo my mate's sentiments. We appreciate your flexibility in these less-than-ideal circumstances. It is a pity Tyfen has shamed us when we'd hoped you would have a beautiful future together."

Tyfen shamed them? He did. But they'd understood he hadn't wanted to be in my Coterie in the first place, and had forced him to be. Had they really hoped we would have a beautiful future given those circumstances?

I wanted to wring Tyfen's neck for leaving me high and dry like this, for leaving me at all. But this wasn't his fault alone.

"Perhaps things would be different had he wanted to be with me in the first place." I cocked my head.

The king cut into a large slab of venison. "We *are* very sorry for the rocky start, Your Holiness. Tyfen's ... unconventional behavior was all due to a bit of anxiety on his part."

That was horse shit, and we all knew it. A proud fae prince wasn't a shy, cowering man riddled with anxiety.

I smiled wryly at the king. "I got to know your son well enough to understand much of him. I've forgiven him our rocky start at the beginning of the Great Ritual. But I have to ask myself what kind of stories I will tell my child in their formative years." I swallowed, allowing myself to make a bit of a scene. "I do not plan to lie to my child, the one who you will someday swear your allegiance to on bended knee. What shall I tell them about my first visit to the beautiful fae kingdom, and how it felt to be missing my fae Coterie member?"

With a calm and assertive voice, he said, "We're doing everything we can to bring him back home. There is only so much—"

"*Is* there only so much you can do? When you've *only now* allowed His Magnificence's troops to assist yours in the search? And so few of them?"

The emperor raised his eyebrows, rather enchanted with his goblet of wine, keeping out of the discussion.

The king straightened, not pleased to be interrogated at a family dinner. "We have our reasons."

I shouldn't say anything. I shouldn't. But I was angry and hurt. I hated him right now. His whole family, everyone and everything. Tyfen had taken a piece of my heart, and they should have tried better to bring him back.

"Perhaps Tyfen has his reasons for not wanting to come here for the celebration," I said. "I would probably stay away, too, had my father told me I was *replaceable*."

King Bretton's eyes fully snapped to mine.

I raised my goblet of water. "Or did I misunderstand when I overheard you tell him that in the palace?"

The king's expression darkened. "You—"

His wife rested a hand on his. Her gaze raked over me, then the emperor and back. It was hard to decipher her expression, but she was definitely assessing the situation.

"Your Holiness," she muttered, "let us please remember there is a time and place for this all." She looked about the room, indicating the others in attendance.

She wasn't wrong. I had no tact or diplomacy in the moment. No matter; I'd made my point well enough. I did feel bad, though, once I noticed one of Tyfen's sisters silently wiping away a tear. The other three younger siblings had their eyes on their plates.

I gazed at the queen again, and her look sparked a reminder in me that she and I were already coconspirators. I'd convinced her to lie to her husband about Tyfen's previous injuries, and here I was humbling him in front of his family.

I nodded. "Of course. My apologies for the timing. I'm sure it's all the travel getting to me."

Don't say it.
Don't say it.
Don't say it.

"And the stress of this *unnaturally* difficult pregnancy."

She pursed her lips at the lie.

Elion coughed. He'd bent me over backward every which way and with plenty of fervor lately. I wasn't frail.

He cleared his throat. "This really is exquisite food." His happy albeit exaggerated smile eased the tension. "My parents always told me your chefs were fantastic, and I wouldn't dare to slight the palace's chefs, but this is quite amazing..."

So far, the king and queen were being surprisingly accommodating to my other Coterie members, likely to compensate for Tyfen's absence.

"The blood is also ... quite nice..." Hadwin added.

I almost laughed at that.

"And I'm rather looking forward to dessert," Gald chimed in.

The emperor dabbed his mouth with a napkin. "I do hope we can all enjoy a sweeter ending to a less than savory day."

He had his quiet and subtle ways of reminding me of my calling, of being my mentor. I wasn't here to conquer or dominate. I was here to keep the peace in the realm.

"I'll make sure to save room for dessert." I offered the queen a more genuine smile.

She nodded, letting the king's hand go.

Elion, my sweet, sweet Elion, spoke again, asking one of Tyfen's sisters a question. Hadwin rested his hand on my thigh under the table. Tension eased as we ate and chatted more.

I kept mulling over my thoughts, and the occasional glance from the king and queen. Dessert eventually arrived. As I reached for a cream-stuffed pastry, I looked at the queen again.

"Your Majesty, would you be willing to take me on a more private tour of your magnificent castle after dinner? I'd like to walk off all this rich food."

"Of course, Your Holiness."

***

I clasped my hands in front of me as the queen led me through the corridors. I'd asked if I'd be permitted to see Tyfen's private chambers. Had he been here, we would have had a hell of a great time in there, anyway…

"He *does* care for you," she assured me. "And I'm sorry his actions have hurt you."

I frowned. I didn't know what to believe anymore. Deep inside, I *knew* Tyfen loved me. You can't be that intimate—sharing jokes and dreams, the looks and whispers—without truly caring for someone. But my hurt pride and confusion were starting to bury that knowledge.

"How can you be sure?" I asked.

Her smile was warm. "I know my son. And he said so."

I swallowed. "He told you he…" He wouldn't have used the word 'love'… "That he cares for me?"

"Of course. You were right there…" She hummed. "I forget. We were in that palace infirmary, and you were keeping him company in his bed. He told me how much you meant to him."

I blinked. "Oh…" I'd forgotten. He'd joked that he'd told his mother he liked my tits and pussy, or something equally silly, but it had been in Fae, so I hadn't really known what he'd said.

"I thought it would work out well for you two," the queen said, her voice full of regret.

"Me too." I had to choke back tears trying to press their way out.

She rested a hand on my arm. "And it may still work out…"

I stopped as we neared the end of Tyfen's private hallway. "Would your husband hurt Tyfen? I was out of line at dinner, but I know what I heard your husband threaten, that he'd cut out Tyfen's tongue. His disappearance…"

The queen shook her head. "My husband may have a temper, but he would not hurt Tyfen like that."

I wasn't so sure. How much of her loyalty had been earned by her husband—her fae mate? How much could a man like that intimidate his own wife into submission?

"Your daughter seemed rather worried when I mentioned your husband's behavior toward Tyfen."

Queen Lourel crossed her arms. "She loves Tyfen. She's worried about him. We all are." Her voice was firm, though not fully cross. "But she's not worried her father would harm her brother. If you'd like, I can show you the dungeon to prove he's not there, though I don't know how else to prove to you our innocence in his disappearance. You may lay the blame for Tyfen's behavior at our feet for sending him when he was not ready to be in your Coterie, but your suggestion of foul play at our hands is insulting and ludicrous, Your Holiness."

She stood unyielding, and I respected that.

"Plus," she added, "I'm sure your mage partner has already ignored our request to not use his magic on our premises…"

I guiltily looked down.

"Exactly... And I trust he hasn't learned more than we have."

I gazed into her eyes again. "If all you know is that he's in your kingdom, why do you keep saying you're getting close? That's not close at all."

She pursed her lips. "We're certain he's in the Dark Forest."

My eyes widened. "Why would he be there?" More oni and unicorns were believed to be hidden in that giant forest than in the rest of the entire realm.

She took a moment to answer. "He knows that forest well from his duties. And he's... Based on previous behavior, we believe he's there. Our Demali has confirmed that region, as she's no doubt more powerful than your mage partner."

Based on previous behavior? My heart stuttered, not sure of the insinuation. "If the royal family is not involved in his departure, and he knows the forest well, does that mean he truly chose to leave me? I don't know whether to be wounded by his spurning or fearing for his life. I need to at least know he's safe."

She frowned again. "As much as it might pain you to hear it, I do hope it's as simple as him leaving you. But all I know right now is that his heart beats, and I want my son returned safely just as much as you do." Tears coated her eyes. "Mother to mother, I want my son to be okay. I swear on my life, we are doing our best. That includes finding him safely and quickly."

I nodded. "I appreciate that."

Wiping away her tears, she sniffled. "Would you still like to see his room?"

"Yes please."

We strode to the end of the hallway, and she opened the door to his bedroom. We walked in together, and I took it all in. Tyfen's room was larger than what he had at the palace, and thoroughly decorated.

The décor hit me in the heart. His room at the palace had barely been decorated at all, despite his ability to furnish and adorn it any way he'd wished.

But the same green tufted pillow sat on his shelf here, holding his crown. I stepped toward it and stopped at the edge of his bed instead. I wanted to sleep here. I craved his arms around me, his skin against mine. I wanted to hear him call me Blantui, or bitch, or greedy cunt, or any fucking thing that reminded me we *were* meant to be together.

I wanted to whisper stories about our childhoods under the covers again.

Wrapping my arms around the bedpost, I stared at the empty bed, my heart echoing that vast space of lost potential.

"He left me," I whispered.

The queen said nothing.

"He didn't just leave me," I said. "He *left* me."

"He cares for you," she whispered.

I faced her, fighting tears. "He sent his things here. Why would he do that if he ever intended to return to my side?"

Her throat bobbed. "I can't say. Don't read into it until we've had a chance to sort things with him."

After another moment of staring at the bed, I peeled myself from the bedpost, continuing to Tyfen's crown.

I carefully picked it up, remembering how handsome he was when he wore it. Especially the time we had sex in our crowns.

'We both wear crowns,' he'd said once, talking about how well we fit together.

I ran my finger over the metal.

"We generally consider it ... bad luck ... to touch another's crown," the queen gently reminded me.

I held the crown a moment longer, focusing on the dent from when he'd thrown it in his room at the palace. "Yes, sorry. I told him to have the emperor's man repair this, but he didn't get around to it…"

She approached, squinting, and I handed her the crown. "That's a shame. We'll have that taken care of."

"Great." I stepped back. "Do you mind if I look more through his things?"

Compassion was written on her face as she put the crown back. "It feels awkward to allow you in here without his presence, because I know you care for each other, but…" She shrugged slightly. "If you're looking for evidence of why he left, nothing here will help you. Nothing is missing, and nothing was added to. He took the clothes on his back and his sword."

I sighed. Yes, I wanted evidence, but I also wanted to simply look around. Perhaps this room would teach me more about the troubled past Tyfen kept hidden from me. I'd like to understand him more. "I won't touch anything."

"Very well."

I glanced about, slowly making my way around the room.

"Do you know how Tyfen's crown got damaged?" she asked from behind me.

I blinked, my focus ripped from a portrait of him as a little boy. "I, uh…" He'd told me when I'd discovered it that way that he didn't care about his obligation to his people anymore. His mother didn't deserve to hear that part; he'd been drinking, obviously in a bad place.

"I don't think he ever told me." I offered her a polite smile with the lie.

She offered no smile in return. "You suspected my husband of harming my son. And I know my son, and have my theories, and understand he's made enemies over his years, but…" She narrowed her eyes. "Was my son wearing his crown when he 'fell down the stairs' at the palace?"

Oh shit. How did this get looped back to that?

"No. He wasn't wearing his crown when that happened."

"I'm not a fool, Your Holiness. While I know my son has a propensity for drinking away his problems and ... other things… He's not physically weak. The timing of his severe injuries and the way things were handled are clearly not in line with your story."

I didn't know what to say to that. She was calling our bluff.

"Who hurt my son?"

Looking away, I shook my head. "It was an accident; we didn't lie about that."

Her voice grew more harsh. "My son is missing. You knew him for two goddess-damned months; I've loved him for more than two centuries. Do not lie to me."

Meeting her gaze again, I wrapped my arms around my growing belly. I didn't need centuries to love fully and deeply. Not with Tyfen, or Hadwin, or any of the people in my life.

"Was it Lord Findlech?"

"No," I ground out. "I swore on my child's life that Findlech never hurt Tyfen, and I stand by that."

"Then *who*? I deserve to know."

I could never be mad enough to betray Hadwin. The fae wouldn't understand, and he didn't deserve punishment for my sexual stupidity. "No matter the why or the how, I swear it again—it was an accident. Not a single person in the palace wants to harm Tyfen."

"I deserve the truth," she implored.

Drawing a breath, I tried to think of what to say. I could understand her fear. If there was another threat out there trying to off her son, perhaps they'd convinced him to go into the Dark Forest alone?

But that wasn't the case. There was no indication the vampire delegation had learned of the attack, and even if they somehow cared, Hadwin had been the aggressor...

"Please, Your Majesty, don't spend your time searching for a threat that isn't there. Tyfen would have remained safe if he'd stayed at the palace." I hesitated. "You keep suspecting Lord Findlech of foul play, though, and I think we both know why. He's not guilty."

"You'll have to excuse me for my hesitation on elf matters." She adjusted some lace curtains in the window.

"Just because the high lord wants your son dead does not mean Findlech does."

The queen's eyes widened. "You know of that?"

"I do."

She approached me slowly, as though I might bite if she rushed. "How much do you know? Who told you?"

How much did I know? As much as I'd just uttered. And there was no use giving her my source. "*Why* do the elves want your son dead? And how likely is it they're connected to his disappearance?"

She nervously eyed me for a moment. "If you don't know why, then it's not my place to say. As for his disappearance, it's possible, though not probable."

Talking with politicians could be so useless sometimes...

"I deserve to know why, Your Majesty. As his partner and as the daughter of Hoku. How can I help keep the peace if I don't know all the facts? About the war that almost happened. I know he was somehow involved. And I'm assuming it's related to the price on his head."

She shook her head. "I cannot say."

I wanted so much to like this woman, and at times I truly did feel a connection with her, but I was tired of people keeping things from me. "I'm powerless without the truth. I won't judge him for whatever he may have done. I'm not like that. I just want to understand."

"It's not the right time. And I'm not the right person."

I wasn't sure which was rising faster—my anger or my desperation. "This is cruel. I love him. He's sworn to me. Even if he does not love me, I won't punish your people for that. But I need him to be okay. And I need to understand the troubles of the realm I'm bringing my child into!"

"Cruel?" She paused, calm and sorrowful again. "It's best for you to stay out of that matter right now." She was starting to sound like Findlech with his ancient arrogance. "And perhaps it's not as simple as kindness versus cruelty. Perhaps the truth is wrapped in both, and I opt to offer the least painful."

I huffed. "Just because I am a young mortal does not mean I am a child."

She closed her eyes. "No, you are not. But the situation is highly nuanced." She opened her eyes again. "Despite what you think, I respect you and your position. I admire Hoku greatly, and the trust she places in you. And I trust that when you say my son's injuries were an accident, you do so out of a good place in your heart and mind. Because I *know* it was a lie. I spoke to the servant who suffered through Tyfen's pain with the feintal magic, and the injuries didn't line up. I understand my son was glamouring his injuries to hide the truth. And you're obviously covering for someone you think deserves it. Please extend me the same courtesy. If the details of Tyfen's unfortunate past with the elves were helpful to you right now, I would share them. But the fact of the matter is, it is better for Tyfen, for you and your child, for the whole realm to let that matter go unnoticed." Her voice and expression held firm determination. "I cannot give you what you ask for. And it is not out of a place of superiority or cowardice or arrogance."

My shoulders slumped at the finality of her declaration. It was like bashing my head against the wall. "You said it's not the right time, and you're not the right person. When will it be the right time? And who is the right person?"

She rested a hand on my arm. "Tyfen would be the one to talk to about that, when he's ready. I hope…"

A haunting memory shadowed my heart. He'd let me in someday? With his self-professed 'dark vault of a heart'?

I blew out a breath. "Why did you force him to join my Coterie when he didn't want to? And if the elves want him dead? Did you think I'd be a shield and they'd simply forgive him his crimes because he was assigned to me?"

True sorrow shone in her eyes. "My husband had the last word on that decision. And while I can understand some of his reasoning…" She pursed her lips. "I convinced myself it would be good for Tyfen. He … could have a chance at love, at a new life. And while we knew it wouldn't be ideal in some ways, I did hope his new status would eventually be to his benefit." She whispered, "I want him to be happy. He deserves to be happy."

I choked down a lump in my throat. Tyfen wanted to be happy, too.

'Maybe I deserve to be happy, Sonta. I deserve to fucking be happy. I've done enough. I've paid enough. I want to be happy! Is that so wrong?'

I was willing to make him happy. He hadn't given me the chance…

"I should go to bed," I said.

"Sure."

"Before I do, I just need to know…" I was tired of getting stonewalled, but I had to try. "A mother can love her son despite his faults, and a politician can lie for their own interests, but I want to know, woman to woman; does your son deserve my love and loyalty?"

"Yes."

"Because he's accused of a crime worthy of death. And I deserve to know the man I've given part of my heart to. Are we talking he accidentally stepped on a sacred beetle, or he tried to conquer the elf nation single-handedly?"

She gave me a pained smile. "My son made a mistake. He may be foolish or hotheaded at times, but he is not malicious. His actions had unfortunate consequences he pays for daily, but we fae would never call what he did a crime, would never sentence someone to death or treat them so cruelly as what…" She stopped herself. "He's a *good* man. Any woman would be lucky to have his heart, even a sacred figure such as yourself, Your Holiness."

That was enough for me.

42
Unresolved Business

Our week in the fae kingdom was both the shortest and longest week of the imperial tour and of my life. I made my public appearances with Tailar and Hadwin, and I felt guilty for the lie, and for the more humble representation for Hadwin and his people. To Hadwin's credit, he reassured me he'd be fine.

But Tyfen hadn't been found. The morning of our last full day, Gald did his usual tracking spell, and we both got excited to see a more definite location under the pendulum. Tyfen was very clearly in the Dark Forest as we'd suspected.

It was hard to watch the servants pack up the next morning. I was all jittery. I didn't want to go, but I understood how this worked.

We stood near the castle's main doors, saying our goodbyes.

"I assure you, we'll send word as soon as he's found," the queen said. "Anytime now."

"Thank you," I breathed.

I gave my required polite farewell to the king—we'd mostly avoided conversation since I'd called him out on his shit the first night.

Turning to Tyfen's siblings, I smiled. I still didn't care for Talphus, but I'd spent some quality time with the others while we were holed up here. The younger four siblings had shared fond memories of Tyfen. Despite telling the queen I'd accepted her decision to not disclose more about Tyfen's past indiscretions, my nosy ass had tried to pry information out of his siblings. I'd been met with shy clamped mouths each time. They obviously knew more but were under the same gag order.

This time, the gates to the Crystal City were teeming with citizens excited to see us off. We weren't going to hide Tyfen's absence on our return to the palace, but our ruse continued. They'd been told Tyfen was staying behind for official business, and he would winnow to the palace to rejoin the rest of the Coterie soon. The king and queen rode out to say goodbye publicly, and Tailar kissed my hand goodbye.

I gave him a hug. Were it under different circumstances, I really would enjoy him as a sort of brother-in-law.

"Be safe, Sonta." He squeezed me tight.

"Thank you." I pulled back. "No offense, but I hope I never see you like this again," I said through a smile people couldn't easily lip-read.

Tailar chuckled, an unnatural chuckle that would never match the face he wore with this glamour, the face of the man I loved. "I mirror that desire."

I kept my false smile and got into my carriage. And our party left, waving out the windows. It was a good hour before the heavy crowds died down.

Heaving a sigh, I settled into my seat.

"I wish I could have stayed just one more day." I frowned. For the first time in a long time, I *actually* believed Tyfen's discovery was right around the corner.

"You know that's not an option," Hadwin said. "They promised they'd send word."

I huffed. Of course I knew it wasn't an option to stay. Had I stayed even one day longer than my expected tour duration, people would make assumptions. Either that I truly was weak with a rough pregnancy, needing more rest before travel, or that I favored the fae, opting to stay in their lands at the end of the tour.

My temper flaring about being reminded of the obvious, and in such a dismissive way, I glared. "The queen knows someone assaulted Tyfen, Hadwin."

His eyes reddened and widened.

"And she knows I'm lying for that person. So don't treat me like I'm *stupid*. I understand we can't stay."

He looked down, not saying a word.

I instantly felt like shit. I had to remind myself he didn't have a ton of experience with romantic relationships, and honestly, this was my first time trying to juggle so many partners. I was on edge, and he often said the wrong thing when he was simply trying to be helpful.

Gald sighed. "I wish they would have taken me up on my offer days ago… He'd probably be back by now."

Gald had made an offer on behalf of the mages to help search for Tyfen in the forest. The king and queen had bluntly turned him down. Magistrate Leonte would have had to approve official human troops, which were a combination of mages and nonmagical humans, but Gald had enough pull within his order that he could have rounded up enough resources separately. He'd even offered to do it under the guise of unicorn research since the Dark Forest was believed to house most of the few remaining unicorns; he naturally crafted his story like the politician he was. He didn't care about Tyfen other than wanting to make me happy.

But the fae wouldn't risk their reputations by accepting mage help aside from their precious Demali.

The ride was quiet and uncomfortable. My heart darkened over the next few days as I waited for word. Gald still performed his tracking spells daily, but the results weren't as precise as they had been that one morning.

I hoped and prayed, biting my nails to nubs.

Two days after we left the fae border behind us, we pulled to the side of the road for a lunch break.

I stretched my legs, nibbling on finger sandwiches and downing a vial of pig's blood; Hadwin and I had barely spoken two words to each other. We weren't exactly angry at each other, but we both recognized we were at odds, and speaking right now only drove us apart.

A guard stirred, sounding the alarm. "Fast approaching!"

Everyone glanced at the road behind us, a small troop of soldiers on swift horses racing toward us. They carried the emperor's flag.

My heart skipped a beat, and I dropped the rest of my food.

They'd found Tyfen. He had been missing for three and a half months, and he had *finally* been found!

I held my hand out behind me. "Gald!" He could take me straightaway to the castle to see Tyfen. "Gald!" My mind raced.

Goddess, I missed Tyfen. Tears pricked at my eyes as my mind went blank.

Gald took my hand, standing behind me.

The soldiers slowed and stopped, and I ran to the one at the front, tugging Gald with me.

"They found him? He's back at the castle?" I couldn't contain my excitement.

The soldier gaped, glancing between me and the emperor as he approached.

"Prince Tyfen has been located?" the emperor asked.

The soldier bowed. "No, Your Magnificence, Your Holiness. We were … sent away. The royal family said they were close enough to locating him themselves and sent us on. We've come as extra security for your return to the palace."

My heart beat rapidly, this time not out of joy. "No. No. They said…"

The emperor pinched the bridge of his nose.

"No!" I wasn't going to accept that shit. "No. They accepted our help. You shouldn't be here until the job is completed. Go back."

The soldier gave me an uncomfortable look. I didn't issue military orders, but I didn't care how stupid I sounded.

"Go back and make them accept your help."

"Sonta." The emperor's tone attempted to soothe me.

I jabbed a finger at him. "Make them go back. They said we could help. If Tyfen isn't home safely, then the job isn't done."

"That is not an order I will make, and you know that."

Gald wrapped his arms around me. "It'll be okay, love."

"No it's fucking not!" I stared at the emperor, fuming. "Make the king and queen listen to you."

I would never go so far as to call the emperor a friend, but we were allies, and family in Hoku's divine lineage. While our personalities didn't mesh all that well, he was one of my mentors, and he had assured me years ago that he took his charge seriously to protect me and guide me, so that I may serve well and raise my child to be worthy of the position they would fill.

I *needed* him to make good on his words, because my Coterie was on thin ice, and it was cracking along with my heart.

Instead of asserting his authority to do the right thing, the stupid pointy-eared man offered me his best approximation of pity or compassion. "We are in a time of peace. An emperor does not march into one of his territories uninvited without a serious reason, Sonta. I do not have such a reason to override the king and queen's wishes in their own lands regarding their own family."

"Callous bastard."

"Sonta!" Gald chastised in my ear.

I couldn't stop the tears as I jerked out of Gald's arms and marched to one of my carriages, slammed the door, locked it, and snapped the windows closed.

I screamed, bawling, and I didn't give a shit if everyone could hear me. I was exhausted from the fae lies. The queen was a lying bitch, and I'd bought her lies and tears about caring about her son, about respecting me. They wouldn't have sent our soldiers away before the job was done had she been telling the truth.

I couldn't keep going on this way, getting my hopes up just to have them shattered time and time again.

Something had to give. A desperate part of me wished I could choose not to care.

But I did. Tyfen had earned my affections so dearly, so deeply I hadn't even understood it before the imperial tour started.

Something *had* to give. But it would not be my hope or my love for him.

43

Lilah's Surprise

I rode alone in my carriage the entire rest of the trip back to the palace. The Pontaii Palace was my home, and I craved its familiarity and warmth to help ease my constant anxiety.

Gald had even stopped doing tracking spells, and I couldn't blame him. I wasn't easy to be around right now.

I strode to the palace entrance upon our arrival, not even managing to put on a decent smile as the servants all stood to celebrate our happy return at the culmination of the imperial tour.

I certainly wasn't in a mood to celebrate.

My mother smiled by the door, Kernov next to her. She opened her arms for a hug. "Welcome home."

My heart stuttered. I couldn't completely fall apart with everyone watching. I'd done too much of that. So, I shook my head and went into the building sans hug.

"Sorry. I need to lie down." I sniffled.

She rushed after me. "Are you all right?" Worry tinged her voice.

Lilah stood, just inside, a frown already on her face. I'd asked her to greet me inside this time, and her gaze shot past me to my Coterie making their way toward us. My *incomplete* Coterie.

I was going to have another breakdown, a proper one, and it was going to be ugly.

As I turned to my mother, fresh tears coated my eyes. "You can tell her everything, Kernov." He would have the latest news, and his frown conveyed his sympathies.

"Everything what?" my mother asked.

I shook my head. "I love you. I'll be fine. I'm going to lie down." I headed straight toward my tower.

Lilah kept pace with me. "I'm guessing…" she started. "Your letters said things were good, but you didn't mention Tyfen…"

I whimpered, hugging myself.

"Shit," she whispered. "Let's get you settled in your chambers."

***

I fully fell apart. Lilah was sweet and great at listening, perfect at holding me as I got it all out. I'd missed her, and I vowed to not keep secrets from her again.

I slept in her arms that first night. Then I stayed in bed all the next day, numb and hurting. After she forced me to eat, I had a servant bring me paper and a pen. I scribbled a note to Queen Lourel, letting her know exactly what I thought of her.

Lilah held the paper after reading it. "I … think we should maybe rewrite this before sending it…"

Scowling, I tried to grab the paper back, but she kept it from me.

"Sonta, no matter how angry you are, you can't call the queen a bitch, fucker, cunt, and asshole all in the same letter."

"Watch me."

She sighed, and a curl dangled innocently in front of her adorable face. "For your own good, I'm overriding your decision." She tore it up, and I grumbled. "How about I pen this one, and I'll help translate how you feel into something more … diplomatic?"

I flopped back in bed, rubbing my growing baby bump.

"Instead of opening it with 'To the Asshole of Crystal City,' let's maybe do something like 'To Her Majesty'…"

Eventually, I was forced out of my misery hole, even if it was only for a little while. I allowed my mother into my chambers the next day, and she consoled me.

Later that day, I invited Haan into my pond, and he was incredibly sweet, not speaking ill of Tyfen, but disappointed in the situation.

Before nightfall, I trudged to the emperor's office for a meeting. It was brief and tense. Magistrate Leonte spoke very little, and the advisors silently took notes.

Nothing was said of me calling the emperor a callous bastard.

Tyfen hadn't been found, though I was assured the tracking spells still showed him as living. I kept fiddling with his leather bracelet as I slumped in my chair.

"We'll let you know if and when anything changes with him, Sonta," the emperor assured. "It would be best if you carried on without him. The rest of your Coterie, and your child, should be your priorities. Do not dwell on a painful unknown."

I stared into my lap. No one had a right to tell me to simply 'move on.' No one in this empire was fighting for Tyfen the way I was; no one loved him as much as I did. He held a special place in my heart, and it wasn't something I could just flip off and on. Why was that so hard to understand? Would they say the same if it were Gald missing? Or Elion?

Still, I didn't have it in me to be cantankerous tonight. "I'll do my best."

The first week was rough, each day stretching to a week long. I only let Haan in to chat for a little bit when he pulled his call string, asking to come in. I allowed Elion to bed me once a day when I got desperate from abstaining, but I had to ask him to not sleep at my door anymore.

Hadwin didn't even try to reach out. Despite my guilt for repeatedly blowing up at him over past mistakes, I was too terrified to talk to him, afraid I'd do or say the wrong thing again. He *could* have tried to reach out, too, but he hadn't yet. Even if he was only in his fifties, which was young for an immortal, maybe he needed more time away from me, and it might take longer than I'd have chosen to be apart. Or so I told myself…

I knew my pain and anger hurt the rest of my Coterie members, but I couldn't help myself. We'd find a way to move on once Tyfen returned, or once I spoke to him at least…

My Coterie limped along, gratefully not in such a bad place any of the others would leave—none of these men would forfeit their place politically, even if they were fed up with my pining over Tyfen and my oft sour mood.

But beyond Haan and Elion, none of the others even tried to visit me, and I was glad of it. I was tired of lashing out at them.

Queen Lourel responded to Lilah's version of my letter, spouting bullshit about how she had Tyfen's best interests, and mine, at heart. She reassured me he would be well. I found no comfort in her hollow promises.

Lilah stuck to me like glue, and my mother gave me space like I'd asked for after our lunch together.

The eighth morning after returning, I lay in bed, staring out my large windows into my private garden. Snow fell heavily, coating everything, and my fireplace blazed in the corner. I'd toured for seventeen weeks, which meant Tyfen had now been gone for eighteen weeks.

My swelling belly now looked more like the six and a half months out of ten I was.

Haan had chosen to winter with us at the palace. I felt bad it was all for me, but I could use his smiles in the indoor ponds and tanks to warm my chilled soul.

Lilah kissed my shoulder, holding me. "I love winter. The crackle of a good blaze. Cuddling under blankets. Warm drinks. I was afraid you'd get delayed in the passes on your final return."

I hummed my agreement. Autumn and winter had been so mild while on tour, but nature seized the opportunity to unleash it all in beautiful white snow now.

Turning, I looked at Lilah, taking in her face. "Is that why you're spending all your time with me? Because my fireplace is larger than yours?"

She giggled, then stole a kiss. "Yes, Your Holiness. You've found me out."

A small smile graced my lips.

She caressed my cheek, and I leaned into her touch.

"I love you," I whispered.

Her smile brightened. "How about we dust off our sorrows and do a few things, just for today?"

I frowned.

"I..." She drew a deep breath. "You need to get some food in you. We could share a bath. And ... I still haven't shown you my surprise I've been working on all these months."

My heart dropped, and I almost cried at the realization. "I'm a shit friend." I'd been so wrapped up in my duties and my own problems that I hadn't made space to consider her. She'd been through a major breakup recently, and she'd been excitedly working on a project. I *had* asked her after returning how she was, but how deeply had I meant it? "I'm sorry."

She offered me a shy smile. "Not a shit friend. A busy and stressed friend." Tucking a hair behind my ear, she cuddled closer. "You are who you are. The Blessed Vessel. You have a unique and busy position, and I understand that. I don't expect a goddess's daughter to dote on me, or for anyone else to. The whole realm places unrealistic expectations on you." She shrugged. "No one expects much of me. I live an easy life here. I'm just the Blessed Vessel's best friend."

Her words hit me hard. She'd never talked this way before, or at least I hadn't heard it this way. "You're not just my friend, Lilah. I love you, and I wouldn't want to do this without you." I gazed into her dark brown eyes. "Friend, lover, or whatever label you take, there's no *just* about you, not to me."

She bit her lip. "Thank you. That means more to me than you know."

My smile recovered. "Let's do all the things—food, bath, surprise..."

Lilah stole another lingering kiss. "I love you."

I hadn't much of an appetite in my depression, but once I ate breakfast and drank some pig's blood, I was more energetic.

It was a little hard to bathe with her, too. Her curves were perfect, and I missed our previous intimacy. But I enjoyed our conversation about the upcoming winter festival. In my heart, I knew I wouldn't fully enjoy it, but I'd try my best not to bring down her spirits.

We braided each other's hair. Her surprise was up in the studio, and I agreed to get dolled up a bit so she could do another painting of me for my pregnancy progress.

We held hands as we strode to the studio. Despite the emptiness in me, it did feel great to be full, clean, and dressed up.

Lilah stopped me at the door, giddy. "I hope you love it. But if you don't, I'd prefer your honesty. Don't lie to me. I can handle the truth."

I nodded.

She pursed her lips. "And ... um ... I did mention this isn't actually a gift for you, right? I just wanted you to see it before it leaves the studio..."

I was thoroughly intrigued. "Whatever it is, I'm excited."

"Okay." She led me in.

The room was chilly, the fireplace empty. But it was bright with my wall full of watercolors. My eyes naturally shot to the empty spot in the green area where Tyfen had taken my painting. A lump formed in my throat, and I looked away.

I wasn't going to rain on Lilah's parade, not now.

Her painting area was stacked with canvases and easels, both empty and full.

"I had a servant help me organize, but I really need to decide where to hang some of these…"

I squeezed her hand. "Yes, they should be admired."

"You ready?" Her eyes sparkled with anticipation.

"Let me see this surprise."

She strode to the other side of the room, where a cloth draped over three canvases leaning against the wall. Throwing me a nervous glance, she reminded me to be honest more than anything.

I was genuinely shocked by the paintings once she revealed them. They were portraits, complete with detailed backgrounds. They were of Magistrate Leonte and his family.

Stepping closer, I smiled. "Goddess, you're good."

"Are you just saying that?"

I narrowed my eyes at her. "Do we need to compare your work to my watercolor blob people?"

She snickered, then skipped to me and held my hand to view the portraits together.

"Everything looks so natural," I said. "And I love how wonderfully you portrayed Leonte's wife." Like him, she was larger in form, and I'd always hated how some artists portrayed people as different than they truly were—different body sizes, hair colors, facial structures—just to fit the vanity of current fashion.

Lilah beamed. "He hasn't seen the finished versions yet. He came and approved them before I did the majority of the highlights and shadows, though." So much pride filled her face. "My first real commission. He's paying very well. I'm … a real artist."

I hugged her. "You don't have to be paid to be a real artist. You've always done great work, Lilah. But I'm excited for you."

She hummed. "I *am* grateful for you, and that I don't have to worry about scraping by like our parents did when we were little. But I do want to make a name for myself, not just … leech off you as your side piece."

I gave her a stern look about the 'side piece' bit. "I'm proud of you if this is what you're choosing to do. I've always been proud of you."

We took a moment, arms wrapped around each other as we admired the paintings. She told me a little more about them. She'd been terrified to approach Leonte on her own. She'd never asked for a private audience with either him or the emperor, but she had made a point of not using me as a crutch, not asking for my referral as the go-between.

"He's nice," she mused. "And his family is lovely. I'm lucky they gave an unknown artist like me a chance." She acknowledged she'd obviously still only gotten the chance because she was my friend, but it was what it was.

Leonte had even encouraged her, telling her he could recommend her to the emperor for consideration as an official palace painter if he liked the final portraits. That was no small deal.

"That's fantastic! I'm glad he's in your corner." I bit my lip. "You definitely don't want *my* referral to the emperor right now. I called him a callous bastard in front of tons of soldiers."

Lilah blinked. "Well ... Hoku chose *you*, of all people. Apparently she thinks the rulers of this realm need a little sass in their lives right now."

I chuckled.

She kissed me. "But could you imagine? An *official* palace painter? I'd be titled like your men."

I pressed my forehead to hers. "I couldn't care less if you had a title as my friend or girlfriend. But I'm excited at the thought of it if it means something to you outside that."

"It does," she whispered.

I returned her kiss, soft and sweet. She was excited yet nervous. This was a monumental step for her, and she'd been soul searching for some time about wanting to make something of herself. Perhaps her breakup with Cataray and her time alone here at the palace had allowed her to clear her head and blaze that path forward for herself.

A simple lingering kiss naturally turned into more as she held the nape of my neck, as my tongue grazed hers. As my breathing picked up and my insides warmed.

She pulled back and whispered against my lips. "Get naked for me."

I swallowed. I wanted to make love to her *so* much. Yes, some of it was my craving for comfort and sex in general, but this was a huge thing, and I wanted to celebrate with her. But I also had my duty and vows. "I..."

"We're still sketching your pregnancy portraits nude, aren't we?" she asked knowingly.

I fought a laugh. "Yes... That..."

After peeling myself away from her, I stripped. She smirked as I did so. "Any requests for poses?"

"I trust the artist wholeheartedly. She's never led me astray."

Lilah blushed, then set to work, positioning me in the bay window area. Her every touch was magnetic, and it took a concerted effort to not start anything again.

"Now stay still." She sauntered to her easel and began to sketch.

Luckily, she announced the sketch was done before I had to slide my dress on and run to the nearest washroom. Hadwin's child loved to jump on my bladder when I sat still for too long.

I returned and wrapped my arms around her from behind. "Good choice of poses."

She hummed happily.

"And you always make my tits look perfect."

Her voice was playful and seductive. "That's because I have a great subject to work with."

I fought the urge to grope *her* tits. Instead, my eyes landed on my belly in the painting. It wasn't like I was huge, but I really showed well.

"I'm such a bitch," I whispered. "Hadwin ... he doesn't deserve this." I *knew* how much being apart from me hurt him. Granted, he'd made no attempt to reach out to me, either. We had an unspoken agreement to let each other wallow right now.

"He loves you," she whispered. "They all do, Sonta."

This was a no-win situation. My heart wouldn't allow me to settle into a comfortable place with my Coterie again, not without Tyfen. I'd even offered supplication to Hoku, and her soft impressions urged me to not give up on him.

"You know, when you went to your room to get some of your things last night, and I let Elion in..." I'd let him take me, and we'd kept it simple—just fucking, just meeting our needs. "He told me when he was getting dressed again that the men want to have a meeting. I'm a coward for not talking to them."

Lilah faced me, frowning. "I promise I won't speak ill of Tyfen, because I really never got to know him well, but you *should* talk to the others. No matter Tyfen's reason for leaving, this wouldn't be so hard if he'd just ... talked to you, right?"

"Yeah." I looked down sheepishly. She could always put me in my place in the most loving and gentle ways.

"You can do this." She held my chin. "And I'm always here for you." After another peck on the lips, she blew out a breath. "We're up, washed, and dressed. I refuse to go lie down in your chambers for the rest of the day. What do you say to a visit with your mother? Or we could bundle up and take a stroll in the snow?"

I considered. Perhaps I'd find the strength to visit my mother later today, but right now, I wanted something more peaceful. "I love that decorative window. What if we watch the snow fall for a while? I'll order some snacks and warm drinks."

Her smiles would never lose their charm for me. "I'm all for it."

"Good. And let's get a goddess-damned fire started. My breasts were so cold when I was posing, my nipples could have cut someone."

Her grin was wicked. "I didn't complain."

44

Hajba Partners

After starting a fire and ordering snacks—I also requested a large blanket, perfect for cuddling in the bay window—we settled down, gazing out.

It was serene, each little snowflake dancing in the sky on its way down without a care. Lilah and I faced each other, our legs touching as we munched and sipped on what a servant had brought.

I kept thinking about what Lilah had said about gaining a title like my men. Amidst her excitement, she'd been uncharacteristically insecure. Granted, that may just be her trying to walk on eggshells around me and my mood.

"Why do you want a title?" I asked, then popped a grape into my mouth.

She sighed. "It would be nice to be important. It's not wrong to want to achieve something, right? Whether earned or divinely appointed…"

I narrowed my eyes. "I'm happy for you to have a title. I don't mean to imply you shouldn't want one or that you're not worthy of one. I'm just curious. I'm worried by your comment earlier that you're comparing yourself to my men…"

Considering, she shrugged. "Maybe there's a small amount of truth in that, but I genuinely like the idea of having it on my own."

I nodded. "Okay." I smiled. "Honestly, when you and Mother escorted me into the paternity announcement, it felt weird to have you simply announced as my childhood friend."

She looked away. "Yeah."

"Tell me what's wrong."

"Nothing's wrong."

"You're lying."

She shrugged again.

I stared at her a while as she avoided eye contact by looking outside. "Other than painting, how have things been while I was gone? What haven't you told me?"

"Nothing exciting."

"Have you been in contact with Cataray at all?" I fished.

"No. It was a clean break, like I told you. It's over with her."

"I bet we could find a dazzling new lover for you at the winter festival."

Lilah shook her head. "I'm not ready for that."

"Okay," I said softly. "Do you want to talk about the breakup?" She never had disclosed the reason for their split, and she was lost in her own sorrow right now. I'd been a shit friend, focusing so much on my own troubles. "I'm here for you, Lilah."

She bit her lip, tears coating her eyes as she faced me. "She broke up with me… Or maybe I broke up with her; it could be seen either way. But she gave me an ultimatum…"

I cocked my head. "Yeah?"

"I told you she wanted to be exclusive."

"I know. And I offered to let her move in, and would have supported you if you'd moved away."

Lilah wiped away her tears. "Trust me, I remember."

I searched her face. "I want you happy."

"And I want *you*," Lilah whispered. "It was exclusivity or nothing with Cataray. I chose nothing."

"Oh…" I picked at my nails. "She knew we were something of an item when you started dating…"

"Yes, she did. But she was jealous, and I was a horrible girlfriend."

"No you're not!"

"*You* wouldn't think so, Sonta. I've always chosen you. You've always been my first choice."

My brain stuttered. "Lilah … you call yourself my 'side piece,' but *I've* always been the one on the side. How many girlfriends have you had since we've been together? And I…" I was so confused. "I swear we wouldn't have sex at all if it wasn't for me… I'm almost always the one to initiate it." She'd been a little frisky since the Great Ritual began, but she'd explained she just didn't like being told what she couldn't have.

She pursed her lips. "Yeah, well… Goddess, Sonta, what do you…" She looked away again. "I try not to initiate because *I'm* the shit friend."

"No you're not…"

She looked me dead in the eyes. "But I am… What kind of friend develops a crush on their friend and then pines after them like that? I was always covering for you when you snuck off with those guys back home, and I was *happy* you were happy to fuck around, but I wanted to be in their place…"

We'd never really talked about *when* we'd started to become attracted to each other, but we'd both made it apparent we were interested after I'd been discovered as Hoku's daughter, before I'd moved here.

Lilah continued. "What kind of person waits to make her move until her best friend is deprived of sex? I felt like a fucking predator, like I was taking advantage of you. I should have stayed your friend."

I looked at her in a new light with that confession. It took me a while to process it all. Lilah was naturally flirtatious, and so was I. Even realizing she'd pined for me for so long, I couldn't see her negatively. While I hadn't moved to the palace yet, I'd had security guards stationed outside my home until I was ready to move. The young men I'd been fucking to satiate my cravings hadn't been anything exemplary, but I wouldn't have pleasure instructors until I moved to the palace. My security staff hadn't thought it was safe for me to entertain those men anymore, and I'd agreed. My brief run-in with the one asshole back in my hometown while on tour was evidence enough of that.

It had been an uncomfortable time, and Lilah and I had spent more time together than usual. Our relationship had blossomed slowly.

I swallowed. "You didn't take advantage of me, Lilah. I wasn't some wounded, sex-starved thing who slept with you because you were the only option."

Her face expressed her disbelief.

"I mean it. If I just needed a hole filled ... there are tools. And if it was all about my sexual needs, I would have slept with you sooner…"

"Still," she whispered, "it's not like you experimented with girls at all until I made my move. The only reason you even entertained my advances was because you didn't have other options at the time."

I gaped. "I was *shy*. I was afraid I'd be bad at it. Lovemaking with men just comes more naturally to me, but I was curious long before that."

She furrowed her brow. "Really?"

How were we this bad at talking? "Yes!" I adjusted my seat. "You had girlfriends when we were teenagers. I had boy— Well, I screwed guys. You think I didn't look at you with those girls and wonder? That I didn't…"

Lilah perked up. "When did you first, you know…?"

A smile instantly bloomed on my lips. "At the lake. You were wearing that magenta suit, and you lost your top."

She smiled back. "Yeah?"

"Yes. That was the first time I stopped just being curious and really … wanted it. I asked myself what it would feel like to press our breasts together. I…" I blushed. "I wondered how much of you I could fit in my mouth. And how soft your lips were…"

She blushed this time. "My hair was a mess."

I angled my head. "Tangled lake water hair is what you think I was focused on? When every other part of you is perfect? Goddess, Lilah, I may be daft, but…" I shook my head. "You have the best laugh, and the kindest heart, and you're just … amazing." I gestured to all her artwork in the room. "Not to mention your raw talent."

"Thank you," she whispered.

I drew a breath, thinking back to Cataray. "So fuck Cataray. I mean ... don't *actually* fuck her, because she's not worth it, but fuck her. You deserve better." Unable to stop myself, I rolled my eyes. "She never would have even met you if it weren't for me, and she knew we were in an open relationship, so it's *her* fault for not honoring that."

Cataray had met Lilah at a ball here at the palace. Her uncle was a high-society tradesman who vended to the palace. She'd only been invited as an extra guest the once.

"You're right." Lilah frowned. "I really wish you could drink right now, and we could get all this sadness nonsense out of our systems."

Sighing, I rubbed my stomach. "After I pop this child out, we're going to get mind-numbingly drunk. We're going to fuck like no one else exists, and cause all sorts of problems."

She giggled. "I'll hold you to your word."

I extended my hands, and she took them. "Good."

For a moment, we sat there, the warmth of our hands mingling. "Where does this leave us?" she asked cautiously.

It was a valid question. She'd said I was her first choice. "I can't be exclusive even if I want to be."

"I know." She frowned.

"Would you want us to be exclusive, if things were different?"

A longing look crossed her face. "Yes and no. I did want that, once upon a time. But then you were announced as Hoku's daughter, destined to bed multiple men for the rest of your days."

That was hard to hear.

She squeezed my hands. "I accept that. I truly do. And I've had so many girlfriends on the side to distract me because I knew I couldn't demand more from you."

"Yes you can."

"You're a busy woman." She grinned.

"One who needs people she loves and trusts by her side, Lilah." As much as I loved my men, I would go positively mad if I didn't have Lilah as a lover, someone without political strings attached.

"True..." She adjusted her legs under the blanket. "I've gotten used to having different lovers. I'm not interested in another right away, not after Cataray, but maybe someday. But I want to make sure they're compatible with *you* early on..." She quickly added, "Not that you have to sleep with my lovers, but you know what I mean."

She pursed her lips. "Not that you *can't* sleep with my future lovers as long as we're all still open to group stuff, because I still want to try that."

I grinned. "I'm game. And I'm happy to help screen future girlfriends."

"And I *do* like your Coterie. More than I thought I would." She clicked her tongue. "You know men don't really do it for me in that way … romantically. But they look like they know how to get it done like Schamoi did. I'm excited to try group stuff with you. But … only with you involved."

I chuckled internally. I wasn't afraid she'd run off with my men, and we both knew who she was more interested in experimenting with in which way. And the men all seemed to understand her place with me and with them. Still, it was good to set boundaries.

"So, I have my men…" I pushed away the thought of Tyfen. "And you. I don't think I could handle more than that."

"And I have you," she replied. "And I'm down to play with the Coterie sometimes, with you. And I may someday take another partner… And we'll see where that goes."

"It's a deal." I slipped my hands under the blanket and grasped her knees. "Would you ever consider moving down to my floor? Because I'd love to see you more often, and things are working out between you and the Coterie…" The irony hit me that Lilah was actually getting along with them better right now than I was… Just in a platonic way.

It was like I'd given her a birthday gift. "I'd love that. But which room?"

The tower was mine to use as I pleased, but my floor was built for my Coterie and our needs. I couldn't promise to exclusively share my room with her. There was no way in hell I'd offer Tyfen's empty room, and Gald and Findlech liked having their own, so it wasn't like I'd ask them to share.

Several rooms lay on the periphery for any children I may bear, both my firstborn and any extras I chose to have. It would be too weird to put her in a child's room.

There wasn't an official 'other lover' room. But there kind of was…

I arched an eyebrow. "Schamoi's old room?" It sat vacant. The other four pleasure instructors had all occupied rooms on the next floor up, but the lead pleasure instructor had a special room on my floor. I'd barely even seen it when he'd lived here, and none of the Coterie's aides had filled it. It had a private entrance apart from the other servant rooms. It was honestly perfect.

Lilah gave me a calculating look. "Are you proposing I take on a new title? A post–Great Ritual pleasure instructor?"

I rolled my eyes. "Yes. You are now *assigned* to fuck me."

She smirked. "Let's take a look at it together. I'm open to it." She then hesitated. "Does that mean you really think you and Schamoi are over?"

Sighing, I nodded. "Our time has passed, and we both know it. Friends now." I did still sometimes miss his perfect ass and icy blue eyes, his sarcasm, jokes, and laughs. But I had plenty of asses and laughs to enjoy. The day Tyfen came home, I'd feel complete.

Forcing myself to stay in the moment, I gazed into Lilah's eyes. "Does it bother you that I don't call you my girlfriend? I know you like using that term, but I feel silly about using it as a woman... And I know not everyone appreciates 'lover.'"

Her smile retreated again. "I'm happy with you calling me anything. Especially once we feel comfortable the public won't judge you for 'straying' from your men."

I eyed her. She was lying if her smile had faded. "Tell me what you want me to call you, and I'll call you it."

"Can I come cuddle with you?"

"Sure. There's enough room." I slid up against the window, and she joined me on my side, leaning her head on my shoulder.

"Remember when we were little, and I tried to get you to play wedding with me?"

I snickered. "Yes. Your brother said you were stupid for decorating the sitting room." I pouted. "And then I made you cry because I told you I would *never* marry you or anyone else." My mother hadn't set that example, and I didn't want to do something my mother hadn't done, despite Lilah's parents having a happy marriage.

"Yeah... Turning down my advances so young, Sonta..." She clicked her tongue in reproach.

I laughed again. "But then you suggested we be hajba partners, and I played along."

To most people in the realm, marriage meant exclusivity for life. Hajba partnership meant an open intimate relationship, but held the same serious commitment for life. Some turned their noses up at it, but most accepted it with equal weight.

"My fantasies of you being my wife someday ... died, after your discovery as Hoku's daughter."

It killed me to hear it, and it reminded me I'd also destroyed our joint dream to open a shop together someday.

"I'm sorry," I whispered.

She took my hand under the blanket. "But I don't consider a hajba less than a wife..."

My heart skipped a beat. "You want to take hajba vows with me?"

She wouldn't look at me. "Just something to consider."

"Yes."

Her gaze snapped to mine. "I don't expect a decision right away; you can take some time..."

"I don't need time, Lilah." I'd never realized how serious she was about us before. How much she'd held back for fear of ruining our friendship or causing problems with my calling as the Blessed Vessel.

How many times had she joked that I should run away with her, and she'd secretly meant it?

How worried had she been that my new men would edge her out of the palace and my life?

How hurt had she been that I'd easily told her I'd be okay if she and Cataray were exclusive, if she and I stopped being intimate?

I was fighting for Tyfen. I'd fought for Hadwin. And I would fight for each of the others.

I would fight for Lilah, too.

I caressed her cheek. "I have never once wanted you gone. When I accepted the idea of you leaving me to be with Cataray alone, I only did it because I thought you were happier with her, because you spent so much time with her. And I *want* you happy."

Her lips twitched into a half smile.

"Look at me."

She did, coy.

"Why would I hesitate to agree to hajba vows when every vision of my ideal future has us growing old together as crusty old grey-haired menaces?"

She giggled.

"I mean it," I said softly. "I wasn't always certain what men I'd be paired with, and how things would work with them, but I always envisioned you there."

Her eyes filled with tears again.

"I would trust you with any children I have," I added. "And if you changed your mind and wanted children..."

Her lip curled. She liked children, just not the idea of carrying one or having to be responsible for it around the clock.

"Well, I'm just saying... We'd have a hell of a time no matter what."

"Thank you," she breathed.

I couldn't forget Hadwin's offer of immortality. I'd warmed up to the idea of being cold. "Would you still love me if I were a vampire?"

She wiped away a tear. "I don't know. Would you learn blood play for me?"

"Fuck," I panted. I hadn't considered that. My craving for blood and sex hit me like a stampede. "Absolutely."

"Even if you didn't, I'd still love you." She bit her lip. "But if you're immortal, do you still see us... I'd be willing..."

My smile grew. "You'd accept an eternal bite?"

She nodded.

My heart warmed even more. "That's forever away, if we do it." I nudged her. "And I know you're not ready to find another girlfriend yet, but Hadwin *did* mention he knew some former Suck and Fuck workers..."

She showed me her teeth. "We'll meet them together."

"When the time is right. We don't have to rush into things." I intertwined my fingers with hers. "So, what do you say? Be my hajba?"

Her eyes welling with tears made my own do so.

"Yes."

I leaned in and kissed a salty tear that ran down her cheek. "I love you."

She lifted her lips to mine. "I love you too, Sonta."

I pressed my lips to hers, savoring this special moment. The way my heart raced, my insides warmed.

Her kiss was more firm with each pass, her tongue wrestling mine.

"I love you," she whispered again as she shifted and straddled me.

Lilah was going to be mine. Officially. As official as any of my men with their vows. Recognized by the law and empire.

I melted in that moment as she tangled her fingers through my hair, as my hands slid up her dress to her ass.

She took the invitation to slip my dress sleeves down, her lips roaming my neck as her hands grasped my breasts.

Goddess save me.

I slipped a finger under the band of her underwear, and she shuddered, arching as I aimed for her pussy. She was as wet as I was.

"No, Sonta," she whispered, pulling back.

"Please?"

She frowned. "I'm sorry I keep doing this—tempting you—but I won't be the reason you break your vows."

I refused to accept that answer. I didn't care about those vows right now; I cared about the ones we'd just agreed to take together.

Staring into her eyes, I slowly rubbed one finger inside her. "I love you. My hajba and my talented painter. And I want to celebrate."

She licked her lips, then took my hands, pulling me out of her, and held them in front of her. "I *won't* be the reason you break your vows. I miss you too. Like hell. But we can wait a few more months."

I choked down a lump in my throat. "The divine edict is open to interpretation…"

"But you wanted to follow the strictest interpretation."

"I don't care."

She released my hands and gently slipped my dress straps back up. "You may regret it later, and you have enough on your plate right now."

"I won't regret it. I want to make love to you." I grasped her waist, peering into her perfect eyes with those perfect long lashes. "Please?"

Kissing my forehead, she sighed. "You can't know now if you'll regret it. We have time. We have forever. We can wait."

My own pussy still pulsed with anticipation, and I hated this.

"Remember what you said? We'll get stupid drunk and fuck like crazy in a few months. I'll hold you to that. We don't even have to do the drunk part." She winked.

My shoulders slumped. "Fine."

Sweet and sensible as ever, she smiled. "Let's hit the washroom, then visit your mother. Don't you want to share our news? Write a letter to my parents? Talk about dates and decorations? Who we'll invite?"

I relented. They weren't horrible ideas. "Let's do that."

45

The Scholarly Approach

My mother was ecstatic for Lilah and me, giving us each a giant hug. Kernov was initially a little embarrassed, having been found in her room, but they were both dressed and sitting down to eat. He beamed, congratulating us. I was grateful to have him here to discuss the divine edicts as we planned things out.

Lilah and I would have to wait to take our hajba vows until after the birth, which we both understood. And our planning should probably be done quietly, without us making any announcements publicly yet. Even entering an engagement to become hajba was as questionable as having sex right now.

We'd keep our plans quiet, though we should inform the Coterie.

I wanted to tell them together with Lilah, but the men had already requested a meeting with me, and it was to be an official Coterie-only meeting.

The next afternoon, I sat with them in the common room, a place I rarely went anymore. It made me nauseous to think the last time I'd had sex with Tyfen had been in this very room, and it had ended in spilled blood and months of torture.

I did my best to be calm, though we were all clearly on edge.

The meeting was nothing more than horseshit. Elion, Hadwin, and Haan barely spoke, but the politician duo—mostly Gald—had planned an intervention.

They insisted I should accept that we didn't know if or when Tyfen would come back.

I should learn to move on, and accept the men who *hadn't* walked away.

Tyfen had disappointed me time and time again.

He'd *left* me.

I was making everyone miserable by prioritizing him…

The meeting was nothing more than an attack that made my blood boil.

"Very big of you, Gald, to tell me who I can love, and to vilify someone who isn't here to stand up for themselves!"

He glared. "You act like Tyfen's one of your mates. He's not."

I couldn't be Tyfen's mate. Fate hadn't chosen to pair fae and humans as mates for centuries.

I stood, done with this meeting. "What does that say of your loyalty to me, Gald? Or to Findlech? I didn't realize you valued the mating bond so highly."

He rolled his eyes. "Obviously, you don't *need* a mating bond to love someone deeply…"

No, I didn't. A mating bond made it easier to explain away such intense and irrational loyalty and yearning, but it wasn't a requirement.

Tyfen had once said something that reverberated in my soul right now.

'The heart wants what it wants. The body craves what it will. Even when the fates deal you an unfavorable hand…'

My life would have been easier if Tyfen had never come into it. If I had never fallen for him. If I had it in me to give him up. But I *couldn't*. And I couldn't even explain to myself why at times.

I gave Gald a stern look, and the others. I knew I was irrational in some ways, and I didn't know how to change that. "I will not accept more negativity about him until he has a chance to speak for himself. Until everyone has gotten a chance to *actually* know him the way I do."

"Sonta," Gald softly pleaded.

"You can fuck off." I turned and left. They had their 'evidence' of his character, and I had mine. And honestly, they were being shit political allies right now.

My happy moment with Lilah had to be tainted this way. I didn't even deign to tell the men about my news with Lilah.

The truth hurt sometimes, though. I *was* making everyone miserable.

After the intervention, I steered clear of the common room and dining hall again.

Day after day, I watched the snow fall, I received no updates on Tyfen, and my hope paled a bit more.

It wasn't fair for them to demand I give up on him. I shouldn't have to. It wasn't fair for them to judge him when he wasn't here to defend himself. There was something bigger happening that he was wrapped up in.

I wrote to the queen again, and she gave me the same useless response. How could they possibly not have found him? It was warmer in the Dark Forest with it being so far south, but that didn't mean the temperatures hadn't dropped. The situation was getting more bleak with him in there.

At this point, I'd sell my soul to have him back. I truly would. When I let Elion bed me, I made a concerted effort to focus on us, but when I resorted to my tools, I always pictured Tyfen or Lilah.

Days turned into weeks. My cravings for Hadwin were agonizing, but I couldn't look him in the eye at this point. Nor did he make an effort to reach out to me. I ate enough to keep myself going and to keep my child healthy, but found little joy in food. Lilah tried to cheer me up, and I did my best to put on a happy face when we talked about our hajba ceremony. Her parents had replied to our letter—they were over the moons.

I tried to tell myself so many times that I needed to separate my love for Tyfen from my love for the others, but it wasn't an easy thing. We were a unit, a package deal.

I tried to tell myself I could find some kind of closure like they'd suggested. I had only known Tyfen for all of two months. Two wild months, but still only that. I should easily be able to let him go like I had Schamoi.

Tyfen was no Schamoi. No matter how many times I tried to convince myself Tyfen had just been a chapter in my life, that it would be okay to move on in my heart, and deal with the political repercussions as they came, his hold on my heart wouldn't budge.

I often found myself daydreaming of being in his arms, or wishing we could have an argument just to make up again. Without fail, I always cried when I pondered the vision Hoku had given me that reminded me of him—dewdrops on grass the color of his eyes, somewhere in the elf nation during the autumn.

Hoku continued to send me visions, and I accepted the distraction, painting them. My eyes would always wander to the empty spot for the one Tyfen had crumpled. I should repaint it, but I couldn't bring myself to do it. I even added to the green section, leaving that spot more obviously open.

Before I knew it, I was already seven months pregnant. Two months with Tyfen, five without. The longer he stayed away, the more I started to doubt my resolve.

Was I a fool to cling so much?

'I like my Sonta,' he'd once said.

My heart had fluttered. I wasn't just Sonta; I was *his* Sonta.

He'd then asked me how I felt. His hand had lingered on my waist, a thumb stroking my stomach after he'd fucked me three times in the playroom. I could almost feel him at times, his whispered praise, his understanding of how much I needed to surrender control sometimes. He understood me in ways none of the others did…

The winter festival was beautiful, and we all put on a façade, but I found little joy in it. I decided that night that I *needed* to dispense with the moping and do something more.

I had once sworn to Hadwin I would use the emperor's forces to scour the realm for him, to do anything to save him if I ever needed to. Why wouldn't I do that for Tyfen? It didn't matter he wasn't my mate, that we didn't share a magical bond. He was in my Coterie.

But the emperor kept shooting me down, refusing to get involved, telling me we needed to wait it out. Queen Lourel also stopped responding to my letters.

Without their cooperation, I had no recourse. In military matters, I didn't truly have a say without the emperor's approval, and the only way I could take control was if he died.

I was losing my mind a little more each day, but wasn't *quite* at assassination-level madness yet.

So... I took the politician's route. I started studying. I journaled about everything I knew, everything I'd learned from Tyfen's time here and while I was out on tour.

The elves wanted him dead. Though the queen had told me emphatically in her last letters that she was confident he was safe, it still had to matter that Tyfen had committed a crime the elves deemed worthy of execution if she would not tell me more about it. And if Findlech wouldn't tell me.

I strode to the library one day, ready to tackle dull reading. Even if I didn't find my answer, I'd satiate my guilt and fill my time.

And I *would* have more time to myself. Leonte had *loved* Lilah's paintings. The emperor had agreed to assign a more experienced painter to mentor her before fully considering her as a palace artist. I was happy for her, and it softened my anger for the emperor.

No sooner had I shut the library door behind me than Gald startled me.

I clutched my chest. "Fuck, sorry."

He held up a book. "I was going to read here, but I can go back to the common room if you'd prefer."

I frowned. "You're fine here. This is your home too."

He bit his lip. He was always cute when he did that, with the way he did it over his lip ring. "Hasn't felt like a home for a while, Sonta."

My frown deepened. "I'm sorry we're at odds, but I won't apologize for my stance."

He gave me a single nod. "Fair. I've always appreciated your spirit."

I rolled my eyes.

"I can't offer compliments now?"

"Compliments or flattery?"

Looking down, he shook his head. "I'm not looking for a fight today."

I blew out a breath. "Neither am I. I'm here to find a book." As if that wasn't obvious from my presence in the library...

"Picking up a hobby in your free time?" He offered a hesitant smile. "I could make some recommendations."

I wrung my hands. "Nonfiction, actually. And I don't really know where to start."

He set his book down. "I'd be happy to help."

I appreciated his civility. "Okay... I want to know the differences between elf and fae laws."

Gald wrinkled his nose. "I'm sure there's a ton, but those thick tomes aren't likely to be in your personal library. Perhaps in the general palace library?"

"Yeah, probably..."

"But that's a hell of a lot to sort through, depending on what you're looking for. Is there something specific you want to know?"

I hesitated. I couldn't tell him it had to do with Tyfen. "I'm looking for information on a possible crime…"

He gave no reaction.

"And I think it would only be a crime according to elven law, not fae law."

He arched an eyebrow.

I sighed. "I don't have a lot of information…" Queen Lourel had said Tyfen *had* made a mistake, but he'd not done it maliciously, and that she and King Bretton would never punish *anyone* for doing what Tyfen had done. Whatever he'd done had to be a crime to elves but not fae. There was no other way to interpret that.

"Maybe you can speak with one of the emperor's legal advisors?" Gald suggested.

And get stonewalled more? No thank you.

"Or what about a law that's ridiculously harsh for elves?" I asked. "Do you know any of those?"

Gald shrugged. "Findlech would be the better person to ask, as a member of parliament."

Again… Stonewalled.

"Come on, Gald. You're brilliant. You've been fascinated with elf culture your whole life; surely you know something…"

He angled his head. "I studied public policy and politics, not law. I'm not that kind of public servant."

I couldn't resist for old times' sake. "Do lawyers not screw their way to the top like you did?"

Gald belted out a laugh, his curly hair swaying. "Fuck you, Sonta."

My smile was brighter than I'd allowed it to be lately. "I miss your laugh."

He wore a look of longing, walked up to me, and took me by the hands and pulled me back. He sat on a table, spreading his legs and tugging me close.

"I miss your laugh too. We all miss it."

I looked down at our hands, at our matching wrist tattoos.

His voice was soft, filled with a warmth I also missed. "We're all hurting, Sonta. Please work with us. Hadwin barely leaves his room, and Haan barely leaves the common room, he's so bored."

Like I needed more reminders of how shitty this all was… Even so… "You're the most adamant against Tyfen."

"Because the others are too afraid you'll lash out at them further."

"But where is your pain, Gald? You still have Findlech. Your bed is still warm."

"Yes, and you still let Elion bed you, so…?"

I couldn't deny that; we hadn't been trying to hide it.

"All the same… My absence isn't much of a loss to you, so you push harder for me to forget Tyfen because the consequences don't touch you like they do the others."

Gald huffed, holding up his wrist. "Friends, lovers, allies. Which of those three am I missing the most? All of them."

We could keep this up, tit for tat. I could point out he'd only included those as *intentions* when forming the magical bond, not promises or guarantees. Then he'd probably say Tyfen's vows hadn't been genuine, or some other shit.

Gald rested his hands on my hips. "I promised to please you in bed, and I'm not keeping that promise right now."

I shrugged, craving him at the reminder. "I haven't died yet."

His fingers gingerly felt for my underwear. "I promised to make you laugh every day, and I haven't been doing that either…"

"Then maybe you should stop being an asshole." The words slipped out casually.

He smiled wryly, then glanced at my other wrist, where Tyfen's leather bracelet had taken a permanent place in my wardrobe. "How many lovers do you require to be satisfied?"

"Only those in this palace plus one."

He grasped my waist and pulled me against him. His sharp blue eyes always mesmerized me, his freckles disarming me. "You were obviously into some harder stuff with Tyfen in the bedroom. I … can do what you want, Sonta. Let me make you happy in that way. We both know I like more flavor in the bedroom than the others here. Ask me for something, and I'll do it."

Gald could be so full of himself at times.

"You think you could take Tyfen's place in the bedroom?"

"I think I could fill your needs if you'd let me."

I caressed Gald's shaven face. "His cock is a lot bigger than yours."

Gald's jaw dropped. "That … was a comparison I could have happily lived the rest of my life without you vocalizing."

I gave him a cruel smile.

"It's how you use it, not how big it is," he defended through clenched teeth, pressing himself against me.

I kept my patronizing smile. "He knows how to use it pretty well. He's got almost two centuries on you."

Gald glared at me. "Now you're just insulting me."

I rested my hands on Gald's chest. "You're a great lover, Gald. And you can be a great friend. But sometimes you let your political mind get caught up and forget what matters. It's not just the sex I miss. It's his soul. His smiles. His stories. All the things you didn't get to see."

Pursing my lips, I tapped above Gald's heart. "It's this I miss. Not the cock or the cocky attitude. I miss this, and you can't take that place."

"And you really think you got to know him that well in such a short amount of time? You fought for the entirety of the first month he was here…"

I drew a deep breath. "I knew enough of him." I slid my hands onto Gald's shoulders. "Would you want me to give up on you so easily if you went missing? Or would you give up on me so quickly? What if Findlech went missing?"

"Sonta," he whispered. "You talk as though he were abducted. He walked away without a single explanation or goodbye. It's not the same."

I didn't need such a hollow reminder. "And I wouldn't fight you so much if you'd just allow me a goddess-damned speck of hope, Gald."

He chewed over that a moment. "I'll try to be less vocal about it."

How giving… "I appreciate that."

His hands still rested on my waist. "Let me make love to you. Right here, right now."

"And what would that accomplish?"

He caressed my ass. "Release, love. I miss being inside you. I miss the little noises you make."

I had to blush at that. It had been so long.

He continued. "And despite my fear of you slapping me again, I'll level with you: you're a hell of a lot less bitchy when your needs are met and you've been under a man recently."

I didn't know whether to laugh at the truth in that or scowl at the insult. My expression was caught somewhere in the middle.

His hand roamed up my dress to my underwear, hooking a finger on the waistband and tugging it down. "Tell me you're not already wet."

I hated how he knew me, how desperately I missed my regular sexual routine.

He took my hand and pressed it against the crotch of his pants, where his hard cock pulsed his own desire.

I loosed a breath. "If I say yes, it doesn't mean I forgive you."

"That's fine."

My body was more in control than my mind. Perhaps I'd be more effective in my search for answers with a clearer mind… "Okay."

We took our time undressing each other, as though we were shy strangers. Gald cleared off the table. "Lie down, your head near the other end."

Smiling, I let him take the lead. I trusted him to know how to maneuver around my growing belly, and he didn't disappoint me as he joined me on the table, kneeling in front of me.

He placed his hands on my belly, then dragged them down my thighs. Grasping my knees, he pulled me toward him, my ass on his thighs, my pussy easily accessible. "Cross your knees and rest your calves on my shoulders, Sonta."

Gald guided himself into me as I followed his instructions, as he brought me as close as possible. The penetration was deep, the angle *beautiful.*

I raised my hands over my head and grabbed the edge of the table for leverage. Gald held my legs and stared at my breasts. They were perfectly perky with my arms over my head.

"I won't lie. I'll miss tasting and playing with those gorgeous things."

Things would inevitably change while I nursed my child. "I'll make it up to you."

His grin was feral as he drove into me with his first thrust. "I'll hold you to it."

Goddess, it was amazing as I pushed and he pulled. The friction, the depth, the special attention he gave my clit with one of his hands.

His every skilled thrust reminded me how great of a lover he was. I let free, moaning and gasping the way we both liked. My tightness had me on the edge, and I leaned into it, squeezing down on him as hard as I could. That always motivated deeper plunges, the kind that made me question the stars and the sun and the purpose of life, and nothing at all as I focused on the beauty that is nerves and cum and sweat and excruciatingly magnificent release as the thickness and full length of a man filled me to the perfect rhythm.

The orgasm left me speechless for minutes as I lay there, as he held my hips, still inside me, our hearts beating rapidly.

But in the end, I had to come back to my senses, and admit sex wasn't a fix-all. That craving had been satiated, but my desires for Hadwin's blood and Tyfen's presence lingered.

Still, I savored my time with Gald, cuddling and kissing naked on the table after he withdrew himself.

"Thank you, Sonta," he whispered against my temple.

I didn't know what to say, so I thanked him back.

After peeling ourselves apart, we cleaned up and redressed. I was already dreading my search. He was right that the law books would be immeasurably thick and in the main palace library. What if Tyfen had broken an obscure law that had been established a millennium ago? It could take a proper scholar a lifetime just to find it. I'd die of paper cuts before that.

Gald was right. Findlech knew his own laws, and he knew Tyfen's offense. But Findlech wouldn't speak to me about it.

I eyed Gald as he did his belt back up, a grin on his face. He thought he was protecting me, mitigating damage by trying to make me let go of Tyfen. He'd thought he was doing the right thing by lying to me for five weeks about Tyfen leaving. Maybe he needed a taste of his own medicine.

I slid my arms around him. "I'm sorry about what I said earlier, comparing your cocks."

He rolled his eyes, wrapping his arms around me in turn. "I told you I enjoyed watching the others claim you in the bedding chamber. You think I didn't notice anything about the other men?"

"Good point." I palmed his ass. "You said you'd be willing to do *anything* for me?"

His expression oozed charm. "I dare you to say something I haven't tried. It may not be my favorite, but I'd be willing to do it for you."

He spoke of sexual favors, but I'd happily use his own words against him.

I batted my lashes. "You want to fill my needs?"

"Yes, beautiful."

I stared him straight in the eye. "I need information. And Findlech won't talk to me."

Gald's expression dropped, a scowl now covering his face. "I said sexual favors."

"For a man who likes to mince words and use double meanings, you left that rather open to interpretation. I need information, and you said you'd do anything for me."

Gald sighed. "Is this about that legal question?"

"Yes."

"Findlech is happy to share his knowledge. Give him another try."

I pouted. "He won't. Not with me, but *you* share his bed. If this law is some obscure 'secret knowledge' thing…"

Gald released me and shoved me away. "You call *me* a snake? I'm not that easily manipulated, Sonta. We don't push each other on things we ought not to. We respect the boundaries we each require to serve our people." He huffed. "Do you really think we're planning war strategy and swapping secrets about the various royal families' private matters as pillow talk?"

"You could just ask him a question. He doesn't have to realize it's…"

"About Tyfen?" Gald continued to scold me. "Of all people, you want *me* to help with Tyfen? After the shit you've been pulling? After I did my best to protect you from his actions? After I performed tracking spells daily for months? After I offered to rally my allies to help find him and was not even given consideration?"

His face reddened. "*I've done all I can.* And it's a shit move to try to use me to get to Findlech. How would you like me to do that to you with one of the other men?"

Of course I wouldn't have liked it. And I hated myself for what was about to come out of my mouth, but I was desperate, and it wasn't like he was above such behavior, either. "Call us even if you'd like. I'm not proud of asking you to get Findlech to talk, but I…" I swallowed, standing tall. "I don't like to pull rank on those I love, Gald, but you *do* answer to me. You've sworn your loyalty to me in the Great Ritual. For life. Findlech is your lover, but that relationship is…"

Looking down, Gald pursed his lips. "Wow…"

My nerves were frayed. Sometimes, mingling love and politics really did suck. And while I sometimes had fun goading Gald about his arrogance with sex, I found no pleasure in reminding him of his place.

"Sonta…" he said softly. "Your Holiness."

We were fucked if he was calling me by my title…

He continued. "I respect your position, and I reaffirm my position. You're right. I do owe you my loyalty. No matter my relationship with Findlech, you do come first."

His level-headedness was a little unnerving.

He met my eyes again. "Findlech won't talk to me about Tyfen. You don't think I've asked? That I've wanted to understand the situation myself? He doesn't think either of us should be dragged into that matter, and I accept it. You should too."

It really had been pointless to go this route… "You're sure he wouldn't…?"

"I'm certain."

"Okay," I whispered. "I'm sorry I did that. That I..."

He held out his hand, and I took it. "We're fine. I'm forgiving, and I love you. And I do sometimes need to be reminded of my place..."

His somber expression morphed into a smirk as he pulled me close again. "I'm even a little impressed. You're more of a politician than you allow yourself to think. You play your part well, so unassuming..."

I clenched my teeth. The intention behind his words and my reception of them were a mixed bag, and we both understood that. It was a compliment of my competency, an insult of my integrity.

"Confusing, isn't it?" He leaned down. "Wondering if you want to kiss me or slap me?"

He didn't need magic or the title of grand master to do his job well, as our fight so quickly melted to a gentler tone.

I hugged him. Goddess, he gave the best hugs.

After a minute, I spoke again. "I'm going to go. I still need answers."

He grasped my chin. "I hope you find what makes you happy. If you need help with books, let me know."

46

Losing It

I wasn't going to waste what would inevitably be hours, days, weeks, or even years of my life scouring through ancient law books, tracing a vague clue about Tyfen's supposed crime. I was going to the source, someone who *knew* what was going on.

I found Findlech in the common room, writing letters like he often did, probably about matters of business back in his home territory. The room was empty beyond that. It gutted me that Haan wasn't even here. He'd wintered at the palace for me but had been giving me space. Hadwin was supposedly hiding out in his room, so they weren't swapping stories like they used to, and Elion was probably taking a brisk jog outside—he liked to run off his energy, often in wolf form.

"Findlech?"

He looked up and set his pen down. "Sonta…"

"We need to talk." I approached, pulling another chair up to him.

"All right." He ran his hand over his papers, and they disappeared.

I sat, telling myself this was going to be dignified. I *was* a mixed bag. *Hoku* had chosen a woman with a temper, but one who was usually kind… One who had so little experience with these elite politicians and rulers, who constantly fought to keep her duties straight, but had managed to survive a far-less-than-ideal imperial tour. I could level with Findlech. He didn't like rash emotion, so I would be logical.

I cut to the chase, my tone formal but not overbearing. "I need to know what's going on with Tyfen. I'm not playing games. I respect you have your reasons to withhold information you deem sensitive because you think it's best for your people. I appreciate your love and service for them. But I need to remind you your loyalty is also to me. Hoku trusts me. This empire trusts me."

"Sonta—"

I held up a hand. "I *also* want what is best for your people. For everyone in this realm. I swear I can balance whatever truth you give me."

He turned his chair, crossing his legs. "Firstly…" He met my tone as if we were equals, as if we didn't have more than eight hundred years between us. "I cannot give you what I don't have. I need you to understand that."

"But you *do* have information that could help me."

Findlech shook his head. "I have information that could *hurt* you."

That sent a shiver up my spine. "Hurt me? How?"

He pursed his lips, his dark brown eyes focusing on mine. "Let's start with what I cannot give you. I don't know where Tyfen is. Or his mindset. Or his motivations. I barely know him. Nothing I know will actually give you hope or help you discover his location. That is why I trust the emperor and Tyfen's family to do their jobs."

"But *I* know him. I know his heart… What you're hiding from me may help us locate him and bring him home safely."

Findlech shook his head again.

I tried to cool my growing anger. "Give me *something*. I should know the crimes of my Coterie. The fact one would have a death sentence on them is astonishing on its own."

For the most part, neither I nor the emperor or magistrate had a say in who my Coterie members were. The territories each got to select their best, who they thought could win me over and who would ideally represent their people by my side. But there were some restrictions, for my benefit and for the good of the empire. It wasn't like we gave free rein to serial killers or abusers to sign up and bed me.

What could Tyfen have done that deserved death but hadn't excluded him from my Coterie? Even if Tyfen's family had tried to hide his crimes, why had the elves not protested his place?

"I have nothing to offer you, Sonta. It's not mine to tell. Someday, I trust you will thank me."

Thank him? Thank him for keeping secrets and reading my private letters?

That anger was bubbling up, all right…

I straightened. "I'm not asking. I am *commanding* you to tell me what you know. You took vows of loyalty to me. I don't give a shit how smart you think you are. I am your goddess's daughter, and I will not repeat myself. As the Blessed Vessel, I demand it."

His expression didn't waver. "I understand my vows perfectly, Your Holiness. But you are not the only person who holds my loyalty. My allegiance is also sworn to my high lord and my emperor. And when there is a conflict of interest, I must choose which I bow to and how I manage my actions and words. I have done so, and I will continue to do so."

Conflict of interest?

"Telling me about Tyfen doesn't change anything, Findlech. There is no conflict. I wouldn't *do* anything other than try to find him. I don't plan to send an army to your borders because I'm upset your people want a man I love dead…"

Findlech looked down into his lap, clasping his hands. "I have chosen my path. Where the future is unclear, I abstain from actions that may cause harm, and I will not be swayed."

What kind of immortal 'I can wait it out because I'm ancient' bullshit was that?

What was my recourse? I was tired of this fight.

Drawing a breath, I stood. "You disappoint me greatly. I thought we were friends, but now I'm forced to seek the emperor's council about any conflict of interest that may hamper my duties and the performance of my Coterie as a whole. I have no desire to break up my Coterie, but I must do what's best for my child."

It shattered my heart to utter the threat. Broken Coteries happened all the time. It was rare for all to stay housed at the palace for years on end, but that had been my dream.

"Do as you must." He looked at me again, his expression barely wavering, a hint of sadness crossing his face. "I *am* your friend, and always will be. Whether at this palace or not, I understand my vows and will be at your service."

Tears flooded my eyes. I didn't realize how much I'd genuinely miss Findlech's presence until now, and I wasn't sure Gald would ever forgive me if I kicked him out. "Give me a reason, Findlech," I pleaded. "*Anything.*"

Tyfen could have been a lot more vile toward him during his time here, given Findlech's people wanted Tyfen dead for something that may not be that big of a deal. Tyfen knew Findlech's secret about loving men—a secret which, if shared, could not only ruin his reputation with his people because they'd question his state of mind, but one that would shatter his people's trust in him.

He'd lain with me to try to conceive a child, sure… But he knew damn well his lack of attraction and romance early on had lost him chances to conceive a half-elf child. His people would resent him for poor representation—that truth could sink him and his family's legacy.

I would never stoop so low as to threaten to reveal his secret, but the fact Tyfen hadn't either had to speak to his character.

Findlech chewed on his thoughts a minute. "I would like to stay, obviously. And the only thing I can say to defend myself is that the emperor trusts my judgment, and so should you."

I sighed. "You've given him no reason to distrust your judgment in general. And it's not like he knows what's going on with Tyfen, to assess that part of this situation."

I'd told the emperor the elves wanted Tyfen dead after I'd learned, in case that knowledge could have helped with Tyfen's disappearance and whereabouts. The emperor had been just as dismissive of my worries since all the tracking spells pointed to him being safely behind his own borders, nowhere near elf lands.

Findlech's throat bobbed. "He knows what I know. And the fact we agree this is the best course of action should speak volumes, Sonta."

I gaped, every thought swept away with a torrent of realization.

He knows what I know.

"The emperor *knows* why your high lord wants Tyfen dead? What Tyfen has to do with the war that almost broke out?"

"He knows," Findlech whispered.

The betrayal cut deeper than I could have imagined. My heart raced as a tear slid down my cheek.

My emperor had betrayed me.

We didn't always get along, and I wouldn't even call us friends, really. But the Anointed Ruler and Blessed Vessel had a special relationship. Just as his mother had prepared him to rule this great empire, he had been my mentor since my discovery as Hoku's daughter. He had guided my education and handled so much that I had not been prepared for. He paved the way for my own child to take his place.

He had told me—both he and Magistrate Leonte had told me—that they hadn't known why the elves and fae had almost gone to war a few years ago.

"Darling?" Hadwin peeked in from the Coterie corridor. "Are you unwell?" he asked cautiously.

My heart thundered, and it had called to him. I had no answer. I instead looked back at Findlech. "How long has he known?"

Findlech lifted his hands in response. He wouldn't be adding more to this conversation.

"Sonta?" Hadwin asked.

I waved him off and turned, heading for the exit. It was time I paid the emperor another visit.

I marched down the corridor, my mind stumbling. While I considered the emperor prudish and unfeeling in many ways, I had never questioned his judgment. At least not until lately, regarding Tyfen's situation and his complete lack of action.

And Leonte... Those two ruled in tandem, always swapping information. He had been so kind, and so thoughtful with Lilah and her career.

I halted, questioning myself. How could I risk Lilah's dreams by chasing the truth about Tyfen?

Hugging myself, I hesitated. I couldn't do that to her. But ... if no one would stand up for Tyfen, didn't I have that obligation? I loved them both, but my divine duty did put Tyfen's well-being first... And Lilah had talent. No matter my actions, she wouldn't have that stripped from her.

"Your Holiness? Can I help you?" A passing servant stopped.

I sniffled, wiping away fresh tears. "I need to locate the emperor. Right away."

"Yes, Your Holiness." We continued together on my path, them rushing to consult with other servants on the way to confirm the emperor's exact location.

As though the old man had nothing else to do with his lonely life, he was in his office, in a meeting again.

"I need to see His Magnificence and His Eminence," I told the guards stationed at the office door.

"The meeting should end shortly."

"No. Now. It's urgent."

One glanced at my stomach. "Do we need to fetch your midwife, Your Holiness?"

"No. Let me into that meeting."

The guards exchanged a look, and one knocked on the door and peeked in. "My deepest apologies. Her Holiness urgently needs an audience."

"Let her in," the emperor replied.

The guards made way, and I strode in, barely keeping any semblance of a level head.

There sat the emperor, with Leonte to his right, and a half dozen advisors I didn't even pay any attention to.

"What's the matter?" the emperor asked.

I looked between the emperor and magistrate. "How dare you! The two of you lying to my face! Halting progress and inserting yourselves where you have *no fucking right to*!"

"Watch your tone and language," the emperor warned.

"Sonta, what are you speaking of?" Leonte asked more gently.

"You *know* why the elves want Tyfen dead. How he's involved in the war that almost happened. What else aren't you telling me? I deserve to know these things!"

Leonte scrunched his eyebrows. "What would give you that idea, Sonta? We've been honest and forthright about our lack of knowledge on those matters."

What the hell? Leonte seemed so genuine.

And the emperor gave no response.

My burning gaze landed at the emperor's feet as old memories flooded me. The Great Ritual claimings hadn't even been finished when we'd had a meeting, and Leonte had commented that we should look into some tension, and the emperor had dismissed it as a nonconcern.

He and Findlech were in on this secret together, but for how long? I'd spotted Findlech at the palace some time before he'd been announced as the high lord's son's replacement for my Coterie. Had they started colluding then?

"How long have you known?" I asked the emperor. "Findlech has already told me about your collusion, so there's no use denying it."

The emperor straightened a pen on his desk. "I've known long enough to consider the best path, and I assure you it's important we address one issue at a time. Once Tyfen returns, we can discuss this further."

If *Tyfen returns*...

"*Allister?*" Leonte asked with a tone of warning and betrayal. It was that much more unsettling to hear someone utter the emperor's given name—it happened so rarely I'd almost forgotten he had one.

The emperor glanced at Leonte. "I've done what is best."

"This is unacceptable," Leonte countered. "Something of that magnitude should not be kept from me."

Shaking his head, the emperor didn't cower a single degree. "Later."

"Like hell," I sputtered. "You have *no right* to withhold information from me when it comes to my Coterie, or to meddle with us. It is against the divine edicts."

He could mentor and help with situations and problems that evolved, but his intervention was only allowed with my express permission.

"This is bigger and more nuanced than your Coterie, Sonta. The needs of the realm are greater. I ask you to trust me."

I was tired of people asking for my trust, even demanding it where they had not earned it.

"You have lost *all* my trust, Your Magnificence, with your deceit and refusal to cooperate." We were on dangerous ground. "I question your faithfulness to your appointment, and the judgment with which you rule."

"I am not senile. I still have a sharp mind and superior knowledge, so I caution you when you border on traitorous words, Your Holiness."

I waited for Leonte to speak up, to back me. He kept glancing between the two of us.

I pushed further. "Senile or not, you have not sat with honor in your position. I should have trusted Queen Lourel when she questioned your impartiality when it came to the fae. She worried your elf parentage swayed you, and she was right."

He gave me a stern look as he stood. "She questioned me when Tyfen was gravely injured, which I will remind you was an unrelated matter, caused by your own carelessness."

I swallowed. "Still. Colluding with a member of the elf parliament. Hiding things from me and Leonte. I'm not the traitor here, and I beg you to give me a reason to not lodge a formal protest."

The laws had been written ages ago by the hand of Hoku and the council of goddesses themselves. Hadwin would rule with me until our child was old enough if the emperor was not fit to rule. Normally, that condition was only filled by the early death of the Anointed Ruler, but formal protests and investigations for improper behavior could force him to renounce his place early. It had to be a serious matter, and since I didn't know how deep this deception ran, I couldn't say if this even qualified to actually dislodge him.

The emperor was not fond of the threat, his glare boring right through me. "I do not cower, Sonta. Your protest would only harm the delicate balance of peace we cling to." He gestured to me. "And you really think things would fall in your favor? When your *mate*"—he glanced at my stomach—"nearly killed another Coterie member, one who is currently missing? When you rashly try to order my troops to invade a territory they have been dismissed from?"

The truth stung, and at least he had the kindness to not point out how truly inexperienced both Hadwin and I were.

"Perhaps," Leonte finally interjected, "we should recess and discuss this matter more in depth." His focus landed on the emperor. "You will tell me what you know."

After a moment of consideration, the emperor nodded. "A recess."

Their advisors stood to leave, and I caught a glimpse of Kernov. He frowned my way.

"We'll call you back when we're ready to discuss things further," the emperor told me.

"No! I refuse to be cut out of another goddess-damned meeting I should be included in!" I wouldn't let these two rulers enjoy their boys' club while I was swept under the rug again.

"Sonta, I swear we'll call you back in to discuss things shortly," Leonte reasoned.

"No! This involves someone I love, someone who has been missing far too long. Someone you gave up on because the emperor is a lazy fucking coward!"

The emperor raised his voice. "Someone who, I will remind you, has no legal obligation to return to you, as he's not the father of your child. Whether he loves you back is immaterial and unknown. This is a matter of state, not of the heart."

Bile rose up my throat.

"Get out, Sonta." The emperor's words were final and firm, and the advisors started to stir further, collecting their meeting notes and avoiding eye contact with me.

I tried another way to appeal to him. He'd always spoken highly of his mother, the previous Blessed Vessel. "Would you do this to your own mother?"

His expression didn't waver, but he did pause before responding. "Yes."

"You think so little of us? This realm's Blessed Vessels? We are mere surrogates for Hoku? It does not matter that we have hearts and minds of our own. I didn't realize you've always considered yourself so much higher than me."

"You're putting words in my mouth, Sonta," he uttered through clenched teeth.

"Then give me other words," I pleaded.

"Get out, Sonta," he repeated.

Kernov held out a hand, offering to escort me out.

I crossed my arms. "If I leave, it will be kicking and screaming. I don't cower either."

The emperor took me at my word, reaching back and pulling a call string. The guards opened the door again.

"Please see that Her Holiness is detained in the foyer," the emperor ordered.

My jaw dropped, and if there had been a chain bolted to the floor, I would have grasped it. Instead, I looked over my shoulder. "Don't you dare touch me."

"While she's in the foyer, fetch her midwife to do a checkup. She's far too stressed," the emperor said callously.

The guards each grabbed one of my arms.

"Your Magnificence!" Kernov protested.

The emperor jabbed a finger at him. "Your personal affection for her should not interfere with your duties."

The guards pulled me back, and I dug my feet in, though I was easily overpowered.

"If you kick me out of this meeting, then you won't find me in the foyer when this door opens again," I threatened.

The Blessed Coterie

Both the emperor and magistrate looked at me, searching for my meaning. All the advisors save Kernov had exited the room.

"I'll leave this palace," I said. "You can sit on your asses and trade secrets. You can have the troops sit on their asses because you're afraid the fae royal family will be offended, but I will be gone. You cannot restrict me from my own resources. I'll take my carriages and my security staff, and we will find Tyfen ourselves. My Coterie will find him within a week between all their skills. We don't need you."

The emperor angled his head. "A weak and impulsive plan. One that could irreparably damage the fae people and Tyfen himself."

"Better to do something than *nothing*!"

Looking at the guards, the emperor changed his orders. "Detain her in her chambers, a full watch."

My heart stuttered. "No. You have no right to detain me."

Kernov protested again. "Your Magnificence, she's pregnant!"

The emperor glared at him. "You think I don't know that? She's unstable. She's threatening to cross borders uninvited and trounce around in an oni-infested forest in the winter. She's a danger to herself, her child, and this realm."

Tears pricked at my eyes as I covered my stomach. I would *never* harm my child, and I couldn't believe he would say that.

Kernov gestured at me. "And she is desperate. Her ... hormones are affecting her. Being so harsh cannot be good for the child. Let us call for the midwife, and I'll personally supervise her as she cools her head."

I resented the excuse, him blaming this on hormones. I was the daughter of a fucking goddess, the most worshiped of the goddesses. She chose me. She knew my spirit and she nurtured me in her own ways. I had a place no man could hold, entrusted with the future of this realm in a way no other living being could lay claim to.

How dare anyone suggest I was fragile. I'd been taught to stand up against immortal bullies and I would *not* be dismissed so easily.

Kernov looked to me, pleading with his eyes. "You won't cause problems, right, Sonta?"

I softened the smallest degree, recognizing Kernov's words and actions for what they were. He was giving me an out. If I couldn't be in the meeting, I'd take Kernov's offer any day over being locked up for madness.

"Yes, I'll behave if I'm with Kernov."

Thoroughly displeased, the emperor grumbled. "Very well, but the guards will still supervise."

Leonte flashed me a pathetic forced smile. "We'll talk shortly. All will be well."

47
Kernov's Question

"He has no right," I mumbled through clenched teeth. "I am Hoku's daughter."

The mage midwife kept to herself as she kindly and unnecessarily did a reading on me and my child.

Kernov's voice was soft, his handsome expression compassionate. "And he was born of one of your divine sisters, Sonta. He is as much your family and Hoku's family as your own child is. There should not be so much strife in such a family."

He was right. Biological family, divine family connected by direction of the stars and council of goddesses…

I slumped in my chair in the foyer, two guards keeping a watchful eye on me.

Kernov ran a hand through his salt-and-pepper hair, his sage green dress shirt rather fetching against his dark skin. "I *am* sorry, though. That got out of hand." He wouldn't openly speak ill of either ruler, wouldn't offer a more specific criticism.

"Thank you for sticking up for me," I said. "I hope you won't get in too much trouble."

"I'll be fine," he whispered. "His Eminence would be lost without his head advisor." He winked, and it softened my mood.

The midwife took her time, inspecting me more thoroughly than usual.

"Tell me, Kernov, do you often blame a woman's emotions on *hormones*?" I asked. "Many would resent that."

He grinned. "I learned that lesson with my first marriage, I assure you. But it *did* work, did it not?"

As pathetic and drained as I felt, I still cracked a smile. "It worked."

He'd been married and divorced years ago, and even had a son a few years older than me from the union, who visited his father here at the palace on occasion.

The midwife pronounced me in perfect health—*shocker*. She urged me to drink more water and to try to exercise more for enrichment. Before she left, she also asked about my blood cravings. I almost started to cry again because I'd been suffering more than not without Hadwin's blood. I told her I'd stay on top of my cravings and that would no doubt be beneficial for me.

After she dismissed herself, Kernov offered his hands to help me up. "She ordered exercise. You're not detained, so let's take a stroll."

I glanced at the closed office door, where two new guards now stood.

"They'll fetch us when the private meeting is over."

I pouted as I stood. "Just to tell me nothing. Mark my words."

"Even so, they'll fetch us." He wrapped an arm around my shoulders, whispering, "And I'll see what I can get from Leonte either way."

I consented, and we made our way outside after a servant fetched us each winter cloaks.

My warm breath rose on the moderate winter day. It did feel good to have some sunlight on my skin. The guards walked several paces away from us, supervising but giving us privacy.

"I'm sorry this has been troubling for you, Sonta," Kernov consoled me.

"Thanks," I muttered. "Be honest. Am I crazy? Unreasonable?"

He drew a long breath. "You are young, and inexperienced, and passionate."

"So that's a yes?"

He chuckled. "You're still learning."

"I'm nearly twenty-six, and I feel like a helpless child."

"Even a man my age learns daily, Sonta; at least a self-aware one does." He nudged my arm. "And you've only been aware of your position less than a decade. You still have some catching up to do in the formal sphere."

"I guess so…"

"Would it offend you if I offered you some advice?"

"You've never once offended me, Kernov."

We strolled and chatted about decorum and how to better word a few things. How to hide my anger when I was ready to blow my top.

The light, nippy breeze whipped at my hair, and I wrapped my fur-lined cloak tighter around myself.

"Would…" Kernov hesitated. "Would it be helpful or insensitive to share good news with you right now?"

I raised my eyebrows. "I suppose I won't know until it's been shared…"

He took a moment. "Well … I suppose it's less news, and more a question for you."

"Okay."

He stopped, facing me. "Your mother has … agreed to move into the palace permanently."

My eyes grew wide. "Really?" It would be so nice to have her here all the time, so much closer than her tiny cottage. She'd mentioned she would consider it when my child was born, but hadn't committed.

Kernov was uncharacteristically shy. "Yes. Under one condition."

"What's that? Lilah's moving into Schamoi's old room, so Mother will have that whole floor to herself."

He winced. "We were actually considering *my* chambers…"

I contained a squeal. "It's not like I haven't figured you two were…"

"Right." He looked properly embarrassed at my mention of him screwing my mother, but I wasn't ashamed in the slightest. She deserved a good man who made her happy.

"Your chambers are closer than her cottage. I'll take it!"

"Great."

I cocked my head. "But you said there was a question, not news."

"Well…" He stuttered. "The thing is… Her condition to move here…"

It was cute seeing such an elegant politician fall to pieces over sharing a room with my mother.

"She wants to move in after the wedding."

I narrowed my eyes. "You mean Lilah's and my hajba ceremony?"

"No… *Our* wedding, if you consented to me … marrying her."

I lunged at him with a hug. "About fucking time!"

He belted out a laugh as he returned the hug. "Does that mean I have your permission?"

I pulled back. "Of course! You're adults. You don't need *my* permission."

He pressed his lips together. "It seemed respectful. And you *are* a rather important person in this realm…"

In the moment, I had only been Sonta—Vesta's daughter. But his reminder gave me pause. I was also Sonta—Hoku's daughter.

And he was the magistrate's head advisor.

I swallowed. "Bustling public life is stressful for my mother."

"I know," he said softly. "She's been warming to it, and I'll be here for her."

"And what of her past?" I asked. She had been the lowest form of prostitute. Service elite members of society like my pleasure instructors had, and you were revered. Lie under any dirty man for a few coins to feed yourself and your illegitimate daughter, and you were somehow less worthy to people.

Kernov spoke confidently. "She is the Blessed Vessel's mother. And would be the proper wife of the magistrate's head advisor. Even if the realm someday learns of her past, her reputation would be untouchable."

Tears stung my eyes. He didn't know how much it meant to me that he didn't even address how her trauma may make their relationship harder. He didn't imply he accepted her *despite* her body having been used by a thousand men before him.

He just wanted to take care of her.

The Blessed Coterie

"I love you, Kernov." A tear rolled down my cheek. "I'd be disappointed if you *didn't* marry her."

He beamed. "I've always had a soft spot in my heart for you, haven't I?"

He had. He'd gone above and beyond to guide me from the day I'd arrived at the palace. As the magistrate's advisor, that was not his job at all.

I got a little choked up, and maybe it was awkward, but I didn't want to let it go unsaid. "You know I've never had a father, and I don't want to make things uncomfortable with titles you don't want, but I really appreciate you."

"Call me anything you like, Sonta."

"What does your son think about this?"

Kernov wrinkled his nose. He hadn't told his son yet, though his son had met my mother before, and Kernov was certain he would approve. Maybe not as emphatically, but things would go well.

We continued our walk as we discussed specifics. Leonte was only eligible for one more term in reelection. Kernov's job wasn't secure for life. He assured me he had avenues of income, and plans, as well as healthy savings. When the day came he was no longer serving the empire in an official capacity, they had my mother's cottage or a family estate of his, back in human lands.

I made sure to offer them a private floor in my tower should they need it at some point. Either way, they had options.

Eventually, we were chilled to the bone and hadn't been fetched to speak to the emperor and magistrate. Kernov suggested I go warm up and congratulate my mother while he waited for word from the rulers.

"Okay." I glanced at the guard behind me, then returned my attention to Kernov. "Can you send word to my Coterie that I'm fine? I know, at the very least, Hadwin will be stressed. I left in a bit of a state…" I wasn't ready to explain myself to my Coterie, not when I didn't have more news. For all I knew, I may be detained indefinitely, popping out my child under the point of a blade for my defiance.

"I'll see to it," he assured me.

I held up a finger. "When I say Coterie, I also mean Lilah. You know, unless it's for official legal things she can't be in. Granted, only if she's in the common room or if she looks worried…" She might not even know about my blowup.

He smiled knowingly. "Of course. I understand when you speak of your Coterie you also mean her. I'll make sure she knows you're all right if she's gotten word of this incident."

We'd already chatted about timing. Kernov and Mother planned to wait to wed until things had calmed, sometime after the birth, and after Lilah's and my hajba ceremony.

It took some convincing for the guards to allow me out of Kernov's sight once we went to part ways, but I swore I wasn't a flight risk, and Kernov vouched for me. The guards took me straight to my mother's room.

I knocked, and she answered with a smile. "Sonta. How are you today?"

I was in such an odd place… On the upside, Lilah and I were engaged, and so was my mother. On the downside, a man I loved dearly was missing, and I had just threatened a teeny bit to overthrow the emperor.

I mirrored my mother's smile as I entered, leaving the guards out of sight at the door. "Good. I thought I'd spend some time with you. We can plan my hajba, and your wedding."

She beamed. "He asked?"

I practically knocked her down with a hug. "Congratulations, Mammi."

We sat and shared a fuzzy blanket, talking details. Easily an hour or more passed, and I leaned my head on the back of the comfy sofa.

Knowing the guards were still stationed outside tore into my sense of safety in my own home, but being in my mother's soft presence gave me so much comfort.

How was this so hard for people to understand? I felt safe and happy when my people were safe and happy and near.

Was I really that unreasonable to be distraught about Tyfen?

Eventually, Kernov showed up at the door. He gave my mother a kiss and told her he'd return. He wanted to 'escort me to a meeting.'

"So late?" My mother frowned.

I put on my best face. "I have meetings day and night. I'll never stop being Hoku's daughter, or yours."

Kernov and I were cautious as he led me back to the emperor's office. He hadn't gotten a chance to speak with Leonte privately, so he had nothing to report. My heart raced, but Kernov's wise words prepared me.

I'd hoped dearly he would be in the meeting with us, but it was to be closed door. The emperor, the magistrate, and me.

I followed Kernov's advice, bowing, using titles and not swearing, biting my tongue so much it almost bled. To the emperor's credit, he was calmer. Leonte was more certain of his position, and diplomatic.

Keeping my cool, remembering Kernov's words that it was better to abstain and process than to say something that could not be unsaid, I listened as they *both* said the knowledge I had of the war situation was sufficient for the time being.

Leonte had been betrayed by the emperor, too. But he now agreed with him and Findlech.

As a human, Leonte was loyal to me even more than my elf partner and half-elf emperor were, at least in theory.

I nodded a lot as my eye contact dropped. They reassured me things would be sorted once Tyfen was found, and that they would petition more fervently to the fae king and queen to allow extra troops back in to aid in the search.

Leonte tried to let me down lightly. "If it helps, I personally—not formally speaking in my station, of course—do not believe Tyfen deserves any punishment from what I've learned. He may not have been the right fit for you or the Coterie, but his actions are not so severe as to warrant his exclusion from the Great Ritual."

Tears blurred my vision. *He may not have been the right fit for me?* Goddess, people misunderstood him. Tyfen was the perfect fit for me in so many ways. In the way our bodies met when we made love, in our temperament and sense of humor. Even our sense of adventure and kinks.

I rubbed the leather bracelet on my wrist. "Glad to know he doesn't kill women and children for sport." The bar was rather low for exclusion from the Great Ritual, normally self-governed by wise rulers.

I asked them why they chose to not intervene with the elf high lord if they both deemed Tyfen innocent. A member of my Coterie shouldn't have a price on their head, especially if the highest rulers didn't agree with the high lord's ruling.

'It's complicated' was their simple response.

Even more uncomfortably, the emperor addressed my threats, and his. He spouted off the laws and bylaws, the divine edicts. He welcomed my protests if I still felt them necessary.

How could I when he had Leonte's support? I sat there asking myself if I was portraying a more mature version of myself, or a pathetic puppet.

"I'm sure we can work things out," I said weakly.

"It's for the best," Leonte said.

They conveyed their concern about my outburst. The subtle reminder they could detain me hung over my head. There wasn't much one could legally do to a Blessed Vessel. In many ways, Hoku's daughters had free rein. I didn't get to make laws and command armies because I hadn't been raised from birth for that responsibility. But I did get to travel anywhere in the realm I wanted. Granted, if I didn't want to make enemies, it should be with invitation.

I wasn't free to lop off heads for sport, but short of heinous crimes, I was untouchable. I could walk into a goldsmith's workshop, demand something for free, and I would walk away with a token 'May Hoku multiply your blessings' because it was beneficial for the empire.

But the emperor and magistrate could imprison me in my own home if they deemed me a threat to myself, my child, or anyone else.

I swallowed and gave them my word I would not be a danger and I would not leave the palace grounds.

Kernov had kindly waited outside the meeting for me. I hugged him, drained of so much of myself.

"How can I help?" he asked.

"I just want to go to bed."

It was well past dark as I plodded back to my chambers.

A figure sat on a chair next to my door in my private hallway, light from a sconce catching the curves of her curls.

"Lilah?"

She jumped up. "Hey!"

I leaned into her embrace. She smelled divine, her squeeze perfect.

"I worried about you," she said.

"Why? I'm fine?"

She leaned back, raising her eyebrows. "A servant stopped by my room to tell me I didn't need to worry about you. And since I hadn't been and didn't think I had a reason to be worried, I naturally *started* to worry."

I rubbed my face and chuckled softly. "That was helpful."

"You look like you're ready for bed." She tucked a strand of hair behind my ear.

"More than you could imagine."

Lilah snuck a kiss, and we entered my room together.

I immediately strode to my bed and flopped onto it.

She went and stoked the fire. "Hmm… Looks like you have an admirer."

I balked. "People think they love me, but then they get to know me."

"I'm going to ignore that comment." She approached me with a fresh-cut red rose and a folded letter. "It was just inside your door from the common room."

I sat up and sniffed the rose. It brought a sad smile after a rough day. Whoever it was from must have dropped by the greenhouse. I opened the letter and melted back onto the bed.

Hadwin.

I hope this brightens your day in some way, darling. My door and heart are open whenever you're ready.

I clutched the letter to my chest, crying.

Lilah frowned. "Good or bad tears?"

"Both." Sniffling, I glanced at the rose. It was as red as his enchanting eyes got sometimes. As red as blood.

The baby kicked, and I drew a sharp breath.

"You okay?"

I reached for her hand, and she crawled onto the bed. The baby kicked again once I rested Lilah's hand on my stomach.

Her smile was encouraging. "Do you want a boy or girl?"

"I want a happy and healthy family."

She stole another kiss. "I'm excited to be part of it." She glanced at the rose and straddled me. "We should talk flowers for our hajba."

I realized I hadn't shared the good news. "Kernov proposed."

Lilah squealed. "I need all the details!"

I was getting sleepy. "Tomorrow. I just need rest."

"All right. Let's get changed."

I closed my eyes, shaking my head. "Too tired. I'm sleeping like this."

"I can strip you down," she said seductively.

"Have your way with me, Lilah."

She giggled and playfully grasped my thighs, then did strip me down, but did little more than cuddle up to me.

48

Back in the Bedding Chamber

Over the next week, I did my best to sing a new tune. Every morning, I swam laps in my pool, and invited Haan to join me. He was so sexy, charming, and friendly. He even offered to swim through the cold channels to go pay the elf high lord a visit, to try to spy for information if I thought it would help. I didn't want him going somewhere he detested, and I didn't want either of us getting in trouble. But I loved swimming with him; he even had me wrap my arms around his neck from behind once, and he took me through one of the water tunnels. It was harder to hold my breath with the baby taking up more space, but it was still safe. And exhilarating.

He also did a *hell* of a job meeting my sexual needs in the mornings. I continued to crave his unique barbed cock pounding into me, and was excited to learn gill play, but for now, we both loved what his mouth and hands could do to me. Lilah watched a couple of times, though she was starting to leave earlier in the mornings to meet with her new art mentor.

I also made it a point to go for a stroll outside each day. Elion and I walked hand in hand. I let him take me in the garden after a good chase. A couple of times he shifted to his wolf form, and I threw snowballs at him while he dodged them or caught them in his canine mouth. Those silver lycan eyes warmed my insides as we shared our moments outside. Then I let him vigorously rearrange my insides back in my chambers…

I also took tea with my mother daily, and we talked hajba and wedding things, and she was of course happy to give advice about the baby.

I hadn't found the courage to visit Hadwin yet, but I stopped by the greenhouse each day, plucked a flower, and had a servant send it to him. He kept sending me flowers, too. Each with a small note about how much he loved me.

Things were still too complicated between us to have the conversations we inevitably needed to have, so I downed tons of pig's blood to manage my cravings, and let the sweetness of our notes and flowers warm us back up to each other for now.

I passed Gald and Findlech in the hall only once. Gald gave me a hesitant smile and a cordial "Hello, gorgeous," and Findlech nodded, though he wouldn't make eye contact.

In addition to Lilah and me spending all but two nights in the same bed, we also painted together more. We had a charmed music box in the studio, and played it in the background. Lilah was so cute as she scrunched her face, practicing new tips and techniques her mentor had taught her. As for me, I continued to have my occasional visions, so I painted those as they came, and I spent a lot of time just staring at my painting wall.

With my back to Lilah, I let myself cry in those moments. I was doing better. I was trying to accept Tyfen's absence. I didn't accept *any* sort of finality, but I needed to find peace amidst the never-ending waiting game. The fae king and queen sent their reply to the emperor and magistrate, *sincerely* thanking them for their repeated offer to send more troops to help in the search. They cordially declined, stating Tyfen would be home *any day now*.

Those words no longer held meaning after the way they'd abused them for months.

I slouched in my chair, staring at the paintings of my visions, fervently praying to Hoku. The goddesses *could* intervene if they wanted to… They could find Tyfen, save his life if need be. They could have ended my suffering months ago, but they so rarely took such a heavy hand with the living.

Maybe I was acting entitled, but shouldn't I get more than passive visions? I was Hoku's own…

Still, I did feel peace in my prayers, a calm assurance from Hoku, especially as my eyes landed on my most recent painting—a giant waterfall I'd jumped from and magically survived.

I glanced from one painting to another, and then it dawned on me—Tyfen had been gone for five and a half months, and in all that time, Hoku had only sent me pleasant visions. Not a single one of my new paintings during that timeframe were scary.

That made me cry, too. I so looked forward to experiencing Hoku's biggest gift to her daughters, though I worried how it would feel if the time came and Tyfen was still missing, but I hoped for the best. Either way, she had been trying to soften the blow of his disappearance.

Of course, I could have just been reading too much into the visions, but the thought of it made me happy, so I accepted the notion.

I rubbed my growing bump, and my child danced in there. I smiled, and Lilah hummed behind me at her easel.

The song changed on the music box, and my eyes focused on the blatantly bare spot on the wall.

I swallowed hard. I was doing everything I could right now to be happy, to be whole despite a piece of my heart and soul missing. But I felt brave in the moment.

Maybe... Maybe repainting the vision Tyfen had stolen would help heal the wound he'd left.

I set out a fresh piece of paper on my desk and dipped my paintbrush in water, then went to work. With each stroke, I recalled how I had sauntered through the dewy, wet grass in my vision. It had been autumn in the dream, the grass clinging to its summer vibrancy while the trees had already started to change colors, shedding leaves.

Wiping a tear out of the corner of my eye after I finished a tiny orange leaf, I contemplated how this vision had always felt a little melancholy. There was something somber about it. Had it been the dew on the green grass that had reminded me of Tyfen's green eyes and the way they'd teared up when he'd begged me for another chance? I'd always kind of thought so.

But maybe it was the slight chill in the breeze, and in the sign of autumn itself. Autumn symbolized change, a transition from warmth to coldness. The trees gave up their leaves.

I sniffled. If there was one parallel to make, it wasn't this, not the giving up part. Tyfen and I were an evergreen, at least until the day he explicitly told me to my face that it was over.

Dipping my brush in grey pigment, I focused on the massive stone wall with the ornate iron gates, which had been locked. It wasn't exactly *foreboding*, but it was certainly unwelcoming. Sad and deserted.

My life felt like that right now. The iron gates were locked, and I was all but imprisoned in my home. Despite all the good news and the upcoming excitement to meet my child, I fought the dull grey of my numbness.

Tyfen had said his heart was a dark vault. Perhaps there was a vault beyond the iron gates. He'd never fully let me in...

Perhaps everything in the vision made me think of Tyfen when it had absolutely nothing to do with him.

Nonetheless, I finished my painting, using a questionable technique for the moss and lichen on the stone, crying more than I ought to.

"Sonta..." Lilah whispered.

I looked to my right, startled to find her right there. The music had stopped playing, too.

"You've been staring at that thing, crying, for a solid ten minutes, love."

I frowned. "But I finished it."

She offered me a sad smile. "It's beautiful."

"It's painful."

"Those two things aren't exclusive."

Sitting back in my chair, I drew a breath and wiped away my tears. "I guess so."

"Can I ask you a question?" Her tone changed, slightly more cheerful, though still soft.

"Sure."

Her luscious lips formed a brighter smile. "How did you manage to get a giant blob of greyish green on your face?" She dipped her thumb in my clean water basin and wiped under my eye.

I bit my lip. "I'm weird…" Suddenly, I remembered biting Tyfen in bed, having fun to make him feel better after he'd hurt me during rough sex.

Lilah swiped at my paint smudge again. "Being messy isn't weird. It just happens."

I gave her a pathetic frown. "I dabbed my brush to my tears to paint the lichen."

She pressed her lips together, and I couldn't tell if it was out of pity for the ridiculous creature I was, or to stifle a laugh at my sentimentality.

"Lichen's clingy like I am, apparently. And I was already crying…"

Lilah didn't respond.

"I know, pathetic."

She kissed my forehead. "Sweet, not pathetic."

She reminded me her mentor was dropping by any minute to check out her progress, and I was grateful for the reminder. I'd barely met the woman, and I didn't need her seeing me like this.

"I'm going for another walk."

Lilah hugged me, her arms molded to me, her scent sweet. "Have a good walk, love."

"Love you too."

***

The bedding chamber was silent, only the faint glow of a sconce I'd lit casting shadows in the alcove.

I hadn't come here since the beginning of the Great Ritual. It was eerie in a way, with no witnesses, no attendants, no people below in the ballroom.

Conflict and craving warred in my heart. I couldn't stop thinking about Tyfen, like usual, but my mind replayed each of the claimings. Hadwin had been immeasurably sweet, Elion ferocious, Gald playful and thoughtful, Findlech … dutiful, and Haan wild. I missed the connection I had with Hadwin, the uncomplicated start with Gald, and Haan's inhuman pounding and snaking cock.

And then there was Tyfen… His cock and ass had been perfect. He'd been a bit of a jerk, but he'd also confused me. To this day, I still didn't understand that lingering look he sometimes got, like the one he'd had before gliding himself into me. He'd rested his hands over my womb, a longing or lost expression on his face.

I swallowed hard as I recalled one of Gald's arguments.

He left you as soon as he could after finding out he wasn't the father.

Perhaps our love really had only been one-way. I'd read into things. He'd never actually used the word with me. I was clinging to wisps of a relationship that hadn't been the way I remembered it to be.

I rubbed my leather bracelet. Maybe it meant *just as much* as I remembered, and it was easier to tell myself it hadn't…

"Is it comfortable for napping?" Elion's soft and sexy voice rose behind me, and I turned to face him.

"How'd you know where to find me?"

He shut the door behind him and crossed the room. "My mate went missing hours ago. What kind of tracker would I be if I couldn't find her in the same building?"

I smiled at him. "Sorry. I don't mean to insult your skills. I sometimes forget when others have talents I don't."

He crawled onto the bed and straddled me. "The bed is rather firm, isn't it?"

"It's intended to take a beating, not for sleeping." I couldn't hide a smirk.

Elion ground against me. "That it is." He had his way of instantly making me wet.

I panted a breath. "It would be sacrilegious for you to take me here again."

His eyes silvery, his desire already pulsing along with my own, he leaned down. With his lips to my ear, he whispered, "If I planned to take my mate right now, my pants would already be off, and you would already be gasping."

Unable to stop myself, I playfully glided my hands up his inner thighs, and he growled.

My smile was wide, and I was grateful for the distraction.

Elion sat back, still straddling me. "Are you all right?"

I tried not to let the high of flirtation and stimulation flee. "I'm fine. I was just feeling nostalgic." I grasped his thighs above the knees. "How much do you remember about when you claimed me?"

His narrow eyes squinted further. "*Everything.*"

"But you were pretty deep into your mating fever…"

He rested his hands on my baby bump, then glided them sensually to my sides. "*Everything.* The way you felt, the sounds you made…"

I had to blush at that.

"Goddess, Sonta, everything. I'd sooner forget my own name. That kind of memory is deeply imprinted."

I beamed. "I love you, Elion." The first time he'd said it, I'd doubted the sincerity, and I'd returned the declaration without a full resolve, but I really did love my mate now.

"I love you too." He cocked his head, assessing me. "Are you getting anxious about the birth?"

I'd be birthing Hadwin's child in this same bed, again with witnesses. "I think my mind is too preoccupied with other things to stress about the birth yet, so I guess that's a pleasant side effect…"

He nodded knowingly. "If my people were invited to search the Dark Forest…"

"I know," I whispered, frowning. The high alpha and his mate were generous and skilled. It might take a mere week for their packs to search the entire Dark Forest, despite its dangers and size.

But each territory held its secrets and sins, especially the immortals, and the fae were not open to intervention, even on Tyfen's behalf.

"You watched Tyfen claim me here," I said. "What were your thoughts at the time?"

Elion bobbed his head in thought. "I was excited to see you naked, but jealous he got you first. Granted, he barely touched you, so I liked that."

My smile tried to recover.

"He confused me, though," Elion admitted. "His behavior was inconsistent."

"I know… He didn't want to be here, but we … we belong together." I choked down a lump in my throat. "I can't do much about it if he doesn't agree…"

"Anyone would be a fool to not love you, Sonta."

I grinned. "You're the least impartial person to speak on that."

His hand found its way to his claiming bite mark on my inner thigh. "You might have a point…"

I adjusted under his weight, blowing out a breath. "Sorry for bringing him up again. I promise I haven't been sulking about Tyfen the whole time I've been here."

"What else do you have on your mind?" Elion asked. "I have damned good hearing… Might as well use it to listen to the woman I love."

My heart folded in half, another pain rising to the surface. "I want to be with Lilah," I said. "I hate waiting until after the birth. We're going to take hajba vows after the Great Ritual ends." I yearned to feel her body and be the one to make her lashes flutter as she gasped. I craved the connection of intimacy now that we had taken the next step in our relationship, now that I really understood what I meant to her.

"I look forward to your hajba ceremony," Elion offered.

"I know," I replied halfheartedly.

"She already shares your bed most nights lately…"

"But we're being good. I took my vows in the temple."

Elion looked me dead in the eye. "Who would know if you allowed yourselves what you want behind closed doors? No one." A grin played on his lips. "Did anyone ever find out how many times I took you before we all shared your bed that first night?"

I blushed again. "No, they didn't. But that was different. It didn't break any divine edicts; it was just inconsiderate for the rest of the Coterie."

Stretching out, Elion lay beside me, and I turned on my side to face him.

"The edicts can be interpreted differently. I understand your intent when you took your vows, but look at the spirit of the law," he said. "You're not allowed to take another lover outside your Coterie until you've given birth for two reasons. So you don't bear their child, which I'm fairly certain Lilah does not have seed to give you, and even if she did, you're already heavy with child…"

"I know."

He caressed my cheek. "You're supposed to be as dedicated to us as we are to you during this time, so we have the best chance to get to know each other." His touch was as soft as his voice. "You're not supposed to have another lover right now so you're not distracted, so the Coterie is strong and united."

My heart strained. "And I've done a good job tearing apart the Coterie. One of the first to lose a member and alienate the others so quickly." I frowned. "So, I should throw in the towel? If I'm going to fail with my Coterie, then it doesn't matter if I try to keep the rest of the edicts around my calling?"

Elion rubbed his chin. "That's not what I was trying to say. I mean that we've never resented Lilah. We accept her, so you lying with her isn't a distraction or something that divides us." He reasoned with me more fervently. "You were together before the Great Ritual, and you will be together after it. Hoku chose your soul and gave you gifts to serve the realm but also to make *you* happy."

I wanted to give in so badly, but I clung to rules. Rules were safe. "She also set forth the edicts about the Great Ritual…"

"She had female lovers, too. And she didn't have to participate in the Great Ritual herself. I'm certain if she would have thought of this scenario, she would have been more clear in her instructions."

I huffed, closing my eyes. Here I was, torturing myself again, and it felt like a no-win situation. "I understand it's a technicality. I like technicalities—they help me know I'm doing things right. I know I don't have a right to complain when I refuse to break the rules to make myself happy, but…" I let out an exasperated sigh.

Elion leaned his forehead against mine, slowly breathing with me. "Technicalities may be your answer, mate."

"How's that?"

He kissed me. "Look at me."

I did.

"Why don't you both get yourselves off, just not directly…?"

"We tried doing that. It's not the same, just lying next to each other. It's too tempting, and not fulfilling."

He grinned. "What if I'm your buffer?"

I furrowed my brow.

"Neither of us can be with Lilah," he said. "But the law says nothing about her using a tool to get herself off. And no one could say *she* got you off if I'm inside you while the two of you enjoy each other."

I blinked. A threesome with Lilah and Elion? Technically, he'd be the one bringing me to completion, and Lilah's tool would finish her. In a tangle of flesh and lovemaking, who could say whose touch and thrust had really done the job?

"You'd be willing to do that for us?"

"Why else would I bring it up?"

Fuck, I wanted it so badly, the image dancing in my mind. Her touch, his firm grasp. My soul ached for that connection with Lilah. But could I allow one technicality to overrule another? And could I let Elion offer himself that way? He was the most giving and forgiving of my loves, and I didn't want to take him for granted.

"I can't do that. I don't want to use you, Elion."

His look was tense, his tone final. "Use me, Sonta. I am yours. I understand the law and the offer I'm making." He grasped my chin. "My body and heart are yours. And I want this for you."

My insides warmed, my desire and hope growing. "I'll need to talk to Lilah. And the others. I won't risk it without the Coterie's permission." Too many secrets already tore us apart.

"I'm ready whenever you are."

49

Asking Permission

Lilah greeted Elion and me back in my chambers. Her hug was tight, her smell divine. Elion allowed me to make the suggestion as I felt comfortable. The three of us stripped and dressed for bed. One glimpse of Lilah's full breasts as she changed had me flushed.

She didn't seem to notice as she excused herself to use the washroom.

Elion, however, knew exactly how desperate his mate was for pleasure. He stood behind me, his thick cock pressed against the back of my nightie. "If you want to wait until you've talked to the others, then I can take care of you before bed…"

I resisted. "Maybe in the morning."

"You're sure?" he whispered in my ear, his hand sliding up my nightie and parting my labia. He stroked my pussy, and I melted back into his arms.

"Please don't," I choked out.

He halted. "What would you like?"

I felt stupid admitting the reason behind my hesitation. I wanted release so badly, but a part of me justified that if I deprived myself of that pleasure now, it would make up for any infraction I committed with Lilah later, technicalities or not. "I just want to sleep tonight. No sex this time."

His lips grazed my neck, the mating bond tugging at me. "You're sure?"

"Yes."

He pulled his finger out of me, made a point to lick it clean, then rested his hands on my hips. "Just let me know when you change your mind."

I elbowed him for teasing me, and he chuckled.

After Lilah joined us, we all went to bed. The two of them enveloped me, but I found no rest. My mind wouldn't quiet. Someday, when I properly made up with Hadwin and Gald, they'd share my bed more. Would Elion be sad to lose so much access to me? What about Lilah? What about when Tyfen came home?

My heart twisted at the reminder of his empty room. Had he really considered the Pontaii Palace his home, he would have left his things for his return.

I kept my focus on Lilah. The moonlight kissed her dark brown curls. Her lips were soft and pouty as she rested easily. Her hand cradled my breast. Goddess, I loved her.

Elion was right that no one would know what happened behind closed doors, and nothing I did with Lilah would change how I felt about or acted with my Coterie.

Pressure, warmth, and desire swirled in my belly. I tilted my head and pressed my lips to hers. She let out a sweet, sleepy moan.

My hand traced her curves, from her round breast to her waist and hip, to her ass.

She stirred more, smiling and returning my kiss. I was seconds away from reaching for her pussy when I stopped myself.

"I... Sorry." I swallowed.

"I'm not," she whispered.

I blew out a breath. "I'm going to use the washroom." I got up and did just that. My child made me regularly get up now, and that pressure often intensified my cravings. This time, though, relieving myself only eased things a bit.

Lilah was standing there, leaning against the wall in my dressing room when I exited the washroom.

"Hello..." I said.

She smiled. "Washroom's not a bad idea." She passed me and went inside.

The vision of her pinning me against the wall and fucking me quickly died.

I returned to bed, desperate after Elion's teasing, after that quick warm-up with Lilah. After I slid under the covers next to Elion, he grabbed me again, pulling me to him.

His erection poked my lower back through his shorts.

Fuck, I should have just taken him up on his offer.

Elion's breathing grew heavier, and he started to grind.

I panted. "Elion?"

He gave no response, his breathing becoming more of a growl as his fingers dug into my side.

"I thought we agreed to sleep," I said.

With one swift motion, his shorts were off, and his cock had found its way to my entrance.

"Shit," I whispered. "Elion?"

He snarled a full-on growl as he plunged into me.

I gasped, surprised and sensitive, swollen and wanting. His cock reached deep, his hands holding me firmly in place.

He was warm, slick, and full of instinct as he knotted inside me. I called his name once more, but he didn't respond.

Elion was fucking me in his sleep.

There was no pause, no easing into it. Elion thrust, needy and greedy, and every bit like I wanted. He was thick and long, his knot rubbing me perfectly.

I moaned as his hips met my ass as he plunged into me, as I tightened around him, as my heart and lungs raced to the finish line that soon came.

I tried to contain myself for Lilah's sake, but the sensation of Elion's cum filling me sent me over the edge. He didn't stop thrusting right away, his breathing still feral as a few goddess-damned noises escaped my clenched teeth.

He clutched me, keeping himself inside me.

Panting again, I cooled, blinking. I shifted the smallest amount, relaxed in that post-orgasm euphoria. His knot was still deep within me, and I wasn't mad in the slightest.

Lilah quietly returned to bed, not saying a thing. Elion's work had done its job, loosening me, relaxing my mind. I gave Lilah a peck on the lips as Elion also relaxed, his knot and cock eventually shrinking and slipping out, his breathing hushing.

My bladder woke me again in the morning. After using the washroom, I returned to bed, but the two of them had already woken.

I smiled bright, sliding between them. "Two of my favorite people."

Lilah sat up, using a pillow for her back. "I know I sometimes like watching you guys, but maybe I'd rather not for a while." She averted her gaze. "It's making me jealous."

I took her hand. "Sorry." She must have at minimum heard us last night.

"That's fine, Lilah," Elion said. "We can schedule to have sex before or after you join us, like last night."

She gave him a knowing look about him taking me in the middle of the night.

He replied with a confused expression. "What?"

I suppressed a laugh. He still had no idea what he'd done. "Elion, you took me during the night."

He narrowed his eyes, reaching a hand down to his bare cock. A grin bloomed on his lips. "That's what my mate gets for denying herself."

I looked at Lilah. "He fucked me in his sleep. He didn't realize he was doing it."

Her eyes grew wide. "Oh, well…"

I slid a hand onto her thigh. I'd wanted to wait for a more romantic moment, but this would have to do. "Elion has made us an offer, so we won't have to wait to be together…"

We spoke of the technicalities, and how we wanted to go about it. She was cautiously enticed. In the end, Lilah agreed to our proposal, but only if I got the approval of the other men in my Coterie. She was as hesitant as I was about the leniency of my vows, and she wouldn't dare damage relations in the Coterie further.

I agreed to speak to the men and gain their approval. She left me with a kiss and a smile before she departed to get ready for the day in her own room.

I lingered a bit longer with Elion after she left.

"See, perfect solution," Elion said.

Smirking, I straddled him. "I forget how clever you are sometimes."

His lycan eyes practically glowed.

"And last night was something new…"

His cock was hard underneath me. "It's a shame I don't remember a moment of it."

I traced his abs. "You've taken me in my sleep, and now in yours."

He lifted my nightie over my head, then tossed it to the side. "All we need now is for *you* to take me in *my* sleep."

Soaking up the challenge, I leaned forward. "I'll take you up on that. But for now…" I reached back, guided his cock to my entrance, then slowly eased him into me, each glorious inch a blessing as his knot grew.

He growled. "When my mate is happy, I'm happy."

I rocked my hips, my breath hitching as he reached beautiful depths inside me. "Then let's have a happy morning."

His gaze and hands rested on my stomach as he gently thrust up. "Let's have an *amazing* morning."

***

I was nervous for how conversations would go the rest of the day, and I planned to tackle them one at a time. Starting with the easiest.

Haan wasn't in the common room when I went looking for him, nor did he answer his call string at his room. I ended up tracking him down, though, and opted to chat away from the rest of the Coterie.

We swam in a larger indoor pool in the center of the palace, a place often used by the merfolk delegation for meetings. Being in the water did wonders for taking the baby-weight stress off my body.

I sat on the stairs after several laps, and Haan leaned next to me.

He glanced at my belly. "Had my seed won, you'd have already had the child, and we could have shared more spins in the water."

I blushed. "The wait will make it more worthwhile." Honestly, the saying was rather trite, and it was a little hypocritical of me to spout, given why I'd sought Haan out today.

We chatted a little more about official business and plans for the future. Mermaids obviously birthed in the water, but some land-walkers chose to birth in pools, claiming it made things easier for them.

I offered Haan a polite smile and a lie. "I'm not sure if it's for me, but I'll consider it." Doing so would probably be more dangerous for Blessed Vessels, since we went into a bit of a trance during labor, though the details surrounding that were our most closely guarded secret.

Drawing a breath, I rested my hands on Haan's strong bicep, admiring all he was as a man. His skin was dark brown with a metallic shimmer, his scales turquoise, his eyes purple, his voice airy and husky. His mind was sharp, his heart good, his curiosity top level.

"You know how Lilah and I are together?"

He nodded.

"I have news, and I have to ask your permission for something…"

I still hadn't gotten the chance to share my hajba news with my Coterie other than with Elion. Haan was supportive. He was still wrapping his head around the differences in land-walker bodies and affection, so two women taking vows and having sex were foreign to him, but it didn't bother him.

I was grateful, in a way, that Haan and I hadn't been able to have sex more than the once. Our friendship had bloomed without complication. Our intimacy was something we could experiment more with over the years together.

Having gained his approval, and ready for lunch, I kissed him, and I went my own way.

After lunch, I dressed sharp, my heart thumping in my chest as I approached Gald's room. He didn't answer. I waited a while, not willing to walk in again in case he and Findlech were sharing a bed and hadn't locked the door…

I knocked again, but there was no answer. I'd asked servants, and they'd stated they'd last seen the pair hovering around the common room.

Sucking in a breath, I moved on to Findlech's room.

I knocked and stood there, forcing myself to stand tall. A single glance at Hadwin's door made my mouth water. I hadn't tasted his blood in *so* long.

Findlech opened his door, wearing a robe. "Sonta…"

"Hi…" I stood straight. "Is Gald here?" I figured I'd try my luck. It would be easier to get it done with both at once.

He opened his mouth, taking a moment to reply. "Yes. He's in the washroom. I can have him come out to speak with you once he's out."

I fidgeted with my hands. "I actually need to speak to you both."

Findlech averted his gaze, his expression hinting at worry. "Perhaps we should speak in private, then. Please come in."

"Okay…" I'd never once seen his room after he'd moved in.

He shut the door behind me and gestured to a chair in his front sitting area. "If you'd like."

Standing still, I glanced at the décor in the little reception area. It brought back fond memories of Findlech's home in the elf nation. He had an entire estate back there, but he decorated this small room like he'd planned to keep his promise to be here for me. "It's beautiful in here."

Findlech's throat bobbed. "Have you made your decision?"

"My decision?"

"Am I to be dismissed?"

It was a knife in my heart. Here I was casually remarking on his décor, and he thought I'd come to speak to the pair about sending Findlech away. I was still angry with him, but my steam had been stolen by the emperor and magistrate. How could

I send Findlech away when the two most powerful men—my mentors—trusted Findlech implicitly?

"I didn't come to send you away, Findlech."

He let out a breath. "I appreciate your forbearance, Sonta. I obviously care for Gald, and it would jeopardize my station back in my lands to be sent home, and..." He looked me in the eye. "I *do* care for you. It may not be romantically or sexually, but I have always tried to look out for you."

It was my turn to avert my gaze. "We'll continue to agree to disagree on how you show your kindness." I could still send him away. While the emperor would likely discourage it, Findlech's and my relationship and his place in my Coterie were private, at my discretion.

I held my head high. "I do want to make it clear, though, that I didn't suggest I'd like you to leave to try to use your relationship with Gald against you. I just ... don't like being lied to."

Findlech nodded. "Fair. And appreciated."

We stood in silence a moment.

"I'm assuming the emperor called you into his office and told you what happened?" I asked.

It was awkward. "He shared a portion of your conversation."

How much was 'a portion'? Did he know I was under house arrest? That I'd essentially threatened a coup? I didn't dare ask. "Did you get in trouble?" If they'd been colluding for months, possibly even years, the emperor likely wasn't happy to have Findlech out him for his part in this.

"I'm fine," Findlech answered.

A noise came from the main bedroom area, and Findlech took the out. "Gald, come here."

"Yes, my sex god!" Gald chimed.

I pressed my lips together, holding back a snicker.

Findlech's jaw worked. He still hated letting anyone beyond Gald see into their more intimate side. "Sonta's here," he mumbled through clenched teeth.

Gald rounded the corner, a surprised smile on his face, a towel around his waist. "And there she is, my god*dess*."

Findlech huffed.

Gald gestured to me. "You can't get mad at me for that. She's never been in your room before. Why would I think she'd be right here?"

"Anyway..." Findlech deflected. "She needs to speak to us."

Gald gazed at me, expectant. "Sit."

I did, ready to tackle the topic at hand.

Findlech took a seat in the chair opposite me. Gald glanced between me and Findlech's lap, a smile on his lips, then sat on the ground in the middle.

"Well..." Them half-dressed and in Findlech's room hadn't been part of my plans, but at least it was private. "I'm actually here about Lilah. Me and Lilah. We're planning on taking hajba vows shortly after I give birth."

Findlech wore a soft smile. "Congratulations."

Gald's vibrant blue eyes lit up. "That's fantastic!" He looked between himself and Findlech. "This is the kind of news we dress up for, that we put together a feast to celebrate."

"True, a feast would be fun..."

Gald's smile was so warm, as was his tone. "We could really use something like this, Sonta. Something that brings the Coterie together again."

I bit my lip. Bringing the Coterie together was *my* job, but I'd done an abysmal job, even before Tyfen had left. With the injured rib debacle with Haan and then Hadwin's assault... "Yeah, Lilah's great." She really had done well befriending my men and being neutral when necessary.

I drew a breath. "But I didn't just come here to announce our intention to take hajba vows. I want your permission to be intimate with her before that." I swallowed hard. "I love her, and waiting won't change that. We've been sharing a bed but not fully, and I miss her." I looked down at my hands. "I know many interpret the law in a way that prohibits that, and I used to want to follow that strictly..."

"You deserve to be happy," Gald replied softly. "And we've never had a problem with her." He cleared his throat. "And the two of us have no room to judge you, given the way we started things..."

Findlech remained quiet.

Our friendship would have a hard time recovering if he didn't agree with Gald, didn't approve of me being with Lilah before the birth. I had the power to divide him from someone he loved, and he had the same with me. I didn't want to be at odds with him even more.

After a moment, Findlech nodded. "Anything of this sort—a feast or intimacy—should be kept quiet."

I tried not to be annoyed at his usual stiff, analytical admonition, as if I were a toddler needing a reminder to not touch a hot stove.

"I understand that."

"I'm only looking out for you, because many *would* still see her as a distraction, given your calling."

"Do *you* consider her a distraction?"

"Quite the opposite," he assured me. "Having relationships outside of duty can be crucial to one's well-being."

Gald blushed. It was cute. Technically, their relationship was still very duty bound, as representatives of their respective territories, but I understood how they saw it differently. All Findlech's relationships with the mothers of his children had been politically motivated, had been planned and created.

Findlech met my gaze. "This Coterie is obviously good at keeping secrets, otherwise our frayed edges would have been reduced to a pile of broken thread already... The important question you have to ask yourself is: can you look at yourself in the mirror knowing you've changed your mind and acted out of character?"

"I've prayed about it. I've considered it in depth. And ... Elion is going to be there with us. The technicalities of how we'll be intimate will ... absolve us of any remaining guilt."

Gald grinned knowingly. He'd offered group activities with anyone I wanted, and he'd even directly offered them to Lilah back when she was sketching us fucking. The three of us had planned to experiment down the road. Hopefully he wasn't offended I'd chosen Elion for our first time.

"Then it's safe to say you have our blessing," Findlech replied. "It takes wisdom to know when to break the rules, and this is obviously important to you."

My heart felt that much lighter. "Thank you. We'll be discreet." I stood. "And we'll see about a feast with us all together."

The men stood as well, and Gald pulled me into a hug. "Love you."

I molded to him, digging my fingers into his curly red hair. "Love you too, Gald." I pulled back, a desire to properly rekindle things in my heart. "We should plan a date, you and me."

He smiled. "I've got some ideas up my sleeve. Name the date and time, and I'm there."

I ran my hands over his bare chest. "You have no sleeves."

He chuckled and stole a kiss. I thanked them both, and apologized for invading their privacy.

The last stop was one I both looked forward to and dreaded.

50

REUNION

I stood outside Hadwin's door for far too long, just staring at it. I didn't know how to have the conversation we needed to have. He'd hurt Tyfen before Tyfen had left, and I still clung to the anger that festered over that. But I also knew this wasn't all Hadwin's fault. If he truly was the reason Tyfen had left the way he had, it would only be Tyfen's immaturity to blame.

Granted, Hadwin hadn't come to see me since the end of the tour... He could have tried harder. We were supposed to be a team.

I rubbed my belly, leaning back against the wall in the Coterie corridor. Hadwin's child grew within me. It was moving more, and my blood cravings were so bad I was downing several vials of pig's blood daily.

Hadwin's door opened, and he stood before me.

Swallowing, I met his gaze.

"Would you like to come in?"

My cheeks flushed. He must have sensed my heartbeat, and his child's, while I stood here trying to scrape up the courage. "Yeah, I'd like to talk."

Goddess, he looked good. That pale skin with his thick blue veins, his blond hair and beard, his hazel eyes.

Hadwin moved aside, gesturing for me to enter. I slipped past him and clasped my hands.

"Sitting area?" he asked.

I nodded, and he led me into the main part of his room. Memories flooded me of us sitting here together, discussing some of the most horrifying things in his life. He'd been impaled and chained in a cellar for two decades, tortured in various ways.

He'd been abandoned and left alone.

Gald had said recently that Hadwin barely left his room anymore...

Sitting, I allowed more guilt to settle into my gut. How could I have stayed away from Hadwin so long?

With a gentle smile, Hadwin joined me, pointing at a vase of flowers, the brightest thing in the room. "Thank you."

"Thank you for yours."

He sat on his own chair, facing me. "How are you?" His gaze dropped to my stomach. "Both of you?"

"He or she is right as rain. I've been better and worse."

Nodding, Hadwin searched my eyes. "And which brings you to me today?"

My heart yearned for Hadwin, a part of me that had been numb and hiding. I couldn't stop myself from tearing up. "I'm sorry for being an asshole."

Hadwin shook his head. "You're not. You're hurting, and you have every right to safeguard your peace." He pressed his lips together. "I just wish I weren't such a threat to your peace."

"But you're not."

He raised his eyebrows high. "But I am, Sonta. I understand how hard it must be to look at me, to be happy with me, when I hurt Tyfen. When you've had to conceal my crimes as well, and I know how much you want to fulfill your duties uprightly."

I picked at my nails. "Well…"

His voice was soft. "I hope and trust I know my mate well enough that she still finds me a suitable partner, and father for the next Anointed Ruler."

My gaze shot to his. "Of course I do. You're…" I thanked the stars for him. To me, Hadwin was so pure, so kind. A lost soul yearning for connection. His desire for partnership and for family superseded any political alliance we held.

I dared to follow my heart, standing and walking to him. "Can I join you?"

He sat back, opening his lap. "My room, life, and heart are always open to you."

I eased down onto his lap and rested my head on his shoulder. His cold arms wrapped perfectly around me, one hand on my stomach.

Closing my eyes, I leaned into him, soaking up the warmth of his soul that always overpowered the coldness of his skin. We sat there, recharging together.

"I don't know what to say," I whispered after a while.

"Nothing, if you don't want to."

I *didn't* want to. I just wanted us to be back in that happy place we'd had after first meeting. But I still needed to clear the air.

Looking at him, I ran my fingers through his short soft beard. "You know I love you?"

Pursing his lips, he nodded. "It can be hard to trust that when I'm left alone for so long, but I reminded myself what we mean to each other every day. And the future we hold, even if the present is rocky."

That eased my worries a touch. "Are you at odds with the others?"

He wrinkled his nose. "Darling, you've been upset with all of us. And I… I don't know what to do when things like this happen. When you get this way. I want to help you, but I don't know how to without making things worse."

I didn't have an answer. He didn't have much experience with romantic relationships in general, nor was he all that adept in the political arena, and I was still trying to navigate having a Coterie. Regardless, I felt bad he'd self-isolated to disassociate himself from the others. With the way I'd lashed out at Gald and Findlech, I didn't blame him.

I interlaced our fingers. "No matter what, you don't have to hide away in your room. You deserve to still associate with the others. Haan is definitely starved for your friendship."

Hadwin acknowledged that with a small smile. "I'll pay him a visit. But how do I help *you*? A simple attempt to console you often pushes you further away…"

Something else I didn't have a great answer for… In the future, things would ideally go smoother. In the *truly ideal* future, Tyfen would be home, and the festering worries and anger would dissipate.

I had to remind myself that each of my relationships had to be handled differently, individually. "I'll make you a promise if you make me one."

"Anything."

I wiggled my eyebrows. "Dangerous precedent…"

He chuckled, and I couldn't have loved him more if I tried.

Blowing out a breath, I adjusted on his lap. "I promise to keep working on our relationship if you will. I understand I'm not always easy to deal with. And you have your own hang-ups… But neither of us wants to just keep away from each other."

He swallowed. "It's the last thing I want."

I kissed him, and his lips followed mine as I pulled away. "You'll never go wrong with sending flowers to my chambers…"

His smile was bright. "Should I have done it sooner?"

"I'd rather look forward than backward."

He paused, considering. "Hard to do at times. You don't like to be protected, but I will always want to protect you. It's difficult to know how to move forward when I keep thinking back to how this problem started."

I shook my head. "I want to be protected. I don't blame you for what you did to Tyfen. I can't." I fought fresh tears. "He chose to leave without a word. He could have stayed to work things out, just like you and I are."

Hadwin rubbed my knee.

"I honestly don't even think it had anything to do with that," I admitted. "And I sure as hell can't be mad at you for wanting to protect me when I'm under lockdown for my own good."

Concern covered his face. "What have I missed?"

I told him all of it. About how Tyfen was wanted dead by the elves. About Findlech's collusion with the emperor, and how the emperor had kept information from the magistrate, yet the magistrate still sided with him. How I'd kind of lost it and almost put forth a formal protest, volunteering myself and Hadwin to rule the empire until our child was old enough to.

His eyes grew wide in terror at that part, and I loved him for it. Hadwin did not seek power; he sought love, justice, and goodness. If needed, he would rise to the occasion, but neither of us were chomping at the bit for rulership. We were happy to form a family and nurture new life who would be wiser than us combined, with the help of the Coterie.

"I wish there was something I could do," he offered. As a duke, he had money and a certain amount of power, but nowhere near enough to fix this situation. As a representative of his people, with direct access to the countess, he still didn't have cards to play in this hand. Adding the countess to this drama would likely do more harm.

I nuzzled up to him again. "Just be with me. I can get through this." I hesitated. I'd initially been worried to tell him about Lilah and me taking the next step, fearful he would think I was replacing him. But he was in a better place, a more mature place than I'd expected him to be.

"You can help me celebrate," I said.

"What is there to celebrate?" He was all confusion.

"Well, first of all, my mother and Kernov are getting married."

His handsome fanged smile was wide. "That's great to hear."

I met his gaze. "And Lilah and I have decided to take hajba vows after the birth."

He nodded. "I enjoy her sense of humor. I support you, darling."

"She's moving into Schamoi's old room," I added.

"It'll be nice to have her closer."

I rubbed his hand, looking down. "I'd like your permission to be intimate with her soon… I know it's questionable, but Elion will be there, and the technicalities will be sorted, and…" I glanced at him, questioning.

He took a moment, then nodded his approval. "Our secrets are embedded in our hearts, hidden by our vows to each other."

I kissed him again, soft and sweet. "Thank you." Interlacing our fingers, I held his hand to my heart. "I know things can't go back to normal, if there is such a thing as normal, with Tyfen still gone, and things at a standstill with the emperor, but I want my people to be as happy as they can be. I'm not going to forget about Tyfen or stop missing him, but I'm making an effort to do better. We're going to have a private feast tomorrow, celebrating Lilah and me. And I want to have group meals again."

"I'm grateful to be a part of it."

"And I want to mend things between you and me. We have plans to make." I rubbed his hand that rested on my stomach.

He beamed with pride.

"And my cravings are killing me."

He glanced at my love bite. "I've been missing your blood as well."

With feeding came sex, and we both knew where this was headed. His eyes tinted red. "Is there anything else you've been missing?" His free hand roamed to my thigh.

Goddess save me. I wanted all of him.

"Nothing else I can think of," I lied playfully.

Hadwin squinted, his hand slipping up my dress, up my thigh. His eyes betrayed him further, as did his hardened cock under my ass. "Not a *single* thing I can do to help us get back on track?"

My mouth was dry, my pussy the opposite. "I don't know…"

"Do you have dinner plans? Plans for this evening?"

I smirked. "Nothing yet."

His finger slid to my underwear, and I opened my legs for him. He quickly found the opening in the crotch. "Allow me to change that."

Fuck.

"Yes," I panted.

He slipped his finger into me, his cool lips grazing my neck. "Don't ever let me be apart from you this long again." He rubbed me inside.

"I won't," I whispered.

His lips covered my neck, his fingers working. I grasped the arm of the chair with one hand, keeping myself in place.

His voice was sensual, needy. "Can I taste you?"

As much as I wanted him, I also had to start thinking logistics about comfort with my growing size. At nearly eight months out of ten pregnant, some positions weren't as great as they used to be.

"On the bed you can."

Without a moment of hesitation or a hint of strain, he lifted me, carried me to the bed, and set me on the end. "Tell me what you want."

I reached for his belt, not answering. After making quick work of it, I dropped his pants and shorts to the ground. "I want you. I miss you." I stroked his erect cock, and he shuddered.

"Kneel for me," I said, much more calmly than I felt. I wanted to shred our clothes and savor each thrust, but I also wanted to take our time to reconnect.

Hadwin dropped to his knees, his irises fully red now. He gently spread my legs, dipping his head down.

I giggled.

"What?"

I grasped the top button of his shirt, undoing it. "I just wanted you naked first."

"Oh…"

We didn't drop eye contact as I undid each button, as I leaned in to reach the lower ones. I kissed him as he shrugged free of his shirt, his tongue wrestling with mine. I nicked my tongue on his fang, and sucked in a breath.

"Sorry," he choked out, straining to control himself at the taste of my blood.

I swallowed, wincing at the pain. Elion would happily see to it to help it heal later. "It's fine."

I backed onto the bed and rested more comfortably with some pillows to support me.

Every bit the predator he was, Hadwin crawled onto the bed, following me. His hands grasped the band of my underwear, and he tugged the scrap of silk off me. I liked how rough he was with desperation.

He slid my dress up, and I lifted my arms to help.

Now bare, I sat here. "Taste me. Take me. Do whatever you want, because I trust you."

Hadwin straddled my legs, looking at me head-on. His hands savored my stomach a moment—his pride and prize. Sweetly, he kissed my stomach. "I love you both."

My heart fluttered.

He moved to my side, palming one of my breasts, holding the other to his mouth. The way he looked at me...

His tongue circled my nipple, its chill making me even harder. He nipped gently with his regular teeth, and my core tightened further. After he'd had his fun there, he worshiped my neck with his lips. "I love you, Sonta."

I was wordless, limp with ragged breathing as he placed his fangs over his love bite mark. His cold finger reached down to my clit, and we were suddenly back in that bedding chamber when he'd first claimed me as his mate and partner.

"I love you, Hadwin."

He bit me, and the pain was shocking, but only for a brief moment before the numbing took hold. The moment he started sucking, he also started stroking my clit.

Blood trickled through my veins up to his mouth, stimulating me. His finger worked magic below, and I moaned.

He liked that, sucking even harder.

I couldn't help but grind against his finger, my pussy so tight, my core on fire. With the tiniest extra pressure from him, I careened, softly gasping, my legs shaking.

"Fuck," I whispered.

He stopped sucking, instead kissing my neck. "You enjoyed that?"

"Yes." But I wasn't anywhere near done with him. "Can I have you now?"

"Of course." He grabbed a spiked ring from the side table and offered it to me.

"Is that really what you want?"

He searched my eyes, questioning.

"Lie down," I ordered.

Hadwin didn't need to be told twice. Goddess, I wanted my mouth on his cock.

Instead, I returned the ring to his side table, and opened the top drawer. A smile danced on my lips as I found his dagger and unsheathed it.

He mirrored my smile as he realized what I was doing.

"Tell me where," I said, my craving wild.

"Anywhere."

Picking our trusty old spot, I slid down, straddling his legs. I dragged the blade to the base of his proud cock, but didn't pierce. Instead, I teased Hadwin by sucking on his tip.

He moaned, already tight.

His flesh was salty, his cock engorged, and I wanted to taste him both ways.

I also wanted to have a little fun, edging him. I released him, licking my lips and staring into his eyes.

His hands rubbed my thighs as he waited for me to act, but I didn't. "Please?" he asked.

Grinning, I placed the tip of his dagger to his flesh where groin met thigh. I pierced him, then set the dagger aside and pressed my lips to him.

The moment I started sucking, I knew the joy of the stars. That salty sweetness of his cold, thick blood coated my mouth, and satiated something deep and primal inside me.

I sucked hard, taking long gulps, all the while grasping his cock and stroking him with my free hand.

I could drink him all day, could make love to him all day.

I could spend an eternity with him.

Hadwin moaned, his breath tight as he arched his back, as he built up. I forced myself to stop sucking on his leg, and slipped my mouth back onto his cock, taking him in deep. Grasping his base with both hands, I sucked, and he came quickly, his cum pouring down my throat.

I took my time licking him.

He blew out a breath, rubbing his face. "I suppose fighting isn't so bad if we make up like this."

Batting my lashes, I angled my head. "So you'd rather not go back to sharing my bed on a regular basis?"

His half grin was full of censure. "That's not what I meant, and you know it, darling."

I smiled, then pressed my lips to his open wound again and took another couple of sips to satisfy me.

He was still firm, having fed from me, and I could go another round.

"Either way..." I wiped my lips. "I'm up for making up a bit more if you are."

"I'll always have enough energy for you."

I rested my hands on his chest, avoiding his large scar, and pulled myself up. I lifted my hips enough for him to guide his cock to my entrance, then lowered again. Every inch of his vampire cock rubbed perfectly, reaching deeper and deeper as I rocked into place, as his hands held my ass.

"I don't know about that, Hadwin. I have *a lot* of stamina right now. You're sure you can handle me?"

Accepting the challenge, he slid his hands to my hips, supporting my stomach, and thrust.

And it was a hell of a ride.

The rest of the afternoon and evening followed in like manner. After cuddling and ordering dinner to his room, he took me against a wall from behind, he sucked me off by piercing my nipple, and we worshiped each other.

He was my partner, the father of my firstborn, my mate. One of the most special people in my life and a companion to my soul as much as he was a companion in my bed.

Finally tuckered out at night, we rested easily, him spooning me. We talked baby names again, and upcoming plans.

"What are your current thoughts on Coterie access to our baby?" he asked, his fingertips grazing my shoulder.

I sighed, more confused than ever. "Obviously, Elion will be fine. And Haan won't have much to do with them until they're old enough to swim, but I trust him."

Hadwin hummed his agreement.

My heart hurt to vocally acknowledge the rest of the group. "As much as I love and trust Gald and Findlech, I have a hard time imagining leaving our child alone with either until I understand what Findlech's involved in."

Hadwin kept stroking my shoulder. "We'll figure it out. I'm sure they mean no harm…"

"I know. I just don't like lies and uncertainty."

He kissed my bare shoulder. "I understand."

And then there was Tyfen. Granted, his position was the most uncertain of all, depending on when or if he came back, and the reason behind his departure.

I quieted, nervous about starting a fight. "When Tyfen returns, we'll have to see… I … I know he's good. I want you to get to know him like I do, Hadwin."

Hadwin was quiet, sliding his hand down to my belly. "I think…" Each word was slow, deliberate. "He will have a lot of explaining to do. And we'll have to assess his position. We've gotten to know Gald and Findlech much more, so when I imagine Tyfen near our…"

It was like he could sense my heart straining, and stopped. Tyfen was imperfect, but he had regularly stressed his allegiance to me and my child, and had shown concern for its well-being multiple times.

Hadwin pressed his forehead to the back of my neck. "As parents, we'll have to regularly assess how this Coterie is working out. Let's tackle Tyfen's inclusion when it becomes a possibility."

"Thank you," I whispered. I prayed that would be a discussion we could have soon. I could not ignore the threat to my nerves fraying further, as my pregnancy steadily progressed to its completion…

The rulers of Colsia had an open invitation at the palace the last month of my pregnancy, and they could trickle in at their leisure. Unlike the beginning of the Great Ritual with the claimings, we couldn't precisely plan the time my child chose to arrive.

The palace staff was under a gag order about Tyfen's disappearance, but how long could we keep up a ruse when the palace was bustling again for the birth? Tailar—Tyfen's younger brother—could take his place by glamouring again, but the idea of it made me nauseous.

Hadwin adjusted positions behind me, kissing my head. "What's on your mind?"

"I'm choosing to be happy," I whispered.

51

Breaking the Rules

The next evening, the Coterie all gathered for a feast at dinnertime. We gave no reason for the celebration to the staff. Lilah and I had considered inviting my mother and Kernov to celebrate with us, but we decided to keep it a more intimate affair.

For the first time, we changed up our seating order. Our table in the dining hall had always had an empty space, with me at one end, Haan's waterway ending at the other, and three places on either long side. Sentimental as I was, I left Tyfen's space open, to my left as I sat on a long side, and Lilah sat next to me.

"Thinks he's the emperor himself, doesn't he?" Gald kidded, gesturing to Hadwin, who now sat at the head of the table.

Hadwin grinned, swirling his drunk-man's-blood punch. "Something like that."

Not an inch of the table was open, rich foods and drink taking up the whole of it.

"This is good wine," Elion said. "But not as good as the mead at Findlech's."

I nudged Lilah. "He had a bit much that day…"

Elion chuckled.

"I could have my delegation bring some when they come soon," Findlech offered. "It's a well-kept secret from my region."

I appreciated the offer. "I'd love that. I can't wait to try it."

"Me too," Lilah said. "I've decided I'm not drinking again until Sonta can."

I pouted. "You don't have to do that."

Her dark brown eyes sparkled. "There's a lot I don't *have* to do."

A servant squeezed in one more cloche. "Specially requested by the chancellor for Her Holiness and Miss Lilah."

I glanced at Haan, who wore a bright smile.

The servant removed the cloche, revealing a memorable fish dish.

"Oh." I pointed. "I got to try this on tour. I like it."

Lilah examined it, one eyebrow raised. "It doesn't look cooked…"

I took a fork and speared a small piece of fish. "It's kind of cooked in the citrus juices. Just give it a try."

She opened her mouth, and I fed it to her.

"Mmm, this *is* pretty good."

I plucked out a different kind of fish, and fed it to her too.

She closed her mouth and chewed. "We need to have this at the formal celebration. My father would love it."

I stole a kiss and turned to Haan. "Thank you."

"I figured she didn't get a chance to try it since she didn't go on tour."

My heart warmed. This dinner really was a fantastic way to bring us together, and, honestly, to highlight the good memories despite the drama and trouble.

Haan glanced at the servant. "What of the other dish I requested?"

The servant's eyes grew wide. "My apologies! I forgot to grab that. I'll be right back." He rushed out of the room.

I raised an eyebrow in question, and Haan just smiled his reply.

Lilah and I ate more of the fresh fish dish while we waited. Haan said it wouldn't be the same with the cold-water fish we had locally that this version was made of, but that the seasoning had been adjusted a little to match it. Either way, it was divine.

The servant returned, offering a bow, holding a small cloche. "Specially for Her Holiness?" he double-checked with Haan.

"Yes. She can share if she likes, but it's for Sonta."

Squinting, I took off the lid. I picked up the strand of tiny little green orbs. "Are these…"

"Sweet sea grapes?" Gald finished.

Haan's husky, airy voice couldn't have been sexier. "Yes."

I busted out laughing, and slapped a hand to my mouth. But I couldn't stop laughing. "Haan!" I wheezed.

Everyone glanced between us, completely clueless as to how a strand of sea grapes could be hilarious. I'd never told anyone he thought my pussy tasted like them.

I dropped the sea grapes back onto the platter, trying to catch my breath. After taking a moment to calm myself, I stood and crossed the small distance to Haan. "You are wicked."

His smirk only widened.

I stole a kiss. "I'll remember this."

His voice was enchanting. "You better."

Chuckling, I returned to my seat, and took a bite. I'd never actually had sweet sea grapes. They were mild—half-sweet, half-salty like the waters they came from.

I held up the rest of the strand, and fed it to Lilah.

"Ooh, I really like that."

Choking back another laugh, I replied, "So does Haan."

Goddess, we had fun. Findlech even smiled, and with enough wine made a flirtatious remark to Gald. Hadwin was relatively quiet, but a soft smile graced his lips for most of the meal, his eyes on me. My mind kept drifting to all our lovemaking the night before.

After I was positively full, I stood to stretch my legs. Gald had already stood, holding a goblet while studying the paintings on the walls.

I nuzzled up next to him. "Lovely painting."

"Hmm. Maybe we'll hang some of Lilah's someday." He winked. "Perhaps one of your nudes."

I chuckled. "I don't think we need to see that while we're eating."

Gald leaned in as if to whisper, but instead sucked on my earlobe. "Why not? Do you think it will make us all too desperate for the dessert we're craving?"

I laughed again, then sighed. I couldn't remember the last time I'd been happy like this. "Do you think you'd like to take hajba vows someday? Or are you still too much of a wild stallion to imagine that?" I asked.

He clutched a hand to his chest. "Is that a proposal, Sonta? It's not traditional for Coterie members to enter hajba, and it may be seen as going overboard, but I'm utterly flattered!"

I rolled my eyes. "I think we both know that's not what I mean."

He threw a glance toward Findlech, then shook his head. "I'll be lucky if he ever holds my hand in public."

I frowned. "You could remain secret lovers and still make hajba vows. Have it in private, or just with the Coterie."

Gald shook his head again. "If I ever make hajba vows, I want it to be public. I'd want my family there, and his, and…" He sighed.

I brushed my thumb across his lip, across the lip ring I always found so stylish. "He might be okay with going public sooner than you think…" I firmly believed the only reason Findlech had betrayed the emperor's secret had been out of fear of losing Gald when I'd threatened to dismiss Findlech from the palace.

Gald wasn't his usual bubbly self. "He's immortal. They think differently than you and I do."

"Not so differently that he doesn't love you…"

Findlech glanced at us, then went back to conversing with Hadwin.

Blowing out a breath, I rubbed my stomach. I really had overdone it with dinner. "Have you given more thought to the idea of immortality…?"

Gald looked down, not answering right away. When we'd discussed it before, he'd been adamantly against turning into a vampire. He was fine if I did, but he would be drained of his magic and a huge sense of self if he ever accepted an eternal bite.

"Tonight's not about me, Sonta. Tonight's about you and Lilah."

I nodded, not pressing the matter. Luckily, Baylana's mage partner had lived a rather long life, and she believed it had to do with the magic bond tattoo he'd given her during their Great Ritual, that he benefited from greater longevity in part by their life-bond and her becoming immortal. Even if Gald never chose immortality, my choice to become a vampire might buy him more time with us.

He cleared his throat and took a drink of his wine. "Are you excited about tonight?"

I raised an eyebrow. "You ask like there's something weighty and virginal about tonight."

He shrugged. "It's been a while for you two."

"Yeah…" I bobbed my head. "But I'm also massively pregnant, and we won't be alone."

Gald whispered into my ear, "I still think you're perfectly fuckable, despite those two things…"

You'd have thought I'd been drinking by how much I was laughing tonight.

Eventually, the night waxed late, and I'd digested enough to feel normal again. Lilah's hand rested higher up my thigh the later it got. I glanced at her, and her look told me everything I needed to know.

"I think I'm calling it a night."

She smiled at the group. "Me too. But first, I just want to say thank you. I'm … nobody, in the grand scheme of things. I never aspired to even meet a duke or chancellor, or a lord, or anyone really all that important. And then Sonta was discovered as Hoku's daughter."

I hid a frown at the reminder I'd stolen some of her dreams.

"And I was worried I'd lose her to all of you, but you've been more than gracious by welcoming me. And I'm grateful."

I almost teared up. "You're not nobody."

Gald sighed, gesturing at her. "And it's not like you're competition, Lilah… You couldn't put a child in her, so we can't really be jealous."

Elion grinned, slouching in his seat. "Speak for yourself. I still want to lock my mate up and have her to myself."

I stood, and so did Lilah. "You're *so* generous to share her, Elion," Lilah trilled.

Gald snickered. "Don't pretend the wolf's a saint, Lilah. He only shares Sonta to fuck her more often."

Elion didn't deny it one bit, still grinning.

I took Lilah's hand, intertwining our fingers. "Don't be too smug, Elion. We might lock you out tonight."

Lilah giggled as she trailed after me.

"I'd swim through Haan's tunnels if you did," Elion called as we passed through the door.

My chambers were on the other side of the tower, but we made haste and shut the private entry door behind us, but didn't lock it. Elion was going to give us a few minutes to warm each other up.

"You're sure?" Lilah asked, wary.

I didn't even answer, instead kissing her and undoing the tie on her shrug, then taking it off.

Her lips were soft against mine, her breath sweet and sensual with each pass.

She slid her hands to the nape of my neck, deepening the kiss as she backed me up against the wall. I took her skirt off next and let it drop. I expected underwear, but there was none.

I hummed my approval as I cupped her ass.

Lilah pulled her lips from mine, panting. "I love you."

How was she so beautiful and passionate? "I love you too."

In one fluid move, she tugged my dress off, then undid my bra. I was bare before her, quickly removing her shirt.

She pressed against me, and giggled. "It's hard to get over your stomach, love. It's still so weird."

It *was* different. I missed our hips meeting, our breasts crashing together the way they once had.

I frowned. "Sorry. We could wait."

Grasping my chin, she shook her head. "We've waited long enough."

I tipped to the side, getting a better view in the mirror wall opposite us. "I love your ass."

As if we were dancing, she grabbed my wrists and spun me around, putting herself in my place. She held me from behind, my ass to her groin, her tits to my back as she held my breasts. "There we go—nice and close."

I bit my lip as we looked at ourselves in the mirror. She'd done her makeup extra special for dinner, even more seductive than usual. I loved the way we complemented and contrasted each other. Her darker skin tone, my darker hair. Her fuller lips and long lashes.

"There are perks to you being pregnant, though," she whispered as she kissed my neck.

"Yeah?"

"Your womb isn't the only thing that's gotten larger." She groped my breasts, grinding against me.

I was wet and thoroughly hers. But I didn't want to rush just because Elion would be joining us in a while. "Let's get under the covers."

"Okay."

We slid in next to each other, taking a moment to gaze into each other's eyes.

"On your back," she whispered.

I complied, and she reached for a box she'd left on the bedside table. "Before Elion gets here."

She held up a small piece of chocolate, grinning, then straddled my legs.

"Still hungry for dessert?" I teased.

"I never got to pay you back before the Great Ritual started..." She hovered a bit, spreading my legs open.

I didn't have to guess what would come next. I was itching for it, my desire pulsing.

Lilah slipped the chocolate between my labia as I had done with her months ago. The way her hands grasped my thighs built my anticipation as she leaned down. Her warm tongue slipped between my labia, dragging through my center and grazing my clit.

Fuck. I was so sensitive already.

She sat up, eating the chocolate, then dipped back down. Spreading me wider, she licked me softly, almost too softly. Her tongue barely rubbed my clit, back and forth.

My nerves burning with each sensual taunt.

It sent shivers up my spine, and my core tightened. Her hands still on my thighs, she perkily hummed at the tensing of my muscles.

Her tongue explored my clit, then my opening, plunging deep. "You're so fucking wet," she said.

I squirmed at her added attention.

"Aren't you?" I breathed.

"Want to find out?"

"Happily."

She slithered up next to me, smiling.

"How do you want it?" I asked.

Lilah took my hand and guided it down to her pussy. "Have a good feel."

I did, sighing as I glided a finger inside her. She was wet, and I craved her dearly.

We lay there, facing each other in silence as I circled her clit and massaged inside her.

Each pant of breath from her, each movement as she ground against my hand… Goddess, I'd missed this.

She leaned in, and we kissed again. Her lips on mine, my tongue against hers.

A gentle tap on the door took us out of the moment.

"I guess that's it for just the two of us," she said.

I frowned. Was I ruining our moment by inviting Elion for a mere technicality?

"Don't you dare frown," she scolded. "I'm still holding you to your word—I get to be the first to have you once you've healed from the baby… I want to enjoy *everything* about you when we don't have to worry about that." She pressed her lips to mine once more. "I really don't mind it being this way this time. I get to have you, and you don't have to be distracted by guilt over your vows."

Elion knocked softly again, then cracked the door. "Am I still … wanted?"

Lilah smiled. "Come on in."

Elion slipped inside, smiling. "Am I undressing myself?"

"We want a show," Lilah cooed.

I giggled as he happily obliged. He took his time when it came to his pants coming off.

Our desire bounced off each other, and I wanted him inside me as much as I wanted Lilah inside me again. She barely even paid attention to his striptease, instead covering my neck with kisses.

"Where do you ladies want me?" he asked, with not a hint of shyness.

"That side." Lilah gestured to the side of the bed, and she and I scooted over a bit.

Elion climbed under the covers, and the moment his warm cock pressed to me, my insides turned to lava. Finding satisfaction wouldn't be a chore when it came to these two.

Lilah glanced at Elion. "What kind of foreplay do you like?"

Elion kissed my bare shoulder, his finger circling my nipple. "We ... don't really do much of that."

It was true, and I'd never faulted him for that. The mating bond made me ready for him at the drop of a hat, and I was usually happy to dispense with foreplay when it came to Elion.

Lilah tsked. "That ought to be a crime."

Elion ground against me. "My mate's never complained."

I couldn't keep a stupid grin off my face. "I really don't mind."

Lilah wrinkled her nose. "Hmm. I kind of had something fun in mind..."

Elion kept softly humping me, his finger working my now-rigid nipple. "Name it."

She pointed at the bedside table behind him. "Grab that jar of honey, won't you?"

I instantly smirked, and her brown eyes sparkled.

Elion grabbed the small honey jar and handed it to her.

"On your back, Sonta," she ordered.

Beyond giddy, I followed orders.

Uncapping the lid, Lilah looked at Elion. "After this, I want her breasts. Are you okay with that?"

His hand slid to my belly. "I'm okay with that."

I'd still never told anyone how much my being pregnant turned him on.

Her perfect lips grinning, Lilah tipped the jar, carefully drizzling honey onto my left breast. It was room temperature.

Before pouring too much, she halted the flow with a finger, then resumed pouring on my right breast.

As it slowly spread out, Lilah recapped the jar and had Elion return it. She went to lick the honey off her finger, but I opened my mouth wide.

I sucked it off her, taking her finger deep.

"All right, Elion. You get that one."

He didn't hesitate to wrap his hands around my breast, and fit his mouth over as much as he could. He sucked hard, his grey eyes glowing silver.

Lilah caressed under my right breast as she licked more intentionally, first around the edges to stop any honey from straying, then making her way in.

I writhed with them both sucking at once. Elion had a growl in his throat as he humped my hip, his teeth scraping my breast.

Lilah's attention tickled just right, her suction and pressure delicate and sensual.

"Fuck," I whispered, closing my eyes and literally forcing myself to not orgasm yet. I was too tightly wound.

I whimpered.

Lilah chuckled against my skin.

"I…" I panted.

Elion halted, his honey long gone. He stopped humping as well. I'd told him I wanted to make sure Lilah came around the same time I did, and that wasn't going to happen with all this attention on me right now.

"Maybe you should get your tool," I suggested to Lilah.

She enjoyed one more suck and lick, then turned, grabbing her charmed tool from under a pillow.

"Let me?" I offered.

"Sure."

I rolled onto my side again, facing her. Lilah lifted her knee, wrapping her leg around my hip. My eyes didn't leave hers as my hand trailed down her body with the tool. The knobbed cylinder slipped into her entrance without a hint of resistance.

"I'll turn it on," she whispered. Her hand met mine under the covers, and she first intertwined our fingers, and kissed me on the lips. Then she let go and reached to the runes on the end of the tool.

The moment it started to vibrate, her lashes fluttered, and she moaned.

I smiled. "You like that, don't you?"

"Mmmhmm…"

"Can I?" Elion pleaded.

"Yes." I answered.

He slid his knee between my legs, lifting my left knee, as well as Lilah's wrapped over me. He eased into my entrance from behind, stretching and rubbing me exquisitely as his knotting cock drove deeper and deeper.

His large hands groped my breasts as he gave a good thrust to get in all the way.

I sucked in a breath.

"You like yours, too," Lilah teased.

Elion growled his pleasure at the truth.

I chuckled. "My mate has a perfect record."

He kissed my shoulder.

Lilah glanced at my chest. "We had an agreement, Elion…"

He quickly removed his hands from my breasts and supported my stomach instead. "Sorry."

Lilah scooted closer. "Love you."

"Love you too."

I claimed her mouth, and her body molded to mine as our tongues glided against each other, as I nipped at her lip, sucking it in. Our hands were happily engaged with each other's breasts and necks.

Both of our breathing picked up, and she rocked her hips to a good rhythm.

Hungry for more and reading the cue, Elion started to gently thrust. Each pull and push was talent and torture as he plunged into me.

My tightness was swiftly building, and Elion struggled to restrain himself.

I hiked Lilah's knee up, pressing my own knee to her pussy, applying pressure that transferred the force of Elion's pounding into her vibrating tool.

She moaned her gratitude. I clenched my pelvic muscles around Elion.

He let go of his restraint, thrusting forcefully, his fingers digging into me.

I gasped and moaned between stolen kisses, clutching Lilah to me as best I could with my stomach in the way.

The closer to climax I got, the more my moans and gasps betrayed me.

Elion went first, filling me, still pounding into me.

I fought for air as I came, my legs rigid and shaking.

Lilah was on the cusp, and I tried to quickly recover to help her, but I struggled to clear my mind.

Being pregnant sucked right now—it was hard to give tits, lips, and clits equal attention.

Elion hiked his knee up, now only gently thrusting through our orgasms. He grabbed Lilah's thigh and pulled her closer. She ground against his knee while I kissed her lips and neck.

I groped one tit, sucking hard on the other.

"Oh, goddess," she moaned, going rigid herself.

I kept sucking, and she kept grinding until she'd ridden out her own wave of pleasure.

Blowing out several breaths, she rolled onto her back, reaching down to tap the rune to calm her tool.

I leaned over her; Elion scooted with me, still knotted inside me.

Happy and glowing, I sweetly stole another kiss, then another. "Not too bad, right?"

She gave me a sleepy satisfied smile. "Not bad at all." She lifted a hand into the air. "Let me see your hand, Elion."

He raised one, and she intertwined their fingers.

"Thank you for the help," she said.

"Happy to," he sighed. "Welcome to the family, Lilah."

They rested their joined hands on my hip, and I was elated to be cradled in their arms, without a stitch of guilt about lying with Lilah or how it had all worked out.

52

THE UNEXPECTED VISITOR

Things were great. As great as they could be with Tyfen still missing... But I continued to try to better nurture the relationships within my Coterie.

Now we had to plan for my mother's wedding, my and Lilah's hajba, and my child's birth.

I threw myself into my work, telling my head aide I only wanted an update on Tyfen weekly instead of daily. It broke my heart to say it, but being told daily there was no update, no hope of his return... It was wearing me down.

So I scheduled dates and dinners with each of my loved ones. Lilah painted me again for a pregnancy milestone. I swam with Haan, and went on regular strolls with Elion outside. I sat with Hadwin for hours to learn more of his people, the people our child would relate to more than the others.

Findlech and I scheduled time for him to teach more about elvish customs and his native tongue. More often than not, the whole group gathered in the common room, our furniture surrounding Haan's tank and the fireplace, to learn together about the most aloof of the races.

Lilah joined us constantly, though Findlech would give her his reprimanding looks when she'd ask how to say something vulgar in Elvish. I fought to keep back a laugh.

One day at breakfast, Elion offered to help Lilah move her things down to her new room. Gald and Hadwin echoed the offer. It wasn't necessary; we had servants to do that sort of thing. But Lilah's face lit up so much at the offer... We spent the rest of the day, the five of us, packing her room. In the end, servants *did* carry her things down, but it was fun to pack together.

Gald had no shame packing her underwear drawer and making suggestive comments. With a hint of embarrassment, she met his energy. Elion commented she had too much jewelry to keep track of. She pushed him away to go pack her scarves, because a man who couldn't appreciate her taste wasn't allowed to touch her jewelry.

Hadwin mostly stood behind me, his arms around me. He helped with heavy things, but we also just enjoyed nearness. He was in his element, holding his mate, my heartbeat and that of our child echoing with his own. The baby was rather active, too, and he ate that up.

Gald took me on a one-on-one date to a nearby village nestled in the mountains around the Pontaii Palace. He was confused as to why we needed special permission from the emperor. I gave him the abbreviated truth about my agreement to not stray from the palace after my confrontation with the emperor. In the end, it was a refreshing breath of air, and a beautiful rekindling of what we had.

***

I sat in Tyfen's room as I had off and on for the last two weeks. Despite throwing myself into my duty and happy relationships, I allowed myself a bit of time each day to mourn. I missed him, and nothing had taken away that sting.

I spent that time praying to Hoku and writing letters in a diary. I wrote to Tyfen as though he could read them. I told him how much he'd hurt me by leaving the way he had. I begged him to be safe and to return, to explain his actions.

I told him everything I loved and missed about him. His voice, his wit and charm. His strength and sense of duty. How handsome he was and how much I missed him in the bedroom. Honest and open, I poured my heart and soul into those letters, then would leave the diary on his bed before I returned to the rest of my people.

Today was no different, with me pleading with Tyfen through ink and tears.

I don't care why you left. I'll forgive you. I love you, even if you don't return my feelings. Please, PLEASE, don't make me do this without you.

I was nine months pregnant, due in a month's time. No rulers had shown up for the birth yet, but they would begin to trickle in. Tyfen had been missing for seven months, taking a portion of my heart with him. Beyond my heartache, I also had to consider duty. It would be hard enough to give birth with an audience, but I couldn't imagine how I could continue to keep it together if the fae delegation arrived and I had to endure another ploy to hide his absence.

Don't make me pretend you're here by my side. I can't pretend to love your brother, can't pretend I'm okay. I need you.

For all the might and wealth I held in this empire as the Blessed Vessel of Hoku, I needed Tyfen.

After baring my soul on paper, I closed the diary and clutched it to my chest, sniffling. For several minutes, I stared at his empty bed. I finally blew out a breath and stood. I rested the diary on the mattress, then used Tyfen's washroom to splash my face with cool water. As I faced myself in the mirror, I gave myself a pep talk.

"You can do this. He'll be back. Things will be fine."

Someday, I might just believe those words… Because after a month of reciting the same thing, it felt no truer than it ever had. Saying I could simply move on from

Tyfen was like telling a puzzle enthusiast they could wholly enjoy their favorite puzzle despite a piece having been permanently lost.

The hole gaped.

But I put on a brave face and emerged from Tyfen's room. I was greeted by kind smiles—it wasn't a secret I went into Tyfen's room for private time each day, but it was never discussed.

Gald and Elion had been sharing a couch, chatting. They stood.

"Off to the gallery?" Gald held out his arm. We were all going to see Lilah's first piece in the primary palace gallery. It was only there on a temporary basis since she hadn't yet been named an official palace artist, but we were all still excited for her.

I smiled, hooking my arm through Gald's, and taking Elion's hand. "Of course."

The others had already agreed to meet us there.

Chatter was loud as we reached the gallery, and my smile became more genuine and bright. My mother and Kernov were here, as well as Lilah's whole family. Hugs and congratulations were exchanged as we reunited and celebrated Lilah's accomplishment.

She was all nerves, fidgeting with her hands. I kissed her cheek. "He'll love it." The emperor would be joining us soon.

Magistrate Leonte approached. "I agree."

A panicked whimper escaped Lilah. I wouldn't dismiss her nerves. She had Leonte's full support, but it was the emperor's she craved now.

The room quieted as the emperor strode in. He acknowledged us with a single nod, then faced the covered painting. It was a smaller canvas, but not too small compared to those around it.

I squeezed Lilah's hand. She gulped, then dropped my hand and walked to the front of the crowd.

"Your Magnificence." Her smile was forced as she curtsied.

"Miss Lilah. Let's see this painting." He stood tall and formal as always, his half-elf ears pointed as if at attention.

Her new mentor's smile was especially bright and encouraging.

Lilah lifted the velvet drape from the painting, and all eyes fell on the canvas. My cheeks instantly heated, and Hadwin squeezed me from the side. I'd known the painting would be of me, but it still felt odd. This was a new one, specifically for the gallery. It wasn't a lover's portrait, but a motherhood one with me tastefully clothed.

She shyly glanced at me before returning her focus to the emperor.

He took his time reviewing it, and Lilah's mentor leaned in to point out some features of the artwork. The emperor turned to Lilah, quietly discussing the painting.

After a bit of nodding and talking, Lilah's whole face lit up. "Yes!"

He extended his hands, and she took them.

The emperor faced the rest of us. "A lovely piece. I look forward to seeing more." He gestured to a table in the corner of the room. "Fine wine to celebrate our newest apprentice's fine work."

The energy of the room was warm as we all whispered. Lilah and the emperor walked to her family, where she started to introduce them.

A servant handed me a nonalcoholic drink, and Hadwin kissed my head. "I bet she's grateful to have you."

I leaned into Hadwin, sipping my sweet drink as another servant handed him a blood cocktail. "My position helped get her in front of the right people, but the work is her own. She earned this."

Unable to stop smiling, I watched as the room bustled. The emperor's introduction to Lilah's family was brief, cut short as his head aide walked into the room and whispered into his ear.

His face was unreadable as he nodded and whispered back. He excused himself, then tipped his head to Leonte. The magistrate straightened, and excused himself, too. With a glance in my direction, Leonte followed the emperor out.

My heart thudded at their abrupt departure. Were those conspiratorial glances?

"Kernov?" I turned to my left.

Kernov approached. "Sonta?"

"Do they have a meeting today? I thought they'd stay a few more minutes…"

Hadwin rubbed my arm.

Kernov looked at the door they'd left through. "There are always unexpected meetings and fires to put out. Don't let it get to you."

Lilah came up to me, her hands shaking, her smile wide. "He likes it! He wants me to redo it full-size in time for the Grand Ball!"

The Grand Ball took place three months after a Blessed Vessel gave birth to her firstborn. That gave Lilah about four months for that big of a painting.

I took her hands. "Congratulations."

She let out a little squeal.

My heart and curiosity still lingering on the abrupt departure of the emperor and magistrate, I couldn't stop myself from inquiring, "Did you hear why His Magnificence and Eminence left?"

She shook her head. "It's a shame they had to leave like that. Do you think they'll come back? My parents didn't even get a chance to properly meet Leonte."

I shrugged. "I have no idea…"

I glanced at her family, where my mother had easily slid into conversation with Lilah's mother. Forcing myself not to worry, I kissed Lilah on the lips. "Congratulations," I repeated. "If you change your mind about alcohol, make sure to grab an extra wine in my stead."

"Very thoughtful of you, Your Holiness." She winked.

Nothing's wrong. Everything's fine. Stay calm.

I fought my racing mind flooding with worries. What if they'd just gotten news Tyfen had died?

Get a grip.

I couldn't spiral like this, not again. Not each and every time the rulers were whisked away on important business. There were a great many matters in the empire that didn't directly affect me or my duties, and I should remember that.

Luckily, no one allowed me to fall apart, and I accepted the abundant distractions of socializing. If anyone deserved my undivided attention right now, it was Lilah.

Our little reception lasted over an hour, then my Coterie conspired and invited my mother and Kernov, and Lilah's whole family back to the common room.

There was ample seating in the common room, and Lilah's family loved it. The fire crackled in the corner, and Haan happily engaged in conversation with Lilah's older sister.

My anxiety hadn't eased. The emperor and magistrate had never returned to the celebration. I reminded myself it had been a quaint little formality for Lilah, not an important matter of state.

Gald massaged my shoulders, and Elion and Hadwin sat on either side of me. It was moments like this I felt sorry for Gald and Findlech. With Lilah's family and mine here, they wouldn't even sit next to each other. It wasn't like the two men were *always* together, and or that Gald wouldn't naturally be showing me affection and attention right now, but the forced distance still pinched my heart.

Findlech sat across from us, legs crossed, answering Lilah's father's questions.

A servant quietly entered from the Coterie corridor and approached Findlech. He handed him a paper. Reading it, Findlech arched an eyebrow. "I'll be right there."

He stood, bowing to Lilah's father. "I'm so sorry for the interruption. I have business to attend to."

"Of course, no apologies necessary. Who am I to command the time of a lord?"

My heart thudded again. "Is everything all right, Findlech?"

He offered me a soft smile. "I'm sure it is. Were my personal estate on fire, I imagine there would be more haste. I'll update you when I return."

Elion rubbed my knee. I needed to stop being so on edge. Findlech had more meetings with his aides regarding his duties than any of the others. For all I knew, there was a pressing matter of an illness in the herds around his community.

The problem was … Findlech didn't return all night.

Not as we conversed for hours. Not when we all squeezed into the dining hall for a celebration in Lilah's honor.

Not when Gald and Lilah joined me in bed.

"I'm sure it's nothing," Lilah soothed as she climbed in next to me.

I'd only been able to hide my anxiety for so long.

"Gald? Are you keeping anything from me?"

He returned from the dressing room in his shorts. "Only the unending depths of my infatuation with you, Sonta." His charming smile attempted to disarm me.

"I'm not playing games. If you know something…"

He cocked his head. "Hoku as my witness, I don't know why any of them were called away. I'm sure they're separate matters, and you don't need to stress yourself."

I frowned, choking down my worries. "Yeah…"

Lilah wrapped her arm around me, and Gald cuddled me from the other side, snuffing out the candles with his magic.

"You just need some good rest." Gald kissed me.

"You're right."

"Congratulations, again, Lilah," Gald whispered.

She hummed sleepily. "Thanks, Gald."

By morning, Findlech had not returned to his room nor the common room. I spoke to his aide, who confirmed he'd been in meetings all night, but wouldn't or couldn't tell me more. I wanted to reach out to Kernov to inquire about the emperor and magistrate, but stopped myself. If I checked now, I'd only validate their worries about my mind being unstable. If I'd needed to know why they all had meetings, I would have been included…

At least that was what I told myself as I fed on Hadwin, then met up with everyone for breakfast.

"I think we should all take a walk," Elion suggested as he cleared his plate. He awkwardly glanced at Haan. "By the lake?"

Haan grinned, grateful to be included. "We always keep the shoreline ice-free by the walking path. I wouldn't mind a brisk swim to invigorate me."

We all went on a stroll. Spring was just around the corner, and several little bright flowers poked out despite a dusting of snow on the grounds.

After we were chilled to the bone, we returned, handing off our cloaks and coats to the lobby servants as we entered.

We went straight to the common room; I was anxious to sit in front of the fire.

The moment I opened the common room door, my heart stopped working, and my legs froze in place.

All alone, Findlech and the fae queen sat there.

"You have our deepest gratitude," she told Findlech.

I blinked. Never had I imagined the queen sitting in my common room. And *never* had I imagined these two calmly sitting together and her thanking him. Hadn't she accused him of trying to murder her son months ago?

Findlech noticed the buildup of onlookers at the door. "Sonta…"

I swallowed and marched in as they stood. "Do you have news of Tyfen? Tell me he's all right." The words spilled out of me, full of worry.

What if she'd only come in preparation for the birth?

What if she'd come to deliver bad news?

"He's fine," she assured me.

I couldn't believe a word out of this heinous woman's mouth. She'd lied to me countless times and had given up on finding her own son.

"I know he's *'fine,'*" I spat. "I keep getting updates on tracking spells of him in your kingdom, *alive*. That doesn't mean shit. How dare you come here after ignoring my letters, after sending away our soldiers, after refusing help because of your pride!"

She swallowed, then replied much calmer than me. "He came with us."

Time froze as that sentence sank in. Tears sprung to my eyes. "He's here?" I squeaked.

"Yes." She gave me an encouraging smile.

"Where?" I glanced past her to the Coterie corridor. Either Findlech or Tyfen must have invited her into the common room, right?

"I'd like a moment alone with you first," she said.

"No." I shook my head, my heart swelling. "Is he in his room?"

"Please," she implored me.

"Later," I insisted as I took a step forward.

She blocked me. "Mother to mother, *please.*"

Findlech spoke up. "The rest of us will give you some space." He ushered the others back into the hallway.

It was torture as they filed out, as my eyes darted between the queen and the doorway behind her.

The door to the main hallway closed.

"What?" I demanded, hugging myself.

Her smile was hesitant as she glanced at my stomach. "I'm happy to see you're doing well."

"You're not here for pleasantries, Your Majesty. Say what you need to."

She nodded. "He's been through a lot." Her frown prodded at the pain in my heart.

Why did she need to preface her answer with that information?

"But you said he's fine…"

"Yes. He's physically fine, and I think things will go well…"

"Okay…"

She pursed her lips. "I pray you'll give him a chance to explain. I pray you can forgive him and accept him again."

My throat was dry. That … didn't sound promising. "If he doesn't want to be in my Coterie…" I wouldn't force him. It would fully break my heart to let him go, but we at least needed to have that conversation.

"He's here by choice this time," she said. "I just wanted to ask you, mother to mother, to go easy on him." She cleared her throat. "We shouldn't have forced him to join your Coterie in the first place. He wasn't ready. And my husband and I are sorry for any pain that decision has caused you."

I wiped away a tear. If she wanted my forgiveness, I didn't have that to offer.

"And we hope you can forgive us our deception, Your Holiness."

Her lies had been paper thin at times.

She continued. "He's been home, at *our* home, since right after you left the Crystal City."

My eyes widened. "Three months? He's been with you for *three months,* and you didn't send word?"

She winced. "We had our reasons. And we beg your forgiveness."

"Did the emperor know he was safely home?"

"No."

I didn't pity what she and her husband faced for lying so blatantly to the emperor, to us both.

"He is your son, but he is in *my* Coterie. You had no right to keep him from me." She didn't answer.

"Why?" My face warmed. "Why did you lie?" I could have been there for him. I could have saved myself and those around me months of torture.

Queen Lourel lowered her head. "He'll explain. As his mother, I just wanted to ask you to fully hear him out. This hasn't been easy for him, either."

"I'll hear him out," I promised. "Can I see him now?"

"Yes, Your Holiness."

I would deal with her later. For now, all that mattered was seeing Tyfen.

Nearly sprinting down the corridor, I wiped away my tears. My mind raced, my breathing and heart wild as I stood at his closed door.

Tyfen had been missing for seven months. Three of which he'd been safely with his family.

Seven months. My hand rested on the door handle. What if I'd been too quick to confess my love for him, had fallen too deep and fast, and he never really had been the man I'd thought I'd known? What if he was only here for the birth and formalities, and not for me?

There were a thousand what-ifs, and I would die of old age if I stood here, pondering them all, instead of facing him.

I probably should have knocked, but my mind wasn't right. I opened the door and quietly entered. Rustling came from the bedroom and sitting area. I fought fresh tears; not a sound had been made in this room for months that hadn't been my own.

I glanced into the bedroom, then stopped.

The room had life to it. The bed was made, Tyfen's crown was on its shelf, and a couple of servants bustled, arranging things in his closet and washroom. The walls even had decorations, unlike before; some I recognized from his room in the fae castle.

Tyfen sat silent, reading the letters I'd written him in the diary I always left here. His expression was thoughtful, his brown hair perfect, his pointed arched ears just as I remembered them.

Memories flowed, all crashing back. The tattoos on his neck, chest, and hands all reminded me of us making love on this bed, of us sharing intimate moments while I traced them. Of him telling me stories of his childhood.

Of him deflecting many questions, not ready to answer.

My heart was in a vise as I stood, frozen.

One of the servants spied me and stopped his work. "Your Highness…"

Tyfen kept his eyes glued to the diary, flipping a page. "I don't care where anything goes. I can rearrange it later if I need to."

"It's Her Holiness," the servant replied.

Tyfen's gaze snapped to mine. His devastatingly beautiful green eyes pricked at my heart further. And in that familiar voice I loved so much, he breathed my name.

53

THE NEW TATTOO

Tears pooled in my eyes at the sound of my name on Tyfen's lips. He set down my diary and stood. The servants took the cue and exited through the back servants' door.

Tyfen crossed the room, and I stood in place, still in shock at *finally* seeing him.

He examined me from a few paces away. "You look amazing," he muttered.

I swallowed. He looked every bit the handsome and healthy man I remembered, the lover who'd stolen my heart against either of our better judgment.

My pain came to a head. "You lied. About everything. You left me."

He frowned deeply. "I'm sorry. I can explain." He took a step forward, holding out his hand.

I retreated a step. "You're *sorry*? I told you I loved you, and then you lied to me to get me to go away. You said you were going to figure your shit out, Tyfen. But you left me, without a single word." I jabbed a finger at him. "I've been worried about you for *months*. Lied to. Humiliated. Having to lie to cover for you. Pretending with your brother when *you* should have been there! For me, your family, the Coterie, and your people! How selfish are you?"

Tyfen's throat bobbed. "I needed to set some things straight, Sonta. And I… I wasn't ready to…" He struggled, all hesitation. "I couldn't say I loved you. I did love you. I *do*. But I couldn't give you what you needed, not then. I needed to leave the palace."

I shook my head, barely softened by his confession of love. "Why am I so hard to love? Why is that so scary a thing that you had to run away instead of facing me like a man?"

With tears in his eyes, he slumped his shoulders. "You're not hard to love, Sonta. You're easy to love." He pursed his lips. "*Too* easy to love. Because I was in a bad place, and I wasn't ready for that. If I didn't leave, I would have only kept hurting you."

What kind of shit logic was that? "People who love each other talk things out. Maybe they take a break, but they don't abandon each other without a word."

He loosed a breath. "It's more complicated than that. I'll need some time to explain."

I wiped away a tear. "And how many times will I hear the word 'pass' when I ask you questions?"

Tyfen closed his eyes, grimacing. "None. I swear it." He looked at me again and stepped closer. "I'm an open book."

A whimper escaped my lips. My heart had become more guarded. As much as I loved him and had promised his mother I'd let him explain, I couldn't imagine his reason for leaving the way he had ever matching the pain he'd caused me. I'd challenged the emperor for him. I'd pushed away people I loved for him. I'd cried countless tears for him.

Tyfen opened his arms to give me a hug. Every part of me wanted to be in his arms, but shreds of pride, dignity, and pain had me shaking my head.

He sank to his knees as he had once before. "I'm not ashamed to beg." He slid his hands onto my legs, cupping my calves. "Please, *Nil Blantui*. I need you."

Blantui—'strength' in Fae. Nil—'my' in Fae. He'd only ever called me Blantui before. But I was *Nil* Blantui? His nickname for me always softened me, and his warm hands now touching my skin only helped.

"I'll listen," I whispered. "I expect the full truth."

"All of it," he swore. His handsome green eyes searched mine. "Let's sit."

I sniffled and nodded.

Tyfen rose, grasping my hand. Why had his touch always felt so right? He led me to the sitting area, and we each took a chair.

"I thought you were in danger. That you were dead," I confessed.

His face somber, he replied, "I nearly did die."

My eyes widened. "But you're … okay?"

"Yes."

I breathed easier, waiting for him to speak while I picked through my questions. "You weren't forced to leave, right?" He'd admitted he hadn't been ready to say he loved me… None of his words thus far indicated he'd been coerced to leave.

"Not exactly," he said. "No one made me go, but that doesn't mean I only left because of you. I didn't feel safe here."

I furrowed my brow. "Hadwin was on tour with me. Why would you be afraid of him hurting you again?" It made no sense.

"No. I wasn't afraid of Hadwin." Tyfen rubbed his face. "People saw us. All those onlookers when you were getting ready to leave on tour… They saw you call on a guard. They saw you in hysterics. They saw me cause that, and then they watched me kiss you."

His explanation still had me lost. "I shouldn't have had that guard stop you, but it's not like it was that serious. And no one knew what we were going through. Why would they assume you hurt me?" The same question from before bubbled up. "Why was it so important to hide that we were together when people would naturally assume we were?"

"It's complicated."

"Complicated? So complicated you packed your things and sent them home? So complicated you couldn't write a letter?"

He balled his fists. "I wasn't in the right frame of mind. I shouldn't have done that, but I panicked. Just as much as I was terrified of my feelings for you, I was terrified of what would happen after you left on tour. I told my mother to send the delegation home as soon as she could, and the moment I was healed enough to go, I left." He blew out a breath. "I tried to write you a letter, but couldn't find the words. And I didn't think about how sending my things back to the castle would look. I know it sounds stupid, but I was also worried about my father's reaction when he found out I'd left my things for people to possibly steal."

I screwed up my face at the weak logic. No one in the Coterie would have stolen his things had he taken a leave of absence, and the servants were all highly vetted.

Tyfen held up a hand, acknowledging the lack of logic. "Complicated. And I wasn't really thinking properly."

It was hard to logic your way through someone else's panicked state of mind.

He attempted a smile. "I know I broke promises, but I kept some, too." His voice was encouraging. "I haven't had a drop of alcohol since I left."

That was promising.

He continued. "And I *did* get my shit together, which is why I'm back."

I hugged myself. "That's good, I guess."

His eyes were piercing, soft and deep. "I wanted to drink myself to oblivion, especially with the way I hurt you after you said you loved me. Instead … I turned to something else to clear my mind."

"What's that?"

He huffed a laugh. "Duty and killing things."

I arched an eyebrow.

"I left with hardly more than the clothes on my back and my sword. I went straight to the Dark Forest and set to work hunting oni."

The confession didn't settle quite right. "I understand you have something in your past that haunts you, and I've tried to give you your space. And I can respect that you have a different way of sorting through that. But *hunting*? A hunting trip to clear your mind was more important than being there for your leg of the imperial tour? I wasn't the only person hurt by this, Tyfen."

Why was a man of more than two centuries so fragile? His whole family had borne the weight of his decision. The rest of the Coterie, the emperor, and magistrate were complicit in lies to protect him. The fae people had lost out on much of their celebration because of this.

He hung his head in shame. "I lost track of the days, but I fully intended to be there. I planned to return in time. But there's a reason I normally take a dozen men on my hunting parties." He rubbed his knee. "I ran into a pack of oni, rather nasty ones."

My heart froze as I remembered the pack that had attacked us on tour. Without Hadwin, we would have suffered several casualties, and that was with the emperor's finest soldiers.

"I almost died out there," Tyfen admitted. "I don't always make the wisest choices."

My fears for his life had been justified. I surveyed Tyfen, my humbled commander. Something clicked. He'd been hard to track, even when we were inside the wards of the fae boundary walls. "Were you using your masking magic the whole time?"

He nodded. He hadn't wanted to be found. Between his glamour magic, masking, and winnowing, he would be a fantastic spy and soldier. "When I got hurt, that's when I gave my location away. I couldn't keep it up."

He must have been gravely injured to drop masking magic to refocus it elsewhere. "The blip," I whispered. "Right before we left your castle, Gald did a tracking spell, and we confirmed you were in that forest."

Tyfen nodded.

"We sent the emperor's soldiers..." We should have been reunited ages ago. He could have been saved faster.

"My parents told them to search in the wrong area, fearing what I may say. What the emperor might learn."

My ears burned. I hated the fae king and queen. "And then they dismissed them and lied about continuing to search on their own when they instead snuck you back to your castle?"

"Yes."

I imagined him lying in bed, his family and servants secretly tending to his fresh wounds. "I would have dropped everything to be by your side." Hadn't I done so after Hadwin nearly killed him?

Tyfen leaned forward, wrapping his large warm hands around mine. He looked me directly in the eye. "I love you, Sonta."

My heart warmed at the earnest and direct confession. "I love you too."

His throat bobbed. "But you were the last person I needed to see. I *needed* to be away from you to heal, and I don't mean my oni wounds... I know I hurt you by leaving, and I know it's not pleasant to hear me say this, but I needed time and space to clear my heart and head. I *asked* my parents to lie about finding me."

I fought tears. It did truly suck to hear that, but he was healed now... Clearly in body, and presumably in mind and heart. I forced myself to nod.

"You were going to get hurt either way, but I knew what I needed, and I knew you had enough people with you here to be okay." He rubbed my hand with his thumb. "I already told you I didn't choose to join your Coterie. And I was an asshole. And I planned to be more of an asshole." He flashed a guilty grimace. "But I felt bad, and I liked you a hell of a lot more than I ever expected to." He sat back in his seat, taking his hands back. "And liking you made things worse."

Why did it feel like I was more of a punishment than a gift?

He continued. "I told myself it was just sex. I just wanted a distraction, just wanted to enjoy my time."

I bit my lip. It wasn't like I was a prude, and I hadn't been delusional about us starting off as more than a sexual pair, but hadn't we grown far beyond that?

"My heart wasn't open," he said.

Tyfen rolled up his sleeves, averting his gaze as a glamour on his forearm shimmered away.

I choked on air as a tattoo filled his forearm. Only one kind of tattoo had a place on fae forearms—the mark of an accepted mate.

Gaping, I struggled for words. "You have a mate…" An *accepted* mate. The mark only showed up once both parties accepted each other as their life partner.

"No," Tyfen softly lied.

I pointed at it. "You left me to go find your mate?"

"No," he repeated emphatically, albeit weakly.

I searched his face. How could he lie? I'd traced every tattoo on his body, and it hadn't been there before.

Then I remembered an overheard conversation months ago. His father had been an asshole in the hallway during the paternity reveal ball. 'Have you been keeping it hidden?' his father had asked.

"You glamoured it away this whole time?"

"Not by choice."

"Like hell!" His heart hadn't been open because it had already been claimed—fully—by the fae mate fate had given him.

Tyfen pursed his lips. "As Hoku's daughter, you should know as much as anyone that glamouring magic can be involuntary."

I blinked, still confused. "Hoku has nothing to do with this. You've had a mate all along, and you lied to me, Tyfen. You told me you didn't worry about finding a mate. You swore there was no one out there for you but me."

"She's dead, Sonta," he blurted.

I held my breath as his eyes filled with tears. "My mate is dead."

I choked back my own tears. Now I understood what he meant about Hoku and glamouring. In rare circumstances, extreme trauma could glamour something away on a person who held that magic.

Tyfen had responded to his father after he'd asked if Tyfen was hiding his mating mark, and I'd forgotten that part. 'You know I don't even get a choice in that!'

"I'm sorry," I whispered.

"Thank you." He wouldn't make eye contact.

We sat in silence as he mourned, and as I worked through my thoughts. No wonder his heart had been closed off. Fae mating bonds were like Hadwin's special kind of Blessed Vessel mating bond—they extended beyond death.

Tyfen was a widower, and he would *always* miss his lost mate.

I thought back to things he'd said about his lifetime, and the stories he'd shared. How long had it been since he'd last slept with a human woman? Twenty or so years…

It was an indelicate question, but I needed to better understand his pain. "How long has it been since she passed?"

He crossed his arms. "Seven years this upcoming autumn."

My heart dropped. I'd never lost someone that close to me, so I didn't know how long it took to recover from that kind of pain, but to an immortal, that was like the blink of an eye. "Your parents forced you to join my Coterie so soon?"

He nodded. "I was already committed to this position. And given everything that happened… Or rather despite it… They pushed me to fulfill my obligation."

I swallowed the lump in my throat, but I was still confused. He'd only been assigned as a future Coterie member forty years ago because his uncle had found his own mate. Why hadn't they chosen another candidate when Tyfen had found *his* mate?

"How long were you with your mate?" I gently asked. "And why does no one know about your union and her death?"

He was a fae prince—a well-loved fae prince—and finding one's mate was a major cause for celebration. The whole realm kept track of that kind of royal gossip. A royal family member losing their mate, we would have heard about.

Tyfen rubbed his arm, and sniffled. "I only got to meet her twenty years ago. We only had a few short years together. But, uh, our relationship was secret. That's why it was never announced." Pain laced his every word. "The match wasn't approved."

I narrowed my eyes. To deny someone a life with their mate was unfathomable, and as much as I hated Tyfen's parents right now, I couldn't imagine them doing it. "Was she … that low in class?" Had she been a lowly whore like my mother had been?

"No. It was a poor political match, but not in that way."

He was holding back, and I tried not to rush him. I knew the pain of hiding a relationship, hiding what I had with *him*.

Tyfen reached into his pants pocket and pulled out two pieces of folded paper. "I took a *couple* of things with me beyond my sword…" He looked at me cautiously, handing me the first. The creases were well set, as though he'd opened and folded it dozens of times.

I carefully opened it and blinked. It was the note I'd scribbled for him when I'd left him after our first night together in his room. A simple thank you for a perfect night.

Tyfen offered a shy smile, then glanced at the leather bracelet I wore. My heart melted fully. He was more observant and sentimental than I'd regularly given him credit for. Of course he was. He knew without instruction what I liked in the bedroom; we'd always been on the same wavelength in one way or another, the push and pull undeniable. I'd been wearing his bracelet daily since he left, and he'd taken a note I'd written, something so small and insignificant, as a token of me despite his panicked mind as he'd fled.

I said nothing, at a loss for words.

Tyfen then handed me the other folded paper, his expression more nervous.

I unfolded it, again shocked. With the tear and crumple marks still on it, I stared at the painting he'd ripped off the wall in my studio months ago. I'd thought I'd never see it again, that he had thrown it away, or that his servants had packed it up when they'd shipped his things back to his parents' castle.

Eyeing Tyfen, I flattened the paper. "What does this painting mean to you?"

I'd constantly questioned why Hoku had given me that vision when she had. Why it brought pain to Tyfen. He'd startled like a ghost had crossed his path when he'd seen it, saying I was the *last* person who should see this place.

His green eyes matched the dewy grass from the vision, and the somberness of the place had echoed his mood shortly before I'd had the vision.

The iron gates of this location had been locked, so I couldn't enter, and I'd told myself it might have just been me reading into things, that it symbolized Tyfen struggling to open his heart.

But there was something more to it. Findlech had also said I shouldn't know of this place.

Tyfen finally responded, his voice quiet. "Do you know what this place is?"

I shook my head. "I know it has something to do with the high lord's family."

Tyfen nodded. "I'm sure you've heard about Lady Malaya?"

Narrowing my eyes, I nodded in return. Lady Malaya was the elf high lord's youngest daughter. She'd died in a tragic accident some years ago...

"That painting is of the sacred burial grounds for elf royals," Tyfen said. "That's where my mate is laid to rest." He choked on his words. "And I'm the one who killed her."

The truth took my air as I stared in disbelief. The political implications and ramifications shattered the lies and false realities built around me.

Fuck.

54

A Gift from Hoku

"Lady Malaya is your mate?" I confirmed.

Tyfen nodded. "Yes."

The elf high lord's daughter was his mate? My mind reeled. Goddess, this must have been hard for all parties involved, to stand in the same room and pretend like they didn't hate each other.

"When I was on tour, her brother confronted me. He asked me if I liked you."

"I'm sorry," Tyfen murmured.

I'd fucked and fallen for the man who had been mated with his dead sister, the one they blamed for taking her life. No wonder he'd been so anxious to confirm if I was fond of Tyfen.

"He was assigned to be in my Coterie, too."

Tyfen nodded again. "But Findlech took his place."

"Shit." Had Findlech not stepped in, war would have *absolutely* broken out. Tyfen *and* his former brother-in-law both assigned to bed me? Assigned to be lifelong allies when one would happily prefer the other dead?

Findlech had stepped in and saved us all. I stared at the bed, working through things in my mind. Both the emperor and Findlech had expressly warned me not to mention Lady Malaya when we were on tour. They'd stated it was too sensitive to bring her up. They'd done it so casually along their list of warnings that I hadn't given it a second thought. But how hellish would that be to have your dead daughter or sister's name uttered by the woman replacing her? And so soon…

"Your parents knew you were hurting. They knew keeping you in my Coterie would be a death sentence. Why did they insist you still participate in the Great Ritual?"

Tyfen blew out a long breath. "They were angry I stirred up trouble. They wanted me to pay for what I cost them." He pursed his lips. "They'll say they'd hoped a union with you would protect me, and that they hoped it would help me get over Malaya's loss sooner, but I'm not enough of a fool to believe that was their main motivation."

The queen had admitted privately that she'd gone along with her husband's request to send Tyfen despite his protests, and she'd convinced herself it would be good for Tyfen.

A wry smile crossed Tyfen's lips. "Keep things quiet. Keep the peace. Don't shame the family or our people."

Always about appearances…

My train of thought took an abrupt turn, and I cocked my head. "I'm confused… Lady Malaya is an elf. Elves and fae haven't been mates in centuries."

"True," Tyfen admitted. "But the fates are in charge, not us. I'm sure many more fae and elves are still compatible that way, and just don't realize it because we've become so separated by land and culture over time."

I conceded the point. If two societies have gone their own ways, what kind of sampling do you have to really know that sort of thing anymore if they barely associate?

Full of questions still, I tackled the glaringly tricky one. The elves clearly blamed Tyfen for Malaya's death. Findlech and the emperor had each separately mentioned it would look bad for people to see or accuse Tyfen of harming a woman. Tyfen had just told me he'd killed his own mate.

I rejected the claim. Other than oni, Tyfen wouldn't willingly harm anyone, especially not his mate. And the emperor and magistrate didn't think Tyfen was guilty enough to have been excluded from my Coterie…

"What happened?" I asked cautiously. "With Malaya?"

Tyfen looked down. "It's no secret I didn't have a lot of ambition when I was younger. I fucked around and partied. I led hunting parties in the royal guard. Eventually, I wanted to make a bigger name for myself. I'm not likely to inherit the crown, but I could still do *something* more."

I settled into my chair.

He continued. "I begged my father to give me extra duties, and he finally relented. He sent me to the elf nation with gifts to renew our friendship." A sad smile tugged at his lips. "We fell for each other so quickly. She had such a spirit…"

Swallowing, he sniffled. "Anyway… We kept our relationship secret for a while, afraid of disapproval, but I stayed a whole season in the elf nation. We knew we were meant for each other, so we promised ourselves to each other and planned to tell our families. Only when we planned on forever did the tattoos show up." He looked at me. "How much do elves respect mating bonds?"

I gulped. They actively denied the bonds the fate gave them, choosing to proudly forge their own marital alliances.

"Yeah," Tyfen said. "We shared our intent to wed, and it didn't go over so well…"

"With either of your parents?"

Tyfen wrinkled his nose. "Hers were *adamantly* against it, forbidding us from even seeing each other again. My parents weren't so harsh, but they still didn't want it. Perhaps they'd have permitted it if one of my younger siblings had been her match, but not their second-born, the spare should anything happen to my older brother."

There was tension, sure, but I didn't see how this had led to her death.

"We refused to be split up," he continued. "We snuck away and saw each other when we could. And then, one day we had an idea. A horrifically misguided and arrogant idea that only fools in love would consider…"

He took a moment. "Most people don't believe fae and elves can still be mates, right?"

"Right…"

"But the fates granted us a miracle, and we believed we could have another."

I was still confused.

"Fae and elves rarely marry. Why is that?"

I shrugged. "Like you said: there's a massive gap between your lands and cultures now."

"True. But what do many people in love want, Sonta?" He glanced at my womb.

My mouth went dry. He couldn't possibly be telling me… "Many couples want to have children. But fae-and-elf mixlings…"

"They die. And if they survive, they don't last long." His eyes flooded again. "But we were *different*. The first fae–elf mating pair in *centuries*. The fates put us together, and in our arrogance, we believed they would give us a healthy child, too."

He wiped away a tear. "We wanted to share that part of ourselves with each other. And selfishly, we knew if we had a child together, we'd become a family that couldn't so easily be dismissed by our parents and societies. So we agreed, and I got her pregnant." His voice shook. "I put a child in her, and it killed them both."

Tears pricked at my eyes. "But she's the high lord's daughter. Surely with the magic and skilled nurses at their disposal…"

Tyfen shook his head. "She went into hiding, lying to her parents about touring the countryside to try to get over me. We planned to show up with a babe in our arms. And I tried to sneak away to see her, but my father noticed I'd started going missing suspiciously, and laid more work on me, and had me watched."

Pain was etched into his haunted frown. "She lied to me about her symptoms, not wanting to worry me. She was terrified of her parents by that point, and made the lady's maid who'd traveled with her swear to keep all of it quiet.

"Only when she was in agony did the lady's maid send for me. But it was too late to save her. I didn't even get a proper goodbye by the time the high lord himself arrived with a full crew of helpers."

I cried freely, unable to imagine a pain so deep. I couldn't even let myself go there in my heart, couldn't picture losing Hadwin and our child. And that was with the mating bond dampened on my end as a Blessed Vessel…

So many things made sense now. In the bedding chamber, Tyfen had hovered over me and had hesitated to claim me, his hands over my womb. I'd wondered if he was performing magic, but he'd been in a much darker place. His parents had served him up like a prized stallion for breeding, callously ignoring the pain of him having lost his mate and unborn child.

'I hate how much I love being inside you,' he'd said. 'I hate all of it.'

I had given him a brightness in new love that he hadn't expected, but I had been a crucial part of his torture, too. No wonder he'd needed to be away from me. He must have felt like he was betraying his mate each time we were together, fighting to not hurt me in the process.

Goddess, he really was misunderstood. He'd tried to keep his distance from me, had been angry at the realm, and he'd had every right to be.

He'd felt like shit for accidentally hurting me before.

He'd been devastated when he'd accidentally called me 'my dearest' before… That had been what he'd called Malaya, and in the blur of a nightmare, he'd confused us.

I glanced at him. "This wasn't your fault."

"Yes it was."

I shook my head. They'd agreed upon it, and had been forced into secrecy. It was the cruelty of nature and pride that she had paid the price. He'd been left alive to suffer the never-ending guilt.

'I just want to be happy. Is that so wrong?'

He'd been in his own private hell, not ready to talk about it with me, and likely ordered not to.

"You said once that you didn't want to be here at the palace, and you didn't want to be back in your kingdom…" He'd passed on his answer then, but he'd promised to be an open book now. "Where did you want to be?"

His gaze dropped to the painting, and my heart was hollow.

"I didn't want to *be*, Sonta. I hadn't wanted to be around for some time."

I wrung my hands. "If it hurts too much to be here with me, I understand." My heart broke as I said it. "If you need more time away, we can work it out…"

His gaze snapped to mine. "No! I'm not leaving you again. I'm here to stay." Less passionately, he added, "Assuming you want me here…"

"Of course I want you here!"

His voice was strained. "Thank you, Nil Blantui."

My strength.

I stood. "Can I have that hug now?"

Tyfen jumped up, scooping me into his arms. I melted there, that missing piece of my heart clicking back into place.

He held me so tightly, one hand on my back, another threaded through my hair. After a long moment of silence, he spoke first. "I knew you would be okay. You have so many who love you. I'm sorry I had to hurt you to get myself sorted."

I squeezed him tighter. "You're back, and that's what matters. And if time away was what you needed, then I'm glad you took it."

We eventually pulled apart, and I wasn't sure where to go from here.

He smiled. "I wasn't ready to see you, but I was happy to get reports you were doing well. And that your child was doing well."

I frowned. "Is this going to be hard with me pregnant?"

He glanced at my stomach, then rested his hands there. "I've made my peace with it. I'm here for *you*."

I slid my hands onto his. While it had been a reckless choice, he and Malaya hadn't been completely faulty in their logic. If he had been the father of my child, our relationship may have been more validated, keeping him safer from the high lord. It might have backfired in its own way, but there was no way to know.

"Do you regret it's not yours?"

"No!" he blurted. "No, Sonta. I... I begged to bed you only out of guilt because I knew my duty to my people. But there was a reason I always pulled out so quickly. I felt like I was cheating on both you and Malaya, and every time I imagined my seed taking, I..."

No harm would come to me if I bore his child; I'd been designed that way by Hoku. But I wouldn't invalidate his fear of getting me pregnant after what had happened with Malaya.

It now made sense why he'd finally thrown me over his shoulder and taken me to bed, really starting something, only *after* my pregnancy had been confirmed.

I felt like shit, remembering how many times I had reassured him that even though he'd lost a few chances to impregnate me, his seed might still win. My reassurances had only fed his worries. Those worries that had bubbled up so much before the paternity reveal.

And how many times had I thrown it in his face that Elion and Hadwin were my mates, when his own had died?

I caressed his face. "You don't have to worry about me when it comes to pregnancy. If you never want children with me, that's fine. And if you change your mind, then I'm open to that, too. Either way, Hoku blesses me."

He furrowed his brow. "She confuses me."

"How so?"

"The fates and their cruelty. Her part in all this."

Theology and conviction varied across the realm, but in general, most believed the goddesses lived amongst the stars in the night sky. They were sometimes called the Divine Fates, or the council of goddesses, or the council of fates.

Tyfen sat back down. "The fates chose poorly with me and Malaya." He glanced at the painting I'd set on a small table. And when I begged you for sex, they mocked me by sending you a vision of my mate's burial site the same night.

My jaw dropped, and I understood why he'd been so bitterly startled by the sight of my painting. That vision had been sent to *me*, of all people.

But I had never seen it that way, and I still didn't.

"Hoku isn't cruel, Tyfen." I picked up the paper and dared to gingerly sit on Tyfen's lap. He didn't hesitate to wrap an arm around my waist.

I explained my own impression. "Hoku sent this vision to *me*, not you."

"Exactly..." He wasn't following.

"My visions are vague, but they're intended to teach *me* how to navigate and judge this realm, how to teach my child to choose well." I distinctly remembered the night Hoku had given me the vision, and the feelings connected with it.

My curiosity had prodded me to try to look beyond the wall, to unravel the mystery within. The sad autumn leaves and the dew on the grass that matched Tyfen's eyes had reminded me of his tears as he'd begged to bed me for the sake of his people.

"I was ready to give up on you," I confessed. "I was ready to cut you off completely for the way you treated me in the bedding chamber and in the ballroom. *This* vision gave me compassion for you. It lingered in my heart and gave you another chance."

"Really?" he asked cautiously.

I smiled. "Yes." It rang true in my heart and in my mind, the soft touch of Hoku's confirmation warming in me. He'd thought Hoku had sent the vision to punish him, but I knew better.

"I think she's more of a romantic than we give her credit for." She was the goddess of unity, though she hadn't historically been a matchmaker.

Still hesitant, Tyfen eyed me, rubbing my knee. "You're *certain* she approves of us?"

"Yes," I breathed.

He looked down. "So she wasn't just torturing me again?" He spoke to himself more than anything.

I pressed a hand to his heart. "No. The vision was never about hurting you."

He glanced at me, those bright green eyes locking with my own. "I'm not talking about the vision."

Now he'd lost me. "Then what are we talking about?"

He pressed his lips into a thin line. "I wasn't sure..."

"You can tell me anything."

"Look at my arms," he said.

He still had his mating bond tattoo on his forearm. I turned and examined his other arm, astonished at a new tattoo there too.

Startled, I jumped up. "What is that?"

"You know what it is."

My jaw dropped as I stared at a swirling pattern I'd never before seen, yet it spoke to my heart.

"Fae only get one mate," I said. I'd always thought it looked odd to have a singular arm tattooed, but it was their way to honor the bond.

"I'm not the only fae in history to have a second mate, though, am I?"

I blinked, acknowledging the truth. Ancient lore spoke often of wilder magic that could do something like this.

"You know who could have done this," he said. "I thought she was continuing her cruelty, but now…"

Hoku. Hoku had performed absolute miracles in her lifetime before ascending, blending magic and forging new paths. She *was* capable of doing this.

I still had a hard time believing it. "I'm a human."

"And Malaya was an elf. Neither bond should be possible anymore." He stood and reached a hand out, his eyes soft. "And you're not just a human. You're a Blessed Vessel. You're different."

I took his hand, intertwining our fingers as I looked at the magical ink. "I didn't get a matching one."

"Your side of the bond with all your mates is dampened, to keep you impartial."

"You're right." I ran my free hand over the tattoo. "When did it appear?"

He kissed my temple, and it sent shivers down my spine. "I was packing my things, ready to come back a month ago, and it showed up."

"A month ago?" I could have had him here with me a whole month ago? "What stopped you from returning?"

Pain narrowed his eyes again. "I had *just* healed from my wounds and gotten the help I'd needed to accept Malaya's loss. I'd just barely accepted you into my heart as a new life partner, Sonta. I was startled and confused by the new tattoo." He averted his gaze. "I stepped back and sought the opinions of temple priestesses. They assured me it was from Hoku, based on her history and our connection. They're not sure when you were assigned as a second mate, but the bond snapped into place once I was ready. It meant you'd already accepted me."

I had. He'd had my heart long before I'd even told him I loved him.

He was still shy. "It was unnerving, seeing it there. I … already had a mate."

Understanding his hesitation to accept me as a mate, I grasped his chin and met his eyes. "She is a part of you. Wear her mark with pride. I would never try to take her place."

He pressed his forehead to mine. "I know, Nil Blantui. I just needed more time."

Goddess help me, I loved him. I'd known his heart more than anyone around here.

Unable to hold myself back from the pull, I angled my head and pressed my lips to his. He mirrored my tenderness as he kissed back. His hands reached around to my lower back, and I lost myself in the moment.

Our kissing wasn't rushed, but the passion and love behind it was as soft as the caress of his familiar lips on mine.

Taking a break, I pulled back and rested my forehead against his. "I love you, Tyfen. You are also Nil Blantue."

He blew out a breath. "There's more we need to discuss. About what happened after Malaya died. About the almost-war. About what we should do from here on out."

I stood tall, preparing myself. "I want to understand it all." *Let me in.*

"Open book, including what I've discussed with the emperor and Findlech since my return."

Finally.

55

Mind Your Scars

Tyfen and I must have talked for at least another hour. His tale was harrowing, his torture far beyond losing his mate and unborn child.

He'd refused to leave Lady Malaya's side after she passed, even after the high lord arrived. The high lord in his rage imprisoned him and charged him with his daughter's murder.

Tyfen got off easier than her lady's maid. As punishment for lying to the high lord and lady, and for her gross neglect of her charge, she was executed.

Tyfen, however, was a prince, and his handling required more nuance. Yes, they beat and bloodied him, all while he already hated himself for getting her pregnant and keeping it a secret, but they did not execute him. Instead, the high lord bartered with his life.

The fae king and queen paid a hefty price to keep the incident quiet and to get their son back alive. Tyfen's father resented him for the shame and cost.

Tyfen was undeterred, devastated by his loss. He winnowed away from his parents' castle and snuck into elf territory, just to try to visit her at her final resting place to have a proper goodbye. Before he reached her grave, elf soldiers neutralized his magic enough to bind him and drag him to a dungeon.

He'd been warned to never return to the elf nation. And they reminded him with each blow as they tortured him.

When the fae rulers petitioned for their son's life, they were denied. Tyfen had been warned, and was now to pay the full price for his actions.

King Bretton and Queen Lourel prepared their army, as did High Lord Elout and High Lady Marsone.

That battle, had it ever happened, would have encroached upon shifter lands, would have disrupted trade and peace agreements across the realm, would have gone against treaties and the emperor's rule. They should have turned to the emperor to mediate, but the cousin races were too proud and hotheaded for their own good.

Eventually, when the shifters bulked up their own packs at their borders, sensing the threat, and the emperor sent out his own forces to investigate, the cousin races backed down. But not until the fae king and queen had paid dearly with land and irreplaceable treasures, and Tyfen had paid with his shattered heart and body. The elf high lord had beaten the mating bond mark that represented his daughter off the man he blamed for her death. Tyfen had been so broken, his pain and fear causing his glamouring magic to repress the bond mark for years.

He barely met my eyes as I sat on his lap, listening.

"You're safe now," I reassured him.

"Am I? Findlech's not so sure of that."

Findlech was in as precarious a place as Tyfen right now. I loved him for what he'd done to help, but it wasn't a simple matter. None of this was simple.

Findlech had it on good authority the high lord and lady still wanted Tyfen dead. Despite the agreement they'd made, and despite Tyfen being in my Coterie, they may very well stage an accident, especially if they ever caught him close to their borders.

That was part of why Tyfen had behaved so erratically. He and his family had been nervous but glad to hear Findlech had replaced the high lord's son as my partner, but Findlech wasn't all that well known, other than being a lord in the elven parliament, hailing from a smaller rural region. They'd feared he had ulterior motives, that he hadn't just come to impregnate me, but also to kill Tyfen.

Findlech had given Tyfen the benefit of the doubt, having more liberal opinions on mating bonds than most of his peers. He believed in a wider variety of love, and had hoped Tyfen's actions had been as they were—unfortunate and misguided, but not malicious. Despite trying to give Tyfen his space, Findlech had tried to talk to him before he left the palace. Tyfen hadn't been ready to talk to an elf, especially one close to the high lord.

Findlech's faith in Tyfen had waned from time to time. He formed his opinion based on Tyfen's behavior.

Tyfen had been placed in a no-win situation. If he disrespected or hurt me, that made him the evil villain the high lord believed him to be. And they'd had their proof, hadn't they? He'd humiliated me in front of a thousand witnesses in the bedding chamber. He'd insulted me constantly in front of the Coterie, even after we'd actually been seeing each other secretly.

So why hadn't he just opened up about being in a relationship with me? He was damned if he did and damned if he didn't. Disrespecting me made him the villain, but so did loving me. How could a man love another woman so soon after killing another? It was proof he'd never really cared for Malaya, that he was callous, and she'd meant nothing.

We'd kept our relationship a secret because Tyfen hadn't wanted Findlech to think he was happy with me after what had happened to Malaya.

There wasn't an easy way out of this. And I hated being caught up in this nightmare of politics, but I now understood why I'd been kept in the dark.

I was the Blessed Vessel. My calling was to bear the next ruler and to be impartial. How could I have been impartial after the claimings if I had known all this? I knew myself, and I *wouldn't* have been impartial. I would have resented being used as a pawn between the two in their secret feud. I would have pitied Tyfen for his loss, and given him more space to mourn. I would have resented Findlech for what his people had done to Tyfen.

Or maybe it would have been different... Either way, I wouldn't have been impartial and free to make my own judgment about either man's character.

The simple truth about the not-so-simple matter was that knowledge and the lack thereof had fueled this disaster far longer than needed.

After the high lord and lady saw Tyfen and I fight and then kiss, Tyfen had panicked. Not only had his heart been in conflict, but he'd feared for his life again. Not thinking straight, he'd left as soon as he'd healed enough to survive in the forest alone.

No one had been able to strategize how to fix the situation because *no one* had known why he'd left or where he was. If he'd been secretly coerced, or if it had been a matter of the heart.

The rest hinged on what the emperor had long known, and what he'd only recently discovered. On what the king and queen *thought* he'd been ignorant of, and what the high lord and lady *still thought* he was ignorant of.

This was going to be a hell of a political storm, but we were going to press forward through the storm together. This conflict would never be properly put to bed as things stood; it required a united Coterie to handle this issue, to tamp down escalating conflict.

I worried about how my Coterie would accept Tyfen after his abandonment, but I hoped we could be united. We were such a blessed Coterie already, full of so much love and talent and wisdom between us. We just needed to come together.

After more reassurances and some stolen kisses, Tyfen and I emerged from his bedroom. The rest of the Coterie had to be dying to hear from us.

We entered the common room, hand in hand. The queen had long since left, and the Coterie all sat together.

Elion and Lilah smiled first. Everyone focused on us as they stood, and we approached.

Findlech's smile was soft, and I let Tyfen's hand go. I barreled into Findlech with the tightest squeeze possible. "Thank you," I choked out.

He returned the hug, rubbing my back. "I've always been your friend, Sonta. And I always will be."

There was no truer statement. Findlech could lose his position and be tried for treason for what he'd done—Tyfen had explained his involvement more in detail.

Despite how beloved Lady Malaya had been, and how little the elf parliament cared for mating bonds, a few had privately shared concerns about the escalating issue. They'd narrowly escaped war a few years ago after Malaya passed, but the cousin races had still been headed on that trajectory with Tyfen and the high lord's son both established as my future partners.

They'd been on a collision course, neither willing to back down.

With the wisdom of over eight hundred years under his belt, Findlech had kept quiet, not being too vocal. How could he tell his high lord his daughter's life wasn't worth a war? He couldn't.

Instead, he'd sought out the emperor, betraying his high lord's command to keep the conflict a secret as has been agreed upon by the rulers. None of them wanted the emperor involved, even now.

But the emperor knew, at least the basics, and had betrayed the magistrate and even his own oath of impartiality to work with Findlech to change things.

Findlech, with the help of the emperor's connections and other more vocal lords in the parliament, had suggested sending himself as my Coterie member instead. He'd leaned on their pain, reasoning the high lord's son was hurting, too, and a member of their family shouldn't have to be anywhere close to the murderous fae prince. He'd said as part of the Coterie he'd inform them of Tyfen's behavior, though he'd ended up giving them very little.

He'd never wanted me as a romantic or sexual partner. He'd never wanted to be in my Coterie for the power and prestige. He hadn't really even cared much about siring the next ruler for his people.

He'd simply wanted to stop a war, and to try to protect me from the fallout.

I loved Findlech, and I didn't care that everyone stared in silence as I cried, filled with gratitude.

"We'll make things work," Findlech soothed.

I hoped we could. The battle had been thwarted, but the battle of wills was far from over.

Stepping back, I wiped away my tears.

Gald frowned. "Are you okay?"

I nodded, and hugged him too. He really had been clueless. Findlech had kept him out of the loop for his own good.

After Gald released me, Findlech took Gald's hand, giving him a look. Humbled, Gald stepped forward. "Welcome back, Tyfen."

Goddess, my heart melted to hear that. It had been said with hesitance, but it was still nice to hear him make the effort, given he'd been so vocal in the 'Tyfen only left you because he's an asshole' camp.

"Thank you, Gald," Tyfen said as he held out a hand.

Gald took it in both his hands and shook. My hope grew.

Elion glanced at me, a question in his eyes. I smiled my answer.

Taking a step forward, Elion greeted Tyfen next. "Welcome home."

"Thank you, Elion." Tyfen was still reserved, and he had every right to be. He hadn't exactly been on great terms with any of them before leaving, and he'd left quite a wake when he had. He earnestly wanted to make it work with the others, but he understood it would take time.

"Glad you're in one piece," Haan said from his tank.

Cracking a smile, Tyfen strode to him and shook his hands. "Something like that. I think the glue holding me together is still drying."

Haan chuckled.

Lilah fidgeted with her hands, and Hadwin continued to eye Tyfen.

Drawing a breath, Lilah spoke first. "I know I'm not in the Coterie, but I'm glad you're back."

His voice was soft and sweet. "Thank you, Lilah, and congratulations."

She narrowed her eyes, not sure exactly what he knew. I'd told Tyfen in my diary of letters that she and I were engaged to be hajba partners, and that she was on her way to being appointed as a palace painter.

"Thank you…" she said.

Shoving his hands into his pockets, his arms rigid, Tyfen winced. "I never had a problem with you and Sonta being together. Not really. I know I said I did, but I was angry about other things, and I dumped some of that on you. I'm sorry."

She shyly shrugged. "It's okay. We have a chance to get to know each other better now, right?"

"I hope so."

"Great, because Sonta thinks you're delightful, and she's rarely wrong about that sort of thing."

With a grin more like the Tyfen I'd fallen in love with, he turned to me. "Did you say that? I'm *delightful*? I don't think anyone's ever described me that way…"

I matched his grin. "I don't think I said that *exactly*. Maybe that you're my favorite asshole."

His grin grew to a full-on smirk as Lilah laughed. I'd missed our banter, and his devilish smiles.

Our levity faded at the realization Hadwin had yet to speak, and all eyes fell on him.

"I'm … sorry I attacked you," Hadwin said. He'd promised me he'd apologize first thing when Tyfen returned.

Tyfen replied. "I told Sonta I was angry you two knew you were the father when that happened, but that was a lie, too. I can't hold it against you for protecting her the way you did when you walked in on us."

Hadwin nodded, clearly not done. "Good. And it seems easy for you to win hearts and forgiveness, but I don't forgive so easily."

"Hadwin!" I chastised.

His eyes reddened as his gaze landed on me. "No, Sonta. He treated you like shit, and he left you hopeless. You've been miserable for months. I don't have to forgive that just because you did."

My face warmed, and I balled my fists. "Mind your own fucking scars."

He furrowed his brow, confused why I would bring up such a private and painful thing for him.

"No one in the Coterie demands to know how you came by them. They accept you as you are. But *I* know how you got those, and I love you despite your decisions that led to them, and despite your actions after you got them."

He had been unwise, just like Tyfen. He never should have fawned over a stupid girl and gone to work for a sketchy vampire. Unlike Tyfen, it hadn't cost him his love's life, but it had cost him his own mortality and twenty years of suffering.

He had murdered his sire and many of his servants, feeding his master alive to an oni.

But I still loved him.

Hadwin pursed his lips, eyeing Tyfen.

"I'm sorry I hurt Sonta," Tyfen whispered.

Elion perked up, cocking his head. "You have new tattoos, Tyfen?"

I fought a smile. Both at the new discovery of a third mate, and at Elion's attentiveness. He always observed, and was smarter than people gave him credit for because of his friendly nature.

Tyfen rolled up his sleeves again so his tattoos were fully visible. "Yes. And they're what you think they are." He gently rubbed Malaya's mark. "This belongs to my first mate." Shyly glancing at Findlech, he added, "She passed a few years ago."

Elion frowned. "Sorry for your loss."

"Thank you." Tyfen's voice was more strained. "The second is for my Hoku-given mate, Sonta."

Elion smiled. "Welcome home," he repeated. He oozed warmth. Shifters revered mating bonds across the board. Despite wanting me to himself, he'd always respected Hadwin's bond with me.

Hadwin's eyes calmed, returning to hazel. He couldn't deny the bond, either. Somewhat begrudgingly, he gave Tyfen a nod. "I'm willing to listen."

Tyfen held out a hand. "And I'm willing to talk."

Hadwin extended his hands, and they shook. My heart almost burst.

"We have a lot we need to discuss," Findlech said, his arm now around Gald.

"A lot," Tyfen echoed, the weight of our situation sinking into his voice.

"And the emperor is waiting to hear from us," Findlech added.

"Let's talk first," I said.

Lilah wrung her hands. "Official Coterie stuff? I guess I'll go to my room?"

That broke my heart. It was as official as it could get.

I glanced at Tyfen, a question in my eyes. I wanted to exclude her as little as possible, but she *wasn't* a politician. I trusted her implicitly to keep his secrets, but it was *his* choice whether he wanted to air his dirty laundry to her.

He mulled it over. "You won't be permitted in the bigger meetings, but when it's just the Coterie, I don't see why not. If a man's going to have to confess to his mistakes and pain, better to get it done with in one go."

56

The Secret Meeting

Our entire group sat together in the common room. Tyfen held me close, like he'd never let go. Hadwin sat possessively on my other side. Everyone else took places, prepared to discuss the matter of Tyfen's disappearance and return.

Gald sat across from us, his expression and posture not quite as welcoming as his earlier handshake with Tyfen. Findlech had his arm around him and leaned in, whispering in his ear. Gald smiled, and Findlech's free hand squeezed his knee. That smile turned into a blush as he rolled his eyes.

He noticed me watching as everyone situated themselves, and he frowned, glancing between me and Tyfen. "Sorry," he mouthed.

I offered a half smile. "I love you," I mouthed back.

He winked. He was begrudgingly accepting Tyfen's return, thanks to Findlech's assurances we were all on the same side.

"So…" I started. "We need to come up with a plan."

We weren't on the brink of war, but the wrong misstep may take us there. It had been utterly wrong for the cousin races to drag me into their feud, but they'd done it, and I loved Tyfen, and I wouldn't give him up for the realm.

I wasn't okay with a lingering threat on his life, nor was I okay with the treatment he'd faced, and the depths to which the conflict had reached in secret.

We talked for at least two hours, ordering lunch to the common room at one point. Hearts quickly softened once Tyfen shared his story. He owned up to his mistakes, and didn't leave anything out. One look at Lilah and it was apparent she was happy to not be a politician. But she was so empathetic to Tyfen's plight.

Eventually, we had to say goodbye to her as we left to meet with the emperor and magistrate. She went to our studio to start on her newly commissioned portrait, and I promised I'd send for her once we were done.

Never before had my Coterie spoken so frankly and privately with the emperor and magistrate. I loved what we were becoming. We each brought something to the table, and each proposed solutions to handle the grievances. We discussed the matter through the evening, and finally adjourned around sunset. There had been some give and take, but we were as confident as we could be. We had to be prepared for the inevitable pushback.

I sent a servant to fetch Lilah, and she met us in the common room again. Hadwin accompanied Gald to pay some friends a visit, using a travel spell. Elion accepted the help of another palace-employed mage to visit his parents for their support. Findlech was nervous, preparing for his part more privately.

Tyfen and I cuddled on the couch. Lilah joined us as we chatted with Haan, who didn't have time to consult the sea king, nor would he winnow or allow a travel spell to help him seek him out. Ideally, we *would* have consulted the sea king on a matter this large, even with Haan having the authority to act in his stead, but we'd agreed to swiftly take action on this conflict.

Tyfen's arms were so warm and strong around me, his scent and touch familiar. I kept tracing his new tattoo, the one that represented his love for me. I loved him. I loved them all in my own way.

The night drew long, the soft crackle of the fireplace in the corner our constant companion.

I startled awake at one point.

"Sorry, darling." Hadwin had covered me with a blanket, which had slipped off.

Groggy, I reached for his hand. "I love you."

He smiled. "Love you too."

I took in my surroundings and smiled. Everyone else was fast asleep. Tyfen looked so peaceful as he held me, my head on his lap. Haan had even stayed, balled up in his tank, his gills softly working away. Elion slept on the floor in front of me, having shifted into his wolf form. It warmed my heart to see Lilah next to him, lying on a blanket and pillow I recognized from his room. She had her arm around him.

Gald and Findlech spooned on the couch facing us, Findlech acting as the big spoon. It made me happy in a new way to see them together. I only had so much real estate and time to share, and I was content they both had someone else they could turn to. I didn't want any of them to be lonely.

Hadwin lifted my feet, sliding under my legs to hold me as I slept. "Would you prefer to sleep in your bed?"

"No," I whispered, taking his hand and moving it to my stomach. "I have all I need right here."

***

The next morning, things were not as peaceful and calm. We were all on edge. I asked Lilah to not worry, and to check in on my mother. And to conceal the truth of our chaotic circumstances from her.

The Coterie filed into a large room to meet with the emperor, magistrate, and others. Kernov gave me an encouraging look from the lobby, and I gave him a hug.

Tyfen held me back from the meeting room, his hands on my waist. "You're sure? You didn't sign up for this."

I smiled, my stomach in knots but my heart still confident. "I'm sure. And I *did* sign up for this. I could have rejected my calling as the Blessed Daughter in the first place. But I never would have met you, and you're worth the fight." I stood tall and pressed a kiss to his lips.

He softly moaned.

Footsteps clacked down the hallway. His parents approached for the meeting. Tyfen and I exchanged a look. His parents wouldn't walk away from this unscathed, either. As much as they were victims, they held blame. Tyfen was angry with them, but also loved them and didn't want to completely burn his bridges. It would be tense.

I squeezed his hand. "I'm going inside."

He stole another kiss and greeted his parents as I slipped away.

Each seat assignment had been planned. I took my place next to Findlech, and Hadwin stood behind me, resting his hands on my shoulders. He rubbed them and placed a kiss on my head.

As a group, we exchanged pleasantries; other than that, we were quiet.

The fae king and queen entered, bowing to the emperor and magistrate. "We appreciate you taking this matter to heart," the king said.

The emperor gestured to two open seats. "Of course. I wish you would have come to me sooner." The king and queen still weren't aware he'd known much more for much longer, and he was content to keep it that way.

The couple seated themselves. "We're so very sorry about that," Queen Lourel replied. "We acted as we thought best."

I gritted my teeth and forced a smile. Perhaps what was best for their son was *not* to force him to fuck a woman while he was grieving…

Tyfen sat between them and me at the giant table, taking my hand and flashing me a knowing smile. His mating bond tattoos were glamoured away for the time being.

We all waited quietly for two of the five remaining guests to arrive. My heart fluttered when the emperor's head advisor entered and whispered to him. The emperor gave me a nod; our three surprise guests were here and waiting.

Finally, the elf high lord and lady arrived, their eyes wide as they were ushered into the room.

"What … is the meaning of this?" High Lord Elout said.

"Just a discussion," the emperor said, gesturing to their seats. "Please do join us."

High Lady Marsone fiddled with her dress sleeves. "We weren't expecting a Grand Council…"

"Not a Grand Council," Magistrate Leonte said. "A friendly discussion of important matters."

The elf couple took their seats slowly, the high lord's eyebrow arched. "A rather unconventional meeting to be held in private…"

Grand Councils required all the territory rulers to be in attendance. We had not invited the vampire countess and her mate, the sea king wasn't even aware of this meeting, and Elion's parents had not come, busy dealing with their own matters.

In Grand Councils, everything was also written down for the history books.

Hadwin's voice was smooth and seductive. "Would you prefer to have my countess here? We could delay this to turn it into a formal Grand Council if you'd prefer. She does *love* a good intrigue, especially when it comes to our immortal counterparts."

The countess would be the *last* person I would go to for help, and the last I would trust. She thrived on secrets, on finding weaknesses and manipulating things to her benefit. She liked things her way, and was chomping at the bit for reasons to hate the other immortals more.

High Lord Elout assessed the offer, recognizing the threat it actually was. He surveyed the lineup at the table. My mate, the father of my child and his future ruler, stood behind me, above the rest, protective of me. Findlech was on my right to show his favor in my eyes. Tyfen, the man they wanted to destroy, was on my left.

Elion was seated past Tyfen's parents, though it was abnormal for a shifter mate to be pushed to the side.

"I'm sure there's no problem here," Elout answered. "Won't you take a seat, Your Grace?"

A smile sharpened Hadwin's voice as he acknowledged the three empty chairs. "I'm quite content where I am. Thank you."

The emperor cleared his throat. "Let's dive right in. Grievances have come to my attention that need to be settled."

High Lady Marsone's gaze flicked to the king and queen.

"I would first like to extend my condolences for the loss of your daughter, again," the emperor said.

Marsone's eyes glazed over. "Thank you."

Her husband echoed her sentiments.

I squeezed Tyfen's hand under the table as his expression wavered.

The emperor was the pinnacle of regality and decorum. "It has come to my attention her life was lost due to complications during pregnancy with her mate's child."

"She had no *mate*," Elout growled. "And there were no complications. It was neglect and murder."

Tyfen's breathing picked up.

"That's still your story?" King Bretton challenged.

"It is fact."

The elf rulers stared down the fae rulers. They had agreed to keep the conflict quiet and beneath the emperor's notice. Now, we all knew.

"It's not fact," Tyfen asserted. "And you know it."

"She would not have lost her life if she had not been brainwashed by you. You took her life by putting that child in there and forcing her to lie to us."

"*Forcing her?* She died because she was so afraid of *you*. We wouldn't have done it in secret had you given your approval!"

"Malaya was bright," Marsone said. "She would have never done something so reckless. She didn't even consent to what you did to her."

Oh, shit… They're really going to accuse him of that?

Tyfen stood, slamming his palms onto the table. "I *never* touched her without permission, you *fucking*—"

"Tyfen," the emperor barked. "Sit down. I understand this is a sensitive issue, but we *will* control our tempers here."

Swallowing, Tyfen obeyed. "Yes, Your Magnificence."

The emperor nodded, then turned to the elf rulers. "Murder and nonconsensual impregnation are both very serious claims. Do you have proof to offer?"

"She is dead," Marsone said. "That is proof enough. He disrespected our traditions and disobeyed direct orders to stay away from her."

The emperor remained silent as if waiting for more, because all they could really prove was that Tyfen had trespassed on their lands after being sent away.

"Her character was well known," the high lord added. "She wasn't one to risk her life like that. She wasn't reckless."

It wasn't my place to speak of Malaya much, or even to defend Tyfen. Not when they'd dragged me into this in the worst way possible. But I did have something to say. "Love sometimes makes us irrational, Your Lordship and Ladyship." I smiled at Findlech like an intimate lover. "It didn't take me long to get to know Findlech, and I would do anything for him." They had to approve of that alliance.

Findlech returned my smile, and I faced the elf couple again. "And mating bonds run deeper."

Elout's lip curled at the mention of mating bonds in a positive light.

Hadwin was as level as the emperor. "You don't have to approve of them to understand them. You cannot claim ignorance on the effects they have."

The high lord cocked his head. "I am not ignorant, but we're missing one key fact here, aren't we? He claims to be her mate, but when was the last time an elf was fated to a fae? Answer me that."

Tyfen put his arm on the table, unglamouring his mark. "She had a matching one. That is your proof."

"It was a lie you forced on her! Not a genuine mating bond!" Elout spat.

Gald took a turn, seated next to the magistrate, his leader. "Forgive me, Your Lordship, but it sounds as though you believe you're an absolute authority over how the council of fates works. Do you command their attention and rule their decisions?"

The high lord glared at him. "I do not pretend to be, but the facts don't lie. It's not even possible anymore."

The emperor didn't move a muscle save his eyes as he gestured to Magistrate Leonte. The magistrate stood and pulled a call string on the wall.

"There are a great many things we must confess to not understanding," the emperor said. "When it comes to magic, and when it comes to the realm of the stars, and how they mingle."

The door opened, and in walked Baylana; Mallon, her elf partner; and Duke Velant, her vampire mate.

My heart sang at seeing them. It was a huge deal for her to reveal herself. She'd felt bad for being so reclusive that she'd been unaware of the conflict and hadn't been able to offer assistance earlier.

Baylana smiled and curtsied to the emperor. He stood and shook her hands.

"Your Magnificence."

"Baylana." True warmth radiated from the emperor. "It's a pleasure to meet you. You're always welcome at the palace."

It felt good to hear and see his warmth toward her. And toward me. He'd admitted in private last night that he'd distanced himself from me because of his own self-doubt about the way he'd handled this whole debacle, but he truly did respect Blessed Vessels, each of us.

Baylana's smile grew. "I appreciate the invitation. Sonta has issued me the same invitation."

The emperor sat, and Baylana took her place, both of her men claiming a seat on either side of her.

She sighed. "It's great to see you, Sonta."

I couldn't hide a smile at my divine sister. "You too."

"And you as well, Elion, and Gald."

They both returned the greeting.

"And of course Hadwin."

I loved how much kinship they held for each other with her as his mentor.

"Always happy to see you," he replied.

Haan offered a greeting, and she told him she'd heard lovely things about him. Leonte was excited to meet her, too, calling her enchanting.

The elves and fae, however, stayed silent as the grave. It was their turn to have been kept in the dark.

"Mallon?" High Lord Elout said.

"Your Lordship..." Mallon had been the son of a lord when he'd volunteered to join Baylana's Coterie, a promising future leader. But he'd fallen so in love with her that he'd abdicated his position under the guise of grief at Baylana's (faked) death, and had left his people, fading into obscurity. He held no official power, but he still had connections.

"Does my brother know you live?" the fae king asked Baylana.

She smirked. "Let's not pretend the two of us got on all that well, Bretton. I prefer my privacy, and I trust everyone in this room can respect that when we take our leave."

Still spooked by her appearance, King Bretton nodded.

High Lady Marsone examined Baylana, her vampire pallor and fangs. "You died."

Baylana chuckled. "I don't feel very dead, Marsone. But yes, I did make it seem that way, didn't I?" She folded her hands on the table. "Surely you're not opposed to me choosing this life for myself…"

A challenge. Would the high lady show her distaste for vampires? Or more deeply for the mating bond?

Marsone's polite smile was anything but sincere. "Who am I to tell a daughter of Hoku what she can do with her life… I'm just confused at this being possible, that you've become a vampire."

Baylana shrugged, at ease in her place after having spent time with these immortals back in her day. I was jealous of her wisdom and ease, at her pure confidence. "Sometimes, we are surprised by things we deem impossible or improbable. No one expects to see one of Hoku's daughters walking around long past her mortal expiration date. Nor do they expect to see ancient mating bonds assigned by fate as she chooses."

Delicately, she added. "When it comes to love, we act with our hearts as much as our minds. You have fought for a daughter you love, and I can't blame you for that. Bretton and Lourel have fought for a son they love. And sometimes we take the ultimate risk. I did not know if an eternal bite would grant me favorable immortality or if I would die, or become an oni. I weighed the risks and followed my heart. I imagine the fae prince and your daughter also weighed the risks and did the same."

Tears pooled in Marsone's eyes.

"The situation is wholly different," Elout protested. "Do not reduce the violation and murder of our daughter to your perversion of an extended life."

"Elout…" The emperor's shock seemed genuine enough. "A man of your station uttering such distasteful things about another race…"

My ears burned. "You will *not* speak of vampires that way in my presence again, Your Lordship. I caution you to remember who you sit with. And who will be your better in a few years' time. Perhaps you have become too comfortable with an elf mixling on the throne, and you forget your place."

He didn't reply with words, but his casual eye roll and averted gaze told me enough. He didn't respect me or even fear me and my child. And why should he? We were mortal. All he had to do was outlive us and hope for a new emperor or empress down the line who favored his agenda more.

"You snub me and my child for our mortality. But you neglect to appreciate the influence we have. Not for decades, but for centuries. I have a private library with dozens of books penned by Hoku's Blessed Daughters, even penned by Hoku herself. We share our truths and secrets where no outside eyes have ever seen, where your influence is moot. You may have immortality and carry a grudge for centuries, but your arrogance causes you to overlook the sacred trust in the holy line."

Baylana smiled softly, and it made me remember something she'd written there. *A Blessed Vessel bows out of courtesy, not in submission.*

I continued. "And do not forget the succession." I glanced at the emperor, grateful we'd smoothed things over after I'd threatened his power. "His Magnificence has mentored me. And we will both mentor my child. My child will then mentor the next Blessed Vessel, and the line continues. Your actions and their repercussions will be remembered or forgotten to time according to how *we* wish them to be."

Baylana's smile slid into another smirk; she was well aware I seriously considered an eternal bite myself. She raised a brow at Elout. "Plus, I'm evidence enough that Hoku's daughters have a way of sticking around. I faked my death because I prefer privacy, not because I lost all my allies and friendships."

"I will not be intimidated," Elout growled.

The emperor could have interrupted at any time, but he hadn't... "I'm sure they mean no harm, Elout. Blessed Vessels are here to keep the peace, to ensure balance and impartiality in the rule of this land. Not to interfere in your territory's business or pick favorites."

Baylana and I agreed. We would surely *never* try to intimidate or threaten a Colsian ruler... We only wanted to ensure he understood our perspective, and we *must* have misunderstood his intentions. He couldn't have *possibly* meant to dismiss us.

"Of course not," he said shortly.

"Back to the allegations at hand," the emperor said. "Your claims against Prince Tyfen are severe. I am inclined to give him leniency regarding the unfortunate passing of your daughter without further proof it was malicious. Do you have witnesses of his coercion? Letters demonstrating she took the risk against her will?" He angled his head. "It's a pity her lady's maid was executed, so I could not hear her side of the story."

"She was guilty of lying to us and of gross neglect of a royal family member!" Elout rebutted.

The emperor held up his hands in concession. "As is your right. I do not interfere. I'm only reiterating the matter may be clearer had this issue been brought to me earlier, and had I all the evidence before me."

I took mental notes on the emperor's smoothness and cunning. He commanded the largest army and navy in the realm. He could force submission, but he would not. Hoku had not sacrificed so much to bring us peace for us to fight again.

Not only would he not force submission here when it was not necessary, but he would not implicate himself in his own interference. He'd broken a vow by interfering with internal elf politics.

I couldn't fathom Leonte ever executing someone for what Malaya's lady's maid had done. She had been deceitful and neglectful, but it had been at her lady's orders. Human law was more forgiving, but each territory had its own laws, and the elves had stronger punishments when it came to offenses against the royal family.

Even the emperor didn't have a leg to stand on if he tried to condemn that ruling. It was not his place to interfere unless the law was more cruel than Hoku had set forth, or unless it spilled over into another territory's matters unjustly.

The emperor addressed Tyfen. "Do you have evidence to the *contrary*? That Lady Malaya indeed *did* consent to have a child with you?"

"Yes." Tyfen looked Elout in the eyes. "I have letters from her." His firmness wavered, his voice breaking. "She wrote about our ... child."

I fought tears and rested my hand on his thigh.

Tyfen swallowed. "I can provide them. I brought them with me."

The emperor was soft. "I understand the invasion of privacy that is, but I should like to see them. I will handle them with the utmost care."

Tyfen nodded, his lips pursed.

The emperor turned to the high lord and lady. "Indelicate as it is, I must ask if you have something of Malaya's my mage can use to verify the validity of the letters. My aides will do their best to be discreet and gentle."

The elf couple hesitated. They wouldn't be allowed to return to their castle to fetch something. It may give them the opportunity to hide evidence. They likely didn't want to provide something of their daughter's out of their grief, but also because they didn't want to be proven wrong. But they couldn't very well refuse the emperor's request.

Marsone's voice radiated her sorrow. "Her best tiara still sits in her old room."

The way she spoke broke my heart, and it forced my compassion. I struggled to be impartial because I loved Tyfen and because I'd grown up under human law, but the elf royal family had lost someone they dearly loved, and I needed to respect their grief. Even if they had gone too far, there was a part of them that truly sought justice for their daughter.

"Thank you," the emperor said. "I'll dispatch my aides to retrieve that, and I'll call on my best mage." He glanced at Tyfen. "Please produce those letters after we adjourn."

57
The Coterie's Influence

We all filed back into the meeting room after our break. No amount of rest could prepare us for the sheer stubborn-headedness we expected to deal with. Hoku had been wise in her creation of mortal heirs, her Anointed Rulers—these older immortal rulers were far too used to people fawning over them and bowing to them; they were out of touch and pigheaded.

"It has been confirmed the letters were written by Malaya's hand, and they speak of wanting a child with Prince Tyfen," the emperor said.

High Lady Marsone whimpered.

"That doesn't disprove he brainwashed her into consenting," High Lord Elout retorted.

The emperor sighed. "Some things, we cannot know. But now that we've arrived at the conclusion she did of her own free will take the risk she did, which led to her death, it's pertinent we address other matters that have come to my attention."

Elout averted his gaze. It would be easy for an outsider to think we were all assholes for ganging up on a pair of grieving parents, but there was more to their actions. They had taken things too far. *Much* too far.

"First," the emperor said. "I understand Tyfen was rather severely harmed."

"He disobeyed my orders and trespassed," Elout defended. "And we still believe him culpable for Malaya's death." He gestured at Tyfen. "He lives."

I clenched my jaw. I wanted to rip him apart for how severely he had threatened and beaten Tyfen. Glamour magic hiding an essential part of you was *not* a normal response to regular trauma. Only the deepest of mental, emotional, and physical pain could do that.

There wasn't much I could say about the matter, though. I couldn't cite my relationship with Tyfen as a reason for him to have not been beaten. He hadn't been my partner at the time. It had been rash to imprison and punish the son of another ruler, but they had *not* killed him.

But there was *something* I could say…

"I'm under the impression he still has a death sentence on his head."

"He understands he's unwelcome in our lands."

"That is a different matter. Do you or do you not still wish to kill Tyfen? He is in my Coterie."

Marsone lied. "He received his punishment, and things have been settled, Your Holiness."

Her deceit made my skin crawl. "You deny you wish him dead? That you would take the opportunity were it given to you?"

Elout threw the quickest glance at Findlech before looking away. He'd been mighty quiet.

"Who makes these claims?" Elout asked me.

Mallon shifted in his seat next to Baylana, leaning forward with his elbows on the table. "Your Lordship…" No other words were necessary; his tone implied he might have heard the rumor himself from old associations back home.

"I don't have to hear rumors," I said. "I'm not daft. Your son cornering me and pressing me about my relationship with Tyfen was more than enough to confirm my worries. And I will not tolerate an active threat against one of my partners."

"There is no order to kill Tyfen," Elout insisted. "But we cannot be held responsible for my people should they learn the truth of our daughter's death. She was much beloved."

"You *will* control your people," Queen Lourel threatened.

"You should have controlled *your son*," High Lady Marsone returned with equal fervor.

The women had been friends as young girls, and it was sad enough that time and duty had taken their toll on their relationship. But this had ended it completely.

"I should like to visit your beautiful nation again," I told the elves, then smiled at Findlech. "Findlech's region especially is quaint. I loved my time there."

The elf rulers smiled softly at the tangent.

"And my child will of course tour and get to know their subjects. Right, Hadwin?"

He squeezed my shoulders. "Of course. It's important the Anointed Ruler gets to know the people. I rather enjoyed the elf portion of our tour. I look forward to returning."

"You are always welcome in our lands," Elout said.

"Is my entire Coterie invited?" I asked. "We travel together much."

Elout's face hardened. "Tyfen will never be welcome."

I rested a hand on the table. "My problem is this… Tyfen was not allowed to have a proper goodbye with Malaya. I'd like to accompany him to her resting place."

"Unacceptable!" Elout's face reddened.

I straightened. "I am the daughter of Hoku. A part of her soul lives in mine. This realm is hers, and I do not need your permission to enter *any* part of it." I jabbed the tabletop with my finger. "I will respect your sacred grounds, as will Tyfen."

"We plead with you to leave that area alone," Marsone said.

I swallowed. "I have already been there."

They both looked shocked.

"Hoku sent me there through vision. I will respect it, as will Tyfen."

Elout shook his head. "Being your partner does not entitle Tyfen entrance into our lands, and certainly not into our sacred burial grounds."

"You cannot deny me a security team of my choosing. The law dictates I'm allowed to have a private security team."

"He is not your guard. He is your lover."

"He is a highly trained commander in the fae royal guard."

Elout gestured at Tyfen. "Exactly. His allegiance to his own military is a conflict of interest in itself."

"I'll resign my position," Tyfen blurted. "Immediately. I just want to be near Malaya."

Tyfen's parents looked utterly shocked, and the offer to resign his position as commander also caught me off guard. He loved his duties, even if they were on pause while he was in my Coterie.

The king and queen were clearly unhappy with the offer; it wasn't like they'd been that fond of Malaya. But they didn't protest.

Marsone locked eyes with me. "Your Holiness. What you are asking is a cruelty to us. Surely you must see that."

Tyfen responded bitterly. "The cruelty lies with you. For denying me one. Fucking. Chance. To say goodbye."

The emperor cleared his throat. "Perhaps we should shelve the concern of Tyfen being allowed a visit. I'd like to hear more about something you said, Marsone. You said Prince Tyfen's punishment has been served and things were settled." He drank from a glass of water. "If this meeting proves anything, I'd say things are not settled, but emotions aside, I do understand there were a great many important things paid to you as ransom for Tyfen. More than once."

Elout held up a finger. "Not ransom, Your Magnificence, reparations."

The emperor narrowed his eyes as he flipped open a notebook. "Reparations? *Before* he was released? As a *condition* of his release?"

"A difference of opinion."

"Like *hell*," King Bretton growled.

This. This was why Tyfen had sent his things to his family home when he left. He knew his father would never forgive him should something go missing in his absence. The elves had all but pillaged the fae with their ransom demands.

"The value of these items is incomprehensible, Elout." The emperor raised an eyebrow.

"What price do you put on your child?" Marsone asked.

What price indeed? No amount of wealth could replace my child. The elves had demanded through the nose for Tyfen's life, and the fae had grudgingly paid their price.

"The Hilta Bow?" the emperor asked.

Baylana gasped. "How dare you!" Her shock was as genuine as mine had been when I'd learned of it.

Hoku had formed our government before she ascended, but she hadn't tamed the realm and done it all on her own. She'd had her own sort of Coterie, a plethora of lovers and allies at her side. To each, she'd left something special, an ancient relic each territory cherished.

Before her victory, Hoku had gifted the Hilta Bow to her fae lover, and it had remained in the possession of the fae ever since. The king and queen had already lied to their people about the temple it was usually displayed in, pretending it was under renovation to conceal its loss. Had Tyfen not been absent for his leg of the tour, that would've been a planned stop.

"A concerning precedent," I commented.

"This is a fae and elf matter," Elout said. "This doesn't even concern the rest of you, as the offense and payment were in the past."

Water sloshed in Haan's tank as he adjusted himself. "It prompts concerns for the future. What if one of our adolescents accidentally drowns one of yours? It would of course be unintentional, but I have to ask… Would you demand the Radiance Stone from the sea king as reparation?"

"Of course not. We respect the sea king and would not demand that. Accidents happen."

Hadwin spoke. "What of the True Blade? Would you demand that of the vampires if we accidentally killed one of yours? I do not think you respect my countess the same as you do the sea king…"

I fought a grin at Elout's panicked look as he surveyed the table. My Coterie was circling, and there was blood in the water. If he could be so cold as to demand of the fae an ancient relic of Hoku herself, who else would he do that to?

I didn't have to be capable of reading minds to know what coursed through Elout's mind at the moment.

Fuck. Fuck. Fuck. Fuck. Fuck.

Findlech's voice was firm. "My high lord would *never* be so foolish or harsh as to take a relic that did not rightly belong to the elves."

"As if you're an unbiased character witness," Gald countered.

"You doubt my ability to think and judge for myself?" Findlech argued defensively.

Gald shrugged. "I doubt the man whose political views are questionable, and the rulership who keeps so much to themselves. Population statistics, for one."

"Privacy and secrecy are different things, and we are allowed—"

"Findlech," I reprimanded. "Gald…" I fought with all my heart and soul to not smile knowingly. There wasn't a shred of doubt in the Coterie's minds that these two were going to have some hot sex after their fake fighting.

All of us—my Coterie, the emperor, the magistrate—were playing our parts to keep the right people out of trouble, to imply and implicate and craft the right narrative. Even now, me silencing Gald and Findlech's manufactured squabble reminded the fae and elf leaders I had control over my Coterie and the alliances forged within.

I continued, addressing Gald and Findlech. "You've gotten to know each other enough during the Great Ritual. You're both honorable men, and we do not fight amongst ourselves like this." I turned to Elout. "I like peace and order. It's a pity my entire Coterie had to be dragged into this."

"Respectfully," Elout said, "they do not need to be. This is a matter for elves and fae."

"This is not an exclusive matter when I still feel Tyfen's life is threatened. And your son's behavior during our visit on tour made me feel unsafe."

"I'll speak to my son," Elout grumbled.

Findlech rested his fingertips on the table. "But you *didn't* actually do that, did you? You didn't take the fae's Hilta Bow, surely?" His voice was full of soft betrayal. "My Lord?"

Goddess, I loved Findlech. I would never question his cunning and friendship again. He knew when to keep quiet, when to be seen as defending his high lord, and when to be witnessed as the one betrayed. As if he hadn't first conspired against his high lord to stop his son from entering my Coterie…

Findlech wasn't just now learning this, but he genuinely hadn't known all the demands his high lord had made until the king and queen had shown up with Tyfen, their list of grievances in hand.

The high lord and lady showed proper guilt. "Perhaps we were hasty in our distress after losing Malaya," Marsone said. "As a gesture of goodwill, we will return the bow."

"We'll make the arrangements," King Bretton quickly replied.

"Progress," the emperor said. "Now about the rest of this ransom…"

He listed off a handful more items the fae had paid to get Tyfen back before the high lord begged him to stop. Elout urged him to continue reviewing that list in private. It was true the other precious treasures long held by the fae and the regular payments of gold didn't really concern the rest of the races as much.

But the question begged to be asked… When would it be enough? When was a list of demands a reasonable punishment, and when did it become a child snatching at another's toy and smashing it to drag them down? To make the other suffer as much as they had suffered?

The fae royal family had paid dearly for Tyfen and Malaya's decision. They had paid for Tyfen's life and reputation. They had all but emptied their coffers to do so. The financial repercussions hadn't hit the fae people yet, but this could cripple them.

The emperor faced me. "Sonta, the choice is yours. Do you wish to go over all these items now? Or would you defer to me?" There was warmth in his usually cold and formal eyes.

"I wish to discuss the final item on the list, but I'll allow the others to be dealt with more privately." I gave him a smile. "I trust you completely, Your Magnificence."

A tiny smile tugged at his lips. Not that long ago, I'd declared I had zero confidence in him, but now I better appreciated the delicate dance he did, and our divine kinship in Hoku's line of successors.

"Very well. The last item." The emperor furrowed his brow. "The fae forfeited Kaibu Island…"

Baylana and her partners blinked in shock, a look of *holy fuck* plastered on their faces. Hadwin and Gald hadn't had much time last night to go over every single detail with them, and it was fine. Their surprise only helped our cause.

"Yes," Elout said curtly. "They signed it over. The miscreant trespassed again after we released him. The penalty had to be more severe to drive the point home."

"Kaibu?" Baylana said. "Really?" She glanced around at us, still disbelieving it had happened.

Kaibu Island was one of the largest islands in the Southern Dalia Sea. In *any* of the seas. Very few fae inhabitants lived there, but many merfolk used its shores for basking, and the fae utilized the island for a good portion of their crops.

Elion strategically took his chance to speak. "My people take offense to this."

"It's not a *shifter* island," Elout said through clenched teeth.

"No. It's not. But you cannot be surprised at our anger to hear of land stolen by our neighbors to the west."

"Not stolen."

"This is not reparation. This is extortion. That island is not yours, and we do not accept the transfer of ownership."

"You have no say."

Elion pursed his lips. "Perhaps not. Nonetheless…" He pulled a sealed scroll from his lap and reached across the table, handing it to the high lord. "This is our response."

Goddess, I loved Elion. He looked sexy in this role, and I loved that his parents trusted him enough to negotiate in their stead. They'd drafted and signed the scroll, but they knew Elion wouldn't choke.

The high lord unrolled it, and he and his wife read it together. "You cannot be serious."

"The high alpha and his mate did not mince words, did they?"

One of the most important trade routes rested on the border between shifter lands and the elf nation. Much of it was in shifter territory, and for centuries, they had freely allowed others to use it.

Now, they were demanding extremely high tolls, only of the elves. Otherwise, elves would be prohibited from using the shifter portion of the route and would nearly be cut off from the rest of the realm.

"Your Magnificence, this cannot be allowed." Elout handed the scroll to the emperor. "The trade route may be on shifter lands, but it negatively impacts the rest of the realm."

The emperor read it. "They have not expressly *prohibited* elves, there's just a toll to pay. It's on their lands, and they're allowed to do that."

Elout gawked at him, exasperated. "You chastise me for making a comment about the vampires, yet this is unfair. What would it say to the other races when we're the only ones being targeted?"

"What *would* you say to that, Elion?" the emperor asked.

Elion waved a hand through the air dismissively. "Make no mistake. This isn't discrimination. This toll is *reparation*."

"For what?" Marsone screeched.

His eyes flashing silver, Elion leaned forward. "When armies gather at our borders, we are not unaffected. Many of our smaller shifters relocated inland a few years ago, fearful of a growing conflict. Many wolves were torn from their crops and cubs to strengthen our packs in case we were attacked. Your hot heads disrupt our way of life."

"You were never the target," Elout said.

"How were we to know? And would it have mattered when my people are directly between the elves and the fae?" Elion leaned back. "Even now, our packs are growing on our borders, as an extra precaution. Unpredictable neighbors do not make the best neighbors."

High Lord Elout wouldn't accept it. "You do realize you'll be harmed by these tolls in the end, right? We'll charge more for our goods to make up for the cost."

Elion casually examined his nails. "We're a simple people. We won't be affected much."

Elout's face reddened again. It was probably wrong to enjoy this part, wasn't it?

"Sorry for the interruption," Leonte said. "Bretton, your people still do not know of this loss? Has Kaibu been evacuated?"

The fae king responded. "Correct. Many workers were forced to relocate, and we've had to conceal the truth from our people about why our citrus harvests have been so little. We can only blame blight for so long."

Tyfen's siblings had awkwardly and shamefully clammed up on tour at the mention of citrus...

"It's not like you don't still own land," High Lady Marsone derided him. "Cut down the Dark Forest and turn it into farmland. Take care of the oni hiding there while you're at it. Problem solved."

My loveable Gald chimed in. "Isn't the Dark Forest the primary known habitation for unicorns? Destroying the forest would be unacceptable."

"I hate to interject," Magistrate Leonte said, holding up a finger. "I do love imported fae citrus. Are you already selling it now with an elf vendor, Elout?"

"Well ... not yet. We haven't established new workers on Kaibu yet. We will soon."

The audacity of the elves continued to astound me. They hadn't set foot on that island, and we knew why, but they still wouldn't fess up to it.

Leonte tsked so genuinely. "Such a pity, all those wasted crops." He scratched his chin. "I would like to say, apart from this whole ordeal with the shifters adding tolls, I independently did some research once this matter came to light, and the humans may be forced to make some drastic changes as well."

Marsone's shoulders slumped.

Leonte continued. "Having been one of the most oppressed races over the course of history, humans *do* have reason to fear a conflict between the immortals, don't we? I'm prepared to send soldiers to our borders, as a precaution."

"That is *not* necessary, Your Eminence."

"I pray you not tell me what is necessary for the safety of my own people." He drew a breath. "Furthermore, this disruption will inevitably affect our economy as well. We would not deny the shifters their right to raise tolls, but it would affect prices for the goods we get from elves. We may need to reconsider where we get our goods. And prices for crops will only increase on what we import from the fae, so that adds to the problem." He glanced at Elion. "But the high alpha will not make humans pay the toll, correct?"

"Of course not," Elion answered casually.

"Your Eminence," Hadwin interrupted. "Just to clarify, you said you'd position soldiers at your borders. Do you also mean your borders with the *vampires*? I would be obligated to inform my countess."

"Oh, goddess no, Hadwin. We have no quarrel with the vampires."

The elves did not hide their anger well at the obvious alliances.

Leonte gave them a quick smile, then glanced at notes he had before him. "Oh, yes, and if we feel there's a potential conflict, and prices are skyrocketing, and we're having to pay for more soldiers at our borders, then we will need to look at our workforce. I'm having my cabinet assess our mines and quarries in the mountains. We may not need your goods."

Elout's jaw dropped. The elves practically owned the mountains; most everything mined in the realm came from there, and it was a huge source of industry. But the humans had their side, too. "That is a bit much, Leonte. There is no conflict between our peoples. Our work is superior, and our goods the best out there."

Leonte eyed him. "Your work is *superior*? Are you saying humans are less?"

It was hard to keep a straight face. I knew Leonte far too well to buy his innocent and hurt act.

Elout sighed. "That is not what I meant."

"Leonte?" Hadwin spoke. "I can't speak for the countess, as she's not here, but I imagine you'd fetch a fair price in vampire lands for your goods from those mines. I've heard human-mined marble is the best in the realm, and if you have a surplus, we will pay well for it."

Leonte smiled. "That's great news."

"*Best in the realm?*" Elout snipped. "It comes from the same *fucking* mountains as ours!"

The room sat in stunned silence. The elf rulers forbade swearing in their own court, and it was shocking to hear him utter a curse word.

Leonte was gentle in his response. "We all have to look out for our own, don't we? I'm not trying to punish the elves. Most of them did nothing wrong here. But I have to put my own people and economy first. I'm sure the elf workers who lose their livelihoods can learn new skills."

High Lady Marsone stared at him as if he were the most out-of-touch ruler there ever had been. "Surely you know it doesn't work that way. The elves in the mountain regions have done that work for centuries. They're skilled, and you cannot just trade chisels and hammers for plows, and expect great results. Especially given the soil and erosion in some places."

Leonte knit his eyebrows as though he considered her point. "I think our people are adaptable. And you just told Bretton and Lourel their people can plow down a forest to start new industry. Are the elves not… I don't want to say not *competent* enough… I'm just struggling for the right word."

"Your Magnificence…" Marsone protested. "Surely you can see this is getting out of hand. Your silence is stunning."

How was I enjoying this? *Fuck… When did I start liking the political part of my calling?* I knew Gald was secretly eating this all up.

The emperor nodded. "This obviously is concerning. All economies may struggle." He tapped his finger on the table as if considering his options. "The palace could be more conservative with our budget, to weather the economic storm brewing. And if your workers are forced to learn new skills, and the strain on your workforce and resources is too much with tolls and whatnot, we would not wish to strain you further. Here at the Pontaii, we *do* have flexibility with whom we hire and where we get our supplies. You don't have to worry about us ordering as much as we have in the past."

Now Marsone's jaw dropped. That was the opposite of what she'd hoped for.

"What would your father say?" Elout chastised him at the obvious passive aggressive answer.

"My father would say I am Hoku's anointed, an emperor of the realm, not a lapdog to the elves. I was not born to favor my paternal side, and I trust you would not want Sonta and Hadwin's child to favor the vampires…"

The elves threw a glance our way.

I spoke softly, leaning forward to look at Haan. "You've barely spoken, Haan."

His handsome purple eyes acknowledged me, but his expression was grave as he faced the elves. "Why have you not set foot on your new island, Your Lordship?"

Elout swallowed. "Haven't had the time."

"Is that all?" Haan's husky and airy voice made his words just as much a threat as they were.

"Yes…"

"It's not because the merfolk who frequent Kaibu would notice the change in ownership? Or because you'd illegally pass through our protected waters?" Just as we land-walkers had territories and borders, the merfolk had been assigned safety zones where fishing and even sailing were not allowed.

"We will not pass through your protected waters," the high lord vowed.

Haan's gills worked. "I am unconvinced. But I suppose that does not matter. My people are often confused by land-walker behavior. We cling to the safety of knowing the established trade routes within the seas. Were you going to formally establish trade routes with the empire?"

"Eventually…"

"How does that work when you hid the change of ownership?"

The high lord had no answer.

Haan's turquoise scales gleamed in the light. "Like the shifters, my people are simple. If your boats cross waters—protected or not—and veer off the known paths, we're likely to perceive them as a threat. I would hate for elven boats to be sunk by accident as they travel to their newly stolen property."

"Do not threaten me," Elout bit out.

"Not a threat. A likely outcome. We're so easily confused. So few of us even speak or read the imperial tongue. You cannot fault so many for such a misunderstanding."

Marsone was quick to respond. "We will file the charter with the empire posthaste."

The emperor drew a long breath, then sighed. "You will continue in this absurd claim to Kaibu?"

"We are owed for Malaya's death, and the boy needs punishment."

"His pain is punishment enough," I whispered. "And your torture was already excessive."

Tyfen shook his head. "Malaya never spoke of Kaibu Island. Or the Hilta Bow. Or of riches. She didn't want my people to suffer. She *wanted* to be happy with *me*. She wanted to start a *family* with me." Tears filled his eyes. "None of your greed will bring her back. You shame her name by hurting my people and disrupting the entire realm."

Findlech barely spoke above a whisper. "Far be it from me to disagree with my high lord and lady's wishes. And I would never aim to dishonor Lady Malaya. But I am also obligated to the Blessed Vessel, and I offered myself for this position so our royal family could mourn in peace. I plead with you to choose peace."

"Hoku gave the fae that island when she made the borders," the emperor reminded.

The high lady took her husband's hand, a resigned sigh escaping her lips. "We … renounce our claim to the island."

The fae king smiled to himself. "Once our crops have recovered, we'll send you a basket of citrus as a thank you."

What an arrogant ass.

The emperor lost his cool. "Do not be so quick to celebrate your victory! Much of this mess could have been avoided had you not sent your son in the first place, and you'll find I am rather protective of Her Holiness."

Elout swooped in with his own pride. "It's true. We were *astonished* Tyfen was not replaced."

Like fucking hell they were. They'd planned on sending their son until Findlech's conspiring changed their plans.

The emperor turned to Elout. "How *fortunate* you were able to find a better suitor for Her Holiness."

"So…" Leonte interrupted again. "If the island is returned to the fae, and the bow is returned, I suppose that means we have no need for these tolls and further disruption of workers and soldiers and economy…" He smiled. "Where does that leave us?"

"Do you swear Tyfen is safe?" I asked.

The high lord mumbled, "He's safe."

"Good." I couldn't stop myself… "I want you to know that if Tyfen so much as stubs his toe on a stone and I suspect you may have had any part in putting that stone there…" I let the threat hang in the air. "My Coterie is united. As should this realm be."

"We will not harm him, but he's not welcome in our lands," Marsone said.

"Not even for a visit to the royal grave site?" Elion asked.

"No."

Elion stood, pushing his chair back, then marched to the door.

"Where are you going?" the high lord asked.

Elion rested his hand on the doorknob. "To call a council of our alphas. Which will result in a formal demand for a proper Grand Council." He looked every bit as affronted as his tone radiated. "You do not respect mating bonds, but it is the highest honor we hold. My mate is not satisfied with the results of this meeting, nor am I." He glanced at Tyfen. "And a man deserves to visit his mate's final resting place."

Hadwin squeezed my shoulders. "I also want my mate happy. I will be speaking with my countess. She's elated to have the next Anointed Ruler be one of us. She will go to any lengths to ensure my child and mate's happiness and safety. We will also want a Grand Council."

Gald stood, straightening his shirt. "I have no mate, but I stand with the Blessed Vessel, and this Coterie."

Baylana and her partners stood. "When did it become a sin or crime to love?"

Tyfen's parents awkwardly joined the protest by standing, though they said nothing.

"I'll clear my schedule for a Grand Council," Leonte said as he stood. "I find no pleasure in it, and it seems an easy thing to extend compassion instead of recording this travesty for future generations to analyze. I fear you will not be viewed favorably."

Tyfen looked down, swallowing. The high lord and lady looked down, too.

"I'll accompany him," I whispered. "You don't even have to know he's there."

Findlech cleared his throat. "I will escort them. To the graveyard and back. I will ensure he's respectful and brief."

The silence was deafening as we waited for a response.

"Once," High Lord Elout declared. "And we will hear no more of this."

I could finally breathe again, my heart filled with hope. It wasn't a time for cheering, but so much pressure dissipated with that acceptance.

"Thank you," Tyfen said, his voice broken.

I squeezed his hand. "I thank you as well."

The emperor spoke. "This has all been undesirable, but I'm grateful we can come to an agreement. Let's discuss the rest of the reparations at another date, shall we?"

The elves and fae agreed. We were all drained.

"Your Holiness?" the emperor asked. "Do you have any requests?"

My mouth went dry. I didn't want to do this next part, not at all. But it was inevitable, and it was better things went this way now. "I'd like a more private word with His Lordship and Ladyship."

The emperor offered me a nod. "So be it."

"I request Hadwin, Findlech, Tyfen, and Baylana stay."

They agreed to stay behind.

"Very well." The emperor stood. "The rest of us will leave you in peace. May Hoku multiply her blessings on us all."

All in the room echoed him.

This next part was going to hurt like hell.

58

Broken Ties

Every bone in my body screamed this was wrong, but I *knew* it was right. The high lord and lady still sat across from me. Tyfen and Findlech still sat on either side of me, and Hadwin and Baylana sat together a few seats away. Around the large oval table, we made a sort of triangle. I hadn't wanted it to appear it was five against two.

The high lord and lady had conceded in the larger meeting. As much as they deserved to be humbled, I had never wished to be cruel. But I was about to be cruel, or perhaps it was kindness…

Queen Lourel's words echoed in my mind. *Perhaps it's not as simple as kindness versus cruelty. Perhaps the truth is wrapped in both, and I opt to offer the least painful.*

The elf rulers did not know Tyfen and I were mates. And I was completely the wrong person to tell them. But who would? Should they learn through whispers? Tyfen and I had agreed to not hide that part of ourselves. Soon, the realm would know about us, just like it would know about Lilah and me.

"Thank you for your … flexibility and compassion today," I said.

High Lord Elout looked as worn down as I felt. "One doesn't have much choice when they're threatened into submission, do they?"

I frowned. "Our society is but a web—territories and races spread out but connected. If one suffers, we all suffer. It is a delicate thing."

"I fail to see anyone else in this room suffering because of this meeting's outcome, Your Holiness."

I pursed my lips. "I fear my child will suffer. Suffer your wrath for something they had no control over. Suffer the lack of your people's vibrant culture and landscape, should you choose to turn your back on your future emperor or empress."

"We are loyal to the empire and your divine mother. We will find a way to look past this."

I hoped so. "Thank you for that reassurance. We all understand in this room that wars are not necessary if we can first use words. I pray we can move past this."

Marsone met my gaze. "You wished to speak to us more privately. Please…"

I drew a breath, my tone soft. "Earnestly, did you not believe Tyfen and Malaya were mates?"

"There is no logic in it. Not when an elf–fae mating pair hasn't been assigned in centuries."

Tyfen slid his arm onto the table, Malaya's large tattoo facing up. "You have proof. And she had matching proof on her own body."

"Put that away," Elout warned.

"No." Tyfen remained firm. "You beat it out of me before. My choice was stolen. And I will not be silenced again. I will not hide my love for your daughter. This would not be here had she not accepted me as her life partner."

"*Life* partner?" Marsone asked, tears pricking at her eyes. "Or executioner?"

I clasped my hands. "It is apparent we may never see eye to eye on the matter, but you *must* allow for the possibility of them being mates. You have all the evidence you need, and you are not masters of the fates."

"And why does it matter?" Marsone asked.

It mattered a great deal… The next few minutes may go terribly wrong if they couldn't believe the simple matter of Tyfen and Malaya's bond.

"It matters."

Neither ruler would ever verbally admit to that, and I needed to accept it.

"I don't wish to injure you further." I choked down the lump in my throat. "But it's necessary I inform you of something the rest of the realm will soon know."

Elout narrowed his eyes.

I glanced at Tyfen. His vibrant green eyes locked on mine, and I nodded.

He rested his other arm on the table. "Hoku… The fates, really… They … have…" He faltered. "Sonta was given to me as a second mate." He unglamoured his second mark.

The couple looked horrified.

"Further proof of Tyfen's lies."

"It's not." I frowned.

Elout spoke first. "We're to believe he's matched with an elf *and* a human? *Two* mates? Two *impossible* mates?"

"See with your eyes, Elout," Baylana urged. "A couple of hours ago, you believed me dead, incapable of immortality."

"Where is the Blessed Vessel's matching mark?" Marsone challenged.

I cringed internally. "Because of the way I was created, I do not have one, but the temple priestesses agree the bond is true." I held a hand to my heart. "And I *know* it."

Baylana's voice was smooth. "You may be astonished at the secrets Blessed Vessels keep. Our birthright is beautiful."

My heart warmed as I touched my stomach. My excitement grew by the day about our little secret.

"And what does being a Blessed Vessel have to do with anything?" Marsone asked. "You are capable of lying."

I'd toiled over this conversation all evening and morning. I could tell them how I believed I was a blessing to Malaya, that I had been sent to Tyfen as a second mate to respect her wishes for his well-being and to honor their union. I truly did believe that. But how would that come across?

'Your dead daughter chatted with a goddess amidst the stars, and she pitied her, so she decided to send someone else to warm her mate's bed.'

No…

I could have been cruel. I could have used this against them in our earlier negotiations. With Tyfen as my mate, I could have forced them to *immediately* accept our proposal to visit the grave site.

But I hadn't wanted to rub it in their faces. I would never.

I spoke emphatically. "I do not need to offer you proof beyond what I have. But I swear on my life, this bond *is* from Hoku, and it is genuine. Wild magic may be rarer by the day, but it still exists."

I'd questioned why Hoku would have gone that far. Tyfen and I would have loved each other the same. But old stories had a way of teaching us things… And Hoku knew how stubborn the elves were. She'd sent the bond as extra protection for Tyfen.

Elout eyed us. "A Hoku-blessed mate?"

"You know her story as well as I. You know the miracles she was capable of. Do you deny it?"

Elout's face hardened. "Do you wish for a prize, Sonta? A celebration? Like divine mother, like divine daughter? Hoku *was* a great deceiver in her day…"

"You dare blaspheme your goddess?" Baylana screeched. She bared her fangs.

There was a reason I'd requested Baylana's backup for this conversation.

"And in front of her daughters," Baylana added, her eyes reddening.

"As much as her miracles are known, so are her war tactics," Elout rebutted. "Do *you* deny it?"

No one had ever accused Hoku of being a shy, unassuming woman. Her legacy had been built on death and pain, her victory won through swords and sex and secrecy.

I loved Baylana's spunk and frankness. "We do not deny it. But what has Hoku's work done for you? You sit at the head of your people. She gave the power *back* to the people. She honored each of us. She gave you prime land where you thrive. You cannot judge her actions while benefiting from them."

Baylana leaned forward in her seat. "If you deny Sonta's bond, you deny Hoku herself. Her story is shared in the temples. She herself proclaimed that a *forged bond* was no less than a fated bond. And if she walked the land still, she would cut your tongue out for your defiance."

Her face terse beyond words, Baylana plopped back in her seat. "If you continue this nonsense, old friends, I will do the cutting. The True Blade rests with the countess. I'm sure she would let me borrow it."

Well, fuck… I hadn't planned on going that far…

Marsone looked at me, the strain of her defeat apparent. "Pray your new mate does not move on so quickly when you pass. How can you proudly stay at his side when his first mate is barely cold in her grave? How much does a mating bond truly mean to you people if you happily share a bed so soon?"

I swallowed.

"I never wanted to love Sonta," Tyfen admitted.

The elf couple glanced at me to see if I was offended.

"Neither of us would have chosen the bond," I volunteered. "But we do love each other. And we will not hide that anymore. We deserve to be happy."

"As happy as possible," Tyfen whispered. He still ached for Malaya, still blamed himself as much as he did her parents.

"We're not asking for your approval or permission or anything of the sort. We do not tell you as a cruelty or to dismiss your daughter. We will *always* honor her." Tears pricked again. "I never heard anything but good about her, and I regret I never met her."

Elout stood. "It is not right for you to speak of her when you willingly share a bed with the man responsible for her death. And it is not right for us to be at the birth of your child when the man next to you took our daughter's life by putting a child in her."

Marsone hesitantly rose next to her husband. "We … will not be at the birth."

My heart broke. Not because I wanted them there. I didn't want any spectators there, let alone ones who had beaten and tortured my mate. But elf rulers had never once missed the birth of an Anointed Ruler. Not once.

I glanced at Hadwin, and his frown mirrored my own. This was not a way for our child to begin their journey to rule the realm, with a blemish, a formal act of no confidence on their service record.

Choking back tears, I remained calm. "We would not force your presence. We thought it a kindness to warn you ahead of time. I hope you and your family can heal during this respite."

"The countess *will* notice," Hadwin gently reminded them.

"Let her," Elout said.

In a desperately sad part of my mind, I consoled myself: at least I wasn't faking with Tyfen's brother as his body double…

Findlech took my hand. "The sea kings only ever attend the births of emperor or empress merfolk mixlings. But the chancellor will be here in their stead." He smiled at me. "I love my people, and this empire, and Sonta. I will remain at her side. There will be at least one elf at the divine birth."

I squeezed his hand but feared the worst. Given the high lord's irrational nature right now, he could charge Findlech with treason. He definitely would if he ever learned Findlech's true part in this. Findlech could lose his land and title. He could be cut off from his community and his own children.

So I smiled back. "Thank you, Findlech. I love you too."

I waited for the worst, but the high lord and lady were too defeated. "Do as you wish, Findlech," Elout said. "May we leave now?"

"Yes," I whispered. "Thank you for your time."

They left the room, and I sniffled, tears streaming down my face.

"They will calm, Sonta," Findlech soothed.

"Perhaps in a century or two?"

He gave me a half smile. "Miracles happen. We have evidence enough of that."

I blew out a shaky breath.

"Thank you, everyone," Tyfen whispered. He didn't like accepting help, and he was as humbled as the elves were right now.

"You will always have my support," Hadwin offered.

We all stood, and I hugged Findlech before sending him away.

Baylana hugged me on her way out, too. "Glad I could help. It felt nice to be useful after all this time hiding away."

I smiled. "You brought me Hadwin. You could never be anything but useful to me."

"I'm a travel spell away." She caressed my cheek. "And if you wish us here for the birth, we will be here. Mallon will make a second elf in attendance. Third, if you count the emperor…"

I glanced at Hadwin. "I think we'll discuss strategy with Findlech, but the offer is tempting. You know better than anyone what I'll experience."

She gave me a wink.

"But you won't be able to hide your existence after that. Too many eyes…" Glamours were trickier with vampires.

She rolled her eyes. "You don't honestly believe I'll still have my privacy after showing up today, do you? I'll be fine."

I hugged her again. "Thank you."

And then there were three.

Tyfen faced me, his hands on the nape of my neck. "I love you." It was still so new for him to utter those words.

I kissed him. "I love you too."

"You are *Nil* Blantui," he whispered, his dazzling eyes locked with mine.

I savored his touch.

"But you'll keep your promise?" he asked.

Sighing, I nodded. "I'll do my best."

He wrapped me in a tight hug, then finally let me go. "I'll be in the common room."

Hadwin approached and took my hand. I found the coldness of his touch calming. "Here with you every step of the way, darling."

We emerged from the meeting room, met by the fae king and queen. I had asked them to stay in the foyer.

"Thank you," Queen Lourel said. "It will be a bumpy road back to where we need to be, but we're grateful for the changes already."

I had promised Tyfen to not be too harsh... We'd see how this would go...

"And thank *you* for finally getting Tyfen the help he needed to heal. I can't say I've forgiven all your lies yet, because he could have been found faster had you not been so worried about reputation and the emperor finding out about your conflict with the elves."

Hadwin's arm was around my waist, reassuring me.

King Bretton responded. "But as you see, we were unable to go to the emperor before. Do not forget that."

I narrowed my eyes. "You should have more faith in your emperor. As I hope you will have in my child." I balled my fists. "And I will try to forgive you, try to nurture good relations with your people, but it will be hard to forget this ordeal. Your choices will color my opinion for as long as I live, as will the elves' choices. What will Hadwin and I tell our child about the imperial tour? About this day? About why there will not be proper elf representation at the birth?"

Lourel averted her gaze. "They won't be here?"

"No. And that is on you."

Bretton glared. "We are not responsible for this!"

I turned on him, my expression dark. "Are you or are you not a king capable of negotiating?"

"Of course I am. If I weren't, Tyfen wouldn't still be alive."

"If you were competent and caring, this may have never happened in the first place! You knew they loved each other. You knew they were mates. You two could have supported them. You could have courted Elout and Marsone, coaxed them to approve of the match. *You are mates* and know that yearning. Why the hell wasn't your son worth more effort?" I huffed, my ears warming.

"You assume—" Bretton started.

I raised my voice. "Better to shower the elves with gifts of your own choosing to convince them to allow the union, and make your son happy, than to have more than you bargained for extorted from you and harm your son, people, and your Blessed Vessel." I clenched my jaw. "Reckless, and shameful at your age and with your breeding. You berate Tyfen for bringing you shame, for costing you a fortune. It was your own *fucking* fault!"

"Tyfen was difficult to manage, and we will not take your censure when you barely know anything of our ways," the king defended.

"He partied. He drank. He ran away," I said. "Perhaps he was searching for meaning and happiness..."

"Everyone can learn and grow," Hadwin said. "I see much potential in Tyfen."

"You did not know him back then, Your Holiness," Bretton said. "Frankly, what happened years ago is not your concern. We thank you for your assistance and pray we move forward."

I wasn't done. "We will move forward when *I* say we move forward. The *only* reason I'm even trying to forgive you is because your son still loves you." More tears surfaced. "I cannot fathom my own parent *knowing* I had lost my mate, had been beaten and tortured, and then forcing me to bed another so quickly against my will. To make a lifelong commitment to that stranger. To lie and pretend as if I'm okay. To try to conceive a child when his own had died and killed his mate. What the *fuck* were you thinking? Where was your heart?"

Lourel swallowed, looking down. At least she'd admitted before that she'd been wrong about sending him.

King Bretton was his usual self. "You have another mate now. How can you be angry with us when you have a fullness in your heart because of it?"

I blinked. "You justify your decisions so easily and weakly. You disappoint me. And you offend me beyond imagination by sending him here to slight the elves. You used him as a weapon, and I was collateral damage."

"All it did was allow the issue to come before the emperor," Bretton defended.

"And what if the high lord had insisted on still sending *his* son?" Hadwin asked.

"Luckily, he didn't," Bretton said.

I gaped. "*Luckily?* You know the truth of it. It was not luck. You owe *everything* to Lord Findlech."

"I owe nothing to an elf."

I cocked my head. "Is your kingdom so starved for good men that you could not find me a more suitable match? You have no virile, palatable men who would *not* be inflammatory? Your other sons could not even fit the bill?"

"Listen, you mortal bitch!" Bretton barked.

"You will *not* speak of your Blessed Vessel that way," Hadwin growled, his eyes red as he stepped forward and grabbed the king's shirt. "You will crawl into a hole and be silent. You will learn respect."

Lourel stared at the two, wide-eyed. As did I...

The king kept his cool. "A vampire duke with no notable accomplishments or battle training does not scare me. Get. Your. Hands. Off. Me."

I gave Lourel a look. She and I had had multiple chats, mother to mother. She had conspired with me to hide Tyfen's injuries before the paternity reveal because she knew her husband was hotheaded. She knew how to at least admit to some of her mistakes. And she needed to learn to tame her own husband.

No words needed to be exchanged.

"Bretton, go back to our room."

"No. I'm not—"

"*Go back to our room, Bretton.* Now!"

Hadwin let him go and stepped back. "Our mates tend to want what is best for us. I'd listen to yours."

Bretton's nostrils flared, and he turned.

"One last thing," Hadwin said.

The king returned his attention.

"I cannot imagine *ever* telling my child they are replaceable."

I rubbed my stomach. Hadwin would never. He cared too much. He was going to be such an attentive father.

Hadwin continued. "And your future ruler may *just* be mortal, but they will know their uncle Tyfen is *not* replaceable." I adored how fiercely he protected Tyfen now that he understood the situation.

The king looked like he was going to speak again.

"Bretton," I said. "May Hoku multiply her blessings on you. You need them."

He gave me a wry smile and left.

After he was out of earshot, I turned to Lourel. "You need to do better. He's as out of control as the elves."

"It is hard for him to see his family legacy ripped from him over this ordeal."

"And what is he adding to that legacy, Your Majesty? I pray you don't speak of only the wealth you lost…"

She pressed her lips together, her expression sincere. "We'll work on it."

"I hope so," I whispered. "I once thought I saw a friend in you. And I enjoyed getting to know your children … your eldest excluded."

Hadwin held me from behind. "We would like to see your people thrive. But we expect to see changes, Your Majesty."

She nodded. "Thank you again for helping my people and Tyfen. We'll forever be in your debt."

I smiled. "I do like citrus. Perhaps I'll come try some once your crops have recovered. I've never been to an island."

59

Reconnect

Hadwin and I hugged for ages back in our tower, just in the hallway, to decompress before joining the others. I had added stress about the upcoming birth, but at the same time, so much weight had been lifted, and so much air had been cleared.

The common room was bustling as we entered, Lilah actively listening to the others recount what had happened. Tyfen was fairly quiet, staring into the fireplace.

Haan smiled. "Sonta, Hadwin."

I returned the smile. I got ample hugs and was ushered to sit down. Worn out, I perched on the sofa next to Tyfen. He slid an arm around me. "How did that last part go?"

I honestly didn't know... I'd let them have it, but really only the abbreviated version. "It's done. And there was no bloodshed, so I call that a win."

Hadwin took a seat on my other side, and Tyfen glanced at him. "Considering Hadwin was involved, no bloodshed *is* a win," Tyfen said.

Wide-eyed, everyone stared between the two.

Tyfen chuckled. Goddess, I missed that sound.

I narrowed my eyes. "So charming."

"I never claimed to be charming, did I? What did Lilah say you called me? 'Delightful'?"

His grin was sexy, his eyes tired.

I stole a kiss, and almost told him he'd pay for that...

How easily we fell back into place.

"I *am* sorry I hurt you, Tyfen," Hadwin said.

"Don't be. If anything, I'm curious if you'd like to participate in sparring practice sometime. It would give me a chance to recover some of my pride, and in case I'm actually going to have to resign my position in my royal guard, I'm going to need all the exercise I can to stay in shape."

I frowned. A lot had been laid on the table, but now that I thought about it, we hadn't set *exact* terms.

Lilah leaned into Gald on the sofa they shared with Findlech and Elion. "You're worried about staying in shape? We have the ponds, pools, and lakes. Stairs and tons of land to walk and run on. And time with Sonta in the bedroom can get rather gymnastic, can't it?"

My jaw dropped, and I blushed as Elion and Gald laughed.

Clearing my throat, I looked at Haan. "What did you think of the meeting? You've been rather quiet."

His purple eyes were mesmerizing, his brown hair handsome. "There's no such thing as victory in what happened today, but I suppose it worked out…"

We all sobered a bit. It really wasn't something we'd ever truly celebrate. It was a messy version of justice.

Elion adjusted his position, sitting cross-legged on the sofa. "Would your people really have sunk the elven ships?"

We all listened intently, especially Findlech. We'd coordinated a lot of bluffs, but there had to be an element of truth for a bluff to really land well.

"Isn't it nice we won't have to find out?" Haan replied.

A politician's answer…

Haan smiled. "I was *this* close"—he made a pinching gesture—"to saying I'd heard a rumor that our younglings being netted led back to the elf royal family, and that someone had spied a mounted tail on a gallery wall."

My eyes widened. "Tell me there's no truth in the rumors!"

His smile grew. "Would it have mattered? We all *know* nobles hide privileged indiscretions. The emperor would have gone along with it and commented about the need to increase the rate of raids the empire conducts."

I blinked in shock. It was a *little* cruel, given the high lord and lady were genuinely still in a great deal of emotional pain, but they *were* less-than-ethical assholes, too… "I should like to have that conversation around the countess, and see the look on her face when vampire nobles' basements are raided."

Hadwin gave me a shocked 'why did you just say that' look, and I winced.

"What do vampire nobles keep in their basements?" Gald asked.

Hadwin smiled. "Don't most people keep wine and cold storage down there?"

Elion cocked his head, narrowing his eyes. "He didn't ask about most people. What do you keep in your basement, Hadwin?" His voice was full of cunning curiosity.

I deflected. "Speaking of basements, what's in Findlech's?" I smiled wide.

He crossed his legs, his eyebrows raised high. "Perhaps our friendship will keep growing enough for you to learn someday."

Gald grinned. "What a silly question, Sonta." He winked.

Lilah pulled her hair back into a ponytail. "I really do want to know what Hadwin would keep in a basement, though... He seems so very sweet and innocent."

He smiled, fangs and all. "You haven't had the pleasure of seeing it yet, but for you, I'll be honest. There is *nothing* spectacular about *my* basement at all..."

"And other nobles?" Tyfen asked.

Hadwin yawned. "I'm so very tired after today's business. Isn't it time for bed?"

It made me yawn, too, and a couple of others in the room. "Good deflection." I drew a deep breath. "And a good point. It's been a long day. Sleep sounds divine." I forced myself to stand. "I love all of you."

It got a little awkward as I stood there. We all knew Tyfen and I needed time to reconnect in private, right? I wouldn't have to dole out bedding instructions?

"I'd like ... in a few days ... if everyone wants, to share my bed again with everyone like on our first night together?"

The smiles and nods were unanimous. "There's enough room for Lilah, too, right?"

Gald's smirk was on brand. "Let's not pretend there's not *a lot* more body contact between us now than there used to be." He ran his hand up Findlech's thigh. "There's definitely room for one more." He puckered his lips playfully at Lilah, and she playfully returned the gesture.

I glanced at Haan. "And if you want to..."

His smile always reminded me of the treasures of the sea. "I might take you up on it this time."

I glanced around, not all that keen to be the center of attention at the moment. Stepping back, I reached out to Tyfen. "Let's go. Good night, everyone."

He grasped my hand and stood, and we strolled to my chambers.

Why is this so awkward? It's not like they won't know we're having sex...

Or maybe we wouldn't... We'd been away from each other for a while... And he'd been through a lot.

I led Tyfen into my bedroom, then closed the door. He took in the room, his face unreadable. He hadn't seen it in seven months.

I gestured to the chairs next to the fireplace. "Take a seat." The fire was a little low, so I bent and grabbed a log.

"I can do that."

Turning, I eyed him. "Sit your ass down. Pregnancy does not make me weak." I instantly regretted saying it. I hadn't meant to imply his former mate had been weak in her tragic ending. "I mean, I still don't want to be babied."

He didn't seem hurt, and he sat. His gaze flickered to my bare wrists—no leather there, and it lit a fire within me that he would even think of that. "So bossy, Sonta."

I tucked the log into the glowing embers. "You signed up for it... And I'll take pampering, but not babying."

"Noted." He removed his shoes. "I *assume* I am staying the night, right?"

"No…" I faced him. "I wanted to show you a few new dresses Madam Gaffey made for me while you were away."

He rolled his eyes, and I smiled.

Tyfen held out his hands, settling back in his seat. I took the invitation, easing down onto his lap. He pulled me in tight, and I nestled up to him, his arms around me, my face in the crook of his neck. In unison, we sighed, and he rested his head on mine.

We said nothing for the longest time, just sharing breath, calm, peace, and unity.

"I missed you like crazy," I finally whispered.

He rubbed my back. "I missed you too."

"How are you doing?"

His contemplative groan reverberated in my head. "It's been a day…"

"It's been a year."

"It's been a few years."

"It's been a lifetime."

He lowered his voice to a barely there whisper. "What are we talking about now?"

I smiled. "I don't know. We were just talking about bigger stretches of time as we went…"

His chuckle was soft and perfect. "You've always been a weird little human."

Pulling back, I gave him a pouty face.

Caressing my cheek, he added, "One I'll never let go."

I leaned into his touch, taking in his handsome eyes. Those green eyes may always remind me of grass, but I now thought of the spring—fast upon us—and new beginnings.

"I love you," I said.

Warmth filled his expression. "I love you, too."

There was one conversation we hadn't had yet, and perhaps it wasn't the right time, but I wasn't sure when it would be…

I swallowed. "Would you still love me if—"

"Yes."

I rolled my eyes, and he smiled.

Poking him in the chest, I continued. "I'm serious. And you don't have to answer right now, and I haven't made a final decision, and if I do it, it wouldn't even happen for years…"

"What is it?"

"Would you still love me if I was a vampire like Baylana?"

His expression changed, more sorrowful, and it twisted my heart.

"I know I'll be cold, and I'll eat different and everything, but I'll still be me… And like I said—"

He pressed a finger to my lips. "You understand why I … resisted … falling for you, or at least part of why. But I also struggled to give you my heart because I've already lost someone I love." He teared up. "After having her for far too short a time."

I wiped away a tear that rolled down his cheek.

His voice was quiet and sincere. "I didn't want to give all of myself to you just to lose you so quickly, too."

My heart melted. "So you *would* be okay if I accepted an eternal bite?"

He leaned in and pressed his lips to mine with the softest touch possible. Just the feel of him made me wet. His lips were strong and supple, grazing mine perfectly. With each pass, my core heated and breasts ached.

My breathing was ragged when he stopped, forehead to mine. "I want you every day for the rest of my life, Sonta. Immortality couldn't ever look bad on you."

Goddess, I wanted him. All of him. But I didn't want to push him if he needed more time.

"Okay. We'll see how the next couple of decades go. No rush to make the change…" I panted. "And … no rush for other things, either, if you need more time."

I didn't have to clarify my meaning. He understood perfectly as he slid me even closer and pressed his erection against me.

Why did it feel like I had no bones? Like I could melt into a puddle and let him do as he wished and thank him when I'd regained my words and thoughts?

"Unless you're too tired," he said. "It's been a long day. I can wait till the morning."

I flashed him a coy smile. "You're not going to make me do *all* the work, are you? I *am* only a month away from giving birth…"

His grin was feral. "I'll always have enough energy to make up for what you lack."

His cock thrummed against me, and my core was tight with anticipation as I undid the top button on his shirt. I worshiped his neck with my lips as I continued to undo them all. With his muscled chest bare, I rested my hands on it, admiring those tattoos I loved so much.

I dragged my fingers up his neck, wanting to reunite with and memorize all of him.

Tyfen dipped his head down, and I kissed him again. His large hands found the hem of my dress, slowly sliding it up as he opened his mouth wider, begging for more. I moaned at his taste as his tongue caressed mine.

He pulled my dress up past my hips, touching as much of my skin as he could on the way. Once he tugged it high enough, we broke apart so he could get it over my head. It hit the ground, and I took a moment to catch my breath.

My heart pounded as I examined Tyfen's naked chest again. "Where did you get hurt? When the oni attacked you in the Dark Forest?"

He pointed to his left arm. "Pretty deep there."

I pushed the shoulder of his shirt down and freed his arm from his sleeve. "Your healers did great work." There was a fine scar, likely because it had taken a while to get to him while he fought to stay alive.

"They took good care of me."

I pressed my lips to the scar, hurting a little more that this was the arm Hadwin had shattered already. I kissed the scar again, covering the whole of it. "No pain, right?"

"I'm fine, Sonta." His tone was gentle and full of reassurance.

"Where else were you injured?"

He pointed to his side. "Those dirty claws can sink in deep."

I slid off his other sleeve, letting his shirt fall, and shifted on his lap to kiss those, too.

Coming up, I searched his eyes. "Anywhere else?" I undid the button on his pants.

He smirked. "Unfortunately, no."

I loosened the tie strings of his pants. "I think you mean *fortunately*, no…"

He chuckled softly. "True."

He took a turn, kissing me again as he undid my bra, then let it fall to the floor. He didn't even try to properly remove my underwear; he just snapped the band.

Tyfen slid a finger to my clit and massaged me. My whole body tensed, so utterly, desperately ready for him.

I let out a whimper, and he dragged his finger lower and massaged me inside. His groan of approval at my wetness only added to the torture.

"We should take your pants off," I exhaled.

"If you're ready…"

I couldn't be more.

He lifted his finger to his lips and tasted me, closing his eyes and cherishing it.

How could I not love this man? Our bodies and hearts had been made for each other.

I glanced at Tyfen's slightly pointy ears, smiling, then grazed the tops with the gentlest touch.

"Fuck, Sonta," he whispered.

My smile grew.

His look darkened, more feral as he wrapped an arm around my back and the other under my legs, and stood, sweeping me up. He marched to the large bed and dropped my legs, having me stand. My back was against a bedpost.

Tyfen seized the opportunity to palm my breasts as I reached down and dropped his pants, then shorts. I glanced down, then swallowed. I'd remembered he was big, but… He was BIG.

"It's been a while," he said. "I'll be careful."

My cheeks warmed as I ran my hands down his pecs, then abs, then south to the tattoo he'd earned by taking a vow to enter my Coterie, right above his cock.

"I always liked this, the pattern."

He shuddered as I brushed up against his base. "Is that your favorite part of me, or is this?" His large warm hands took mine and rested them on his cock.

So many memories flooded me as I held him, treasuring the girth. "I could never choose a favorite part. But give me a moment to reinspect you, and I could give you a list of my top five." I winked, then lifted my hands to his neck again.

"Not bad..." I slithered down. "Good shoulders." They really were...

I felt his biceps, and he subtly flexed. And then my hands slid to his forearms.

I quickly pulled my hand away from Malaya's mating mark, and looked down.

Goddess, this was going to take some getting used to. I was familiar with every inch of his body, but I truly wasn't. This had been here all along, but I hadn't known, hadn't understood. It felt so disrespectful to touch her mark during intimacy like this.

Tyfen was silent a moment. "Do you want me to glamour it away when we're intimate?" he whispered.

I could never ask him to do that, not after all he'd been through. We just needed to communicate and work through this.

I met his eyes. "Would you like to glamour away *my* lovers' marks when we're intimate? Hadwin's love bite? Elion's claiming bite? Gald's bond tattoo? Do they bother you?"

He wrinkled his nose. "Sharing mates in *any* of our races is uncommon, but it comes with the territory of loving you. I accept them for what they are."

I held a hand over his heart. "As do I. You never have to hide part of yourself from me again."

His smile was warm and grateful, and he moved my hand back to his arm. "And for the rest of our lives, all of me is yours."

I nodded, and Tyfen caressed my waist, guiding me to my left, to the edge of the bed. When he stopped, I sat, then lay back. He grasped my knees. "Comfortable?"

"Yes."

Spreading my legs, he stepped closer, then pressed his cock to my entrance. Shivers ran down my spine, and I strained my neck trying to watch him penetrate me. My pregnancy had been marvelous so far, but it certainly limited some things in the bedroom this late in the game.

Tyfen didn't continue, only surveying me. He stepped back, then cast his gaze about the room. Without a word, he set to work, swiftly shifting the daybed to the side, where I could more easily see myself in the mirror on the far partition wall. Then he grabbed a footstool from the sitting area.

That tight ass... How had I forgotten his perfectly curved ass?

He set the footstool near my feet, then crawled onto the bed from the side. Without warning, he yanked my legs so I lay perpendicular to the bed.

I let out a scream in surprise. "Fuck, Tyfen." I blew out a breath. "I'm capable of moving myself..."

He only grinned and grabbed some pillows, then tucked them behind my back.

Realizing what the stool was for, I draped my leg over the edge of the bed, supporting myself with the stool and opening myself for him.

"How's that?" he asked as we both looked into the mirror. "You like what you see?"

Was Lilah too busy to take another commission? Because I saw the perfect side view of his ass and cock, every muscled and tattooed part of his body. Even his ears. I didn't look half bad either… "I love it."

Half kneeling, half standing, Tyfen held me in place again, pressing his tip to me. "Make sure to tell me what else you love…"

I watched every glorious inch of him slowly enter me, savoring the stretch from his massive cock as he grasped my hips. I moaned. "I love *this*."

He eased the last of his length into me, his base kissing my pussy. "You're so tight."

I squeezed my pelvic muscles, and he gasped.

I finally stopped watching in the mirror and met his gaze. Goddess, he looked like he was ready to destroy me. I already knew I'd ask for seconds.

"Ready?" he asked.

I rolled my hips in reply.

Tyfen pulled himself out, then slowly reentered. The friction was so good it ached.

He pulled halfway out again, then thrust with more speed and force. I sucked in air, clenching my hands around his.

Each thrust was intentional, rhythmic, and absolutely possessive. I tightened and burned for him, my core on fire, my release already building.

Each time he plunged deep into me, it hammered into me the fact he was really home. That my lover, my Coterie ally, and my mate was home. My heart could not be fuller.

His eyes didn't leave mine for even a second.

Our breath became thick and heavy, as quick as our hearts beat, as quick as he thrust.

Tyfen came forcefully, loudly, and I loved the vulnerability of it, and I loved the extra few thrusts he gave me that pushed me over the edge, too.

My knuckles were white as I squeezed his hands, as my legs trembled, as I all but screamed.

Panting, we cooled. He lovingly tickled my thighs. "Tired? Or would you like to go again?" He was still fully erect, still buried inside me.

I grinned. "How about in the pool? It helps with the baby."

I didn't have to ask him twice. He scooped me up again, and I didn't give a damn his seed dripped everywhere—plus, the pond cycled fresh water regularly. Soon enough we were both inside.

He kissed me, and my hands landed on his forearms again.

"How would you feel about me getting a tattoo that matches yours?" I asked. "Neither of us asked for the bond, and we don't owe people anything to prove we're mates, but I'd like to … have that on me…"

His confident grin was every bit that of the cocky prince I loved. "It'll take up the most space on your body."

My jaw dropped. "Is this a competition?"

He lifted me higher in the water, crouching low. We were both so wet with each other, he slid into me easily as he pinned me against the pond wall. "No competition. I know what I have and what I have to offer."

That he did.

We made love three times. The pool was a nice reprieve for my back, and then we fell asleep after the third time, tangled up in each other on the bed.

I woke at morning's first light, my lashes fluttering.

Tyfen held me from behind as I lay on my side. He whispered words I did not know, all in Fae, stopping every little while to press a kiss to a different part of my shoulder. I *did* recognize Nil Blantui.

I remained still, smiling at the sweetness until he finished, his forehead pressed to my skin as he softly sighed.

"We'll need to start up lessons again, so I understand your sweet nothings next time," I whispered.

He hummed, and I turned to face him. "But those were not sweet nothings," he said.

I arched an eyebrow. "No?"

Circling my nipple with his finger, he smiled. "No. Prayers to Hoku."

That surprised me. "I never took you for a devout worshiper."

He cringed, applying more pressure to my nipple. "Don't you dare accuse me of being an upright temple boy."

I giggled.

"I prefer to worship in the bedroom." His cock pressed against me, already hard again, confirming his truth. He wrapped his lips around my perky nipple, and gave it more attention.

We were going to have a hell of a reunion period. A hell of a lifetime.

A hell of a good time for eternity.

He looked at me again. "I don't pray as much as I probably ought to, but I know how to give thanks where it's deserved."

I caressed his cheek. He was so soft and sweet, and I'd always loved this side of him. But I had to ask myself how much he had changed in our time apart, during his soul-searching and recovery. No matter what, I would take him as he was.

"Is this the new you?" I asked. "A sweet and gentle lover?"

He lowered his head, looking away. "Is that … what you want?"

My smile was crooked and my heart happy at his apparent disappointment. I loved this softness, but I would miss his ferocity and dominance if he had lost that side of him. "I don't have any plans to get rid of the bracelet you gave me."

His gaze slid back up to mine, his expression hungry and happy. He rested a hand on my throat, stroking me with his thumb. "Once this child is out of you… There's a hell of a lot in that playroom we never got to try."

I blushed.

His other hand made its way to my thigh. "For now, why don't you be a good girl and open your legs for me?"

Without hesitation, I obeyed.

60

Soft & Sweet

I joined my Coterie. We gathered at Haan's tank in the common room as we chatted, digesting our rich lunch. I rubbed my enormous pregnant belly, ready to burst any day. It didn't help I'd eaten an extra serving of the fresh spring vegetables.

Things had been so busy in the last three weeks that we didn't share as much time together as I would have liked, but we made it a priority.

Meetings were our constant companions, about the fae–elf conflict and about regular business. Lilah and I had spent loads of time with mother and Kernov, excitedly talking wedding details, at least when Lilah wasn't busy in our studio.

My visions came as they normally did, and I cherished them, but I looked forward to Hoku's secret gift to her daughters.

Tyfen and I were insatiable, but I made time for all my people.

So far, Findlech had not seen any personal fallout for his place in the ordeal. He kept in touch with the high lord and lady, and they were still boycotting my child's birth.

I didn't wish to have them here for it. I didn't want that negativity. But I did wish I could do something to help heal their hearts. We all agreed the best I could do was give them space and time. An offer of money or a grand gift of flowers and fruits wouldn't be right, coming from Tyfen's new mate. Nor would a letter conveying my condolences. Sometimes, the best thing you could do was let someone sort out their grief on their own.

The elf delegation would be absent, but I would have Findlech in attendance, and Mallon—Baylana's partner. Baylana and her partners had recently arrived for the birth, just as most of the other rulers had.

I loathed breaking bread with the vampire countess, but I had to work on my mindset. Although there were questionable things about her and vampire society,

The Blessed Coterie

there was still much good to be found. My child was half vampire. One of my mates was a vampire, and I couldn't do this without him.

I sat on the common room floor, stretching my painful back as the group chatted. Tyfen sat behind me, his legs spread to either side of me.

"How does that feel?" He dug his thumbs into my back, massaging.

I moaned softly. "I could kiss you."

He leaned forward and rested his chin on my shoulder. "Then I must not be doing it right. I only get a *kiss*?"

I chuckled.

Hadwin and Elion each massaged one of my feet. I wouldn't complain about the pampering one bit.

Findlech and Gald sat on a sofa, hands on each other's thighs. Lilah had just left to go fetch a surprise.

"Any word from your father about Kaibu?" Haan asked Tyfen.

Tyfen huffed. "Not to me. I don't expect to hear from him for a while. At least not personally." He ran his thumbs down my spine.

Tyfen and his mother had asked the king to leave the palace, and not return for the birth. I was grateful to have one less person I disliked there for the special moment. And it wasn't even going to look all that scandalous. The king and queen had always been in attendance for previous Anointed Ruler births, save when the queen herself had given birth around the same time a previous Blessed Vessel had, but they had a valid excuse to keep it from looking like there was something wrong this time.

Having reclaimed Kaibu Island, the fae king was now there, assessing the damage of neglected crops, trying to jump-start it. For all the people knew, their king was being more hands-on about the fictional 'blight' that had destroyed all their crops on the island.

It was as good of a lineup as I'd get for a public birth. Thank the stars any bonus children I may have someday could be delivered in private.

Hadwin kept smiling at me, and at my stomach. I was still elated for him to become a father.

Lilah strode back in, a large canvas in her hands. "Ready for the surprise?"

My smile was wide. She'd painted me a gift in preparation for the birth.

"Absolutely!"

She glanced at everyone. Findlech and Gald shifted for a better view. "It's kind of a gift for all of us. I hope you like it."

Lilah turned the canvas around, and I almost immediately cried.

It was breathtaking—the background featuring the current spring weather with the Pontaii Palace behind us, the massive mountains further behind that.

Trees blossomed, wispy clouds hung in the air, and the grass grew green.

All the Coterie stood there, her included.

"I love it," I choked out. "It's so beautiful."

Elion cocked his head. "I think you made me too short…"

She glanced at it. "No, look at you compared to Tyfen. I was careful about the proportions."

"You made my ears as pointy as Findlech's." Tyfen's lip curled.

Findlech cracked a smile.

Lilah gaped. "That… You…" She huffed. "Your ears are not *that* different!"

"What's with Sonta's arms?" Gald wrinkled his nose. "Not the most natural position…"

She scoffed. "If you paid attention, she's also not massively pregnant in the painting. Her arms are cradled, and I'll be adding the baby once we know what they look like!"

Gald furrowed his brow, nodding.

Hadwin spoke next. "Not to be too critical, but you painted a bright spring day, and I'm not wearing a cloak… My skin would be blistered, Lilah."

Lilah grunted. "Artistic license, Hadwin! I didn't want to hide you under a blanket or make it a dreary day." Exasperated, she scowled. "You all suck. I can take criticism, but you're a bit much…"

Hadwin belted out a laugh. "Come on, Lilah. We're having fun with you. It looks *amazing*."

"It does," I said.

She pouted, until the others confirmed it *was* masterfully painted.

Haan spoke up. "In earnest, though, it's a pity you can't see my tail."

"I know…" She moved closer to his tank, showing it to him close up. "The angle just didn't work well with the surroundings. But look: I made sure to include your favorite starfish earrings!"

He smiled. "It's lovely."

She mirrored his smile. "I was thinking about hanging it over here, in the common room where we can all enjoy it." She hopped past Hadwin and Elion, and strode to the middle of the room, gesturing to the wall. "What do you say?"

I let the others vote first. They agreed with her, and so did I.

Lilah beamed.

I suddenly realized my ass and thighs were wet… My eyes grew wide. "Shit."

"What's wrong?" Elion asked.

I took a closer look. I sat in a puddle of my own water…

Gald pressed his lips together. "It happens to some pregnant women…"

Glaring at him, I threw him a vulgar gesture. "I went to the washroom after lunch. I didn't just piss myself."

"It's time?" Hadwin breathed, his eyes reddening.

I didn't want to be wrong, but I *knew* it was time. The constant backache made more sense. "Yes."

Elion stopped massaging my feet and jumped up. He bolted to the main hallway door and opened it. "IT'S TIME!"

Well, that was one way to go about it…

"Shit," Lilah whispered, setting down her painting. "Let's do this."

Everyone stood, Tyfen helping me up. Findlech gave me a smile. "I suppose we should all get dressed in something more appropriate for the event."

I had a special birthing gown prepared, a beautiful flowy thing, and the rest would want to wear something befitting their stations. Lilah even had a special dress. We'd all been in casual clothing for the afternoon.

Elion rejoined us. "How can I help?"

I smiled through a spasm in my body. "We've gone through all this. Stop stressing. Just get changed."

"Right…" He kissed me, then darted to his room.

Findlech left much more calmly to his room, and Gald gave me a kiss before heading back to his. Haan splashed away to go find his people.

"I'll be back soon." Lilah kissed my cheek and squealed, then sprinted away.

My midwife entered with two servants. "I hear we're needed."

I sighed. "I think so."

She did a quick reading and smiled. "We don't have to race around. These things still take time, even for a Blessed Vessel."

Hadwin and Tyfen lingered.

I gave Hadwin a hug and kiss. "Go. Join me in my chambers when you're dressed."

"Okay." He hesitated, so protective and nervous.

I caressed his cool cheeks, admiring his honey-hazel eyes tinted with red. "I'll be fine. You'll be fine. And the baby will be here, happy and safe, before we know it."

He kissed my forehead. "Would you like some blood beforehand to strengthen you?"

My lips quirked up. We certainly weren't about to have sex, and it wouldn't hurt for me to top up before hard labor set in, but I understood his question on a deeper level. I wouldn't crave blood after the birth, and he'd miss me feeding on him. "In my chambers after I'm changed. Go on."

He nodded and turned.

One of the servants quietly worked to clean up my water while I addressed Tyfen. He bit his lip, and my heart twisted at his hesitation.

I kissed him, brushing his gently pointed ears as I dug my fingers into his hair. "I'll be safe, and you'll be there for every moment of it."

His throat bobbed. "Yes I will be."

Had Malaya's lady's maid called for help sooner, for Tyfen or a physician, Malaya's life most likely could have been saved. Tyfen couldn't turn back time, couldn't save her, and this was going to be hard for him. But he had to be there as a member of my Coterie. And he wouldn't leave even if he were ordered to.

I took his large warm hands. "Today, you're one of my strengths, Nil Blantue."

He cracked a smile.

Before sending him to his room to change, I gave him one last reminder. "I'm Hoku-blessed. Even if I don't respond, I will be fine."

Blessed Vessels fell into a trance as labor developed, barely conscious of the world around them as they birthed their firstborn for the realm. I'd already instructed my loved ones so they wouldn't fret or be confused.

"Okay," he whispered.

Elion returned, looking absolutely handsome in his formal wear. I couldn't hide a smile.

"Go on," I told Tyfen.

Hadwin had waited for Tyfen at the door to the Coterie corridor, and he rested his hand on Tyfen's back as he joined him.

"I bet you might look sharper than Elion for this affair, but that dusty old crown of yours won't outshine me."

"Hey!" Elion protested.

Tyfen chuckled. "Fuck off, Hadwin." The two entered the corridor to their rooms, and I followed my midwife to my chambers to ready myself.

The pain was steady as we changed and prepared me. My mother and Lilah joined me in my chambers, then Hadwin. I did feed off him, and we savored the shortest moment alone as a couple in the nursery.

I cried as we glanced at the crib. We were going to be parents.

The Coterie reassembled, and we made our way to the bedding chamber, now renamed the birthing chamber. Most rulers and witnesses who were invited to attend in the alcove had already arrived, full of smiles and excitement. One of Tyfen's sisters now accompanied his mother, wearing a glittering tiara.

The countess's greeting was as warm as it had ever been, and I tried to believe it was a genuine and kind gesture, not just a politically motivated one.

The emperor and magistrate arrived, greeting everyone in the birthing chamber, and the ballroom below started to fill. The unpredictability of a pregnancy meant there would not be a thousand spectators, and there would not be a ball tonight, but many still came to herald the birth of the next Anointed Ruler. The palace was packed with dignitaries and noblemen waiting for word, and the inns of the nearest villages in the mountains had sold out long ago. Many citizens had even camped in the mountains, waiting to participate and celebrate.

I chatted with the people in the alcove while pacing and breathing, the spasms in my body steadily growing larger and closer together. I drank water, ate fresh fruit, and chatted as I occasionally rested on the bed.

My mother held my hand, sitting next to the bed. Several chairs lined the bed, mostly for my Coterie members. Lilah stood as support from the sideline as a personal witness again. She visited but didn't hover, not ready yet to announce to the realm we were a couple. She did wear the beautiful ring I'd given her as a symbol of our upcoming union, though. I couldn't stop smiling after I noticed that.

"How do you feel?" my mother asked.

I squeezed out a breath through a rough contraction. "Fine, Mammi."

She was so young to become a grandmother, but she was excited and dedicated. She gestured for Baylana to come over, and Baylana happily did.

"You said she won't even feel it?" my mother asked.

Baylana's smirk spoke volumes, but only to me. "Barely. She'll be well."

"No pain..." Tyfen said. "And you don't even need that gel Findlech likes to use."

My eyes widened, and I smacked his arm. He coughed to hide his fit of laughter. Findlech in his regal circlet pretended he hadn't heard the jab.

Goddess... Nearly ten months ago, all six of my men had fucked me in this room, all but Haan on this very bed.

I glanced at Baylana again. "Is it really as amazing as they say?"

Her fangs showed this time as she smiled. "Possibly more."

No one really knew what we meant, our secret our own. Motherhood would have its ups and downs. Just like rulership did. But an Anointed Ruler's birth was blessed.

The crowd below continued to grow as people from the mountains and villages trickled in, and my contractions got rather intense and quick, so the emperor made the official start.

He stood on the lifted platform, welcoming the people and reciting all the divine edicts and traditions. He announced the important people here today, simply citing the elf high lord and lady and the fae king were unfortunately unable to attend due to matters they were overseeing in their lands.

Hadwin and I got up there, doing our part and thanking the people for coming to celebrate with us, to welcome Hoku's next heir.

The pain hit a point where I didn't want to keep pacing. The emperor took the cue and made a request for the attendees to please respectfully wait in silence. "May Hoku multiply her blessings on the Blessed Vessel and upon us all."

The crowd recited the blessing, and I was on the brink of tears. For my place in this realm, for the loved ones surrounding me, and for the blessings I had out of sheer luck in my birth. I was also a little terrified...

I was about to push out a whole other person...

Baylana's smile calmed me.

Trust the process.

61
The Blessed Vessels' Secret

I chose to do most of my hard laboring on my knees. I had three mage midwives attending to me, and comforting words and caresses from my Coterie and mother.

During a particularly painful contraction, my face was warm as sweat beaded, and I blew out a breath.

And then it all faded into a calm whisper—the world around me, the pain, and my sense of time. I was caressed with Hoku's greatest gift to her daughters, the Blessed Vessels' absolute secret.

The future was uncertain, and things could still change. Our gift could be used inappropriately, which was why we guarded the secret, even from those we loved most. Hoku gave us crisp visions during the birth of our firstborns, dulling the pain of childbirth and replacing it to thank us for our service to the realm.

The haze of my mind soon solidified into the first vision, and it was as if I were truly there.

I was in my chambers pond, not a stitch of clothing on me, nor did Hadwin have a stitch of clothing on him...

Wrapping my arms around him, I kissed him.

Goddess, I forgot how it feels to not have a huge bump between us.

Hadwin backed me up against the pool wall, our kissing rather passionate, and his hard cock giving me an idea of where this vision intended to go.

His lips changed course to my neck, worshiping my love bite. "I really do miss you feeding off me," he said, his voice thick with desire.

My future self's body was very happy to be with him at the moment... "Does that mean you changed your mind?" I glanced at his deep red eyes. "I'll give you another one, and you'll get ten great months of me feeding off you."

He laughed, palming my breasts. "I think I'm still good with things the way they are." His fanged smile warmed my heart. "Right now, at least, I want to give my girls my everything."

I couldn't tell if I was crying in the present day, but I was in my mind. A girl. I was currently giving birth to a little girl.

Future me didn't catch on that detail, instead happy to continue with our romantic moment. "You want to give me *everything*?" I grasped his cock and guided it to my entrance.

Hadwin paused, his gaze flicking to the back door of my chambers.

"Nursery?" I asked. Present me couldn't hear anything...

"She's up," Hadwin said.

He can still sense our daughter's heartbeat.

A little knock sounded at the door that led to the maternal suites, and I blew out a cooling breath.

Hadwin sighed as well, rubbing my arms. "I told you that room is too big for her."

"The nursery is full, and too small for her anyway. She'll get used to it."

The nursery was full... I would have at least one more child. It had to be the cub Elion wanted so badly.

"I'll get it." I hopped out of the pond and threw on a robe.

Hadwin also left the pond, and dashed naked to the dressing room.

I opened the door and was met by the sweetest little child.

I crouched. "And what would you be doing up at this time of night, my sweet one?"

Her hair was black like mine, her eyes hazel like her father's. Her complexion was standard for a vampire mixling, paler than my skin but not quite as much as her father's. She had to be three, perhaps four years old.

She pouted. "It's scary in there."

"But Uncle Tyfen added all those lovely fae lights to ward off the monsters and beasties for you."

"The fae lights *should* do it," Hadwin chimed in behind me.

I would never forget the way her eyes lit up. "Father!"

"Hello, my little darling."

Fuck, I had to be crying in the present. The way he called her that, the way she was *so* excited to see him. It made sense she was surprised. She may never know which partner I shared my room with each night...

Our daughter ran to my now-dressed mate and leaped into his arms.

"What's this I hear? Your room is scary despite all those lights?"

"I heard an oni," she whispered.

I closed the door, and Hadwin settled down on a sofa with her on his lap. I joined them.

"The palace is safe, Alana," I said, tucking her hair behind her ears.

Alana had been Hadwin's mother's name, too.

Hadwin twisted his lips. "And oni are far too large to fit under the bed of a little girl..."

She frowned. "It's a baby oni."

Oni didn't have offspring, nor were there any little ones I'd ever heard of...

Hadwin sighed dramatically. "Those dastardly things. We're working on getting rid of them. Perhaps Uncle Gald can perform a protection spell in your room to better scare them away?"

She nodded fervently.

"But it's a little late to wake him. We'll have to ask in the morning..."

Alana had such big doe eyes as she looked at her father. "Can I sleep here?"

"Hmm..." Hadwin glanced at me, a plea in his gaze that told me all I needed to know. She had her father wrapped around her little finger.

"Sure," I said.

She beamed.

I poked her side, tickling her. "But Uncle Gald is going to take care of the rest of your room monsters tomorrow, and you'll sleep in there tomorrow, won't you?"

She nodded.

I kissed her forehead. "Okay... I was about to change into my nightclothes anyway." I stood and strode toward my dressing room.

"Why are your eyes reddish, Father?" her little voice asked.

I halted to hear him explain that away.

"Oh... Well," he answered quickly, "I just stubbed my toe on a side table before you knocked, and I was very cross at the naughty thing for trying to trip me."

I choked on a laugh.

"Everything all right, *darling*?" he asked.

"Of course, Hadwin." My voice was all play at him having to hide why his eyes would be so red as we headed to bed.

The vision faded as swiftly as it had started, granting me a brief moment where I could sense a bit of pain, could hear the reassurances and comforting touches of my loved ones in the present.

Then I slid into a fresh vision.

A charmed music box played a song as I perched on the edge of a table in a medium-size sitting room in my tower.

Alana stood before me, perhaps eight years old. She was so charming, and giddy at the moment. I caressed her face. "I think that is a lovely gift for Uncle Gald's celebration. He'll be surprised."

She beamed, her sharp fangs having grown in.

Findlech spoke from my right. "And if we're going to have a ball to celebrate him achieving *grand* master in his order, we ought to make sure our dancing is also *grand*, don't you think?" He held out a hand, and she nestled her little pale one into his large dark one.

He led her into the middle of the room. "How confident are you in the dance steps we practiced last time?"

She shrugged. "Confident?"

He furrowed his brow. "One cannot shrug and reply that way and *actually* be confident. Either you are, or you must pretend to be." He pursed his lips. "Or you *can* be honest. Luckily, we have plenty of time to practice, don't we?"

"Yes." She followed his direction as he led her. It was a nongendered dance with no designated lead. The symmetrical style was beautifully rhythmic.

I watched as they danced, content as the music spoke to my soul, grateful to see my friend had stuck around and was teaching my child. I was also so proud of Gald for having achieved his goal to become a grand master. It wasn't an easy feat for mages, and while joining my Coterie gave him prestige and influence, it would make it harder for him to find the time to study, practice, and prove the necessary skills to advance.

The handsome devil himself strode into the room. "Here we are!"

Alana smiled as she continued dancing. "Hi, Gald."

Gald glanced at me, holding out a hand. "I won't take no for an answer."

Future me readily accepted, standing and joining him in the center.

"How excited are you?" I asked Gald.

His hand slid to my ass, pulling me against him. I loved that passion and closeness.

"You mean excited about our getaway this weekend?" He whispered in my ear, "How could I not be excited about that?"

His sensual delivery sent shivers up my spine. I too leaned in, cupping his ass, my lips grazing his ear as I whispered playfully, "You know that's not what I was talking about, but glad to know."

He chuckled and stole a kiss. "How could I not be happy?"

I took in his freckles, his septum and lip piercings, his dashing blue eyes and that familiar curly red hair.

When the song ended, a new one slowly began.

"Partner change?" Gald asked.

Alana happily accepted the offer, running to him.

Findlech offered me his hand, and I took it. We danced and chatted for the entirety of the song, mostly discussing politics and updates from his home. One of his sons was getting married, and the Coterie was invited to come.

The song ended with a big bang, and so did Gald, sending up a shower of flames that Alana giggled at. Without a doubt, he would be the fun uncle.

Gald glanced at Findlech and me. "Partner change?"

Findlech bowed to me, then joined Gald at the start of the song. Alana and I practiced together. I loved that Findlech and Gald weren't hiding their relationship from her. They both looked so elegant in each other's arms, Findlech tall and dark with pointed ears, Gald pale and pierced with great posture.

Gald had left the door to the sitting room open, and I heard a mumbled voice. A blurred figure stood at the door, likely a servant. In these special visions, I was only granted clear insight into the most important people in my life.

Findlech and Gald stopped dancing, but their arms were still around each other; they weren't hiding their relationship from the servants anymore either...

"Tell them that's no problem," Findlech said.

Another mumble.

"It's quite all right, thank you."

The dancing continued until the end of the song, Gald stealing a kiss at one point.

Once the song ended, we bowed to our partners.

Alana grabbed a glass of water. "How many songs will I dance with you at your ball, Gald?"

He smiled. "As many as you wish."

She returned the smile.

"And how many songs do *I* get?" I asked, puffing out my chest.

His smirk was mischievous. "As many as *I* wish."

"And what of me?" Findlech asked, cocking his head. "How many dances do I get with the grand master?"

Dancing in public? My heart soared at the prospect because I understood just how much that meant to Gald.

Acting disinterested, Gald examined his fingernails. "Oh, I don't know... I'll see if I can even find the time for *you*."

Findlech pulled him in by his belt loops, then whispered something in his ear. Gald chuckled, then whispered back.

Findlech laughed. A full, deep belly laugh.

Present me had never heard him laugh before, and it warmed my soul deeply. He was happy, and he deserved to be. I still doubted Gald would ever choose to take an eternal bite to become immortal, but even if he didn't, both of them were loved, and they were not ashamed or afraid to show it.

Before I knew it, my body ached a bit, and the vision collided with the present, then flowed to the next.

62

SIBLINGS

All my visions during labor featured Alana. All of them gave me a glimpse of how things could be. They weren't in any particular order; they covered the gamut of her childhood years.

I saw the terrified look on Tyfen's face when he felt courageous enough to hold her for the first time. I watched her struggle to learn to read, especially when it came to the Fae and Elf tongues. I sat with her as she cried about a fae boy she liked who used her interest in him to gain popularity. She must have been around sixteen.

Like with my regular visions, I had more questions than answers, but I trusted I was granted the visions to aid me. It wasn't a warning to never let her have a crush on a fae around that age, but an early introduction to what it meant to be the mother of a future ruler.

I hadn't prepared for her to date. She hadn't even been born yet; I was currently pushing her out... I'd always lived under the rule of Emperor Allister, and he had never married or even had a serious partner during his reign from what I understood.

Perhaps the vision was to help me prepare for how hard romantic relationships would be for her as a ruler. Or I needed to teach her how to accept rejection with grace, or put on a smile and continue her duties for the good of the realm—I certainly did my fair share of that. Maybe it was to help me prepare Hadwin so he didn't rip off the head of a young fae boy someday, given how protective he could be.

Another vision came.

The sun was bright, the air warm on a summer's day. I sat on a picnic blanket with Elion, Alana, and two little boys who looked so much like their father with black hair and grey eyes.

My heart was as warm as the air at seeing that. Alana looked perhaps six, and the boys just a couple of years younger.

He gets his cubs—twins.

Before Alana sat a small empty plate with breadcrumbs, and a short glass with obvious blood residue. As a mixling, she was able to enjoy the sun unlike her father, but her eyes were still sensitive. She wore shades as she drew quietly in a notebook.

The handsome little boys munched on their food, and Elion only looked better with age. Fatherhood looked good on him, too.

"We're still spending the night with Mamaw and Papaw?" one of the boys asked.

Elion swallowed a bite. "Yes, you are." He glanced at Alana. "You still want to attend the sleepover, too?"

She smiled but didn't look up. "Yes, please. They tell the best stories and bring the best gifts from your lands."

"What are you and Mammi doing tonight?" my other son asked.

Elion cleared his throat. "We're having date night, remember? We're going to stroll the gardens."

My future self's lips tugged up at that.

"You two always have date night in the gardens," Alana commented.

"Shifters love nature most of all," I responded, selecting a cucumber slice from my plate.

One of the boys was particularly fidgety. "But the palace gardens aren't very exciting. I like hunting in Mamaw and Papaw's forest more."

Elion gave me a glance like he was going to devour me whole. "I like a good chase, too. Trust me, when you have a mate of your own someday, you too will enjoy a good stroll in the gardens."

I felt myself blush in the future, and the present me couldn't forget him tackling me and taking me against a tree. I looked forward to that after healing…

The boys got rowdier as they finished eating, and fought over a glass of juice.

"Boys…" I warned.

But it was too late. One yanked the glass enough to splash Alana and her sketchbook. She screeched. "You brats!"

"Alana!" I scolded.

Elion snarled at the boys, and they frowned.

"Sorry."

"Sorry, Alana."

She pouted, trying to wipe her drawing dry on the picnic blanket. "Sorry doesn't fix it."

I gently held her chin. "No, but remember what we've talked about? We have to take into account intent. It was an accident."

She gave her brothers a side eye, her irises still tinged red, then grumbled her forgiveness.

"How about you two go run off some energy," Elion suggested, ruffling their hair.

They hopped up and ran into the open field behind us, shifting into wolf form. Their fur matched their father's—that silky grey I knew so well—but they were rather small in wolf form compared to their peers, an effect of being a mixling.

They chased and tackled each other.

Elion scooted closer to Alana. "What are you working on?"

She showed us her sketch of several basic figures. "The family. Well, the children's family. I'd need a bigger paper to do us all." She pointed at each of us. It was adorable how she'd made Hadwin's fangs stick out; she had herself between him and me, then the boys and Elion.

"I left room on both sides in case I get more siblings."

Elion and I glanced at each other.

"Do you want more siblings?" I asked.

Her gaze shot to her brothers. "Are shifter *girls* less annoying?"

As an only child, I had no concept of the struggles of siblings, but it wasn't hard to imagine...

Elion simply smiled, more at me than anything. "You'd prefer another *shifter* sibling, huh?" He looked hungry enough to knock me up right then and there if she said yes.

She shrugged. "Or a mermaid sister. Or a fae or mage sister, but it depends on the magic they get."

I laughed. "First of all, this family is not a democracy. We don't get to vote on which man I have a child with. Secondly, sweet one, I can choose the type of mixling, but cannot guarantee a boy or girl. Plus, I will remind you that not all magic is hereditary."

The boys ran back to us, shifting into human form last minute. "Race with us, Alana!"

I took her notebook. "Go on," I encouraged.

She stood, her eyes returned to their natural hazel, and they lined up. Elion counted down, and they darted forward. Just a few footsteps into it, the boys shifted, bounding on all fours.

"Not fair!" she yelled as she ran her fastest. With vampire blood in her veins, she ran faster than I could, but the boys were faster still.

I flashed Elion a look as he scooted next to me. "Those boys..."

He shrugged. "We're supposed to teach her the need for precise language, right? She *didn't* state they had to stay on two feet... It was open to interpretation."

He had a point. She had to learn a lot at a young age.

I slid a hand onto Elion's thigh, stroking his cock through his pants. "I wonder if I left anything open to interpretation about our date night tonight..."

He growled, his lycan eyes glowing silver. "I'm going to fuck you raw. Any questions?"

I chuckled, kissing his neck to further taunt him. "I suppose not. But are you even capable of waiting till tonight?"

He narrowed his eyes, removing my hand. "You're cruel."

I hummed. "I love my mate."

"I love my mate, too."

I gave Elion a hint with meaning. "Maybe we should also teach Alana mistakes and oversights can be fixed with a little help…"

Elion tried to tame his erection. "Good point. I think I need to run off some steam, anyway…"

He jumped up and shifted, then bounded after the children. The boys were far in front of Alana, but she didn't give up. Elion raced up to her, barked, then ducked to get between her legs, scooping her up onto his back.

She grasped his fur and giggled, riding him. They'd done it so smoothly, they must have done this dozens of times before, and it soothed any worries I'd had about mixing my children and fathers. The Coterie was a unit, a family.

At the finish mark at the edge of the tree line, Elion just barely got in front of the boys. Alana whooped their victory, and they had fun tackling each other and laughing. As they raced back to me in like fashion, I smiled.

The vision faded, and I felt myself actively pushing in labor.

"You're doing great," my mother coached.

The pain dissolved, the noise of the birthing chamber gone as I stood in the common room.

Snow fell past the window, and a blaze crackled in the fireplace. Haan was in his tank, chatting with Tyfen. I could see the back of Tyfen's head over the back of his chair.

Without a word, I urged Alana forward, a hand on her back. She looked to be ten. She sauntered up to Tyfen's chair. Haan flashed me a smile from his tank, but I put a finger to my lips so he wouldn't say anything.

"Hello, little one. How were your studies today?" Tyfen asked.

Alana smiled. "Good. We talked a lot about Kaibu Island."

"Is that so?"

She clasped her hands in front of her, standing on her tippy-toes. "Yes. And Mother said I could ask you about going on vacation there sometime."

"I don't see why not. We went there once when you were a baby."

She seemed to love that answer. "Mother said I should ask you about Kaibu Island and why the lower beaches are reserved for merfolk only."

Haan's slitted purple gaze darted back to me, and I felt myself smirk.

"Oh…" Tyfen was clearly uncomfortable. "Well … centuries ago, fae were meaner. And … the merfolk, well, we hurt them in a lot of ways."

"What kind of ways?"

"Well, you know…"

She cocked her head, clearly confused.

He looked past her, to Haan. "Is this even age appropriate?"

Haan's smile was wild, the merman in on my torture. "I don't know, is it?"

Tyfen tapped her arm. "How about I sneak you extra dessert tonight if you go find Uncle Findlech and ask him about *elf* war crimes on *their* islands…"

Haan piped up. "Come here, Alana. I'll tell you all about Kaibu Island."

"Okay." She smiled, and stared at Tyfen's chest a moment, moving her hand as though she was straightening his shirt. Then she turned and joined Haan at the tank.

I finally strolled forward, peeking around Tyfen's chair. He gave me a scowl, and I snickered.

Future me was so nonchalant as a young babe in his arms noticed me and flapped its arms and legs for attention.

A little girl—just a few months old—who had grass green eyes and fae mixling ears.

My heart almost burst. Tyfen… Tyfen and I ended up having a child together.

I smiled and picked up the little girl. "Always ready for more of me, aren't you?"

I sat on Tyfen's lap and opened my top to breastfeed our daughter.

Tyfen pulled me tight to him, a hand on my thigh, the other fondling a brown version of our leather bracelet on my wrist. His breath tickled my ear. "You're going to pay for that, you know."

My expression sultry, I met his gaze. "Is that a threat? Or a promise?"

His eyes darkened, sexy as ever as he caressed my thighs. "Keep it up, Sonta…"

I leaned in and pressed my lips to his. "I will if you will…"

He glared, his fingers digging into me. He was going to absolutely wreck me later, and I would beg him for seconds.

Glancing between my two daughters, he spoke through clenched teeth. "So … how were lessons?"

I grinned. "Fantastic. How were things here?"

"No big deal."

Shifting on his lap, I settled in further. "I don't know… You're still awkward about teaching Alana things."

He pinched me, and I yelped. "Teaching a young girl about war crimes is different than burping and changing my own child."

I blew out a breath. "True. Still, I trust you to know what she's ready for."

He rubbed my leg, contemplative.

Just then, the door to my chambers opened, and Lilah walked out.

"Hey," I said.

She instantly looked guilty. "Oh, hey…"

I narrowed my eyes. "Searching for something in there?"

She wrapped a hand around her wrist. "Not at all…" she responded, comedically guilty.

"What are you borrowing?"

She strode to me, showing me a bangle bracelet of mine. "I meant to ask and then forgot, and then you were busy with Alana, and I have my meeting in a little bit…"

I swiped a dismissive hand through the air. "Go for it."

Lilah's smile was beautiful. "Thank you. I've always admired your fashion sense. Well ... after you came into money, that is." She winked.

My discovery as Hoku's daughter had definitely catapulted my mother and me into a safe financial situation.

Lilah brushed my bare shoulder with the back of her hand, gazing down at my baby. "I love that blouse."

"Thanks."

"I love all your blouses and dresses. The styles are always on point."

I raised an eyebrow, suspicious of the additional compliments.

She smirked without a hint of shame. "I love them as much as your children have. Quick access to the tits."

I smacked her leg, and she laughed. Tyfen slid a hand into the wide and draping arm hole in my blouse, tickling the side of my breast. "She isn't wrong…"

Alana turned around. "Lilah! Come here!" She was such a happy girl, and it meant the world to me.

Lilah joined Alana, leaning on Haan's tank. "At your service. How can I help you?"

Alana giggled. "Haan's telling me stories."

Lilah wrapped an arm around her. "Haan does have rather exciting stories, doesn't he? What are we learning about today?"

"He's telling me about fae war crimes!"

Tyfen grumbled quietly, but I only smiled. I'd been half paying attention to Haan, and he was discussing things tactfully.

Lilah faced me, exasperated. "War crimes… *Lovely.*" Her every word dripped with sarcasm. "I *never* get tired of politics and stories of *war crimes*…"

I shrugged.

"I think we all need that vacation sooner than later," Tyfen whispered in my ear.

"I think you have a point," I whispered back.

Lilah bent, looking Alana in the eye. "We should spend more time in my studio, and in the big gallery… It's less … bloody and sad."

I cleared my throat loudly, and Lilah glanced at me. I gave her a pointed look. "She has a natural curiosity, she needs to learn, and she was not *born* to be a painter, love."

Lilah stuck her tongue out, then whipped around. "Please continue with your *riveting* story, Haan."

He grinned. "I do believe there's a large painting of this massacre in the gallery. We could take a look while I share more…"

I stroked my little baby's soft face and chubby cheeks. She'd fallen asleep nursing. "She's such an easy baby."

Tyfen held my hips. "Makes up for the trouble her father causes…"

I wore a toothy smile. "Just a little tit and rocking, and she's out."

We both stared at our daughter, her breathing so soft in slumber, her ears so delicately pointed.

I was so blessed, or at least I would be.

"You look tired," Tyfen said.

I frowned. "I do?"

He shrugged. "Maybe she's got the right idea by taking a midday nap. A little tit time and rocking did the job for *her*..." He suggestively rolled his hips with me on his lap. "And I'm willing to help with some tit time and rocking of my own."

My face warmed. Luckily, Alana was distracted, and our voices were low. "You're wicked."

He wore the censure like a badge, his smile broad. "I'll never deny that."

I didn't want the vision to fade as it did. I wanted to cling to the warmth of my child I would have to wait a full decade to meet. I wanted to stay in that place where Tyfen had healed enough to want a child with me. I wanted to savor that happiness.

But the vision did fade. I felt the echo of pain, the encouragement of my head midwife coaching me through pushing. We weren't quite there yet, and another vision started to come into view.

63

The Unexpected Child

Based on my glimpse into the present between visions, I knew my time was short, and I wanted all the sweet moments. For now, I embraced this next one, drinking it up.

It was a warm summer day, not too hot but fairly sunny. I stood in the outside pool, chatting with Haan. He looked as handsome as ever, with his short brown hair, slitted purple eyes, his dark metallic skin and shimmering turquoise tail.

"What's that smile for?" I asked.

His sexy husky voice responded. "You're wearing the earrings."

I couldn't see myself in the vision, but future me felt my earrings. "Of course." They were shell earrings just like his.

He slid a hand to my hip, his thumb seductively hooking over the band of my bottoms. "We're still on for tonight?"

He was getting good at this foreplay and stimulation thing…

I wrapped my arms around his neck, pressing my chest to his, careful to not rub his cock scale. "Gald and I would *never* miss a standing appointment with you, Haan."

Fuck, I miss the feeling of his unique cock, the fight for air, the way I had to cling to him. The way he bashed me into the side of the tank, and I wanted more…

We kissed, and he held my waist, his thumbs now slipping under the hem of my top, brushing against my underbreast beneath the water's surface.

"Haan!" Alana yelled.

We pushed apart, smiling.

Alana ran up, dressed in a cute swimming suit, now perhaps five years old. She tossed her shades onto a lounging chair and squinted, then did a cannonball into the pool, splashing us. Trailing far behind her were other people I loved.

"Swim lessons it is," Haan said. "We'll continue this later."

My smile was feral. "I'll hold you to it."

"Haan!" Alana shouted, swimming up to us. "Mother and Father let me swim in my bigger chamber's pond last night!"

He smiled. "Nice to have a bigger one, right?"

She nodded.

"Come on. Let's have a good swim." He gestured with his head, and they took off, away from me.

I turned my focus to the others joining us. "Just in time! The staff should be here with a fresh fruit platter and some chilled blood any minute."

After pulling myself out of the pool, I toweled off, then sat on a lounging chair.

My mother eased down on a lounging chair next to me, and Kernov next to her. I was elated to see them together, though it was odd to see Kernov in swimming shorts. I'd always seen him dressed so formally. But by the rings on their fingers, they had married, and he was important enough in my life to fully see and hear in the vision.

"You seem to be missing someone," I said.

My mother rolled her eyes. "She waited until we stepped outside to say she needed to use the washroom. She'll be here soon."

Lilah sat next to me, resting a hand on my bare thigh. "Hey, love."

"You're missing someone, too. So much attrition for an afternoon at the pool…"

She puckered her lips. "She'll be here any second."

I kissed her.

"She'll be here right now," an unfamiliar voice said.

I glanced at the owner of the voice, a beautiful blonde with shaded glasses and pale skin. She carried an umbrella to protect her from the sun, then collapsed it as she took a seat next to Lilah under a shade.

Future me thought nothing of this stranger, and naturally wouldn't since she somehow became important enough to me to see and hear her so clearly in this vision…

Who the hell is she?

Despite the discomfort sun gave her, she wore a rather skimpy bathing suit, and I kept glancing at her curves. She looked a bit younger than Lilah and I had to be in this vision, but that didn't really say much. That only told me she'd been envenomated in her twenties, but she could be hundreds of years old…

Whoever the blonde was, she rested a hand on Lilah's thigh, just like Lilah had on mine.

Fuck… Lilah does get another lover down the road. I wasn't jealous, just surprised. It wasn't against our hajba vows.

The woman looked at me, lowering her shades enough to show me her chocolate brown eyes. "I found that missing earring of yours. The fancy dangly gold one."

I gasped. "Where? The servants turned my chambers upside down looking for it!"

She bit her lip with a fang, and her reply was silky smooth. "Under my bed."

I laughed.

Lilah grinned. "Now how did it *possibly* get there…?"

For a moment, present me wasn't completely sure… I didn't know what kind of relationship I had with this woman in the future. Did she and I…? Or had Lilah just borrowed my earrings?

The blonde continued. "You have a date with Haan tonight, right?"

"Yes."

She replaced her shades, easing back in her lounger. "And tomorrow? I think I'll hold that earring hostage until the three of us have another date…"

Hell yes… Lilah and I finally get to have group sex with another woman…

"I'll clear some time in my schedule," I said, my voice sensual.

I watched Haan and Alana in the pool for a minute. She had wrapped her arms around his neck, clinging to him, and he was swimming fast. She looked like she was having a ball.

A blur of a person mumbled something past Kernov, likely a servant. They seemed to dip as if to curtsy, then left after dropping off another little girl around Alana's age.

Future me casually said hello. Present me was completely lost.

The girl was maybe a year younger than Alana, at most. Instead of jumping into the water or coming to see me, she climbed onto my mother's lap… She had to be *my* child, right? To be important enough to be visible in my vision…

She looked fetching in her grandmother's arms as she wrapped her arms around her.

But who the hell… How could that be my child? Lilah didn't want children, and I couldn't imagine the girl being hers. The little girl also had much darker skin than mine.

Who was the father? Findlech had the darkest skin of my men, but her ears weren't pointy at all, and we had no plans to have sex again… Haan had the next darkest skin in my Coterie, but the little girl had normal human eyes and no patches of scales…

Wait… When would I have even had this child? There wasn't really space between having Hadwin's daughter, a year's healing break, then having my boys with Elion…

Future me closed my eyes, casually soaking up the rays. Present me was totally lost.

"Mammi? Can Alana and I go to the unicorn stalls tomorrow instead of riding lessons?" the little girl asked.

I said nothing, basking in the sun with my eyes closed, savoring Lilah sweetly drawing circles on my thigh.

My mother answered her. "I don't see why not, but you'll have to ask your sister."

"Sonta, can we see the unicorns instead of riding tomorrow?"

VENUS COX

Fuck. She's... Fuck! Sister? I have a sister? Shit! She has darker skin, and so does Kernov... She wasn't much younger than Alana... My mother had become a teenage mother with me, so she wasn't too old to have more children, but I hadn't ever imagined it!

Future me was utterly unfazed, her eyes still closed, and I wished they were open to examine the little girl better.

"I don't see why not. Alana mentioned something about wanting to go. Double-check with Gald, though. He's happy to have people learn about his breeding program, but you can't get in the way of any workers."

"Okay!"

I wanted to linger here a bit longer, but the vision was ripped from me.

"There's the head," Hadwin whispered. "You're doing great!"

My last vision came into clear view, the most astounding of them all. I sat in my throne like I had at the beginning of the Great Ritual.

Alana, a full-grown woman, sat in the middle throne. She was barely an adult, but her posture was immaculate, her black hair curled, her wine-red dress stunning. A middle-aged woman sat in the third throne, a new magistrate.

The ballroom was packed, and I had a moment to glance at everyone around me. Hadwin was closest at the base of the stairs, proudly watching his daughter. Next to him were the rest of my Coterie, every single one of them. Even Lilah and the new blonde. My twin boys were so dashing next to their father, and my little fae mixling so fetching next to her father.

My mother and Kernov were close by, my new sister smiling brightly at the Anointed Ruler niece she'd grown up with.

Every single delegation took their place, even the fae king and the elf high lord and lady. They weren't exactly beaming, but I doubted they would have been even if we hadn't faced the nightmare we had with Tyfen.

The important thing was: they'd come. When this day arrived, they'd pledge their loyalty to my daughter, to Hoku's anointed.

Alana glanced at me, a sweet smile on her lips. I loved her so much, that lovely girl I'd had these blessed glimpses of. Then she stood, and the room completely hushed.

"I stand before you, prepared to take the mantle of Hoku as her heir. I appreciate each and every people in our beautiful realm, and vow to serve to the best of my ability for the duration of my life."

She spoke with such authority. "I will safeguard the peace that was sorely fought for, recognizing the rights and rich cultures of each territory, and I do so with confidence, with the best people at my side—with honorable rulers both mortal and immortal, and with my family."

My heart was utterly full.

"May Hoku multiply her blessings on us all," she said.

The people bowed their heads, reciting the blessing.

I stood, and Hadwin climbed the stairs to join us. His smile was subtle, but tears pricked at my eyes at the pride that shone there. He took my hand, squeezing it.

Two Demali priestesses climbed the steps, carrying a glistening jeweled crown. Once at the top, they handed the crown to Hadwin and me, then they took a place on either side of Alana.

"Today, we celebrate Hoku's grand victory for Colsia, and the centuries of peace her empire has thrived through," one priestess boomed.

The other spoke. "Finding our empress worthy, Hoku bestows her full authority to govern this land."

"We present to you Alana Gwynriel, daughter of Her Holiness—the Blessed Vessel—Sonta Gwynriel, and His Grace, Duke Hadwin Gwynriel of the vampires. Hoku's Heir. Your Anointed Ruler. Keeper of the Peace. Guardian of the Six Territories. And Empress of Colsia."

"Empress Alana Gwynriel."

Save Alana, the priestesses, Hadwin, and me, every single person took a knee. A thousand people—packed in a room—bent the knee, pledging loyalty to my firstborn daughter as their ruler.

Hadwin and I carried the crown to Alana, both beaming and misty-eyed. She smiled at us as we placed it on her head, and then we, too, bent the knee.

Demali mages, by law, had no obligation to bow to *anyone*—a promise made to them by Hoku herself when she reigned as the first empress of Colsia. But out of respect and tradition, even the two priestesses bowed.

Her voice clear, one of the priestesses boomed, "May Hoku multiply her blessings on Her Magnificence."

The people's recitation was solemn and thunderous, and my heart burst.

A baby cried, *my* baby. My sweet Alana as I swiftly slammed back into the present, the searing pain of childbirth coursing through my body.

I gasped and blinked.

Hadwin held my hand as I still knelt on the bed in the birthing chamber. My knuckles were white from squeezing so hard.

"Are you all right?" he asked.

Tears flooded my eyes as our daughter cried, and I sank onto the bed. "She's beautiful," I sobbed.

My stomach and pussy hurt like *hell*. It was worth it. I would heal quickly, and I'd felt hardly any of the process.

Hadwin and the others helped me settle more comfortably on the bed. All the while I kept thinking of her at all those ages, but especially as a regal and confident woman. "She's beautiful," I panted.

The midwife brought her to me and rested her on my chest. "You're right. It *is* a girl." She'd said it as though I'd just made a lucky guess, and to the world, I had.

"A girl?" Hadwin said, tears filling his eyes as he stared at her. Between my Coterie and mother surrounding me, and Lilah off to the side, there was hardly a dry eye in the room.

I stared at my little girl, brushing her wet black hair from her face—she had a good deal of it. Her eyes were red from the excitement of being born, her skin paler than my own. No little teeth yet, of course. And thank the stars vampire mixlings didn't develop fangs until they were past the nursing stage!

I offered her my breast, and she latched and calmed quickly. I cooed, being showered with love by those closest to me while rulers stood on the sidelines. My mother invited Lilah over, and her smile stretched from ear to ear. "You really were so calm!"

Hadwin kissed my sweaty temple. "You were amazing, darling."

I glanced at a grinning Baylana, the only other living soul to know my secret. "Hoku's amazing," I said.

The crowd below was full of whispers, Alana's cries having no doubt stirred them.

The emperor approached, a soft smile on his lips. "Congratulations."

Goddess, she felt right in my arms. As right as it was to have Tyfen tearing up and clutching my hand, or Hadwin massaging my shoulder, or to have each and every person smiling back at me.

The emperor addressed me again. "Take your time. When you're ready, we'll recall the assembly."

I still had to deliver the afterbirth, and I had fruits and water to give me strength. We'd clean me up, and we'd have more privacy for a while before I was expected to stand with Hadwin—briefly, of course—and present our daughter to those in attendance.

I nodded, and Hadwin pressed his forehead to my temple, caressing his daughter's cheek. "I love you. Thank you." His voice was strained with joy, and it only made my tears flow more freely.

The emperor stood on the birthing chamber platform, addressing the people. "We'll reconvene in a few hours. At which time we'll present Colsia's next Anointed Ruler, your future empress."

Cheers rose from the crowd about the news of a little girl. The curtains closed, and everyone but my midwives, two guards, and my loved ones filed out of the birthing chamber.

Tyfen smiled, meeting my eyes. "An empress."

Gald cocked his head, staring at Alana. "She looks so much like you two."

I glanced at Haan; he wasn't able to be quite as close. "Here, Lilah, take her for Haan to see, won't you?"

Lilah's eyes grew wide. "Uh…"

I let out a silent chuckle, regretting it at the pain in my core. "Please tell me you're not going to be terrified of holding my child…"

"I don't want to drop her…"

My mother's voice was soft and friendly. "I can take her. I've got plenty of practice, though I'm a bit rusty."

As I handed Alana to her, all I could think was that my mother could use the practice again... For my little sister she was likely already carrying.

Everyone doted on Alana, and on me as I went through the messy, painful ordeal. I drank a tea that helped with the pain.

"Any plans for names?" Findlech asked.

I would try not to influence *too* much based on my visions.

Hadwin looked to me. "We've discussed a couple of names for girls..."

I smiled. "I still think our first choice is the right one." We both liked Alana for a girl, and I loved that it honored Hadwin's mother. He worried it was too common for such an important person, because his mother had died a commoner human.

But that was the beauty of Hoku's choices. She chose whoever was best at the time for her Blessed Daughters, be it the daughter of a rich human family, or the daughter of a lowly whore.

"Alana," Hadwin whispered, holding her tiny hand.

Fresh tears pooled in my eyes at the rightness of it. I would never forget how reverent his voice was, or the joy on his face. I would never forget a single detail from my special visions.

I would never forget how it felt to crown my daughter, the entire realm supporting us, as all the people I loved stood by.

Elion looked so happy as he watched Hadwin pick Alana up. He would be elated to learn he'd be a father, too.

Life could be rough, the mantle heavy. But it could also be beautiful and blessed.

I had so many loves, and I got to keep them all.

EPILOGUE

Hadwin and I stood at the top of the stairs in the grand ballroom, holding three-month-old Alana. Our smiles were wide, his fangs on display. We'd just made our grand entrance, and everyone had bowed again. It was hard to not be choked up about that.

This was her first big introduction to the realm. Technically, her birth had culminated the Great Ritual, but people *always* looked forward to the three-month Grand Ball celebration.

The emperor had introduced us and recognized each of the territories' rulers in attendance. The fae queen was once again in attendance, her husband missing. Shockingly, the elf high lady had been coaxed to show her respect. We would have to be delicate about the announcements.

I gave Alana to Hadwin as we prepared for the rest of the introductions. My loved ones waited near the base of the stairs.

"The Blessed Vessel bears a huge burden for this realm," the emperor said. "And Hoku's heir will be nurtured and guided by many." He stood tall, his posture never betraying his age. "First, Her Holiness would like to recognize her mortal mother, Vesta Gwynriel. Hoku entrusted her divine daughter to Vesta, and this realm has been blessed."

Her smile strained, my mother ascended the stairs. She'd been torn about her mention at this ball, but it really felt right. Now that her engagement to Kernov had been formally announced, she couldn't really escape a more public life. And she *deserved* to be recognized. Hoku had seen something in her worth investing in. I would be no one without her.

She reached us, a more genuine smile emerging once Alana's eyes lit up, spotting her grandmother.

My mother curtsied. "May Hoku multiply her blessings on this family."

"Thank you," Hadwin whispered as we both gave her a simple bow.

She squeezed my hand, then took her place at the side of the top stair.

My stomach twisted at the next introduction. Save Hadwin as Alana's father, my Coterie would be introduced in the order they'd taken me in the bedding chamber.

Everyone watched the emperor; he was prepared to handle this, and had prepared the high lady.

"This topic needs no reminder, but I will issue it this once. The Blessed Vessel, her family and her Coterie deserve respect and privacy where they wish it. This goes for her mortal mother, and for any of them." He stared down the room.

I rubbed the new mating bond tattoo I'd gotten to match Tyfen's.

"Today we honor His Highness, Prince Tyfen. Her Holiness's Coterie partner from the fae kingdom and her mate."

Prince Tyfen took the stairs, both of his mate tattoos visible, as I hiked up my sleeve to better show my mark. The room understandably erupted into whispers. The high lady's gaze was far from us, her lips pressed together.

The emperor cleared his throat, getting the room's attention as Tyfen finished climbing the stairs. "It has been confirmed at the temples. It is a forged bond, Hoku-blessed, and His Highness's second mating bond, following the tragic loss of his first."

We wouldn't turn this into a carnival where people gawked for entertainment, whispering and making guesses. They would, but we would try to stamp it out. And we wouldn't dare mention Malaya's name. It was still too fresh for the high lady, and she was barely able to abide being here.

Eyes stared at Tyfen as he bowed to the emperor, then met us.

Tyfen looked nervous. "Thanks, um, Hadwin, for everything," he whispered.

Hadwin held out a hand. "Brothers."

Tyfen took his hand. "Brothers."

I smiled at Tyfen, understanding his anxiety. "I love you."

"I love you, too." He kissed my hand, then turned to take his place on the steps below my mother.

We prepared ourselves for the scrutiny and insatiable curiosity the people would have for some time.

The emperor continued. "We honor Elion of the shifters, son of the high alpha and his mate, Her Holiness's Coterie partner and mate."

Elion smiled and approached.

One by one, we went through the formalities before the dancing would begin.

The merfolk tunnels led to a small tank beside us at the top, so Haan could also participate in the honor. He then swam back through the tunnels to take his place at the base of the stairs.

The people expected the culmination of the introductions, for the dancing to commence, but we had one more person to announce.

Lilah was surprisingly calm, the smallest smile on her lips as she stared at me, her matching hajba ring on full display. We'd shared our vows with those closest to us. Her family was also in attendance today.

"Today, we also honor Lilah Casten," the emperor announced. "Hajba of the Blessed Vessel—"

I couldn't hide a smile, and Lilah's only grew.

"And the Pontaii's newest resident artist."

My jaw dropped as Lilah started climbing the stairs. She beamed.

"Her latest portrait is in the public gallery, should you wish to see it on your visit," the emperor added.

I had to contain my excitement and surprise as Lilah met us at the top of the stairs. I wanted to give her a huge hug. "Why didn't you tell us?" She'd only said the emperor had liked her painting enough to add it to the gallery, but not that she'd officially been appointed as a painter.

She smirked. "Your surprise was worth it."

"Congratulations," I whispered. "You're amazing."

Lilah kissed me on the cheek, then gave Alana some attention.

"Congratulations," Hadwin added.

"Thank you." She remembered, and quickly curtsied.

We honored her as we had the others, with a small bow.

As Lilah walked down the stairs, everyone assessed her. This was the formal announcement that she was not only a fantastic artist, but that she was my lover, my hajba. We had not made an announcement until now.

Each of my men in turn offered Lilah a bowed head as she passed and took her place at the bottom of the stairs.

It was controversial to announce our relationship so quickly after Alana's birth. People may assume I had been distracted during my pregnancy when I had vowed to give my Coterie my full attention.

Let them assume. Let them question.

In rulership and politics, at least in the peaceful empire of Colsia, our beauty was not found in the armies one could command. Public opinion was not won by oppressively restrictive rules or intimidation. Not everything needed to be spelled out.

Approval and submission were often won by subtle caresses. It was the order in which things were done. The exact wording one used. The intentional *omission* of the right word or action.

The emperor had announced her as my hajba. Ergo, he must approve.

Hadwin and I had let her caress our child's cheek when the public could not. Ergo, we *both* found Lilah trustworthy.

Each of my men honored her with a bow as she descended the stairs. Ergo, they accepted her. And if Hoku's divine descendants and the entire Coterie respected and accepted Lilah, not a soul in the realm would have a leg to stand on were they to criticize us.

Lilah's introduction *did* have to be last, as she was an unofficial member of my Coterie, given the political nature of the unit, but it also hopefully pulled some attention from the announcement of Tyfen's and my mating bond. Let the people focus on the latter surprise while the earlier was still more tender.

Schamoi and his mistress had come at our invitation, and he gave Lilah a friendly smile as she took her place.

Baylana and her partners were in attendance as well, at the biggest non-vampire event they'd attended since her faked death.

Let the realm chase the gossip of it all, and let us celebrate new beginnings together.

"May Hoku multiply her blessings on us all," the emperor said, and the people echoed. "And I welcome you all to partake in the festivities of the grand celebration of your future empress!"

He bowed to the people, and the orchestra struck up a tune.

I breathed a sigh, and Alana stirred, hungry again. I eased down on my throne and fed her as the room bustled with excitement.

My mother and Coterie descended the stairs to the public, save Tyfen, who came back up.

"Am I a coward for rejoining you to hide from speculators?" Tyfen asked as he crouched next to me.

I caressed his face. "I don't mind being a shield."

Hadwin stared at the giant merfolk tank that lined the ballroom. "Luckily, we *do* have plenty of distractions today, don't we?"

Just as a crowd surrounded Baylana, and a smaller group congratulated Lilah, eager to get to know her better, a plethora of people gathered at the merfolk tank.

My heart warmed as Haan took his place next to the sea king. I'd finally met the man, and it was not often he left the deep sea, but he had come at Haan's request. We had needed the extra assurance, the extra display of approval and support from rulership because we'd been afraid the elf high lady would snub our invitation again.

"I don't mind the distraction one bit," Tyfen said.

Haan smiled at me in the distance, and I fidgeted with the white shell earrings he'd gifted me, smiling back.

The three of us at the top of the stairs conversed while Alana fed, the room loud with music and chatter and dancing in the center of the room.

After Alana had her fill and fell asleep in my arms, the four of us joined the people on the main floor.

Our private section was heavily guarded for Alana's sake, but not so much that it was stuffy.

I sat between Lilah and my mother. Lilah's hand slid onto my thigh as she kissed me. "I thought that went well."

I kissed her back. "You're in trouble for surprising me like that, you know?"

Her grin was fresh and challenging. "I'll take whatever punishment you want to dole out to me."

We carried on and ate, all discussing the event. Haan joined us, his sexy grin reminding me of our second successful time having sex a few days ago. Goddess, the man knew how to ram into me. Gald had magnificently kept me alive with his elemental magic.

Hadwin handed Alana to Elion at one point, and he was the cutest, proudest uncle ever. The shifter high alpha and his mate came over to visit, and I allowed them to hold her.

The vision I'd had during her birth danced in my mind. Alana would never want for an aunt or uncles, but grandparents were few and far between. I had no father. My mother had never reconciled with her family, though Alana looked fetching in Kernov's arms. Hadwin's family had all died long ago.

But someday, not that far down the road, Alana would have shifter mixling brothers, and the three of them would spend time with their shifter grandparents. The high alpha and his mate would have obviously preferred Alana to be born a shifter mixling, but they accepted her into their pack in their own way.

Lilah sighed, rubbing her stomach. "This food is good, and Elion wasn't wrong about the mead."

Tyfen stared at his glass of water. "I still think it's odd to drink *mead* at such a formal event." He'd told me he wanted to avoid alcohol for a while, but didn't want to make a big deal of it.

I shrugged. It was only being served at our table, imported by Findlech for us from his region.

"I missed alcohol," I confessed, swirling my goblet. "And I had them add just a little sweet wine into mine." I glanced at my mother. "Have you tried it? What do you think?"

She held her water glass. "Oh… I'd just prefer water today."

I suppressed a smile. She had to be pregnant, but still hadn't fessed up to it.

"You're sure?" I took another sip of my drink. "It's divine. Let me order you some."

"No, Sonta. I don't need to drink tonight…"

I couldn't stop myself from wearing a knowing smile. "I suppose I wouldn't either, if I were you."

Her eyes widened, and she and Kernov exchanged a look. "What do you mean, Sonta?" Kernov asked.

How could I possibly know he'd knocked her up? I would not betray my greatest secret. "What do you think I mean, Kernov?"

He pursed his lips. I didn't want to worry him. He loved my mother, and it did not matter one iota to me if he'd proposed before or after getting her pregnant, if it had been planned or not.

"I love seeing my family grow," I simply said. "And I'm glad you're part of it, Kernov."

He relaxed a little. "It's an honor."

"Look at that," Lilah whispered, gesturing to a table across the ballroom. The fae queen had sat with the elf high lady, and they were softly conversing.

I blinked. It gave me hope they could mend things. They had been friends as young girls, separated by time and duty, completely torn apart by Tyfen and Malaya's bond and tragedy.

Tyfen swallowed, staring back at his water. Findlech noted both actions as I had.

"I wish I could express my condolences," I told Findlech.

He shook his head. "Still too soon. I'll let you know."

I nodded, and Hadwin approached, bouncing Alana. "Let me know whenever you're ready to dance, darling."

I downed the rest of my drink and stood. "How about now?"

Lilah held out her hands for Alana, and Hadwin handed her over.

I pointed at Tyfen. "Get ready to dance. You're next."

He smiled. "I'll be ready."

A vampire song began as the last ended, and the floor cleared to give us space.

As always, Hadwin was elegant as he led me. His every touch and smile reminded me of how much I loved him. He had a way of melting away my worries lately about the never-ending tasks ahead of us to raise Alana right, to keep the peace despite tensions.

Right now, I was just a woman in a pretty dress in the arms of a handsome man. We were not dignitaries; we were parents, mates, and lovers.

We ended with a kiss. After a glance at Alana, we parted, and he returned to the table to hold her.

Tyfen approached and took my outstretched hand.

The orchestra struck up the tune of a well-known fae song, and Tyfen furrowed his brow.

I pulled him closer to dance. "Come on, now. I thought you were a better dancer than this…"

He straightened and smoothly rested his hand on my lower back. "I thought we were going to dance to the song we've been practicing…"

I beamed. "We can dance more than once tonight, right? I asked the orchestra to play this first because you love it so much."

Tyfen's glare was the sexiest thing in the realm. "Yes… You know how much I *love* this song…"

Unable to help myself, I chuckled. It was the traditional fae song we'd first danced to, the one he most certainly hated. I stroked his strong bicep with my hand. "I thought you'd like it. It's *our* song after all, isn't it?"

He pulled me even closer, leaning down to whisper in my ear. "Just because the bracelet I gave you isn't fancy enough for this event doesn't mean I won't make you pay for this in the morning."

No one could instantly heat my core the way he did. Could we sneak down the washroom hallway, as Elion and I once had, for a quickie?

Instead of goading him on, I stood tall and kissed him. His lips were perfect, his grip on me divine.

"I love you," I whispered against his lips.

"I love you, too, Nil Blantui."

I danced with each of my loved ones as the night went on, Haan obviously excepted, though I made sure to spend quality time with him as well.

I couldn't have been happier to be in Lilah's arms when our chance came.

"How does it feel?" I asked as we spun on the floor. "Everyone knows."

She glanced at Tyfen. "I'd imagine like you and Tyfen feel. When you love someone, you want to shout it to the realm. And now I get to."

My heart was full. "Sorry it took so long... And that I still can't offer you what you hoped for."

She cocked her head. "I will never have a wife, but could I complain when I have all this? You, the Coterie, my position as a painter?" Her grin was mischievous. "And that doesn't even hold a candle to the free jewelry I get by being with you..."

I returned her grin as I glanced at her necklace, a nice chain with a sparkling pendant nestled between her breasts. She knew how to make my mouth water.

"I agree. The *jewelry* definitely makes us both *perky*, doesn't it?"

She laughed, and the song soon came to an end. I savored a kiss on her perfect lips before we went our own ways.

Gald had hung back for once, and I held out a hand, my eyebrows raised.

His charming smile answered me as he accepted.

We danced to a more familiar human tune.

"Why am I getting you last?" I asked.

"My penitence for being your first at the start of the Great Ritual?"

I bit my lip. "Consider your penitence complete, Gald."

He snuck a kiss, his hand caressing my bare back.

I thought of a fond memory. "During that dance, you told me you liked watching Haan take me, liked my ass to the tank glass."

His smile was wide, his lip piercing gleaming in the soft light. "A memory I'll always cherish."

"The different setting of my chamber pond didn't change your enjoyment of it last time, though, did it?" My tone dripped false innocence.

His look darkened with desire. "Better than *seeing* your ass is *holding* it, Sonta."

Fuck, I wanted him again too. Right after Haan had taken me, Gald had fucked me. My voice had been hoarse that day from the gasping between those two.

It didn't hurt one bit that Gald now had a pierced cock...

I snuck a kiss. "I look forward to a repeat."

As we danced, I couldn't help but notice Findlech's longing gaze on us. He and I had kissed at the end of our dance together, too. I was happy to keep up romantic appearances for Findlech for as long as he wanted. But it had to be hard for them both to know I only stood in Gald's place for Findlech.

The Blessed Coterie

"We've shocked the realm plenty tonight," I said. "Baylana, Tyfen, Lilah, the sea king in attendance… I think they could handle one more thing…" I glanced at Findlech. "Any plans to dance with another partner tonight?"

Gald looked down. "Let's not kid ourselves. I'll be lucky if he's ready for that before I die of old age."

That wounded my heart, but I recovered. Hoku had blessed me to glimpse the possibilities of my future. A future existed out there where these two could openly be partners, could comfortably dance in each other's arms as he and I did now.

"The day will come," I said.

Gald wrinkled his nose. "I wish I could speak with such confidence."

My conviction did not waver. "I find great strength in Hoku's example. The heart has a way of winning out. Love finds a way to tackle that which we originally find insurmountable."

Gald's smile was soft. "Thank you. I'll remember that."

I rested a hand over his heart. "The day will come, and the support you've given others will be repaid in full."

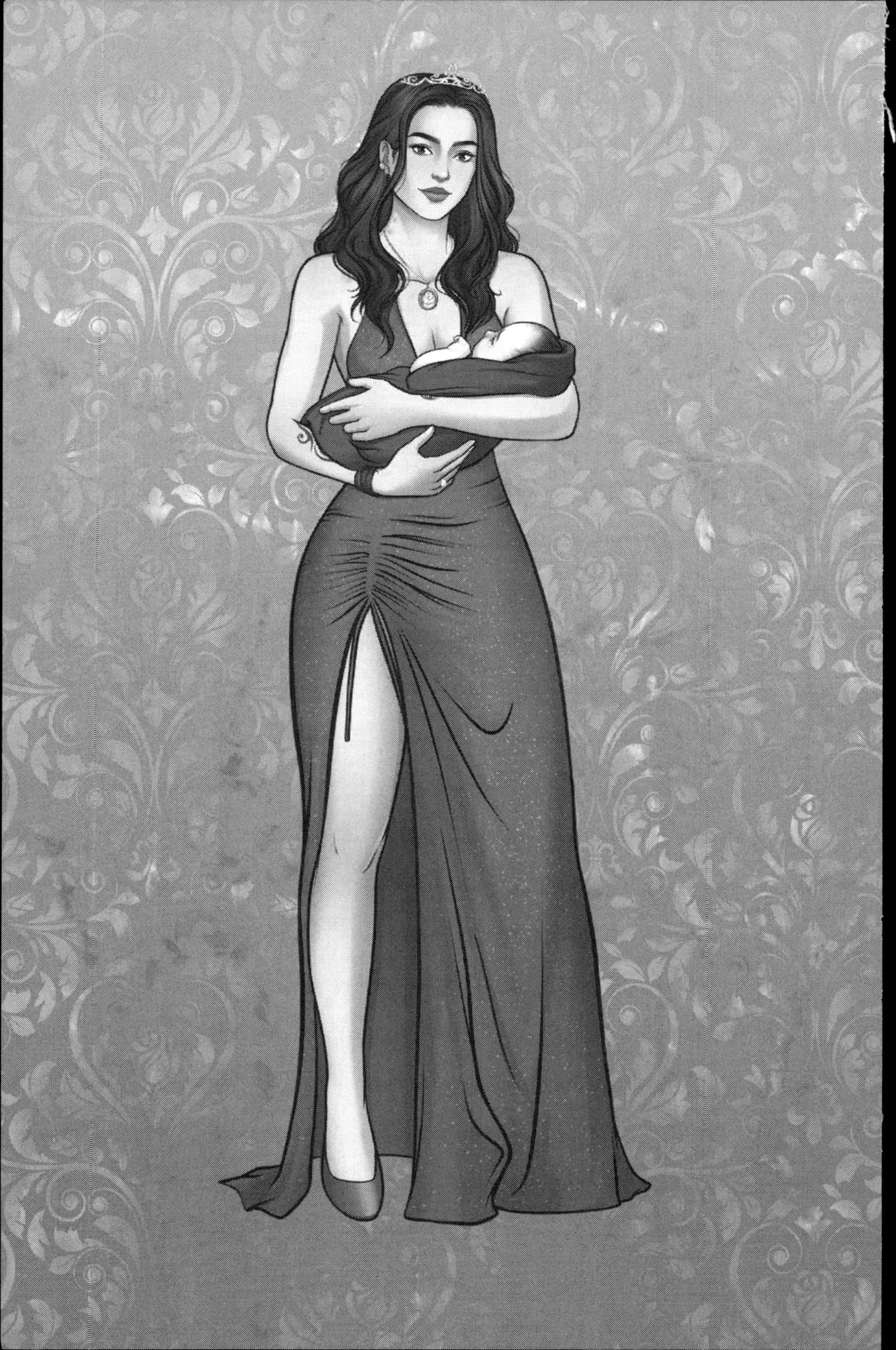

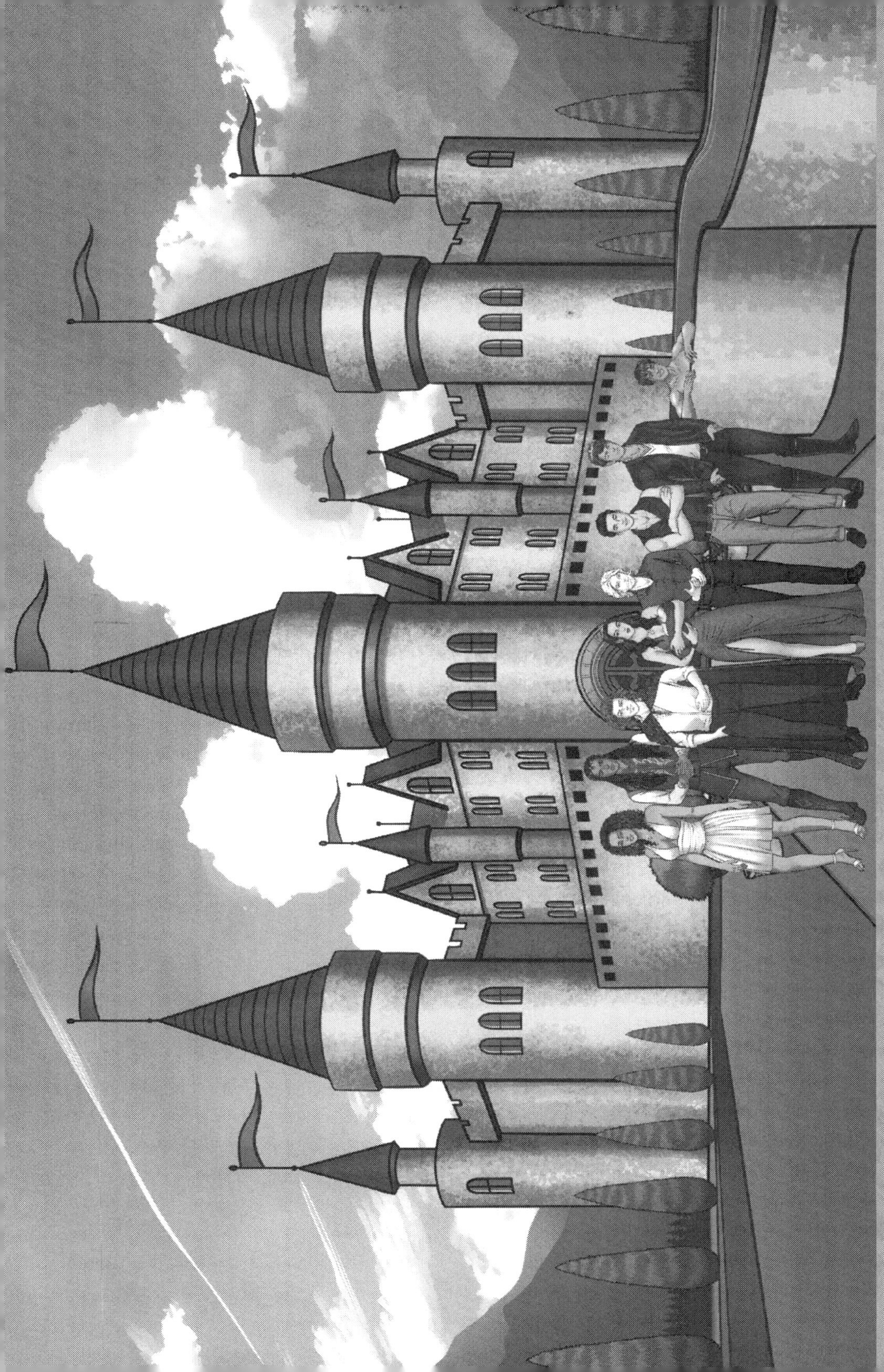

More by Venus Cox

Wishing we'd gotten another time with Sonta & Haan? How about all three mates taking her at once? What about what it's like to visit a Suck and Fuck? An inside glimpse of Vesta & Kernov's relationship? More about that blonde? And all the behind-the-scenes fun for Gald & Findlech?

These stories will all be posted to Kindle Vella first, under the title *Beyond the Coterie*!

You'll even get a brief sneak peek into Goddess Hoku's story ;)

Remember to leave a review for
The Blessed Coterie!

Sign up for Venus's newsletter for more book updates!
VenusCoxBooks.com

Follow her online @

- https://www.facebook.com/groups/venuscoxbooks
- https://www.instagram.com/venuscoxauthor
- https://www.tiktok.com/@venuscoxbooks

Steamy Character Art & More!

Looking for steamy *Blessed Vessel* art?

Sign up for the author's newsletter for more information and access to exclusive offers!

Made in the USA
Las Vegas, NV
30 December 2023

Epoxy Resin Art For Total Beginners

Randall .P Mcneil

All rights reserved. Copyright © 2023 Randall .P Mcneil

COPYRIGHT © 2023 Randall .P Mcneil

All rights reserved.

No part of this book must be reproduced, stored in a retrieval system, or shared by any means, electronic, mechanical, photocopying, recording, or otherwise, without written permission from the publisher.

Every precaution has been taken in the preparation of this book; still the publisher and author assume no responsibility for errors or omissions. Nor do they assume any liability for damages resulting from the use of the information contained herein.

Legal Notice:

This book is copyright protected and is only meant for your individual use. You are not allowed to amend, distribute, sell, use, quote or paraphrase any of its part without the written consent of the author or publisher.

Introduction

Welcome to the fascinating world of epoxy resin art, a realm where creativity knows no bounds, and stunning works of art come to life through the alchemy of resin. Whether you're a curious beginner eager to explore the artistry of resin or someone seeking to expand their crafting horizons, this guide is your gateway to unlocking the potential of epoxy resin.

Our journey commences by demystifying epoxy resin. You'll gain a comprehensive understanding of this versatile medium, exploring its unique characteristics, applications, and the endless possibilities it offers for artistic expression.

Before diving into your resin art endeavors, it's crucial to equip yourself with the right tools and materials. We'll walk you through the essential supplies and equipment required to embark on your resin crafting journey, ensuring you're well-prepared to create your masterpieces.

The world of resin art beckons with a plethora of project ideas, each brimming with potential. Discover a curated selection of easy resin art projects designed specifically for beginners. These projects will serve as your creative playground as you hone your skills and explore the magic of epoxy resin.

Creating flawless resin art requires attention to detail, including preventing the dreaded bubbles that can mar your masterpiece. We'll share invaluable tips and techniques to help you achieve bubble-free resin creations, ensuring your art shines in all its brilliance.

Not all epoxy resins are created equal, and selecting the right one for your specific applications is essential. Dive into the world of epoxy resin choices, understanding the nuances that make each type suitable for various projects. Armed with this knowledge, you'll make informed decisions about the resin that best suits your artistic vision.

Adding color to epoxy resin opens up a world of creative possibilities. Explore the art of coloring epoxy resin, discovering techniques and pigments that allow you to infuse your creations with vibrant hues and captivating designs.

Safety is paramount in resin artistry. Learn essential safety precautions and best practices to protect yourself and your workspace while working with epoxy resin. Prioritizing safety ensures that your creative journey remains enjoyable and risk-free.

Unleash your creativity with a collection of easy resin crafts that you can create in the comfort of your own home. These projects offer a perfect starting point for honing your resin art skills while producing stunning pieces of functional or decorative art.

Dive deeper into the world of resin crafting with a curated selection of the best project ideas. From jewelry and home decor to unique gifts, these crafting projects offer endless inspiration for your resin artistry.

These specialized guides will take you on a journey to create captivating resin rock art and mesmerizing resin geodes, expanding your repertoire of resin crafting techniques.

Embark on this artistic adventure with epoxy resin as your medium, and let your creativity flow. Whether you're a novice eager to explore the possibilities or a seasoned crafter seeking fresh inspiration, this guide will be your trusted companion on your journey to mastering the art of epoxy resin. Get ready to unleash your inner artist and craft stunning resin creations that will captivate and inspire.

Contents

CHAPTER 01 WHAT IS EPOXY RISEN? 1

CHAPTER 02 RESIN ART TOOLS FOR BEGINNERS 10

CHAPTER 03 TOP 8 EASY RESIN ART PROJECT IDEAS FORBEGINNERS 29

5 TIPS TO AVOID BUBBLES IN EPOXY RESIN 29

CHAPTER 04 HOW TO CHOOSE RIGHT EPOXY RESIN FORYOUR APPLICATIONS 50

THE COMPLETE INFORMATION SOURCE FORRESIN 50

CHAPTER 05 COLORING EPOXY RESIN: HOW MAY EPOXYRESIN BE DECORATIVELY COLORED? 60

CHAPTER 06 EPOXY RESIN SAFETY PRECAUTION 70

CHAPTER 07 EASY RESIN CRAFT TO MAKE AT HOME 82

CHAPTER 08 BEST RESIN CRAFT IDEAS: RESIN CRAFTINGPROJECTS 92

CONCLUSION 109

How To Resin Rocks: Guide For Beginners 111

How to Make Resin Gems How to Make a Resin Geode? 117

CHAPTER 01
WHAT IS EPOXY RISEN?

Everything You Should Know About Epoxy Resin Art

Epoxy resin is a simple way to learn. You'll be astounded by the stunning artwork you can produce, even as a beginner, and it's a beautiful way to explore your artistic side. The best aspect is that you'll always have new projects, methods, and ideas to try. Once you grasp the fundamentals of working with epoxy resin, you'll discover there are countless options!

Epoxy resin is unmatched in its adaptability and possesses an alluring beauty. It can create anything from 3-dimensional artworks and home décor to brilliant jewelry and unique furniture. Everything you'll need to start making resin art is in this introduction to epoxy resin.

When you get to the end of the chapter, you'll be well-equipped to answer any questions about epoxy resin art. Are you prepared to impress your friends—and perhaps even your clients—with some original epoxy resin creations? For inspiration, keep reading!

What Components Make of Epoxy Resin?

A transparent liquid plastic, epoxy resin, is composed of resin and hardeners. Let's examine the definition of "resin" first. Resin comes in two types: natural resin and synthetic resin.

What is natural resin?

Natural resin is a viscous liquid that plants exude for defense and therapeutic purposes. Natural resin's key characteristic is its ability to solidify and change into a translucent substance, utilized in various products like jewelry, fragrances, lacquers, and varnishes. Natural resin is costly because it is so hard to find.

What is Synthetic resin?

In the form of viscous liquids that solidify into a plastic surface, synthetic resin, also known as liquid plastic, is an artificial and more cost-effective alternative to natural resin. Epoxy resin, which is often comprised of polyester, silicone, or polyurethane, is the synthetic resin that is used the most widely. Because it is affordable, adaptable, and successfully mimics natural resins' liquid and solid qualities, epoxy resin is widely used.

Without a hardener, the synthetic resin cannot harden into a solid. Hardeners act as the resin's curing catalyst. They are epoxy's curing agents and are frequently made of amines and polyamides. The chemical reaction known as curing occurs when the synthetic resin is combined with an appropriate hardener.

At standard temperature, we are curing converts the two liquid substances into a complex, firm, and lustrous solid in a few hours. A high-gloss, crystal-clear surface is the result.

Resin art is a term used to describe art made with Epoxy Resin.

What is Epoxy Resin Art?

Epoxy resin is nearly universally mentioned when craftspeople and artists discuss the "resin" they use to make "resin art." Epoxy resin was initially employed in industrial settings. That is until photographers and painters realized that a glossy resin varnish gave works of art a sleek, contemporary finish and made the colors jump. Today's artists, designers, craftsmen, and DIY hobbyists are all completely obsessed with resin art, which has recently experienced a meteoric rise in popularity.

Many techniques can be employed with epoxy resin to produce artwork with outstanding depth and beauty. Here are a few of the most well-known works of resin art:

- Coasters & Trays
- Resin Castings
- Epoxy Countertops
- Abstract Art
- Flow Art Projects
- Jewelry Resin
- Resin Wood Lamps
- Sculptures
- Mosaics
- Resin Geode Art
- Resin Pens
- Charcuterie Platters / Serving Boards
- Flowers Preserved in Resin
- Epoxy Art Paintings
- Resin Tumblers
- Wood River Tables
- Resin Bar Tops

Epoxy resin can also be used as a topcoat to give drawings, paintings, and photographs a polished appearance while shielding them from harm and the damaging effects of UV light. The products produced by the addition of resin colorants and inclusions are intriguing. When dealing with epoxy resin, experimentation is essential whether you're a novice or an expert artist.

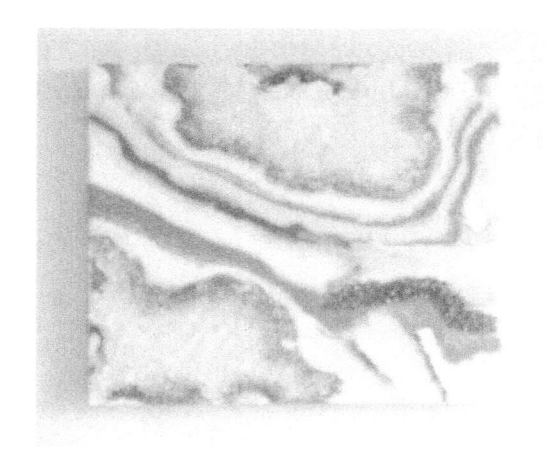

Is it Safe to use Epoxy Resin?

Different brands of epoxy resin have other qualities. To stretch the product, many brands use hazardous solvents and additives in their formulae. They have ominous warnings on the label and present the user with significant health hazards.

Fortunately, there is a brand that is non-toxic and has undergone the necessary testing to guarantee that your health and safety won't be jeopardized. For artists and crafters, ArtResin® Epoxy Resin was created. When used as instructed, this pure, low-odor product is secure for use at home. It doesn't make any fumes or volatile organic compounds (VOCs) that can irritate your lungs and doesn't contain any dangerous solvents.

Unfortunately, this is not the case for the majority of epoxy resin brands, so before you begin, always check the Safety Data Sheet for the resin brand you are using to make sure the product is safe or to make sure you are using the appropriate PPE, such as safety goggles and respiratory protection, to protect yourself.

Follow these common-sense safety precautions to avoid skin irritation, which can occur with any epoxy resin, regardless of brand:

- Use disposable nitrile gloves.
- Be sure to dress in long sleeves.
- Working in a room with open windows and doors will help you stay healthy.
- When working with resin, avoid food and drink.
- Keep away from children's and animals' reach.
- Never flush out any unused resin.
- Using a paper towel and isopropyl alcohol removes all resin stains from equipment, work surfaces, and clothing.

Which Resin Should I Purchase?

You may be tempted to purchase the cheapest epoxy resin when you begin working with resin. This is the kind of resin you want to avoid using! Inexpensive epoxy resins weren't made for artistic purposes. They frequently include harmful substances, release unpleasant smells, and turn yellow, damaging your artwork and costing you money. The adage "You get what you pay for" applies.

Ultimately, it's worth spending a little more to protect your health and artwork with a product like a premium, crystal-clear, non-toxic epoxy resin.

What Colors and Dyes Work Well With Resin Art?

Epoxy resin is colored using a wide variety of colorants by resin artisans. Each one has distinctive characteristics and outcomes that will influence the result. Among the most widely used resin colorants are:

- Mica powder
- Acrylic paint
- Powdered pigment

- Alcohol Ink, the specific colorant required for petri dish art
- Richly saturated ResinTint, explicitly designed for use with resin
- Glitter is not a true colorant but still provides a colorful effect

Solid colors, metallics, neon/fluorescent effects, and pearlescent effects are just a few options for resin colorants. You have a choice!

Before adding your favorite epoxy colorant to color epoxy resin, combine the resin and hardener. Once the resin and pigment are appropriately blended, stir softly yet thoroughly.

The First Time Maker's Guide to Epoxy Resin Art

Have you thought about a project or a design you might start with, along with possible color schemes? Your first work of art made of epoxy resin is particularly remarkable, as we are well aware. We've developed a thorough 6-step tutorial that explains how to make resin art for the first time because of this.

1. Get your work area ready.

It's crucial to have a spotless, dust-free, and adequately ventilated environment when dealing with resin. To ensure that the resin cures uniformly, the surface you're working on needs to be completely level and protected with a plastic drop cloth. Can use a drop sheet to shield the floor from resin spills.

Before measuring and mixing, ensure that all the necessary instruments are available and that your piece is prepared and ready to go.

To ensure you have the necessary personal protective equipment for the resin you use, consult the Safety Data Sheet for the wax.

Disposable gloves must be used when working with Art Resin, but other resin brands may call for respiratory protection or even safety goggles. Always read the SDS before you start, and be safe!

2. Measure the amount of epoxy resin you'll need.

To find the proper mixing ratio, refer to the instruction booklet. This is crucial because different resin brands may require different mixing ratios. When handling wet resin equipment or the resin bottles, and before you measure and mix, put on a pair of disposable nitrile gloves to protect your skin. Measure carefully because if you add too much resin or hardener, the chemical reaction will be changed, and the mixture won't cure properly.

3. Mix

While imagination and originality are crucial, patience is a quality from which epoxy resin artists and DIY producers benefit. Slowly combine the resin and hardener until they are thoroughly combined. Slow stirring is essential to prevent adding too many bubbles to the resin mixture.

Check the instruction handbook before mixing because mixing times can differ from brand to brand. For example, Art Resin epoxy requires a minimum of three minutes of mixing. As you stir, scrape the mixing bowl's sides and bottom. A reagent that has been mixed incorrectly and is left on the bottom and sides will not catalyze well, creating sticky stains that won't dry.

Even if you've mixed slowly, the resin mixture probably contains some bubbles. Don't worry; these bubbles will be dealt with after the resin is poured.

4. Beginner's Guide to Resin Pouring

The resin mixture should next be applied to your artwork. Before you pour, make sure your piece is dry and dust-free. The resin can be worked on for about 40 minutes before it gets too thick to run and distributed with a flat tool, such as a plastic spreader, to position the resin. Self-leveling art resin will begin to spread independently, but applying it will guarantee that the entire surface is equally coated.

Several options exist for how to handle the edges of your piece.

- Toto has the Art Resin sit domed on top of their piece; they should tape the sides and direct the resin to the edges. Remove the tape at the 24-hour mark to reveal the clean sides.
- Tape off the piece's bottom and let the resin drop over the sides before spreading it evenly with a foam brush or your gloved finger.

5. Finish Your Epoxy Resin Work

A quick pass of a flame torch can quickly eliminate air bubbles. Even though many tiny air bubbles may spontaneously pop, a clean, glass-like surface will result from an artist's torch pop.

Use a toothpick to remove any dust or hair that may have gotten stuck in the wet resin. B Defects can be seen by placing a light source on the spread-out resin.

The best tool for this is the flashlight on your smartphone. Your artwork should be protected with a box or tote made of plastic or cardboard. Ensure the lid is clean and within easy reach before you start to resin. If you do it this way, you won't have to leave your wet piece while looking for one.

6. Await Curing Of The Resin Artwork

Give the resin artwork at least 24 hours to cure in a place free of dust. The resin will become thick and tacky in 3 to 5 hours when you can pour a second coat.

The resin will be touch-dry and 95% cured in just 24 hours. You can hang your item on the wall or show it after 24 hours without worrying. Within 72 hours, it will be cured entirely, and you can ship it without risk.

CHAPTER 02 RESIN ART TOOLS FOR BEGINNERS

Using the proper tools for the job is a wise maxim when dealing with epoxy resin. To maximize your time, effort, and financial savings, it's critical to employ the appropriate equipment for the job at hand. Each resin tool has a unique function. You might not know where to begin, though, if you've never dealt with resin before:

- What equipment for resin art should a beginner buy?
- Which resin-related tools are necessary versus desirable?
- What stores sell resin tools?
- Do I have to spend much money on materials for art resin?

The good news is that simple resin art supplies are conveniently available online or at your local hardware store. They might even be lying about your house right now.

The prerequisites for using epoxy resin are as follows:

Supplies for Resin Art for Beginners

1. Epoxy Resin
2. Disposable Gloves
3. Butane Torch
4. Apron/Old Clothes
5. Plastic Drop Sheet
6. Masking Tape
7. Plastic Stands
8. Plastic Spreader
9. Toothpicks
10. Level

11. Plastic Measuring Cup
12. Plastic Stir Stick
13. Butane Torch
14. Dust Cover
15. Alcohol and Paper Towel
16. Butane Torch

The Value Of Plastic Resin-Based Tools

For a good reason, I advise using plastic equipment while working with resin, including stir sticks, spreaders, and plastic drop sheets. Who doesn't want rapid cleanup? Epoxy resin won't stick to plastic, making cleanup easy.

When it comes to degreasing equipment made of plastic resin, you have two options:

- Wet tools should be sprayed with isopropyl alcohol and dried with paper towels. To get rid of every last bit of resin, repeat this process as frequently as necessary. Tools should be properly dried before use after being washed in hot, soapy water until no more resin residue is visible.
- To allow the resin to solidify, leave wet tools on a plastic surface overnight. The following day, the resin will easily peel off.

In either case, plastic tools are a wise choice for dealing with resin because they can be used repeatedly.

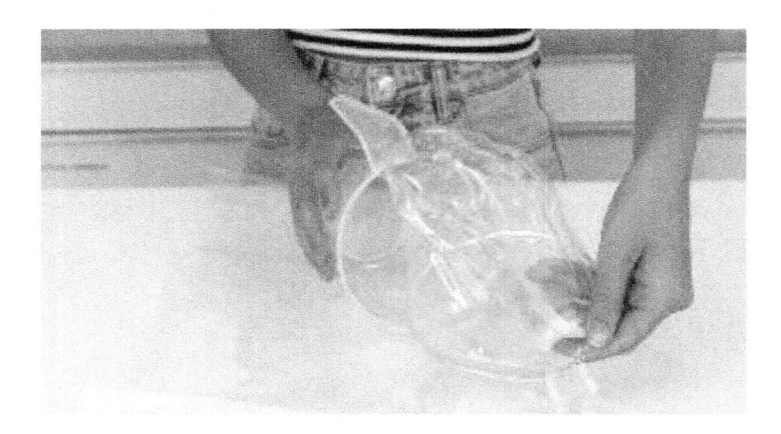

The Significance of Dry, Clean Resin Tools

It's critical to have the appropriate equipment for the work, but it's also essential that your resin tools are dry and clean:

- Dust, fragments of previously cured resin, solvents, or greasy substances can all contaminate resin from dirty instruments, preventing the resin from healing correctly.

- Water can result in a murky resin cure, so make sure your work area, measuring cups, tools, and the object you're resining are arid.

Essential Resin Art Tool Needs

A simple method to begin with epoxy resin and get a feel for it is to apply a coat on a piece of art. There are a few straightforward (but necessary) tools when working with epoxy resin. Let's look more closely at the supplies you'll require to use epoxy resin as a surface coating:

1. **Epoxy Resin**

Depending on the scale of your project, epoxy resin materials are available in various volumes, from 8 oz to 10 gallons. Uncertain of the quantity required? Resin Calculator (you can find it on Internet) will precisely calculate the amount of resin you need and which kit to purchase once you enter your dimensions.

A Remark on Respirators: You may have heard that using epoxy resin requires a respirator. This is accurate for many resin brands available today. However, a toxicologist who examined resin found that it is a clean system, meaning that nothing in the formula reacts and leaves any dangerous emissions that can be discharged into the air and ingested.

2. **Gloves**

Disposable gloves will protect your hands. Resin is sticky when liquid; thus, wearing gloves will keep your hands clean and prevent potential skin irritation. When working with resin, ensure you have several pairs of gloves that prefer nerves since they resemble latex but are much more robust and don't include any of the allergic substances typically connected with latex. You may find nitrile gloves in your accessory kit and the paint department of your local hardware shop.

3. **Old Clothes/Apron**

Wear an apron, a smock, or old clothes while working to shield your clothing from resin drips. If you unintentionally spill any resin on your dress, there is no easy way to get it off. If you have long hair, ponytail it to keep the resin out and the hair out of the resin.

4. Plastic drop sheet

Use a plastic drop cloth to prevent resin spills or drips on your work surface and floor. Paper towels and isopropyl alcohol can be used to clear resin drips, or if left too dry, they can be scraped off the next day. A clear, smooth vinyl shower curtain offers a cheap, durable liner that can be used repeatedly. Kitchen parchment paper is ideal for little jobs.

5. Masking Tape

Suppose you want to resin the piece's sides and tape off the bottom using premium painter's tape. This will prevent drips from ruining your artwork. Falls begin to build up around the base as resin drips down the sides due to gravity. The tape will catch these drips; you can remove the video and the beads together after the resin is touchably dry.

TIP: If you want to let the resin rest on top of your artwork or form a dome around it without spilling over the sides, you can tape off the bottom for extra stability.

6. Stands

Extra resin can collect on the plastic-lined work surface when plastic stands to support your item. I use painter's pyramid supports; you can purchase them separately or as part of your Accessory Kit. You can get them in the paint area of any hardware store. Large plastic shot glasses or toy building blocks also work nicely; both can be found at the dollar store.

7. Level

Make sure your work is horizontal by checking it with a standard level. Due to the self-leveling properties of epoxy resin, if your object is tilted, it will run off the edges at the lowest point.

8. Plastic Container For Water Bath

If your resin is excellent, a warm water bath will bring it to room temperature and make it easier to handle. Choose a narrow container with high edges to prevent spills and keep the bottles uprights. The capped bottles should soak in a container half-filled with warm water for 10 to 15 minutes, approximately as long as you do with a newborn bath. You are now prepared to measure and combine after properly drying your bottles.

9. Stir Stick

The most excellent stirring device for resin has a level surface; resin that isn't well combined won't cure properly, so be sure to scrape the container's edges and bottom as you st ensure that all of the resin and hardener are blended. The container can be squeezed much more successfully and stick with a flat surface than t can with a round object, like a spoon. Tongue depressors made of wood can be used, but they must be thrown away after each usage.

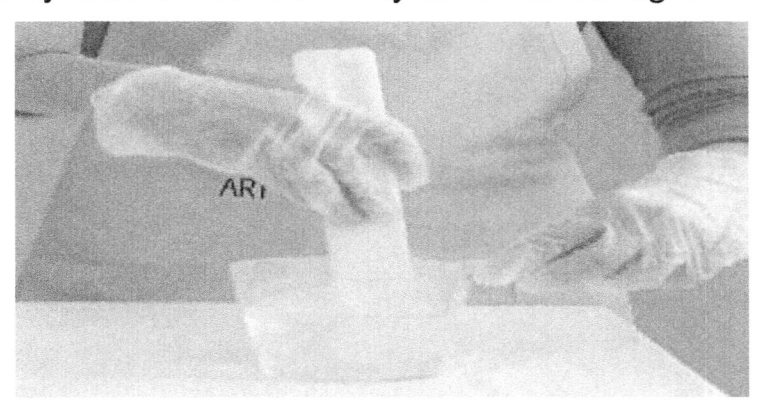

10.   Mixing Container

Use a plastic, graduated measuring jug to correctly measure and mix your resin because poorly measured resin and hardener won't cure. This makes it crucial to use a cup with clearly delineated lines to prevent guesstimating. As long as all the components weigh the same, it doesn't matter whether you consider weigh the resin or the hardener. Pick a plastic mixing cup, and when you're done, flip it over onto a surface covered in plastic to allow the resin to collect. Once the resin has dried the following day, you can peel it off and reuse your cup.

11.   Spreader

Pinning epoxy resin will naturally self-level, but a flat plastic spreader evenly distributes it over your work. To direct the resin, use a plastic spreader with a flat edge.

If you want to cover a particular species of your object, you can apply epoxy Resin there using a toothpick, a popsicle stick, or an old paintbrush.

If you want the resin to sit perfectly in a dome on top of your artwork without spilling over the sides, a small spatula or a plastic takeout knife works amazingly to push it up to the edge without spilling over.

You can apply resin to the sides of your item with gloved hands or a foam brush.

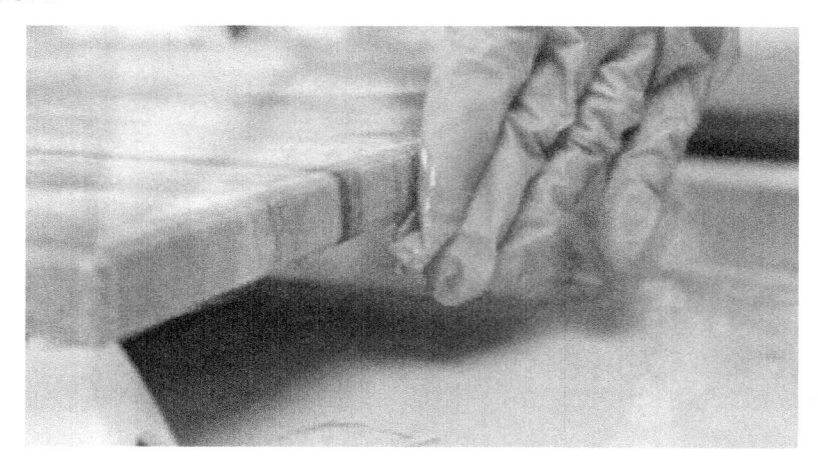

12. Torch

A flame torch is the most acceptable method for obtaining a flawless, bubble-free finish. Numerous bubbles are produced when the resin is mixed; if not eliminated, these bubbles will cure into your sculpture. They cannot be expelled by blowing into a drawing pricked with a toothpick. Hairdryers don't heat up to a hot enough temperature, which will blow your resin around and add dust. When working with silicone molds or resin that contains alcohol ink, a heat gun is a suitable option.

Nothing beats a flame torch for removing bubbles from most resin work.

A small butane torch, works well for most applications, except for liquid alcohol ink dropped into liquid resin, which is combustible. A propane torch is tough to beat for larger objects! Any hardware store will have tanks for butane and propane.

TIP: Please don't be anxious about using a flame torch. You'll wonder how you got along without one after using one.

13. Toothpicks

When resining, toothpicks are a necessity. After torching your item, hold it to the light at eye level to check for stray bubbles and fish out any hair or dust particles. They come in handy if you need to move tiny bits of resin or precisely position inclusions like jewels or gold flakes.

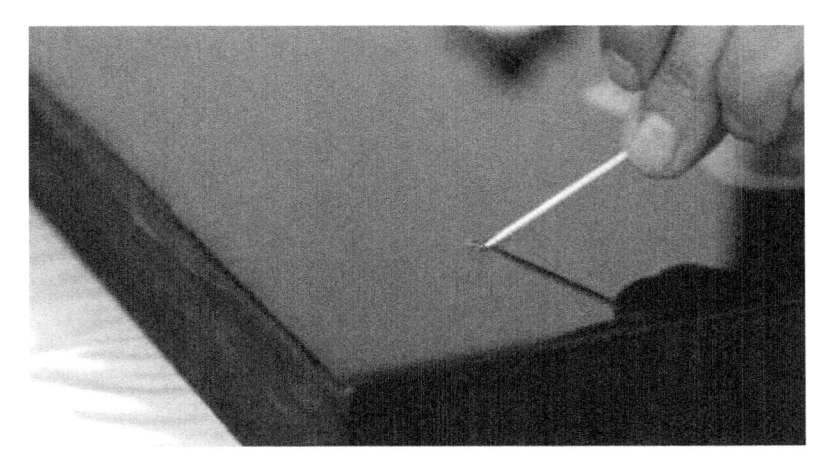

14. Dust Cover

Before beginning to resin, prepare a dust cover since you never want to expose your newly resined artwork while searching for a cardboard box or plastic tote. Wipe the cover surface to prevent dust from getting into your wet item. Since plastic totes are easy to clean, I prefer using them. Make careful to remove the flaps from the cardboard box you use. You don't want When you awaken the following morning, you don't want to find that a flap has fallen and cemented into your resin

15. Paper towel and alcohol

For spills and cleanup, paper towels and isopropyl alcohol are needed. Wearing gloves, remove as much wet resin as you can with paper towels before misting your equipment with alcohol to eliminate any remaining residue.

Repeat this procedure until there is no residue, then wipe dry with an extra paper towel. Resin should never be flushed down the toilet! After removing all resin residue from your instruments, wash them in hot, soapy water and allow them to dry thoroughly before reusing them.

TIP: Since alcohol destroys resin, you should avoid using it to remove resin from your hands because your skin can absorb it.

16. Hand Cleaner

Use an exfoliating hand cleaner to get rid of sticky hands. If Resin unintentionally gets on your skin, wash it off right once to prevent potential skin sensitivity. The hand cleanser with an exfoliation from the hardware shop is excellent. In a hurry, dry rubbing your hands to remove resin can be accomplished using a few poppy seeds and liquid soap. Give your hands a thorough water rinse after that.

Nice haves: Trying out resin

Here, you are free to showcase your talent! When you have a firm grasp of the principles, you'll be ready to experiment with new resin projects. Here are several places for novices to start:

- Create coasters and other small castings using silicone molds.
- Pour resin into alcohol ink to create petri dish art.
- Pouring several tints of colored resin results in flow art.
- To make ocean art, layer resin dyed with various colors of blue and white.

You'll need to upgrade your resin toolbox with the following items to complete these projects:

1. Silicone Molds

Unlike rigid plastic molds that could shred or deform, silicone molds are flexible and straightforward ove from the resin cast, making them perfect for little resin art projects. You can use them again and time again because it returns to their original shape.

Molds are available ly every size and form, but using a cast like this to produce resin coasters is straightforward. Beer caps, shells, vibrant stones, diamonds, crystals, and other inclusions are all possible.

A 2-part silicone substance called Mold Making Material enables you to make custom molds.

2. Alcohol Ink

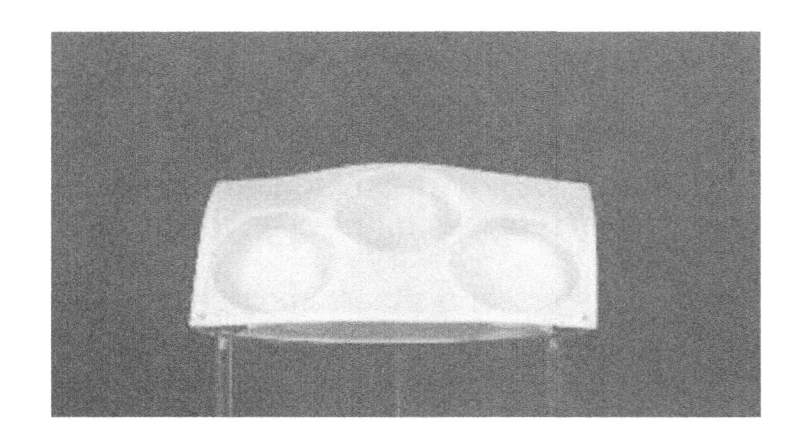

You can also make petri dish resin art using a silicone mold. Pour a few drops of Alcohol Ink into some epoxy resin and put it in a silicone mold to produce tendrils, squiggles, and other fantastic effects. The colors are then forced down through the resin by a white ink sinker!

Please Be Aware: Alcohol ink is flammable, so avoid using a torch when working with it. While the liquid resin is not flammable, adding alcohol ink changes this. Most resin bubbles will usually pop due to the alcohol in ink, but if you need an extra boost, use a heat gun.

3. Colorants

When colored, epoxy resin has a lovely appearance; for optimal effects, always use a colorant made especially for resin, such as ResinTint liquid colorant. Once the resin has reached a single, uniform tint, stir in the colorant.

TIP: No matter the kind, colorants shouldn't be used on more than 6% of the resin and hardener mixture's volume. If you do, your resin might not cure properly.

4. Stirrers and Plastic Cups

If your resin art project calls for colored resin, Mix it as follows using popsicle sticks and transparent plastic drinking glasses:

- You should combine all the resin you'll need for your project in one sizable batch.
- Depending on how much resin you need for each color, portion it into separate cups. For each hue, use a different cup.
- Add the tint to the resin and thoroughly mix it to get a uniform hue. If you start with less color than you think you'll need, you can always add more later.

- You can check the color's intensity by pulling a small quantity of tinted resin up the side of the plastic cup; if more tint is needed, add it immediately.

5. Metal Trays & Wood Panels

Epoxy resin weighs a lot. Therefore, when working with resin, wood panels are the best option. The most excellent substrates for holding resin weight are solid ones. Mount prints, images, or even paint directly onto the panel and cover with resin for a modern style. Cradled panels are an excellent option for pouring colorful resin into ocean art since they have a lip to keep the resin. For this use, metal serving trays are also ideal

TIP: To prevent the stretched canvas from sagging and causing the resin to cure in a pool in the middle, the back must be reinforced with cardboard before resigning.

6. Heat Gun & Hair Dryer

Though I usually advise using a flame torch, there are three exceptions: Use a hair drier and a heat gun to create flow art on silicone molds.

- **When using alcohol ink:** A flame torch can cause a fire since alcohol is combustible. If you need an extra boost, please use a heat gun. The alcohol in ink usually pops many resin bubbles on its own.
- **When utilizing silicone molds:** A heat pistol is a good substitute when dealing with molds because a flame's intensity runs the risk of harming silicone.
- **For making cells and incorporating them into flow or ocean art:** Push the colored resin layers lightly with a heat tool or hair dryer set to low to produce entertaining results. Finally, swiftly eliminate any bubbles from the surface by fast passing a flame torch over it.

7. Inclusions

Include gold leaf, crystals, decorative stones, charms, glitter, and other fun small embellishments in your work to add shine, intrigue, and texture. "inclusions" refers to all the charming small accents you may incorporate into your resin product. Gold leaf flakes can be suspended, crushed glass or crystals can be added to imitate geodes, glitter can be used to create depth and brightness, and dried flowers, shells, or bottle caps can be used to construct coasters.

There are a million items you can add to the resin at the craft store; always ensure your inclusions are completely dried, and I recommend testing first to ensure you get the desired outcome.

7. SandPaper

You might occasionally discover that your resin has hardened but still contains a bubble, some dust, or even hair. Don't worry; this may be quickly repaired by applying a new resin coat. To prepare the initial coat so that the new resin has something to stick to, you must sand it down first. Using a piece of sandpaper, a sanding block, or an electric sander, sand the entire surface with coarse sandpaper, such as 80 grit. Pay special attention to sanding out the trouble spot. It will appear to be a mess, but don't be concerned. It will seem new once you remove the sanding dust and apply your fresh coat.

I sincerely hope this was useful. The bottom line is that having the proper instruments while working with resin assists you in producing better results.

CHAPTER 03 TOP 8 EASY RESIN ART PROJECT IDEAS FORBEGINNERS

5 TIPS TO AVOID BUBBLES IN EPOXY RESIN

8 Easy Resin Art Project Ideas For Beginners

Do you want to attempt to create some resin art for yourself? Epoxy resin has many creative uses, such as coating artwork, pouring coasters, flow art, trinket dishes, and more! Here is a list of ten original resin art concepts suitable for novice and seasoned artists. Which one are you most eager to try?

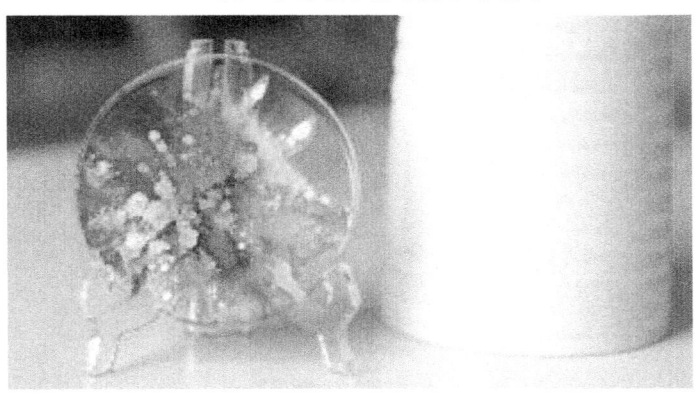

1. Petri Dish Art

Alcohol ink is mixed with resin to create Petri Dish Art, cast in a reusable silicone mold. As the ink penetrates the polish, bright ribbons and multicolored "petrified" squiggles are produced.

How to Make A Resin Petri Dish

Before starting:

- Before combining, reheat the resin and hardener bottles in a warm water bath. Any bubbles that later try to escape will be helped.
- Put on gloves and measure your resin and hardener equally by volume while working in a well-ventilated location.
- For at least three minutes, thoroughly combine the ingredients while scraping the sides and bottom of the basin.
- Each mold component should contain half of the resin.

You're now prepared for the enjoyable part!

Step 1:

- 5–10 drops of Ink Sinker should be added to the Resin.

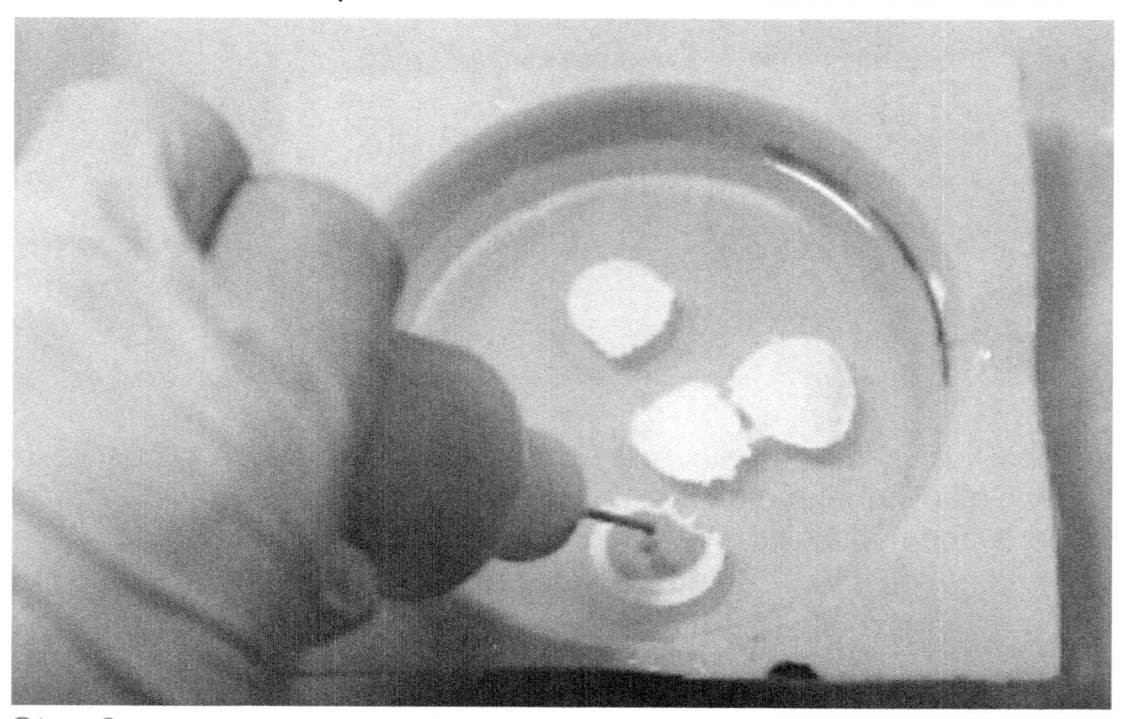

Step 2:

Add 5–10 drops of pink or red alcohol ink to the white.

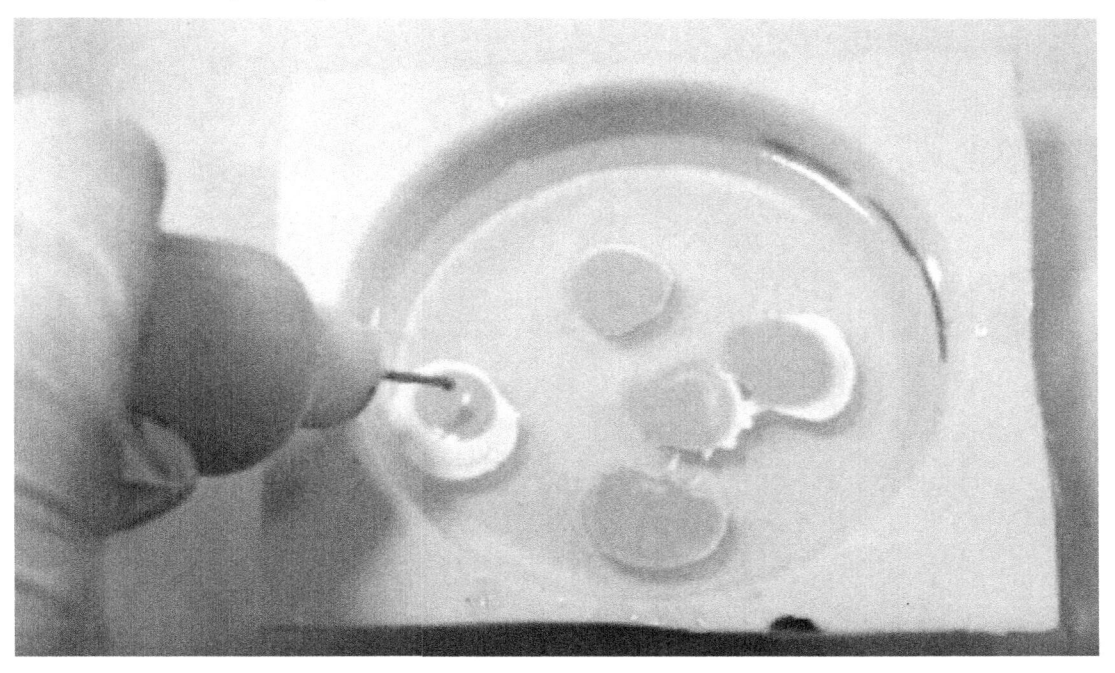

Step 3:
Apply 10-20 drops of gold alcohol ink on top of the pink/white drips you applied in Steps 1 and 2 and over the remaining resin surface.

Step 4:

• Add five drops of whitening, 10–15 drops of pink OR red, then pink or red.

Peel the silicone mold of your resin petri dish after it has been curing for 24 hours.

And It's Ready

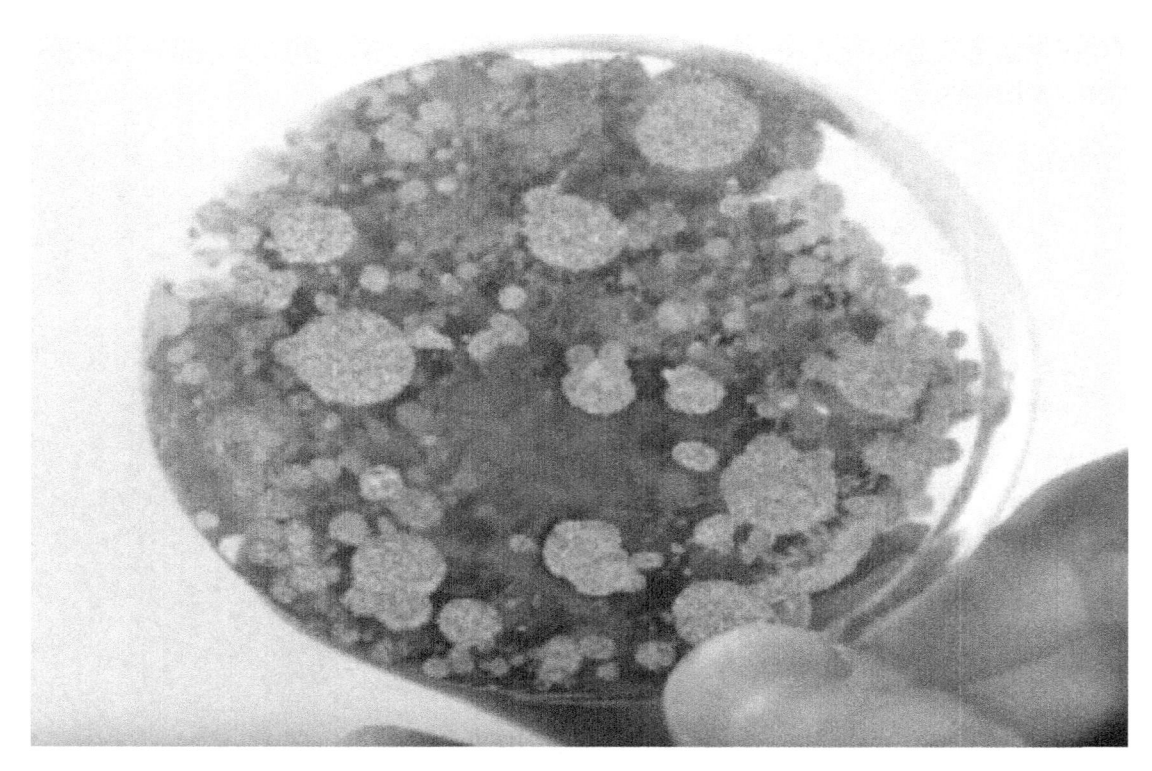

2. Bottle Cap Coaster

Why not put your beer on a cap rather than a cap on your beer? While there are many other styles and hues of coasters, a resin coaster filled with your favorite beer caps will surely attract everyone's attention. Use your preferred soft drink caps if beer is not your thing.

3. Flow Art Tray

Flow with it!

Add some colored Resin on a cheap serving tray to make it seem better! They are helpful and lovely and make for interesting discussion pieces.

How To Create A Resin Flow Art Tray:
   1. **Before you begin, assemble your materials:**
Before you begin, gather your tools and make sure your dust cover is nearby.

When creating your design and selecting your color scheme, keep in mind the color of your background. For instance, if your location is white, you can get away with translucent colors, whereas a dark or metallic background will benefit from opaque colors.

2. Get Your Resin And Tints Ready:

The resin and hardener should be mixed well for at least three minutes while scraping the bottom and sides of the mixing container in equal parts. Give each color its miniature plastic cup, then sprinkle the resin equally.

Each cup of resin should be tinted with a few drops of ResinTint, which should be added in small amounts and thoroughly mixed. Don't be scared to mix and combine different colors to get the colors you want.

3. Pour The Resin

The enjoyable part now! Pour the darkest color first—in this example, navy blue—on the tray's side closest to you.

Pour the white over the opposing side next.

If desired, you can overlay the two whites to add depth and a marbled appearance by varying the opacity of the white. Use a spreader or tilt the tray to reposition the tint and alter its shape.

In addition to the blue, add a turquoise ribbon by applying some to the tray and some over the dark blue. Finally, add gold to the vacant spot. To ensure no bare places, tilt the tray or use the spreader.

The Artist's Torch can be used to blow bubbles away. Before blending, let the resin sit for around 15 minutes. This will slow the movement and maintain the integrity of your pattern by allowing cells to grow and the polish to thicken.

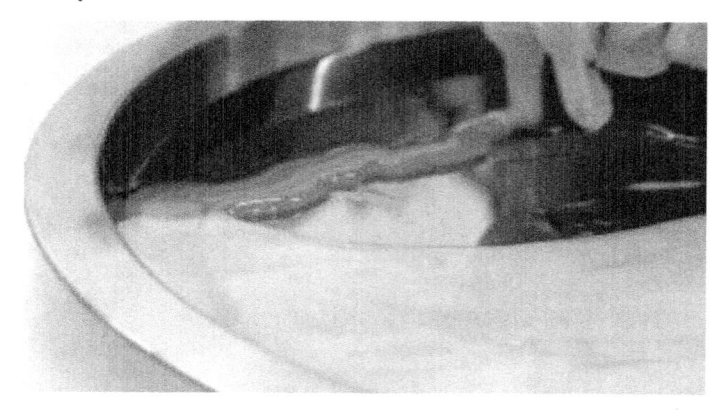

4. Create Your Design:

Before beginning to build your pattern, ensure the resin has had 15 minutes to settle and thicken. The resin is too fluid to blend straight away; you'll get muddy colors and lose your design. To make a pattern in the wax, carefully and organically combine the colors with a spatula.

When pulling the colors out so they can combine, use gradual movements but don't be afraid to go a little deeper. The shape you design will be preserved because the resin has thickened.

5. Torch, Cover, And Wait:

To eliminate any last bubbles, lightly run the torch over your artwork. When your item is dry to the touch, cover it with a dust cover and cure it for 24 hours.

Now It's Ready.

4. Puzzle

Puzzles are enjoyable, beautiful, and require no disassembly. After you've finished the last satisfying piece, choose a puzzle you'd love to display on your wall and cover it in resin to preserve it so you may keep enjoying it.

How To Resin A Puzzle

1. **Choose a puzzle**

Select a game that you like. Find a high-quality puzzle with sturdy pieces that fit tightly and have the image firmly attached without lifting, even though numerous variations are available. These problems could cause the resin or sealer to leak into your puzzle pieces, causing dark stains to appear along the seams. Poorer puzzles contain thin, usually misshapen parts that don't fit together and occasionally even have graphics peeling away at the edges.

2. **Assemble your Puzzle**

Put your puzzle together and use your preferred brush-on sealer to seal it. I suggest using a brush-on glue like ModPodge rather than a spray sealer since it will allow you to get in between the puzzle pieces and prevent the resin from seeping in. Use a gloved hand, a brush, a foam brush, a plastic spreader, or another tool, as I did. Be sure to cover the outside edges of the problem as well.

Allow the sealant to finish drying.

TIP: If the conundrum is of lower quality, you may want to apply 2-3 coats to ensure the problem is thoroughly sealed. Between coats, the sealant must be entirely dry.

3. Place a Thin Coat on

Apply a tiny layer of ModPodge or glue to the back of your sealed puzzle while flipping it over, ensuring it covers the entire surface.

4. Mount the Puzzle

Place the puzzle on the board. To ensure the puzzle adheres to the board, brayer the entire surface and then place a piece of paper on top to protect it. We are focusing primarily on the borders. Give the adhesive time to dry completely.

5. Use plastic stands to support your artwork.

Use plastic stands to support your item once the adhesive has dried (I used turned-over plastic cups.) Now that you are ready to begin!

6. Determine how much resin is required.

Use Resin Calculator to enter the length and breadth of your project to determine how much Resin you'll need. For a typical 1/8" coating, a 12 by 12" piece of artwork requires 5 oz of resin (2.5 oz resin and 2.5 oz hardener).

7. **Stir Thoroughly.**

Wearing gloves, measure out precisely equal amounts of resin and hardener. While stirring for 3 minutes, carefully scrape the sides and bottom of the mixing bowl.

8. **Pour the Resin**

Pour the resin into the middle of your piece and spread it to the edges using a plastic spreader or a popsicle stick. Before the resin becomes too thick, you'll have around 45 minutes to work with it.

9. **Put your artist's torch to use.**

Just long enough to cause the bubbles in the resin to pop, hold the flame of your Artist's Torch a few inches above the resin surface while continuously moving the torch from side to side.

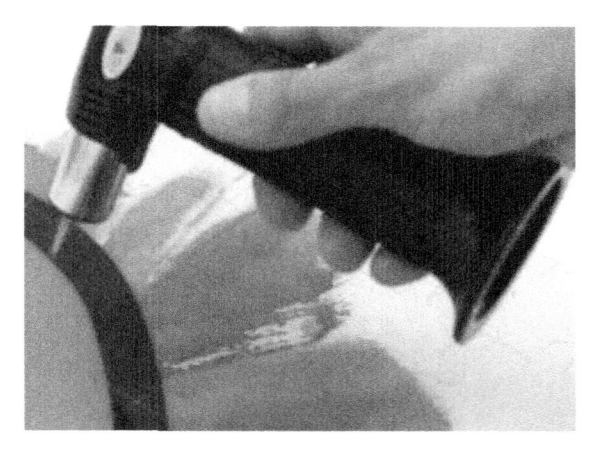

10. Check your work

Using a toothpick, search the resin in the light after the item has been torched for any missed bubbles, hairs, or dust particles.

11. Wait 24 hours while you cover your puzzle.

For 24 hours or until it feels dry, cover your piece with a plastic bag or a cardboard box (with the flaps removed).

After 24 hours, make your content public!

TIP: The resin should feel dry to the touch after 24 hours. Your artwork is yours to hang and enjoy, but if you want to pack it up and move it, you must wait at least 72 hours for the resin to be correctly set.

5. Add A Resin Accent

Add a Resin "accent" to a work of art that is already created or one of a kind.

To add some more oomph, choose a tiny or large area of the sculpture and decorate it with resin. It lends depth to a flat piece and is shiny and smooth.

6. Upgrade Your Art

A little paint or a glossy layer of resin may transform a work of art! When you find an item that is *almost* perfect but needs a little something extra, it's a fantastic alternative.

7. Trinket Dish

Where do you put your change? Maybe your earring? Possibly paper clips?

Making your trinket dish is fun, easy, and has such a unique appearance that you'll find yourself placing them all over your home or place of business. It is priceless art!

How To Create Trinket Dish Art

1. **Pour warm water over the resin and hardener.**

Start by soaking your hardener and resin bottles in warm water for approximately 10 minutes. Removing them from the bath when they are still warm will allow you to measure equal amounts of resin and hardener for your mixing cup.

For each trinket dish mold, you will need roughly 2 oz—1 oz of resin and 1 oz of hardener. For at least three minutes, whisk the mixture gently. To prevent creating many bubbles, try to stir slowly.

2. **Put your silicone mold into the cardboard container.**

Repackage your silicone mold in the kit's cardboard box so that it can collect any spillage. Pour the mixture into your silicone mold once the resin and hardener have been properly blended. Each mold should be filled.

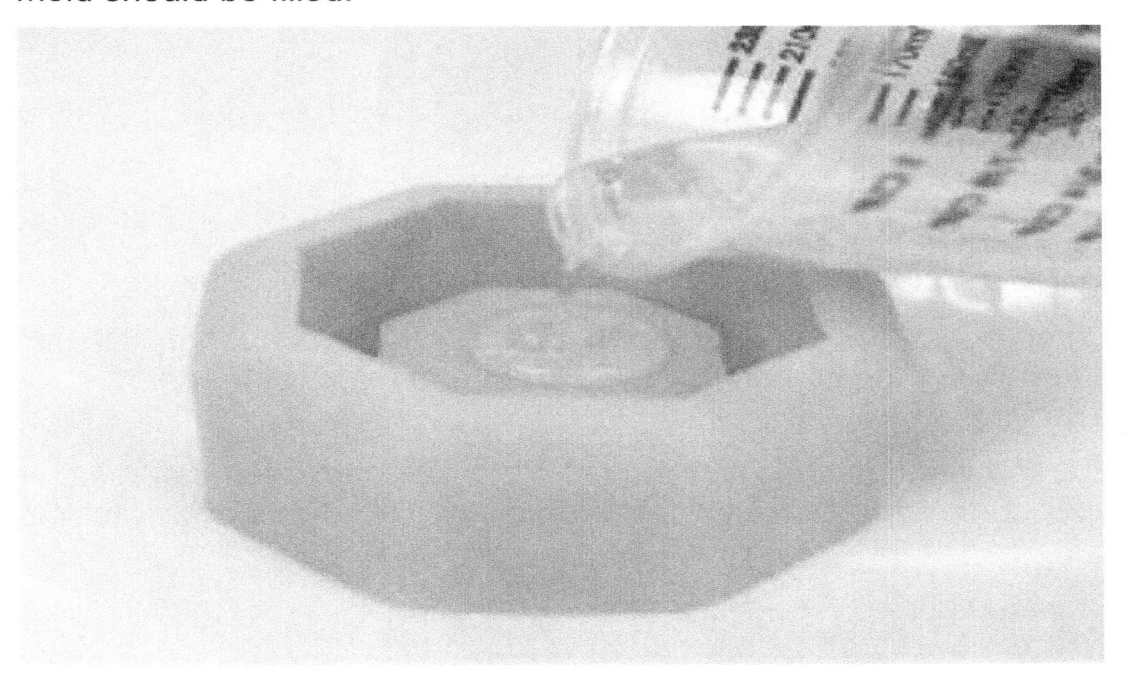

3. **Use the alcohol ink**

Now is the enjoyable part! Drop your chosen colors straight into the resin from the alcohol ink bottle. After using the stain, place a white Alcohol Ink Sinker over each color drop. Continually alternate between color and ink sinker until you're happy with the design!

Tip: When blending paint, use about two drops of color to one depth of ink sinker. This facilitates adequate stain penetration into the resin. For the resin to catalyze correctly, you need only 75–100 drops for each mold.

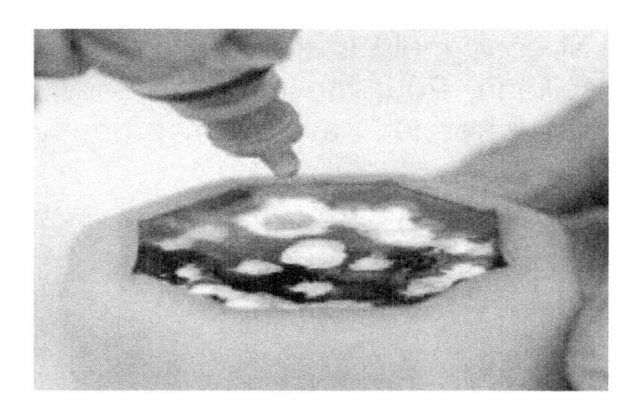

4. Close the cardboard kit box

Complete at this time! Cover the mold with the cardboard kit box after adding the ink, and allow it to set overnight (between 12 – 24 hours).

The following day (or after around 10 to 12 hours), you can remove your cured trinket dish from the silicone mold to see how it turned out.

Prepare yourself for a stunning color surprise!

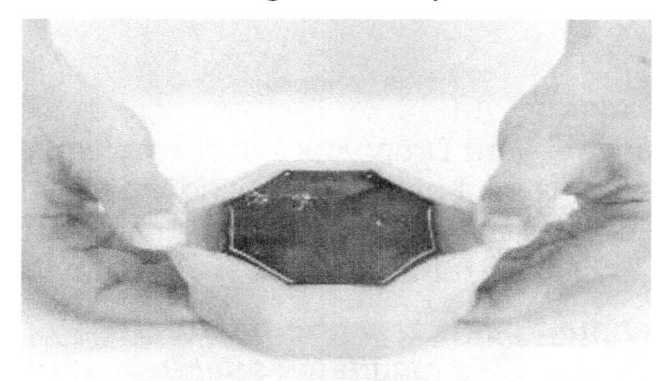

You've just made your functional trinket dish!

8. Jewelry Pendants

Sometimes all you need to level up your outfit is something easy and trim to make. Jewelry pendants are the ideal approach to display your originality and artistic flare to the world.

5 Tips To Prevent Bubbles In Epoxy Resin

Bubbles might be one of the most significant obstacles when using epoxy resin.

There are four primary causes of bubbles in resin that you could encounter:

- Not adhering to recommended epoxy resin processes
- Cold conditions
- Too thick of a pour
- There may be trapped air released by the artwork (this is often the case with paper and organic materials like wood, leaves, dried flowers, etc.)

When using resin, follow the following guidelines to help prevent air bubbles:

- **Use a Torch:** A torch is the best instrument for removing bubbles. The flame instantly heats the resin surface, thins it out, and causes bubbles to release.
- **Work in a Warm Environment:** For a resin with a crystal clear look and honey-like consistency that flows and spreads quickly, Ensure that your workspace is a little warmer than ambient temperature (75-85F or 24-30C). Epoxy resin enjoys being warm. When the resin is thick, murky, and appears milky due to hundreds of tiny bubbles that you won't be able to burn out, the temperature is too low.
- **Pour in layers of 1/8":** If the resin is poured thicker than 1/8" because bubbles won't escape to the surface, the resin will cure.

Tip: The resin will cure if it is poured thicker than 1/8" because bubbles won't be able to rise to the surface.

- **Seal over natural objects:** To prevent animals from breathing and blowing air bubbles into the epoxy resin, seal them with a brush-on or spray sealant before applying the epoxy.

How Easy Is Resin Art?

Epoxy resin art may seem scary at first. Still, if you try it, you'll understand why it's such a rewarding, imaginative activity for creative types like artists, crafters, and DIY enthusiasts. Once you master it, you'll be motivated to take on more challenging tasks and experiment with novel ways.

CHAPTER 04 HOW TO CHOOSE RIGHT EPOXY RESIN FORYOUR APPLICATIONS

THE COMPLETE INFORMATION SOURCE FOR RESIN

Epoxy resin is more resistant to heat, chemicals, and mechanical stresses than other resin forms and has a wide range of industrial applications. Epoxy resin is applied in layers over a substance or poured into a mold when liquid to provide a protective outer covering. The meaning becomes solid, durable, and structurally sound after curing.

Epoxy resin is very helpful in various applications, from industrial tools to creative endeavors and the production of automobiles, thanks to this mix of properties. The fundamental properties of an epoxy resin formula will vary depending on the precise chemistry and polymerization techniques used.

What is Epoxy Resin?

Epoxy resin is a form of artificial resin that has several applications. Epoxy is created by combining two complementary components. A chemical reaction usually lasts many hours when the liquid resin is mixed with the proper hardener.

After the components are joined, the material changes from a liquid to a solid and produces heat. For the material to fully cure, the resin to hardener ratio should be either 1 to 1 or 1 to 2.

According to the manufacturer's instructions, several synthetic or epoxy resins can be employed for various applications and have varying qualities. Different kinds of resins significantly affect how long they take to cure, how hard they are, and how sensitive the finished surfaces are.

Heat resistance and the maximum layer thickness that can be applied to the substance are other factors to consider when selecting the best epoxy resin.

Epoxy resin's various qualities in various product varieties:

- Viscosity (flowability)
- Heat-resistance
- Electrical insulation
- Anti-corrosive
- Chemical stability
- Low moisture absorption
- Durable adhesive bond
- Low shrinkage after curing
- Absence of VOCs (volatile organic compounds)
- Excellent fatigue strength and flexural strength

What is the Purpose of Synthetic or Epoxy resin?

Epoxy resin, in general, is adaptable and can be used for various art and craft applications. The following things are possible uses for epoxy resin:

- Acrylic bar tops
- Soil Sealing in residential areas
- Resin-based Wood Stabilization
- Model construction projects
- Production of resin jewelry
- Shower tray shelves made of resin
- Kiteboards can be built on your own.

- Quick fixes using a specific UV resin
- Indoor and outdoor stone carpet repairs
- Waterproof epoxy coatings for garage floors
- Putting small parts together and repairing the
- Constructing one's terrariums and aquariums.
- Epoxy resin artworks, including resin art paintings
- Epoxy mold casting and many types of figurines
- Kitchen resin countertops sealed to prevent cutting
- Ideas for modern rehabilitation of historic structures
- Items for decoration like resin geodes and Petri dishes
- Synthetic resin can be used to cast objects and artifacts.
- Useful items made of wood with epoxy resin, such as cutting boards
- Furniture that endures, like river tables constructed of epoxy resin
- Artificial resin used as a topcoat or Gelcoat while manufacturing boats

What to Look out For When Purchasing Epoxy Resin?

Epoxy resin is available from several specialized dealers and most home improvement stores. The selection is considerably more extensive, and the supplies are frequently less expensive if you order online. Numerous internet retailers likely provide the broadest assortment of high-quality items .for all conceivable purposes.

The relatively high cost of many synthetic resin components may deter you if you begin working with synthetic resins. But it would help if you didn't look for the cheapest deals. Very inexpensive goods may be of worse quality, which might be visible in the outcome of your labor and demoralize you.

Some products might also include solvents that are unhealthy for the body or that evaporate during the curing process. This may cause the substance to cure or make it challenging to combine partially.

Additionally, some less expensive epoxies process somewhat brownish rather than being transparent and crystal clear. A little sunlight can subsequently amplify this yellowish tint.

Tip: To make sure that your job is practical and that your results are satisfying, you should buy the best resin components you can afford even after completing a careful pricing comparison.

Which Epoxy Resin is Best For Your Project?

The ideal epoxy resin for your project will be determined by the material qualities that define a particular epoxy resin combination. You should be able to infer how the resin can function in its liquid and cured phases based on the manufacturer's specifications.

Casting resins / Low Viscosity Epoxy Resins

Viscosity describes a liquid's capacity to flow. But take note: A liquid is said to have low viscosity if it is delicate and freely flowing. If you want a low-viscosity casting resin, choose an epoxy resin. For a variety of uses, like the casting of molds or the construction of river tables, an almost watery consistency can be essential.

The cure for these extremely low and low viscoelastic epoxy resins is relatively slow. There should be more time between the future processing steps on your calendar. However, you also have a lot more processing time and less stress as a result. The typical curing time for low-viscosity synthetic glue is between 12 and 24 hours. Since the exothermic chemical transformation process is so slow, relatively little heat is generated. As a result, compared to epoxy resins with high or medium viscosities, thicker layers and larger quantities of the resin can be processed fast in one step.

Applications for casting resin include:

- Casting of several mold types
- Jewelry made of epoxy resin is made
- Molding of parts for the model-making industry
- Furniture creation, including resin river tables and epoxy resin tables
- Epoxy for wood crack and hole filling
- Production of epoxy resin for use in garage or living space floors

Epoxy resins (highly viscous), laminate resins, and countertop resins

Honey's stiff texture is reminiscent of extremely or moderately viscous synthetic resins, which are much denser. The many items in this category are frequently referred to as resin or laminating resin in the trade. They function best when applied to coated surfaces.

They can also be utilized to carry out undertakings in the areas of resin geodes and resin art. When using highly viscous epoxies, you must adhere to the manufacturer's recommended maximum layer thickness for each step. A maximum layer thickness on topo centimeters for trouble-free processing is frequently needed.

Laminating resin used for the following purposes:

- Epoxy resin is used to cast paintings as resin art.
- Petri dishes made of resin and resin Geoden are decorative pieces.
- The completion of all kinds of paintings and art pieces.
- A few types of jewelry made from epoxy resin.
- Surface sealing for tables or worktops.

Overview of the Various Viscosities

Layer Thickness

Due to the resin's lower thermal conductivity during curing, thicker layers can easily be cast using low-viscosity epoxy resins. You can gently remove air bubbles from the epoxy resin layer using a hairdryer or a Bunsen burner that is suitable for the task, if it does include any.

However, you shouldn't pour more than one centimeter thick (such as laminating resin). Due to its thick viscosity, it is challenging to induce air bubbles to rise and escape from the resin.

> ***TIP: The most crucial details are often listed under the manufacturer's information on a product's box. Most of these items also reveal how much material is usually a single process.***

Processing Time

When working with epoxy resins, the processing time—also referred to as the pot life or open time—is essential. The period before processing epoxy resin combined with a hardener is specified. The resin thickens and toughens after a certain point and shouldn't be used any longer (except in exceptional cases). After t that, it can no longer be colored consistently and cannot level out into a flat surface.

Short Processing time
Pros:

- Distinct epoxy compositions can provide different impacts while a person is dying.
- Quick layer buildup because more layers can be placed on top of one another more often.

Cons:

- More bubbles are produced as the venting scenario becomes more complex.
- When exposed to UV light, yellow coloration is possible.

Long Processing Time

Pros:

- You can combine various colors and complete your work in silence.
- The transitions between the layers are hardly noticeable when several transparent layers are stacked on top.

Cons:

- More unusual materials are required to cast numerous layers (mixing cup, spatula).

Curing Time

In the case of synthetic resin, the curing time is the period after the components have been mixed before a condition of complete totals and insensitivity has been attained.

In most circumstances, processing time and curing time are correlated: If processing time is constrained, the resin usually cures completely, even quickly.

What degree of variation exists between the processing times for the various products?

The curing phase for items lasts about 24 hours, while processing takes 20 to 1 hour on average, with processing times of up to 12 hours and a complete cure time of up to one with whether the rein can be processed and used for more complex effects.

Properties of epoxy resin at a Glance

Synthetic resin production and sales have significantly increased in recent years. This astounding growth can be attributed partly to the fact that more and more people are becoming aware of the exceptional properties of this astonishing substance.

Advantages of resin

When people first see epoxy resin, they often have questions. Listing the specific characteristics of the resin is the best method to respond to this query. The features listed below best define the solid state after solid-state curing.

It could take up to a week to achieve this condition, depending on the company and product. You can frequently find precise information about the curing time on the packaging instructions for your components. The resin can seem fully cured, but the chemical transformation typically takes much longer than expected.

Once the epoxy has thoroughly dried, practically every product has the following benefits:

- Extreme resistance against abrasion.
- Superior material toughness.
- Resistant to impact (does not shatter or splinter).
- Most of the time, minimal shrinking happens when a substance changes from a liquid to a solid.
- Densities of about 1.2 grams (per cubic centimeter).
- Products of excellent quality with exceptional UV resistance.
- The vast majority of materials adhere well (for example, also on wood).
- A hot environment to reflect heat. Insulating effect on the electrical current.

- Strong acid resistance.
- The epoxy resin virtually ever splits with proper substrate preparation.
- Excellent outdoor degradation resistance.

TIP: When the liquid, high-quality epoxy resin is rarely or never flammable.

Nearly unbeatable Durability

Premium synthetic resin creates surfaces that are solid and abrasion-resistant when fully cured. Significant mechanical loads can be applied to the material without it deforming. Additionally, it is corrosion-proof and resistant to acids. As a result, kitchen worktops are coated with high-quality epoxy resin to make them cut-resistant.

Possible Negative Effects of Epoxy Resin

Even though epoxy resins' advantages outweigh their drawbacks, there are still some drawbacks to this substance:

- Acids in large amounts can still damage epoxy resins.
- After skin contact, the raw liquid may trigger allergies or skin rashes in some persons.
- Some items may turn yellow because they are not entirely UV lightfast.
- Epoxy that has already been set is challenging.

Are synthetic resins harmful or toxic?

Ingredients in liquid resin and hardener shouldn't be applied directly to the skin. Similar to many other medications, direct skin contact may irritate the skin or trigger allergic reactions. When dealing with epoxy, I encourage you to do so in areas with good ventilation. You should also always use eye protection goggles and, if possible, a breathing mask with a filter. You must follow the safety guidelines provided by the manufacturer, which are specified on the packaging.

Precautions:

When using epoxy resin, you should practice the following safety precautions:

- Wear eye protection that shields your eyes.
- Dress in shabby attire with long sleeves and legs (or a protective suit).
- Only operate in a space that has enough airflow. Put on complete nitrile gloves.
- Putting on an air filter-integrated breathing mask.
- Avoid filling the vessel to the top when combining the ingredients because the mixture could easily spill over as it mixes.

When manufacturing epoxy resins, no significant issues or risks should develop if these fundamental guidelines are followed.

CHAPTER 05 COLORING EPOXY RESIN: HOW MAY EPOXYRESIN BE DECORATIVELY COLORED?

Epoxy resins are typically wholly transparent and colorless. As a result, casting artifacts or collectibles into them is a common practice. Additionally, translucent epoxy resin is frequently used to construct aquariums and terrariums. You could want to tint the resin for a variety of other uses.

People of all ages and professions are now dabbling in resin art, which appears to have gained enormous popularity in recent years. The resin creates various unique objects, including jewelry, cutting boards, coasters, sculptures, and even containers. However, the resin is usually straightforward, so adding color is ultimately up to you. However, how can color be added to epoxy resin? Let's examine a few epoxy resin coloring agents and how they work.

What Can be Used to Color Epoxy resin?

You will need to add a colorant, preferably when the epoxy and hardener are mixed, as epoxy resin frequently cures entirely clear. What compounds, though, can be used to color resin? Epoxy resin can be colored with alcohol ink, mic powder, food coloring, acrylic paint, resin dye, and even eyeshadow. Here is a closer look at each of these coloring substances and how they function to give your epoxy resin color.

1. Using Resin Dye

It takes a scientific technique to use epoxy dye, also known as a resin dye, to add color to your resin castings. You may easily and quickly add color to your resin creations with little effort.

If your neighborhood store doesn't have it, you can usually find it online or in most craft stores. What is the way the dye works? Contrarily, resin dyes are signed to color resin as effectively as possible, dyeing the epoxy at the molecular level rather than just saturating it.

Resin dye's main color aesthetic is opacity, even though it still enables some light to pass through liquid resin and solid castings. Without limitations like glare or magnification, the epoxy dye gives polish forms the appearance of stained glass. In light of this, resin dye might be a good option if you search for a slightly opaque tint.

2. Using Mica Powder

Mica powder is another coloring component that novice and experienced resin artists consider the proper approach to tinting resin. Stone flakes are pulverized into a thin powder to create mica powder. These powders are frequently colored and sparkly because the stones used to make them are often pigmented and shiny. Mica powder can be compared to glitter but lacks reflective qualities. When mixed with epoxy resin, mica powder spreads its color evenly.

Mica powder is completely light-opaque and creates a thick finish. This is ideal if you want to produce solid resin forms or an excellent

with an excellent color finish. The enormous variety of colors that mica powder can produce is its most alluring quality. The most important aspect is that mica powder is typically inexpensive, making it possible to stock various colors in case you need to dye some epoxy resin or any other materials or surfaces that mica powder may color.

3. Using Eyeshadow Dye

Compared to other plastic composite materials, the resin is a straightforward material to color. It's simple to color your resin with some leftover eye shadow. Surprised? Since the color tone resembles adding mica powder to resin, it's a trick that knowledgeable resin artists are familiar with. Therefore I don't blame you.

All you have to do to give your resin a lovely look is to add some eyeshadow and stir it with a toothpick.

This is a practical workaround to be aware of in an emergency, and it also serves as a solid justification for purchasing some excellent eyeshadow shades. They do the job and, if necessary, can even be blended with other color agents. If you had added some mica powder, the result would have been more spectacular.

4. Using ink dye With Alcohol

Although alcohol-based ink is relatively successful at adding color to resin, due to its power, it is often not suggested for novices. Compared to other coloring ingredients, alcohol-based inks are very pigmented and offer a lot of "bang for your buck." They cannot be added to the resin and hardener as they are being combined, which makes using them for the first time challenging.

To prevent alcohol ink from interfering with the resin's initial chemical interaction with the hardener, it is best to add it while it is still curing.

After the resin has been poured into the mold or placed on the tabletop is the ideal moment to add the alcohol ink.

As a result, it can tint your resin without impacting how it bonds and cures. Resin can be colored using additional dyes. Even still, alcohol-based ink is one of the best solutions because it requires very little shade and offers a wide range of brilliant colors.

5. Using Acrylic Paint

If you're an artist experimenting with resin for the first time, chances are you already have some acrylic paint on hand. The good news is that acrylic paint is one of the only graded paint for resin use because the base materials are compatible. It's important to note that acrylic paint's lack of intensity may disappoint you if your goal is to make your resin "pop" with color.

Why? Due to the paint's frequent use of resin castings to create swirls and an overall impression of movement, the color's intensity isn't powerful.

High-quality acrylic paints typically offer a brighter color than those you can pay less for, though this relies on the type of acrylic paint you are dealing with. Because there are so many colors and brands to choose from, you may choose a tint and finish for any occasion when coloring your resin castings with acrylic paint.

6. Using Glitter

Glitter may be used for much more than the occasional birthday card or party decoration, so if the mood strikes, you might add some to your resin casts to give them color. Even though glitter rarely adds color, if you use enough, your resin workpieces can gain from cat a fraction of the cost of most of the coloring techniques we've discussed thus far.

Selecting the proper type of glitter is crucial because the wrong kind will sink to the bottom of your container. Finer glitter dust can be mixed with resin to ensure that your color is applied evenly because it will stay suspended within the resin.

The benefit of utilizing glitter is that you may create works of art in multiple colors, combine various shades of glitter dust and add them to your resin before or during the casting process for an utterly stunning appearance.

Using this technique, you can color epoxy with minimal mess and use glitter that might sit unused in your supply cabinet for years.

Processing of Epoxy Resin

In addition to the resin and hardener, you will need additional equipment and supplies to process epoxy resin. Here, I have provided you with a summary of the most crucial ones.

Mixing smaller quantities of epoxy resin
There are specialized cups with measurement scales for use in epoxy resin art or other applications requiring small amounts of resin. The use of spatulas with a straight edge is also advised.

Mixing larger quantities of epoxy resin
Use a large container and a drill attachment with an emotional attachment to swirl the mixture for several minutes if you want to combine more than one liter of resin and hardener at once.

Drill epoxy resin

Drilling is difficult with epoxy resin because it is difficult. Choosing the right drill is essential for creating suitable holes. You have a choice of two materials, depending on numbering places and the budget you have available:

- HSS: High-performance, high-speed steel is a more inexpensive option for drilling holes in epoxy resin. However, after just a few drillings, the material turns dull.
- HM: Tungsten carbide drills comprise 90% tungsten carbide and 10% cobalt. This increases their hardness and resistance to temperature while also making them slightly more fragile. Therefore, tungsten carbide drills are much better for frequent use or drilling multiple holes.

Sanding Epoxy Resin

You can wet sand epoxy resin or dry sand it. Sanding with dampness is frequently carried out by hand because wetness can cause short circuits in electric sanders. You'll need a wet sanding block and a hard rubber sanding block. The surface is sanded in circular motions, from coarse to fine grain. This method can be used on arp edges, such as those on tables composed of epoxy resin.

Polishing epoxy resin

Depending on the form, texture, and resin used, the resin's surface may appear slightly rough and matte after application. This is where polishing the surface can help. Using a polishing machine and an appropriate polishing paste for larger surfaces is advisable.

With this, the epoxy resin can be easily polished to a high-gloss surface according to your preferences. To manufacture smaller objects like resin jewelry or casting molds while keeping both hands free, utilize a drill and drill stand. You have complete control over the polishing procedure, thanks to this.

UV Resin Processing

A unique resin called UV Resin becomes rigid when exposed to UV radiation. The best way to cure is with a UV light or UV torch because the sun doesn't shine strongly enough and frequently enough at our latitudes. As a result, the epoxy resin may be treated very fast, and the UV resin has already begun to solidify after one to two minutes.

Epoxy Resin is poured using Silicone Molds.

Epoxy resin can be painted, used as a coating material, and poured into molds to produce three-dimensional things. There are numerous options, ranging from geometric forms and coasters to more sophisticated shapes and jewelry.

Many silicone molds are available, and epoxy resin casting is best accomplished with these molds. After hardening, you may easily mold the item by covering the mold with non-adhesive silicone. If you want to create silicone molds, replicating silicone simplifies the process.

Remove the Epoxy Resin

You will quickly discover that removing epoxy glue is not that simple if you ever need to. Removal of the casting resin after it has been set has been accomplished using a hot air dryer and a scraper. Isopropyl alcohol or vinegar is appropriate if the resin is still liquid.

What Distinguishes Liquid Resin Dye from Pigment Powder?

The easiest ways to tint epoxy are liquid resin dye and pigment powder (similar to mica powder). On the other hand, their approaches to coloring resin differ just a little. Pigment powder is a mixture of innumerable smalltinyicles casting cast the resin color.

Due to its homogeneous distribution throughout the casting's interior volume, the resin seems to have the same shade as the powder. Both are liquid dyes that produce solutions diluted in resin; it then acquires the dye's hue. But the way that liquid resin dye and alcohol-based inks operate is different.

Dyeing is excellent, but unlike pigment powder, dyes tend to fade over time when exposed to direct sunshine, which is unfortunate because castings tinted with liquid resin dye look beautiful outside.

Due to their lower susceptibility to UV deterioration, pigment powders undergo substantially less decomposition than resin dyes, which is what you want if you use epoxy resin to create items like baby mobiles or wind chimes. This demonstrates that the question you ask most frequently is What to Color Resin With, not How to Color Resin.

When choosing a coloring agent for your resin, consider the location of your workpiece, the resin you'll be using, and the pressures acting on it.

How to Color Epoxy Resin

It is all well and good to know what an excellent product looks like, but what counts most is learning how to color epoxy resin with it.

In light of this, we've produced a brief tutorial explaining how to apply liquid and pigment dyes to resin. When using dyes to resin castings for the first time, go carefully to get a sense of the strength of the dye and how to make your resin lighter or darker.

Get your resin ready.

Combine your resin and hardener in a 1:1 ratio for consistency. By doing this, you may prevent resin from being either excessively fluid or too lumpy. To ensure that you can always see the color of your resin and the quantity you have on hand, I advise performing this technique in a clear container.

Using Pigment Powder

When compared to alternative techniques for applying epoxy colors, utilizing pigment powder is simple and enjoyable. Wears a mask and some gloves to avoid inadvertently breathing in the fine pigment powder that is there and can get everywhere.

Add the Powdered Pigment.

Add the color confident when you are sure that the resin and hardener have been appropriately combined. I advise using a small spoon and filling it to the brim with pigment powder before adding it to your resin container.

Using a mixing stick, stir the resin and pigment powder combination until the powder begins to bind to the resin mixture. As you combine, the color should change.

Add extra color dye to the container if you're unhappy with the intensity. When is the resin ready, and how can you tell? Once the color powder and epoxy resin have been thoroughly combined, there shouldn't be any powdery residue left in the container.

How To Use Liquid Resin Dye

Using liquid dye may have a high learning curve for beginners, but as long as you are cautious and watchful, it shouldn't be too difficult. Utilizing liquid pigments for epoxy resin gives you great value for your money because they create vibrant color palettes for epoxy colors.

Get your resin ready.

Before pulling out your liquid dye, you need resin to color. In a clear container, combine your resin and hardener. This will enable you to keep an eye on the resin's color and consistency as you add the dye.

To achieve the ideal consistency before adding the liquid color, ensure your resin has been diluted exactly 1:1.

Add Your Liquid Resin Dye

Get a pair of sharp scissors and remove the sealer cap typically found behind the twist-on/off caps that are included with liquid dyes. Please ensure the container's snout is pointing upward, and avoid squeezing it when you remove the safety cover. After the cap has been successfully removed, combine the resin and dye in a bowl.

Working gradually and slowly is critical in this situation. Squeeze out the tiniest quantity and mix it into the resin container. As you combine the resin and dye, observe how the color changes. Continue adding paint until the containers are the desired shade. Always start with a modest amount because once resin color is applied, it can't be taken out, meaning you'll have to start over if you put more than you told.

It's time to put your newly acquired knowledge to the test. Knowing the differences between pigment powders and liquid dyes and the best product for each color, you should go out and put your knowledge to the test. When dealing with resin, always wear gloves and a face mask, and make sure your workspace is sufficiently ventilated.

CHAPTER 06 EPOXY RESIN SAFETY PRECAUTION

Entropy Epoxy Resins: Safe Handling

Working with epoxy will become more enjoyable, fulfilling, and safe with the help of these safety measures for epoxy resin. Although most epoxy-related health issues are minor, I want you to have no problems. The good news is that avoiding these issues with a few precautions is simple.

The risks associated with using epoxy resins made by Entropy Resins will be discussed, along with some typical shop risks. Follow the common sense guidelines to protect your security, efficiency, and pleasure from the extraordinary and spectacular things you can create using Entropy Resins.

Topics Of Epoxy Resin Safety Precautions

- Why you should prevent Overexposure: Overexposure prevention
- Working Clean
- Disposing of Epoxy Safely.
- Epoxy-related Hazards

Why You Should Prevent Overexposure

The majority of chemicals have a safe exposure threshold. The overexposure threshold of a chemical is reached faster, the more hazardous it is. Health issues are brought on by exposure levels that are too high. Your immune system and general health may impact your ability to tolerate a chemical.

The Entropy Resins product line's epoxy resins and hardeners are created with the best physical qualities while posing the fewest environmental and human health risks. This keeps the number of dangerous substances in these products at a level where you can easily avoid overexposure using sensible work practices.

Hazardous compounds can enter the body through ingestion, inhalation, or skin absorption. The usual route of a chemical depends on its physical characteristics and everyday uses.

Epoxy Hardeners And Resins

When liquid, resin, hardener, and combined epoxy are more susceptible to exposure. Epoxy interacts chemically to form a solid as it dries or cures. Sanding dust, which we'll talk about next, is the only other possible route by which solidified epoxy could enter the body.

Skin contact is the most frequent method of exposure to resins and hardeners. Minor skin-to-skin contact that occurs frequently can provide health. Occasionally, hazardous substances may be absorbed through prolonged or recurrent skin contact.

Exposure through inhalation is uncommon because epoxy resins have a sluggish rate of evaporation. However, this risk rises if you are heating the epoxy, working in a confined space, or if your workspace is not adequately ventilated.

Epoxy Dust That Has Partially Cured

Epoxy that hasn't thoroughly dried when sanded emits airborne particles that can get on your skin, in your mouth, or get breathed. The epoxy may take up to two weeks to properly cure, even though it can be filed after only a few hours. It's possible that the epoxy dust still has hazardous components present that haven't yet reacted. Never undervalue or disregard this sanding risk.

Effects of Epoxy Exposure on Health

Let's examine the most typical health issues related to epoxy use. We can almost all steer clear of these problems. Even people with health difficulties can typically continue using epoxy with a few extra precautions.

Dermatitis

Less than 10% of people exposed to too much epoxy resin or hardener respond. A severe case of dermatitis is the typical outward sign of the reaction. Rashes may develop after using epoxy resin or hardener. Even the discomfort could be terrible; symptoms usually fade once adhesive contact is broken. On the other hand, constant contact may result in contact dermatitis.

Typically, this is milder but lasts longer. It may involve swelling, blisters, and itching and can develop into eczema if not treated over an extended length of time. Contact dermatitis can also result from sanding dust from partially-cured epoxy that collects on the skin.

Allergic dermatitis (Sensitization)

Less than 2% of epoxy users will experience allergic dermatitis, a more severe condition brought on by the body overreacting to an allergen. Sensitization, a type of allergy, emerges after repeated exposure. The strength and frequency of your epoxy exposure, immune system, and risk of getting allergic dermatitis are all factors.

You will be more susceptible if you have already developed an allergy to an epoxy chemical or have been seriously overexposed to epoxy. Fair skin, prior exposure to other sensitizing chemicals, hay fever or other allergies, or stress all raise the risk.

Epoxy might make you sensitive after several exposures or only one. Some people become hypersensitive in just a few days, while others may take years. Since there is no way to estimate how much exposure you can withstand before developing an allergy, the best action is to prevent all disclosure. Epoxy allergies can cause skin rashes or breathing difficulties. Skin irritation is by far the most frequent side effect.

It frequently has a poison ivy appearance and can cause swelling, itching, and red eyes. The symptoms may be sudden or chronic and may be moderate to severe. Your respiratory system may become irritated if you inhale epoxy vapors regularly or for extended periods.

Chemical Burns and Severe Irritation

On their own, many epoxy hardeners have a mild caustic flavor. Burns caused by hardeners are uncommon, whereas burns caused by mixed epoxy are sporadic. If hardener comes into touch with the skin, it can cause significant chemical burns and severe skin irritation. These gradually manifest and start as little pain and irritability. The burn may leave a faint scar on the skin.

The area of the skin and the hardener concentration determine how quickly epoxy hardener will burn the skin. Hardener is less corrosive because of the dilution caused by mixing it with resin. While mixed epoxy is less corrosive than pure epoxy, Never let it sit on your skin since it quickly hardens and is difficult to remove.

Respiratory Anxiety

The epoxy vapor that has been significantly concentrated has the danger of irritating and sensitizing the lungs. At room temperature, epoxy vapor concentrations shouldn't be too high. However, even to little amounts of vapor can cause an allergic reaction if you already have an allergy to epoxy. Epoxy vapor concentrations rise in hotter environments and without adequate ventilation.

Sanding epoxy before it has fully cured might have detrimental effects on one's health. When stuck in the mucus lining of your respiratory system after inhaling, epoxies chemical particles can cause excruciating itching and respiratory allergies. Epoxy chemicals are reactive until they have been cured.

Preventing Excessive Epoxy Exposure

General Epoxy Resin Safety Instructions & Precautions

These recommendations cover both professional and recreational epoxy use. They'll shield you against epoxy and other dangerous substances if you follow them.

- Use the product that will complete the task with the fewest risks. This lessens or even gets rid of the sources of danger.

- Create a secure store. Install safety measures and adhere to protocols to avoid or decrease exposure. Adequate ventilation comprises everything from low-tech floor or window fans to sophisticated air-filtration and exhaust systems, depending on your workshop. This applies to a variety of gases and dust. Exposure can be decreased by designating a specific cabinet or separate space for storing hazardous materials.

- Wear protective gear for the project, such as respirators, gloves, safety glasses, goggles, and protective clothing. Gloves, eye protection, and protective gear are a must when working with epoxy. A respirator with an organic vapor cartridge will protect you against epoxy vapors. A dust/mist mask or respirator provides the best respiratory defense against noxious dust, wood dust, and epoxy dust.

Minimize Exposure to Epoxy Resins and Hardeners

The US government has not established any exposure limitations on the epoxy resins made by Entropy Resins. These guidelines are based on the appropriate dosages for the raw components I use in my formulations, as specified in the SDS for each product.

Avoid Using Epoxy Products on Your Skin

- Avoid getting resin, hardeners, mixed epoxy, and sanding dust from uncured epoxy in your eyes or on your skin. When working with epoxies, wear safety gear such as gloves and jackets. Remove any resin, hardener, or mixed epoxy that may have accidentally come into contact with your skin. Use a waterless skin cleaner to remove resin or mixed epoxy from your skin because the resin is not water-soluble. You can remove hardeners from your skin by washing them with soap and warm water because they are soluble.

- After using epoxy, including sanding, wash your hands thoroughly with soap and warm water. If epoxy gets on your clothes, you should replace them right away. To get epoxy off your skin and clothes, use skin cleaners. Wearing garments with epoxy on it is not recommended. If the item is mixed with epoxy, you can re-wear it after it has fully hardened.

- Avoid using solvents to attempt to remove epoxy from your skin. The chemicals in the epoxy can penetrate your skin when exposed to solvents, even safe ones like vinegar, increasing the likelihood of overexposure.

- If you get a response, stop applying the epoxy. Work should only be resumed until symptoms subside, typically after several days. When you consistently avoid lengthy exposure to epoxy, its fumes, and sanding dust, improve your epoxy safety precautions.
- Stop using the drug and see a doctor if the problems persist.

Protect Your Vision and Eyes

- Protect your eyes from resin, hardeners, mixed epoxy, and sanding dust by wearing safety glasses or goggles.
- If epoxy unintentionally gets in your eyes, rinse them immediately with low-pressure water for 15 minutes. Obtain medical help.

Protect your respiratory system and lungs.

- Prevent inhaling epoxy vapors and sanding dust. All epoxies have minimal volatile organic contents (VOC). However, fumes can still build up in closed spaces. In small workshops or other restricted areas, provide enough ventilation.
- If you cannot adequately ventilate your workspace, use a respirator with an approved organic vapor cartridge.
- Wear a dust/mist mask or respirator and allow adequate ventilation when sanding epoxy, especially partially-cured epoxy. Sensitization risk is increased when epoxy dust that hasn't thoroughly dried is inhaled. Even when the epoxy has hardened sufficiently to be sanded, it may

take more than two weeks to cure at room temperature fully.

Do not ingest epoxy

- Wash your hands well after using epoxy, particularly before eating or smoking.
- If you unintentionally ingest epoxy, drink much water but resist the urge to vomit. Hardeners are corrosive and can get worse if you vomit them. Contact Poison Control or a doctor right away. Consult the SDS for the product for first aid instructions.

Work Clean

- Maintain order in your workshop to avoid accidental contact with the epoxy resin. Avoid touching doorknobs, light switches, and epoxy containers if your gloves have epoxy residue since you might feel them again after removing them.
- Use a scraper to remove epoxy spills and gather as much debris as possible. Utilize paper towels afterward.
- To control large spills, use absorbent materials like sand, clay, or other neutral substances. To absorb hardeners, AVOID using sawdust or other fine cellulose materials. Reclaim pure resin or hardener for your use.
- Acetone, lacquer thinner, or alcohol are good cleaners or mixers for epoxy. Observe all safety instructions on solvent container labels.
- Hardeners shouldn't be thrown away in garbage cans with sawdust or other fine cellulose materials since they could catch fire.
- Use warm, soapy water to remove any remaining hardener.

Safety Measures for Epoxy Resin Disposal

- Puncture the can's corner to release the resin or hardener's residue into a fresh container.
- Resins and hardeners should never be disposed of as liquids. Waste resin and hardener should be combined in small amounts and allowed to cure into an inert solid.

CAUTION! Epoxy curing pots can heat up to the point where they release dangerous gases and ignite neighboring combustible things. Put containers of mixed epoxy away from construction sites and flammable items in a well-ventilated area. After the solid epoxy mass has thoroughly cooled and hardened, you dispose of it. Observe any municipal, state, or federal disposal laws.

Epoxy-related hazards

Uncontrolled Epoxy Curing

Exothermic chemical reactions that produce heat are used to cure epoxy. Epoxy can heat up to the point where it melts plastic, burns your skin, or sets adjacent combustibles on fire if left to heal in a small area, like a mixing pot. An epoxy mass produces more heat, the more significant or thickens a hundred is. One hundred grams of mixed epoxy can weigh up to 400 grams.

Pour the combined resin and hardener into a roller pan or another wide, shallow container to prevent heat accumulation. Epoxy should be applied in multiple thin layers instead of one thick one when filling vast spaces. Heat buildup and uncontrolled curing are rare in bonding and coating applications because spreading the epoxy into thinner layers dissipates heat.

Hazardous gasses like carbon monoxide, nitrogen oxides, ammonia, and probably certain aldehydes are created as the combined resin and hardener thermally decompose. When warmed, such as using a flame to remove a cast or an implanted object, these gases are cured overheated. Work in an area with good ventilation, and only use a flame as a last resort. Set the container aside where you can keep an eye on it while the remaining mixed epoxy cures. Vapors can be spread out and directed away from people using a fan. Respirators that purify the air might not be sufficient for these vapors and gases.

A fire may start if hardeners are mixed with sawdust, woodchips, or other cellulose. Heat is produced when the hardener is poured on top of or combined with sawdust due to the amine's reaction with the air and moisture. This can ignite the sawdust if it is not extinguished soon. Never attempt to clean up a hardener spill using sawdust or other cellulose material. Don't put hardener that hasn't been utilized in a garbage bin alongside cellulose items like sawdust.

Periodic Entropy Since epoxy resins and hardeners have flash points of more than 200°F (93°) and disperse slowly; they are categorized as non-flammable chemicals. In the presence of epoxy fumes, furnaces, wood stoves, and other heat sources do not provide a significant fire risk.

Spraying epoxy

Epoxy spraying carries significant dangers to one's health and safety. Hence I never advise it. AA little mist of epoxy is released from a spray gun nozzle, making it too easy to breathe in. Other health issues, as well as severe lung damage, may result from this. Your skin may become sensitized and experience an allergic reaction if this mist settles on it. Your eyes could become injured if it determines there.

Compared to other application methods, spraying releases more dangerous volatile components. Health and safety issues increase when solvents are used to thin the epoxy. The flammability and health risks are the same as any spray painting job. You can reduce dangerous vapor and mist when spraying epoxy by using isolation and enclosure, such as a ventilated and filtered spray booth. Wear a respirator that delivers air and full-body protective clothing at all times.

Removing Unused Hardener And Epoxy

Follow these steps to dispose of any leftover resin and hardeners properly.

- Save any leftover resin and hardeners for upcoming projects to reduce waste. When kept in sealed containers, epoxy materials from Entropy Resins have a long shelf life.
- Unwanted resin and hardener should be combined before allowing the mixture to dry and cool to a non-hazardous solid.
- Draining is more superficial in warm vessels.
- Attempt to empty the container owing away any empty resin or hardener containers. At the time of disposal, the container's inside should contain no more than 3% of its total weight.
- Recover any uncontaminated epoxy that has been spilled or leaked. It is waste if it is polluted. If you clean up a spill with solvent, the contaminated epoxy-solvent mixture may be considered a controlled hazardous waste.
- Do not ever release hazardous waste into the air, water, or ground. Many localities organize periodic waste collections and accept domestic waste for proper disposal.
- The preceding disposal recommendations might not align with your location's rules and ordinances. Consult your

local, state, and federal laws if you're unsure.

Epoxy Safety Overview

You are responsible for your health and safety. By being knowledgeable about the items you use, following the safety instructions for epoxy resin, and adopting shop safety precautions, you can safeguard your health and safety when utilizing Entropy Resins epoxy products. Each Entropy Resins product label has the necessary hazard warnings and safety instructions.

CHAPTER 07 EASY RESIN CRAFT TO MAKE AT HOME

Incredible Resin Art Ideas You Won't Believe Are Doable at Home

Combining epoxy resin and hardener produces a stunning, rock-solid finish over nearly any material. Even though the resin is simple to work with, preparation is essential. Set up your workspace and equipment before mixing the first batch. A dust-free room or garage (preferably 65°F-70°F) should have heavy-duty plastic covering the floors and work surface.

Use disposable cups and stir sticks for simple cleanup, and wear old clothes and latex gloves. For flat tasks like artwork, you should also have a level on hand to ensure that the resin distributes evenly. It's time to play now that your room is ready, starting with easy tasks like coasters and glossy artwork. You'll have enough resin because most packages are large enough to use for several projects.

1. Glossy Impact

Easy art may be created with art paper, a canvas, and resin mixture, like the enormous succulent in this wall gallery. Attach art paper to a canvas, such as this 10x10 Inch Wrapped Canvas, while working on a level, safe surface.

More decoupage medium should be applied to the paper, smoothing out any air bubbles and letting it dry. Use your finger to round the edges after pouring the clear resin into the center and allowing it to flow down the sides of the sculpture. Give the artwork 24 hours to dry. To prevent dust from gathering on the artwork's surface, I advise placing a big box or plastic tub over it.

2. Rocky Coast

These simple-to-make coasters resemble split geodes and are the ideal introduction to resin painting. Using a glue gun and glue sticks, pipe the contour of a rock shape onto a silicone mat to create a form for each coaster. When building up the edge, add some more layers and, if you like, some rocks and glitter.

When dry, combine a few drops of purple, gold, blue, and white acrylic paint in each cup of clear resin, swirling to ensure a uniform tint. Pour a small amount of one color in the center and then repeat with the remaining shades to create the appearance of rings. The colors will spread and meld. Add some sparkle.

Finish with the white paint, giving it a swirled appearance using a stir stick, then use a heat gun to melt the color and remove air bubbles. To protect your furniture, line the bottoms with felt and paint the edges with gold metallic paint after giving them 24 hours to cure.

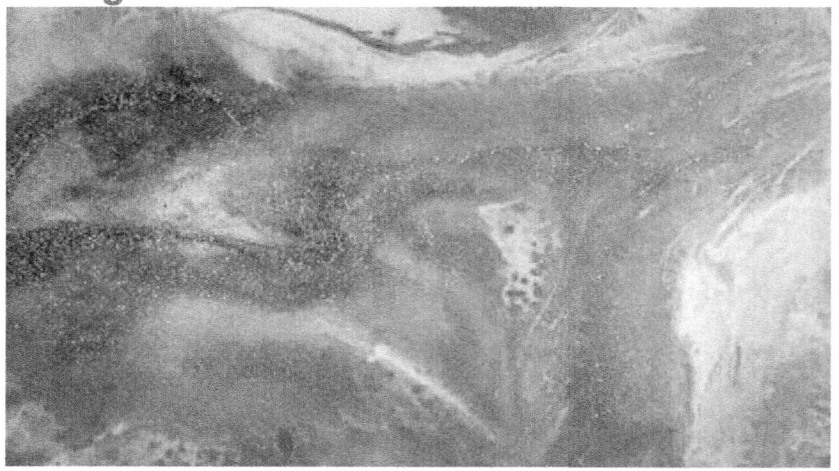

3. **Making Waves**

Resin mix, a blank artist canvas (ours is 24 x 24 inches), and a few craft paints produce resin art that is so beautiful you can almost hear the waves breaking. Combine resin with a few drops of each of the following paint colors, using a different plastic cup for each color: The colors used are deep blue, teal, light blue, and white with some clear resin. Utilized a total of 32 ounces of mixed resin for this canvas. Pour the transparent resin into the form of a canvas's stripes or waves.

Pour the blues and teals over the canvas while moving in the same direction (and keeping the colors apart), blending if desired with a gloved finger. Use a heat gun to continue combining the colors. Sprinkle some blue or teal glitter on the canvas to make it shimmer. Spread thin white resin stripes to resemble foam, using heat to combine the colors. Cover with a sizable box or tub to keep the surface free of dust as it cures flat for at least 24 hours.

Tip: To conceal drips at the canvas edge and give your DIY artwork a polished appearance, trim it with a thin frame.

4. River Still Life

Use this simple concept to capitalize on the river rock table trend. Wash river rocks with soapy water, then allow them to air dry (or purchase a set from a crafts store). Arrange the stones inside a lamp with a glass base and a detachable top. Then, add resin to the center of the rocks, allowing them to fill in around the pebbles. Spray some polyacrylic spray on a fake flower, let it dry, and then place it over the rocks. Before utilizing the lamp, give the resin 24 hours to dry out.

5. Resin Photo Art

Use resin art to carefully preserve images in a location where you'll see them every day. Resin art isn't merely comprised of abstract designs. I utilized clear resin and a sizable family portrait to personalize this wood jewelry box. Trim your photo to fit within the resin mold of your choice to create your own, then pour and spread the resin over the surface until it is completely coated. Heat the resin using a heat gun to eliminate bubbles before allowing it to dry.

6. Cubist Design

When enclosed in resin art, dried and synthetic greenery doesn't deteriorate. Center it in the bottom of a square resin mold if you're working with a single large object (like the fake air plant and silk flower I used). Use a heat gun to reheat the resin mixture to remove bubbles before adding it to the mold. Pour over the item and leave it for 24 hours before taking it out of the mold. Fill the mold with clear resin to the brim for smaller flowers, attach the foliage and blooms into the resin using a sharp stick, and allow it to cure.

7. Doodle Craft

Decorate a tabletop with resin drips in various colors and a marking pen. Draw natural forms like leaves, berries, and flowers to cover the surface with patterns. Use stamps or stencils instead of doodling if you lack confidence in your abilities. Filling certain portions of the way with colored resin using an artist's brush and gently tapping will give it a three-dimensional appearance.

8. Sweet Accents

Amplify the charm of commonplace items. A wooden napkin ring is given a sweet touch by a candy mold that is capped with resin and filled with sugar sprinkles.

9. Resin Buttons

In just a few simple steps, you can create your handcrafted buttons. Add buttons to sweaters, throw pillows, and other crafts to enhance the homemade look. Purchase a resin button mold, epoxy resin, polyamine hardener, and acrylic paint in the colors you like for the buttons before continuing. Add a little bit of the acrylic craft paint to the resin and mix to color. If the button holes are covered in resin, take the button from the mold when it is still rubbery (a few hours later), and insert a pin to reveal the holes. If not, wait 24 hours before removing the buttons from the mold.

10. Napkin Rings

Add resin accents to simple napkin rings. To make these chic flowers, I employed a fondant mold. To manufacture it, mix acrylic craft paint into a 1:1 mixture of epoxy resin and polyamine hardener before pouring the mixture into a rubber mold and letting it dry for 24 hours.

Remove the ornament from the mold before the resin can fully harden if you wish to curl it around the napkin ring. The flexible resin should be gently bent around the ring's curvature, hot-glued to the ring, and then let to finish drying.

11. Cabinet Knobs

Add playful flowery resin knobs cast in contact lens cases to spruce up cabinet doors. Place a piece of vintage jewelry upside down in the mold after spraying the case with mold release and adding resin. Top with a machine screw that has been put at a 90-degree angle once the resin has reached the consistency of gel (after about 20 minutes). Before removing the knob from its mold, let it dry for 24 hours. Before mounting, provide a space between the knob and the cabinet door by threading a machine nut onto the screw.

12. Door Knob

Something as straightforward as a doorknob may be given a little glitz and beauty! Add resin to complete the look of a practical concave-face doorknob in a few easy steps. To create a circle that fits the knob's curve, punch a piece of scrapbook paper to fit the knob's face and cut a slit from the edge to the middle of the article. Apply two coats of decoupage material on the doorknob after attaching the form.

After the decoupage mixture has dried, center a beautiful ornament on the handle. Pour a 1:1 combination of epoxy resin and polyamine hardener on top while working on a level surface. Before installing the doorknob, wait 24 hours.

13. Picture Frame

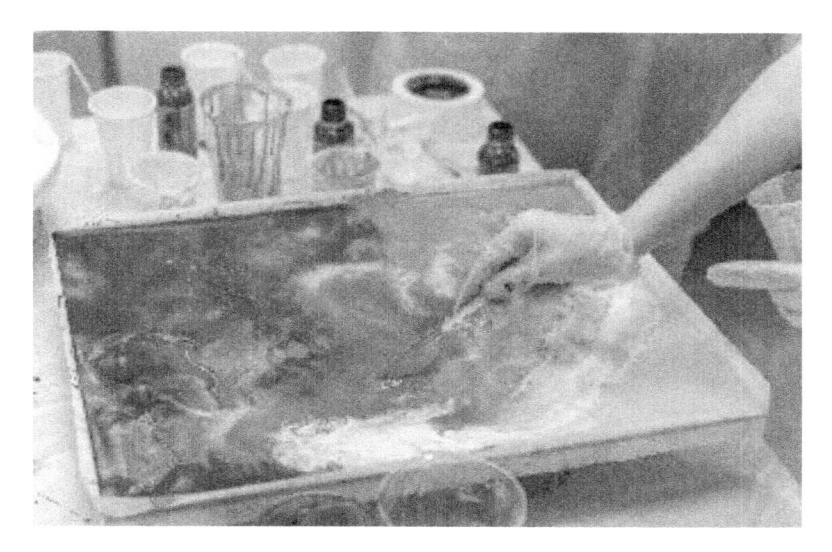

Put a particular photo on display with this simple frame. Cut off the picture. Cut a second paper circle and attach it to the back to give the image weight. Decoupage medium is used to seal both sides; allow to dry. Spray mold release within a soap mold.

After that, put the photo on top of the resin. Insert the picture facedown into the resin using a toothpick. Before removing the frame from the resin mold, let it for 24 hours to dry. Cut some lovely paper to fit the back of the frame, then fix it with spray glue to complete the look. Use a small easel to display the finished photography project.

14.   Floral Paper Weight

Who would have imagined a paperweight would be valuable? Create this attractive paperweight to hold errant papers on your desk or work surface. All you need to add a fashionable touch is resin, a bowl for a mold, and dried flowers. Fill a plastic paint mixing cup with resin and top it off with mold release. Using a toothpick, "float" dried flowers—I used dried baby's breath—at different levels in the resin to add dimension. Before removing the paperweight from its mold, let it dry for 24 hours.

15.   Suncatcher

To reflect light and color throughout the room, hang this sea glass-inspired mobile in a bright window. To create this vibrant design, you need some resin, water-bottle ice cube trays, and a few drops of food coloring. Epoxy resin and polyamine hardener should be poured into the rubber ice cube trays in a 1:1 ratio. Each resin mold should have one or two drops of food coloring added before being stirred.

After they have dried, take the reflectors out of the mold and screw an eye into the top of each one. The fishing line should be tied to the hooks before suspending the glasses from a metal ring at various heights.

CHAPTER 08 BEST RESIN CRAFT IDEAS: RESIN CRAFTINGPROJECTS

What Is Resin Crafting?

Resin craftsmanship can be viewed from many angles, but what is it at its core? Construction or reproduction of forms using a variety of molds is known as resin crafting. Epoxy resin in liquid form is poured into these molds to fill them. After that, as the liquid dries and hardens, a flawless reproduction of the negative from the mold hold is created.

The idea is that resin can be used to duplicate everything found in a mold. Why would you want to do this? You might want more of a particular item, have a favorite ornament, or wish to utilize your imagination to make something unique and one-of-a-kind. Whatever your motivation, there is something for everyone in epoxy resin crafts, and there are several types of epoxy resin for various uses. Why is resin available in such wide varieties?

Several resin kinds are available for different applications since some resins are plain, others are colored, some are multicolored, and some are plastic for additional rigidity. How many uses for resin are there? The wide range of resins available is well justified when you consider that epoxy resin is employed in every aspect of modern civilization, from crafting to automotive engineering to the construction of Jewish artifacts and even tool insulation.

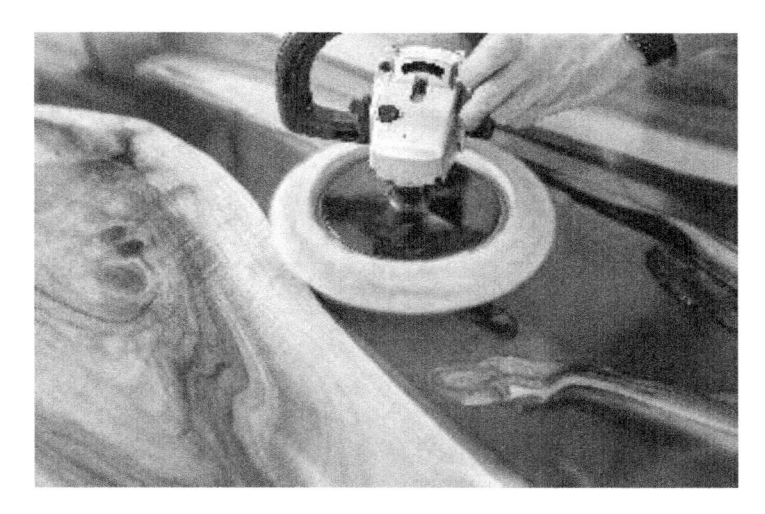

When Was the First Resin Made?

Although you wouldn't be entirely mistaken if you assumed that resin was a relatively recent discovery, the first synthetic resin was produced in 1909. Because it was pliable and thus versatile, the first resin iteration—Bakelite—could be utilized for thousands of diverse purposes.

Various naturally occurring resins were previously available, but they might be challenging to grow and even more difficult to work with. This is why the invention of Bakelite at the start of the 20th century marked the beginning of the "plastic" age.

You may remember the Tupperware craze of the 1970s when several homemakers and television commercials urged purchasing this innovative, cost-effective, and durable line of containers that could be used to store almost everything you could think of.

Even though there are tight restrictions governing which plastics can be used in mass manufacturing today and that this type of plastic isn't particularly beneficial for the environment, back then, firms saw dollar signs in the research and development of resin-related items.

Plastic resins are essentially a by-product of the cracking process used in oil refining. As a result of this procedure, the substance is changed into either propylene resin or ethylene resin, which can subsequently be reused, molded, colored, and sold to the general public.

Like other polymers, epoxy resin is created through a reaction between epichlorohydrin and bisphenol-A. By changing the chemical makeup of the finished plastic, several varieties of resin can be made.

Although it may appear complicated, there are several straightforward techniques to work with resin to get the desired outcome. There are countless possibilities because some materials are so powerful that they can even be used in place of metals!

In light of this, I should probably return to crafts made from epoxy resin. As we've already indicated, the resin may create various objects. However, you do not need to use the readily available molds in stores or online. If you were to make your manufacturer, you could make a mold of whatever you discover and reproduce.

Many people take advantage of this by purchasing resin mold-making kits, replicating desired forms, personalizing them, and then selling them as a hobby or side hustle. Considering what you can make with these resin mold kits with imagination and perseverance, they are accessible and reasonably priced.

Toys for kids, electronic parts for cars, jewelry, food molds, and even shoes might all be cloned! However, if you decide to go this path, Be careful not to use anyone's artwork or intellectual property without that person's permission.

What could be included in resin?

Resins can be tailored in several ways to suit your preferences. Here are some intriguing accents you may use to add personality to your epoxy resin projects. These upgrades are cheap and straightforward, but they scratch the surface of the potential.

- Glitter
- Little things
- Coloring agent
- Dyes
- Flowers
- Clothing beads
- Photographs
- Wood shavings
- Sequins

What kind of materials can you use resin on?

If you use your imagination, the resin may be applied to practically any surface. When people talk about resin, they often refer to the castings you can make using the molds they come with. Here are a few daily applications for resin. It's usually a good idea to do some research on the materials you're working with because some surfaces can require extra prepping.

What Materials Can I Use Resin On?

- Metal Surface
- Wood Surfaces
- Mortar Surfaces
- Plastic Surfaces
- Canvas Backings
- Glass Surfaces
- Paper Surfaces
- Ceramic Surfaces

What Materials Can't I Use Resin On?

- Wax
- Polyurethane (PU) Surfaces
- Grease or Oil
- Silicone
- Polyethylene
- Polypropylene
- Painters Tape
- Parchment

What Kinds of Molds Are Appropriate for Resin Casting?

Molds exist in various shapes and sizes, allowing people to use them to make many incredible things. Molds can also be made from different materials, incorporating various casting materials and resin kinds. Here are a few illustrations of the other molds you might encounter during resin casting.

Plastic Molds / Store-Bought Silicone

These mold varieties are more frequently purchased. Why? Because they are simple to make and inexpensive to generate in large quantities. However, not all of them are built of recyclable materials, making them not necessarily environmentally friendly.

These molds can be used to create a variety of molds that are usually seen in starting kits or children's toys. They are frequently affordable.

Since there isn't much surface friction, which would otherwise cause the resin to attach to surfaces, they frequently have a smooth surface. They also have the advantage of being easy to clean, allowing frequent use.

DIY Latex and Silicone Molds

You are not required to utilize the molds manufacturers sell because they come with resin and harden. Although you do have the option of producing your molds using kits for either rubber or latex, the majority of people prefer the simple fun of generating unique forms.

In essence, some substances can be combined to create a particular kind of putty that can duplicate a form by leaving a negative imprint. This was the standard procedure for reproducing objects in resin before 3D printing, and plastic molds were invented.

Prepare and shape the mold-making materials around the item you want to copy; remove the silicone or latex of the object after allowing it to dry for the amount of time recommended by the manufacturer. You are now prepared to begin making resin castings.

Which Projects for Resin Crafting Are Best for You?

It would take a very long time to list everything made of resin. Check out a few resin crafts projects that you can finish in two to three hours instead, whether you're working on them alone, with friends, or with family.

1. **Resin Tabletop**

If you enjoy DIY home improvements, this is a great first project. You can utilize resin tabletops to add essential aesthetic touches to your house or go all out and construct something unique. The experience will be a ton of fun in either scenario! Before you start, gather the following materials: a tabletop, a base coat, the resin colors you want to show up in your workpiece, a paintbrush, a heat gun or blowtorch, a short PVC pipe, and several cups to mix them in.

The first step is to blend and apply the base coat of resin to your tabletop. Depending on the resin colors you have chosen, this color may either stand out sharply or blend in beautifully. After the foundation layer has been put in place, use a paintbrush to evenly and flushly apply the resin to the surface and let it dry.

Use a blow torch or heat gun to eliminate bubbles and expedite drying. Combine the various resin colors in their cups once they have dried. After blending the colors, place the PVC pipe on the table and pour the pigments into the cylinder.

Slide the cylinder in the desired pattern after they have been poured in to finish creating your tables. Apply the final clear coat on your piece of art after the resin has dried, then take in the beauty of it.

2. Resin Jewelry

This is one of the unique venues for beginners to start their resin casting experience. When it comes to jewelry casting, there are a ton of creative paths you may go down, and the most significant part is that you can wear your creations later on! Jewelry castings are simple to create and straightforward to find their molds. If you went to the store to buy one, you would undoubtedly find that jewelry resin molds are sold in packs of multiple molds.

Hair clips, rings, earrings, bracelets, necklaces, and even chokers are standard accessories that you should be able to construct easily. This is the most straightforward resin craft for beginners because you must combine the resin and hardener before pouring the mixture into the mold of your choice.

To make your casting more appealing, add grains of rice, individual letters, glitter, or color swirls while the resin cures. Attaching a pin or chain plug is also optional. If you want that effect, you may incorporate these modifications into your resin as you combine it with the hardener. Anything you can wear technically qualifies as an accessory. As a result, endless items can be turned into jewelry using epoxy resin crafts.

3. Resin place mats and Coasters

Is there anything more advantageous than a hobby you can practice every day? The capacity to create products that can be used throughout your home is one of the characteristic aspects of renin making. Despite this, castings for placemats and coasters are some of the more popular beginner resin crafts.

Jewelry-related popular beginner resin crafts are not the only ones available. Why, if I may ask? These castings make a fantastic birthday or holiday presents for your friends and family because they are simple to manufacture and can be personalized.

The possibilities are unlimited; you could design a set of coasters or placemats using family photos, make one for each family member using their favorite color, or incorporate something special into a set of coasters to act as a constant reminder of your friends and loved ones. These molds are fantastic since they are strong, versatile, and straightforward.

If you wish to reproduce the shape of a coaster or placemat, mix your resin and hardener, pour the mixture into the mold, and let it set. Aside from the contents, keep in mind that resin may also be cut and sanded, allowing you to market your creations.

Like jewelry, coasters and placemat molds are frequently supplied in sets, giving you the extra benefit of producing multiple separate units at once. This mold is ideal for people who want to offer their houses or the items they plan to give others a personalized touch.

4. Resin Light Bulbs

I frequently overlook a practical use as significant as light production when considering epoxy for crafts. Although it may sound a little absurd, the resin can be used to make light bulbs that are beautiful to look at and effective in illuminating the area around you. Given that resin is not glass and does not refract light, how is this accomplished? Well, it is simple.

It just so happens that when an LED (light-emitting diode) is inserted under the lightbulb cap, crystal resin that has been molded into the shape of a lightbulb with the proper chemical composition makes a usable lightbulb! The correct shape/form of light is perfectly absorbed and reflected by crystal resin!

Epoxy is frequently used for crafts as an exercise in aesthetics, and this does fill a rustic, relaxing niche that is currently very in demand. To begin with, casting like this, you don't need to be a rocket scientist. As we did with the previous castings, combine the resin and the hardener, then pour the mixture into the mold. All that's left to do is add the LED to the top of the dried-out light bulb casting, remove it from the mold, add the lightbulb cap, and you're good to go!

5. Using resin and alcohol ink together

There are hundreds, if not thousands, of resin crafting ideas accessible, but some might get more difficult the further you go down the rabbit hole. If you're searching for a quick and simple trick, try adding alcohol ink to your resin casting.

What distinguishes alcohol ink from ordinary ink? Consider the impact of resin dye and regular ink as being more subdued than their alcohol counterpart on a casting. Alcohol ink is frequently used with crystal resin because it enhances the resin type's overall glassy appearance. Additionally, it distinguishes itself from other coloring agents by preserving the resin's clarity.

Alcohol ink's key selling point is that it keeps the resin translucent after the added dye. This indicates that you may achieve the same result by mixing a small amount of this ink with a clear resin, which is a little less expensive than colored resin.

Because it is affordable and can produce some intriguing effects, which few people are aware of, many individuals prefer to employ this approach in their DIY resin projects. You may drop anything made of resin without shattering it into a million pieces. The appearance is comparable to stained glass without the hassle of dealing with such a delicate material. Consider objects like "stained glass" bowls, drinkware, placemats, and coasters.

6. Resin Paintings

This isn't exactly what most people consider an "entry-level" DIY resin project, so I should start by stating that. Resin paintings are relatively new, and if you are skilled at creating them, you might be able to sell them for a reasonable price.

They can be a little challenging to create outside of the commercial market. Painting requires considerable talent (any fine art); however, working with a medium like resin can be frustrating if you don't have the correct temperament. Please persevere; resin painting can be enjoyable, a great way to express oneself, and an excellent indicator of the creator's attitude.

Their best feature is that designs made with resin on canvas or another surface are frequently surprisingly good. It could take one or two tries to get the hang of things if you're trying to construct anything specific. It can be expensive to purchase resin in the numbers required to create paintings of a standard size, but this doesn't preclude you from making a smaller piece of art specifically for you.

A peaceful afternoon alone with your thoughts and a lot of resin and hardener in the colors of your choice could be seen as rewards in and of themselves.

To ensure that the paint is permanently kept, you can add a glossy clear coat after you finish. Using a blowtorch or heat gun is preferable on the workpiece's surface. Could you make sure there are no bubbles in it?

7. Using resin to fill wood voids

Most resin enthusiasts like this process, but it could be daunting if you don't know what you're doing. There's a strong possibility that if you have a Pinterest account, you've seen resin used in this manner. Before resin became available to people like us, hardwood tables with sizable parts missing or that had merely deteriorated over time were thrown in the trash.

Some people may have recently spotted intentionally removing pieces of their larger tables to fill them with colorful resin. Is this decent? Is it important?

No, I don't believe that at all. The end effect is impressive and even somewhat strengthens the table. It might take a little longer than a weekend to accomplish this. Just pour the resin into the cracks. That sounds easy. Before you can start running, you must first make sure your surface is level and sand it to make it flush. Additionally, ensure you choose the right color combination and have enough resin to give the impression of flow.

Since this void filling needs a significant amount of resin, I suggest starting with a smaller workpiece and increasing your level over time. For the whole family, especially on larger projects, filling gaps with wax is a fun way to give old furniture new life.

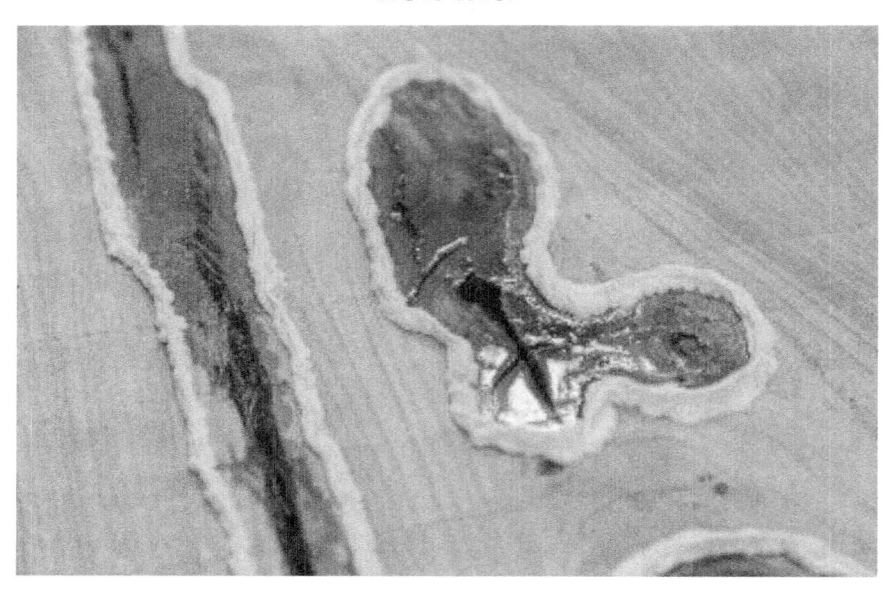

How Are Resin Castings Made?

Even the simplest castings might be frightening if you have never worked with resin before, even if knowing what you can make with resin is excellent. You can use the following tips to ensure your resin workpieces' creation goes as quickly as possible. It would help if you worked in a well-ventilated area when mixing and pouring your resin and hardener since resin is hazardous once it has hardened.

Set Up Your Work Area

Working with resin may be dirty, regardless of whether you create large or little casings. Setting up your workspace is essential since, once the resin has set and solidified, removing it off surfaces can be difficult. You want to begin by laying out a tarp to keep any resin from coming in contact with the neighboring surfaces. To protect your hands, lips, and face, gather paper towels, gloves, and a cloth face mask.

Next, depending on the size of your workpiece and the number of colors you intend to use, prepare your mixing containers and sticks for each color. Finally, prepare your molds by slathering them in a thin layer of baby powder or anti-adhesive coatings similar to those in stores.

Mix the resin and hardener.

Time to get filthy now! F This can be a little nerve-wracking for beginners because you must mix your resin and hardener at a 1:1 ratio to produce the best resin casting results. You can experience mixing the resin and hardener and working within the mixture's pot life by beginning with small epoxy resin projects. Combining a little amount of resin and hardener to obtain a sense of the viscosity and dry time of the solution will help you determine how long you have to pour the resin before it completely cures.

Try to pour the resin and hardener together as gently as possible; this will lessen the amount of trapped air brought on by the change in the liquid's surface tension and the possibility of leaks. It's a good idea to practice this method if you're new to resin casting before attempting to remove these air bubbles from the resin later on with a torch or a heat gun.

Small resin casting projects are perfect for beginners because they let them practice working quickly and efficiently while also introducing them to working with resin, which is slightly different from working with other crafting materials.

Prepare Your Mold

You can save time by preparing for mold over a long period. Why? Most new users of resin casting discover that getting their castings out of the mold is only half the challenge. Various molds and resins have different best practices for ensuring a painless demolding process, which will prevent damage to your mold and casting during removal.

It's usual practice to use an anti-adhesive spray to prevent resin castings from sticking to their molds. To speed up the demolding process, you can quickly add other friction-reducing ingredients to the interior of the mold, such as baby powder. These are commonly available online and at the majority of merchants.

Other anti-adhesive substances shouldn't be used since they can interfere with the chemical composition of the molds you want to employ. Manufacturers may add anti-adhesive sprays explicitly designed for use with mold-specific molds.

Fill Your Mold

Even though this process is simple, there are a few tips and tricks to remember to get the most out of your resin molds and create flawless castings. Pouring resin and hardener into your mold is not sufficient. Remember that your castings may have air bubbles due to the resin's surface tension being different from the mold's, which might cause imperfections.

When using epoxy for crafts, place a small amount of resin within the mold to form a thin coating. After this layer has been run, let it settle before slowly pouring the remaining rein into the mold.

Before allowing the resin to dry, ensure the mold is tightly shut once it has been poured into it (if you have a two-part mold). If your mold has two parts, ensure the connection between them is strong and consistently upholds its integrity.

Take Off Your Cast

The molds that come with epoxy for crafts are often built to work flawlessly with them, but if you want to use a different sort or brand of epoxy with your present molds in the future, it may be difficult to remove the epoxy once it has been set.

As I previously mentioned, one effective way to ensure that your castings don't stick to the mold interior during the demolding process is to apply anti-adhesive materials to the interior of the mold before the resin is poured inside.

However, if you are excessively forceful when extracting the casting from the mold, you risk accidentally harming both the casting and the mold. When taking the casting from the mold, it would be beneficial to try to pop it out of the cavity rather than peel it from it. Try heating pieces of the mold if your molds are difficult to work with or have weird shapes. This will cause the mold to expand and release any casting that has been trapped inside.

It's time to put your newfound knowledge to the test now that you are aware of how resin was created, what it is made of, how to cast resin on your own, what it can be used for, which forms it can be used to create and which ones are the simplest. Always operate in a well-ventilated room, wear personal protection equipment, and make sure your workspace is appropriately covered.

CONCLUSION

A liquid substance called epoxy resin is blended with different color pigments and additives to form resin art, a blend of distinctive patterns and textures. In the unusual painting technique known as resin art, no conventional brushes, acrylic, or oil paints are used. For the new generation of creatives, it is regarded as a sophisticated painting. Ordinary artists can be distinguished from resin artists by the distinctive materials they use to create their works.

I hope you learned "what is resin art?" and found this book valuable. Try out all the techniques and tools suggested. Order a resin pack immediately to start creating something of your own. Slow and steady wins the race. Try out various pigments, colors, and creative materials. Consider posting your designs on social media if you perform well. Before beginning your epoxy resin business, always choose a quality resin art kit. Working with resin is easy and versatile. Impressive resin art is possible with general knowledge and basic skills. The possibilities for using resin in the craft are endless.

The process of creating a unique resin painting is relatively tricky and sophisticated. In addition, preparations must be made before the work can start. However, producing a resin piece of art is worthwhile for any hobby artist since the stunning end product is worth the effort. When different color pigments and additives are mixed with a fluid substance called epoxy resin, it produces a variety of distinctive patterns and textures. Epoxy resin, a synthetic material created to simulate the desirable qualities of natural resin, is used in resin art. The two components of epoxy resin are synthetic polymer resin and a hardener. A chemical reaction occurs between the components of the resin mixture, progressively hardening it (when combined with a hardener) to a solid plastic.

It can be simple to jump in without conducting any research. However, resin art has unique difficulties, and there is a lot to learn, which can be intimidating. Beginners are encouraged to practice the straightforward methods used to produce stunning resin artwork to master them eventually. Due to its unique properties and compatibility with a wide range of materials, epoxy resin offers countless creative possibilities. Depending on the size of your project and how thrifty you are when buying the necessary tools, the cost of starting to experiment with resin art will vary. The cost of your new activity increases as your ideas grow. Your imagination will thrive in this secure and simple hobby!

BONUS:

How To Resin Rocks: Guide For Beginners

Resin can be easily applied to rocks (and other embedded objects). Resin elevates embedded artwork to a whole new level. In addition to acting as an adhesive to mount your materials, it also adds a glossy sheen that accentuates the texture of your collage and compels you to reach out and touch it. - You may mount the piece of art and pour the resin right on nel! Clean and smooth edges are made possible by panels with a raised lip that helps hold resin.

Your rock collage will transform from good to stunning in 24 hours by measuring, combining, pouring, spreading, covering, and waiting.

Supplies:

- A wooden art panel measuring 12 by 12.
- Ornamental rocks.
- Epoxy resin
- A spreader, a stir stick, and a set of nitrile gloves.
- A grade.
- A measuring cup with precise measurements.
- A mixing vessel.
- A small torch, such as our Artist's Torch.
- Toothpicks.
- A container to protect your object while it cures, such as an empty cardboard box or a plastic tote with the flaps removed.

Steps:

1. Put Your Rock Collage Together.

Put together your rock collage first. Before you begin, you can either freehand your design or create creating outline into the wood panel (like we did). Use resin or a very minimal adhesive to attach your rocks to the board (resin is the most potent adhesive in the world.) Allow your collage to set and dry for at least 24 hours once all the rocks have been mounded, and your collage is finished.

TIP: *Because wood is an organic object, it can have trapped air that eventually escapes as bubbles in your resin. Gas bubbles can be affected by a wide range of factors, including humidity, the type of wood used, and the degree of drying of the wood. A technique to stop bubbles is to pre-seal wood using a spray or brush-on sealer. But before resining your finished project, I always recommend testing with your specific materials so you know what effects to expect. I've had enough success with these wood panels to know that they don't need to be pre-sealed. Again, pre-sealing is always a good idea if it makes you feel more at ease.*

2. **Determine how much resin is required.**
   Enter the length and breadth of your object into an online resin Calculator to determine how much resin you'll need.

   TIP: *5 oz of resin is required for a standard 1/8" coating on a 12 by 12" panel (2.5 oz resin and 2.5 oz hardener). The lip of your board should be measured because it may differ.*

3. **Stir well**

Measure out precisely equal amounts of resin and hardener while wearing gloves. You should stir quickly for 3 minutes while scraping the mixing bowl's sides and bottom.

4. **Pour the art resin in.**

Using a disposable foam brush, distribute the resin from the piece's center to the perimeter so you can work around the pebbles. Before the resin becomes too thick to spread, you'll have around 45 minutes to perform.

TIP: *Because resin makes things appear wet, it can darken natural objects like rocks, wood, and other raw materials. You can* *accurately predict the appearance of your products once the resin is applied if you test them first with water.*

5. Put your artist's torch to use.

Just long enough to cause the bubbles in the resin to pop, hold the flame of your Artist's Torch a few inches above the resin surface while continuously moving the torch from side to side.

6. Final inspection of your work

After burning the item, examine the resin under a light to search for missing bubbles, minute hairs, or dust, and use a toothpick to get rid of them.

7. Wrap up your Artwork

Allow your item to cure for 24 hours or until it feels solid to the touch then wrap it in plastic wrap or a cardboard box (with the flaps cut off)

8. Wait for 24 hours

You are releasing your artwork after 24 hours!

***TIP:** The resin will be touch-dry after 24 hours. You can certainly hang your artwork now to enjoy it, but if you're thinking about packing it up and shipping it, give the resin at least 72 hours to fully cure before doing so.*

Which resin works best with rocks?

The type of project you are working on and the desired output will determine the best resin for rocks. Epoxy resin is an attractive option for decorative applications since it offers a clear, glossy, long-lasting, and UV radiation-resistant finish. Polyester resin is a better option for structural uses since it is more durable and flexible.

What benefits can resin have over rocks?

Compared to conventional materials, resin for rocks has several benefits, including greater strength, increased flexibility, and a smooth surface. It is a fantastic option for outdoor projects because I

also more UV radiation resistant. It may also be used rapidly and is reasonably simple to deal with.

What Safety Measures Should You Implement When Using Resin for Rocks?

To shield your eyes and skin from the resin while working with resin for rocks, you should always wear safety goggles and gloves. The directions for the specific resin you are using should also be familiar to you, and you should make sure you are working in a well-ventilated location.

How to Fill Epoxy with Crushed Rock?

Jewelry makers and other crafters sometimes use epoxy resin mixed with finely crushed stone as an inlay material. The resin-stone mixture can readily fill cast or carved voids in work. When the resin dries, it looks like intricately inlaid stone. To help you obtain almost any look, from turquoise to granite, there are numerous possibilities for stone type and resin color.

Supplies You'll Need

- Sandpaper Grits of 220 and 400 for Hand Sander
- epoxy resin
- Use paper or tinfoil
- Hardener for Epoxy
- Buffer in Felt
- Toothpick
- Finished Crushed Stone

Step 1

On a sheet of paper, create a pile with the crushed stone you intend to use for your inlay. Your inlay will appear denser as there are more stones used.

Step 2

Epoxy resin and hardener in two equal portions should be applied to the paper. What you'll need to fill the hollow in your inlay should roughly be the combined volume of the two.

Step 3
To get the density of stone you want for the inlay, quickly combine the epoxy resin with a toothpick, then stir in the crushed stone.

Step 4
Use toothpicks to scrape the epoxy-stone mixture off the paper and work it into the inlay. Make sure to fill the inlaid area om bottom to top. A sufficient amount of the mixture should be added, so it mounds just above the inlay cavity's top and extends past the cavity's edge. Any excess should be removed right away.

Step 5
Follow the manufacturer's instructions and let the epoxy completely solidify.

Step 6
Using a hand sander and 220-grit sandpaper, sand the hardened epoxy until it is flat with the surface of the inlaid piece.

Step 7
Change to 400-grit sandpaper and smooth off the epoxy.

Step 8
Apply a felt buffing wheel to the epoxy and buff it to a high luster.

> ***Tip:** A more excellent range of color effects can be achieved by adding epoxy colorants or colored caulk dust to the epoxy. Choose your stone's texture based on the size of your inlay. You can use stone chips to cover a sizable area. It would be best to use incredibly tiny stone fragments for fine jewelry.*

Cautions

When working with two-part epoxy, always employ adequate ventilation. Avoid letting epoxy dry out on your skin. It is preferable to combine less epoxy than not enough. After the initial inlay has dried, adding more epoxy to fill the space will leave noticeable fractures and seams.

Conclusion

There are numerous varieties of resin on the market right now, which makes it challenging to find resin of high quality. Resin can be easily applied to rocks (and other embedded objects). Embedded artwork is brought to a whole new level by resin. You must expect beautiful things to enhance your rock's beauty. We sincerely hope you found this to be both educational and useful.

How to Make Resin Gems

How to Make a Resin Geode?

I can assure you that manufacturing these wonderful small gems couldn't be easier or more enjoyable if you require resin gems for jewelry making, crafting, or decorating. And the best part is that finding the materials you need to construct them is simple. You can have a mountain of gems at your disposal with just some resin, a mold, and extras like glitter. Here are various methods to create beautiful jewels and spice up your upcoming creative project.

Using UV Resin to Create Gems

UV Resin is the best option if you need these gems quickly or want instant gratification. Instead of the 24 hours that 2-part epoxy resins require to cure, this resin uses a UV light to cure, allowing you to have jewels ready for use in only a few minutes. Even though UV resin is more expensive, it is worthwhile if speed is of the essence.

Materials Used

- UV Resin Kit from Mr. Resin
- UV Light Curing (mine came with the above kit)
- Paxcoo Resin Molds for Making Jewelry
- Rubber Mixing Cup (Came with Mr. Resin Kit)
- Craft Sticks or Silicone Stirring Instruments
- LEOBRO 16-Color Epoxy Resin Mica Powder
- Glitter (For the opal-appearing gem, use giant flake glitter).
- Large Glitter Flakes.

Optional:

- The Silicone Work Mat

- Tweezers

1. Plain Clear Gem

1. Put together your work area and put in your UV lamp. Then, fill the gem mold of your choice with UV resin. Don't overfill the mold, please.
2. Verify that the resin has reached all of the corners.
3. Pop any bubbles on the resin's surface with your grill lighter or heat gun.
4. Turn on the lamp, then position it above the gem mold. Depending on how thick the resin is, this could take a while.
5. Turn the mold over and continue curing it from the front after curing from the rear.
6. Test the resin to determine if it is sticky or soft after the light has gone out. Remove it from the mold if it is challenging.
7. You can put the gem under UV light if it seems slimy to the touch. If you contact it when it's sticky, fingerprints will be left on your finished product.

2. Ruby Red Gem

1. Add enough resin to the little mixing cup to fill the mold's gem holes however often you want to.
2. A little bit of the red mica powder, added to the mixing cup, will go a long way. Stir to combine the color thoroughly.
3. Verify that the resin has reached all of the corners.
4. Pop any bubbles on the resin's surface with your grill lighter or heat gun.
5. Turn on the lamp, then position it above the gem mold. Depending on how thick the resin is, this could take a

while.
6. Turn the mold over and continue curing it from the front after curing from the rear.
7. Test the resin to determine if it is sticky or soft after the light has gone out.
8. Remove it from the mold if it is challenging can put the gem back under the UV light if it seems slimy to the touch. If you contact it when it's sticky, fingerprints will be left on your finished product.
9. Put your silicone mixing cup under your UV light to cure and clean it. The mess can then be obliterated from the cup.

Note: It is advisable to use tiny amounts of colorants when combining them with glitters. Adding too much can prevent your item from curing, leaving you with a runny middle and an outside shell.

3. Add-in Gems

1. One of the gem molds should have UV resin squeezed into the bottom of it. Just enough should be added to cover the mold's bottom.
2. Add some small embellishments (I used tiny heart-shaped glitter embellishments) while ensuring they are where you want them to be with your tweezers.
3. Turn on the UV lamp and place it over the mold; let it on for roughly 45 seconds.
4. To finish filling the mold, add additional UV resin.
5. Any resin bubbles on the surface can be popped using a grill lighter.
6. Under the UV light, totally cured.

4. Glitter Gem

1. One of the gem molds should have UV resin squeezed into the bottom of it. Just enough should be added to cover the mold's bottom.
2. Add some glitter on top of the resin in the mold (I used some bright, opaque, white large flake glitter to make it look like opal). Push the glitter just a little bit into the resin using your tweezers.
3. Turn on the UV lamp and place it over the mold; let it on for roughly 45 seconds.
4. To finish filling the mold, add additional UV resin.
5. Any resin bubbles on the surface can be popped using a grill lighter.
6. Under the UV light, totally cured.

Note: Another way to make this is to combine the resin and glitter in the cup, then pour the mixture into the mold and allow it to set. It does have a slightly different impact as a result. You can determine which you prefer after trying both.

You may go wild with making these gems because it is a delightful and simple pastime. See what magnificent little beauties you can make by using your creativity and experimenting with different colors, glitters, and additives.

Producing Resin Gems using 2 Part Epoxy Resin

Materials Used

- ARTISAN RESIN Kit for Epoxy Resin.
- Paxcoo Resin Molds for Making Jewelry.
- Blending Cups (One for plain and one for each color).
- Craft Sticks or Silicone Stirring Instruments.
- Glitter: Small or large glitter is acceptable. Here is some glitter in a large flake form.
- Grill lighter.

Optional:

- The Silicone Work Mat
- Tweezers
- The Timer

Instructions:

1. Set up your workspace, wear gloves, and don your safety glasses. Make sure you have easy access to all of your supplies.
2. Combine a craft stick and resin in a small cup as directed on the packaging. It would be best if you used an accurate timer to time this. (When you are mixing and your hand starts to pain, time moves more slowly.) It would be best to combine this in small batches unless you work exceptionally quickly because your workday will only be between 30 and 45 minutes long.
3. Once the resin is blended, you may pour some of it into the silicone molds that are fashioned like jewels to create clear gems. Don't fill the mold with too much material. To remove any surface bubbles once the resin has been poured, wave the flame of your grill lighter back and forth over the resin. Then, put the mold aside.
4. With a brand-new cup and craft stick, sprinkle some glitter on the cup and then drizzle some resin over it. With the craft stick, stir this mixture just long enough to incorporate the glitter.
5. Put your gem molds with this mixture inside. Work the variety into the corners of the mold using your tweezers or a toothpick (something pointed, of course!). Don't overfill once more.
6. Clear the uncured gems' surface bubbles using your lighter.

7. Until you run out of clear resin or it gets too thick, you can repeat this procedure with different glitters, additives, and mica colorants (whichever comes first).
8. Your resin-filled mold must be set aside to cure. The ideal temperature is just above room temperature. It won't heal and may even get rubbery if your curing place is too chilly (below 70 degrees).
9. You can take your jewels out of the mold after the recommended curing time (for me, it was 24 hours). Not your good sewing scissors! If there is any overfill on the stones, you can carefully remove them and smooth them out with an ordinary nail file.
10. You may now incorporate your finished jewels into various craft projects.

For this two-part epoxy resin, the same additives that you used with the UV resin can be employed, including confetti and mica powders. Although it takes 24 hours to cure, the UV resin is slightly more expensive. Therefore, you might want to try this resin if you have the time and many things to build. Ultimately, it comes down to desire and the kind of project you are doing. Both types of resin produce high-quality goods.

What is a Resin Geode?

You can envision what a resin geode may look like if you can visualize a geode. To be precise, geodes are geological structures that house colorful mineral stuff inside sedimentary or volcanic rocks. The rocks' beautiful crystals are exposed when broken or cut open. Of course, a resin geode is not a genuine geode.

It's a creative take on a geode made of resin, a substance with a hard, polished texture when it cures. To enhance the effects of your resin, you can also add colors, glitter, sparkles, crystals (either real or fake), and metallic paint.

You'll like creating your resin geode if you adore arts and crafts and bright, shiny things. These can be done as relatively flat pieces on a canvas or board, as slices that can serve as coasters, or as more significant, more sculptural pieces.

How to Make a Resin Geode?

Consider taking a tutorial on using resin if you've never worked with the material before. Even for relative beginners, it's not too harsh, but there are many crucial details to remember. Before beginning, it's critical to understand how to handle resin because certain varieties are hazardous, and all call for protective equipment like gloves and a respirator.

Step 1: Compile Your Materials and Prepare Your Work Area

You'll need the following materials to create geode art with resin on canvas or board:

- Parts A and B of the resin
- Safety equipment: an apron, drop cloths, and latex gloves (a respirator and safety glasses are highly recommended)
- Stirrers and a spatula
- cup or jug for measuring
- tape masking
- Use isopropyl alcohol with wet wipes
- Canvas or wooden panel (not a stretched canvas)
- acrylic colors
- Crystals, foils, glitter, glass globules, and as are examples of decorative objects.

Before blending the resin, prepare everything (always according to the instructions on the label). Put on an apron to protect your clothing, long sleeves, gloves, a respirator, safety glasses, and gloves to protect your skin. Cover your table and flooring with safety drop cloths.

Tape up your canvas's four edges to make it easier to mop resin spills.

Lastly, check to see that your work surface is ideally level (use a level marker, if you have one, to prevent this). In case your surface is uneven, the wet resin will dry unevenly.

Step 2: Draft your Geode Shape

Look through geode pictures to choose the one you want to copy. On your canvas, sketch out the contour and primary forms of the design while keeping track of the colors that should be placed near one another for the most significant outcome. Of course, if you'd prefer to use your resin and ornaments more haphazardly, it's OK.

Step 3: Paint on the Canvas

Fill in any lines or areas you sketched out earlier with acrylic paint by painting straight onto the canvas. This is the moment to embellish your geode pattern using metallic foil or glitter.

Step 4: Incorporate crystals or other embellishments

Once the paint has set, you can add crystals made of glass or acrylic to your design. To prevent them from moving when the resin is added later, secure them with a small amount of regular craft glue.

Step 5: Add Resin Layers

Mix the two components as directed on the resin bottles. To reduce waste, mixing in smaller batches is a brilliant idea. You might now choose to resin by mixing in some paint or powder. You must mix up several resin containers individually and pour them over your canvas surface in stages if you want to have different colored resins next to each other that don't combine. It's up to you if you enjoy the effect of blending various colored resins because some people do. To move the resin where you want it, use wooden sticks.

Step 6: Add Glitter Layers

It's preferable to apply any layers of glitter-embedded resin to your canvas at the very end when the sparkles are closer to the surface. Repeat preparing a small batch of clear resin, stirring in some glitter.

Step 7: Optionally apply a clear coat

You might want to add a final transparent layer on top of your colored and glittery layers because clear resin creates a shiny and flawless finish. The resin geode can resemble an agate piece that has been polished if you do this. The texture of your resin geode may be diminished, though, if you've added a lot of glitter or gemstones. So it's entirely up to you if you apply a final clear coat.

20 Best Crystals & Gemstones For Resin Art

These suggestions for adding crystals and gemstones to epoxy resin are the best. You're in luck if you love to create geode resin artwork or river tables but need some inspiration on what to use for crystals or gemstones. Here, you'll find the BEST geode resin art inspiration with gemstones and crystals! We are completely enamored with the geode art and epoxy resin crafts sweeping the DIY community.

Epoxy resin, glitter, crystals, gemstones, and anything else to mimic the appearance of agate or geode, such as gold leaf or pens for producing lines detailing separating the various hues, are all used to make resin art.

What Gemstone Embellishments Could You Apply to Epoxy Resin Art?

When creating resin art, you can use various materials for your gemstones and crystals. For geode resin art, rose quartz, amethyst, and crystals are frequently used as gemstones in epoxy resin. There are a wide variety of materials available. Choose the finest solution for you with the aid of expert gemstone photography.

Read on to find our beautiful suggestions for making the gemstone or crystal component of your resin crafts, epoxy projects, and jewelry. These resin components are necessary to get dazzling embeds that appear as floating or genuine geodes.

To avoid getting hurt, you must wear the appropriate safety gear before performing any of these techniques. Using the proper respirator, eye protection, and gloves is essential when dealing with resin.

Crystals & Gemstones For Resin Art

1. Resin for Bulk Gemstones

You can use a wide variety of gemstones in your geode resin artwork. The materials you require for resin crafts, geode resin art, and other projects can be purchased bulk from gemstones. Any creative project benefits from the luxurious touch that raw gemstones bring, and they can be used to make one-of-a-kind, breathtaking pieces of art.

2. Rose Quartz

Rose quartz is a stunning, functional stone that may be utilized in many resin arts and crafts projects. Its delicate pink color makes it ideal for use in geode resin artwork, and its rough gemstone form works well with more realistic designs. Rose quartz is perfect for anyone wishing to add a touch of refinement to their resin creations.

3. Bulk Amethyst

Bulk purchases of gemstones like amethyst are frequently far more affordable than individual purchases. This implies that you can use high-quality materials for your resin projects while saving money.

Amethyst is one of the most widely used stones for this purpose. When cast in resin, the gorgeous violet color of raw amethyst looks spectacular. It makes sense why this stone appeals to so many artisans. Adding natural amethyst to your next resin pro will give it that wow factor whether you're a novice or an expert.

4. Crystal Quartz

Bulk crystal quartz is the best option for artists who wish to give their resin crafts a touch of luxury. This refined form of quartz, often known as rock crystal, has a beautiful sheen that resembles diamonds.

It gives the appearance of a natural geode when used in geode resin art, with its sparkling crystals snuggled inside a smooth outer shell. Quartz and other uncut raw gemstones are becoming more and more common in resin crafts since they enhance the beauty and worth of handcrafted objects.

5. Crude Amber for Resin

Raw gemstones can provide a dramatic touch to resin jewelry and geode resin art, which might appeal to those who enjoy resin crafts. Amber in bulk is a magnificent material that may be used to make beautiful objects.

The translucent nature of amber resin can assist in highlighting the distinctive shape of the uncut gemstones, and the golden hue provides a cozy and cheery element. Additionally, light, weight, raw amber is perfect for resin jewelry. Further, crafters of all skill levels can benefit from utilizing it because it is so simple.

6. Turquoise Crushed & Tumbled

Turquoise that has been crushed and tumbled is ideal for resin crafts. When utilized to make geode art or jewelry, the raw jewels' vivid blue color is breathtaking. It also makes a beautiful present for resin artists because you can use it to create many resin crafts, including jewelry, geode art, river tables, and ornaments. Crushed and tumbled turquoise is ideal if you're looking for a one-of-a-kind gift for a friend or a unique accessory for yourself.

7. Stone Box Mixes

In this store, you may find bulk raw stones for resin artwork. Some people favor buying large quantities of natural rocks to smash themselves. Any resin creation can benefit from the stunning and individual touch that rough stone crystals can offer.

8. Gemstone Kits

This store has many fantastic kits for jewelry and epoxy resin crafts that you can use if you need smaller gemstone pieces and want a more polished finish. Just be mindful of the size of the project you'll be working on, and whether this kit contains enough jewels to complete the entire piece you're working on.

9. For Geodes, Crushed Glass

Crushed glass is essential for anyone who enjoys using resin in their projects. Beautiful jewelry, accessories, and more may be made using it that imitate actual jewels. The best aspect is that it is reasonably priced and simple to locate in large quantities. You can mix and match the many hues of crushed glass to make your unique designs. When handling it, be careful because the shards might be sharp. Wear safety goggles and gloves.

10. Sea Glass For Embeds in Resin

Sea glass comprises pieces of weathered glass polished by the ocean's lapping waves (doesn't that sound so soothing?). So it's fantastic if you live close to a beach! You can look for sea glass, gather it, and possibly begin a geode resin sea glass project. Sea glass typically comes in pale blue and green tones.

11. Shells for Resin Art in Geodes

Thinking about geodes with white wave crests scattered throughout and turquoise waves as inspiration while we're on the subject of beaches? So romantic, no? Wouldn't real seashells look stunning in place of gemstones in your geode resin artwork?

We are referring to the interior, which is reflective and iridescent, like a section of an oyster shell or a mussel. Here are some dreamy shots for crafts that you can buy for a fantastic price if you want to imitate the beach in your geode resin art for some peaceful and tranquil emotions.

12. Mirror tiles

Your geode resin art will have you oohing and ahhing after you add those reflective bits since they add dazzle and sparkle.

13. Shiny Flat Marbles

These are the ideal way to provide an exposed, "gemstone"-like vibe. You recognize them because you frequently encounter them in fish tanks and flower vases bottoms.

They come in a wide range of colors, and again, depending on the effect you're looking for, you can crush them into tiny bits or keep them whole or partially whole. Every resin artist has to have this on hand!

14. Round Marbles

These bring back memories. As children, we would play with other kids from the neighborhood to see which marbles I could grab while collecting these. But there was always a select handful I refrained from playing with out of concern for failure. Can you identify it?

Because they are all different and unique, those vintage marbles are a fantastic find for your geode resin pours. You can get marbles in solid blocks of color or the original marbles of clear blown glass with colored swirls inside. If you cannot locate your old marble collection, don't worry. I wouldn't want to ruin my early memories and go crazy! (hehe) Grab some instead at a discount.

15. Crystal embellishments in jewelry

If you can find a jewelry-making kit like the one below, you will have many materials. Your imagination is the only thing that will restrict you, from the tiny metal clasps and rings utilized for some attractive and distinctive elements to the beads and stones used.

16. For Geode Resin Art, Gold Leaf

Perhaps you've previously considered incorporating gold, silver, or rose gold leaf in your geode resin artwork. But bet you didn't imagine it being used in this manner: collect some little stones and pebbles from the road or yard, and lightly coat them with Mod Podge or a glue stick. Then cover them with gold leaf, being sure to get the leaf into every nook and cranny of the rocks with a stiff-bristle paintbrush. Now it appears that the pour contains tiny genuine chunks of gold!

17. Decorations for fish tanks

Mainly blue or gold embellishments for resin, fish tank accents provide lovely touches. Fish tank bottoms are frequently coated in a stunning rocky material that would be wonderful for a geode resin art piece. Green, hot pink, blue, and shiny black are all available. You can choose from a wide variety of colors.

18. DIY-Polished Stones & Rocks

Polishing your stones and gemstones is another option. National Geographic is the source of this rock tumbler. Additionally, it starts with half a pound of unpolished, uncut gems. Create your jewels from rocks for geode resin artwork.

19. Swarovski Crystals

Your artwork will become even more collectible thanks to the shine and dazzle added by these stunning crystals. You may achieve the intense glow you're striving for by sprinkling Swarovski crystals here and there.

20. Fire Glass

We've saved the best for last and are putting an exhilarating, high note on our list of gemstone and crystal suggestions for your geode resin art. Have you heard of fire glass? Imagine one of those stunning contemporary fireplaces with the bottom made of sparkling, brilliant glass. The glass is incredibly reflective and luminous since we located a supplier who doesn't tumble it before delivery.

Furthermore, it is tempered and offered in 10-pound jars, allowing you can use it for large projects. Additionally, you can select either 1/2 or 1/4 size pieces. Alternately, you can use both to create a ring made of more significant reflecting bits and a call made of little geode sections to make it appear more uniform.

Conclusion

It's simple to understand why resin is one of the most often used crafting materials. Resin is a flexible, strong, and simple material; it dries transparent, allowing you to make beautiful objects that glitter and shimmer. You can make gorgeous resin crafts for every occasion with just a little effort. A rock with colorful crystals inside is called a geode. While some individuals are passionate about finding geodes in the wild, making your resin geode art is a great indoor pastime.

Printed in Great Britain
by Amazon